EQUATOR *a novel*

WAYNE ASHTON

Gotta mix, gotta mingle,
hup two three,
over the hungry mountains and over the hungry seas.

Book club notes available from
www.fremantlepress.com.au

EQUATOR *a novel*

WAYNE ASHTON

For the new custodians of the oceans

Contents

I

A summer afternoon brings alive
a new pair of wings

Golfo de Valencia

Anything over thirty-five and Pinski goes to pot. Today was touching forty. He lay on the floor, open lips flat as the air. A passer-by, like me, could have walked in and made off with everything, including the household's memory. Transported it off to the place known as The Exchange.

Now on the bump of mid-afternoon Pinski flattened his stomach to the cool cement, paws splayed out, snout stuck off into the cool air dropping from the washing above his head, hind legs out crook like a bike's handle bars. Who knows, Pinski might be dreaming of ripping the snorkel off the face of a snorkelling racoon.

A racoon who sneaked up underwater to make off with the household's basket of sardines caught under the moon.

But any crippling idea of protecting the place had evaporated with the hot wind. Pinski couldn't care less. Hell was arriving, a very nasty form of hell, and Pinski did not care. His dog spirit said, 'Me? Shoo away.' Pinski said, 'This God created dog.' Pinski said to himself, 'Pinski cannot care less today.'

In a place where the best couldn't care less today, Ellie-Isabela stood barefoot at the bench, and nothing mattered more to her than the children who might drift inside while the butterflies drifted in the trees outside.

I always liked her special place at the bench. If you'd wish to take a journey from that bench on the coast, dear butterfly, far off to a different set of benches in Broome, be my guest.

Assume you are flying first class on one of the placemats, in order to conserve your energy, a pleasant journey, a comfortable, safe journey of seeing just a little bit more than Pinski going to pot. Not a long journey, say off to the moon rather than the great lumbering distance to Pluto. A steady flight, calm, drinks, meals, conversation, good views. If you accept, I can remove the mystery once and for all, and take you to that unknown place, known as The Exchange. I can maybe answer the question you asked yesterday: Who are they? Who are these custodians of my nectar? I see them everywhere up and down the coast, but what are they?

Let's go, dear butterfly, let's find out what they are, these custodians of your nectar. I can show you a bit of yesterday, but mostly I'll show you what they are today, in the contemporary climate. The comparison can bring into sharp relief how they have changed, their transformation. Fresh, new, different surprises in store at The Exchange.

We can start here, dear butterfly: Ellie-Isabela worked in the smaller room located past everything, at the end of the main room. Ellie-Isabela's special little place, a box, dimly lit, just two small windows, yet it was a box where the brightest concentrations of her ancestry were found on the coast.

Memory is like water. Flow, calm, shine, evaporation, and then condensation, soft water riding the hot air, it might bring a mist. You will see this at The Exchange, if you choose to fly, dear butterfly. Over the treetops of fresh new leaves and fresh new lives, a new leaf a new life, that's just private, secret, not for the outside where a bigger fact heats up the road at the beach: all memory is like water.

A Private Room for the Tree of Bones

Everyone in town rightly believed the back room was the headquarters where Ellie-Isabela grew the children's bones. But the business of growing their bones was for the main room towards the house proper. In here, at the bench, nothing mattered more to Ellie-Isabela than the kids who arrived to hang around, because here she grew the other useful body part, their minds. Their sensibilities and their possibilities were grown in here wild as tender herbs. This was done mostly in the afternoons when the activity around the place had slumped away so that the pervasive quiet would make the game exclusively about delicacies and not much else. In here it was delicacies, not survival.

Incomplete understandings were not for the inner room, they were for the crass life outside; the halfway understandings that brought only frustration and other pressures were not for the special quiet of the inner room where she worked. Phone call understandings were for elsewhere. She felt sometimes a sweet pity, for the world of blunt arrogance, for the world of no nuance, she felt, in higher moments, the emotion she could only explain as confirmed sweet pity.

So much of that world relied on fast responses, betraying perceptions that were no more nuanced than Pinski's explosive barking when he was up to protecting the place if it was under thirty-five, protect the bright possessions, and the inhabitants, or even just the fading possessions, like memory rounding away into smiles along the beach.

In here it was slow delicacy, or, as she would say, as full an understanding as might be available in the quiet drift of afternoon, not the pleasant abbreviations of cut and thrust survival. Her belief in the full understanding was strong and supple. While it could throw danger in the way, it might also provide delight.

The abbreviations of survival, she believed, could not provide delight for the kids. Not much, what could it do, make em into giant men and women of immense survival. What good would it do, that outside world of abbreviation.

A Temptation in the Private Room

Today all the kids in the place were at the ocean, and a solitary boy wandered aimlessly inside. He wore his best shorts and his best shirt because he was expecting visitors, but the shorts were torn at the side, and the shirt was torn in the armpits. The boy came up and leaned his survival elbows on the timber bench to see if Ellie-Isabela was really doing anything.

At the boy's footsteps, Pinski slid his eyes to the bench, but nothing else on his wiry body moved much at all, and he went back down to the floor. Ellie prepared soup. But soup was twin survival, so when the boy strolled up to the bench Ellie lifted the bowl off the placemat and put it aside to make room. To fly you see, to fly. To wait, but to fly soon.

Ellie-Isabela had waited patiently for a long run of many weeks. But even without the tension of waiting she knew the boy was now more or less at the age where it was time for a whiff of guidance, old enough to understand the magic she wanted to show him on the empty placemat. She'd waited maybe two months, and around here on the gulf that's a long time even if stars swap places upon a handshake like men taking time on old phones.

'I have a magic wand,' Ellie-Isabela said in slow, gentle Spanish.

'I don't see any magic wand,' the boy said, irritated, in Spanish, 'show me.'

'I have a magic wand,' she said again, 'and it is called Giving.'

'You're just bullshitting again,' Carlos said impatiently and swung off the bench, and he walked gruffly away, running his hand along the lemon-coloured walls of the bigger room and then drifted back outside to the fountain to hang around and wait for the visitors who were due to arrive.

As he walked he swore in the slang Spanish he'd taken from truck drivers: 'Shit, Fuck, What a Fucking day,' and then he kicked a box off the steps, kicked it hard and his foot swung right up into the air to the height of his bony shoulder.

Flying Outside

Ellie-Isabela also went outside to look for fine material to kick, but she did it without moving away from the bench where she had work to finish, work she wanted to do, this was work she desired because she knew it was giving new power to the kids. The big eyes, sparkling in a round face, drifted over the view from the small window.

From where she stood inside, the dry landscape, with sunlit glimpses of the meandering river, may have reflected her inner world that afternoon, flapping the inner magic of quiet skills that she possessed for the art of giving, for the flow of giving, skills that faced up to possession head-on.

The gullies where the light reflected off the river fell away from the back of the property twice and then started to rise into the distance until the hills met the sky in a seamless fold, which, to her way of approaching life on the coast, was a radiant fold, the limits of the farms that had once belonged to her ancestors. Radiant also her inner world, for after forty-seven years living on this coastal landscape, Ellie-Isabela's inner world knew the facts better than anyone.

The ancestral farms had all gone, and the house she was born in, at the hinge of two centuries, in 1900, the house where she was raised, this house, had also gone. It had all gone.

Her mother, her father, also gone. With everything gone there was scarcely much to protect, even possessions like memories, so that on the days below thirty-five, days when the Jack Russell was alert, his explosive highsprung policing made Ellie-Isabela smile away the dullness.

And with everything gone, the dark little room with the wooden bench had become hers, and also Pinski's, the corner where her ancestry glowed the brightest after it had flowed downriver against the parched landscape and out into the lost expanse of the Golfo de Valencia veil of things.

When he was alive Ellie-Isabela's father had said of the river: 'Memory is like water. Boil the tea, or freeze the juice.'

Naked to the Creek

These days Ellie-Isabela was celebrated as the best guide in the district, she moved on gut instinct and grew on giving. No sooner than a traveller arrives at the doorstep to ask for directions up the river, and no sooner than Ellie obliges by carefully drawing a line of instinct charting the walkable riverbanks on the convenience of the page of the traveller's map book, no sooner than you ask, the river changes course. And since it's a fact of life around here that a river is a poem, the direction might change again, and yet again.

This is the same with locating that other cruiser of quiet drifting afternoons, that other poem—for Lee Glass-Darlington certainly was, to friends in the know, a poem—Lee Glass-Darlington of Sydney, future granddaughter of the young Scotsman who lived in this large hacienda with Ellie-Isabela and the twenty-six children. But to locate the Scotsman's dearly loved granddaughter strolling naked and traumatised down the hillside at Tenmoon Creek in Sydney, the children need directions.

For the fuller understanding, the children need guidance, need the signs, a little help at least, maybe Pinski's highsprung protection, if he hadn't gone to pot. To locate Lee, somewhere along her own river, the children need to take a moment on a previous heatwave afternoon, starting with the young Scotsman, David Darlington, sweating beside his lover in a musty cottage of ferns and moss.

David Darlington and his lover in the cottage may have been a vivid dream, like Pinski on a snorkelling racoon sneaky as a suntide. It may have sounded a bit too real, far past real, or not real enough. But memory doesn't care much, for memory is like water, and water has at least three realities, maybe thirty, maybe three hundred, and you can't pin down three hundred realities easily, especially if the afternoon is as hot as this one today on the gulf. Mendoza said the sun had grown, overnight, got bigger, that's all.

Maybe Three Visits

The lovers lay in the cool sheets. Muttering softly after a random fuck, one of the many beautiful random pieces inside their never-ending variety of love since they had met. It was a difficult random fuck for there was a guy running around outside with a rifle.

But they lay together. Gun or no gun they had loved now. Arse exposed, his, and her arse protruding too. Round worlds, two pairs, smooth with new sweat, one pair white, alabaster white, Scottish drifter, the other pair brown, golden brown, Indian, a fine maharaja's daughter, also a drifter.

Faces up together. Voicing concerns, but really just muttering slow words, so slow as to lift into the humid air no concern at all, slow for the pleasure, words for the fear, always words for the fear.

'They'll find us, we've blown it, everyone downtown knows this place.'

But they were in fact very far away, a four hour drive behind the city.

He'd parked in the shade that gathered round the front door. The shack maybe a hundred years old, swinging its small rooms round an old well, guarded by extinct curtains on mud windows, while the outward windows searched across the abandoned landscape rising behind the shack, searched for evidence of intruders. She humps her backside in to turn closer.

'Nobody will find us.'

'And her, outside?'

'My most trusted, she loves me, my most trusted of them all.'

'Someone could ride past the car, and they'll spot the car.'

'Nobody comes here any more. I want to show you something, something you have never seen.'

The maharaja's daughter started to move again, and then the afternoon stopped.

The young Scot, David Darlington, woke gradually, no longer hidden in a mossy shithole in the hills behind Calcutta, he was on his back, alone in his room in the hacienda in Spain. Blap.

He could hear Ellie-Isabela at work in the kitchen, soft cluttering, distant. He got up and opened the window, slowly, expected the fierce glare. It had remained hot out there, the rolling sunbleached hills of the coast vibrated in the haze. For David, this landscape was to commence a kind of future, for Ellie-Isabela it spoke of a respected past.

The sea breezes, the updrafts, the tides, would carry David Darlington forward just as they carried Ellie-Isabela around backward, along the Catholic generations that had worked this landscape as a prize from God. But for the agnostic mystic David, the place around here on the coast would propel him into a pending life.

His granddaughter Lee Glass-Darlington would emerge from that pending life, strong, powerful, intelligent, and yet, on the collapse of her bold project, she would be sighted strolling naked and traumatised down to the groves of Tenmoon Creek in Sydney. And the younger great-granddaughter Laura would immortalise David over a week at the Edinburgh Festival, and then Laura would fly away to Margaret River, to Yelverton where she'd soak up warm rest in the sunshine of Cowaramup Bay.

Ride the placemat if you will, dear butterfly. We shall travel treetop to treetop if you like. Leaf after leaf, new juicy leaves, new flowers, high great bastards to love.

The Tree of Surprises

From the window David Darlington could hear the Spanish children on the beach, calling and shouting, still too young with the world to be interested in a siesta.

David Darlington made small Carlos a big promise for his birthday, but around here spooky intentions amount to nothing, so Carlos couldn't care less about David Darlington's promise. Shit is shit, Carlos spat to himself, a new tide brings a new prawn and so fucking what, hm.

Carlos walked outside to wait on the fountain, and he couldn't care less for the fountain.

It never flowed like you want a fountain to flow, nobody ever knew water in the circular cement two feet above the dirt, and across the road there was water in the ocean without bothering about a cracked old fountain. Besides, with everything else on the coast gone the timing was true, the fountain was at least punctual. Carlos could hear the kids over the hacienda wall, screaming and shouting as they dived off the jetty into the sea, nobody stayed here at the front of the hacienda to care about a dusty old punctual round tub of concrete, they were all at the jetty because the afternoon was burning hot shit off your nose like a man at a cooking steel plate stewing a cow slice.

Anything over thirty-five and Pinski just went to pot these days, unlike when he was younger, when he'd be out on the jetty and swimming in the sea, with the kids to take care of, barking at the sharks and loving the sea like the sun.

Carlos then sat on the wall, where he could examine the inner wall of the other side. A line of ants moved up the cracked white paint like ink on legs. A string wrapped around his finger, and on the end of the string was a rusted key.

He swung the key round and round in the hot air until he felt he was hanging from the key like a bat. But, the thing was, hanging around and watching the sea breeze get into things, Carlos had no clue he was sitting on his bony backside two steps from the fattest inheritance anyone on the gulf had ever seen, heard of, or dreamed could be handed across the wings of a calendar. The biggest surprise a sea breeze ever carried.

The Tree of Love

The heir to a new world was hotwired out, blank. He watched the ants, with a rusty key swinging round and round. But the problem was this: where the heir sat, the bony jetty-reject, may as well be two thousand same calendars from anything. Where he sat, with his drifting mind accepting and discarding the thoughts and smells of mid-afternoon, a whole village fast asleep—who the hell cares what they might be dreaming—was a place of slim pickings, so nobody entertained even an idea as available as a teapot shot through with holes. It just wasn't a subject, inheritance, no, not here on the gulf, where Ellie-Isabela grew the kids' bones from the bigger room beside her own small room of concentrated ancestry junked off and loved, not here on the coast, where the pickings out of the world were zero. Ample fresh water in the river, a lot of honey for no reason, but barely enough food. It was a good afternoon to hang around watching the salty breeze getting into things while the other kids were at the beach swinging their lives at God.

He swung the key round and round. And then you, dear butterfly, chose the journey, but Carlos was not aware that you chose to discover what The Exchange was, what Carlos simply saw was that a butterfly played from a green cavern in the tree, drifting on the sea air, like the soldier he'd seen yesterday, a crumpled marching. He did not know that the butterfly was now commencing a search for the place known as The Exchange. Nice joint, check it out. Carlos cared more about the gate that the butterfly played into, marching up the sky of the beach, because he waited for the visitors to bring a zing to his day.

But he began to care about the butterfly, certainly it was grand. A deep orange butterfly, large as two teacups, now marching on the hot updraft, clear of the fig tree, so that the rich orange bellowed against the blue of the sky. How the hell did that butterfly get so big? He flipped the swinging key to a stop. He fixed his brain on the butterfly.

Swearing at the Stranger from the City

Instead of aiming his useless afternoon riddle at the butterfly's meals, a butterfly heading for The Exchange, Carlos might have asked a different question. Let's say a dirty trustee from the city had travelled down to the village, stood at the front door, told Carlos he was about to inherit a song and dance of no small consequence—Carlos might have squinted, señor? From whom?

But Carlos wouldn't even reach the question, that plain point of understanding, not around here, the chances of reaching that question around here are nil, nada.

No, instead Carlos would have said, like anyone would have said to a suited stranger from Barcelona standing at the glare of the door and making absurd promises, in a full sweat, making cruel promises to obtain a day of fun, ridicule; no, instead Carlos would simply have said in the hard, truck-driver Spanish used on the gulf, Piss off. Take your ugly sense of fun with you and piss off to France. If that didn't work, and if Ellie was in the doorway beside him Carlos might have tried a slightly different tack on the sweating man in the suit: 'I love everyone here. Just please go away, you are making me have a bad time, go away.'

Ellie-Isabela's father would have nailed it home a lot further, he'd have told the Barcelona creep: 'Fuck off, leave my household alone, and fuck off.' Her father understood the river, had known it all his life, and so he knew lightly, that of all the riches of any inheritance anywhere, the river was the greatest or just sweetest, or ugliest, but it was the best.

Memory, her father always liked to say from the escarpment, is like that water down there, it is honourable. You can screw the life out of anyone but you will want to screw us down there, down that bend, what a nice beach, your mother loved it down there, dear Ellie, wow, she loved us.

A Memory in Motion

Memory is like water, home to many creatures large and small. Home to many creatures miniscule or invisible, and a single drop of the river under the microscope teems with life. The ancestral river behind the hacienda brought abundance to the valley for many generations, and the waters that flowed underneath the leaning trees transported enough nutrients to feed the coastal towns of the gulf ten times over. Water moves, travels, through three states, liquid, solid, gas; a stream, a cloud, a glacier. Interchangeable, depending on the temperature. Memory is like water here too. Around the landscape of gullies, and the old farms halfway down the coast of the Golfo de Valencia, memory has three states. Cherished and loved, forgotten and lost, bitter and destructive. Often interchangeable depending on the afternoon temperature, and depending on circumstance, on a visitor, or on a passer-by, like me. The bitter memories, however, no, they were not really water, Ellie-Isabela's father dismissed them as 'bitter as goat's piss.'

Water can be found lurking everywhere, migrating tirelessly along its three states. And, like water, memory lurked on every escarpment of this corner of the Golfo de Valencia landscape that unfolded out of the window from Ellie-Isabela's small room where Pinski had gone to pot. Patterns of memory that migrated round and round the crests and gullies, dissolving into siestas, condensing out of siestas, like David's moments in the mud shack behind Calcutta.

A Scent of Give and Take on the Sea

David Darlington stepped outside because his head felt hot, into the afternoon air of memories, and Ellie-Isabela came outside into the same air filled with the gulf's memories.

Carlos hopped off the fountain and went over to see if he could get a sip of David's coffee, he could smell the aroma from the distance of the fountain. He sat between them on the steps. The coffee smelled good. Ellie-Isabela smelled good, she smelled like the sea in his mind. Of all the aromas his memory had room for, it was the scent of the coffee, and the scent of the sea on Ellie-Isabela's dress, that Carlos could not escape. Any coffee anywhere, any scent of dried sea on cloth, quietly placed into his mighty mind a full picture of that afternoon when everyone else had gone to the beach while he waited, with the giant orange butterfly, for the gate to be thrown open to the world.

'Same as it always was,' Ellie-Isabela said, 'some give, some take,' and she lifted a folded newspaper off her knees, slapping it lightly against Carlos's mighty head, breaking his aimless thoughts on butterfly food. Around here a paper was always out of date, but the good thing is, a paper was pressed into more than the one use, and so nobody threw out an old paper, not really, nobody much, not under the watch of Ellie-Isabela.

'Señorita Ellie,' Carlos moaned as he re-smoothed his hair that he had carefully combed for the moment when the gate would burst open, 'you are telling shit again, just shit.'

'Me telling shit? I do not think so: colonel, does Ellie-Isabela tell shit?'

'Never heard Ellie-Isabela telling shit, no she does not,' David the colonel said. He was no colonel, but round here they called him colonel, in the house, around the house, in the village, because he was a mixture of far-off places. Scotland he'd come from, India he'd come from, he'd been to Madrid, Barcelona, he had sailed to America and London, so they greeted him with what seemed right for the times, colonel.

Carlos was getting shitted off with Ellie-Isabela's magic wand bullshit, so he insisted. 'How can anyone do giving all day long, giving forever and ever, or just do taking forever?'

They sat waiting on the steps, six knees, side by side, Ellie-Isabela wearing the thin cotton dress her mother bequeathed with the other things in the brown suitcase, the inheritance that lay under the bed in the dark room beyond the kitchen, far from the sun. The afternoon was now very hot, giving the impression of vacancy around the place wherever you looked, bareness.

Everything is in scarce supply around here, money especially. The only thing in abundance around the bare village is the flavour of that summer ecstasy of dust. If you could re-use the tea, then, according to Ellie-Isabela, you re-use the paper, not that the paper was ever known to bring us anything that looked like good news. Not since the Germans, and the English, and the Italians, and whoever else joined in, had used up most of the money conducting what Ellie-Isabela called their 'activities.'

The house rambled across the courtyard to the stone walls of green vines, a big place. These were old vines from a long time ago, and colonel David, being the newcomer in the village, had wondered how such a thick abundance formed against the stone in such dry heat. A place of big big rooms, above the beach, the house was built on a wave of extravagance nearly a hundred years back, in the 1850s, when the village was a vast farm interconnected on the rolling hinterland and the house its headquarters you saw over hills. Ellie-Isabela was given to understand, from that ancestry, the fig tree in the courtyard was planted around the same time as the farmer's crazed vision had converged upon the coastal valley to build the farmhouse. Most likely planted by the farmer himself, her grandfather's grandfather. But four generations along in summer '47 it was no longer a farmhouse. As David the colonel would say, the house is now 'the happiest orphanage on the Golfo de Valencia, full of leafy shade thanks to the trees, and cool relief thanks to the handsome vines, and care of the best kind thanks to the generosity of the people of the village and the sailor's shop.'

The kid, one of the kids, was just two simple steps away from inheriting the prize of all prizes, and this inheritance would depend very, very much on colonel David's memory of an impatient boy on a cracked old fountain. It would depend on David's memory during a moment of destiny, when David would be helping out a friend, in Calcutta, helping the friend apportion what he euphemistically termed 'the family jewels.'

'Carlos has a point,' the colonel said to Ellie-Isabela, 'giving or taking forever and a day, it certainly would be tricky.'

'He certainly does not, I say not, have a point, no señor,' Ellie-Isabela said to her employer. 'He has what I call the empty head, how can there be a point in the empty head, and from where he got that empty head, who knows, from somewhere, just like I got my green eyes, from somewhere. If the head was not so empty he would understand that some give, some take, that's all. And if now he is big enough to fly away on these big outings then we say he's big enough to learn from old green eyes that some will love to give and others will love to take.'

Then she said to Carlos, 'Besides, what would this colonel know about it, he's not much older than you.'

'Si! He is dammit, he's old,' Carlos said.

'Our colonel? When were you born señor colonel? 1920? This makes you twenty-seven last month, still a mere boy, still desperate to understand the mysteries of give and take.'

Ellie-Isabela turned to Carlos: 'What do you wager our colonel has inherited? He inherited the Give? Or maybe you think, O la la, he inherited the Take?'

Carlos turned to inspect the colonel. 'I don't know what the señor has inherited, you're just talking shit.'

The coffee smelled strong. Carlos could also smell the honey drifting out of the mug.

'Look at those ears, he has inherited big ears our colonel, yes colonel?'

'Yes,' the colonel turned his head to Carlos square-on, 'I also inherited a long head, see how the head is very long?' And he placed a hand on his chin, and a hand on the top of his head, and then swapped the hands around.

'Like me,' Ellie-Isabela said in Spanish, 'look, here, I have inherited a lovely fat arse those fishermen like Mendoza would kill to squeeze. And beautiful feet, look at my long, elegant feet, these feet have kicked nothing, they are not for kicking, they are for laying out in the sun for men to look at and maybe understand.'

'Are you ready for your visit to the Mendozas?' the colonel asked.

'Yes,' Carlos said. 'Can I have some coffee?'

'But if you're ready, where's your fishing rod?'

'We are not fishing this time,' Carlos said. 'Can I have some coffee?'

'Oh?' Ellie-Isabela said. 'Then please do tell us, what will you be doing out there with señor Mendoza and his sexy little daughter Rosa Mendoza?'

'Don't know. Tell you when I get back. Can I have some coffee?'

'Just tricking,' Ellie-Isabela said. 'The colonel and I have no desire to know what a zero-headed boy does today, do we now colonel?'

'This is very true, we do not care,' David the colonel said. 'Here, careful, it's hot.'

The boy was called Carlos Luque. David the colonel had renamed Carlos, as a birthday present for turning eleven. Carlos Luque was thereafter called Kieran Leeft.

'I wish,' Carlos Luque had said last month when asked by the colonel what he wanted to do when he grew up, 'to become a traveller like you, señor colonel, and travel the world, will you give me a name that means "traveller"?'

'Into the sunrise, or into the sunset?' the colonel had asked.

'Er, si, two, sunrise and also the sunset.'

'Then I shall give you the name Kieran, which means sunrise, and Leeft, which is sunset. This will be your birthday gift, Sunrise Sunset.'

'Thank you, señor colonel.'

'You're welcome, but until that day you are Carlos.'

'Si!' Eagerly.

Eager because the world past the butterfly was now his like light, the zing for which he'd yearned a long time. Given the zing from colonel David the traveller, and Carlos here cared a hell of a lot, because the colonel, well, Carlos respected him the most out of all the lost travellers he had seen scrape into the village. One after the other, burnt out men, never spoke a word, even when Carlos would walk across the road to ask about the world out there, not a word, maybe they might look over at the boy, maybe smile badly, and then shuffle away down the road looking for a truck going south to the city of Almeria. They all walked on past. Only one of the burnt out men stayed, and he opened a shop.

Carlos cared that the colonel's gift was real, cared it was true, and from that moment he peered forward like hell and high water to his eleventh birthday, for the gift. When he would become Sunrise Sunset and be able to say to himself, whispering with an angry fury out behind the house alone, I am a traveller!

He'd light a fire to the fury. Stamping the hard dusty ground with his bare feet, and glaring downwards and saying with the hard Spanish he'd learned from the truck drivers, 'You fukkin bet, I am a traveller, fuck!'

The colonel had asked him, 'Will you travel on foot?'

'No, señor colonel, by boat, I'll buy a boat.'

'Santa Maria,' Ellie-Isabela had whistled, 'he wants a boat.'

Now, tho, at eleven and a month, watching the breeze get into things and waiting for the visitor who was due to walk through the gate, he couldn't care less. He gave the mug back to the colonel, saying gracias. He walked back to the fountain, swinging the rusted key round and round. It flew off his finger and landed at Ellie-Isabela's elegant bare feet.

'What's this?' Ellie-Isabela said.

'It's a key.'

'It can't be one of my keys, it's rusted like hell. Is it one of my keys?'

'No, it's mine, I found it in the stones under the jetty.'

'You want a useless old key washed up by that useless old bay?'

'Si.'

Carlos walked back to the steps. Ellie-Isabela handed over the rusted key.

'Why?'

'It's the key for my boat.'

'It might be a magic key.'

'It's the key for my boat,' he insisted, and he walked aimlessly back to the dry fountain, moving his aimless arms and legs like a lost soldier to see if this would convey the shit aimless day to Ellie, make her move, make her bubble into life, make her take notice, he swung the arms away and away. The dog instead got his mojo.

Pinski and Henry

Pinski walked out the door, no doubt strolling in satisfaction from his dreams of turning a snorkelling racoon into a snivelling racoon. Racoon pleading for mercy. Pinski sat next to dear ol Ellie, his own dear ol Ellie, and he stretched his mouth back with afternoon satisfaction, stretched it far behind his eyes, and then blinked and then smiled, and he sat smiling out into the haylight of the hot afternoon, with the pinkness of his tongue bringing round a couple of flies, and Pinski did not want the presence of flies. They wrecked his life here, if they were elsewhere he was sure he would have a better life here. Every dream he had was of being dropped into hell by a party of five thousand flies lifting him by his pink tongue and lowering him into a horrible pit of something, he never got to see what the something was in the dreams, but the flies buzzed him into it anyway, and the pit always seemed to devour his legs, or his happiness, he could never be certain which.

Put it this way. Pinski had a friend next door, a little kind of a dog, not even a small dog, very tiny, nice friend, he looked like a housefly this dog Pinski felt, and Pinski liked him, but Pinski was too whacked out, and too hot, to try the housefly for fun round the pace of today. Housefly doggy. Little thing, legs like small sticks, eyes bound outward bung-ho like a fly. Pinski never got into pity. Pinski liked him so much that he felt the housefly wings might have been real or true, a fly that looks like a dog, a furry mammal fly dude, Pinski liked him.

His name was Henry. Pinski liked Henry because he just liked him but Pinski is a great protection liar and so he liked Henry really because Ellie did, Ellie liked the housefly doglet very dearly. Pinski didn't care anyway, Pinski was a chomper, he always dreamed of eating a racoon, heroically throwing the racoon in the air like a sock, or his dreams of eating a shark, but he never recalled dreaming of eating a housefly.

Henry was the sweetest dog you ever met, full of life and fun, thin paws out barking for joy, jumping the jaw this way and that way, barking with no actual bark often attributable to a dog, just a sharp chirping yeck-yeck! If Henry any time was very concerned or rampant he finished up making noises that were beyond chirping, Yeckreh, yeckreh! Yex yex! Yeckreh!

Henry and Pinski were friends, but it was Pinski, not Henry, who did the work of barking at the sharks. To help out, Henry barked at shells. The shells were often located above the water line while Pinski was in the shallows seeing off the sharks, but Henry barked at the shells as if they were killers and would kill anything, so Henry waited until Pinski started out in the shallows, keeping his big fly-eyes on the moment out there in the surf. Then Henry would fly round the sand, his little bony head jabbing around the place looking for shells, and when Pinski began to bark Henry would immediately pounce so fast he looked like a dart, and the bigger shells were never much smaller than Henry, so that he felt equally matched. He felt he could conquer this beast if he just gave it what he stood for. He'd air-jab the living daylights out of the shell, back and forth on his small legs, with magnificent almost-bites, Yeckreh! Yex-rr … Yeck-reh-reh!

Pinski in the surf barking at a big shark, Henry killing an empty shell, they were friends. They were good friends. Henry&Co. It is very probable that Henry thought of them as Henry&Co. They were, day in day out, just as busy as the fishermen who brought fear to the gulf every night: Henry&Co were busy every day looking after the kids at the hacienda. But more really than the kids, they were keeping an eye out for their queen Ellie. Someone from the hacienda soon would make Ellie break badly, they would hurt Ellie, and Henry&Co would not like it. Henry&Co would take it badly.

It was not only Henry&Co that would become filled with colour in the face. It was also Pinski&Co. Pinski&Co would definitely take it badly. Chomper would make racoon dreams arrive just by focus. Flat out at forty. Flat out at thirty. No matter, make a dream occur, and then get the creep who hurt Ellie. Get em good. Fekking idiots, get em.

Pinski and Henry ran the village. They dictated what went and what didn't. They never agreed on the 'Me&Co' point of destruction and construction, but they barked at sharks and shells and that was good enough to protect queen Ellie, even all the kids. Other smart dogs ran the rubbish tip behind the village, and still other dogs ran the highway behind the rubbish tip, and yet far away dogs ran the other village whom nobody had ever seen, so it was assumed it didn't exist, or it existed as a shadow to this, and so all was well and no trouble drifted off the dirt into the air. Odours, as they say, remained safely in their place.

Three dogs from very far away sent a message. Our rubbish tips are known to be more sweet and friendly than Henry&Co but that's not hard to do because running a village on the coast with Ellie is a small game, our game is a big game, please come see us soon. Pinski smelled the note in the air and he just fell back and let it go, he flapped back inside under Ellie's bench and let his lips dribble on the cool cement, his answer was saliva and bye-bye. Henry objected but he also could see it, and Henry too stuck out the sticklegs to sleep, little paws big as a curry leaf.

But days change and the kids at the hacienda are restless when days change. In a house kids are different, in a proper house kids are restless when days are the same. One way or another, kids are restless, and the dogs are running the village. After the war a new century might be born of kids, and Henry&Co, and of the dogs at the tip, and of the dogs far away, and of the dropdown from the tree of a butterfly, and of Ellie-Isabela when she asks for the guy from whom she wants unspeakable things.

The Tree of Peace

The lost soldier who stayed around town for a few days in silence did eventually ask about the shed; he kept quiet on his intentions but he did enquire about the structure out at the beach. It stood hollow at the jetty in the sun, away from the trees of the hacienda and the other houses, so that the ocean came gleaming through like a blue torchlight of gases and dreams made long before his running had started. It was just an empty hut for old men at another a time, but you knew it became good at a point because legends seep from it today, every few days, like a tap that needs a man who understands water stoppage and water flow. You could also see the gulf's horizon through the shaded interior, and it was no shed, just a square piece of tunnel someone had put up. When nobody claimed the shed the soldier opened his shop there. Henry sat next to him in the afternoons. Henry&Co head office was maybe the little dog's idea of the place. Now that the old shed had a person sitting in it, Henry walked his small legs across the beach to see what he could do to keep the village safe out here at the extremities, the north end where nobody goes anyway, what a fool, new guys are always fools, wonder why that is, let's go see. Henry sat by the guy's feet.

Turned out he was not a soldier, he was a sailor. His shop sold and rented goggles and snorkels, in stock lay exactly eighteen pairs of goggles and snorkels on the floor, but none of the sailor's goggles sold, a few were rented now and then. David would treat the kids every week with half a dozen pairs to share, and fights broke out early in the piece but by month's end the kids had worked out how to share them round in a more or less agreeable way, since you heard less fighting, and you began to hear laughter and splashing, nowhere does laughing attract more goggles if a sailor has made a place for kids better than it was before.

The sailor would sit in the shade of his shop playing a harmonica, unconcerned that the village seemed to offer nothing much in the way of customers who came by to say please let me have that, barring a dog looking for all the uneven sightlines like a fly. The sailor also sold shots of whisky upon the floor, until the four bottles ran out, but by then he'd made enough to wait until he could buy a couple of bottles from someone else wandering through needing the money. He also sold boxes of matches, these were kept in his pockets. He also sold two inch tins of tomatoes, these were on the floor in small stacks. The tomatoes had no labels, just a plain tin, but everyone soon trusted they had a tomato inside them once the first few were bought and cut open for inspection, especially Ellie, she was suspicious of a tomato brought round to the table like that. She came, she looked, she hated him even more for he had not lied, and there were red bulbs in juice, beautiful red bulbs in tasty juice.

But these were items of slower stock; the sailor did most of his better trade selling bright new spoons to the fishing community, who had thousands of hooks but few spoons, especially shining spoons that you could see your eye in, your face if you held it just so far off. The spoons were the smartest thing the sailor did for the shop. Great big fishers had never seen spoons like them, and a spoon gave them the sense that it was a new way of talking to the kings.

The sailor played his inner glidings on the harmonica in the afternoon, you could walk down to the jetty and see the silhouette face the sea. He was shifting side to side with the tune's tide, and a thin-legged creature was busy sitting on the floor beside him raising the head every so often to see if the man was still there. Henry would be glad to be looking out at the sea, and then suddenly his little head with his big eyes would pop upward quick to check, and back newly sustained to a view of the sea where he would wait for another pop up of the head to check again that the man was still there.

The Tree of Wishes

Ellie-Isabela's father once told her that the technique of giving sometimes involves no giving at all; it involves, simply, not joining in the combat but dissolving the combat, and a good place for this was the tree of wishes.

The hundred year old fig stood central, between the house and the gate. A dusty path swung across the expanse, leading from the gate to the hacienda. But a second dusty path looped under the tree without going anywhere, no destination, looping round the huge trunk, the path of wishes, to walk round and make your mind up.

Everyone thought it was Ellie-Isabela who'd called it the Tree of Wishes, but she hadn't, it had become the Tree of Wishes long before anyone could remember, back in the time of the vast farm of her ancestors. Ellie-Isabela wasn't shy of it, the Tree of Wishes, she loved it, and she used it, and she helped everyone else use it. She would help loudly, leading a visitor on the outside into the loop of the inside: 'Once and for all, once and for all, make your mind up; what is it you wish.'

A large butterfly dropped from the leaves into the hot air and bounced towards the house. Colonel David watched the butterfly as it tacked closer, and Ellie-Isabela followed it too. Henry&Co were watching and yawning. Ellie was about to make a wish, but the wish appeared at the gate with a suddenness that caught her breath, and she coughed, not knowing which way the air was going, in or out, or round and round.

Rosa Mendoza's father walked through the gates with a share of his catch, a basket of sardines for the house of twenty-six children, two fish for each kid, and two each for Ellie-Isabela and the colonel.

Carlos suddenly got nervous. He put the key into his pocket

in case it looked stupid, certain it would look stupid.

Mendoza had done the loud invasion of rough, grandiose giving twice a week for a long time, bellowing off the Golfo de Valencia and striding through the gate like a giant that had walked out of the sea. A head of brown seaweed risen from the waves, pants long enough to be thrown over the stern and dragged along as two commercial nets, boots like the trunks in Ellie's room. But today Mendoza strode across the dried grass, ignoring the meander of the pathway, with something special as well as the sardines, an octopus.

Ellie singing high, rolled across the hot air: 'Good afternoon, señor Mendoza, good afternoon,' as the giant rounded into the compound with his daughter Rosa, 'what a beautiful day of sunshine!' Then a small cough that fixed the air problem for good.

'Yes Ellie-Isabela,' Mendoza howled back in his coastal Spanish, 'it would be, if those fucking English and fucking Germans and Italians and Americans, fuck em all, if they all went home and left the fucking sunshine to light the gulf to grow more of these tasty treats. I hope you have the mood to prepare octopus señorita Ellie-Isabela, sweet rubber from God himself, if you have the mood I shall rub your feet with octopus slime.'

'I do wish,' the colonel said quietly to Ellie-Isabela, 'the man will one day stop swearing in here, the place is full of kids.'

'No no, it is nice,' Ellie-Isabela whispered as she smoothed down the cotton dress and threw the paper over the shoulder. 'It is the good energy of the sea he brings with all that healthy foulmouth dirt.' Coughing definitely gone.

Sweet rubber from God himself. Said by a vibrant, generous Catholic in a colourful coastal Spanish. Half a century later the full count of tongues in the Catholic realm of a billion faithful would be sixty-three. The grateful statement of fact could be stated in sixty-three different languages by hard-working men and women that were as robust and generous as Mendoza.

Then she called out to Mendoza in a different pitch, 'Si señor! I was dreaming last night of octopus, too many hands, so many so many!'

'Jesus Ellie,' the colonel sighed quietly.

Mendoza was not a quiet guy. To be a shy Catholic was not his way, he was a boisterous guy, a celebratory Catholic. The louder the better, booming across the hearts of all the lingerers looking for fun but way too undecided as to how to locate it as hotly as Mendoza did.

'Nice dress, señorita,' Mendoza said as he walked up, 'I have not seen it before, very tidy style, like a dress from France, Paris maybe.'

'This dress, señor, this is untidier than you think, señor, much, much untidier.'

'Glad to hear it.'

A sturdy pitch: 'Good catch today señor, look at that damn bag in your handsome arms.'

'Jesus,' the colonel said.

'This is the Golfo de Valencia, señorita, it is the sweetest water in the whole of Europe, all the creatures come here to die. Did you enjoy your ride in the plane last week?'

'Very much,' Ellie said. 'You were right, what a handsome view. I could see along the beaches a mile out where the deep shadow starts, the line where you say you all fish.'

'It is the shadow of God on earth, señorita. But now with those fucking English and fucking Germans making so much noise, the creatures have found other places to gather, but, si, we have enough to feed the children and ourselves.'

'You're a good man, señor Mendoza,' David said.

'Around here a good man is a poor man, colonel, but I thank

you for your confidence in my morality.' Mendoza laid the bag on the step. It bled onto the cement with brine and blood.

'And Carlos? Are you ready?'

'Si, señor Mendoza.'

Mendoza strolled down the dusty ocean road with his daughter Rosa at one side and the boy at the other. The other kids were out on the jetty, pushing each other off, running, hitting, screaming, diving for the round river stones collected behind the hacienda.

'So Carlos, they are treating you well at the hacienda, those two clowns?'

'Si, señor.'

'That's good, and I have to say with higher pride than I have in my crew, you seem more happy than last month, what has happened?'

'Si, now my name is Kieran Leeft since you last came to take me out, the colonel has given me a new name for my birthday.'

'Really? Why?'

'Kieran Leeft means traveller, I am going to be a traveller.'

'How will you travel?'

'By boat, I will go to many islands by boat.'

'Do you think you will become known as this, this, Kieran Leeft?'

'I hope so.'

'Shall I call you Kieran today?'

'Si.'

'And you, Rosa, do you agree to call him this Kieran?'

'If Carlos likes his new name Kieran, then I also like the name Kieran.'

Nobody knew what Carlos Luque had inherited deep behind his skin, but the hole of knowledge was a gap as natural as night and day because nobody had known his mother or his father. But that didn't matter; Sunrise Sunset was going to inherit something grand anyway. After Mendoza had taken Sunrise Sunset away for the day, Ellie-Isabela went back inside to the bench to work the smells and scents and juices into a meal for the evening.

Opening the Teak Box

David retired to his private room where he had spent the siesta hidden in the hills behind Calcutta. He'd already taken his siesta for the day. He had a good reason to return to the room.

Compared to the other rooms of the hacienda it seemed like a broom cupboard, so small that a foot would be in hell's matchbox. David's broom cupboard contained nothing: a bed, a chair and a chest of drawers. He'd chosen it, preferring to return the previous manager's stately seaside room to the twenty-six children for the fresh breezes. On the stone floor of David's small room lay a thickly woven mat, a gift from the trustees against the gulf's brittle winter.

On the chest of drawers lay a teak box, and the stuff inside the box was never to be seen by anyone; it was strictly under David's lock and key. He was a generous guy all up, but not with this teak thing here on the battered chest of drawers.

David inherited the box from his wild singer aunt Lee in Glasgow who loved wearing very little when she sang, and who everyone felt was just too crass to visit, and who claimed

Charlie Chaplin saw her sing in Soho one night and they went off to his hotel together. She concocted a new song from that 'meet' and performed it for the next year in the Soho pub, 'I Seen What Charlie's Got O Yeah Baby'. She left all her songs in the box, but during a long summer the songs went missing, stolen she claimed. Aunt Lee got the box from her father who had worked in Rangoon. It hailed from the decimated Burmese goldrush of teak, a wood aunt Lee called 'the most illustrious of timbers,' and a wood that she claimed, 'Were it given, this wood, a chance to sing, this teak, it'd be the most dangerous tenor in all Scotland, and let me tell you right straight you don't fuck with a dangerous tenor, or the dangerous tenor will fuck with you.'

David went to the box, communing with a secret society, and he picked out a bell, no bigger than a pear, which aunt Lee also inherited. He held it up to the light at the small window.

But as David was aware, because he'd tried it many times, tho not yet here in his new country on the gulf, the bell was capable of moving aside key hindrances in order to send a peal journeying into the countryside for mile upon mile. Whether the resistance was teak forest, heavy air, thick cloud, impenetrable mist, or blue rock, the bell brushed them all aside for what seemed to David one reason, and only one: for a clean ride into the past, present and future. David lifted it high into the small room against the suffused afternoon light of the small window, and he said, without ringing it, he said quietly, whispering with a comfortable intimacy, 'Ding-dong, and how's the time?'

The bell was said to be the same bell that the famous and proud Rangoon stationmaster, the great-great-uncle of Aung San Suu Kyi, enjoyed using as the final call for passengers on the Mandalay train. The box and the bell had arrived together as an inheritance that David treasured deeply, one item from his aunt's father, the other from a stationmaster of whom David had heard only vaguely around aunt Lee's bath. The bell's outward surface was a mass of scratches and dents, gained from the station's hectic bustle in the time of teak, gained, that is, from the frustrations of those who felt they failed miserably to demonstrate, to the world of international trade, the beauty of the organised Rangoon mind. The scratches came from the frustrations in four ways: clanging against the wall where the bell was thrown to hang; or falling on purpose off the desk where it occasionally sat, onto the cement floor; or flung in a burst of anger against the iron signal when the train was late; or flung across the room at an incompetent car attendant. Today it nonetheless glowed dimly with a hell of a lot of nonplussed delirium, for as a cup bell goes, it was sturdy.

He returned the bell into the polished box, and the movement he chose was very slow, was filled with care, with honour. He crouched over as he replaced the bell, and in the stalling of that slow movement the box was lit by a brass handle at each side. The handles seemed to him, in the lost intimacy of the moment, like wings that sprouted off the woody edges, wings that were catching a moment of sunlight from a faraway time that he cherished. When he leaned over a bit more he looked directly into the box. It was an empty box, he knew that, he wasn't searching for something else besides the bell, but he knew what he was looking for, and he started to see a trail of recent memories emerge from the box, ones that filled his heart with the sweetest, wildest happiness. Memory has three states: cherished and loved, lost and forgotten, bitter and destructive. That afternoon, David's teak box forwarded him the cherished and the loved memories. The same teak box, dear butterfly, you rested upon when you floated through the window into David's room. Resting on the box you asked your question: Who are they, these custodians of my nectar, why do they destroy my nectar?

Now that you are flying with me, let me do you the favour by attempting to give you an answer.

II

Many new wings are found,
attached to the strangest things

The Tree of Dusk

It's just as Ellie-Isabela claims. Some give, some take, tide in tide out. Mendoza gives. Golfo de Valencia gives. When her own inheritance, the leather suitcase, had combed its way across the gulf of night and day, she was also given a set of wings. Won't matter if Ellie-Isabela inherits ten unbombed houses or just two pebbles off low tide.

Or perceptive green eyes that could turn a confusing world into the black and white of give and take.

Or just an enviable arse. The flow of stuff across the second equator is what counts, the north–south equator, and chances are the flow will give away wings. The second equator, that burnished line of day and night moving across twenty-four time zones. Giving the body its circadian rhythms.

The second equator. Racing east to west, across the oceans and across the continents, creating past and present.

The sun rises in the east, and goes west, sunrise moving west, and further west, always west. The hazy line of the second equator is dusk, and directly opposite dusk the second equator is creating dawn. Dusk and dawn. Existing somewhere all the time, every moment of every day. But the sun doesn't move, the earth moves, rolling and turning away from the sun, creating night, then turning towards the sun, creating day. The earth also travels forward as it turns, in an orbit around the sun, a journey of three hundred million kilometres every year. Which is a distance too absurd even for your tireless cousins dear butterfly, the teeming clouds of monarch butterflies that fly all the way down the American continent to Mexico every year, spring to winter, winter to spring.

But down at the coast beside the hacienda, dusk and dawn are the slowtime when the octopus is hunting the fish, and the shark is hunting the octopus. When Mendoza goes in search of the catch that has been scared off to other gulfs by the war.

The Wings of Give and Take

Accept the inheritance and, as Ellie-Isabela rightly claims, a fresh traveller like Carlos begins to sense the beating wings of give and take fluttering around an old rusty key. But it lay in the present that the dancing was at its most unseen. Every time a butterfly like you dropped into flight from that fig tree, it always looked like the present floating about in search of that second equator. The present bumbling about, unable to pursue the second equator, unable to pursue it with the same speed or unable to care to possess that speed, fumbling instead on the dance floors of warm currents left between dawn and dusk. I am orange, I have wings, I am the present.

'Look at that butterfly,' Ellie-Isabela said to the colonel after Mendoza collected Carlos, 'what is he looking for?'

Ellie-Isabela could never know back then during the settling dust of what she called the 'activities' that far beyond her own lifetime the give and take would arrive in a modified form: those who would pick and choose what they give to inherit.

Heirs to choice.

They'd design, like the florals of the tidy cotton dress she wore that afternoon, they'd design what to pass on. For after all, like the butterfly dancing in search of the past and the future, a person would prefer to choose from the past what to have delightedly in the future. Choosing from the limbs of the family tree, picking, selecting, saying thanks, and then tootling off to harvest a fine life.

This is the first part of the answer to your question dear butterfly. The custodians of your nectar are inheritors, they cannot avoid being inheritors, genes become family trees, and so they become inheritors of activities good and bad, outlooks of give and take. One impulse may wish to destroy your nectar, one to create it. Let us fly another mile for a touch more of the answer.

David Darlington's Attempt at Rest

David Darlington had arrived the previous year, '46, from Calcutta, to run the small orphanage at the request of his father's friend, the grave but stable monseigneur Aballte. David Darlington's telegram replied to the monseigneur with a characteristic mix of vigour, brevity and politeness: 'Yes, course, would love to.'

David's vigour was always gently compacted into politeness. But it was never a lesser vigour than Mendoza's or Ellie-Isabela's or Sunrise Sunset's. He looked plain but he burned bright. David always had the appearance of being still, but on the inside he was always in full flight, the agnostic mystic. The monseigneur had warned him in a second telegram that the hacienda would not be easy work. David had replied: 'The tastebuds of the soul mean we all have a different take on the same piece of cake dear monseigneur. I shall arrive next month.'

From his birthplace in Scotland, David had travelled widely, and settled in what was then Calcutta where he chose what he regarded as an enlightened new way of life, swinging with great elegance almost overnight into the halls and timerooms of one of the great faiths, Hinduism. Naturally enough, the young Scot had to be contented with prevailing attitudes, with being an 'expatriate Hindu,' an 'outsider Hindu,' a 'slightly Hindu,' or 'colonel David-the-Scot' as the local Calcuttans called him fondly with their considered intelligence and inclusion. 'Slightly Hindu' was his own term for himself because he always felt success at being a Hindu was an elusive thing, that there were simply too many forms of Hindu jostling for supremacy. But the gap did not scuttle the intensity he carried around in his quiet way; his concentration on the faith was far from balanced, and his fixation with Maheesha the buffalo demon of chaos and evil became more excessive as the calendars of Bengal gathered their dust. By the time he arrived at the orphanage in Spain he was heavily into the great Hindu deity, formally known by the spiritual leaders of the faith as Maheesha the buffalo demon of chaos and evil.

Yet the fixation had no effect on the growing love and respect that everyone round the village felt for the young Scotsman; the give and take was good and strong. The love and respect came from every corner of the village, from Ellie-Isabela, to the trustees, to the kids, and to the fishing community. Pinski didn't know about any buffalo, but he liked the colonel, and in his Jack Russell way he protected the colonel just as he highsprung protected everyone else in and around the hacienda. Nobody in the house or around the village needed protection, but Pinski's worldly perception was protection.

These days the twelve boats, Mendoza's included, became the main source of whatever income might blow into the village; most of the money of the world had gone to the 'activities.' For the Spanish villagers, David's Indian buffalo demon was a way of keeping the evil and chaos of the German and English activities at arms length. Instead of feeling threatened by David's fixation with the buffalo demon, they felt safer for it. In turn, David liked the village, and he very much enjoyed running the orphanage. For the present, he didn't entertain the slightest idea of a return to his beloved Calcutta. Only many years later was he drawn back to the revered old Indian city, where sadly he would live permanently in the belly of one of the opium parlours by the docks. But before his ruin at the dockside came a time back in Scotland where he would marry and raise a daughter.

So David had five lives, none planned in the slightest way, each brushed with the lightness and darkness of discovery, plenty of give and take. Six, counting the final days of addiction to the buffalo demon. Six adventures, he'd prefer to say. First, a happy childhood in Scotland. Then, a teenage thirst took him to America. Then a Calcutta sojourn where again and again he would drive his Indian lover to the old stone hut in the hills; then a fourth life, another happy adventure, here at the orphanage in Spain. Then a life in Edinburgh married to a great woman where they lovingly raised their daughter Rachel, Lee Glass-Darlington's mother; and sixth, a return to Calcutta, by himself, where the opium parlours placed their claim upon his lights in 1966 as a forty-six year old husband and father.

His wife Enid endured a week of fury before feeling any approaching of grief. When they cremated his body in Calcutta, the proprietor of the opium parlour expressed his life perfectly for all the Calcutta friends 'our favourite partial Hindu.' The friends arranged for David's belongings to be sent back to his wife in Scotland. All up it was just a suitcase of clothes.

But the teak box was swiftly taken by a wealthy industrialist, along with the bell inside it. The industrialist claimed that David was the 'greatest and wisest' friend he'd ever had. With David, whether he was in America, India, Scotland, Spain, or temporarily in the middle of seemingly nothing and nowhere, say travelling on a long train journey, he was liked right away. And, with time, was either loved or honoured. He had a certain tilt, a light moved behind the eye, and it smiled back at the listener, nobody had ever seen him glaze over.

David's daughter Rachel had two daughters, Lee and Meryl. Around three decades later the younger one, Lee, would be holding court on the equator for a week, bringing her crisp intellect to bear on a widely respected project that had the attention of powerful policy makers from Washington to Beijing to London to Berlin.

Then she'd leave the equator only to be found strolling naked and traumatised down a hillside of burnt grass and dust, just metres above Tenmoon Creek in Sydney. If she had Pinski for protection at the Sydney house, the Jack Russell might have been dreaming a different concoction. Instead of protecting the place from a snorkelling racoon sneaking up to steal a steak, Pinski might have cooked up, inside his crazy brain, a snorkelling wombat to shoo off.

They claim she inherited that smile behind the eye, that light, from her grandfather. Therefore it was right that for the girl's name, well, the choice was direct: David's favourite aunt in Soho from Glasgow, whom nobody, except David, liked to visit because they felt she was too crass, was called Lee. So Lee was the name given to David's second granddaughter, a descendant destined to become as beautiful and as loved as her grandfather, a fine inheritance in anyone's language.

The moments at the steps behind the Tree of Wishes that afternoon, awaiting the arrival of the second equator, awaiting dusk, are significant for two reasons. I was there that afternoon as you know, hidden. But what you may not know was that the evil master of taking, Bakks, he was there too.

I got there first. Bakks the evil fucker rode in second, a gross second, because Bakks is always gross. Ellie-Isabela on the steps in the inherited cotton dress, had she clapped the keen green eyes on Bakks, even across a country mile of Spanish dust settling after the war, she'd've picked him right off: a taker. An evil taker of the highest order. He was going to take from David, from Sunrise Sunset, from Ellie-Isabela, from Lee, from her sister, from Lee's friends, Bakks was gunna take it all.

Ellie-Isabela's Fine Suspicion

A knocking came to David's door, slight.

David was stooped over the private teak box, and his eyes shot up, fixed in terror on the door.

The knocking came again, slight.

'Yes? Yes?'

The door moved aside; it was Ellie-Isabela. 'Señor?'

'Yes Ellie, what's up?'

'It is Carlos, señor.' Ellie-Isabela had come to her employer with a suspicion. Mendoza's nose for a storm would have called it foresight.

'Yes?'

'I have the feeling this boy, he is to cause much bad damage.'

'No, not Kieran, he likes it here, this is a happy place, Ellie, happy, he knows this.'

'Señor, the boy has got it from somewhere, mother or father,' Ellie shrugged. 'You and I, we cannot say from where, we do not know,' shrugged again, 'but he has got it from somewhere.'

Maybe Ellie-Isabela didn't catch sight of Bakks, but it seems she did smell a small something in the air basking round the hacienda grounds in the heatwave that afternoon when the other children were across the road at the beach. Maybe those green eyes missed Bakks altogether. But what she did encounter, give the good woman, either very smart or very wise, give her credit: what she caught was a faint whiff of Bakks's evil influence on the kid, so early, so early in his life, upon the kid Carlos Luque who'd strolled out the gates for the day with Mendoza and his daughter Rosa, past the other kids diving off the jetty, past the two shops, past you dear butterfly, stamping the present with your hefty orange manoeuvring.

'He truly has got it from somewhere, señor colonel, I am saying it again like I said last month,' she shrugged.

'No Ellie, I do not believe so.'

'You know, señor.' She fell silent.

'Yes?'

'You know, señor, one thing I have not told you,' and her voice cracked, 'I love this child.'

'Dear Ellie-Isabela, dear dear Ellie-Isabela, oh, oh. You love all the kids in here, so do I.'

'No señor, this one, he is special, you are right to give him the name Sunrise Sunset, I want for him to do good for this shit world, but I fear he will cause much bad damage.'

Ellie-Isabela closed the door and walked away down the corridor to clean Mendoza's octopus for dinner. As for the employer's innocence, she shook her head as she strolled away into the hacienda. Just gone twenty-seven, what the hell would he know about it, this Scottish Maheesha.

Memories Spilling from the Box

David, palm against the closed door, breathed deeply and slowly, taking his time. He turned to the box, and the starlit nights began to emerge like the start of quiet songs, those recent memories that filled him with the exquisite happiness. For him, the teak antique was a beautiful window into those afternoons back in Cal, had always been a window, ever since he inherited it from Glasgow aunt Lee.

He could easily, gazing into it, find the good times dancing round the world like butterflies up and down the old stone walls of the hills behind Calcutta. As he stood bent over, peering into the box, he was drawn into a moment back when he was twenty-five, just two years ago. Pleading for the dream to come back, but the pleading went ignored, and the teak box called up a different memory instead.

He was idle on the walls outside the musty cottage beside the maharaja's daughter, a woman hopelessly shot through with all the qualities her friends wished they had in gallons, friends who called everything illicit. The maharaja's daughter was riddled with the best glows and flushes: she was vain, unruly, hungry, disobedient, tough, soft, gentle, a seeker of illicit fun, already a dazzling mezzotint of greatness, a stray within the royals. Her friends were never bored. They were excited with the ways that she invented to run up and down the tree of noble behaviour. They called her The Hooligan. She was the nearest thing to a hooligan they knew. And she accepted The Hooligan. The industrialist moved inside her circles and wanted her badly, almost hunted her down as she bolted up and down the branches of behaviour, file it, week after week at dinners and lunches. Pass the salt please: ignoring the request she'd get up, walk outside, unlock the brass cage on the terrace of the club, fling open a full side of the brass lattice, to stand back and watch as the butterflies poured from the cage and flew into the afternoon at the western side of men's minds. Dozens of butterflies in all colours, crumpling their way off the terrace and down across the slopes and into the butterfly universes of the gardens.

'We,' said the industrialist, 'were protecting those lovely creatures from being devoured by the herons passing through from Siberia this week.'

Like the butterflies she fumbled from those circles and hunted down the Scot. Hooligan had Scot in her sights.

'Let them be devoured by the sweet Russians then,' she said.

As colonel David stood in the sparse room in Spain peering into the teak box, the memory appeared and it grew. He was sitting beside her as she slowly brought up into the air those long fingers stained with henna in the most crowded elegant patterns, lifted the fingers under his chin and brought her mouth to his in the slowly arriving kiss.

'My beautiful foreign man,' she whispered.

'My beautiful man with his long forehead, long chin, so serious, so shy.'

'My father would kill us if he found us like this.'

It was 1945 in the hills behind Calcutta, and his life lay before him. For the lost Scottish Hindu the second equator would roll only until 1966, but it would roll with zest and fire and love. A few years on from '66 the box, and the bell, would be owned by the industrialist Miles Banford.

Emerging from the Shadow of the Second Equator

As we take flight on the placemat dear butterfly, we can see the evolution of other animals, an evolution also guided by inheritance.

For Carlos, who couldn't care less for this or that, the second equator would roll for a longer time, far past '66, into the time of David's granddaughter Lee Glass-Darlington.

Ellie-Isabela's suspicion, or foresight, would furl off like a ribbon round a gift box, because, of those present with the dancing big orange butterfly at the steps that afternoon, it was the boy, Sunrise Sunset, who would stumble into a gulf of inheritance in the sea of give and take. Sunrise Sunset would ride his boat along a string of islands.

Along an archipelago of the descendants of others, driving his boat up a beach here, a beach there, bringing to his travels the air of seeking the fuller understandings, and savouring the delights they gave freely, using the techniques that were given to him as a start in life by Ellie-Isabela at the escarpment window. In the early wanderings Sunrise Sunset would not be aware of the ongoing coaching he had received from the many times he drifted into the back room to see what Ellie-Isabela was up to at her bench. Only to find she was dribbling on about a magic wand. Even tho she was talking what he heard as bullshit. Even tho he would hit the bench and storm back outside full of irritation. He would not be aware that he was instinctively discarding the incomplete understandings in favour of the fuller understandings. But years later, in steering his boat along the sun-filled archipelago, anchoring at the coves with their sandy beaches, he would grow to realise that's exactly what he was doing; carrying Ellie-Isabela's back-room illuminations into the world.

Each beach would become a memory, born from all the three worlds of memory: cherished and loved; lost and forgotten; bitter and destructive. Fond memories, bleak memories, sweet, sour, also memories that would become so twisted out of shape that the loss of recognition would steal from the boy any anchorage of what actually happened.

But the stealing, that was Bakks, Bakks was gunna sit back and take it all, the evil fucker. Even when David met his future wife Enid, Bakks was gunna spill plans to take it all.

Except the key-swinging kid's inheritance—Bakks didn't count on how difficult it was to be, to take the kid's inheritance. Even tho nobody knew the identity of his mother or father, or where they were, or if they were alive today, the inheritance that the kid was poised to receive was spectacular, abundant and joyous.

July 2009

David's granddaughter dear butterfly, sat pleased this afternoon. Lee Glass-Darlington approved, and didn't say so, because at thirty-nine she'd grown to know how to get the most from a moment of poise.

Choosing the pleasant silence, she continued to admire the sleek lines, velvet finish, the illusion of depth, and the sheer presence of the luminous teak. The scent was a rush to behold, hinting at the freshness of a new leather suitcase from duty-free. Up to now it had been safely locked away in the lobby of the hotel, stashed under secrecy downstairs in the care of Tony Chen, the smartest Mandarin supercop in town, who worked full-time, and exclusively, for Lee's office. A long while went by in the cool room before Lee broke the silence of the lingering approval.

'Today it definitely has the essence of,' she finally said, 'dignified *capital.*'

'Open it,' her husband Rudolph invited.

Lee reserved the impulse to open it because the moments were moments to savour. Indeed the whole hotel was a hotel of ambient quiet to savour. From the ground floor lobby to the room on the tenth floor the entire style was a style of bayside equatorial wealth.

The afternoon had been a flow of slow pleasure leading up to this moment. Rudolph brought it up to the room from the vault in the lobby where Tony Chen kept an eye on it, and Lee was not about to give the afternoon's rolling pleasure any excuse for change. For now, while it lay on the table, the enjoyment of the outside surface was more than enough. Size of a shoebox, jetblack interior, velvet. It was the same teak box that colonel David owned in the hacienda, it had travelled, it had first gone to David's friend the industrialist, then to David's wife Enid, then to mother Rachel, and then, now, to Rachel's daughter Lee Glass-Darlington.

She moved away and took up a chair. Rudolph stood where he always stood, at the centre. At the most concentrated hubris, normally into four whiskies, Rudolph claimed the centre shifted with his shifting, it moved according to his position, so that if he stepped from a flight at Frankfurt airport then that's where the centre was located.

After emptying a glass of champagne Lee Glass-Darlington got up and returned to the table. She lifted the lid. Inside was a litter of precious stones, a ruby, two emeralds, six diamonds and twenty-one pearls. In total: thirty gems and jewels and stones. And the stationmaster's bell. She lifted a small gold animal.

'What's this?' she said quietly.

'A buffalo, solid gold, that one's for us,' he said.

'Get rid of it.'

'What? No way, do you have any idea how many carats shine in that little beauty?'

She took the two inch buffalo into the other room.

'Lee? Lee, what the hell do you think you're doing?'

She folded it round and round into a long sheet of toilet roll until it was the size of a baseball so that it would draw enough suction to compensate for the weight of the gold and then dropped it into the toilet and flushed it away.

Lee Glass-Darlington and husband Rudolph Lowenstein were on a roll here in five-star Singapore luxury.

Rudolph sighed. 'Now why the hell did you go and do something as stupid as that?'

'It's a buffalo.'

'So what?'

'We can't keep buffalo figurines.'

A sharp adult, a crisp, elegant intellect, Lee did not believe in demons, but she nonetheless was mindful not to keep any representation of a buffalo in her possession. Too late now tho, a purist would argue. A possession had taken place, brief but reasonably actual. The gold buffalo wasn't even a Maheesha token anyway, it was just a gold buffalo, but Lee's inheritance had her fixated round another way. The second equator had rolled a lot, but not enough.

Rudolph shrugged. Then he walked into the bathroom, and he started to laugh. The buffalo wad was stuck. He flushed again, and the big wad struggled up the loop and then disappeared.

Rudolph Lowenstein's work was indistinct; even Lee could state only thinly what he did for a living, called himself a jewels trader. Certainly he was mighty good at it, he could source fine stones from fine contacts around the world, and he travelled a lot, going right into the hot centre of things where he always preferred to stand for the view.

Lee's work was altogether different, what she did was indeed hot, but easy as a door to describe. Knock first. They spent the evening celebrating the purchase of the jewels, reward for a year's hard work, a year of realignment that Lee had overseen for the firm. She headed up two units in the firm, one in Singapore and one in Sydney. Each team under her leadership was responsible for raising cash from around the Asia Pacific. That was only the start of Lee's work, the really hot stuff came second. Knock first, door opens.

Lee turned to the DVD player to watch the short film she was given at the Singapore office earlier that day. The same film had been distributed to the VIP donors across the Asia Pacific, America, Europe, and the donors loved her work, and the work was the talk of the town.

A field officer from Belgium surveyed a wide, dry field. It lay saturated with crop ready to harvest. Then a dozen men began to cut down the harvest. For each plant the farmer was to be paid five US dollars above the market price. Next, the Belgian counted the crop. Next it was stacked in heaps across the fields. Next the heaps were torched. The Belgian watched them burn, thick black smoke oozed from the lush juicy plants of poppy. The meadows of Afghanistan, where the diminutive Tree of War was now being systematically destroyed. The Belgian paid the farmer a total of five thousand US dollars dear butterfly, a thousand more than the farmer would have earned had he sold his crop of poppies to the heroin makers. Across the length and breadth of the Afghan meadows, a team of field officers were systematically engaged in destroying the heroin that the Taliban, to fund their arms purchases, would sell into the west. After all, Lee reasoned, the Taliban were simply taking money from the addicted kids and then paying it to those select parents addicted to making arms. Lee had placed it on the boardroom table in exactly that language: she'd said to the boardroom, 'Let's stop handing the Taliban the money.'

The vanloads of money, Lee said that afternoon in the boardroom, were very close to having a tricky consequence. Pakistan and Afghanistan, it was feasible, could possibly have a new country lodged between them if the Taliban continued to operate with such large amounts of cash—Talibstan. And she has a point dear butterfly: who except those guys would want a new state Talibstan dedicated to such a grim interpretation of sharia law as to ban just about everything including the potential for girls and women to reach the heights, to create memories of the loved and cherished kind rather than accumulating memories of the bitter and destructive kind.

Lee first put the idea to the partners at Anderson Watson & Milne two years ago. The firm of corporate lawyers understood immediately: the boost to their global profile, plus the boost against the supply of heroin, would be incalculable. Their best mergers and acquisitions lawyer, Lee Glass-Darlington, immediately became the head of a new unit, staffed by ten in Sydney and twenty in Singapore, The Afghanistan Heroin Fund. They chose not to title it the Anti-Heroin fund or anything like that because they reasoned that the headline 'The Afghanistan Heroin Fund' would catch the eye right away, and with a great deal more impact. Two lines later it would become obvious what the fund was all about, yes buying the national poppy crop, but buying it to burn it, and after burning it making regular payments to the farmers at their future times of harvest, of non-harvest, and keeping up those payments far into the future or until the farmer convinced himself to change crops. And Karzai, since he once worked for the US oil giant Unocal, was in possession of an intimate understanding of the relations between addiction and commodities, and he therefore threw his weight behind the project even tho it at first seemed to him like Lee was yet another talented westerner dreaming the naïve dream. He had first opposed the US Congress idea to aerial spray poppy crops. But now, not five years later, he was firmly on Lee's project coz of the income her project was delivering to the farmers as the crops were burned.

To get the unit up and running had been hard work over the course of the two years of 2006–07, but Lee and her two teams soon had hundreds of thousands of dollars flowing into the fund each month, co-chaired by former US president Bill Clinton and Grameen Bank founder, the Nobel prize winner Muhammad Yunus. Single-handedly, Lee Glass-Darlington had made the war on drugs into a sexy corporate beast that worked, instead of a political commitment that sagged under democratic consensus, or that just didn't work at all. She was not yet strolling naked and traumatised down a hillside to a creek in the dead of night.

Around the world were many spiky agencies and political propositions committed to the idea of destroying the source of the Taliban's funding. But Lee Glass-Darlington's Heroin Fund was so downright plain and downright practical that even the field operatives, violence-hardened, cynical men who'd worked mainly as mercenaries all their lives, and who oversaw the destruction, and the filming, were taken aback by the success of the program.

It had brought Lee two years of grind but now, on the tenth floor above Orchard Road, Lee and her husband Rudolph Central were relaxed because the fund had brought up a string of visible successes.

Then the Fannie Mae global crash caused huge losses and sackings around the world. But there was a light burning in the new darkness. With the happy fact of Hillary Clinton as Obama's Secretary of State, the Heroin Fund still had an engine of ding-dong power behind it, sweetly connected up to the top, even tho the top was now a bit low on cash and was forced to start printing money. While they were giving big corporations twenty billion dollars here and fifty billion dollars there, they could manage to divert healthy sums off to Lee's fund. Which meant one simple outcome: while big businesses around the world were sacking ten, twenty, thirty thousand at a time, the Heroin Fund was managing to keep the Taliban out of work too. Nice work if you can get it, ding-dong and how's the time.

Lee and Rudolph enjoyed the next few days out on the bay skiing and swimming in the round heat of Singapore's equatorial sun. The jewels were gifts for each of the thirty staff on her teams in Sydney and Singapore, but the field officers were given, on Lee's insistence, hefty cash bonuses, not happy tokens to take home and swing around the barbeque.

But some nasty and intense piece of taking, some horrible piece of shit, had swung by to crash Lee's celebrations, her success. Days later, at the weekend, Lee went up to the room to find Rudolph. By the evening Lee had searched the hotel, the local bars, the ski club, and the next day the general manager called in the police, brushing Tony Chen aside, but Chen was a smart enough Mandarin coolhead to pretend he'd been brushed aside, and he hung around Lee without being seen. Rudolph Lowenstein was reported missing. Forms were filled out, by Lee, in a daze. Occupation: gems trader.

After ten days of shock, hanging uselessly around the hotel's service corridors, Lee packed the two suitcases, including the box of jewels, and she went back home to Sydney. She immediately placed herself into counselling, with a specialist in Macquarie Street.

One fact dear butterfly. Neither had been aware, when Lee conferred her approval on that box, how could they know, give em a break, that I was present, right there in that grand equatorial airconditioned room on the tenth floor. It's true, Lee flew back to Sydney to the big old bungalow they recently acquired, although she was unable to sleep much, spent the nights waiting for calls from the Singapore Police, and from Tony Chen. But me: I flew to other approvals, from the opening of one box to the next. To offer to help, you understand, not pry, only assist.

Other boxes were being flipped open to private fanfare, certain contents kept, some crassly discarded. Decisions were being taken about what to keep and what to throw out, and I needed, desired, to be present when the keep-it and throw-out decisions were being taken, when the tidal currents of give and take were fighting for dominance in a domain where memory is like water. By young and old, by rich and poor, boxes were being flipped open all over the place as if spring had suddenly bolted into the room of expectation, as if Ellie-Isabela's magic wand of give and take had become the new currency, the trade hinge of excitement. The golden mean of a new spring, fresh shoots, new leaves, mountainside after mountainside of nectar.

Crude Light Sweet

Basically, Lee was shifting currencies around to achieve an outcome, and she also knew how, with panache, to conduct that shifting with the hottest and sharpest ebb and flow of energy. She was the best of the elite dear butterfly.

They were odd currencies, but nothing in the world to Lee was odd, so she worked well with those currencies—opium, cash, arms. Until Rudolph went missing.

In a coming time long after oil, or 'crude light sweet' among those who love the stuff, long after oil runs out, the world will awake to a new kind of crude light sweet. Afghanistan grows ninety percent of the world's opium, nine-tenths of the stuff. If Lee's Heroin Fund fails, the world will awake, obviously, to production levels of opium outscaling anything in history, a new currency to crash entire towns and cities, crash entire countries. They might call it 'smooth light sweet' instead of 'crude light sweet.' The diminutive Tree of War dear butterfly, may eclipse crude light sweet, and may outlast all major forms of currency far into the future. It may appear that, without Lee, the Singapore office was destined for failure. Disband the office and junk the Fund.

But no. That other powerful currency has a destiny too, the tide that Ellie-Isabela's magic wand of give and take can harness like a tree. Take for instance the dining room at the hacienda, observe how the force of give and take swirls around that kindly old room beside the beach, the room that keeps the children fed and loved.

The House Without Shadows

Fair to say dear butterfly, that Lee Glass-Darlington had inherited whiffs and shadows of colonel David, and these shadows lead to another part of the answer to your question: Who are they, these custodians of my nectar? What are they?

It was at dinnertime in that kindly dining room, dusk, that colonel David preferred his speeches. 'All along the equator,' David Darlington said to the girls and boys, 'the waters are warm and are filled with dreams.' The girls and boys sat wide-eyed, listening keenly. Carlos Luque sat far up the back with Ellie-Isabela.

'The dreams that fly free on the warm waves, they are yours, yours for the taking. After you become a fine young adult, on the day when you leave this hacienda in search of your dreams, you will see that they have been waiting for you.'

What the trustees didn't know in the early days was that there was a dubious reason the kids listened with such attention to the Hindu Scotsman. The kids sat intently because the head of the hacienda did two contradictory things before sitting down to the evening meal: he would be rasping out two wildly different stories. One story was to believe in their dreams, but the other tale was the frightening ramblings that made the kids recoil with fear, and that was David's jumpy, edgy cracklings about the violent buffalo demon. The place looked like it was full of kids who were sitting intently, but they were in fact bewildered, couldn't hold the conflicting pictures together as a friend. Then dinner would proceed, and David the colonel's anecdotes would be left behind in the noise of twenty-six children lurching forward into their plates of Mendoza's sardines.

Hope's enough. Spread across the hacienda, seeping into shadows where the buffalo demon of chaos and evil lay in wait. Just on the moment that I was about to show a nice kid, Carlos Luque, Sunrise Sunset of the second equator, into the world of special favours beyond the reach of that buffalo demon, a certain evil creep by the name of Bakks got in the way. Bakks, dear butterfly, he is so energised by his own version of hope that he styles himself as the grand buffalo demon of all buffalo demons. Problem is, hope's a plaything to Bakks, any hope: new hope, old hope, deep hope, shallow hope, Bakks converts it all windward-ho into false hope. Hope's his favourite toy, the ol Bakks. Fair to say a plain fact: el creepo's ill will is a sight to see. Bakks, well, what he thinks of me is just low, says I'm sweet as rosewater. So, yes, it struck the note of a battle royal right from the start, the el creepo and I, beginning on the old road that nobody cared to use any more.

An unused road, face it, is a good place to talk to an evil creep like Bakks. What else to do except get to know the enemy once you've decided to help a kid sail freely into the world of special favours across the roll of the second equator, the world of light and height far beyond the buffalo demons. What else but defend the smell of hope, defend the new scent of hope with feathers combed off the wings of monseigneur Aballte's willing angels.

The road had baked alone for years, and a guy sat on a wooden box. The guy was Lee Glass-Darlington's grandfather, back in the early days, a young guy, long before his time as the agnostic mystic, before the time of becoming a partial Hindu, joins the world's highways in search of his dreams. He was maybe just sixteen at the time, 1936. Another ten years would go before he became the boss at the hacienda juggling advice to his charges.

Now beside the deserted road, five thousand miles from home, which was the tiny village of West Linton under the Pentland Hills south of Edinburgh, David stopped on a vast treeless plain south of South Dakota. South Dakota 1936 was a place of big spaces, not too many towns. The nearest town lay four hours east by bike, sixty miles, and no shop existed. No shade, just the dusty cracks of the badlands obeying the silent commands of the hard summer sun defining mercy for strangers before anything else could even think mercy, except for one stranger. A man on an old black bicycle rode past, mudguard clacking. Up ahead he swung round and came back to the guy at the roadside. The guy on the box stared into the treeless plain, tears darkening his dusty cheekbones. Bakks had come through, no doubt about it, had all the signs of el creepo having been at work: tears, a dusty plain, a wooden box. Young David on the box, young and lost, he just sat still and silent, the only sign of life the tears that came down his long head. The bicycle rider pulled up. He alighted from the old black bike with a good deal of Missouri calm, and he stood a while on the cracked basalt. He brought down the bikestand, leaving the bike out in the middle, and he stepped closer. He knew this plain, he'd been crossing it for years. It had shaken off the world.

'Are you waitin for a lift here?'

The young Scot sitting on the box did not respond right away.

Everyone insists that everything's become fair just lately since the Dark Ages. Become full of hope, and hope's enough. Obvious that the guy with the bike knew it, for he'd seen corners where the world had been shaken off, where all that was left, strewn invisible across the dust, was a baking party of hope defining mercy differently from the sun.

'Would you like a dose of water, I have these two bottles, here, you can have one if you'd like to.'

The young man on the box stared ahead. The tears still came, regular and slight. He seemed no longer like a young man, just a boy, the bike rider could now see it clearly. Just a boy, and maybe not from around here at all.

The bike rider then offered the boy a word. 'This road I'm afraid, son, is not used any more, this here's a done forgotten road, the long route. No gettin a lift here, not this stretch of the countryside.'

The boy on the box stared into space. Unaware that his searching would eventually lead him to a buffalo demon, dockside Calcutta.

The bike rider then asked: 'Where have you come in from?'

No answer.

'Where is you goin to, is you headed up that way?'

No answer.

The bike rider placed a bottle of water into the shade by the box, and rode off to town four hours away; what he'd do is get Bill the cop to drive out and fix it, this hiccup.

The boy screamed, it's all he did, just screamed, large one, open mouth.

For me, I was keen to give young David on the box a chance at that world of special favours, starting right away, but a certain creep got in the way yet again, el creepo by the name of Bakks. To the pleasant guy on the bike the situation seemed like the boy on the box had lost all hope, but to me, well, I already knew Bakks had been to work with his ill will, stewing up his own scarred version of hope.

The hot winds of summer on a dusty road, they shift, and Bakks's ill will can, with effort, be overturned.

Bakks and I caught up with the sixteen year old Scot a few years later when he was in his twenties, in the hills with the maharaja's daughter, and out on the front steps of the hacienda. Also in the dining room when the guy was spitting his fear of the buffalo demon into the air with his speeches for the kids.

Bakks learned from his violations of colonel David how to conduct violations upon granddaughter Lee Glass-Darlington, Bakks had gleaned the whiffs and shadows of inheritance, knew what possession to burn, how to burn it, when was the best time to burn it.

Love and Resistance in Bond Street

Two other inheritances dear butterfly, lock up part of the answer to your question.

Nobody quite knew, but they suspected that Catherine Fekdin put an end to the affair between her brother Remple Fekdin and the London society girl Patricia. At any rate all fingers pointed first at Catherine Fekdin. Inside a fast mind lay the fact of the matter, but she wasn't saying, she simply flew out of London back to Australia once she felt secure that the job of splitting them up was done to guaranteed satisfaction.

Then, with a lot of speculating on every angle from sex to

income, two tides of rampant opinion emerged. Approval, disapproval. One tide of conversation assumed Catherine caused it by design, and the other tide presumed the affair had simply fizzled out like a hope. But even with just two flows of opinion, Patricia's resentment towards Catherine grew to what most would call, at the least, a civil form of hatred. Hate alone, pure, is bad, but a civil form of hatred is less bad, maybe.

Yet pause dear butterfly. Catherine and Patricia, they were good friends. Civil hatred between friends, no way. On the face of it they were smooth professionals who hold one another in high regard. The main difference was that Catherine Fekdin was the smaller art dealer from Perth, and Patricia cut a large figure in London art circles, rolling a universe into bubbles of success. So the behaviour, seeing they were indeed friends, might now have to be, for a good deal of time to come, two equators, roll roll, the new hatred would need to be concealed a bit, or at the very least the new hatred might have to be gently rubbed into a busy gallery life anyway.

Catherine Fekdin owned two small art galleries, in Perth and Sydney. Catherine was unlike her property-baron brother Remple, she disliked corporate business, preferring the smaller business of exhibiting her artists' work. She took pleasure in promoting their work.

By comparison Patricia was a giant. Owned a spectacular art gallery in Bond Street in London, a hundred times the size of Catherine's galleries in worth, in cashflow. But also much larger in the sheer numbers of clients, customers, collectors and hangers-on.

So Patricia knew a lot of people too, perhaps a hundred times more than small Catherine, and one might assume she had a full life, great friendships. True, there were hordes of people around society London talking about the spectacular split-up between their art dealer Patricia and her tycoon lover Remple.

But under all the colours of the hectic heights, Patricia's life was hollow as a copper pipe. The basic position was what gave it the hollowness, scant candour available in a position like hers. You put your foot where your mouth is and your mojo is as hollow as a copper pipe shipping nothing. The people with whom she might be open were not, as they say, thin on the ground, but nonexistent. For instance, how did Patricia talk openly with an artist in her stable, where would the info skip off to? How could she talk openly with another dealer? Openly with artists outside her stable? Openly with the directors of the major galleries like the National? In fact, where if anywhere lay Patricia's turf to drop the guard and have a good time galloping away beyond the fences of the paddock? Every moment of her life had an edit, an agenda, in that way it was one of the hollowest jobs in the world; an MI5 operative at least has a buried invisible world of others, deep beyond the lattice of copper pipes, to drink with in candour and rancour and fun. Patricia at day's end had only herself, so she went steadily unhinged over time, an external state that the crowd of hangers-on would term eccentric. But she was not eccentric, she had never become eccentric, it was simply frustration, and it looked like eccentricity. Floating around were a handful of people that she knew for a fact were just great, trustworthy, fun, but Patricia had no idea how to become friends with them in a way that might brighten her days. All she did was get bigger and bigger in eccentric stature, impressing everyone.

But that's an easy summation of Patricia, for she had one powerful trait that almost no other art dealer had, and this trait made her into a free spectacular person who was capable of having much more fun than anyone else. It was this. Patricia waved along anything her artists wanted to believe of themselves, whatever they felt about themselves, she let them feel it, she entered no debate, no discussion, she just let them go right on ahead into their own lunchboxes and have a good time doing it, even if critics promoted the same stuff. If an artist said he or she was hot, then Patsy let em go on believing it. Cutting edge, go ahead. Brilliant, go ahead. The newest thing, go ahead. She had managed to become the best eye in London without ever having to slip out even the slightest opinion, and from this remarkable piece of elegance she found a pleasurable freedom.

One thing she secretly looked forward to was hanging a new exhibition. The picture-hanging man, Lars, had finished the job. It looked great, bursting with energy. She never allowed the staff to do the hanging, and she banned artists from hanging their work. The staff would lay them out ad hoc on the floor against the gallery walls, but Lars the hangman would walk in fresh, talk to nobody, set himself to work, and up they'd go, and there they'd stay. When he finished, he looked across the room at her form.

Lars saw just one thing.

She was so so heavy.

He said, the hangman said right out, 'Makes you look white, my dear Patricia, fukkin white, this life you have, not a friend in sight ey. Wontoo have a drink then?'

He was always careful to say it when there was nobody else in the gallery, not coz he wanted it but coz he didn't reckon others needed to know she was a lost and lonely piece of high voltage electrocuting herself with hollow copper pipes. That would be unfair.

He was a magician, the hangman, and the reason he had a quiet little potency over the great Patricia of Bond Street was pretty simple. When pictures were hung right for a new show they sold, but when they were hung true by the hangman they sold out.

Patricia said, 'Yeah let's have a fucking drink.'

Patricia had met Remple, a casually dressed thirty-five year old, on a visit to one of her painters in Spain. Remple was in Spain to visit a man raised in an orphanage on the east coast of Spain, a guy who was called Sunrise Sunset, and who had lost a friend, Rosa, but the guy had been a great friend of Remple's grandmother Renata. So Remple was not in a hurry as one might be when on pure business rather than on pure pleasure. He was relaxed. When he and Patricia met, the instant attraction was so great they felt that the sky had caught alight, and, with the day burning and the night burning, Patricia and Remple roamed around the hotel bedrooms of southern Spain for a month and a half.

Back in London they lit up the skies for another six months. Remple had no work-related reason to head back to Perth—Australia not Scotland—he was one of the city's wealthiest guys, he could take his time.

But it ended with a lot of noise, at the centre of which lay the burning, not of sky, but of rancour. It was as tho the entire district around Patricia's gallery in London had caught fire, fed by the flammable oils of loathing, abuse and excitement.

To those who ride the two tides of opinion, I am a stranger. Nonetheless, I am a stranger who happens to know a lot about Catherine and Patricia. And about Remple. By virtue of my strange career I happen to know these movers and shakers quite well.

I decided to go in there, into the noise. Why? To see if I could help Patricia confirm beyond doubt whether the entire burning shitball was in fact of small Catherine's design. But going to the core where that rancour burned like a garbage tip would mean examining a collection of very private powderboxes along the way. Lifting them open one by one as I stroll along, into the decibels, lift the lid, and take a look into the depths.

My strange career certainly helps in lifting them open. It's a reasonable career, can't complain, and most diviners haven't a clue what it is. Some diviners say I'm a meddler. Others say I'm a secret agent. Some have no idea what I am, and so count me as a complete arsehole. Other diviners kind of take a shine to me, claim I'm a doctor, others suspect I'm a Buddhist down here on a break from those putrid generals in Rangoon. But diviners are all like that, speculation and more speculation. What I do is not too important for the moment, it is Patricia who is important, and therefore going to the centre of the fireball is important. Lifting the lids off powderboxes along the way. They're a miraculous place of existence those powderboxes. The depth inside them powderboxes, well, I can say only this: Continue to fly with me for a moment dear butterfly. Powderboxes are a significant element of my nice career. I might add: Rather a very very nice career, juicy.

Jimmy Hazel's Powderbox of Butterfly Prawns

Once in a while the eye is mistaken, taken for a joyride dear butterfly. Is that a snorkelling racoon? No sir, it's a snorkelling wombat. By no stretch can a butterfly become a prawn. No, a butterfly ain't a prawn, and yet ask Jimmy Hazel about a butterfly and what'll he do instead? He'll talk the miracle of prawns all night long, their speed, their finesse, their fear of whales, the crisp design of the big black prawn eyes so far off the head they'd see right round the equator in a blink.

Jimmy's from landlocked Lucknow—Australia, not India—where a snorkelling wombat will not only talk Swahili he'll also talk prawntalk—but that's only a part of the reason Jimmy'll talk the miracle of prawns all day long. Landlocked Lucknow down the road from Orange was once famous for butterflied prawns pink as the moon over Nepal dear butterfly. That was until Jimmy Hazel took up his things and drove, full of hope, out of Lucknow, on through Bathurst, Lithgow, Katoomba, rattling down into the Sydney basin and on towards the city tower in the crimson distance. By dusk he finally pulled up at Kirribilli where he sat on that scrappy lawn under the harbour bridge where you can see the opera house across the water. It was such a bad lawn, it was amazing to Jimmy, what a bad lawn, what a crap lawn, we have lawn in Lucknow, this junk ain't lawn.

Lucknow lay far behind Jimmy's old car, the birds of dusk arrived, and he sat on the grassdust beside the bonnet listening to the three-pronged upward call of a currawong:

Where've they gone
where've they gonnne
where've they gonnnne

The song, the lost homely tone of it, drew him into thinking back on the day's travel. When he left Lucknow he felt sad, true, but he also argued that on the whole, as things come and go, in his life up to now he'd experienced the good things more than once or twice. As he drove east he calculated, that up to now in his life, he had said 'yes' around sixty thousand times, and had said 'no' a mere eight thousand times. Not bad for a Lucknow loper of twenty-four. That's three thousand times each year responding with a yes, that's ten times a day. Ten yeses to take him to the heights of happiness.

Funny thing was, the prawns that he cooked every Wednesday, while they were concocted from the offhand cheer, they arrived in Sydney as a memory, for Jimmy Hazel never again made those butterflied prawns. The offhand decision meant one thing, it meant those hefty prawns loomed larger than ever, for they'd found their way into Jimmy's powderbox. He'd done one of the easiest things in the world, he'd created an offhand memory.

The cheerful Wednesday prawnfest with Jimmy Hazel and his fine Lucknow friends no longer existed out there in the bright blue sky, but yes it did. O yes it did, more powerfully, more truly, because the butterflied crustaceans pink as a moon across the Himalayas were now flapping about in Jimmy's powderbox, a miraculous place of existence where the prawns no longer required a fear of whales in order to survive. He sat on the grass listening to the lone call at sunset, the three-pronged question-song of the currawong: Where they gone, where they gone, where they gone? Into Jimmy's powderbox, that's where. This was Jimmy's first taste of loss, a tincture of loss, and the second taste would be not too far off his right shoulder under the blue sky. Not too many more rolls of the second equator.

It gave Jimmy Hazel the empty. He sat tired from the day's long journey, but he perked up when a brief relief scooted past his tired mind: at least he wouldn't be called 'Jimmy chickname' any more by those stupid high school guys always yellow on drugs and cheapshit bourbon. Their fuckem-off loud upper lips, mossy with their almost-moustaches, and their cheap old bikes, and their shitboards with wheels.

Jimmy Hazel walking to the barbeque from his weekly visit of humility and rounded shoulders to the seafood shop, strolling past the factories, and then, out behind the council rubbish tip, 'Hey girlname! We got prawns for ya, girlname!'

True, Lucknow lost its pinkmoon prawn Wednesdays, but Lucknow bother wasn't excited. Lucknow New South Wales had plenty of other fun things to look forward to on a Wednesday, any Wednesday.

And anyway let's face it, by catching the Wednesday flight out of nearby Orange airport you could kick-start a tour of the entire world if you needed to be busy filling a powderbox with globs of transformation, direct from Orange-Lucknow soil, then returning a year later, on the same Wednesday flight, your senses buzzing with equating and comparing places. A calendar year of memorables and forgettables; let's call it forgettables because just a year on the whole world would mean doing a lot of quick and therefore impressionistic visits. Yet the memorables would linger as longingly as a butterflied prawn afternoon. So bang out of Orange and bang back into Lucknow twelve months later would be good but only so good. Even a yesfactor like Jimmy Hazel would tire of attempting to experience the whole planet's goods and greats in just a year of showering the grime from nameless cracks. That is, unless we put Jimmy into the world of special favours before that evil sonna da bitch Bakks gets warmed up to commence his take take take.

Jimmy Hazel sat on the grim grass under the harbour bridge and reminded himself of one last thing one more time before heading off to Lee's sister's place, Meryl Glass-Darlington's at Pittwater. He'd said yes now around sixty thousand times in his life. He was neat proud of it. Hope's enough.

I can confirm the importance of his arithmetic. Once, he had this bright idea, he'd open a chain of eateries, a Jimmy offhand idea. The eateries would go gangbusters, say forty shops all up. They'd be a BYO type place. Full-tilt BYO: Bring Your Own,

Cook Your Own.

He reasoned it right: the whole mojo's become BYO, so you bring along your own food and then you cook it yourself at the table on a cooker designed into the table. It'd be fun, and the sense of style that the customers would get would be huge, it'd be a powerful success that flew right into the centre of the new mojo.

Lucknow friends fobbed off the concept, but Jimmy said a big city would take it seriously, and fuck Lucknow. He said yes to things so much that the winds ruling his life were the winds of gain. So a chain of eateries where you ferried everything along yourself and cooked it too, a franchise like that, under Jimmy's yes vibe, would go utterly gangbusters, yes being truthfully the most elemental arithmetic to all the ideas history has ever visited or toured. Besides, Jimmy's yeses were always offhand. It's like the time he had said yes to a trip from Wandiligong to Wodonga in north-east Victoria. He walked, took him two weeks, the valleys between the two towns. Jimmy was not a maybe kid, no hoverings of er, um, perhaps: none of that, he was a yes kid up and down. Life was one big offhand yesfactor so it led to nothing less than Jimmy having a good time. For a while, only for a while. Coz the thing is this: if Jimmy watches a falling leaf he may certainly call it a zigzag or a spiral, but if he watches a butterfly fly he might have to accept just a few more complicated occurrences than yes or zigzag or spiral. The first consequence about hope being quite enough is the famous but ugly string of complicated occurrences, especially to a yesfactor like Jimmy Hazel.

'Girlname! Girlname!' The stupid yellow fuckers out the back of the council depot rang like a chime, ding-dong, in the poor kid's head, poor Jimmy could go far away as Brisbane, and the chime'd still ring between his ears. He got up after resting with the Lucknow echoes under the bridge and drove to Lee Glass-Darlington sister's place. Meryl's place, in Pittwater, where he'd soon start work in the garden.

Just like the David on the box in the Badlands, I wanted to give Jimmy a piece of action in the world of special favours. But the creep Bakks bounced in, a battle that took up a bit of speed at Meryl's sloping gardens at Pittwater, that big bay an hour north of the harbour bridge. More Californians live there than anywhere in Australia, beside the palm trees, regularly butter-flying their prawns on a deck on a Saturday, why coz hope in the City of Angels perhaps surged to a low. Like Lucknow to Jimmy, Los Angeles was filed away in their powderboxes, or burning on their barbeques.

Jimmy Hazel arrived to start work at Meryl's. Lunch was in progress, and Patricia the society girl, a day after a long flight from London, was one of the guests.

Meryl's Memories at Lunch. The Tree of Friendship

Lee's sister dear butterfly, Meryl Glass-Darlington, slid open the drawer and lifted out a small, well-travelled box.

Meryl's mother Rachel had given it to her, and Meryl intended to pass it on to daughter Laura, who would become the fifth owner of the box. It was not teak like David's box, but oak. The box was first spotted on a Saturday morning in the bright sunshine at the markets in Piccadilly in 1892 by Meryl's maternal great-grandmother, and it has gone the twentieth century, down three daughters to Meryl today, in good shape.

As Meryl herself would say: 'To continue to keep the box in good shape it lives in the drawer wrapped in a clean cotton cloth. Not sitting about the house in the open, where fingeracid and salty moisture from the bay await to eradicate it in their slow and certain ways.'

She was right about that. A small box is one of the first things in life to be eradicated, so keeping it safe was an important acceptance of give and take. For Meryl the work of keeping it in good shape was crucial because it carried a crucial cargo.

It carried the cascading jewels of the minds and spirits of mother, grandmother, great-grandma. When handed to daughter Laura, the box would also carry Meryl's own spirit and mind, her memory if you like. It carried the give and take of four generations dear butterfly. It would continue to carry the give and take of another four. Forty if the forty-generation line so desired.

To show how, Meryl took it out of the protective drawer and outside to the table on the verandah, where lunch with the three guests was in progress. The gardens, where the new gardener Jimmy Hazel was at work, filtered large amounts of warmth from a breeze, but not just any unknown breeze, for this was the purple-placemat season, a passage of time in which the breezes were familiar friends. They brought with them a special gift. On the green slopes grew two dozen jacaranda trees, and in the final few days of October, in the last gasp of the tenth month, they breathed overnight into purple fans. When Jimmy Hazel had arrived and caught sight of the sweep of the gardens he said this forest of jacaranda trees made the incline of the gardens look like, from the verandah, the wing of a large butterfly with purple spots.

Meryl needn't have heard him say the compliment out loud,

she liked him right off anyway without Jimmy chickname saying anything. She agreed, it was a good place for lunch, and a great place to usher in the early summer warmth. The day by day deepening of purple was a rush to behold. The barest purple tint commenced in late October, until, in early November, it intensified into a rich purple of such pain that when the whole tree turned, well, it no longer looked real. It was just this sphere in the sunlight, a huge ball buzzing with a hyper-drenched purple. To honour the jacaranda trees their performance Meryl chose to use the purple placemats for November. By December the jacarandas were green again, real-looking trees that danced in the early summer breezes, good enough to hide in, play in the garden, play maybe with the employee.

But today, behind the purple, those other guests glittered in the sunshine. The bay swept broadly, making a seaview that spanned the field of vision. As Meryl would hum, 'The sea sparkles blue blue blue as it feeds a wave of monseigneur Aballte's angels with their favourite snacks—hue upon hue of truth and youth.'

Meryl regarded the bloom as a sign of continuity, as a signal of remembering to preserve certain things cherished. So it was at this moment of the year she would bring out the box, the antique wooden work of clean lines and elegant proportion. It was no bigger than a shoebox. It sported spots of purple on the lid, and it indeed did preserve things from the sea of give and take.

'Looks to me like a box of boiled sweets from the 1920s,' Meryl's visitor Patricia said. Here in Sydney Patricia was called Patsy behind her back.

'Yes, it's, er, antique,' Meryl said, stumbling slightly at Patsy's abrupt presumption, and then Meryl finished confidently, as if Patsy were not there, 'but it's not for sweets, no.'

'It's got to be a sweetbox, I had one as a kid, I kept all my pretend jewellery in it,' Patricia said, bright with confidence.

'No, it's not a sweetbox.'

'Expressive little lid, is the painting on the lid a Toulouse-Lautrec picture?'

'It's a butterfly. Big lilac spots on the wings, see, here.'

Patsy swayed drunkenly and then leaned hard at Meryl across the table. 'May I take a closer look, let me hold it.'

'Hang on, I'm trying to tell you about it.'

'Mine was a boiled cherry box, I ate the boiled cherries,' Patsy said.

'This is not a sweetbox.'

To lighten it up Gwen the other guest said: 'Well thank fuck it's only an illustration because if that butterfly flaps its damn dingle of a wing it would cause a hurricane up in Darwin within a week, har har ya ho ho.'

Gwen joked, but within the week certain things would happen. In any case dear butterfly, a wingflap of a kind was about to occur within the next minute, a bam-good wingflap.

Margaret was the first to sense an accident was on its way. She cast a glance at Meryl and then at Patsy.

Patsy swayed and said: 'Meryl, they were all sweetboxes, Meryl.'

'Look I'm telling you, this is not, I say not, a sweetbox. If you let me damnwell explain.'

Patsy sighed and sat back upright.

Meryl proceeded. She started to give the three guests a brief sense of the box's importance, to bring the contents alive. As she commenced she could feel the welcome vibration from inside the box transfer out to the fingers, she felt the contents begin to shimmy and shake.

'If this box,' Meryl said, 'could talk, the highs and lows and hopes and dreams that we would hear about, they would go back such a long way.'

Problem was, Meryl couldn't continue because Patsy was distracted today, Patsy was dedicated to, keener on, conversation relating to who was up whom in Australia this month than in Meryl's earnest feelings about an old box, plus they were on wine. Lunch was concluded and they were on a third bottle of white. Patsy on Meryl's earnest feelings, especially about an antique box, was breezy irritation flapping about in extreme confidence.

So Patsy was again lurching in search of a fun afternoon, fuck the sweetbox, she said. The box in Meryl's hands subsided back to her lap, and the contents settled down. While Patsy pelted out the latest info on fresh new flings in London, the contents of Meryl's private universe fell into a gentle coma just a short ride north of Sydney. Out on the sparkling bay monseigneur Aballte's angels were being fed their hues of truth and youth, but on Meryl's lap the box retired like a loved and fed doggie, like Pinski, like Henry&Co.

Which was a pity for Patsy. Behind that Toulouse-Lautrec butterfly on the lid of the box lay a lot of material on who was up whom, it was packed with data. It was cascading with the data and dangle of a palm tree grand enough to house every butterfly up and down the Pittwater cape. But Patsy was on, lurching and laughing. All the give and take of a century would have to wait. But then, that's a typical lunch with Patsy back in town. And she was only called Patsy behind her back. To the face she was called Patricia. The give and the take. The warm afternoon became a typical Patsy lunch, became full-on central speculation, when the facts are just to the left over there. In this case, in a little box. All the fine facts, deep in a coma, pushed back to sleep by Patsy's tenacity for a loud afternoon of good fun turning upon a simple visit. Meryl didn't mind. She'd wait till Patsy ran out of breath and she'd try again. Give and take: Meryl's tenacity was a different type to Patsy's. As tenacity goes, it was a languid type, a type that sees angels at a feed. The languidly tenacious can look like a wilting flower dear butterfly, but they only appear beaten down. When they return they sport weapons of pollen, colour and surprise, and pollen can itch, colour can hurt, a surprise can delight. So Meryl let the box slide into her languid lap and they all carried on drinking the cold wine while the angels on the bay nibbled on the hues of truth and youth.

Four friends, breezy gardens, boats on the bay, the lunch was good. When Patsy's phone went off she took the call because a buyer was on the other end. She took the phone into the open grass of the gardens and strolled around in small circles talking charm into the purple sunshine, vitamin D, confidence smooth as a tan. Not everyone could take Patsy, but I liked her, she had the guts and the glory. The caller was keen on a series of canvasses of her hottest painter, Jack Black. So the conversation took a while, keeping Patsy out in the sunshine away from the lunch table.

Meryl, pleased, commenced again. Languid lap gave up the box, and the butterfly drifted up, back to the table. Give and take.

'A box like this,' Meryl said, 'is very important. Great-grandma bought it in London in the 1890s. Since then it has served as a centre for all our memories, we pass things on, good and bad, remembered and savoured, we hand it down only after the stories are told rightly enough to be held together as well as a good carpet. My grandmother then accepted, then my mother, then me, and when I hand it on to Laura, I'll recount all the moments that make our line. It's only a box, but we've made it become our album of triumphs and losses, joys and tragedies.'

'That's a good idea,' Gwen said.

'Our lot,' Margaret said, 'we have, oh God, at least twenty photo albums.'

'Yeah we do too,' Meryl said, 'but the box is a gatherer, Great-grandma said the box would gather our moments where photos would dissipate them away to who knows where. Great-grandma was a bit of a mystic when photography was still new. She felt that a photo steals the moment. According to my grandmother, Great-grandma laid down the law: "This fangled thing a photo is a piece of paper, but the box will live, the box will always be alive." That's what we repeat when we hand it down: "The box will always be alive."'

'What's inside it then?' Gwen asked.

Meryl looked blankly across the table at Gwen for the dumb question. But Meryl didn't hold the stale question against Gwen. 'Memories,' Meryl said.

'So there's nothing in it,' Gwen said. 'I mean, no actual bits of anything, like buttons or pebbles, or a ring, things, you know, just normal objects.'

Patsy came back to the table with her glory and guts and vitamin D. 'Are we on that fekking box again?'

'It's a beautiful notion, Patricia,' Margaret said. 'Give Patricia the idea of it, Meryl.'

'Yes go on Meryl,' Gwen said.

But Patsy had come back to the table in a substantial forward motion, so instead of stopping she carried forward and slumped down next to Meryl, collided with Meryl's shoulder, took up the box from Meryl's hand.

Luckily Meryl had a hold of it.

Patsy tried to prise it out of Meryl's grip.

They pulled back and forth until they were again standing.

The box was in the middle of the table when it burst open. A white cloud exploded onto the table. The cloud hit Gwen on the side of the face and down the shoulder. It made a neat line across her face, one side lunch-ridden make-up, the other side an alabaster white sculpture of a fine nose, exquisite cheekbones and a large almond eye, now blinking in shock. The rest of the powder rode the breeze down the length of the table, covering plates and bowls with a fine white sheen. Patsy's forearms were white, and Meryl's too. Margaret's shoulder caught a sweeping drift of it.

Gwen was white. She held her arms out to double check, both were streaked white. She looked down her chest to her stomach. It had drifted down to her lap. Into the wine glass. She was white all over, except for the half-face that the explosion missed.

'It's powder,' Gwen said. 'It's talc powder.'

'Powder?' Margaret asked looking up at Meryl.

'Yeah, it keeps the box dry and safe. Look what you've done Patricia.'

Patsy was swaying and grinning as she examined her arms. 'Yep, I've blown open your powderbox. Oh damn, holy fukka-roondie, check out Gwen's face.'

Patsy started laughing but the laugh got wilder until she stumbled backwards and fell, rolling onto the lawn in the sunshine. She made no effort to get up, and she lay laughing in a hard, loud, helpless way, four waves of it, glory hurting her guts jampacked with vitamin D.

Margaret went to the kitchen to wash. Gwen went far past the kitchen to the bathroom for a more full-blown wash under the shower.

Margaret helped Meryl clean up the lunch table. For just a mere four girls I gotta say dear butterfly, the lunch mess they'd made was very impressive, high enjoyment lay strewn right across the whole gossip-slab. They transported everything back into the kitchen and then wiped the table down. After that Meryl hosed the table, dried it off, and they reset the table with glasses, a platter of cheese and biscuits and a fresh bottle of wine. Truth and youth were still being enjoyed out on the sparkling blue dining table of the bay. I had nicely tap-tapped young Jimmy Hazel along to get him here, and he was out in the gardens working when he heard the shouts and laughter on the verandah. Jimmy kept working. I couldn't help the guy on the box on the old broken road in America, Meryl's grandad; Bakks had really roughed that one up too good with Maheesha the buffalo demon of evil and chaos. Cremated an all back in Calcutta back in '66. His wife, Meryl's grandma Enid, never got back to being right.

Patsy had got up and stood wavering for a moment. She stumbled down the purple slopes a little to put herself back together.

'Did Patsy come up in your car?' Meryl asked Margaret.

'Yeah, why?'

'Did she talk, at all?'

'What do you mean?'

'What's the matter with her today?'

'Oh you mean all this. Yeah, she's a bit fed up. Says she spent the last week non-stop hearing everyone she had contact with go on and on about irritations, someone hates this, someone hates that, can't stand this, can't stand that. She counted about thirty-eight different individuals banging on about what they can't stand, unprompted, just slinged at without being asked, right in her face with all sorts of stuff, inane stuff too. They did the head in, she says, bigtime.'

'Well then let's have a go making fun of them when she

comes back outside,' Meryl offered.

'Good idea, she'll respond well to that. Sorry about the box you know,' Margaret said.

'No, it isn't a problem,' Meryl said.

'So it's a powderbox?'

'That's what Laura likes to call it.'

Meryl's daughter Laura would be disappointed to have missed Patsy's visit. Laura always liked Patsy, looked up to Patsy a great deal.

'Is Laura still travelling in Turkey?' Margaret asked as she reached up the table for a cloth.

'She's in Edinburgh this month trying to fill her head with a great-grandfather she never met,' Meryl said. 'South really, of Edinburgh, in a village my grandad David came from. He had an affair with a maharaja's daughter when he went to Kolkata, her father found them in bed and the story goes he nearly shot him with a Winchester, went straight back out to fetch the rifle and chased him round the house. My grandad had to flee to Spain for fear of his life. You never know with those moments, one can never know. If the maharaja had let them make music, today I'd be royalty. I'd be an Indian royal with a working class grandad from Pentland Hills in Scotland. Patsy wouldn't know quite how to take me.'

The remark Meryl made, innocently, for fun, with fun, with an ample lighted spirit that day, after lunch in the pleasant light of jacaranda sunshine and the pleasant mists of good wine dear butterfly, is the key of ancestry, a family tree, more than memory. It is the genes, the forming of natures, the making of propensities, making of talents and potentials. The potential to become the custodian of your nectar, or the destroyer of your nectar. More than a gene waiting patiently. It shows how a gene prefers to be ferried down the line. By lovemaking. It's by sex, by fucking, that a gene prefers to ride down the line. These days a gene to be ferried across time doesn't require lovemaking, not strictly, not that much, not at all.

But, had the colonel and the princess back in '45 joined the chromosomes in their respective genes, Meryl and Lee may have had their bones built upon Indian royal blood. Bones and brains tend to be made from sex, it's true, but nowadays sex is not strictly required. The joining of the genes remakes the glorious spectrum of potential in ways that are loved and treasured. New talents, new dancing. Flowing up various kinds of rivers, these new potentials and possibilities are carried across the two equators like gifts. New hopes laced with realities are brought into the world, fresh light brims on the treetops. New loveliness is brought into the sunshine, and all the human possibility forms a fresh edifice further out to the new edges of the world. Or just plush lapses in normality. Lapses that ferry into the new world a chance at better music. Longer nimbler fingers for a virulent playing of the piano that sets alight the spirit of freedom, longer feet for the Olympic pool, a bigger yet more sensitive nose for the scent of the cherished memories. And new loveliness to torment the lover of loveliness. Eyes to torment those who like to project all manner of assumption in to the eyes. Skins glowing smooth as a lost lake, skins to torment. Or just flights. Joining the genes can bring flights of irrevocable presence, flights of irrevocable colour, of irrevocable friendship on the verandah overlooking the gardens that dropped to the inlet.

On the other hand, it may also bring about your query dear butterfly: Who are these custodians of my nectar that always destroy my nectar?

The sex can be all things, can be light, can be gruff, it can be horrendously beautiful, and, under cover of the extinct curtains in the shack in the hills behind Calcutta in '45 it was often horrendously beautiful, as we shall see. It was a two-way Scottish–Indian mugging.

'My grandma,' Margaret said, 'told me she had a fuck with Aristotle Onassis on her sixteenth birthday, he was only seventeen.'

It appears Margaret's grandmother mugged mister Onassis.

'Did she say he was good?' Meryl asked.

'She said he smelled, and he was great and was dirty at it like a kind of horse or a pig or something, a cross between a horse and a pig and a diesel engine.'

'But anyway,' Meryl said, 'Laura's researching grandad's hometown, then she's staying for the festival to perform a solo show she's writing, she plays my grandfather as a buffalo.'

'A buffalo?' Margaret said.

'I knew him briefly, as a young girl,' Meryl said, 'but Laura never knew him so to Laura there's a fascination. She visits my grandma at Lee's place, but Grandma won't talk about him. He lived in Kolkata most of his life where he developed a sort of mixture of worship and fear of the Hindu deity Maheesha, the buffalo demon. The Edinburgh festival commissioned Laura, they were taken by the fact that grandad David was the only Scottish Hindu they'd ever heard of.'

'I never know how to say Edinburra,' Margaret said.

'Me neither, I say Edinbruh-huh.'

'Edinbrr-hugga-huh.'

'Hugga-hugga.'

'What the hell are you two grunting about?' Patsy appeared, banging on the wall with an ice bucket.

'We're trying to figure out how to actually say Edinburrah,' Meryl said.

'Edinbunghole,' Patsy said as she put the bucket down with a bottle of gin.

'I was telling Meryl about your week of grizzlers.'

'Gawd, they were just amazing, every single one of them, holy fukkaroondie, about fifty of them, I hate this I hate that, this pall of sameness.'

'Patricia calls it, calls the sameness I mean, monochromatic inanity,' Margaret said.

'Margaret calls it haterology,' Patsy said, 'I like that better, haterology. I mean, it would've been interesting if the grizzling was worthy of their problems, if there were one or two proper problems, but they hated only bits of utter petty shitty nonsense.'

'But it was the consecutive persistence of it, wasn't it, as well?' Margaret said.

'One after the other, I've never had a week like that, never. I couldn't find the tonic, or the limes for that matter, we need limes and tonic, where the fuck do you keep em?'

'They're in the spare room,' Meryl said.

'What're they doing in the spare room?'

'Hiding from us,' Margaret said. 'I'll get them.'

'This is Lee's favourite drink,' Patsy said, 'She'll be furious. Where is Lee today?'

'Lee's in a state,' Meryl said.

'I've heard the exciting news,' Patsy said. 'So is she well?'

'Not so good, she's been getting restless nights.'

'That's odd, I was informed she made partner at the firm.'

'True, she did.'

'Then what's the problem? She's not the kind to toss and turn over a promotion, she'd handle it like a light switch.'

'Also true, Lee is, what shall we say, Lee's one of a kind. She's capable of throwing a hundred switches at a time that girl. No, it's something else, there's been a disaster at the house.'

'I gotta say: I can't stand that guy of hers, they came to

the gallery in London last month, then off they went, off to Singapore, he's an idiot, what's his name, Rudolph.'

'Well, that's the disaster.'

'Duzzn surprise me,' Patsy said. 'Rudolph, what a fekking name, suits him, Rudy, he's rude and he's a prude. Rude-prude.'

And that was lunch in the sunshine of purple and green. An exploding powderbox of give and take among friends linked up to a patch of the Scottish diaspora of Sydney. Reason I recount the lunch dear butterfly, is, since I too am a box, it will be sweet that I too have these, um, contents. Let me show you them briefly, they will help to solve the mystery of locating The Exchange dear butterfly. Where we have the answer to the query: What the heck are these custodians?

Beautiful Wood

Whatsmore we boxes can, and we do, exchange the contents, as it will become horribly apparent, coz what we are, after all is said and done, is we are pirates moving piles of good and bad smells. Not all our contents are the same, by any means, massively varied, in fact horribly so. For instance that nasty box Bakks the Taker on the steps of the hacienda.

His own big strength is taking the smallest negative feeling and whacking it round until it grows into hate. Primary tool? Memory.

Even from a teeny-weeny memory. Bakks can take a single nasty quip, make it into road rage, coz he's made from good and bad smells, make that into divorce, make that into burning down a house. Whether the, um, contents are lurid, putrid, fresh, sweet, we boxes don't mind, for a few of us it is a truism that the more putrid the better, yum. Yep, we don't mind, we swap the, um, um, memories all the time, the memories of these blundering, bumbling, squishy inheritors. And that's in fact our sole purpose. Nothing else to do, see, for a self-respecting box, so we're very, very good at it, hustling memory from here to there, selling the stuff on the open market at wow fuckme prices.

Yep, we boxes are the dudes of the open market when it comes to the business of trading in memory; we pirates prefer the open market, tho no-no, we won't deal in memories if they've been securitised. No, sorry to say, securitisation is a whopping filthy business coz you can't untangle the stuff to check what you're getting and giving, securitisation just fucks up the magic wand of give and take. Any ol box can sell securitised rubbish, but only us better boxes can cause a cherished memory to fly. So, owing to this fine trading ability of us better boxes of good wood, you'd rightly assume you could nip round the corner and hock a box. But just go try it when you're free. The pawn shop guy'd be just as dumb as that Londoner Patsy. I mean, the disrespect she showed that poor damn purple-lidded box at lunch, beggars belief. She'll keep. Wait till vitamin D Patsy sees what's on the cards back at her gallery in London, yep, she'll keep reasonably well, like a salted anchovy keeps after being hustled from the deep by Mendoza fifty years before.

If you treat a box badly it is liable to behave badly, or, put bluntly, if you treat it like shit you're liable to smell the shit, and if you paint it purple you have a purple shitbox: these are the facts of life, specially if life is memory.

Memory ought to be respected, like the farmer used to insist, Ellie-Isabela's father; if you prefer having a pleasant day, memory ought to be respected. Talk, say the people you love, say the people you like. Try telling that to Patsy. I'll agree quickly, Patsy can be this rub-em-wrong plenty rude smartie, but that's Meryl's judgement, not mine. I like Patsy, guts, glory, and a gungho sniggerer of immense confidence. Patsy could run my gallery of boxes anytime if I cared to have a gallery of boxes to run. Plus, my given career was gunna help her out a bit. Unless that evil fucker Bakks got there first, if he got there first he was gunna, he was liable to, take take take.

Hup Two Three

No, a box is one of the first things in life to get eradicated just like Ellie's mind and her old farms, by a bit of sun, a season of salty air. And fingeracid, from fingerers like the London bon-bon Patsy rubbing her vitamin D all over the place. Eradicated. I resent that, yes, but then again, with nothing to do but make use of our primary tool, that is, sling a slice of hatred from here to there, hup two three, we get a lot done before being, um, eradicated. Call it the give and take. I prefer the giving, and Bakks prefers the hustling. Bakks, hatey majora.

Everything, everything, comes in a box—booze, chocolates, bananas—so there's plenty of us, we're everywhere. And once the produce is removed we fill up with those other contents. Sort of automatically, thanks in no small way to what the primdicks in Soho called diasporas, carting lives across the two nimble equators in all manner of nimble boxes. Lee the saucy dancer's nephew, colonel David, was one of a small crew of Scots in Calcutta at that time, the Scottish diaspora of north-east India.

Talk about diaspora, yep, I've had so many different diasporas shoved and loved into the space under my lids that I can say a simple thing like 'no thanks' or 'yes please' in all these wonky ways. To get rid of us: it ain't possible. Eradicate, fumigate, scrub with soda, whatever you like, the gig is we are hup two three, lined with memory. And memory is like water, hup two three, three states: cherished and loved; lost and forgotten; bitter and destructive.

Take a quick look at what I've had stored under my lids dear butterfly. Notes, letters, petals, cards, rings, stones, hoarded bits and pieces from love and loss, plenty of memories. Pencils. Paper. Rudolph used me for his sallow collection of business cards at one point, until Lee threw them back into his briefcase and then threw his briefcase into the pool. And the Rangoon bell, ding-dong. A hundred times a day all over the city, an owner like Meryl might tell a friend like Patsy: If only that box could tell us what happened.

Gotta Mix

So in a simple word, what are we boxes? We are The Exchange of all exchanges. And let me make it huelessly clear from the start.

The open market is by far our favourite, whether it's a guy on a deserted road under a sun defining mercy, or a guy saying goodbye to his butterfly prawn barbeque afternoons in a rather dry patch of dreams where chickname! chickname! rings out from behind the council rubbish tip from time to time. We boxes operate across everything, across the high seas and across the mountaintops we boxes make em happy, from the Golfo de Valencia in Spain to the little bay of Pittwater, free to fly, best job in the world as they say in a moment where humility goes to pot like Pinski&Co. Plus, we have wings, most of us anyway, the double-lid. Wings, so that means? No borders, attitudes, bans, passports, and hup two three no restrictions of state, caste or creed to bother about, just sell the stuff to the highest bidder and bugger even skin colour. Cash it in the bling. Thin-skinned, thick-skinned, crocodile skin, buffalo hide, we care not a jot for bow-wow, or for permission, or fumigation, cash it in.

We are the great unwashed, the very dirty pirates of the high seas and the high slopes. Across the hungry seas and across the ravenous mountaintops. We boxes throw around all manner of stuff—love, hate, prejudices, phone calls—we confuse the shit out of our customers. But then there it is, it's easy to confuse squishy wingless wonders made out of a galaxy of quaint prejudices. We're smarter, we boxes, coz we haven't a single molecule of the ooze of bigotry, high class, low class, racial or religious. Same goes for all the outer oozes, hate, love, laughter, we have no weaknesses, no strengths; well maybe I lie. A tad, I lie. We winged wonders have outer oozes, we do. As it will soon become horribly apparent, we like outer oozes. I try like the sky to give a person a key to that world of special favours in the outer oozes, and the creep gets in the way, Bakks. Ready and eager to crumble young David's cherished memories into bitter chips of recollection. El creepo and I had a chat. Yes it will soon become horribly apparent, the battle of Bakks the creep and I, that started on the old road on the badlands of South Dakota where Bill the cop went to collect that Scottish pre-Hindu sitting alone, a boy in tears under the dusty sun of mercy. The sun has very small power on the outer oozes. The sun of mercy is very small compared to the mercy we pirates can show, we show mercy like a big universe. Example, David.

David Darlington's Cherished Dirt Saved

A final note on the box. As a breed we boxes come up pretty well. Here's why. Nothing can move a memory from a mind to a mind, not like us. We move stuff from a powderbox behind the forehead, to another powderbox behind the forehead, like nothing else. No invention in the cutting-edge high-tech frontier can throw memories around like we can. Not the web, not a satellite, not fibre optics, not a mirror, not a Blackberry, not plane train scooter, and certainly not the customers themselves, fudge fudge; nothing can hurl juicy slices of memory around like we boxes can. Over the seas, over the mountaintops. Wings. I mean, everything's private right?

Take the iPod as a pleasant comparison, a very cool and sweet tool that transfers and stores heaps of good stuff; it sucks, keeps and spits info like a hundred libraries or museums, everything is iPoddable. Everything except of course a memory. A fact as plain as day: you simply cannot iPod a memory from one mind to another mind. Final fact, nail it home: we boxes can, and we do. A lot. With glee. Just like I did in David's room at the hacienda with his memories of the maharaja's daughter in that shack of extinct curtains, memories drifting out of my woody safehold like a scent off a shoulder, drifting up into David's powderbox to bring alive those lost nights behind Calcutta.

So hey-ho and ding-dong the fusty world of boxes, we make

the world of highspeed high-tech look as if they use scrappy fishing nets recycled off a lost beach to catch a memory, to transport a memory. Storing and recalling binary language just ain't memory.

And the reason we're better than the binary bagpipes and their high-tech world at transporting a memory? We're unaddicted to fudging. And we have this, um, special understanding, let's say. We understand, we comprehend, that the sleek world of information, knock-knock, just ain't memory, whatever information: talk, chatter, the one-on-one criminality of the phone, whisper-clatter, bye-bye, hello, hallo, hillo, hullo. They've got the binary language, but we've got all the other diasporic yumyum languages that help the memories burn or rot, or sweeten and fly, because from the things we've had shoved and loved into us to store, from the things we've seen and heard, we've got twanguage, pranguage, haranguage, banguage, ganguage, winguage, slinguage, songuage, and there that's it, that's the reason we boxes are better than the binary bagpipes at transporting a memory. We've got the jungarummy jiddle, they don't. Do the jungarummy jiddle, get the glee, mix the secrets. Gotta mix.

Good Mix, Good Mix

Consider the contrast. You may, for instance, ask my ex-hippy friends at the space agency NASA to ship thousands of tonnes of grand information off to the edge of the Milky Way, and they'd respond with immense excitement. They'd say, 'You betcha we will, we're the experts, man O man, do we have wings, man what a fun job, man do we take cosmic cake for breakfast every day, youngster.'

And they'd be under the exciting impression that they'd be pole-vaulting this valuable cargo across the great chasm of uncharted space, wingless ding-dongs. Rocketing the stuff across the great hallways of time. Blasting off the planet's pull using the power of bucketloads of that Arabian oil. Sending the cargo off into dreamland with high hopes, with all that intent, with sweet, romantic grandeur, moving through the vast empty void, a solitary bearer of info, and the project will rightly fill the hearts of all concerned with an epic sense, an epic sense of homecoming. They'd be giddy with magical loveliness, my hippy friends at the space place NASA. But let's face it, the stuff they're shipping, it just ain't memory. No way NASA could do the quiet stuff: a butterfly hitching a ride with a box of memories to find out who the heck they are, these custodians of the nectar.

For moving memory round the place, it's us, plain ol boxes. We're pastmasters at carting a memory, hup two three, the jungarummy jiddle, glee, glee. I would ask, for example, Jimmy Hazel chickname-chickname to look at it like this. Feeling like shit today? Remembering how they treated you like shit last week? Bakks can help. He'll take last week and jam it into your powderbox so hard you'll want to kill em all, dear Jimmy. To my envious friends at NASA: everything comes in a box, everything, computers, printers, televisions, shoes, tins of soup, matches. Slophouse to shithouse, life comes in a box. A ding-dong winged one. And that, to us boxes, is beautiful. Alternatively, the most beautiful thing in the known universe might be the act of thinking. But I doubt it coz we boxes, we seen, honestly, seen so much of that synaptic brain cell electricity stuff, electrical elegance, electrical privacy, result being, thinking when compared to throwing around memories, thinking seems dull, seems lifeless, solo ho-hum. Gotta mix. I mean where the heck's the mixing in thinking?

Where the heck's the mixing in Jimmy vowing to himself: That photo in the lounge of Meryl's sister, wow, I'm gunna get Meryl's sister, Lee Glass-Darlington, yes I am, and may the carnal forces underneath this garden lend me a very expert helping hand.

Where's the mixing in a mission like that? With us, boxes.

Whenever there's a hint of negative vibes in a powderbox, Bakks can ramp it up until the poor fucker of a target is spitting bile all week. Whenever there's a hint of positive vibes in a powderbox, I can ramp it up, me, Bob the box. We can catalyse. We precipitate. Gotta mix. But we're the opposite, Bakks and Bob. I do my own motto, 'Make Love Not War.' Bakks does his motto, 'Hit em in the Mouth.'

Patsy's Carnal Mission

And anyway, yes it's true that the bonbon Patsy couldn't stomach Lee's guy, Rudolph Central. True absolutely, but that's most likely because Bakks helped Patsy to recall a teeny little thingy: that Rudolph Lowenstein the jewels trader, mister Central, reminded her of Remple Fekdin, or of Remple's horrible sister Catherine, or of both somehow. But that's a peachy prejudice jammed up by Bakks, even for a tipsy bonbon; if a powderbox dislikes, she's showing it, and if she likes, she's also showing it.

I should show the open market exactly the reasons why

gungho Patsy the art dealer wanted to vomit at the sight of Rudolph the bloke who bought the goldrush house a mile from Meryl's place on the bay of calm brimming with a Californian diaspora. Certain key fellow boxes cannot agree with me, like Bakks, but so what, big deal. I make a start, watch, they'll join right in, specially Bakks and his team at work upon Patsy's powderbox in that ugly way Bakks favours. I mean, everything's private in that world of memory, right?

Gotta mix, right?

Patsy ripping off her top and her pants won't exactly happen without some kind or another kind of mixing, right?

Tops and Pants Torn to Shreds, with Gratitude

Start by throwing around a few bits: all will become horribly apparent, and my colleagues are shit at resisting temptation, especially Bakks, O Bakks, he of even less scruples than the rest of us dusty pirates, he of high-wind ill will. He who feels he's the buffalo demon of all buffalo demons, loves chaos, loves evil.

Won't take long, the energy gathers pace and the next moment we're all in it, boxes abuzz in and around The Exchange, floating suggestions from powderbox to powderbox, hup two three, jungarummy jiddle, frantic glee, throwing private stuff around the shores of hopes and dreams. Patsy would belt out howls of thanks if she knew who or what to thank. Jimmy chickname would howl thanks, so would David at the hacienda. Every powderbox everywhere who might be secretly dedicated to a private little mission would almost go purple with the concentration in gratitude burning outwards from the inside, out to the cheeks and the hot skin.

But they can't howl any gratitude at us, because we boxes do not intrude. As you will soon see dear butterfly we boxes vanish. Far into the shadows and cellars of the second equator. Until all the mad rush of the powderboxes dominates. Soon there will be not a box in sight, for that is where, at The Exchange, we turn the jungarummy jiddle generators up high. So that the mixing is maxing. Patsy gets what she wants. Jimmy Hazel steers his mission into just where he wants it. David Darlington may still get what he wants. And David's granddaughter Lee Glass-Darlington may get what she wants. Ellie might get Mendoza the way she wants him.

Before the fingeracid and salty moisture from those shores of luck&calm can sneak along to eradicate us boxes, we simply set off into the invisible distance to do what we do, hup two three, hup two three. Across the seas and over the mountaintops, wings, across the two equators wrapped around the ball in space, ding-dong and how's the time.

Across the equator, and across that second equator wrapped round the globe north–south, bringing day and night all the time, eternally. Bringing with it new mixing, in the moments of its blurry edge, moving along at zero degrees, all twenty-four thousand kilometres of the journey, renewing the journey every twenty-four hours, across the seas and deserts, across the cities and diasporas, bringing intimations of infinity, bringing the gift of possibilities. That lovely old equator number two, north–south, separating now from then. Helping create the memories, nicely creating the past and the present, so that we boxes can conduct our pleasant work in those precious moments of possibility, right there in the blurry edge of the second equator. We boxes fling our stuff across it all. We do. A lot. Most especially we work well in those fleeting moments of dusk and dawn, where the universe is expanded into those sweet longings for this and that, hunger. Feeding time. Gotta mix, hup two three. Do the jungarummy jiddle, mix the secrets. Fling em across the two equators.

Even across the blurry boundaries of what the primdicks at the Soho club Suave's like to think of as the diasporas.

Even across the yawning blurred breath of a daybed or a nightbed.

Even across the blurred shadows of a fumigated pantry in Ellie-Isabela's tiny dark room of ancestral brightness.

It's exactly in there, in that blurry space of remembering and forgetting, that we boxes catch the illuminations. Like Carlos the hacienda kid was to do, Sunrise Sunset. He didn't quite know it yet, but he was taking with him Ellie-Isabela's backroom understandings, her illuminations, out into the world.

And also this: we boxes keep the wave of monseigneur Aballte's angels busy with their favourite snacks, so the truth is, their beautiful intrusions into purple hillsides of carnal hope are minimal. Peaceful yes, but minimal.

O Bobbo

What I call myself is quick to say dear butterfly: Bob, Bob the box, coz I do exactly that, bob round the world making mischief like a foul pirate, and burning the roof off that open market, the market of dreads and tragedies. The one and same, I am the teak box colonel David lifted in his room back in the hacienda, yep.

A window to his cherished days past, including the days with the maharaja's daughter and her friends who loved everything illicit, try this try that, fuck this fuck that, set the butterflies free, the royal stray had a loyal following.

How to blame em, even graciously or gently. Princely offspring desperately need to exit a formal education from time to time, go smell the world outside, go gamble on the glee, get the glee, aromatic and rancid. Plus, I was a nifty window to all the other cherished days that David wanted to travel back to, hup two three, wings. All he had to do was shut the door to his room, and peer quietly into my woody safehaven, and he'd receive anew the pleasures of that old shack with its extinct curtains.

He could even smell the scent of the Calcutta dust upon the weave of their cotton, those paltry curtains, worn out, exhausted by the secrets they'd maintained up in the hills.

Nowadays? Bobbing around at will and whim, O Bobbo, that's me hup two three, with Rangoon stationmaster's dented bell still intact, dangerous as it always was, ding-dong and how's the time.

Nowadays I can safely say I've been around, seen this, seen that, I seen more diasporas than the colonel tasted princess kisses in the green hills behind Calcutta in that smelly shack. There's no such stupid thing as a diaspora anyway. It's just a dumb-arse way for birthright powderboxes to calling-card the implication of sadness or dislocation upon non-birth powder-boxes. Everything's a diaspora, that's what a good wooden box like me can understand over time, over the run of hasty-paste.

The Tree of Togetherness Money

The only true diaspora, the true sadness, if sadness is expected to be the core of a diaspora, is a madness diaspora, when a clan pretends not to have any madness running round the family tree, a fallen seed in the dust is the diaspora. Scientists call it a genetic defect. In labs around the world, across the two equators, they call it a genetic defect, not from displeasure or disrespect, but factually, and they study all manner of genetic defect in order to improve the human potential dear butterfly.

If all the world's presidents, plus all the fucktoid dictators, could work in unison, together, they could explore that potential; well at least they could bandy about quite a large sum of togetherness money to give their scientists. Those bombs and ships and planes are very expensive, what drudgery locking up so much money in metal nightmares when it could be poured upon the dreams of human potential.

Skip a generation, skip two, won't matter, the only true diaspora the universe has ever known is the madness diaspora, including large mountains of metal nightmares staring one another down, and including a broken branch of that family tree lying on the dust in the shade of the tree. No such thing as an ethnic diaspora, an ethnic diaspora is just an imaginary loophole for birthright powderboxes to chuck around. It's just a stupid word for texture and colour, not skin colour, but mental colour, culture colour, a generalisation. A bingo word made to stand for migration and hope and those who therefore must—it is perceived by birthright powderboxes—have a longing or belonging for elsewhere, a memory for elsewhere, a weakening magnet for elsewhere.

In any case the plain fact is that across both the equators the powderboxes have been in solution since the beginning of hasty-paste, gotta mix. At least since gorilla times. In solution, mixing, rivers of memory. If you ain't watching the second equator from where you were born you must therefore be a diaspora, so you an me dear butterfly, we is the wooden box diaspora. Coz we is flying nice across it all. Over the treetops hup two three. Ding-dong and how's the time.

A Hundred Years and More

Made in 1895 roundabout, and the dual lid, the wings, still in top condition, no ding-dong doubt on that, because back in the days when I had those owners they were fine owners. The Calcutta industrialist. David the Scottish Hindu. His glorious aunt Lee from Glasgow, singing her way into powderboxes in London's Soho night after night, wearing very little. The wild singer perhaps the most renowned member of what primdicks round Soho town called the Glasgow diaspora, singing hard and loud but beautifully, with such a force of elegant gusto, enchanting her audience: 'I Seen What Charlie's Got O Yeah Baby.'

And the scratched up dented bell that her nephew David, years later in a dusty village in Spain, lifts into a hot afternoon, whispering: 'Ding-dong and how's the time.' There certainly was keen choice in that little question for David, a knowing choice, a wise, hardcore choice. He didn't whisper what's the time, or where's the time, or who's the time, or even why's the time, no, his choice was how's the time. O yes, how's the time, because that's what O Bobbo slung at the guy's powderbox coz 'how' is the most giving of all. In the stakes of give and take, 'how' is the best for conducting the giving. How's the time says how's life, how's the party, how's the maharaja's daughter, how's things. Saying how's the party does what, it presumes, bigtime, presumes yer havin a party.

David's wild aunt Lee had no problem presuming it was all a party so I don't see why her colonel nephew ought to be deprived of the same ding-dong presumption driving his ol Scottish mojo. Partytime Davo, yep, yer kin say that again. Gotta mix.

Besides, one must encourage the attempt. Avoid falling for the old trap of making the claim: 'Well, that's who I am.' No, not good enough, you may soon need to stroll and learn, grow, adopt changes, dust off the extinct windows of perception, acquire quicker, finer, better ways of seeing things, ways like: 'How's the time.' Yer can't just sit back and mutter, 'O well aunty Lee, this is who I am.'

O well friend, this is who I am.

O well uncle, this is who I am.

O well father, this is who I am.

O well mother, this is who I am.

O well lover, this is who I am.

O well cousin, this is who I am.

O well brother, this is who I am.

O well sister, this is who I am.

No way, not good enough. Gotta mix. Gotta bumble and mingle.

As my hippy friends at NASA would say. Flux man, flux like the world man, underneath every mountain you see is a molten goo, been oozing from that big Hawaii volcano continuous, every day every week, since '83, changing the distance between mountaintops every second of every day, the world changes, man O man, quantum mechanics ain't just a party in space, it's flux, change along with it.

Like aunt Lee always said, 'When you dance nice they hate you, when you dance rough they love you.'

And then there's another thing, the era of blurry rolls before aunt Lee. I was owned by her lofty father, the teak merchant who loved batting bad jokes at his staff to see if they caught his real meaning, and he's the guy who commissioned me in the first place, a commission given to the celebrated Rangoon boxmaker Arnie Colchester.

Arnie Colchester, no less than the most famous boxmaker anywhere, Rangoon to Shanghai, the box business followed the man's shirt sleeve. The decimated Burmese goldrush of teak, a wood that aunt Lee claimed: 'Were it given, this wood, a chance to sing, this regal teak, it'd be the most dangerous tenor in all Scotland and let me tell you right straight you don't fuck with a dangerous tenor.'

Not only did Arnie make the finest box, he made a lasting box, take me. Arnie banged and sawed and bevelled and planed so damn good that even on my hundredth birthday back in '95, a time when I was busy as hell throwing memories across the equator, Arnie's design for the dual lid, my wings, held it all together like pure destiny. Yep, we boxes get a lot done before getting eradicated, specially when you've seen a few things fly hup two three over a span like a hundred years.

David Darlington Runs for His Life

And right there's the nub, the nib, the hub. We teak boxes outlast a line of ten, twenty, even a hundred lives. So it ain't only high-tech that I seen, O no. Lowtech too, seen a lotta stuff come, seen a lotta stuff go. From the telegram the young David used on accepting the job at the hacienda, fleeing for his life from Calcutta, leaving behind all his belongings except O Bobbo and the clothes he had on for the trip, telegram goes, telephone arrives. Gramophone, TV, and space, yep, the wars, the love and the music, right up to those binary bagpipes the computers. Yep, I am one layer upon the next of habits, of slang, of dreams, hopes, secrets; ain't nothin yet beaten the box.

If you ain't yet been eradicated extincto after that amount of the second equator rolling round the goo-ball in space, you get to be proud of a kid like Sunrise Sunset. Okay, he wasn't going to inherit wings, but wow was he going to inherit one hell of a big pot at the end of a rainbow. Like aunt Lee says, no, sings, with all the might of a chunk of the constellations, sings and dances while she grips her thin pants, hitching the pants up her wily bumcrack, the Glaswegian diasporic bumcrack that sends the primdicks in the Soho audience wild, as she paints the Soho stage a darker shade of soprano: 'I Seen What Charlie's Got O Yeah Baby.' Or her other song, 'Youth Mouth'. Aunt Lee, being a healthy Scot, would claim her Youth Mouth song made even greater sense to these tougher audiences round Soho. Following from 'yooth,' she'd sing 'mooth,' and following from 'mouth' she'd sing 'yowth,' pelting it out: 'I Got Mouth and Yowth, She got Mooth and Yooth, Which One Yer Gunna Have Today Ey Buster?' Lee would sing as loudly as she could, dancing like a five-legged festival, blam-blam, ding-dong slap-slap.

New Owner, Fresh Dirt

The Calcutta industrialist lord, Miles Banford, who claims David was his greatest and wisest source of nourishment, his greatest friend, knew of the Arnie Colchester reputation, and so that there's why he kept me after they sent poor David's worn-out suitcase back to his wife Enid in Scotland. The industrialist was a surprise. He understood a bit about boxes, what we store, the layers, the lore. Keeping me was his way of remembering the bright times he'd had with his great friend. He kept on hunting down the royal stray, but the maharaja's daughter was shooting out of the circles and into the smell of the world. She tried hard to score David's teak Colchester, but the industrialist got the better of the princess, and he became the secret but proud, um, owner. Sturdy sleek teak designed by Arnie Colchester, hot dang.

Stick Em Up Baby

But most of all, the biggest reason those binary bagpipes have nothing on a timeless ol teak box like me is my lineage dear butterfly, a lineage that can shoot out one or two obnoxious blobs of info, ping splatter pop.

Imagine for one second what I've picked up after being handed around for a hundred years, owner to owner. Taste being nine-tenths of the task of equating the past and present and future. As colonel David always liked to say when he returned to his favourite Calcutta dockside den: 'The tastebuds of the soul, yes everyone's got a different take on the same piece of cake.'

He had a point, the dearly loved colonel, sitting in his favourite bar, spilling his traveller's romantic wisdom across the table, on the subject of the particularity of tastebuds, to bright new arrivals rolling into town looking for action. The tastebuds of the soul indeed do generate the vast constellation of memories hurling across the two equators, different memories, particular memories. Gotta mix n mingle. Do the sweeter jungarummy jiddle.

So imagine the spread, the tastebuds of the soul that I've picked up after being handed round for a hundred years. In all that haste, imagine the tastebuds roiling with glee at the sweet and the savoury.

First. Made as a Colchester.

Second. Aunt Lee's father, a Rangoon poker man by night and a smart trader by day, mainly teak. Ready to rustle up the hup two three, the jungarummy jiddle. Mixing the secrets, blending the secrets, tasty.

Third. I'm given to aunt Lee. Migrates from Glasgow down to Soho with her songs neatly stored in the teak box her dad gave her, becomes a wily dancer, not a stripper, but what she gladly calls a 'saucy dancer,' creating her own material for the darkened spotlit little Soho stage that paid her rent month after month: 'I Seen What Charlie's Got O Yeah Baby'. 'Mooth Youth, Mouth Yowth'. Soho in the thirties.

The stage where she worked the audience into a frenzy was a fun club full of good sorts who knew how to laugh well at all the haste of the world, and they all loved Lee dancing before and after the jazz bands played. There was fun like fun was a sky: roulette, cards, booze, smokes, and, to give the place a point of flinty difference from the other clubs around Soho, Nigel the owner even let you order a pot of tea if you wanted. It was therefore acknowledged as a civilised place, not a boghole that bullied the pennies from your pocket, a cool, suave little place. Nigel called it Suave's. Suave's of Soho 1936. Packed night after night to the rafters with diasporas from the empire's far-flung post office thumpers and singers ready to be filled with joy and fame and beauty, filled with love and press articles, but it was Lee who got the press.

Fourth. I'm handed to her favourite nephew, David Darlington of the hacienda on the coast. From gentle David Darlington I got a taste of South Dakota and Calcutta and the hacienda of children where giant orange butterflies like you declare, 'I am the Present.' But I also got the past, I got the lingering aroma of a maharaja's daughter whispering out from my lid, my wings: 'My beautiful foreign man with his long head, long chin, so serious, so shy, my father would cut you into nine pieces if he found us like this in his favourite childhood shack.'

Which the maharaja tried, running round the house with his Winchester shooting at the young Scot.

Fifth. Colonel David's friend the industrialist Miles Banford, who followed the princess up and down the calendar of stately lunches. From him I got the dirt on how the timeship of that great slab of lovely timber the north-east seaboard of India was run, governed and protected from crass outsiders with their new, ultra-modern intentions. Goodship Calcutta had its way, and if you didn't know what it was you might as well piss off back to Knightsbridge and bother your favourite cafe every weekend. And from the cool industrialist I got the taste for finance, pennies and pounds.

Sixth. Colonel David's wife Enid, and from dear Enid I got the most wise dirt on desire, on how desire has its own sneaky tricks to ignore a freezing cold climate.

But from the saucy dancer's teak dealer dad I got a couple of extra tips. A month after Arnie Colchester delivered me to her dad, a sudden trip to Shanghai. Her dad got a telegram. He must come to China at once. There was a big deal going down. Hundreds of tonnes of teak were needed. At the Rangoon docks he jumped on a schooner. In Shanghai he quickly found that the project was far larger than he'd even dreamed, and he found he had to live in Shanghai for over a year to complete what turned out to be his life's biggest deal. O Bobbo sailed along, carrying her dad's favourite accoutrements. Today, Shanghai a century later, what glittering changes from the English Shanghai. Today the magnificent gardens of Shanghai city dear butterfly, are a sight to behold. Shanghai's architecture, a sight to behold. The museum is a giant cooking pot, pure white, a massive building in the shape of a cooking pot coz that's what the city is fabled for, cooking its delicious signature meals. A round, rotund cooking pot, what architect thought that up was a clever architect. Today, all the children of the Middle Kingdom are keen celebrators of the achievements of the ancient dynasties, even more proud of the achievements of their great cities, like Shanghai.

So yeah, after being handed around for a hundred years owner to owner I gradually gleaned all the songuage and language and haranguage and ganguage and slinguage and pranguage and twanguage and winguage needed to fling a memory or two round the joint. Needed to do the jungarummy jiddle. The stuff that I gleaned in Shanghai was the very beginnings of all the rich layers that the greatness of the Middle Kingdom had to offer in the last days of the nineteenth century puttering into the twentieth. China. What a blazing hoot. Cusping on the readiness to rock and roll into the world once again after a couple of thousand years of slumbering dynasties gradually replacing each other's tastebuds.

After all, those tastebuds of the soul, what they do, is they brighten up a box. As for eradication, well, what a yuk topic. Expiry date: not known. Extinction be fucked. Extincto may wish to go to pot, like Pinski.

Gotta mix. Gotta hup two three. Do the jungarummy jiddle. If I last another hundred, two hundred, then I'll say right now that those tastebud inputs into my lids are gonna mix together so much that whatever the powderboxes wanna say, wanna indicate, communicate, will be next to unrecognisable, even for my high-tech NASA dudes. For instance. We cannot keep buffalo figurines; flush that buffalo figurine down the toilet. In a hundred years: swim snorter hornhead into yukriver, nada nada keep keep, squish burn melt, ding-dong ye centre melter.

Even the odd genetic miracle might sound different. Happily tho, we're only up to owner number six. In all the haste of a flight on the placemat dear butterfly, we're only up to owner number six.

And owner number seven. Owner seven, naked and traumatised, is just round the corner. Moving step by step nearer to Jimmy Hazel's mission, his urge.

If one looks at the many urges that have fallen into my unprimed abyss, if one glimpses all the impulses spoken, whispered, sung, hummed, shouted and hissed, one would see not just the tangy main branches of fertile diasporas from far-flung pantries, one would also see the sweet darkness of lost pathways and long nights without end, and the width of human hope and human neglect, the give and the take. Ellie-Isabela's magic wand, the Give. Henry&Co shipping shells to the other dogs. Which they bingle off to yet other dogs near the road.

But give and take does more than make the world go round, makes more than the second equator roll round with its blur of dusk and dawn; give and take also lights up the tastebuds, specially when those tastebuds find their way into my unprimed abyss. Nice place, my woody abyss, Arnie made it, and the others filled it, full. Full of the dirt and tang of what the hell's going on round the joint from time to time. Even if it is all a bit too hasty. But the one thing even we boxes can do nothing about, no influence at all unfortunately, is hasty-paste. Nope, we can do nothing about time. Besides, who the hell is supposed to be able to resist the tanged aroma of a teak-lined abyss? Patsy as she rips off her top? Jimmy as he lays a carnal path in the purple gardens? Don't think so.

Oxley

Among us better boxes dear butterfly, is another wooden box that specialises in urges like Patsy's and like Jimmy's: Oxley.

Which is odd, because Oxley likes nuance. Nuance of the give and take, more specifically the nuance of give.

When you have no nuance you have nothing, reason is the dynamic that changes with every passing moment. To catch a passing day requires nuance, observing a change in a friendship, a change, that is, of a memory, requires nuance, Oxley likes the nuance of give. He knows all about the slippery nature of hasty-paste, but he certainly has the grip on the nuance of give.

The nuances of making a deal at The Exchange are, to us boxes, one of the most payable things. Without nuance, no deal. I mean, just because you apprehend a cube it doesn't mean you've seen a box, to see a box you need the nuances of boxworld, of memories mixing like gas in the ether of The Exchange. Blunt bombast might look nice at first blush, but you need nuance to truly impress the powderboxes of the jacaranda slopes where the sun shines dappled purple and green.

It's no good saying 'purple.' Which purple? Or green. Which green? Good ol Oxley.

Oxley is a picnic box from around 1915. Many a picnic box has hosted many an urge, good urges, bad urges, grimy urges, special urges, heady urges, withheld urges.

His wings perform a concertina outwards to fanly expose all manner of picnic comforts that boost the urges. Salt and pepper shakers for stirring nipples, teapot for rubbing the thighs, cups and saucers for catching the gasps and spits, knives for cutting out livers, forks for piercing the neck, spoons for sipping all manner of moisture, tub of marmalade for squelching the armpit, tub for the butter to tan the belly, napkins to tie at the neck, mustard pot for those with a low register, corkscrew to threaten, a steel nutcracker to carry it out, toothpick case, wine glasses, gin glasses, all strapped in tight by leather and brass and pop-down buttons. A lot of thin pewter strips of lining in ol Oxley, so he glitters in the dappled picnic shade, quietly getting filled with layer upon layer of chit-chat spanning the century of hasty-paste. Woes and laughter spill over sweet wines and gin&tonics, Oxley flings the memories around as good as any box, hup two three, jungarummy jiddle.

Oxley's has been a world that rolled more slowly than mine, owner to owner, over sun-dappled picnic secrets, picnic activities and picnic promises where golden moments and tawdry moments were very often rolled into one ding-dong day of pranguage and songuage and haranguage. It would be easy to understand Oxley's entire world of memory trading as the sun-dappled land of breezes and flowers and flowing grasses, a shimmering world of ponds and lakes, but for one owner. Had all the picnics, this owner, strange guy, every single picnic, in a windowless basement. So Oxley's has been a trade of two general varieties of infusion: a dappled sunlight variety, and a dark mildewed variety. But before Oxley commences any hup two three he psyches himself up with the most pleasantly repeated spring of a question that had been asked around him since 1915 when he was first built and purchased like a boiled sweet: 'Like a jink? Let's get jinking,' and off the Oxley trade goes, over the seas and over the mountaintops to give the fretting powderboxes mired in the uncharted depths of hasty-paste a hint here and there of what the hell was going on with their missions and other urges.

It is Oxley that always insists on cyxmix. Cyxmix was it, he says. He says without cyxmix there will be nothing. Cyxmix is even more central, crucial, than nuance. For us boxes to properly service the powderbox urges, we simply have to have a handle on cyxmix. It remains the most reliable of the memory currencies. Along with scent, cyxmix is a powerhouse. Okay, scent can make a ding-dong transport occur in the blip of a second, but it is cyxmix that makes that transport glow into a cherished memory.

Glimmer with reach, extent, saturation, duration. Depth. Distance, to put it simply. Scent can catch the memory, but cyxmix will expand it, smooth it out over those great distances inside a powderbox to make moments like, say, music, or moments like paintings. Holding hands with time just lightly enough so that things are made not destroyed.

Dappled sunlight made Oxley's trade. Certain boxes would say the dappled sunlight corrupted his trade. Without the napkin of nuance the world of the powderbox is an abstraction, like, say, cloth, or like money, or like the money tailor, a bank, a bank is just one of those agreed-upon abstractions. If Ellie-Isabela thinks a bank in Barcelona has money in it, she'd be wrong. Abstract. But the bank is very good at creating a window of perception to counter the abstraction and so it looks like it has money in it, so she'd be right, the lovely Ellie-Isabela, the purveyor of illuminations. But dear butterfly, if you can create a functional sweetie from a total abstraction, if you can give money to the powderboxes off the punch of a button, you can then be smart enough to genius a whole new system. Good ol Oxley, mister laid-back munchoid, grazing on nuance right across the span of a century, grazing upon the helpful intensity of cyxmix, that hot currency that gives a memory its true depth of taste.

But it is nuance for Oxley, the nuance of give. He's got it all over the powderboxes. The average powderbox buys cheerfully into the best wisdom as: Live, listen; reply, retort.

Wrong. Oxley says: 'Just sit back and watch the clouds; nuance.' Oxley long ago understood what the sweet gentle Ellie-Isabela knew from the start, the chief addiction is the addiction to the nuance of give. Which is lucky for us boxes because such a big engine of memory transport makes our hup two three a lot easier. Hup two three, across the hills and across the seas.

And in any case, if I were one of my clients, a powderbox, a human, mired in the hasty-paste I would definitely wish to know what in the hell was going on, coz if I knew, I'd be chilled out not stressed out, but no I wouldn't know coz I was a client, a powderbox. Like the colonel, sweet ding-dong that the man is when whispering, after a siesta, into the teak-lined past.

To put it as politely as colonel David would, being a polite guy himself, if he had the skill to in fact see a butterfly joining up for a journey with a box: one can celebrate as many giant orange butterflies as one likes, dancing around a cracked old punctual fountain in a seaside hacienda announcing, in orthodox

Butterfly: 'I am the present.'

But no, truth is, wastage is just a child of the timeslot. Oxley believes wasting a moment just comes from the ding-dong hubris of not quite knowing the allocated time. But that's hasty-paste for you. If a powderbox was stamped on the nose with an extincto time a powderbox might take to banning wastage. But, generally, powderboxes quite like wasting time in all the gentle ways that Oxley has seen and tasted over the span of hundreds of picnics. Being gentle fuckwits, being gentle liars, being half-arsed, being busy, being beautiful, being ugly, being truthful, being clothed, wrapped in all manner of stupid hats, wrapped in all manner of imposing opinions of minimal nuance. Problem is, when you stick a hat on a powderbox you trap the heat. As the second equator rolls round creating the present, so Oxley will quietly open, fanly open, the option to nuance the present into a past, or to nuance the present into a future of possibility.

The Tree that Grows Upside-Down

Underneath my dual lid, inside the teaky abyss of true wood, also lurk one or two bits and pieces from outside the present, to either side, as it were, of the present.

Which is another way of insisting that we better boxes have an aspect we prefer, and the aspect we prefer is this: to be performing our trade whilst being the right side up, not upside-down. On the other hand, the powderbox world lives completely upside-down, and seems to enjoy it. I've seen it again and again. Me an Oxley, we're convinced powderboxes go about their days sailing through the hasty-paste upside-down. Can't say why. Can show proof. Common sense morphs into stupidity all the time, as eternally as the second equator rolls and rolls to create all manner of fuel to burn.

Exactly how it morphs into ding-dong stupidity is fuelled by just the one impulse: the aggregation. Check out any aggregation, it'll say and do things utterly upside-down, fuelled by conviction not seen since kings and queens believed the earth to be flat as a plate, flatter, a pancake. Power-packed aggregation. There is nothing else upon the treetops that generates harm, just aggregation; take a single, individual powderbox and join him up with others to form a committee. Next thing the committee decides, in its wisdom, the committee encourages the notion, that graffiti may be defined as vandalism, and, Lo, Behold, yars, before too long a situation is neatly created where graffiti—no nuance required—is taken as vandalism. Now that's just upside-down, because what truly is vandalism is the committee's vast battalion of two-stroke leaf blowers dangling off a limb and buzzing up and down the streets of the powderbox communities across the two equators. That's the upside-down life in a nutshell dear butterfly.

Oxley: 'Bobbo's right, and it's quite a regular posture, one sees it across the two equators all the time, the upside-down caper, or the upside-down mojo, as Bobbo calls it. For instance, your habitat dear beautiful butterfly: what the powderboxes call growth is in fact a destruction of your habitat. The birth of nuance dear butterfly, occurred with the ascent of you and your kind. Bobbo and I, we have seen very much the insides of powderboxes for quite a while now, and we happen to know that you and your kind have given light and freedom to their apprehension of nuance. It is like this. Your forms are the same. But within this form of two wings and an abdomen, it is your thousands of shapes. The thousands of patterns on your wings. The huge numbers of colours, and the even more numbers of hues, it is the discovery of these immeasurable variances of hues and patterns that gave first glimpse, gave birth, to the newly evolved looseness inside the powderboxes. The joy of colour has allocated itself inside the collective powderbox dear butterfly, so may I say: well done. And as for growth: for a millennium, powderboxes have moved from the birth of nuance into an adolescent phase. It is unfortunate that the adolescent phase will continue to live upside-down for some time to come, calling the destruction of your habitat "growth." Another example of the upside-down predisposition takes us to Italy.

'When Christopher Columbus set sail from Genoa, he announced he was off to the New World.

'New to him perhaps, for in fact this was a world that was quite old, millions of second equators had rolled over the mountaintops of this world prior to mister Columbus's visit that afternoon when he finally decided to take a shave to celebrate his breathtaking depth.

'All the tumbling and bumbling is of course none other than the clammy touch of perception and nuance. To those who never shaved, like the sages who got kicked out of Byzantium and hermitted themselves to the hillsides of Rhodes, it might have looked like mister Columbus were attempting to cut off his own head.

'He would no doubt have craved for a meal of that famous lobster that the clever Genoese fishers often caught from those sweet Genoese coves, but rumour at The Exchange has it that the man's perception and nuance led him far into a different dish, and he quickly acquired a taste for racoon, though not a snorkelling racoon.

'Which to mister Columbus was a new meal in the New

World, but had for a long time been an old meal in the old world. He discovered America dear butterfly. But Bobbo says a Chinese chap discovered America, is that so Bobbo?'

'Yep. Naval commander, guy by the name of Zheng Ho.'

Oxley: 'And he had no testicles?

'That's right, Zheng Ho was an imperial eunuch, a Muslim eunuch, one of the emperor's most trusted commanders, very powerful guy, an organiser, a high dignitary, a smart courtier, a diplomat.

'He was sailing his armada of sixty ships a time across the oceans a hundred and fifty years before Europe's commanders, before Queen Elizabeth's Francis Drake. Zheng discovered America a century before jaunty racoon Christopher Columbus did upon shaving. But thing is, with the bad communication back then, I'd say America was discovered two hundred times, heck, three hundred times.

'Any brave seadog who bumbled ashore would've told his friends and patrons he'd discovered America, so it was discovered by outsiders again and again until everyone settled on the Spanish guy. For Zheng's discovery to be today's currency, he would need to bounce the news westward immediately on his arrival home to fanfare. Westward into the Silk Road, deep into the Takla Makan Desert, and the Gobi Desert, and then onwards west past today's northern Pakistan and on through Afghanistan, into Persia and then Byzantium and then Rome. But important dudes like Zheng, and certainly his emperor, the Son of Heaven, thought of the Silk Road as a total shithole that brought barbarians eastwards into China, so his news of discovering America went bouncing nowhere except round the serene walls of the imperial palace of the Middle Kingdom.

'The landscape of the Silk Road, eerie and stunning, is of long deserts of ghostly beauty surrounded by towering mountain peaks covered in glowing snow. Water in frozen flakes, like memory waiting to flow. It lies north of Tibet, and north again of the majestic Kun Lun mountain range. But this beauty abundant and stark didn't matter: the imperial world in China thought of the Silk Road as a shithole of disease and thuggery. The lords in China thought of the Silk Road as a lost world of barbaric tribes and backward peoples who did nothing creative about the sewerage in their wayside inns. But the emperor kept the road open for those who didn't mind the filth, as a pass for trade; it's just that Zheng probably felt that his massive American accomplishment had no need to go scootering down the yuk of the Silk Road, and for good reason. Zheng was an imperial lord, he was lofty and arrogant, felt he was clean and superior, so he didn't like the Silk Road. Mention of it would make him steady his feet to regurgitate.'

Bouncing Back and Forth

Today dear butterfly, a phone call to an office in Melbourne can obtain a train ticket on the Silk Road for twenty-three thousand dollars. The ride goes from China to Russia, and along the way enters the ancient cities of the Gobi Desert, the Silk Road stalwarts whose fame echoed round the old world—Urumchi, Turfan, Tun-Huang. The train also stops at Tashkent, Samarkand, Bukhara in Uzbekistan, then up through Kazakhstan into the Russian city of Volgograd, ending in Moscow. Or a passenger may choose to go the other way, Moscow to Beijing. But in March 2009 the Silk Road trade shocked the world yet again.

Stunned the world anew. This particular trade cuts an eastward-bound line on the old Silk Road that Zheng loathed so much. The trade runs at high volumes, but it is a deadly trade. Across Afghanistan, across Pakistan, over the top of India and Nepal, into the ancient towns of the Silk Road in the deserts of Takla Makan and Gobi, on to China, across China, and then shipped out to the western drug dealers of unrelenting ugliness as heroin, fooling Lee's Heroin Fund. Which makes a change from when the west sold opium into China, a swap. But more to the point, the stuff that Lee's office in Singapore missed, or from farmers they could not yet convince, was being trucked along the same route, the same landscape, stern, stark, beautiful, flat deserts, of the ancient Silk Road that Zheng reviled.

Mind you, if Zheng and his emperor had no such ill taste for the Silk Road, the news of Chinese landfall in America may have freely reached Genoa a hundred years before Columbus set off. Which today may or may not matter since America is American in everything except money, proper cash, which it borrows from China. But still, sending Zheng's news back along the inns of smell and rot, of flies, rats and cockroaches, Zheng had no wish to do that. Today it would be like taking big news, say the Chinese Sovereign Wealth Fund actually buying a crown jewel giant like Rio Tinto, and then taking the news to the open sewers behind Manila. I mean, why would you want to do that?

Oxley: 'True. And anyway the upside-down tendency makes our work at The Exchange easier by a country mile. The urges at my picnics are always upside-down.'

It does, the ding-dong upside-down flips that are common to powderboxes, they cause our work at The Exchange to focus on the main game. Cyxmix, for us boxes to set to work on the powderboxes, the nuance of Give performs one item rather well.

It can provide the energy to replace the powderboxes the right side up. But aggregation is a headache majora yukko. Aggregate anything, race it away far from the individual, make it a policy, a religion, and you lose nuance, and when you have no nuance you have nothing, well, you have something, you have the portent for harm. And harmheads, all the different kinds of harmheads, the whole galaxy of em, mired in the depths of hasty-paste, tend to find nuance a toxic substance.

Another powderbox upside-down posture that is liked is war and famine, war and famine is actually more than liked, it is loved. For all the bombs and boats built, the famine could be cured. Take India, it has hundreds of war toys and its powderboxes eat memories. Take China, same, eat memories, Pakistan, same, Russia, America, North Korea the dear Kim and his starving teeming children skin an bone can't eat bombs, take everywhere, bomb bomb bomb but not a cake to take home. Jetfighters everywhere dear butterfly, but no nectar.

The upside-down habit. It comes from wanting to be intense, but intense in a specific way, connected to old ways, stupid ways, ancient, like instinctual ways, gorillas, not that a gorilla is stupid, I like gorillas. But in a powderbox it amounts to a very simple form of intense. Upside-down behaviour is the intensification of stupidity. You'd assume stupidity could not be intensified, but there you go. Powderbox arrogarnta. It's like the arrogance deployed to promote a comfy singular identity, when the reality is closer to entertaining a number of co-mingling identities. Born here, raised there, caned here, schooled there, loved here, loved there, loved everywhere. But powderbox arrogarnta likes to take these co-mingling identities and iron em out into one, always in search of one, one is the king, one. Even the English are drizzled through with Roman matter, English-Italians, you could easily accept that the entire British posture that crisscrossed the planet was one of Anglo-Italo ancestry. And the upright, proud Pathans of the north-west frontier of Pakistan, a Greek mix. Greco-Pathano. Or the whole Mongolian-Chinese mishmash of central Asia when Genghis Khan's men were dating every cherry in sight. But no, powderbox arrogarnta needs One, just one. Squeeze em into one, crisp dry, drain the juice. Oh well, just another upside-down caper on reality. Ding-dong and how's the time.

The Tree of Love and Fucking Em With It

The upside-down mojo in a powderbox, tho, is nowhere near as bright as the upside-down mojo of the bigger identity, a bigger slab, a country. America dear butterfly, has a very big military, a mojo instrument so vast it could blot out the whole earth if it so chose. All the big countries have a very big military—Russia, England, Germany, France, Spain, Israel, Iran, North Korea, even petty pretty Singapore has a big scary military—so it is true that the dudes who run these militaries are packing a very heavy weight, a rather big blunt instrument. This mojo instrument is designed to protect, keep love safe.

It's for the sensible idea of protection, all military complexes push the quaint idea that they are there to protect, and perhaps they do. From what? From the mojo of evil-doer butterflies perhaps, from the great big spirit of evil. Pity they can't protect powderboxes from Bakks. So okay, we have the American military, larger by a hillside than most entire countries, protecting America, protecting the American way. But no.

These days, the decay is wrought across the hallways of Ordinary Folk USA. Decay that has been mighty visible for eighty years, wrought from end to end, from the New Orleans slums of desperate poverty and decay, to the Detroit nightmare of decay and loss, to the junkfest of eastern LA, to the rot of Chicago's burnt out blacklands. It means that, from top to bottom, the military instrument is protecting truly a dream, for today it protects only decay, and the only light in decay is the dream for renewal.

When Australia is America, same. Take Port Kembla. It is a beautiful sunny part of the country, graced with lakes and beaches. It is also graced with being one of the many fulcrum dynamos of Australia's immense wealth. Yet go up the main street of Port Kembla, visit the town surrounds, like Laura Glass-Darlington did to make her documentary before she went to Edinburgh, and Port Kembla is astonishing, ghosted, empty, always drunk on being lost, streets that look like the human spirit has forgotten the sun. Pub windows of no glass just black holes, empty buildings, empty houses, a lone drunk, wasted on the hopes of steel, hobbling up the main road round one o'clock, shift finished. Same as America, which the military works hard and smart to protect. What would it say, this hard-wired military mojo, what might it say as it cruises the shores of the threat-makers, its edifice looming upon sordid plans. It might say: 'Don't you even think it, don't you fuck with us, don't you fuck with our hard-won decay.' Being a sprightly long-lived free market, one could patent the decay thereby protecting it from being copied elsewhere into the future. Same with Port Kembla. Park a fishing boat off the jetties: 'Don't you Kiwis fuck with our decay, don't even think it.' Yes dear butterfly, if one could swing a country round a room like a cat one could watch the false promise fall out like peppercorns—coz the truth of the matter is ordinary folk everywhere want a life not a country and a flag, you can't eat a flag, and a flag don't dance, since when did a flag ever dance, since never.

The Tree of Petrol

Upside-down, it's like the leaf-blowing machines. We better boxes can hup two three blow memories around like filthy pirates but at least we don't blow leaves from nowhere to nowhere with petrol and call it civic yumcha. Any solo, single, individual powderbox might happily choose to devolve the leaf-blowing machines of the world of their rights to gravity and let them float off to Alpha Centauri, but an aggregation?

When you ask an aggregation for the time, just hold, listen, for the retort: 'We have consulted on this and we believe it is in the best interests of all concerned to move Greenwich to Mongolia.'

But Oxley has ways round it: 'If you can't feed a goat, feed a sheep.'

Long ago I asked Oxley what this means.

Oxley: 'In my experience it is not often possible to have a flat world. Powderboxes may try to aggregate their whims and impulses into airy agreements to promote what they call fairness, a level ground of equal potential, but there will always arise a focus place, a tower, a hill, an England, an America, a Rome, a Ming dynasty, a land of honey and possibility. I'd go further to say that wherever the human possibility is perceived to be a real option, the best real option, that'll be the next land of honey, no matter how cruelly they make the honey there, or how stupidly. Take my picnics. One of my favourite picnics was in just such a centrally loved place of focus, a land of honey, Surrey, in the beautiful Mole Valley where the undulating greens have caused powderboxes to see so many deeper worlds that I have simply lost count. No smaller corner of the planet has given rise to more sightings of other worlds than the patiently quiet Mole Valley that apparently lies in a coma saying nothing. I believe the reason is simple: powderboxes might float off their feet a bit in the Mole Valley. Might get a bit light-headed from all that oxygen, from all that greenery, the jammpackery of green in the Mole Valley would be giving off such a hefty amount of fresh, pure oxygen that a powderbox would see things where there wasn't anything to see. If you can't feed the goat, feed the sheep. It was one of my favourite picnics, that day in the Mole Valley.'

I said: 'Your Dorking picnic, yes?'

Oxley: 'Yes, the tiny Dorking in the Mole Valley where that gloriously dirty musician, the composer Vaughan Williams, lived. He came along to this particular picnic, brought his dirty mind with him.'

I said: 'Aunt Lee the Soho dancer went to Dorking with Charlie Chaplin when it was a tiny village in the early thirties.'

Oxley: 'Most did. It was a peaceful place to have a fuck. Talking of Dorking, I must say the jammpackery of green that gave the powderboxes their mystic glimpses into other worlds rather worked well on Vaughan Williams, he jotted down the elementary coda for his hallucinogenic visions for the Fourth symphony, scribbled it onto one of my fresh newly ironed napkins. The napkin, dear Bobbo, is still today exhibited in the Vaughan Williams house in Dorking, bless the Mole Valley souls.'

'So Oxley, the question, forgetting nuance for a second, the question.'

Oxley: 'Which one dear fellow?'

'Where would you say the land of honey is located today? Is it petty clever Singapore where Lee Glass-Darlington set up the fund with Clinton and Yunus?'

Oxley: 'Oh I see what you mean. No dear Bobbo, the lawyer made a mistake. The ambition component of natures is still today drawn to the crumbling old parapets of petty New York or petty London. The lawyer would have been better off establishing the fund in London. Mind you, Vaughan Williams didn't care for either city, and he thought of Singapore as a hotel with a beach at the bottom of its garden.'

'London and New York? Even after hundreds of thousands of bankers have been sacked, evicted, deported, maybe migrated back to their birthplace?'

Oxley: 'They were not quite as required as one would imagine for the depth of human possibility, London and New York retain their land of honey status without the legions of financial people in middle management.'

'Maybe Shanghai, maybe Beijing? Are these the new centres?'

Oxley: 'For the mass flow of millions from western China maybe so, not for the world, not yet.'

'Is Surrey still a focal for possibility in the eyes of the powderboxes?'

Oxley: 'Oh shit no, Surrey's been forgotten, not by lovers of Surrey but by ambition, Surrey has been long forgotten. The last romantic to see things in Surrey was that Melbourne artist Sid Nolan, now there's a nice guy sprung into the world fully formed, like Mozart. No, I'm afraid Mole Valley, and the whole of Surrey has, by the hunger for possibility, Surrey's been dumped, which suits the powderboxes of Dorking no end I can tell you.'

'Do any of the powderboxes anywhere actually know where the true centre is, The Exchange?'

Truly remarkable events occur at The Exchange dear butterfly. At The Exchange a mountain may be cracked into two. Let me guide your gaze to the true Exchange.

Oxley: 'I haven't yet encountered a powderbox who knows where The Exchange is, no.'

'Maybe Rudolph, the guy who takes the centre with him wherever he goes?'

Oxley: 'The gems trader?'

'Lee Glass-Darlington's husband, yeah, has he got the instinct for it do you think?'

Oxley: 'No no, dear Bobbo, Rudolph has no idea where the centre is, Rudolph's knack for the centre is nothing more than a power for concentration and deals, a power for blocking out the rest of the world at the moment of his concentration. Rudolph wouldn't have a clue what the give and take is all about. In fact, dear old Rudolph Lowenstein, funboy that he is, wouldn't know how to deduce the tones of giving in even his closest friend, he has no idea whatsoever what any of his friends are talented at in their giving, no, I'm afraid Rudolph cannot discern the centre.'

'So he lives for the aggregations?'

Oxley: 'He likes them, yes. He wouldn't have a gig without them, yes. With the vast and deeply comprehensive existence of rules and policies and religions and styles and tides and judgements, Rudolph has things to twist or break. The jewel aggregation he needs desperately. If nobody agreed a diamond was expensive, Rudolph would be trying to sell shitty dumb carbon, dear Bobbo, he'd be selling a carbon that doesn't even burn, like coal burns.'

'He's powerful tho.'

Oxley: 'He's very powerful. But while he thinks he carries

the centre with him wherever he goes, the folly is that what he's actually doing is he's following a simple orthodoxy chosen from any number of simple orthodoxies floating about on both sides of both equators. He follows the aggregation; Rudolph's not much more than a follower at best and, at worst, a cucumber sandwich to the tides. In a world—in a past, present and future—of free-floating nuance, the proteins called Rudolph might turn into a jam jar, or the jam in a jar.'

'So where has he gone do you think?'

Oxley: 'No idea, though what I can confirm is he's not a salt shaker.'

'Maybe the buffalo demon of chaos and evil, maybe Maheesha flung him out to the ozone layer to burn.'

Oxley: 'Maybe so.'

'I've never seen a powderbox just disappear.'

Oxley: 'Me neither, dear Bobbo.'

Oxley has enjoyed the company of many owners. Together we hup two three the floating dreams across the mountains and across the seas, those hopes and dreams inside the powderboxes, mixing, mingling, scraping, hustling, from place to place, from cracked old fountain to airconditioned five-star luxury with a spread of gems. Gotta mix, gotta mingle, hup two three, over the hungry mountains and over the hungry seas, keep that delicate sadness out of the glittering trees.

And it is worth remembering the simple things dear butterfly, like nectar, like food, a meal. A powderbox needs a couple of meals a day. And the simplest fact of all the facts in the present is this: powderboxes need around twelve billion meals a day. On a good day, eighteen billion meals get eaten, three a day. Some days, nothing. But if you could, you would see powderboxes despatch eighteen billion meals each and every day. These are the custodians dear butterfly, of your nectar. They eat more or less anything, tho me an Oxley we haven't yet heard of fried chilli butterfly. They eat just about all else, anything that grows, it has to grow, if it don't grow it ain't cooked, and it is worth noting that they do not return the favour.

Globe

Another one of us better boxes dear butterfly, is Globe. Calls herself Flattie. Coz she's from a time when the earth was flat.

She's beautiful. Inlay over inlay, oak, deep grains, slim antique brass work, a stylish lid, and, inside, lo and behold, a globe. The world. A round ball. A ball inside a box. A ball set upon a beautiful brass plinth inside a beautiful wooden box of exquisite design born of a love and passion for wood so profound you'd assume the artisan was a singer of hymns from the time when the earth was flat.

But no. The guy what made Flattie, he was a whopping great transgressor, a heretic. Mad as a cockroach. Terrible haircut, even for an artisan, worse than Einstein's, hair utterly forgotten for the sake of the good work, a head of shock mop gone to pot like Pinski's mojo. His paintings on the little wooden ball, of the countries and the empires and the sea routes, of the continents, of lush islands, of engorged bays, of outsize gulfs, were charmed but of course wonky, far from the actual put across by my NASA friends and their satellites. But what he did put on his globe, lovingly drew and painted onto its surface, was the extent of what the mariners knew at the time.

The Tree of Knives and Whips

The local priest hated him, suspected he was making round earths, and so late one night on his way home he got beaten up by the priest's thugs. The artisan recovered, and he continued his work. When he completed Flattie, he never made another globe box because he deemed Flattie his best ever work. But the following year he started work again and he made many more beautiful globes.

His reward came four centuries later. He would never have dreamed that his earth box that we know as Flattie was, hundreds of years later, almost bought, nearly, so close, by that map-crazed collector, the Perth billionaire Kerry Stokes, but the kindly mister Stokes missed out by the skin of his teeth. Someone else bought Flattie. Flattie ain't big, she's about a ten-inch cube, nifty an cute as they come.

And Flattie dear butterfly, Flattie's the best bet for keeping Bakks the evil twit off Lee Glass-Darlington so that we better boxes can furnish you with the answer to your question.

Oxley: 'My relish jars, dear butterfly, were made by Flattie's artisan's great-great-grandson, who became a glassmaker. Jars for the nectar, powderboxes call them jars for relish.'

Flattie: 'My artisan was full of relish dear butterfly, most of all he relished exuberance, he would never be involved in destroying your nectar were he alive today.'

Flattie's proper name is Flatglut Globe. The name Flatglut might sound to the world outside The Exchange like a name lacking in affection grimly, as if we're saying Fatgut, dear butterfly, but we are not. Rather more than affection, we are giving vast amounts of respect to this particular box. We are saying flat, and glut.

Flat, in honour of the fact that she rode the tides of an ancient revolution, turning the earth from a piece of flat board into a round ball. Confirmed today by my hippy friends at NASA.

Glut, coz she's seen more hup two three than the rest of us better boxes put together, more jungarummy jiddle than all of us at The Exchange, she's seen a glut of owners and their dreams and fears. And a glut of aggregations. When you talk about a glut of hungry hup two three, talk to Flattie, she's had twenty owners of ravenous disposition.

Conducting hup two three from a faraway age of a flat earth, she enjoys a fertile glut of the three states of memories. Lost and forgotten, cherished and loved, bitter and destructive. Twenty owners, hopes and dreams, twenty owners, private jealousies, twenty owners, hurts and losses.

Flattie: 'No, Bobbo, no, I've had twenty-five.'

Oh. Twenty-five owners Flattie has enjoyed dear butterfly, spanning just over four centuries. But catch her now, the present, in the twenty-first century. Coz it's in the lives of the more recent batch of owners that brings Flattie's ability for the best jungarummy jiddle along to our treetops of glittering golden-green light. It is how Flattie ended up beyond the angry swords, ended up in a suburb of Perth, and from Perth it is how Flattie's excellent hup two three had helped Lee Glass-Darlington avoid the truly ugly side of the disaster. Flattie's journey off to Perth was quick, considering. The recent string of inheritance went like this:

Flattie was a member of the Turkish royal house. In 1922 Flattie's owner succeeded as caliph. The caliph resided in the Dolmabahce Palace in Istanbul. How do a pair of English-speaking, Turkish-ignorant powderboxes say that?

With heat, with difficulty, they'd sound like an unresolved feud if they said it in twos. Take two Oxleys trying to say Dolmabahce, feuding Oxleys they'd sound like, tipsy at a picnic.

Doma-hullcie-hullcie, Dollum arch-arch.

But the caliph had run out of humour, and his situation became deadly serious, life-threatening. Two years later Ataturk's troops surrounded the palace to force the royal Ottoman family to leave. They itched to use their rifles, their swords, their knives, swaying from foot to foot. The caliph began his exile in Paris. The nizam of Hyderabad courted the caliph for his daughter as a bride for his son. Her Imperial Highness Durruhsehvar, Princess of Berar, married the nizam's son. When her father the caliph passed away the Turkish princess in exile then owned Flattie. She and the prince had two sons, two young boys who were half Ottoman and half Indian. One son, Mukarram Jah, became the nizam of Hyderabad, and by the early 1980s after a couple of visits to Western Australia he'd settled into the leafy suburb of West Perth. An Indian Ottoman prince came to live in Perth, Australia not Scotland, and he insisted on driving around in a beaten-up Australian Holden because he loved old machinery and disliked ostentation. He also owned Flattie. The nizam of Hyderabad living in Perth became Flattie's twenty-fourth owner.

But that's old, here's the new, the recent. Flatglut Globe in her recent travels had zoomed across the two equators with enough zing for five solar systems. From the last shreds of the Ottoman Empire, the conquerors of Byzantium, to the golden dust of Hyderabad, to be found lurking on a mantle in a pleasant corner of one solar system, a large shady lounge room in West Perth, sharing the fresh new sunsets. With Subiaco and Swanbourne, Flattie shared the roaming of the second equator.

Filled with the original relish for exuberance sustained from the artisan who received a beating from the priest's burly thugs. And so Flattie was beautifully filled with quite a long time of jungarummy jiddle skills ready to poke em at any wayward thug in the employ of any residual flathead powderbox. Not that the current age could possibly harbour a residual flathead who'd beat the crap out of anyone with affection for the two equators, but you never know, you never know, in some parts the powder-boxes were created, it is told, a couple of thousand years ago.

When the nizam put Flattie up for auction in 1994, mister Kerry Stokes took the bidding to where he felt it rightly should be, and then he dropped out, passing ownership of the antique globe box to Remple Fekdin. It was Flattie's shortest journey of all the twenty-four previous journeys, West Perth to Cottesloe, via the auction rooms, a brief drive along Railway Parade that opened, erupted, onto the clear blue vista of the Indian Ocean rimmed with hearty Norfolk pines still singing the songs of golden sunsets.

The Tree of Swords

It's the aggregations that are your real enemy dear butterfly. Me and Oxley and Flatglut Globe, we seen, we have certainly seen, no ding-dong doubt on it, one or two unpleasant aggregations bumbling around the doorways of the last century, and we give those aggregations hell, we give em hell coz they're bad for the human potential. Wings, hup two three. We better boxes at The Exchange, we all together hand in hand, wing in wing, nudge the good stuff along, glee upon glee, the mixing and the mingling, the care, the looking after, the human potential.

Flattie: 'Human potential became very big around the time I was made dear butterfly.'

'Today, Flattie, the human potential is poised to receive another surge over the coming decades, massive, like a vast new world about to be born. One yum thing this will do, dear Flattie, it will activate your relish for exuberance, quite nicely.'

Flattie: 'Can't be so, Bobbo. I cannot imagine anything of potential as significant as señor Galilei showing how the earth was round from his blind spot of a chair and a desk. I well remember the week when the town woke up to señor Galileo Galilei inventing the telescope. By the way, he named it from the Greek: Tele, "far," and scopia, "look," lookfar, lookfar with my new tube of tiny glass plates. Yes, I remember the hot summer night on the twenty-fifth of August in the year 1609, Galilei unveiled the little tube to a group of businessmen in Venice. Nearly a hundred years earlier señor Copernicus had already been busy suggesting the earth was round, and that it lay not at the centre, but señor Galileo Galilei proved it—and so in the last years of his life the church placed him under house arrest. That's how they thanked him for opening up the human potential, and I still cannot imagine anything as significant as that hot summer night when he showed the lookfar tube to the town of astonished eyes.'

'Well, in China these days, I love China, dear Flattie, there are a billion powderboxes. And if you go beyond the cities into the hinterland, far far away into the remote areas where hundreds of millions labour at their tiny farms, then you have the picture of human potential.'

Flattie: 'Growing food?'

'No, statistics and possibilities. Out of hundreds of millions who belong to a single currency, giving them a vibrant confidence, the chances of new Galileos arriving into the world, the chances are very good: statistics and currency and confidence.'

Flattie: 'Oh, yes, I see what you mean, how exciting for the age of renewal.'

'New Einsteins, lurking out past the ozone, ready to bash into Chinese soil, ready to enter the world of hasty-paste. New Hawkings, Newtons. New Mozarts, Beethovens, Shostakoviches, Shakespeares, Austens, Brontës, Rimbauds, Coleridges, Li Pos, new Confuciuses. Utter naturals, born complete. Marie Curies, Picassos, ready and waiting to be born on a tiny little scrub of a humble hillside in far western China, I love China, in the more humble regions that Zheng and his emperor the Son of Heaven rather disliked coz those areas were just a bit too overly humble for their taste. But all great powderboxes, Flattie, don't you agree, have arrived into humble circumstances.'

Flattie: 'In my experience, most have, yes. Some no, Byron, but most have, yes.'

'Like David Darlington. He maybe should have taken his aunt Lee's advice and stayed in London to service his gift of painting and drawing.'

Flattie: 'Yes, like him.'

'But he serviced his other addiction at the dockside inns of Calcutta instead. And he gave his genius to the kids at the hacienda, so we can't hold much against him, he gave his gift to the kids, to Ellie, he gave good.'

Flattie: 'Well exactly—that's what I need to hurry along with his granddaughter Lee Glass-Darlington before she rots away, I'll need to force along a bit of the relish for exuberance.'

Oxley: 'How was her grandfather's powderbox to look after at the orphanage on the beach in Spain, Bobbo?'

'Colonel David, nice chap, bit heated up on the buffalo demon of chaos and evil Maheesha, other than that he was okay, except for the maharaja's daughter, she was ripping off her dresses in his powderbox whenever she could.'

Oxley: 'And the great-granddaughter of the Spanish farming

clan, what's her name?'

'Ellie-Isabela, yep, she was ding-dong on it the whole time, she practically knows exactly where The Exchange is located, but has no idea that she knows. Good ol Ellie's core activity, is giving.'

Oxley: 'Core activity? Where do you pick up these new parsimonious phrases Bobbo?'

'Core activity, let's see ... Miles Banford the business tycoon in Calcutta I think, if I remember rightly. And it's true, Ellie doesn't do much else. Give give give, that's all she ever does, perfectly instinctively, she doesn't even try, she just exists, and by existing she gives, just gives. Whether it's a smile, a peso, a sardine, an illumination out in that teeny back room, she likes giving, I've not seen anything like it: extreme to say the least.'

Oxley: 'A jammpackery of giving, yes, interesting.'

'Very extreme. Do you believe it may be a hereditary trait, Oxley, a deformity?'

Oxley: 'Quite possibly.'

'Hereditary deformities sailing the world day and night, making diasporas everywhere.'

Flattie: 'But Bobbo, you do not subscribe to diasporas.'

'True, there is no such thing as a diaspora.'

Flattie: 'What alternative might you offer?'

'I dunno, I dunno, maybe, let's see, diaspirin?'

Oxley: 'Why diaspirin?'

'Coz diaspora causes headaches for the powderboxes. Loss-ache, melancholy-ache, dislocation-ache, longing, those kinds of headaches, tribal friction from the homeland, all that kind of thing, you know, headaches, so the new name solution? Diaspirin. Lose the ache and get the relish for exuberance, diaspirin.'

Oxley: 'I have an offer for an alternative, let's call it something that goes for potential, goes for human possibility, let's call it The Dunsborough Swing.'

Flattie: 'The Dunsborough Swing?'

'Good thinking, Oxley, come Flattie, we'll show you the Dunsborough Swing, something that our dear butterfly and friends have recently concocted to heighten the human potential.'

The Jungarummy Jiddle for Lee Glass-Darlington

And that's the party, ding-dong and how's the time: that's what we better boxes do dear butterfly, the hup two three, the jungarummy jiddle, across the dark seas and over the ravenous mountains, wings in service of the cherished memories. Flattie in service of Lee Glass-Darlington. Relish for exuberance. Filthy pirates rubbing exuberance everywhere we go, across the two equators hup two three.

So, with wings still in good shape after an eventful little century, what we'll do is start with Meryl's dappled picnic on the verandah, specifically with gungho Patsy's wish to vomit away the vitamin D at the sight of O Rudolph.

Or I could start with Rudolph's elegant lover, that gifted woman who didn't make it to lunch, aunt Lee's great-niece namesake. The beautiful, tough, bright Lee Glass-Darlington who strolled traumatised and naked down the hillside in Sydney, who burned the meadows of Afghanistan with that tough and bright attitude, each shrub of poppies, up in flames, stoned crows doing fly-bys into the brown smoke over the Tree of War. I mean everything's private in that pantry of memory, right? Knock-knock. Lee Glass-Darlington would be mixed in with Flattie's relish for exuberance, and the lawyer might just, and only just, be tilted back from the edge.

Allow my NASA friends their quantum mechanics for space travel dear butterfly, let them have their useless wingless fun, and welcome instead to the mechanics of powderbox lore de lore. Here at The Exchange. Who knows, you might even see why they don't like trees. Me an Oxley can together show you some rather odd powderbox habits. Or, as Oxley says, 'Peculiar predispositions.' The beginnings of the answer to your question. The single question you first put across. About these cloth-wearing powderboxes. Who are they these custodians of my habitat?

Let's be more specific dear butterfly, welcome to the mechanics of the grottier end of powderbox lore de lore, not ugly, just grotty. Well, perhaps ugly too. Haranguage and pranguage yo ho ho.

And from here, fly easy on the backroom placemat, rest your big orange wings, cruise from Ellie-Isabela's illuminations, far away to the corner of Lee Glass-Darlington's powderbox where not only were the illuminations a rare occurrence, but where the lights now went out altogether poor thing. Dear and sweet Glass-Darlington, wishing merely to give.

You've got the unhurried mojo dear butterfly, I suspect the fast-buzzing nectar gobbler the hummingbird might irritate your mojo. Have any hummingbird pals? I doubt it, at eighty wingbeats per second—eighty beats per fukkin second—they'd sorta tire you out, kinda pop you into two pieces.

Thirty-Five Degrees Hot Down at Midnight

It is plum simple, granted, over a sunny luncheon of bursting powder amid the jacaranda, when the new prawnhead Lucknow gardener arrives, for Meryl to observe it was a restless night, but it became burst-open more than just restless. It became vibrant with physical frustration.

Put it like this. Rudolph had vanished and, coz he liked to assume he always took the centre with him wherever he went, we might have to assume he's having a good time, ding-dong how's the time. Or maybe the eager yobs, those nifty hippies at NASA, shipped him off to space, made a memory out of the guy, but I doubt it. Here's why I doubt it. Ugly reason, but here's why.

Lee Glass-Darlington got up and went to the window in search of a breeze, and under the window sat the box of gems, me, O Bobbo, taking in the breeze upstairs in a room on the hillside. Lee Glass-Darlington, owner seven, given O Bobbo by the previous owner grandma Enid, David's wife. Yep, the one and same in the plush hotel room in Singapore, when you took off for a break to explore the orchids. Only difference is I no longer safeguard the gems for good ol Tony Chen the Singapore freelance cheap-shirt cop.

A junior lawyer had grudgingly driven all the way up the northern beaches' shit-run of continuous retail glumness, from the Sydney offices to the Pittwater house. Pittwater is one of the best places in urban Australia, a sparkling bay bounded by green hills of the Ku-ring-gai National Park on one side and hills of houses on the other side, but few Pittwater residents could stomach the one-hour stretch of retail, light industrial and occasional bursts of some of the most ugly shopping behemoths ever built. But it was also broken occasionally with stunning vista of bay and beach, headland and blue sky before arriving at the enchanting subtropical expanse of the Pittwater cape. Great destination, crap on the eye getting there. He thought that the only other endless roadway that might be worse than this horrible drive was Parramatta Road, or perhaps Great Eastern Highway back in his birthplace, Perth. But the junior lawyer drove through the inexhaustible glumness listening to Shirley Bassey, he drove up to bring the gems back to the office and then cart the gems off to Singapore to give to Lee's staff up there.

At Lee's house he transferred the gems from me to his briefcase, leaving the bell behind, not before lifting it up to the light of the window and giving it a two second once-over and perking up his brown legal eyebrows. He rang it to see what it sounded like. He liked the sound, light, clear, fresh.

'Can I make an offer on this?' the lawyer said to Lee, who was sitting slumped in a sofa in the corner.

'No,' Lee said, 'you can't. It belonged to my grandfather.'

The lawyer drove the gems back to the Sydney office to courier them onwards to Singapore that afternoon, the stones would be on a plane by eight that night. The field guys who made the films of burning poppy fields were given big slabs of hard cash, not colourful stones, but the gems were a good idea as a thoughtful bonus for the staff at the Singapore office.

The field guys, a pack of steel-fingered mercenaries who'd seen it all, they would in no way whatsoever dear butterfly, have been impressed by a bonus of a pouch of shiny stones each, they had successfully negotiated hefty slabs of quite colourful paper, money. They screwed the chiefs of the Heroin Fund for so much money that at one point Bill Clinton had to object, and so the steel-fingered guys walked away, and Bill Clinton had to relent and pay them as much as they asked for.

But it was worth it. The films of burning were being made. The world had proof.

A Feral Naked Backside

Dunno why Lee came to the window, but it was same as the other nights she came to the window once she got back from the Singapore disaster, maybe for the breeze, and maybe to think out what she called the Whole Damn Mess. Fat chance tho, for dear Lee, on a night like this to think out the weird Rudolph evaporation. Rudolpho extincto. Centre melter melted away.

Missing husband gives rise to broken sleep. A restless night, yes, but more, a night that hums with worries and cares, amplified worries. The kind of night awake when the loose negativities are amplified enough to make you believe your life is in a great big mess, or fucked utterly, when by morning you realise you'd overcooked your slim concerns: the expensive specialist counselling in Macquarie Street has helped, but not much. It has given her the tools to believe the guy is only missing, just missing for a while, gives her hope he's just busy, somewhere in the world, at the centre, conducting his gems trading, and will be back before she knows it, ping splatter pop.

Far better assistance was to come from Flatglut Globe. Flattie would stew up enough of the jungarummy jiddle for Lee Glass-Darlington to stand away from the edge. Flattie's relish for exuberance. Help at hand.

But in the weeks that she'd been back from Singapore the hasty-paste had slowed right down for Lee, hardly any ping splatter pop, or none at all. Besides, right now the air was very hot on the face, but the perspiration was too heavy for the hot air to cart off.

She'd woken in a sweat, sheets fallen to the carpet, the window thrown open to the heat: everything now ready to be thought out clean, now ready to be made transparent by a gifted powderbox with the intellect of ten. One bit from Flattie's relish, and gifted Lee Glass-Darlington might have a ball sorting out the confusion that had come to the house, fumigate the place. Fumigate it of these contagious, warped and sticky misunderstandings. I mean, who'd do a thing like that to her? All she wanted was to burn the drugs, good idea too. Ping splatter pop those horrid lines of trade along Zheng's reviled backroads up the silk corridors.

And maybe she came to the window to consider sister Meryl's advice. Direct was diviner Meryl's advice: Go to the creek girl, go. Yet even at the window Lee did nothing but swing like a bulb from the ceiling. She'd walked over to the window to dry off and think, but all poor Lee did was put something up and knock it back down. She was busy as a flock of clerks making useless swings and more useless swings. Fine enough to wake up in a putrid sweat and stand at the window to examine the chain of recent events and to put your foot down. Even to work it all out. But to swing back and forth with a vacant mind, well, on a very hot night it may O yes spark a fire in a small corner of certain powderboxes. And in exactly what style does powder burn? On this enigma I can state a simple fact: Lee Glass-Darlington is the one elegant person who has the goods to find out. Unless that fucking putrid Bakks goes around Flattie and gets to Lee first.

What Lee termed the Whole Damn Mess started out only as odd. Lee and Rudolph were to fly to London for a break, via Singapore. Planned it a month ago, bought tickets, mangled the sheets many many times, drank champagne to celebrate her promotion at the firm, so it started off, in the daily flow of ambition, just a bit odd, that's all. I mean, the Heroin Fund was still working, the board members were just waiting until their glory girl got better, even the two chairmen, Bill Clinton and Muhammad Yunus, were confident Lee would be back at work in no time. The two chairmen knew Lee's contribution to the women and children of Afghanistan would suffer no great disruption, they had met Lee many times and they were confident she would bounce back to the task with that intellect of sprung gusto. Little did they guess that this same breadth and width of intellect would also shine as a feral naked backside.

Sweat and Salt

But Lee had to think once again about the whispers at the creek. Now at the window she was considering a walk down the hillside, for good reason, not just to sit by the banks of the clear waters as Meryl had urged.

Meryl was right about one small thing: Rudolph cannot vanish, that's just not feasible. Lee also felt it was just not possible; they had had three of the wildest fucks all month back at that hotel, gruff and rampant. All their lovemaking ranged over all the moods, and the coarse stuff at the hotel was but just one of the many varieties.

But anyway, Meryl told her: 'Go to the creek, consult the presences.' Nice idea but Lee, long way or short cut, didn't take to presences like Meryl did. Then again, once the Whole Damn Mess turns to persistent panic you take to anything at all no matter how gifted and elegant you are, and you stand surprised by what you might choose to believe. That's what the winds of change do, they make you see double, or nothing at all.

The house was bolted onto a hillside, jutting hell too far into open possibilities. It was forever catching the valley in a way that felt like you were lost in flight. But it was the stone wall that dictated the flight, a big, long wall, a beautiful antique that the heritage officials would never allow to be touched with blowhard wallets from the other side of hell.

She stood at the airless window, sweat running down her neck, burning eyes flying with the wall down the steep slopes. Old stones, large and rough, around fifty years ago the wall had been constructed so that the spaces between the rocks grew the established wood of deep-green shrubs, good wood, the type that's used to make we better boxes like Oxley and Flattie. It was definitely a sturdy wall, roaming from the base of the house, down the hill, a two metre high guide, easing into the agreements at Tenmoon Creek that made everything seem nice in the world. Nice place, Tenmoon Creek.

It's one of those more, um, fertile, yes, lush, places to whang around a few memories, pick up a packet of remembrances and get em off to The Exchange. Make a decent contribution to the winds of change. Call it Ellie-Isabela's give and take. Give and take at Tenmoon Creek, rob em good you two bad dogs. Henry&Co barking at Pinski's sharks and shells.

Nice view too. The valley was huge to look at from the window, a full half kilometre, and the gardens vast with untended growth going up and down Jimmy's new mission to get Lee all to himself somehow. Four main slopes careering across the moons and suns, huge sweeps of open grasses cutting across clumps of olives and jacaranda, terrain that so quietly suited Jimmy's loose-shredded Lucknow mind. Vines everywhere, especially at the banks down at the base where those giants the Moreton Bay fig trees had seen out the century of hasty-paste, like me, and like Meryl's Piccadilly box too, good ol Yottick, and like good ol Oxley round near Dorking.

Lee reached out the chin for a smell at the oils hanging on the night like a thin lagoon. The only breeze lay in the rustling down in the gully, but the weak rustling might be the presences, hustling for memory from the night and day, as Meryl had said with ease. Hustling for an exchange. This for that, this for that, hup two three.

Lee had to admit, the trees now did seem alert. They unfolded wood off the line of the creek like another universe on the march. True, they were titans that could resist the winds of change; where a sapling would bend in those winds, the Moreton Bay figs wouldn't budge much. But to Lee they now seemed poised to exchange secret briefings and sail away on those winds of change into another darkness, migrate to a more iron notion of earth. In the daylight they were just trees, giant Moreton Bay figs, but deep into a hot, still night they were airborne hustlers ready to ration air, reeling in the night wind to ration happiness. They weren't just good at resisting the winds of change, they were also good at making shots of change, a whole another universe on the go, hup two three. So Meryl might be right.

It's true the grounds were huge as valleys, but the place on which Lee fixated was the stone wall stopping at the creek, forming a corner of sharp cliffs, low branches and big roots, burls of wood thick as a buffalo torso. This was the grove Meryl insisted on, a subterranean hollow where the old days could be found mixing aloud with those smaller engines of memory, day and night. One of the bigger engines, scent, was perhaps also pungent down at the grove, perhaps. So maybe it lay the other way round, the grove fixated on Lee instead. Glaring back solely at her like a big night animal. Returning her stare, as she protruded naked from the window at the huge house.

Built in the old days by the goldminer's workers, stone by stone, the sturdiest three-storey joint in the whole district, a sprawl of love. When seen from the creek, tho, the house was ready to collapse down that hill in pieces the size of cars. When seen from the grove it looked like the goldminer had played a fast and loose game with the fleagods of gravity. And, being a goldminer, heartily enjoyed it.

The grove was where the old days forged agreements to steal the iron out of things, or the gold. Wrap a day in duct tape and ship it across some kind of second divide. But it had to be hot, very hot. Enough to slow the hasty-paste getting past the powderboxes on heat and horror. Twelve consecutive nights at thirty degrees was certainly good enough to take, from the two smaller engines of memory, a chosen piece of important iron whatever it was: shining key, rusty hinge, old powderbox, new husband Rudolph, red-blooded, full of iron, yep. So it was simple to say, and Lee knew it; if she wanted more she'd need to take a stroll, mix with the greater hustlers out past the rocks. True or false, real or not, what's to lose out of this Whole Damn Mess. What's to lose. I mean, it's private up there behind her forehead right?

That's the moment she'd become a walking shoelace in the night. Walking shoelace Lee Glass-Darlington thought it out fairly right, up to that point. There was not a lot to lose just by heading down the hill to the creek. If the grove wanted to glare back at her with a hundred eyes then let it glare back. The two smaller engines of memory, day and night, gave no impression to the top floor bedroom that they'd come and gone this week. Or the presences at the creek had stolen these vapours that posed as day and night. Like him. He fucking just vanished without a trace. Or they'd stolen him into the bargain, Meryl again. Maybe the lagoon vapours afloat on the hot air were his breath. Maybe he'd become this thin, scented lagoon that floated each night over the grounds. Day and night didn't seem right any more, one was brighter, one a bit darker, that's all, and both hot like hell. Maybe he'd become this lagoon. Aloud: 'So is it, Rudolph, is it you?' No answer. Just a faint echo, probably off the stone wall with all that good wood giving good fear. As a teak box, must say, I love good wood, love it like a song sprinkling from the night-sky.

Trapped inside this useless loop of a still night, the hasty-paste now almost at a standstill, Lee the walking shoelace started to swing more wildly, naked at the window, to swing from Meryl's advice to her own conviction and back to Meryl. He can't just vanish, something must've come up, he'd be back when the business was seen to and completed, he's always like that, a cardinal sign, powderbox Meryl calls him, meaning a mover and shaker who initiates things and gets them rolling.

A powerful guy, true, but then: here it is. Now really is the fifth week that Rudolph hasn't been found. Walking shoelace Lee starts to think aloud again, talking to herself as she watches where she steps through the dark bedroom: 'I could impress myself by giving it another night, maybe another five nights, well, until he's back after doing whatever needed doing. But no, no, get down there tonight, consult, at least listen.

'For anything, a hint, a whisper, what'll I lose if Meryl's right. Standing at the window smelling this lagoon won't do me any good. Get your clothes on and get down there. Or go as you are.

Too damn hot to put on even a bracelet, go as you are. Except the feet, put on gym shoes. Walk down to creek naked, in your gym shoes, that's good, you'll say that's how you went out to find him. One hot night I walked out naked in my gymshoes, and there you were, am I clever Rudolph?'

Gifted, she remembered they called her; at the drinks, at the announcement the managing director called her a 'gifted new partner to help steer the firm into the growth bonanza of the twenty-first century once the global slowdown is history.'

She said aloud more firmly, 'So come then gifted, get gym shoes and get going, be a gifted lawyer loping down the hill naked in the night, check upon the presences, gifted, at Tenmoon Creek, nifty gifty.

'Gifted,' she puffed, 'what a fucked way to tie me up. I mean, if I'm to devote my life to shovelling money into chief sod's pockets at least he could come up with something a little less childish, what a prick he is. Oh well, let's get the gym shoes on and head down to Meryl's haunted corner, can't believe I'm doing this. Jesus Rudolph, where the fuck are you?'

And then, with all the backwards and forwards at the window, the moment: she'd do it, Lee Glass-Darlington the walking shoelace, what the hell. She went downstairs. She slipped on the gym shoes, tied the laces loose and rough. This would be her first visit to the creek since they'd got the grand old goldrush place, and what a reason to visit the creek. A cardinal sign gone missing. A mover and shaker duct taped and shipped off by the invisible whisperers hustling for a bit of fun. Duct taped and shipped off to who knows where. Or why.

She checked the red line on the thermometer that he'd duct taped to the window frame. Right up close, using the dim light the night had on offer, eye right up near the numbers. When she got it, she managed only a low murmur, 'Thirty-five degrees, fuck, thirty-five degrees in the dead of night. There's no way I'm putting any clothes on, the gymshoes'll do, let's go. Visit Meryl's presences. And you, Rudolph Lowenstein, I swear you'd better get a good laugh out of this moonbum gymshoe stroll.'

So there it lay, a good start, Lee began to feel the tickle of a slight optimism. Flattie's relish, a relish for exuberance that Flattie obtained far away when the earth was flat. And yes gifted she is, Lee could mentally wrench a circumstance right round the other way, that's why they loved her at work, loved that robust will, hup two three. Even Meryl's new garden guy said she was gifted, letting a huge garden go so grandly wild was a slick of genius, Jimmy'd said with wide eyes. The second slick was Flattie in service, Flattie getting on with a slim piece of jungarummy jiddle, hup two three.

Tenmoon Creek

Anywhere else there's just the one moon, but Jimmy Hazel swore down at the creek behind Lee's place there were ten moons afloat in the canopy. Juggling their way around branches and clusters of leaves to drop their messages round the boulders and into the sludge along the edge of the creek.

When Lee stepped out the back door in the gymshoes she made a foolish promise. The night was hotter, not cooler, than inside the house, so she felt immediately the torch of heat on her chest and head, and she made a promise. Ding-dong, when was the last time she concocted a promise out of five weeks in hell?

The ground lay spiky with dried grass that crunched, so the gymshoes were a good idea even tho the loose laces trailed along the dust. And she found she felt good wearing only shoes. The body was open to the night. Bum, leg, underbum, nose, overbelly, slight caper, all were open to the night as if a song was being played away by beauty and friendship and joy all at the same time. She felt mad. The storms above her head made her feel mad. Lightning, sky cracking, bold gods taking her for a ride, bold skydogs growling away off into the future, it's all just junk and madness, and she felt in love, the whole sky and material of her life, they felt like a sister and a friend.

When she started walking and crunching it produced a breeze on the skin. Yes, prime case, cooling off was now at least on the cards. Even if diviner Meryl says there was a lot else on the cards down at the creek.

The only other house in the area was the house she should have been at for lunch yesterday, Meryl's, a kilometre to the left along a series of tracks through the forests, so that directly ahead the whole hillside was hers to stroll down alone. Go to the creek, fine. Inspect, listen, open the mind, do whatever Meryl says, fine. But still, prime case, she made herself a simple yet elegant promise of poise. Flattie's relish for exuberance. Beginning to seep through like a thin catch of moonlight on a branch of the family tree. David Darlington, his promise lay all over his granddaughter.

Lee was not given to making promises, she always felt a promise was a cheap way to overstate an objective, and a target was one of the simplest things in the world for her to achieve, it did not need a promise to impose the harmless fears of failure. When she did make those occasional promises they were either without gladness or were grunted inwardly; they were blunt: I won't this, I will that, must, should. But this one, now in the heat of night: it had poise and elegance, she liked it. But it was neither poise nor elegance, it was relish. She rolled it around in silence as she walked on the dry grass, shoelaces trailing behind each step in the dust, and she found that the footfalls were fun, crunch-crunch sounded crisp out into the huge hillside, Lee Glass-Darlington thought it was like walking on pretzels. The husband is missing but the pretzels became hollow fun: sleepless nights had bent the hinges in her powderbox so that the lid didn't close too tight and stuff came spilling out.

She crunched her way over the plateau outside the back door, on past the table and chairs, to the start of the slope where the world she inhabited could be given a poke. Here she stood for a moment looking back at the façade of the large old goldrush house. Examining the dark windows as she stood naked, hanging between the house and the gully like a cream stick of crayon. That's how it looked from where Jimmy Lucknow stood. He stood far down the slope hidden in a clump of trees, good wood's a good thing even for that, a lurking yesfactor whose powderbox forever rang with chickname. Far up the slope he could see a cream little crayon poised at the top. A naked one.

The Trees of Tenmoon Creek

Stars were everywhere, jamming the sky full, giving the house its three-storey shapes. This is where she always came to stand for a moment, at their famous outdoor lunches, to give her life a poke from outside herself, and to stare down into the gully and wonder about the creek hidden from view by the grove of big trees. She'd always wondered about it because she'd never chosen the half kilometre walk down, too busy, soon one-day, soon maybe, poke the creek. And here was a reason now, that one-day had come round. She stood at the edge of the back garden, swinging her head around the skies to confirm the oddness of the week's high heat. From the vantage point out on the edge, the massive view was cloudless, clear, bright, things ought to be cool, but the slope generated its own barbeque air travelling up the rise to the edge where she stood naked. She felt it on her thighs, the heat of that barbeque air. But now it started to feel good, a perch of optimism to climb.

Down the steep slope was impossible for a straight-ahead stroll. She had to lean to the side to make her way down. Scudding like this it seemed a long way to the first forest of shrubs, but now the upward breeze on the skin was evaporating the sweat, the first relief she'd felt since leaving the bedroom window, the first relief since trying to sleep hours ago. She made her way down the hillside with these careful sidesteps, which was a bore, but it was a cool journey, which was fine. At least at the grove it would be cool. Crunching the dead grass became fun again, and she was lifted, a bit, into the night air, felt now a cheer to take to heaven. She came to a patch of discarded cardboard boxes. She stopped. Had a look around, there were at least a dozen. Banana boxes maybe, they looked like those handle boxes, wingless ones. Strewn around the place for no right reason. She had no idea who'd thrown away a stack of empty boxes. Get them in the morning. She continued down the slope. In ten minutes she arrived.

Soon she was pissed off again. At the grove it was one shitty thing after the next. No movement of air, and the temperature was hotter than in the house. It was dark and black too, the Moreton Bay figs blocked the shine of the sky. The material in the grove absorbed the residual light that stumbled in from the hillside. Locating the creek, prime crap, out of the question.

From the wellness of an elegant promise, she went into grunting out abuse. 'Listening, fuck that. Hints and clues, yeah Oh right. Consult the presences, might as well consult the NASDAQ. Meryl-Meryl, you fucking-fucking peanut.'

Then she heard a low sigh. The darkness forced her into slowing right down, but as she moved she noticed there was no more crunching of pretzels. It was soft underfoot. She bumped into something solid. Then she didn't hear her feet. She didn't hear herself stumble into the roots and she didn't hear any more the sounds of the hillside, the brief rustling, the harmless bats, or the sounds of the distant bay that Meryl said was ruffled by angels. What she heard wasn't a sigh, but silence, the matted, thick silence of the grove at Tenmoon Creek. The smooth, gully-captured silence cut out the hillside, and it brought a visitor to her powderbox.

There's a Hat on Lee's Powderbox Today

She then found that she could see, in the blank darkness she could newly see. The-world-is-full-of-silly-hats. It started without warning, neatly on her arrival, that is, when she could hear the silence and see the darkness. It bounced into her mind as a song-like chant, The world is brimming with silly hats, over and over. It sounded loud in the silence that mere slip of a thought. Never quite discovered where it had come from, just somewhere in the far reaches of early childhood, and stuck since, resurfacing for no reason, tonight loudly coz she'd got no true sleep for days, and was out at the edge of things, all things, daybeds, nightbeds, second equators. But even during the times of her life where she was okay and fully rested, it would soon surface for no reason. In the boardroom with a large corporate client, him droning on with an important briefing, the chant would spring into her mind: The-world-is-full-of-silly-hats, tra-lala-lala. Chopping onions. Paying the butcher.

Sometimes it would slip in as a groovy rock track she invented: The wa-waald is f-f-fuull of see-lee huh-hats!

Sometimes as a nursery songline.

Sometimes she'd rap it along: Da-da waald-ah …

Fuck Em All Twice

Mostly it just came along as a statement by a fact. A fact. She often liked the notion that it had come from her funny grandfather David, but verify this she could not. As a box in tune with the open market I could've put her straight with those hat tunes, but what the hell, the phrase was just another one of those millions of particles of powder in Lee's own bent-hinge powderbox behind her forehead. Let her stay confused for a while, I say. Let the walking shoelace bumble, feral backside shining beams of wonder out to a lurking yesfactor in the trees, bumbling's good, bumble into boxes. Nice tune, my tune: 'Boxes boxes everywhere but not a wing in sight.'

What she was able forever to verify, thanks to the phrase the-world-is-full-of-silly-hats, was that on every corner in every town all over the world someone was wearing a silly hat, that the world really is, as Oxley would say, jammpackery with silly hats, Dorking to Durban.

Meaning, what a wonderful place the world really is capable of being after all is said and done. So the jumping of the phrase into her mind always coincided with a profound injection of optimism, that's what it seemed like anyway, that whatever your custom, culture, religion or persuasion you'd be caught out wearing a stupid, silly-looking hat. You'd think your hat was important and someone else would think it just looked fukkin silly. Optimism.

While the well-meaning person solemn as an equinox pleads for tolerance, the silly hat says over and over: 'Found it a thousand years ago.' In many parts of the world they do not tend to wear hats outside occasions, but they're an aimless pack thin on tradition, like herself. But whichever way the phrase bounced it always came at a moment of inexplicable lightness, that much she knew, and since childhood it had grown to become a touchable moment. Grew to become a signal that she was swimming in a state of profound optimism. But here, in profound darkness? At Tenmoon Creek? What kind of optimism creeps up to you here? Chances of any kind are slim when you check out the list of bad news. A cardinal sign gone missing. A dark grove smelling of batshit. A slow-boiling yesfactor hidden down the slope. Creeksludge up and down the way expecting moon messages. A deafening silence. Supposed to be filled with presences. But there it dangled, the singing chant: The-world-is-full-of-silly-hats.

Maybe it was no more than perfectly right anticipation. A connected-to-nothing expectation that was concocted to build those walkways across time. After all, that's all willpower is, bridging unreal gaping holes. And right at the moment that's exactly what she was. She was freshly promoted naked willpower in batshit gymshoes. So with bang for your buck willpower, you find stuff, you do. Especially after you've made an elegant promise, rackadack right away, and please yourself with a pert ol promise.

When she found the creek she found a bank of pebbles that found a bamboo fan of dim light. The light filtered in through the canopy giving the pebble flank a luminous sheen. She was stunned, she'd blundered into a room.

Bumbling's good. She had found a huge room made of pebbles, water, tree trunks, a rockface across the other side—and a vertical curtain of vines back up the creek. The weak light helped the impression because at the edges of the room the glow simply died off. She found a low branch sailing out over the creek. She found the crisp scent of cool water. She found a limousine of orchids. Found a laced raft, afloat on the black sheen, of solid, powerful lilies, more than a raft, a barge. But above all, what she found was the other universe she'd earlier assumed the Moreton Bay figs had marched into. What she hadn't found were Meryl's sentinels from that other universe, the Tenmoon Creek advisers. Us, the boxes. Particularly Flattie. Relish from far away when the earth was flat and señor Galilei was flattened in the old ways.

Lee thought: If Meryl's advisers were hustling for a show and tell, then they were doing it somewhere else. Or, she thought, they were doing it right here but they were doing it very quietly. Or disguised as pebbles.

By now shoelace Lee was hot, irritated and thirsty, not thinking too well, but 'disguised as pebbles'? What kind of unbridled stupidity is that? I mean she's a whack em up lawyer for goodness sakes. Oh well, may she continue.

A round rock beside the water was a fine spot to sit sweet

for a moment. By the time she was resting on the rock she had strolled through a few states of mesh, or states of powderbox, down the slopes of the grounds without anything on: late night panic, to ratty derision, to very shitty irritation. And all the while, conversely, a consistent rising of the perch of optimism had run alongside these states. So that now sitting on the rock, with the dusty shoelaces falling over the sides, she felt pleasant and cool in the dense cave of silence, ready for Meryl's advice. She took off the shoes and got in the creek for a swim. The water was cool and soft. She swam to the barge of lilies. She floated on her back beside the barge, and she quietly reinstated the promise, I shall give the backend of that goldrush place a well-earned coat of white. Then she said aloud as she floated out to the deeper centre of Tenmoon Creek past the barge: 'Yes I'm consulting, I am now consulting please.' And then she waited and listened, fell silent, swam slowly round the creek. A couple of minutes later, when she'd cooled off, she turned back for the rock, but the thing was, the gym shoes, they'd gone. And thing is, we boxes, we do not throw shoes around, no sir-ee, just memories. Lined inside the abyss, layer after layer of whispers, hopes and memories, no gymshoes, in my case, a bell.

The night had started to vanish. As Lee worked her way up the hillside, the second equator was rolling off to the west towards Lucknow. In the shadows of Sydney, Lucknow exists. Lucknow. What a place. Imagine calling yourself Lucknow in Australia when you call yourself Lucknow in a beautiful olden place like India. Luckyum and Lucknever and Luckforever and Lucktomorrow and Luckboo and Luckum nice. Luckshee. Luck. Early dawn, and still hot as barbeque air. Memory is like water.

When she came to the plateau behind the house she sat on the dust to check her feet. They were bleeding, and her ankles and calves were brown with wet dust. She sat on the ledge with her back to the house, looking down at the early morning hillside, tired, pissed off and vacant. And naked.

A figure in a nightgown came outside with a mug of tea and sat at the table. 'Good morning dear.'

'Morning Grandma.'

'You're up early.'

'Went for a walk.'

'Dear, are you wearing anything?'

'No.'

'You went for a walk without clothes on?'

'Yes.'

Lee's grandmother Enid sipped the tea, knowing how different her granddaughter's reaction has been, different to her own reaction in '66. Her own reaction had been day after day of unrelenting fury, horrible fury, hell five times, and then, only after a week did she weep like an ancient, howling far back into herself.

She sipped the tea as she thought how dear Lee had always had David's beautiful smile. Except since Singapore. Since coming home she hasn't smiled. Before Singapore, David's smile had always lived on the glow, right there on the dear girl's jaw.

Then she said, with love: 'He'll be back, dear, Rudolph will be back very soon.'

The Tree of Morning

The morning birds called out in the distance; dawn was now looking beautiful moving with the second equator as it arrived to warm the peninsula of love yet again into a heatwave day. But Lee, bang bigtime sitting on the back ledge, was getting angry. Wow was she getting angry. Walking Shoelace was growing the fume, big-willed granddaughter. She was about to mistake her grandmother's gentle demeanour for a dotty spaced-out past. The fume grew, and it grew. And then.

'I wish you'd shut the fuck up. All month that's all you've said. He'll be back dear, back dear, back dear, just shut your fucked old wisdom up.'

David's widow said nothing, she sat there for a moment, and then she got up and walked back into the house.

Lee made an error of judgement here, for Enid Darlington was no dotty spaced-out nightgown from the thirties, Enid was sharp as Lee, sharper, much sharper, Enid had Lee like a lock. Enid had seen off all manner of fuckwits in her life, lousier fuckwits than her trumped up ex-corporate granddaughter had seen off.

Enid had come to stay at Lee and Rudolph's bungalow to look after her granddaughter, but now she put a call to Meryl and announced she was packing up and going home. Enid lived not far away, St Ives. Meryl pleaded, and Enid stayed. It was more than a month since Rudolph had vanished. During those weeks Enid had observed her granddaughter begin to slide into decay; Lee rarely showered, almost never left the house, brooded over a pot of baked beans that she'd poured from the tin, sitting cold on the stove.

I can see Bakks at work right there on Lee's powderbox; telling her lovely grandma to get fucked was just low as Pinski piss, stagnant in a cracked old fountain. Bakks can hup two three across the seas and over the mountaintops like the very best of us, yep, a first impression of his ill-will is fine. But get to know him, as you soon will dear butterfly, and phew Bakks is a venal memory valve that sorely needs fixing. Buffing up at the very least. Past or present, what the heck, to me an Oxley the whole century is the present, certainly to Flattie. To Bakks the flow of time is a huge opportunity to create abuse and offence. I am pleased dear butterfly, that you are not taking a ride with ugly erratic ol Bakks. For he was now conducting his jungarummy jiddle upon the lost and confused feral intellect Lee Glass-Darlington, ruining her days and nights with the one trick he loved the best of all the tricks: counterfeit.

Bakks the Slimebox, a Grim Game in Three Parts

It's currency if everyone uses it, that's what they claim, right? If everyone agrees to use, say, a shiny pebble like the pebbles at Tenmoon Creek, the world operates on pebbles, and pebbles are counted, kept, exchanged, hoarded, fought over, examined, crushed, ground into sand, securitised, squared, painted, hung, glued together, skipped across the creek, written about endlessly in various pebble theories, macro and micro. Five pebbles thanks, here's your change. Oh keep the change, do.

Or that famous molecule, carbon. A tree draws carbon out of the air and makes, well, wood. Compress wood you get coal. Compress carbon truly heavily and you get Rudolph's idea of things, diamonds, diamonds are nothing else, only carbon. But different from compressed carbon, is the plain ol carbon molecule. Which dumb ol Bakks believes makes wool, it doesn't, it makes wood. Teak, mahogany, oak, pine, jacaranda, wood. And it burns, good ol carbon. Odd thing, making currency out of stuff that burns.

Or if everyone agrees on seashells, ratskins, matches, or the peso, dollar, euro, pound, yen, ruble, yuan, or the Polish zloty. Same for us boxes dear butterfly; memories, heck, they're currency. Plunder the powderboxes behind those foreheads for the lore de lore. Store lore and save up for a rainy day hup two three.

So the grunt of it all? Well ding-dong and how's the time, where there's currency there's counterfeit. Moonlighting printmasters hard at work behind the back wall of every stale tavern of the great cities of the world. So too counterfeit memories. Same with us boxes, we tend to see quite a lot of fake memories. 'What ya pushie-pushie here? Dammit, what're you pushing!' We boxes hear that irritated phrase over and over just outside The Exchange, in the subprime swill of the outer reaches where crap is sold all the time day in day out. But who then is downright responsible for the fakes?

Meet my horrible friend Bakks, the el creepo. Says the fake memories, they're made by brick boxes, rooms. I firmly hold that it is Bakks himself, along with his network, that shonky hoard of cardboard friends who help him successfully blur the responsibility. And to curl the universe's blanket, the main elements of his game? Precious currency, precious counterfeit, precious memory, suspicious accents, suspicious loitering. Missing mail helps, as does strange blips on a monitor, unexpected blips.

Yeah, Bakks has the grim game down pat. Let's spy on how he works the game dear butterfly.

Counterfeit Takes Hold in Walking Shoelace

All he has to do is locate a spot of bother: Lee Glass-Darlington who still hadn't located a lost husband, a cherished and loved cardinal sign, a centre melter. Then coax her into blaming stuff on everyone else for long enough—and the blamer hey presto gets the first scent of bogus memories inside the powderbox behind the forehead. Like Bakks will say, again and again, and with exasperation, 'If you need to see a penguin in the picture then there's a penguin in the picture.' Bakks, he's not too stupid in rugged ways, but wow he's grim, and he's pretty stupid in smoother ways.

Blame it all long enough on someone else and it begins to look like real currency, smell like, taste like, behave like, real currency. Counterfeit high grade, nicely indistinguishable from the real stuff. So for Bakks trade is going along well, no casualties, Bakks is on a roll, Bakks bakes his pies of time. Fucks up David the Scot on that lonely road outside South Dakota, tries to fuck up Lucknow Jimmy driving down the lonely road in his shitheap off to the city, tries to fuck up Walking Shoelace scudding down the hillside naked, busy guy. Violation after violation, pure elation to Bakks and his crew.

But Bakks and I go back a long way, and to tell the truth you wouldn't trust him with a kite let alone a tailwind of memories being flung around outside The Exchange. Besides dear butterfly, fake ones don't fly with that same shimmer: there's a peculiar weightless weight to the way a real memory gets thrown around, and we proper wooden boxes tend to see it, that weightless weight. Dried mashed potatoes like Bakks and his cardboard hoards, they don't got the same feel for it, and you do need the instinct for it. And so they assume-assume, that the rest of The Exchange is as parlous, or just dumb, as they are themselves in the subprime shitpool outside. But, problem: Bakks is this box who just ain't stupid, he's a giddy little flyer, here or there in a flash, over the mountains and the seas once he's chosen his target, hup two three.

Bakks and currency, well they're interchangeable when he's in the mood. He couldn't care less what the agreements are meant to be, he just takes what he wants, and takes with a mood that matches any of the mysterious phenomena floating around beyond the ozone layer. Simple as a whim: Bakks can catch sight of a creepy ol blame-buster of a storm, next thing: new currency.

Yottick, Meryl and a Hammer

Last month he made a whole new currency that excited a herd of cardboard newlyweds, that is, wedded to the Outer Exchange, a new currency that a new pack of fools began to trade. Led by that evil fucker Bakks, they kept themselves happy trafficking in sadness. And they traded with a vigour you won't get on The Exchange proper where real memories are the currency. Now ding-dong that's not too petty an achievement, but it certainly makes eradication into a nasty business for boxes like me. What ought Meryl do if she finds out for instance that her Piccadilly box Yottick is being fucked up by Bakks, being rendered unreliable by Bakks and his cohorts? She'll eradicate it, that's what, out of plain resentment, and who can lay blame on Meryl for that? Bakks is always mixing the jungarummy jiddle with other boxes: bad work, lousy work; mixing the memories between boxes is exactly what changes the dynamic that the powder-boxes can't keep tabs upon.

If Meryl the diviner finds out that Bakks is hurling utter crap at the safely protected box in the cotton cloth in the drawer behind the security of the purple jacaranda gardens, she'll be disappointed, she'll perhaps burn it. Or crush Yottick with a hammer. Jumping up and down on her two fast feet, hammer coming down, bang-bang, not even bothering to hold the box in one spot, just following the pieces around with her two fast feet, bash-bash. All that care, from one generation off to the next, buffed into waffle by Bakks and his newlyweds out at the edges of The Exchange. Not to forget all that precious care that Meryl took to retain the box's quiet authority on the subject of her lineage. All that sweet love she offered. She'd be furious, if she knew. If she knew that her line was being twisted out of shape. Complete with emerging falsehoods and fly-bys. But to avoid that fury, there is always a sneaky line in his hup two three. Bakks makes the work, the violations, slow enough, he makes it imperceptible enough, to keep it from changing colour. He keeps up the work behind those tavern backwalls, and for him it functions very well thanks a heap.

Technique on Meryl? Slow, Very Slow, and Invisible

It's a good technique, that stillness, if you're into trafficking in shit. By using the slow and imperceptible energy in counterfeiting a field of memories, using the technique of partial invisibility, you can assume Meryl would be pulled up short for a reason to crack a temper. Good news connection: no temper possible, no eradication possible, true. But she'd nonetheless have reason to grow lost and confused. And that's what Bakks deals in, he doesn't see memories as belonging to Meryl, he sees them as his trade, rightly, and so the profusion of sadness resulting from bogus memories is not, in the technical sense, his problem.

'In the technical sense,' he'd say, 'it's Meryl's problem, not my problem. What I, king Bakks, must do is simple: I prompt her to start a cracked up cake of blaming, and the rest is hers. Same cake different take. If she needs to see a penguin in the picture then there's a penguin in the picture. Same with that boat-boy, that Spanish kid from '47 at David the Scot's hacienda, but the Spanish kid was definitely a problem for me coz he hardly ever blamed anyone for anything the little squinty shit with his rusty key. Me, I can only use shits who like to blame, so the boy I left alone for a bit, but I can't speak for my crew if they wanna hassle the boy, they're eager, my crew, how am I supposed to control bigtime batfish eagerness in my swelling ranks?'

Bakks has it down pat, fine, but he can't do it alone. He has the crew. He has a club out there in the swill. Groupings, sorted using the vowels. A E I O U, so first he is called Bakks, then the other type of counterfeiter, the group known as the Bex, then the Bix, Box and Bux, numbering in the hundreds of each type, except that the Bux types are good. The other types, the evil takers like Bakks, they lurk in corners the world over, up corridors, down the shelves of shops, awaiting orders from Bakks. An evil crew of deadbeats, smellers, suckers of ratsblood, pure ratsblood leaking from the drains of counterfeit flow. Pongsters, each, smellbombs all of em. Ready to plough their hup two three upon the unsuspecting powderboxes up and down the coast.

Assistant to Bakks, Ratsblood Inch

One pongster in particular is worth keeping an eye on, scrutinise, coz he's keen to make a disastrous hup two three upon Jimmy Hazel. For us wooden boxes like me an Oxley an Flattie that attempt the good work this pongster was horrible.

He's a Bex, and the Bexes generally aren't into amusement, but this particular Bex they call Inch, well he's serious. And Inch is greedy, very serious and very greedy, like a cafe owner who is found sitting at a table in the cafe having a two-staff productivity meeting all day long and punching the odd furious extrapolation into the calculator with his greenback index finger, stippity-tap, pting-ptish, this equals that. Whenever I run into Bakks, Inch ain't far off.

Inch packed a surveillance camera, so he's tinged with a habit or two, bad yuk habits. One habit he'll never shake is that he vehemently insists he's always honing in on what he calls 'the truth.' Plus, it means Inch wouldn't know a real memory from a footpath. It is also fair to say, that of all Bakks's deadbeats, Inch is one of Bakks's more grubby counterfeiters.

But Bakks's entire crew, they are gladdened in one way or another by the shit side of life anyway, and they are excited by the shit of life with powderboxes, so Inch being the most serious and greedy of them all was somehow just another day at work. Thing most insulting to Inch is that he never really was a box, he was just cheapshit cardboard wrapping sort of squared off, and they pong even worse than all the other deadbeats and pretenders and ripe types.

So fact is, Inch should not have made it into the world of memory traders. But Inch made it into the world because he was habitually of it by virtue of the film of the security camera he once wrapped, now bolted to a corner somewhere and trained on a footpath. Which is to say Inch's pie-eyed counterfeiting of memory has no more dimensions than one. One dimension, plus it stinks. Shackled to surveillance footage for an eternity, or until eradication. No wonder the no-shape grunt ended up falling in with Bakks's pong of counterfeiters bouncing from one violation to the next, from Jimmy Hazel to Lee Glass-Darlington. Inch had plans for Jimmy and Lee, for Jimmy anyway.

Rumour goes that Inch waited in the basement of the surveillance camera factory in Guangzhou for quite a while before being shipped off to a surveillance goods distributor across the seas. The factory was located in a district in Guangzhou that was so grim, so polluted and so desperately unsanitary that the rat plagues in these factories were permanent. Inch sat around in the southern Chinese industrial darkness in the midst of these teeming plagues for at least a couple of weeks. Cardboard wrapped around a camera, cardboard that got gnawed every night by passing rats on their way to better meals like cockroaches the size of a baby rabbit. This chewed upon wrapping is nowadays the Bex they called Inch, stuff that still today has an abiding loathing of the poor rat, any rat. Me, I like rats, what I don't like is a termite. Chewed up by termites, no way boxes like me an Oxley wanna be mashed into termite excreta. If I was a fallen tree, yep, fine, return me to fertiliser, but a proper wooden box glossed into life in Colchester's workshop, no way. The frequency Inch wipes himself in ratsblood is almost too much to bear, his whole top, sides, base, his flaps, wings, all smeared in layers and layers of dried, caked, crusty red, every olden layer turning a rusty brown. And that we proper boxes call oxidation, Inch style.

Maybe that's why his second terrible habit is so spooky. When he's concentrating on a gig, getting nearer to the action, to warm up for a spot of trafficking, he starts this low, evil humming, chanting, a mishmash of hum-chant:

Kill the past
and kill it dead
or it just might
kill you instead

From where he got that extremist fundamentalist neo-Marxist shit graffiti about bombing the past I have no idea, except to try and imagine what it must've been like in his own past, in that putrid factory, to be gnawed at by rats all night every night. I too might have embraced neo-Marxist fixit dogma, how can one tell. One must just trust the instinct to feel what it must've been like to belong in Inch's past. Then one sees that it's right he should be such a severe hummer-chanter on killing the past.

So therefore he's got a couple of bling ideas on what makes the present the present, on what makes the now truly contemporary, up to the moment new. What's obsolete, what's in; what's twee, what's hot.

Helping Jimmy into a Violation

For instance, Inch likes the current fashion in security for code red. He loves the fact that the normal locks and systems of the gone old days that created a sense of safety around boxes like houses and banks, well, he loves that they've become petty little curios. Inch adores the fact that nowadays it is no longer about the pleasant concern of safety, nowadays everything has ramped up, to his great pleasure, become a fortress. He's right at least about that, check the list: what was once a dainty diplomatic house for parties, the embassy, has become a fortress, a busy engine of spies running around a house of lockdown aggression. Armed to the teeth with every gun n gadget under the sun. The embassies of yorc, yeah they were always a sinkhole of spies with fuck-all to do except get body odour in the armpit, but nowadays the olden embassy looks like a nice cute club.

Then the airport, once an exciting gateway to see the world and make new friends, has matured into an auxiliary weapon.

Then there's this: the cops now want ordinary citizens to use their mobile phones to photograph suspicious activity and send the pic to the new cop website.

Then there's the ongoing ding-dong of keeping up with cyber theft, ever more software for more and more hardware.

Inch loves the commotion because while the world is fixated with talking machines, with fingerprint recognition, with face recognition, eye recognition, voice recognition, DNA recognition, cameras, bugs, codes and firewalls, he can bounce his counterfeit round the place like an old-fashioned tennis ball, in and out of Jimmy Hazel's powderbox, and the putrid trafficking requires no recognition at all. Then, at the end of a productive day, dusting off with fermented ratsblood, yet again caking himself in that relic from his past. What Inch likes is the vivid stuff. Trafficking in counterfeit crap to him is the ultimate in vividness. He calls it vividity. We better boxes call it violation.

Jimmy Hazel Starts to Taste It

But oo-ee damn, does the fucker Inch stink, under all those layers of ratsblood. But the ratsblood bizzo from way back is his main mistake. As far as a moment of happiness goes, Inch has just the one form of happiness. A furious happy moment is the only one he's into, concentrated, intense.

The thing that got him very happy indeed was the fact that the Scottish Hindu was being hustled and harangued by the great Hindu deity Maheesha the buffalo demon of chaos and evil. But what Inch did not understand was the profound Hindu reverence for rats: a good Hindu celebrates rats, feeds them, sits with them, they are ancestors re-born. Living artefacts of souls that gave goodness and charity. So Inch's layers of ratsblood were really only layers of his own ignorance.

The layer however where Inch is a lot smarter than Bakks, and therefore uglier in his behaviour, is located in that most simple of all the simple facts of life. Inch understands that the free market at The Exchange, the free market of memory trading, is based at its core on a cache of unfree secrets. If these core secret agreements are blown, the market will cease to function.

Inch pushed into use the very same concealment principle in his dealings with his pungent crew of helpers, keep em on a need-to-know basis only, and he started to treat Bakks with the same disdain, which gave Inch regular moments of his happiness, the fury happy moment when he knew for certain he was doing his ugly work on Jimmy's powderbox. We wooden boxes proper, we liked and honoured the free market so we flatly refused to fuck around with it like Inch, but—and this we inside The Exchange all know—an opportunist is an opportunist, and when you see an opportunist caked in ratsblood you just let him get on with whatever he's doing. Avert your startled eyes and walk on by.

So between the code-red ramping up of locks and keys, and the application of the concealment principle, Inch was nicely set up to make counterfeit memories taste credible, even healthy, so his moves on Jimmy Hazel were to become easy, and Jimmy began to smell the urges so well that the gardening work at Meryl's had taken a back seat in the lazy summer days beside the bay.

And Inch was always shrill, except for a low hum-chant, he was shrill as a basement of rats. When he warmed up, chanting away in that shrill ratpitch, it was sickening, just sickening. Oxley felt he was funny, but I found him sickening.

Bakks Out of Whack

I said to his boss Bakks that he couldn't have the title Box in his evil crew because we wooden ones are boxes proper, but Bakks told me to go get fucked. He'd have his team of A E I O U boxes, and that's that. What he failed to discover was that the Buxes were ours, friends belonging to us, not his friends. The Buxes were good, and they appreciated being given good to do here and there round about.

When I asked Bakks why vowels, he said: 'Powderboxes love their stinking varwells.

'Make em choke on their varwells, gives me a laugh.

'Plus, Skinny, varwells are the key spaces—no varwells means gluggy words, and gluggy words means gluggy thoughts, and gluggy thoughts means gluggy memory. So their varwells are like the little princes, see, princes of space and sound.'

When I asked why only he exclusively is allowed the title 'Bakks,' and not the 'Bax' configuration like the rest were, he said, 'Coz you're lookin at the king of them princes, you fukkin skinny idiot. You're lookin at the king, and king starts with K.'

So Bakks wasn't unromantic. But wow was he, um, grim, and was he phew nasty. But complain he couldn't. He held the biggest share of all the counterfeit that got thrown across the seas and the mountaintops, so good luck to his romantic adventures I suppose.

Only one thing needs to be remembered about Bakks. It is not hard to see where his loyal gangs have been at work stewing up fake memories, securitising the cherished memories into evil shots of old porridge. The flavour profile is easy to spot once you're accustomed to it. Look for a certain gloss. Look for an earnest tinge. And keep an eye out for shrillfactor Inch the greedy smellfest with his penchant for ratsblood. Pushing into useage the principle of the not-so-free, free market. Especially when his loyal gangs infested the powderbox of that painter south of Perth, the hardcore merciless painter Dave in Margaret River; Bakks made him crush the life around him so comprehensively that he ended up rather close to crushing himself. Nice work, Bakks.

Jimmy's Liver and Bones

It's all very well for these counterfeit creeps, but a real memory has that exquisite weightless weight: it can exude a quiet magic and fill a day with life's riches.

And ding-dong, even Bakks couldn't figure out the magic of a simple yet complex piece of flight across mountaintops, and seas, and the two equators, such as weightless weight. I mean, how could even king Bakks explain the past and the present travelling duo on a skiff of weightless weight?

The differences between the real stuff and the counterfeit are many and amiable. But difference number one, the simplest point of divergence, is war and peace , is giving energy to war and peace, giving mojo to war and peace; Bakks and the pongsters even love teeny-weeny disagreements created from the counterfeit.

The difference between my trade, and the trade of the great King Bakks, is in the two following central points dear butterfly.

One. We boxes throw stuff around, and powderboxes share the memories, dispute the memories.

Two. Whereas no, Bakks and his crew, the Bexes, Bixes, Boxes (not us woodens), and not the good-loving Buxes, they create stuff that powderboxes like Jimmy Hazel didn't even realise existed. Then they share it thanks to the throwing around conducted by Bakks and his crew, and then they become more and more rattled by these fake slices of light, become so sharply fucked up in the head, that they take a perfectly reasonable dispute and make it slightly larger. Sometimes they take it from a personal dispute to a public war full of memory against memory.

I asked Bakks what he thought about this aspect of his work, and he said, 'In the technical sense it is not my problem, they each have a brain so it is their problem. They've got livers, bones, intestines, pull em apart Skinny, they're all the same, surprise surprise.'

Then he said: 'You ought to be grateful they have a brain,

skinny boy, we'd be out of work if they didn't. How the hell would we throw around their personal stuff if they didn't have a brain each, hm? How would we do this game, this best job in the world, hm? Think of that. Today if you get a moment. If you get a moment blown outside of your bubble of fake humility.'

Then, with a quick slap against his paper sides, Inch the smellbomb greedy, Inch the favourite assistant, turned to Bakks, shrill as a panicked rat: 'May I speak for you?'

'Go ahead.'

Inch turned to me: 'Look here you rotten little fucktoid, you wooden do-gooders give us the shits, know that. We put up with you, we tolerate the mess you create, dante we. But I now warn you, we will not tolerate dilutions of our grandeur. No dilutions of grandeur, period. You wooden do-gooders can't even get a grip on grandeur, you have no idea what it means coz you lot have owners, *owners*, you're all slaves every one of you rotten wooden fucktoids, not like us, we're free, we aren't fukkin well owned, imagine being fucking *owned*, makes me wanna be sick. You wait Bobbo, you see what my freedom can bring to this Jimmy Hazel powderbox, what bigtime liver and bones he gonna do round that house of naked walking shoelace.'

'Nicely told, Inch,' Bakks said proudly.

'Thanks boss. Fucktoid majora.'

I said to Bakks: 'Don't you have even a slight piece of ding-dong regret for all the sadness you cause? Even just a twinge? Lee Glass-Darlington is frightened enough already, sad enough already.'

Inch: 'Twinjj? What the hell is a damn twinjj? Take your fucktoid twinnjjee-winnjjee and go away. We can cash-in any memory we want, cash or stash or mash, even dash it to bits.'

Drop a Wet Box

Bakks carries an old injury. He's been dropped once, when damp, from waist high, by a fishmarket worker. So his injury, a slight crumple, looks like that Federation Square place in Melbourne, a crumpled box: that is, his injury looks actually quite good, has style, dented, carefree, careless, but ding-dong important.

This you could not tell Bakks, he felt he carried a major injury and that was that. So that's how he ran his counterfeit kingdom. Poor Jimmy. With all that wounded logic Bakks ran the deepest wellspring of junk the world has ever known. Poor damn Jimmy. Maybe they should've stuck a few of those stickers, 'Fragile,' to Bakks's sides like they do for boxes of crystal. But I doubt a sticker would have changed anything with Bakks. The game is what he liked, just the game, just the trafficking, just the violations, and he found that the blame lurking in a person's head was by far the easiest game around. Poor poor Jimmy.

Then again, Bakks is no grand old wooden chest decorated with slim straps of brass, borne of Arnie Colchester's beautiful studio-factory of shavings and scents, nor is Bakks a fold-out Oxley all hinged-up and buffed, Bakks is a cardboard box. He's an ex-prawnbox, and this he strenuously denies even tho in today's modern world of highly effective cleaners, there does indeed persist a smell or two that lingers no matter what. And ding-dong: smell's a mighty bigger engine of memory than those bigtime engines day and night, the dark powers of smell can take you home if you let them, to a prawnfarm.

Inspect a home, inspect a shop, everything arrives in a box, edible, inedible, fragile or futile. Only sunlight and moonlight don't arrive in boxes. Still, we boxes take those smaller-than-smell engines of memory, day and night, and we box em good, throw em round over the seas and the mountaintops.

Oxley says the rumour is Bakks was also a baconbox. A trainee butcher filled him with fresh bacon rashers and left him out the back too long. In the sun. The bacon went for a ride into smell hell, and Bakks has forever hated pigs. Me, I like pigs, aunt Lee's teak merchant dad had a back yard of pet pigs, he loved em, I loved em. Sweetest intelligence, full of affection, they talk, they quiz you up with their little eyes, waiting for the games to start, and they play, love it, the play. Wobble round the garden snorting and laughing like old men no longer needing to wake up early and fish for a living.

So maybe Bakks had a bad start. Had he instead done the hup two three as a box of chocolates from the Swiss Alps he might have escaped his crappy fate, but with Bakks you never know. Even if he'd been a box of pure bumble-bee honey from the tame shallow valleys of Wisconsin he'd find a bumble of a scheme to de-sweeten it. Even a box of Moët, he'd pop every bottle and pour them into a mouldy old wine cask, another box, but that he would not do, no sir, never, coz he hated moisture, liquid, water, drizzle, rain. Cardboard, see, cardboard.

The Fear of Relaxation and How It Moves from Cardboard Box to Powderbox

Memory is like water. This basic fact of life put off king Bakks bigtime. The flow, it's like water, a river, a lazy dazzle of light playing on the water's surface. Evaporates, turns to mist, the cloud in the distance speaks of things savoured. There's turbulence in the flow, and whirlpools, eddies, tides. Water can dissolve certain things—sugar, salt—just as memory can dissolve certain things. Water goes forth in three states, memory gathers in three states: cherished and loved, lost and forgotten, bitter and destructive, and Bakks enjoys the bitter stuff, the destructive memories.

Poor Jimmy, he was gonna smell a lot more trouble than he'd ever smelled behind the council garbage dumps back in Lucknow.

Bakks would shout: 'Excellent! Excellent! Get down to Tenmoon Creek and see what you can come up with, go!'

And the Bex or Bix would dutifully, gleefully, leap the seas and mountains, off to Tenmoon Creek, crossing both the equators, hup two three.

Team Odour

Inch could fly counterfeit from powderbox to powderbox with the ferocity of a big bomb, and he always boasted about being a jumbo jet. On that fateful meeting, Bakks also met Inch's cohorts, those nine pongsters who called themselves Centimetre, Metre, Millimetre, Yard, Foot, Mile, Furlong, Kilometre and that creep of all vain creeps, Lightyear. Cardboard blowhards, every one of em.

Vain show-offs too, taking their names from cyxmix, from the depth cyxmix can effortlessly gain, and the distance cyxmix can give, improving the cherished memories with the golden almond oil of love. That fuckface Lightyear was the most vain of them all coz he could hup two three a memory quicker than anything, quicker than smell, odour, scent, quicker than music.

And being quicker with memory transport than a song is really, really bad news.

But since '47 Bakks hasn't changed, O Bakks the king, not a jot, two extra rips down the side, that's all, which is to say he looks as tatty as he ever did, the king of creeps. I mean, yes he can fly in and out of memory's weather like the rest of us boxes, yes he can go on destroying the ache and sweetness of a beautiful memory, but fact is someone somewhere will always be making another violin, locked away by choice in a workshop with all those mingling scents filling the air, the resin from freshly cut pieces, the glues, the stains, and under those swirling scents continuing to tease the wood, slowly as ever, teasing the stuff into life as a violin. So that somewhere, someone, can pick it up and celebrate the sweetness of a beautiful memory, make a minor miracle of nourishing the present with other moments of giving. Unless Lightyear interferes, if that vain cardboard creep Lightyear gets a chance he'll use it. Whether it is loved and cherished, lost and forgotten, bitter and destructive, Lightyear doesn't care, he'll go ahead and use it bigtime. Fuckface's big interface with counterfeit pleasure.

It greatly helps Bakks that his assistant Inch has in tow the grotty crew he can call on to conduct the shittiest work that nobody else in the swill outside will touch. For instance, Bakks needed a simple dirty trick done on Lee Glass-Darlington. Violations, they were his beloved trade, out there in the swill that's all they ever did, violations. He held a meeting on the gig with Inch.

Bakks: 'Be warned, Inch, this idea of her powderbox, this view going round that her powderbox is petty, I don't like it. Her powderbox is one damn smart customer. What about you, do you think her powderbox is petty?'

Inch: 'Me? I dante. I simply dante. She's a lotta things but she ain't petty. She's great. Reckon she's powerful too, and sexy, I dig her vividity, she walks like a world, nobody walks like a world, everyone walks like a pit-pat slingalong, Lee lawyer chick walks like a rolling sexball out in space, talk about vividity.'

Bakks: 'That's your true opinion?'

Inch: 'That's the opinion, yep. I dante see petty when a world is walking, yang-yang wang-wang, nah I dante see petty.'

Kilometre

Bakks: 'Well get one of your crew to fuck with her powderbox.'

Inch: 'Yep, I'll try. But, but whatiff I fail?'

Bakks: 'I shall sack you and your crew, if you swine me off you're sacked, but I'll sack you first in front of your fucked up crew.'

Inch: 'I won't fail. Prefer to work with you boss, dante I. Let's try Kilometre, he's jumpo yes for use in misunderstanding.'

Bakks: 'Fine, go get him.'

Inch: 'Yep, okay, I shout.'

And Inch shouted, shrill as hell: 'Kee-lo-meeeter!'

They waited for Kilometre to show up from the depths down there in the swill.

Bakks: 'Well?'

Inch: 'Hmm ... he's too slow today, hold on, I shout bigger. KULLO-MARTAAR-MARTAAR!!'

They waited for Kilometre to show.

Bakks: 'Well?'

Inch: 'Shit, he's a fukkin-away today the bastard, hold on, I shout bigtime this time. HAA-LAAA-MAAA-TAA!!'

They wait.

Bakks: 'I'll square it off, Inch, your dudes are fucked, useless.'

Inch: 'Boss, no-no! My crew is good, hold on, see, over there. Ah, he arrives now, look.'

Kilometre: 'Hallo Inch, sorry I late.'

Inch: 'Is cool, buster, you grow up quicktime, this here Bakks.'

Kilometre: 'Wow, Bakks, the one, Bakks.'

Inch: 'Yep, now shut up, listen.'

Kilometre: 'Okay.'

Bakks: 'What I want you to do is get this woman down at Tenmoon Creek, this one, see, here, and another woman round here, see, in this gallery in London, and another woman here, see, in this gallery in Perth, name's Catherine Fekdin, put into all three powderboxes a misunderstanding, yes?'

Kilometre: 'Yep, can do, how big?'

Bakks: 'Very small, nothing huge, just one a them petty ones.'

Kilometre: 'Can do, mister Bakks.'

Bakks: 'What will you choose?'

Kilometre: 'Oh um, say fucking a man.'

Bakks: 'No, don't choose that, take a promise, yeah take a promise instead.'

Kilometre: 'Mister Bakks, sorry, promises, too foul with me, I can choose other things.'

Bakks: 'Use their promises.'

Kilometre: 'Um, all right then.'

Bakks: 'To one another, to each other.'

Kilometre: 'Yep.'

Kilometre shot off to Tenmoon Creek, over the mountains and the seas, across the two equators, hup two three.

Inch: 'Boss?'

Bakks: 'Shut up Inch, I'm thinking.'

Inch: 'Why are you look this time at issue small as misunderstanding, too clean, yuk, too pure, I no look small petty stuff.'

Bakks: 'Inch, you truly are quite stupid after all, that's why you ask stupid questions ...'

Here Bakks got it very wrong. Inch was, although pungent and shrill, he was certainly not stupid, he was in fact not too far from the ecstasy of overthrowing piggy Bakks completely, something Bakks would not smell for quite a while. Inch was actually conducting, day by day, night by night, a fairly neatly orchestrated push to bounce el creepo out of the vividity game completely.

I cautioned Inch to take it easy, I mean we all wanted Bakks out of the way, but to do it like Inch was gonna do it might get Bakks on alert; nobody wanted Bakks on alert, and so I gave Inch a minor clue: take it easy O ratsblood. But Inch had his plans, he was gonna do in Bakks like a garbage heap on fire, just like the one that torched the suburb after Patsy and Remple collapsed. Inch was a horrible fucker when we first met and he's a horrible fucker now, taken by some other force. He was never good even in a small way, drunk on bad, so bad luck to Bakks, and bad luck to boxes like me, bad was the thing with Inch's glow of vividity, bad bad bad. This is how bad, how excited, Inch can become in the hotter moments of trafficking: Centimetre once told Inch that in New Mexico one is able to visit the Los Alamos science museum, as the city of Los Alamos is America's ding-dong height of science pride, the peak. Inside the museum you can walk around Little Boy and Fat Man, replicas of the two bombs that destroyed Hiroshima and Nagasaki, and Inch nearly fainted with the extremity of his excitement, that's how bad the fucker is. But, for the time being, Inch was nowhere near as gruesome as Bakks.

The only one of Inch's crew that is a bit different is Yard. Yard is different in a few ways, but the first thing to note is that he started out as a box keeping together a litter of puppies in straw. Yard is the only smellbomb deadbeat who doesn't really belong in Inch's crew; Yard, a Bux, has to pretend being a nasty trafficker. But oddly, Yard has never left the counterfeiters. Why, I'll never know, such a sweet puppy, O Yard.

All the Grim Warping

One day I said to Bakks, very clearly, 'You are ruinous, you ruin memories by twisting them or changing them altogether, you ruin the facts.'

Inch turned to Bakks: 'May I speak for you?'

'Shut up, Inch, shut up.'

When Lee Glass-Darlington couldn't quite recall the sequence of events back at the hotel in Singapore in the hours before and after Rudolph went missing, it was coz Bakks had been to work on her powderbox. The only place Rudolph can today be found is as a clump of binary language on the missing persons database inside the Singapore Police. He is at risk of becoming a distant memory.

When Patricia is trying to figure out the sequence of events that laid waste to her and Remple, as her grip on the sequence becomes looser, less reliable, Bakks has been to work on her powderbox. The warping is Bakks, all the twisting and dissolving, Bakks. So, I said: 'You are in ruination of experience.'

'May I speak for you Boss!'

'Shut up Inch.' Bakks turned to me: 'Listen Skinny, don't you try and swine me off, I'm not in ruination of life, I'm in celebration. How else might you suggest myths get made other than by bending and scrubbing the facts, hm? You wage a losing battle, Skinny, myths get made like it or not, and might you understand why you are losing? You are losing because you're gross, and you're gross because you're negative, stop being so negative.'

Bakks was now warming up. 'All that I do is ... what would your friend the wowfuckme Lee Glass-Darlington that corporate lawyer call it in her jargon, that activity when you avoid a head-on court battle? Mediation, all I do is mediate, and all the world adores a mediator, Skinny. I'm a mediator that helps myths along, so what am I Skinny if I'm the best myth-helper in town, and get it right, I'm an enchanter. Enchanting is what I do. You, you're a bore.'

Grass Turns into Milk

Bakks tilted his tack. 'Look at it like this, plain as a staple, if you keep on telling the fekking truth, what chance myth, hm?'

Then he grabbed at his usual response. 'Be brisk, Skinny, brisk, comprendes the following fact of the world: things morph, Skinny, including memories, everything—everything—morphs, get used to it, boyo. In the sprinkling magic of things, grass becomes milk when you stick a cow into the equation. Likewise, and heed this one Skinny, memories achieve the status of myth when you stick Bakks into the equation. Comprendes? See you around, I'm off to Spain to check the progress on that Spanish kid in the hacienda.

'He's my latest project, Skinny, you'll want to inspect it when it's finished, this one, O yes, gonna be my pissaye de resistonce, and may the gods of eradication help you if your old-fashioned woody wings stand in my way. In fact, if you behave your do-goodie little self I shall consider installing you as my sartorial adviser.'

The finesse of appearance. Bakks likes that I'm a very nice teak box, sleek lines, brass hinges, grain of the ages.

Wood envy: it seems to produce in Bakks that grass and cow logic all the time. His whole damn team of smellbomb dead-beats has that boring fukkin wood envy.

If Bakks wants to see himself as a cow, that's fine, we boxes in The Exchange proper we understand our enemy, and we don't call them cows, we call them counterfeiters. They lay claim to being able to make soup from a leather shoe, but it just ain't soup. Looks like soup, smells like soup, but tastes like shoe. A counterfeit memory, face it, is a counterfeit memory.

Bakks's Hunger for Lee Glass-Darlington Goes Red Hot

The only time Bakks comes anywhere near making an excuse for his frightful behaviour is when he talks about his hunger.

Bakks claims he's nothing more than a box riddled with hunger pangs. Hunger for the game, hunger for the myths, hunger for yesterday, today, tomorrow, and the hunger for excitement. What erotic forces in the universe beyond the ozone layer invented a box like Bakks riddled with hunger pangs I have no idea. And anyway, if you ask me, Bakks's main pang is eroto-pang. He might like to fuck memory but he'd just as soon fuck a brick if he could.

But for all his hunger smarts, Bakks got one hunger gig wrong. He sent a member of his crew to Tenmoon Creek to try to plunder and pillage the powderbox behind the forehead of that walking shoelace Lee Glass-Darlington, maybe mix in Jimmy Hazel, gotta mix. Bakks thought it might be simple to warp and twist her memories. The logic was sound.

His wounded logic went step by step. It said Lee was a corporate lawyer, step two she's therefore proud, ambitious, lots of willpower, hard as nails, supple as a snake, she'd therefore be an excellent candidate for the game. He liked the fact that she spent a lot of time in a box, the office. Or the boardroom, box. Or zoom up, zoom down, fifty floors, a box, whoosh, ding. Plus Rudolph went missing, so for the great king Bakks Lee Glass-Darlington was truly yum, a prime-prime excellent candidate for his subprime game.

Bakks got it wrong; Lee was not only smart, she was also sensitive, most particularly she was sensitive to the feelings of another, and therefore she was often able to touch a leaf of the elegant vine of trust, which bloomed, as trust inevitably does, into reliable information about this or that memory. Lee was able, gifted shoelace was greatly able, to tell the difference between counterfeit memory and real memory, so when Bakks sent one of his Bixes down to the creek to see if he could fuck around with Lee's powderbox, the game didn't work. Her gymshoes were pinched, yes, maybe by the Lucknow jolly so that he could play smell games, fine, tho the Bakks game didn't work out at all. But that's the counterfeiter's central weakness, he tends to have such a good time doing it all that he ends up quickly falling into hunger mediocrity by going blunt, basic bigotry, aiming at the generic, like his currency. Plus, Flattie was in the way with her relish. So Bakks has his shortcoming, but he always loved the game, no ding-dong doubt about that, and he would take his bite at success elsewhere. As it will become horribly apparent after one or two later games of violation. Like he says, 'If you need to see a penguin in the picture then there's a penguin in the fukkin picture.'

I am Orange, I am the Present, but ...

On the Tenmoon Creek peninsula at Pittwater no powderbox lives in the present, which is perhaps why they say There's No Time Like The Present, meaning it. Like Meryl they're dreaming back into their powderboxes, the glow of yesteryear, or making plans and ambitions for next year, nobody actually has a foot planted in the present. In fact, face it, nobody anywhere lives planted in the present, they're all on a drunken roll of hope for tomorrow and a yearning for the sweet bygone days, things gone by like a scent of vanilla in the night. All of which means we boxes are by far the busiest highways in the whole universe when you come to think of it, the amount of work needing to be done, the busiest backlanes this side of the ozone anyway.

Hello, where do you live?

In the past.

And you?

In the future.

Noting the vacancy of the present is all very positive and straightforward, until we realise that a taste for the past and the future also makes Bakks's frightful work of grim warping a whole lot easier. You needn't move mountains when there's already a compulsion available, you just tweak the compulsion and the rest is history.

Kings and Cops

Bakks is forever complaining that his beloved game is spoiled. Says the troops around The Exchange, far too many nosey troops. Eradicate, he says, fumigate. Agreed to with force by mister surveillance himself, the no-shape prince who adores vividity, Inch, O greedy Inch.

Too many troops? Ding-dong since when did anyone run shop without an army in tow, never. King Bakks won't listen, so remind him of another king in another time, a titan who would make Bakks look like a sweet puppy, a Yard puppy, nice way to infuriate Bakks, compare kings, pit em against each other, king upon king, who's the greatest, ey Bakks? Yee-ha, Bakks in a fury.

Start with the thing Bakks hates the most coz it's the thing that makes his counterfeit weak, Bakks's weakest point, water, anything water, even moisture. Cardboard blowhard. The Ming emperor in the fifteenth century sends a fleet of thirty thousand troops to establish Malacca to his own tastes, to create his gateway to trading the Indian Ocean rim, option a bit of his own trafficking.

And then those lard-pushing latecomers, the East India Trading Company, has a huge fleet of armed vessels plying the airconditioned shopping arcades of the age, Java, Calicut, Hormuz, Calcutta.

And then the greatest astronomers of the period, those other sophisticated navigators who could find their way around open seas—ocean, Bakks, ocean—using their starmaps in the night-sky, the betelnut-pushing Arabs, cruised the highways of the sea selling boxes of exotic remedies, with troops in tow. With troops in tow the traders could sail the world in search of what they wanted, gold, slaves, spices and ding-dong surprises by the thousands. By now Inch is panting. Bakks is reaching a pitch of fury. With the help of troops they could protect the hold, and impose a takeover too.

These days troops tend to hang around oil, not boxes of remedies. And these days there is just the one acceptable means to colonise a coast or a city or a country, and it ain't surveillance cameras, hey-ho sorry-o.

Inch is shaking like a leaf, his caked-up exterior taking a fresh crack, red flecks falling to the floor: 'May I speak for you!'

Bakks: 'Shut up Inch.'

While the troops hang around the gulf, do like a gulf-state does—say Abu Dhabi—and buy a big American bank, say Citigroup, which by the way is a moneybox. Start buying other piggy banks, cuter ones like hedge funds, buy a big shop like Harrods, a nice shop chockablock with boxes, buy whatever you can, colonise by true trade, no troops required, just ding-dong oil money, tonnes of it a day, money which the target country gives you in the first place for your oil. Abu Dhabi can dear butterfly coz it has the biggest moneybox in the world, a shiner they call a sovereign wealth fund: the guy who controls the fund, hereditary king of Abu Dhabi, won't say how much, but the best money analysts dug deep, nosey-nosey, and finally they estimate four hundred billion to eight hundred and seventy-five billion American bucks ping around in this moneybox. Abu Dhabi is the capital of the United Arab Emirates. And Abu Dhabi is the owner of eight tenths of OPEC's reserves, a club of dudes that has very little interest in your habitat dear butterfly. Or wait until the house of cards collapses and then buy everything cheap, a penthouse for a penny. Nice view if you can get it. O what a greasy panorama. If this is the age of financial colonisation with all those gigantic piggy banks, the sovereign funds barging through borders like a buffalo demon, then hey-ho the pivotal place of yet another box, the greasy moneybox. Inch's surveillance habits: useful here.

Anyway, point is, our box troops around The Exchange are troops by mere name. In reality they are an unwashed, lazy pack of dreamers who wouldn't know day from night, and knowing that elementary difference is a very large part of a box's business. You need to know day from night if you're in the business of throwing around bits and pieces across the blurry boundary of the second equator. Even sun-dappled Oxley knows day from night. You need to know a bit about that second equator rolling round the planet north–south.

O yes, Bakks was to take a bite at success, troops or no troops, the game is what he liked, hunger or no hunger, relaxed or irritated.

'See you around Skinny, I'm off to check my progress, mine, on that Spanish kid in the buffalo-demon hacienda.'

What he meant was: See you around, I'm off to make a situation. A situation is very important to Bakks. No sooner than you have a situation, every utterance is true. Specially a situation like a dispute. In a dispute it won't matter what anyone says for or against, it all weirdly becomes true. Perfect conditions for Bakks. It's all true, mulch on, mulch till you drop.

And hup two three king Bakks the self-proclaimed enchanter was away. Across the seas and over the mountaintops, across the two equators, to attend to his latest evil gig on the coast of Spain, bringing his wounded logic to bear on all that putrid trafficking, fucking up the memories of the innocent bystander. Not to mention Lee Glass-Darlington, Catherine, Patricia, Remple, Meryl of the jacaranda verandah, and David of the hacienda. Bakks did not go near Jimmy Hazel because Jimmy's powderbox was full of butterflied prawns, but he sublet Jimmy to Inch. Poor poor Jimmy soon to battle an addiction to walking shoelaces.

Give and Take Tucksick and Lucksick

Inch had a niche skill bigger than king Bakks. Inch could cantilever a prospect across to another prospect no matter how unrelated or bogus, the myths were screwed looser if Inch got a hold of the powderboxes, the counterfeit rougher. Even a very small cantilever, one vowel to another vowel, spoke of the portent of Inch's niche skill.

I said to Inch: 'You are toxic Inch, just plain ol toxic.'

Inch: 'Tucksick, what the hell is tucksick you pompous wooden fucktoid, we're tucking a bit of sick into our lids, are we? Fucking slaves, make me wanna be sick.'

But all of us boxes have one skill in common, owned or not owned, wooden or cardboard. We do the hup two three, the jungarummy jiddle.

Put it this way: it might look like we sit idle in a corner, or on a table, or on a shelf, when in fact we are swimming in deltas and rivers and oceans of memories, constantly. Plus, we can be thousands of miles apart and still do the talk, do the trade, hup two three, over the hungry seas and over the ravenous mountaintops.

Bakks can be sitting on a shelf in London, Inch can be lying in the dust in the Western Australian desert—won't matter a jot: they can easily arrange to bring the grim warping to any powderbox anywhere. They'll fling it well past comfortable and safe language into haranguage, twanguage, pranguage, all the grim shit they love so much. Easy as beathing. Or, in your case dear butterfly, easy as drifting on a breeze.

The cardboard smellbomb deadbeats would love it if they could deal in the future, see the future of a powderbox, but they can't, neither can the woodens.

The single saving grace is that memory is a bit like water, and Bakks the evil fucker hates water. His fear of water looms rather large. And since Bakks and I go back a long way, you can bet your last counterfeit dollar, your last violated penny, on another fact of life.

Serious greedy smellbomb Inch was not far behind, making sly and smart preparations to eradicate his enchanter boss, making preparations to becoming the king of counterfeiting out there in the swill, counterfeiting from the hacienda to Meryl's place in Sydney. And sucking on fermented ratsblood as he went, across the mountaintops, hup two three, in search of his vividity.

The bad bad tucksick Inch, flying across the two equators like a jumbo jet, chanting his neo-Marxist mantra, humming and chanting for the birth of a new start, a fresh new order, 'Squash the past and squash it dead or it just might squash you instead.' And he'd get his way, O yes, because his boss Bakks, the king of Taking, never, ever, had learned the simple art of taking good advice.

If he had, he could've taken a chat with Ellie-Isabela. Staring from the window of her tiny room behind the kitchen where she gave away her illuminations, staring across the sunburnt ancestral lands, Ellie-Isabela could've shown lucksick Bakks a thing or two about the give and the take.

Sunrise on Patsy's Boulevard

Ain't just Bakks's beloved game that likes stumbling upon a predisposition to one compulsion or another, bumbling onto a grand view. Every game in town likes a good eye, and one of the best eyes in town is Patsy the fingerer's eye. Sharp as a quill with all that vitamin D in her limbs, promoting gallons of vitamin A to the retina. Back in London after a week in Sydney she woke to a strange tangle of a day, but Patsy was nobody's fool, she could untangle any tangle, she could handle untangling a string of stars if given the task. A night prowler had placed a box on the doorstep. It looked like a plain box the size of a suitcase, which is to say another unpleasant cardboard box. A note attached to the lid read:

A good game ***loves*** *a good eye.*

She took the box inside, lifted the lid, and found nothing but a small card:

> *This is a powderbox, it has the appearance of being empty, but bring a good eye to bear upon that hefty emptiness and watch what happens.*

Patsy lived on the third floor, and she had the gallery cleanly laid out on the second and ground floors. As London's coolest art dealer she could untangle a string of money, a coiled ego, a twisted hardhead, a hedge-fund blowhard, a vulture-fund blowhard, she could even untangle a banker, she could've helped mister Paulson untangle Bear Stearns had he asked, the whole securitised universe, had he asked, but she hadn't yet learned how to untangle a curse. I mean, she was still very busy trying to untangle Catherine's curse on her own beautiful love affair with Catherine's brother Remple. But being a tad ignorant of how to untangle a curse, well so what. That in itself I do not hold against the gutsy gungho Patsy, I mean the country alone is tangled up; calls itself a tangle of things: England, Britain, Great Britain, United Kingdom, British Isles. So how to expect a resident, when her country can't settle on a title as plain as its own name, how's she meant to uncurl a curse? There are two types of curses down round London, and that's dirty and clean, and by far the more difficult one to untangle is the clean curse, much more difficult. But how, tell me truly, could London's smartest art dealer know anything about the difference between dirty curses and clean curses; curses ain't underwear, yep they're tight, but they ain't underwear. How could anyone who treated that box at lunch in Sydney so badly, how can they know anything at all about a curse?

The note in the box concluded:

A good eye is just the sucker a game wants, for what is a game without a sucker? With a good eye comes the habit, and when the habit is established there's no going back, not from the sweet centre of it all. Welcome to the game.

She went back to the top of the note, and because it started with 'This is a powderbox,' she picked up the phone and called Meryl in Sydney. Diviner Meryl Glass-Darlington got up in the middle of the night, took the call, and confirmed that she had nothing to do with the delivery of the box. Over the next month Patsy almost forgot about the box, but it touched her gungho mind every second day. Plus, it wasn't a curse at all. Patsy suspected it to be a curse because, like a good dealer, she was a suspicious bonbon, but it was not a curse at all. In fact, the powderbox that landed on her pukka gallery doorstep might have been a half-century-old message from a flea-bitten boy in Spain. Living in a hacienda where the buffalo demon Maheesha roamed up and down the cool stairwells of siestas, a message twisted by Bakks and the pongsters into an unsuspecting crazy banker tipped over the edge by the melting of the banks.

III

A girl is given an unusual pair of wings, and from this unusual gift she becomes the matriarch

1-1-1, When-When-When. When in Spain, do as the Spaniards do: Ask a Simple Question of the Powderbox

It's a fact with villagers on the Golfo de Valencia coast that David the Scot likes his work caring for the children at the hacienda Zaragoza, so Bakks and Inch got a good start in the plunder and pillage of the coast's smaller powderboxes.

Less known is the odd truth that, on this coast, when a triumph arrives, it arrives in threes: 1-1-1, 2-2-2, 3-3-3 and so on.

For example, the older boys of the hacienda Zaragoza promised the girls of the village 'how to do the best sexing.' But when? By the time the boys finished their talking about it, announcing it, singing it out loud, all the girls of the northern tip of the village had married and had kids of their own.

See, had the boys suggested their trumped-up tuition three times, just three, chances are they might have enjoyed a rubbing and poking party not easily forgotten, an experience even Bakks couldn't destroy. Even with Inch's grubby, caked-up help. But the flea-bitten boys babbled on past the golden threes, those older boys, the golden threes, when-when-when. One one one, two two two. Think three, for a triumph.

The hot afternoon back in 1947 when one of the younger boys, the shy and quiet Kieran Leeft, the newly named Sunrise Sunset, jumped the perimeter wall of David the Scot's gardens of the hacienda, he sought a small triumph. So slight it could barely count as a triumph: he wanted to find his dusty friend. Sling the hot afternoon round her shoulder and maybe together enjoy a cool drink. Kieran was not a club with the older boys with their hurry courage, and he had no wish to promise Rosa any tuition.

Finding Rosa Mendoza would be a simple enough thing to do, for what's complicated about meeting your friend, saying on a hot sunny afternoon, 'Let's go diving off the jetty and wrestle a shark,' and, in a way, the boy was right. For while the village seemed to be a place of busy laneways, at least in the imaginations of the twenty-six orphans inside those shady walls, it was more, outside their imaginations, a sleepy place of dusty trees and three lazy squares. Hardly a thing got done from week to week. Twelve boats of peeling paint fished the Golfo de Valencia. Colonel David raised goats in his spare time. The shops along the ocean road would open and shut, and a traveller or two burnt out from the war would loaf around during the day, and, at night, along the side verandah would weep his broken spirit to sleep.

So the boy was right, Rosa Mendoza would be easy to find, and first he'd check on the other side of the main square because Rosa did not live behind ten-foot shady walls as he did. Rosa lived in a comfortable house with her parents, out near the sunny beach at the southern tip of the village.

The idle moments climbing the shady wall of vines back in '47 still disturb Kieran's powderbox today, mainly because of the great rule on this coast, that when a triumph comes, it comes in threes. Produces a lingering bitter taste until the third part arrives to complete that, um, triumph. Provided Bakks is kept under control. If Bakks could, he'd simply destroy the third part where the sun pours in. Where the sun brings nice big sheets of potential, offering possibilities.

The first part, escaping the Scottish Hindu, was plum simple, for the colonel forever hung in corridors tangled in his fear of Maheesha the buffalo demon. Then, for Kieran to move low between the others in the house, including Ellie-Isabela, who cared nothing about Maheesha, this proved tricky but also simple.

When Kieran made it to the end of the overgrown gardens, it was pure: he climbed the broad branches of the old fig, jumped the stone wall, and, well, he was away, pure. He didn't even look back to see the place from the outside on this, the last day. Straight ahead was the thing now, somewhere out there, out here, in the pure sky where the orange butterfly headed off with his crumpled marching. Kieran's eyes bulged with tied-up glee as he took up the ocean road, and he strained to avoid breaking into a smile. Two-thirds of a small triumph, one part to go.

Now that he had successfully escaped, a spring in the foot made him eager for the dusty friend's fun. Rosa knew the village, the good beaches, the streams and the hillside forest where the old abandoned farms finished, there was a lot to do on this great day when he'd made the decision to climb the wall. And what a sun-filled round afternoon visited the open village in '47, he was right, she'd be easy to find in this happy light.

But Kieran was deceived by the happy light. This, the slower realisation, also hums in his powderbox today more than half a century later. Early in the new freedom he felt certain he'd encountered Maheesha, that buffalo demon of chaos and evil that the colonel had warned them of many times, the admonition done hotly, with flaring eyes and sometimes pops of spit. For the Maheesha speech, or for his other speech about dreams awaiting the girls and boys, the colonel always chose the moment of hunger, before dinner.

The twenty-six children were seated at a plate ready to be

served with potatoes and Mendoza's sardines. In a stream that sounded like another language, and with tears welling in his eyes, the colonel's description of Maheesha the buffalo demon of chaos and evil would run round the plate before the eyes of the children. No food would be served until the colonel once again digested the tale for his own self-preservation.

The colonel's powderbox still carried the moment when he was seated on a box of his belongings on the empty backroad in South Dakota.

The powderbox behind the colonel's forehead was now also rampant with galloping buffaloes, lurking buffaloes, buffaloes gathered in judgement round a swamp electrically charged with the festering alchemy of oxygenated, nitrated mud, Maheesha's bloodsoup the colonel had said, The Buffalo's bloodsoup.

In a small village on the coast dear butterfly, one would think the head of an orphanage would rightly be, say, a good man from Barcelona, a fine Catholic skilled by the gifts that arrive by living the ordered and vibrant life. But the colonel, a good Scot, had lived in Calcutta as a Hindu among many lost Scottish Hindus in that great sprawling city of lost myths confected by Bakks and his crew. The curious thing: back in Calcutta the great city of hope, the Scot's Maheesha reminder was never a daily ritual. The buffalo's gaze became a nightly event only when David relocated to Barcelona and then south to the small village, for the job of administering the house of children. This nightly event created an unexpected thing.

It created a diaspora, a small, tiny, miniscule one, but a diaspora nonetheless, at least in the eyes of the Soho primdicks who knew aunt Lee, those patrons of Suave's who take great pleasure in pointing to any movement whatsoever as a diaspora. David's nightly pops of spit created the Scottish/Calcuttan/Hindu diaspora of the Golfo de Valencia. I don't hold any certainty that the colonel's powderbox was the work of Bakks and his filthy crew, but yes I'd bet on it long.

So the demon Maheesha had galloped across the world, over the seas and over the mountaintops, to run each evening round the meagre plates of Spanish children. Seated obediently behind the shady walls of the old hacienda, the famous little orphanage, vainly called the hacienda Zaragoza by a forgotten patron now lurking in the cardboard dust of nobody's memory. But certain small people, when cut free, can dance over the warm rooftops of towns when the big people are busy ripping off one another's ears over their shutters of perception. And two kids here are about to fill their respective powderboxes by meeting for a dusty swim to slap about a shark or two. All is well: they're about to make a slab of fine, excellent stuff we boxes can throw around, toss across the seas, bits maybe to London in the next century, maybe to bonbon Patsy's pukka doorstep, yep, all's well, har har, ding-dong and how's the time. Get them bumbling, we boxes, we pirates, we like to watch a bumble, O bumble-bumble. Oxley's seen plenty of bumble-bumble, Flattie more.

Jumping into Pesos— Two Triumphs Quick as a Smile

Kieran walked the dusty streets of the small village slowly, a good technique, no need to attract attention, towards where he would try first her sky-blue house. But walking slowly was not working. He walked towards the southern tip of the village faster and faster, eager and shaking. When he rounded the last corner out near the ocean he did slow down, but that was due to a natural panic that the house lay barely twenty paces off. At the front gate of the small sky-blue house he stopped because his heart was beating too loudly. He walked up the little lane to the front door, and it lay thrown open so he stole inside where he was about to make his way up the corridor to the kitchen when he noticed the place was empty. This moment, when he stepped very slowly into the open door to see the landscape of an empty shell of Rosa Mendoza's house, also dominates his powderbox today. Dust lined the empty shell, no chairs, the kitchen table had gone. Also gone, her father's recreational fishing gear always stashed up the end of the corridor like a winter tree.

Powderboxes dear butterfly, are made in all shapes and sizes, and they contain all manner of abandoned bits of life, from torn bus tickets to a moment shared over a mug of re-used tea. One powderbox might be this, one might be that, one can be dominated by starlings, another by fish, or sometimes offal, or sparkling gems, or chickenfeet, in the colonel's case it was Maheesha, the list is long with the powderbox. Variant, that's the key to all powderboxes, the variant. Which is what excites Inch, all those millions of possibilities dear butterfly for his gleeful counterfeit thrown at your custodians. Inch's hup two three across the seas and over the mountains was made bigger and better by the variant. Outside the walls of an old clay house that sits back from the ocean road, a boy is on a stroll over the rooftops of towns. It's a journey that begins to fill his powderbox, but the one moment he would never quite forget is that footstep over the threshold of the front door into that empty domestic landscape of dust.

A man sitting on the porch of the house next door said in a polite Spanish, 'You have come to visit the Mendozas?'

'Yes.'

'He's gone, drove away on Tuesday. Took the family to Almeria.'

'Almeria? Where is that?'

'South.'

Kieran said nothing.

'That way,' the man said.

'Can I walk there?'

'Yes sir you can, if you want to walk for six months. But you're better off going to the main road and getting a lift with the trucks, that should take a week.'

'Why did they leave?'

'These days after the war Almeria has plenty of work. Aren't you supposed to be in the hacienda, since when did that smelly Scottish fellow let you kids out after lunch?'

'I have escaped.'

'Oh? Well good for you. I have never escaped from anything and I'm forty.'

'Almeria? Are you sure?'

'Do I look like a man who would lie to a buffalo boy?'

'I am not a buffalo boy.'

'You're all buffalo kids in there. But you're right, now you've escaped you are no longer a buffalo boy. So what will you do? Now that you have escaped the Scottish Hindu.'

'I'll get on a truck and find her.'

'Do you have any pesos?'

'No.'

'You will need pesos, how will you get pesos?'

'I'll sell pescado.'

'Who taught you how to fish?'

'She did. It's okay, I'll go out to the main road and follow them, I'll find her.'

'Here, I have a few pesos. I'll give you these pesos to help you on the journey down to Almeria to find her, but first you need to convince me that you are no longer a buffalo boy.'

'I am not a buffalo boy, dammit!'

'Do you believe in the colonel's dinnertime warnings?'

'No! That stuff's for the small ones in there.'

'You do not believe in Maheesha the demon of chaos and evil?'

'No, I don't, that's right.'

But Kieran had lied. After two years eating the colonel's teachings it was difficult, and it could be said that the colonel force-fed Maheesha into the children's fig-big powderboxes. Hindu Maheesha for a pack of tiny Spaniards with tiny powderboxes. That's okay, what harm can it possibly bring, a custom crossing the sea, a Hindu cosmos drifting over to the Golfo de Valencia thanks to a shipping container that looked not a little like a Scottish powderbox.

'All right then, here, take these pesos.'

This gift of survival pesos to start the journey from the village was another welcome slice of the second part of Kieran's small triumph, but the third part would elude him for a very long time. For Kieran and Rosa the second equator would roll and roll, starting from the days on the beach, or the jetty, or hanging around on the road outside her house. These were all the flavoured and savoured things inside Sunrise Sunset's powderbox, no problem, but the main thing was the discarded floor of the empty house, the shock, bits of litter all over the place, making it look like the Mendozas had been hunted from the house rather than taking an orderly exit for a new life in Almeria. The second main thing in his powderbox was a lot happier, and even tho the littered empty house drove his nights, it was the happier stuff that drove his days.

Like the time Mendoza had found a ten foot length of thick

plastic floating out on the gulf. He towed it back to the village and bolted it to the jetty so that a good eight feet of it lay out above the water. He then taught Rosa to dive. He taught Kieran too. The standing dive was first, the running dive second. For the standing dive his instructions were detailed. Walk slowly to the end. Keep your toes over the edge, grip the edge, get the toes right over it. Arms up, up, hands together. Now begin your bounce, more, more, now away, and his small daughter would spring into the hot air of the gulf, make a small arc and slip into the water. For the running dive he taught them how to take the foot up and make a big bounce, and the scope of the running dive became the favourite. The last press of olive oil was always handed to the fishermen to help make the slick of blood and oil to bring in the fish, and Mendoza kept a bucket aside for the diving. He said to apply the stuff to the whole body, tip to toe, and see then how the dive goes, see what happens when you hit the water, and the kids felt it. That famous bucket of last-press was stashed and buckled in the boy's powderbox forever, the scent of that last-pressed oil. Didn't matter where he stood, sat or slept, if he caught a scent of that last-press he was bouncing high into the hot clean air of the Golfo de Valencia, 1947. It was just after the world had smashed itself to bits, just after Bakks and the deadbeat crew of counterfeiters got in too much success. But the kids of the hacienda on the Golfo de Valencia were eleven and ten: what they knew was the sun was hot and the sea was cool, not the world had gone into a frenzied orgy of violence. Ellie-Isabela had said they were just activities, they were not nice activities, but they were just activities.

And so Mendoza that summer taught Rosa and Carlos how to dive like kingfishers, and the birds dived almost every day. The other kids who could swim joined in the diving, and the frenzy was judged, to look at from the height of the roadside,

David said to Ellie-Isabela and her cousin, wonderful and beautiful and glorious. Two months of high heat in a long summer. Mendoza would sail back in with a catch only to see the hacienda kids bouncing off that piece of plastic. But when Carlos ran up Mendoza's street and stood at the empty floor of his house, door thrown open, windows open, light splashing around bare walls, bare rooms, and the guy next door handed him a few pesos, that moment was definitely a sorrowful piece of war debris that Bakks somehow stashed into the kid's powderbox.

Ellie-Isabela had been right when she warned colonel David, the kid was going to run away and cause trouble. Cause shit, she'd said.

A banging on the colonel's door. 'Señor señor!'

'What is it Ellie?'

'He is gone, señor,' and the cleaner turned to put her back to the wall for stability but she slid down to the floor and began to let go, a quiet weeping welled up from the shoulders.

David sat down beside her and he brought his arms around the jumping shoulders, trying maybe to set a direction for the give, a direction back into the greatest giver of the village.

Triumph Number Three Rolls Far Away Under Too Many Second Equators

Down the road Kieran picked up speed, then he began to skip over the patterns of shade and light, and then he started running, and he ran all the way over the hill and he kept on running and running, faster and faster. Over the heads of the big people he ran with the wind at his heels. He sailed through the shutters of perception that had ripped the world to bits, he ran across bridges, along highways, through forests, up into lofts and down into basements, he had to, needed to stay running, always running, for it gave his nostrils the air to keep calling out. Rampant energy for the outside is how he arrived at a curl in time he just didn't count on, a curl in time when the windspeed running slowed right down almost to a halt. This is the first part of the question. At what moment in Kieran Leeft's adulthood did he encounter that boy? When exactly was it that he met himself as the escapee he once was; the boy who set out running non-stop in search of his friend? For he did run out into the world from the old hacienda Zaragoza, leaving the place with one less child, and much later, as a big person, he certainly did encounter himself as a small one, Maheesha or no Maheesha, Scot, Catalan or Moroccan.

All dusty small people slow down to arrive at destinations unknown, and Kieran Leeft was no different. Every dust-made kid can, and many do, meet themselves, watch themselves chase a dream, scattering around back gardens, climbing trees to examine, from high above the dust, where the world might begin, helped along by us boxes, us restriction-free pirates, no-rules, burn the rules, hup two three. Like all dust particles Kieran the boy is resourceful when it comes to slipping into or out of shutters, swift, hopeful, and, maybe, just maybe, he gave the half-broken shutters of perception the slip. The way ahead now, outside the locked gates of the orphanage, and down the main road south to the buzzing port Almeria, for Kieran Leeft, is clear as a bowl of their salty ugly soup.

The windspeed journey spent racing through those shutters of perception was to be a rocky one, testing his fine skill at every obstacle, folding smooth resourcefulness into rough cunning, and bending the sightlines of high hopes toward soul-destroying dead ends of thick mud. He was eleven and had lean arms and quick eyes and strong legs. He'd lived his life in the hacienda, and the future outside the old farmhouse now belonged to the strong legs. He was away to seek out, in the colonel's words, his dreams.

Two of the big people were testing their shutters at a table in a cafe. Kieran recognised it, the testing, right away when he ran in to pause for a glass of water. He didn't know who they were, to him they just looked like yet more big people tugging at the ears. He was breathing heavily, but he asked politely at the counter for a glass of water, the man gave him a glass, Kieran thanked him, threw the water down his gullet, and he was on his way again, out the door. Down a cold London road, yes, a different road to the one he'd escaped. He ran down the cold miserable road today, and the other in '47 was hot and dusty. The split seems odd, but only at first, once the powderbox is flung open it is not odd, a hot dusty road one moment, a frosty one the next, not strange at all dear butterfly. Across the seas and over the mountaintops, across both the equators, hup two three, even my hippy friends at NASA would pay a pretty packet. Trouble is, they don't deal in memories like we boxes deal in memories, O poor NASA unhappy to the last.

Brushing Closer to the Third Part of the Triumph: Carlos Runs into Patsy's Hottest Painter

The simple question to ask of the powderbox, in a curious way, was connected to the boy and the two big people at the table who continued to prise open the shutters. When the art dealer Patsy Murray asked her hottest painter Jack Black if he'd been able to 'smell the troubles in the early days,' it was not an interest in Jack. It was altogether an interest in someone else that Jack knew well enough to answer the question directly and with enough emotional authority to cause Patsy to ask in the first place, to cause her to hitch up her nose.

'Some dickhead left an empty shoebox outside the gallery this morning,' she said.

'Why are you telling me this?' Jack demanded.

'Was it you?'

'Why would I do something like that?'

'Don't swine me off, you would do it because of the note.'

'I like you Patsy but I don't send you love notes. It was probably Remple, maybe he's not really over you after all.'

'It talks about a good game liking a good eye. That's you.'

'Well, you do have one of the best eyes in London.' Then he tried to piss in her pocket: 'One of the best eyes in the whole world my dear Patsy.'

Patsy took no notice, she continued unblinking.

'And it talks about powderboxes, that's you as well. You and another friend of mine in Sydney, but she's already said no.'

'You mean your friend Meryl.'

'Yes, Meryl told me she had nothing to do with it. Did you put the shoebox there on my front step?'

'No, I did not.'

'All right. I believe you.'

But Patsy's query about smelling the trouble made Jack bristle with half-thoughts, and the sudden flurry behind his forehead might have looked like a flock of starlings that scattered in ten directions. Patsy Murray was making an attempt to feed from his powderbox, which is the easiest means to mingle two separate powderboxes' contents. Fact is, powderboxes mingle in a thousand other ways, bumping, scraping and hustling, because they tend to be capable of using more than just language, powderboxes are capable of using twanguage, pranguage, haranguage, banguage, ganguage, songuage and, not least, winguage, wings across the mountaintops, best job in the world. And dusting up against one another across the two equators, they spring a leak, as Jack would find out. The Scottish Hindu colonel in the village put it like this: 'Our powderboxes up here *do* leak, oh yes,' he'd tell monseigneur Aballte every Sunday, 'we must never forget this, sir, no, no.'

Smell, Jack then thought with irritation, the trouble in those early days, what a pathetic tool Patsy's using to enter the subject of, what would it be called with Patsy—lost love. A lost Remple.

Maybe like a lost Rudolph, duct taped off to who knows where, maybe to the centre.

Neat batting, Patsy and Jack were seated comfortably in the humming cafe, warm indoors, icy outdoors, and she'd managed to splinter his afternoon forehead with an aside sounding like a contented sigh. One of Jack's scattering half-thoughts: So there it is, yep, a quick Patsy Murray–yawn, that'll do it, open the wounds.

Another quick-thought: And whose wounds she's on about, that I do smell, yep.

In Jack's perception there'd always been a primal colour to

Patsy's abilities. Even tho she held sway as one of the nimblest intellects he'd come to have the pleasure of knowing, a simple sigh like the one at Bernardo's Cafe in Notting Hill was not simple.

Since it was a sigh of carefree sensitivity, it might be contemporary in approach. But he knew that in destination it was more often than not, talking Patsy, it was more often primal, way below the gutter, that sculpted underground river of all the tastiest juices the world has ever squashed from itself. Helped along by Bakks, and by that bad smell, May-I-Speak-For-You, the greedy Inch.

Patsy's always good company, Jack thought.

He thought, Don't quite understand how she does it, the flam-bam, calm and sharp, sedated almost, at the same moment as being able to cut through a London high street's history with her little finger tweaking away from the cup like a little Swiss blade. Glad she's my dealer: that's what I say in gratefulness about the flam-bam. Patsy: my sensitive warlord.

A boy bumped Jack's overhanging elbow as he ran past and out the door into the cold London afternoon, calling out loudly a girl's name.

'Little fukkin pest,' Jack muttered.

'What did you call me?' Patsy said.

'The kid, not you.'

'What kid?'

'The one that just ran out the door.'

'Nobody has run out the door, nobody has even moved.'

So that's the exact second Jack's life took a left turn, the moment on his arm when one powderbox leaked a puff of information into another powderbox. But he had no way of knowing, no possible way at all, hadn't the mind equipped for it, that what slid across his elbow like a heavy jacket was a slice of someone else's memory. Of sixty-two years previous, the moment a boy escaped an orphanage in Spain. To go out in search of his favourite girl. It was the moment Jack would begin to enter a friendship where the powers are slightly different, coz Jack would soon meet the little windspeed runner.

O Bobbo the good box, yes.

One small victory over the evil fucker Bakks.

And those in that world would refer to him not as Jack Black, his real name, but fondly as Jack Verandah because he'd stumbled in from the outside, the bumbler. And Kieran the boy. It took a lifetime to piece together the third part of his triumph. The struggle to keep the evil force of Bakks off his case had its highs and lows, I can say that straight.

Kieran Leeft's windspeed running did find the world, no doubt about it, but he could not find Rosa Mendoza. From the port of Almeria three days south to the towns that lay across day and night, young Sunrise Sunset found the world all right, and then left it. Couldn't stomach it. That's when the slowdown occurred. Slowing down brought him a different life. A few years after the escape from the hacienda he acquired a boat. He was sixteen. The early life of windspeed rushing had come to an end, and in the years that followed he lived on the sea with the rusty key slung round his neck. Feet on land came down to a few days a month. Of the world on land his knowledge evaporated, he grew to know nothing and nobody. Within a few years he knew none of its events, none of the names. In his twenties he still lived on the sea, where even the loudest powderboxes of all had no existence, Robert Kennedy he'd never heard of, Mao, Brando, Liz Taylor, Einstein, Picasso. When the English set off three nuclear bombs on the Montebello islands in the north-west of Australia, he didn't know. Events passed him by. During his thirties, 1967 to '77, he never heard of Mick Jagger,

Bob Dylan, Bo Diddley, Nixon, he'd not heard of his fellow ocean-dweller Jacques Cousteau. He'd not heard the news in '66 that the Beatles were banned by the Israeli authorities from playing in Israel. He'd never heard of the Beatles. Nor did he hear of any of the monsters that Bakks had pushed further than he'd pushed anyone, like Pol Pot, Idi Amin, Pinochet. Sunrise Sunset had not even heard of Margaret's grandma's first sexing tuition conquest with the great boat builder Aristotle Onassis. He hadn't even heard of the greatest inheritance earthquake of them all, doctor Watson when he threw the light on the shape of DNA.

No, what Sunrise Sunset had inherited was far beyond addiction, he'd inherited a nose for the solitary, dear butterfly. Land's events held no interest. He loved the sea and he loved his boat. In his mid-twenties he set off east, and past Italy he came to Paxos. He stayed in its shining blue bays for a month. There were many places he visited like Paxos, places that were still far from anywhere before they became favoured by the jetset. Over time the Sunrise Sunset traveller became less connected to the busy goings-on of the world, more remote from its decisions and concerns. Moving from bay to bay, island to island. He never cast a net like Mendoza had done back at the Golfo de Valencia, but he used his fishing lines to good effect. Fifty years on he'd meet Jack Black, the guy who'd been warned by bonbon Patsy not to swine her off, and instead tell the truth about if he had, um, smelled the troubles.

Answer a Simple Question of the Powderbox

Jack's reply to Patsy's query came only after going for broke, for he'd lend the currents of the early days a good deal of love and dance. You don't just offer the careless reply to a query like that, no, Patsy was asking about a lifetime jammed into a single summer bouncing about in Spanish hotel rooms. When she asks about smelling the troubles, she's really only asking about Remple her lost love.

Besides, Jack Black noted a primal smirk. The smirk showed one thing on Patsy's mind for the moment in the warm cafe. Which was that Patsy comfortably believed that Jack Black was a very large fool for not having been able to smell the troubles. Patsy's favourite painter, yes, no argument, but she openly termed him a 'blockhead' because while he was hot at painting he was pathetic at reading a situation. And right there lay one of the grandest of the grand misunderstandings that continually wafted between the two crooks, which is why neither of their powderboxes recognised the other as even a powderbox in the first place, the pair of dumb ding-dongs.

Patsy Murray thought Jack Black completely inept at casting the unwavering gaze, when in fact her painter was indeed very expert at gauging the thickness or thinness of a skin, if in a bumpy way. But let them bumble, bumbling's good.

Round the other way, Jack thought Patsy sharp as a Swiss knife, yet Patsy was poor at living in the present skin. Besides, she didn't have the position to have any true friendships. This sad fact about Patsy, Jack didn't work out, he was too self-centred. He had no idea that Patsy actually had no friends, at least no friends she could be with now and then in comfortable candour. It was the position. The only person that remained aware how extremely her powderbox listed with clagged-up memory, was her own bonbon self. And me. And maybe Bakks.

So that's how Jack and Patsy worked with each other, stumbling on either side of a fairly substantial misunderstanding of one another's fundamental strengths. Jack had an instinct for the present, Patsy's hollow days of extreme success gave her the instinct for what the past can do to the present. That's a powderbox for you; one of the minor problems with powderboxes is that they forever create all manner of mistakes and misunderstanding when cooking a pot of tea. They're handy, powderboxes, for storage, and handier for scrambling the facts of a day, and, as my, um, friend Bakks insists, for making a myth or the smell of one. The boldest thing to admit would be to say that without powderboxes yeah okay the place'd be mythless. But the rumours about Patsy flattened her powerful strength into the old insult: that Patsy lived too richly in the past. But, then, if Jack believed the rumours that was fine too because he found her conversation always inspired, and that's more than enough, he knew, in any painter's language anywhere, so 'Thanks Be to Patsy' was Jack's loping compliment. At any attempt to diminish Patsy, Jack would cut in: 'Thanks Be to Patsy.' Then he'd walk off into the party. Patsy copping crap was Jack's line in the cement.

The scatter continued, half-thoughts. Jack certainly had been up to his neck in the whole disaster. He thought: Patsy of course knows this, and so she chooses my forehead to hit for it. And Jack Black felt that it was time to own up to one or two moments on Remple and Catherine. Jack thought, half thought, Time to expose. Why? Because of what was said about Patsy. Rumours were that Patsy'd been deeply in love three times, and that Remple was one of those relationships, the other two she'd never quite shaken either. Jack knew all that; Patsy was someone with depth, with secrets, with memories, painful and wondrous. And so what—the whole rollcall of romantic hardbitch yummoes possess similar images of carefree wonder. Well, maybe not quite like Patsy's imagery of her three great loves, maybe not.

And anyway, Jack reasoned, she's an art dealer for chryssakes, that says a bit. But for all that and more I love her a lot, not romantically, but absolutely a lot.

Another half-thought bolted around his powderbox: Perhaps, just maybe, it was Catherine Fekdin's influence on Remple that Patsy needed clarified. That is, was it Catherine Fekdin that destroyed Patsy&Remple? When all is said and done—and remembered.

The scatter of starlings hadn't yet slowed. He knew that Patsy Murray's smirk hung there to provoke him to hunt down the beginning, so he'd taken the two weeks to clarify the memory before he sent the email. He wasn't too certain about what Patsy already knew, so he went for broke. Besides, Patsy had a right to know, and he liked Patsy, especially the sensitivity lurking behind the hardhat warlord, and anyway the easy grudge was he respected Patsy. And if through the honeycomb of her sparkling sensitivity she knew most of it, then she'd wish to have the grubby stuff confirmed. If she knew very little, then she'd want the whole lot patched up properly. Properly to Patsy, Jack knew too well, meant everything from that month before the trouble, everyone, every habit good and bad, that's what Patsy called 'properly.' So Jack took the request, or, as he preferred, Patsy's forced order as a given, and he exploded the powderbox so he could give Patsy a free drift right back to the beginning, free, with his compliments. He'd keep it brief. He'd stay directly in the time he ought to have detected that scent. For that's when all the primal stuff high and low that Patsy aimed for was first located, if a smart enough person with a fine enough nose could only have smelled it, like Ellie-Isabela could smell a rat under the steps of the hacienda.

Jack decided he'd go for broke, properly. He privately decided, behind the forehead, Everyone wants things done properly so what I'll do is give them properly. Even on Catherine's supposed campaign against Patsy&Remple, if there ever was one, a campaign, yuk.

Yeah, he thought, if the Properly Brigade wanna bang n tap our foreheads over and over, then the innocent bystander can expect, eventually, a forehead to strain, creak and then burst, bang, splinter well and proper.

Or, as we boxes prefer: Ping!

Ping: and the album of powdered starling fills the room.

Jack thought, What she no doubt wants is to slow the particles of detail swirling in that room-scale cloud pertaining to, er, encapsulate, yes, define, that relationship of Remple's with Catherine. He knew that slowing down the speed of the detail meant he'd have to start with the old seadog, Kee Leeft. Two maybe three weeks later Jack sent it, the reply, no earlier, for it took him that long to settle down the starlings in the powder cloud in order to keep the reply primal and proper and brief. What a damn question, Had I fukkin well been able to smell the trouble. Little sordid biff she is today. On the footpath outside the cafe they embraced, said bye, and Jack strolled home to start the reply. He did wonder who'd dropped the box at the gallery. He thought it might have been one of the merchant bankers that Patsy forever entertained, drawing them into attractive payment deals: after all, it was now clear as day that the subprime calamity in America had totally fucked up the lives of the merchant bankers. They were being rounded up by the hundreds. Flung rudely out the front door along with their cardboard boxes.

But in truth Jack had no answer for the box that was left at Patsy's doorstep, and so he didn't mention in his reply that it may have been a crazy banker tipped sadly over the edge by recent events. Too true, it might well have been Bakks roughing up a banker who'd been shoved over the edge by the subprime calamity, desperately attempting to roam the Bond Street area in a nicely ironed suit, but instead his powderbox being roughed up—ping splatter pop—by Bakks, being twisted into writing the stupid note in the box on Patsy's doorstep:

> *... and when the habit is established there's no going back, not from the sweet centre of it all.*

O yes, it may have been a crazy banker indeed. Being junga-rummy jiddled by the pongsters and deadbeats.

By the end of the month, Jack sent the email. It was only a couple of night's worth of observations about the dirt and about Catherine, but that's how long it can take, aromatic dirt, an answer.

Mister Kieran Leeft in the Bahamas, 2008

After meeting the seadog's friends in the Bahamas, Jack wanted to follow them directly back to Perth dear butterfly. He wanted to give London a miss. Go straight to Perth, maintain the ping splatter pop, keep the fun and the adventure swirling round his happy powderbox, the painter arrogarnta. But he didn't, he went instead back to his studio in Tottenham, he had stuff to see to, things to do before heading for Western Australia on a long stay, for he intended to stay a month or two.

Anyway, fact is, he had to meet up with his dealer Patsy at their usual café in Notting Hill to set a date for the show of his new paintings. Little did he know dear butterfly that they'd be paintings of your custodians mixed in with the blood and gore associated with inheritance. One painting would be a massive triptych of a butcher, a surgeon and a genetic engineer.

Jack sent the email and then went out to see the Gauguin exhibition.

'Hi Patsy, it's true that the seadog Kieran Leeft warned me, and it's also true that I wasn't listening. But, believe me, it was not the place to hear a warning, anyone could see that fact. During a day on the lagoons the first warnings drifted with lightness, like a mirage, mainly because the pleasure of the day was turned up as high as it gets. The sky was clear as an empty mind, the temperature hot, sea the colour of limejuice, three of pleasure's primal rhythms you'll agree, being a beautiful animal yourself. And they flashed such a sleek amount of primal magic that I had no real way to catch the warning, but warn me he did. Try hearing anything at all when you're up to your neck in hot breezes after escaping London, up to your neck in manta rays, turtles, fine lagoons and mornings lasting a week.

'Or perhaps it's a different form of primal gravity. Perhaps a warning's got that curled way of leading me on. The moment I hear a caution, see, drawn into a basement without lights. We find ourselves turning it into alarm and then we heat it up to menace and then we're well on the way to no going back. To come to that basement though, to Remple and Catherine, we need to start with Kee Leeft, Remple calls him Sunrise Sunset. I first met him in a bar in Georgetown in the Bahamas, by accident really, nothing more.

'He told me he'd squeezed the name Kee Leeft from his given name Kieran Leeft after he ran away from an orphanage in a small village in Spain. He's a seadog of about seventy, indistinct, heaps of rampant health is probably why, fish, fruit, sea, diving, clean air, sunshine, all day every day.'

So the ding-dong memory that brushed past Jack's elbow hup two three came in at sixty-two years old when Patsy and Jack shared an hour in the cafe on the frosty high street back in Notting Hill, prompting a few days in the sun across the Atlantic. Jack Black wouldn't understand, quite, coz he was a bighead, but once he fell in from the outside as the newly formed Jack Verandah, he'd have a slightly better chance. Besides, Jack had that painterly pomp in him, and no way you'd find things out with that kind of pompous streak. Let him bumble a bit, I suggest.

Because he liked Patsy dear butterfly, his email gave her an honest account.

'Later I would come to acclaim Kee Leeft as wise and kind, and I would learn that nothing on earth gave him cause for haste, this slowest moving guy. And yet the speed with which I fell into the wired world of electricity you refer to, was at the howling speed of sound. The world of shysters and wannabe angels I slid into through meeting Kee rumbled and groaned and screamed with their peals of sorrow, cheating, loneliness, ambition, madness and fastness. And there was I, contentedly assuming that my own world, of painters and shysters, was the one that laid bare our civilisation's more cute rorting and hustling, but no. The chink I fell through after meeting Kee opened onto a sadder, madder place than the London art world that you and I know only too well. The world I slid into buzzed with the slapping electricity of expectation, everybody wanted a chunk of something, someone, someplace, and it certainly was a world that buzzed with the belief they could bake a loaf of success. But it was also a world that couldn't touch Kee because it existed on land, and nothing on earth, on dry land, had the power to give this bloke cause for haste. He remained the wise, slow fellow living on the blue and white thirty foot boat, he remained unhurried, a sea labrador browned by the sun that reflected into the open cabin. He was anti-motion to look at, he possessed a sharp eye for avoiding haste, and the world of hurrying gave him the taste of boredom. Kee's hurryisms gained good ground among those I met a month after my chance encounter. Hurrying brings on scurvy. Hurrying whistles out to sharks. Hurrying wears out the wind. And the chief hurrier that I met through Kee, Catherine Fekdin, took to his best one: Hurry over there, that's where the action is, look. And get to the action Catherine Fekdin did better than most, better than you or I at any rate.

'Catherine, I was to learn, celebrated him. She'd often say, factually, Kee has this amazing life force, and a massive warmth. I say factually because at first I couldn't believe such gunk could come out of such an impressive person as Catherine, and she meant it, believed it, even though she's a brutally fast-moving success story, as I'd find out. Bit like you really, oh softly spoken warlord.

'But for me, right from the start, there existed something else too in Kee Leeft, concealed under the magic carpets of kindness, wisdom, life force and warmth, something strange, not right, he seemed rattled under all that finery, the way things feel when a bay is too calm, breezeless. My instinctive suspicion settled on a storm of cruelty for the time being unarrived, that he was some kind of dangerous and bitterly cruel guy who roamed from small port to small port ripping life and cash from their hearts and pockets, but, maybe, I was just wrong. Meeting a stranger in a bar, first impressions, loose hints, the salty atmosphere, barely reliable taste tests. Less so after a year of heavy exhaustion in London, and the long flight across the Atlantic to Nassau and then the overnight mailboat journey south to Georgetown. One is able to smell very little in the way of trouble when assaulted by all that adventure, dear Patsy.

'Kee and I sat around that night exchanging brief stories, we struck it up right away, enjoying one another's company without the slightest effort. Looking back I can now see that even those small anecdotes at the bar contained all the warnings a guy could want, that's where the miniature explosions commenced, and then they continued over the next day out on those spirit-melting lagoons. Miniscule pops and eruptions all through the relaxing day that should have caught my eye, or ear, or nostrils, but didn't, largely owing to the fact that I was then just another dumb, arrogant blockhead of a painter from London, and who'd blown in for a break. The lights of the vessels on the harbour glowed. The night was hot and humid, good for the drinks we shared.

'We quickly found anecdotes of mutual interest, tales of survival, his tales being based on the oceans as he wended his boat up and down the great coastlines. He had no address, he lived on the boat, ever since he was a boy. Mine less vast, though just as curly, as a desperate painter kicking at, and missing, the shins of curators who were too busy to take a glance at my work, boxing their ears would've maybe worked better but I'm not an animal like you are. I told him that I'd just completed an exhibition in London with you that after ten years living on cracked wheat had delivered my first success, so I took off for the islands where I could recover, swim, snorkel, feed, drink and re-think.

'I told him I was under the grand impression this was the

show to change my life, lying under the sun to nut out a course into a life of work. To me the show had the gong of authority as the moment I'd been hunting down for ten stupid arrogant years. But of course I was a blockhead way off the button. Kee Leeft sailed into Georgetown late one large afternoon—and how the hell was I to know if he was shot with a shitbad cruelty or not—but he sailed in, and that lay closer to a moment that hurled my life in the twisted new direction that you politely call trouble. That's what I've always liked about the pungent animal in you, Patsy: when it gives off a grunt it's a nimble grunt.

'Anyway, the missed explosions started with Kee Leeft recalling the night he'd saved the life of a small girl who later I would also hear of as the grandmother of the most nuggetty art dealer anyone could want after you. A clever lizard if ever there was a bright lizard that wore bangles, and who turned out to be my best friend, and your suspected enemy, the heaven part of the world I was hurled into, Catherine Fekdin. Or Fekdin The Fekk Off, as she came to be known by you because you still believe she fucked up your bedside manner with her brother Remple. Anyway, Kee saved their grandmother, as a girl of fourteen, when he was a young man of nineteen on the Spanish coast. He'd already been looking for a friend since he was an eleven year old, but he stumbled onto Catherine Fekdin's future grandmother instead.

'I mean, had I not met Kee that night in Georgetown there's really no way I'd have met Catherine. And had I not met her, it's very difficult to imagine that nowadays I'd be the prime donator to a hospital that specialises in caring for the children of the Diamond City. But a digression to the Diamond City, that place of the weirdest, wildest colours known to humanity or history, is also best for later.

'It was the anecdote of how he'd saved Catherine's grandmother years earlier that introduced me to the depth of Kee

Leeft's roundest attribute, that streak of profound light he carried in himself. A characteristic that I've never been able to term anything else but kindness. It was weird, really strange, to come twisting around to understand that anyone could possess so much plain, natural kindness, and it was worse to see that it came with no trace of nonsense but instead came with humour, clarity, a complete lack of the sentimental. I was to learn that with Kee Leeft, kindness was nothing more than just a way of life, it was done and delivered with no more affectation than breathing the fresh ocean air. Except for that underlayer where something lay concealed, maybe lingering cruelty, I had simply and lightly to enjoy his kindness.

'When he described at the bar that night how he'd saved the girl, who grew through life to become Catherine's grandmother, how he'd swept her up from the threat of outrageous violence, it was only because I pressed the subject after he mentioned it in passing. As if it were another small occurrence of fiddly interest in his travels from port to port. But then, see, yeah, it constituted a significant part of the warnings. And I missed it. Heard the tale, missed the point. Dumb blockhead arrogant painter.

'And that was in fact the best result from not heeding the warnings. The world that I fell into on meeting him succeeded in changing me from a blockhead arrogant painter, succeeded in taking me from the narrow world of London painting circles, succeeded in returning me to a broader world, a bigger place, where I became human again. Meeting Kee destroyed the layers of conceptual detritus that had built up over my skin and skull, dearest Patsy; what lay on the horizon destroyed a huge part of my personality, shovelled the art out of me and then breathed something kind of like life into that trench—and for that I remain grateful. When I pressed the subject of him saving the girl, he pleasantly got on with it.

'His account began when he swung his boat up to the jetty of a sleepy place, on the west coast of Spain, of no more than a hundred shacks to where the girl had directed him as a possibility of locating her mother and father. It had been nearly ten years since he'd escaped the orphanage.

'But after the anecdote he stopped.

'"Well," Kee said to me when I pressed for more, "you say you're a painter. My friend is meeting me here at the inn tomorrow, she's involved with painters, so here's a line of information you might find useful about her, an anecdote about her grandmother," he said. I bought us another drink.'

A Clear Memory

'Nineteen year old Kee had picked up the girl three days before, and together they followed northwards the hunches that she'd offered on where they might find the parents. She said she had travelled with them on the road south, past the hills behind the plain, so this meant home lay north. Her hunches were reasonable and Kee found that she could hold her shoulders up while she offered the ideas. With a reasoned fourteen year old manner, the girl was showing, he felt, hope and courage. There'd be no way she could have recognised her town from at sea, so he followed each hunch into the jetties or beaches with care and patience. It was now almost dark, and this meant they would spend the night at the jetty and set off again next morning—if it turned out that the place was not the girl's home.

'Walking up the jetty she knew it was not her town. They

wandered to the shops to ask had anyone seen or heard of the parents. Kee bought a box of food and they strolled back to the boat to prepare dinner.

'At night a woman visited the boat, and she brought along a bottle of wine, and a lump of chocolate for the girl. She'd heard that a young unknown man, say twenty, had a girl with him, say fourteen, she was curious. After the girl fell asleep, Kee and the woman shared the wine while they sat on the stern. It became clear to Kee that she was a pleasant person, mid-thirties, had lived her life here, but had never grown fond, like most coastal dwellers, of being out on the ocean, and this made the young Kee suspicious. By around seven, the sky of stars and the wine drew them into conversation. The woman asked Kee Leeft about the lost girl. They spoke in Spanish.

'"I found her three days south at the edge of a small outpost," Kee said to the woman, "a place where I stopped for supplies. She was sitting alone on a crate in the morning sun, she sat with an air of confidence, yes, that's quite certain, but I noticed a crack, then I saw a trembling underneath the air of belonging. She wanted to show everyone that she was all right, that this was her regular patch, and maybe she wanted people to believe that she was just out for the morning, but the imitation of being grown up was too pronounced for me, so I approached. At first all we did was talk idle observation about the day and the weather maybe for two minutes. Then she asked what I was doing in town, I told her, buying supplies, she asked where I was going, I said that I had been travelling the coast. Then there came a long pause, when she blurted out the fact that she'd lost her parents in the crowds of a festive night in the square the night before. She said they'd probably driven home thinking she'd already taken a ride home with family friends. Ever since that morning on the crate, I catch the look in her eyes and the language of her body. This fear and trembling underneath, yes it has subsided, but we will locate the parents, of this I have a simple conviction. I have been travelling without haste, until now by myself, for many years, and for two months now northwards along this coast, experienced a few things, but not the tight grip of this kind of certainty, so we have nothing to worry about."

'"So you have not been north of here?" the woman asked.

'Kee had not. He'd lived north, in the hacienda Zaragoza a decade before, but had not sailed the coast until now. "North along this coast will be new, yes, I look forward to it, and in the morning we'll set out to continue searching for her village."

'"Did you report the lost girl to the police?"

'"The place I found her was very small, very much like the place I grew up, it would not even offer a postal service, there were no trees, maybe forty dwellings, we know the kind you and I, a daydream on a streetless patch of dust. Different to this place, these wooded hills and the treeline along the estuary. Anyway, she said the town next morning lay deserted. Except for an old man, he'd told her that the town had taken itself to a harvest wedding to an inland village, which they tell me is about right for this part of the coast at this time of year, as you'd know. For an occasion a town will either burst or empty out, leaving behind only an old man and a few dogs."

'"We have phones, I can call the police."

'"Yes, good idea, nobody down the coast seems to have shown the least interest in a lost girl."

'"Let her sleep, I'll phone in the morning for you."

'"Thankyou."

'The woman was about to get up and go, but she turned to Kee. "Let me ask you something. What made you so certain you could locate the parents' village?"

'Kee told me that as a nineteen year old he remembers himself as a guy keen to show a wisdom of the sea, that was the prime thing. He told the woman, "I am not normally one for conviction. The grip of a tight mind, I've always suspected that it achieves no more than lend energy to feuding, but in the last three years I've given away conviction. Out there on the sea, I am learning that conviction is not quite the thing one wants, it's more like an ebb and flow of instinct one wants, which is a more useful attribute than iron conviction. But when I picked her up three days ago, a sturdy conviction of sorts fell back into my mind."

'"She could well be using you."

'The young Kee Leeft was mildly shocked.

'"Making use of me? For what exactly?"

'"It is not uncommon for a girl on this coast to make her way up to Barcelona, for the dreams."

'"I cannot see that, would not the roads be easier than the open sea on a small wooden boat?"

'But the speculation had shaken Kee's conviction.

'"Has she said what village she's from?" the woman asked.

'"She told me she would know it from a beach or jetty, which is the reason we have been stopping in at each place on the way up the coast for four days."

'"Well, it's all right anyway, I'll make the call in the morning."

'Kee said he was alerted to a false note. This in turn made him feel that the woman's presence had shifted from pleasant to sharp. Her care, expressed in the offer to contact police, now seemed to him like a concealed mistrust. In the dim light he thought the earlier face of warmth she'd extended was now an expression of ugly forcefulness. He noticed that her mouth strained to make a welcoming smile, but conversely her eyes in the dim light were sort of manic. He began to shake. It was yet more evidence of what he termed "sick caperology." He used the words "sick caperology" a lot, I've no idea what it means.'

For we better boxes dear butterfly, sick caperology is a good way to identify the powderboxes who were successfully being jungarummy jiddled by Bakks and the pongsters. And so what do we better boxes do? We give Sunrise Sunset a couple of quick words to spot any approaching danger of haranguage.

'I did ask Kee a few days later, and what he told me was great. He said sick caperology is sickening mean-minded blobs pretending to be human, blobs pretending to sport an ear capable of listening let alone sport a head to fasten it to, and a love of a kind perhaps inside the head. Blobs pretending to have knowledge of the tides. Pretending to be able to fish, or swim, or even to have an eating habit in the first place, he'd blundered into them a hundred times. And here sitting before him was another sick caperologist. One caper after the next, they just couldn't help it. Between the abrupt change of mood and the two glasses of wine and the gauze of the night, Kee's sudden flare of irritation prompted a flow of opinion he couldn't avoid.

'He said to the concerned woman, "It is not new or unusual. When I'm in I pick people up all the time, drop them off later, passengers that to me are a source of talk, we set off, we're in the sun, we fish, we eat, drink, swim, and then we bid farewell; what the girl has done is not new. An example: one day I picked up a baby and a pirate, he was mean and bleak about the world, down on his luck, boatless, I'd say no more than a mailboat thief, but he was keen about the baby."

'Kee could see the woman had not let her smile drop away, and this told him she was pretending now even more. He continued.

'"I discovered he had taken the child in order to annoy the

mother, by his account a vain and cruel person in the extreme, and whom he decided should be rattled around for a day or two only because he believed it might loosen her metal mind. He got off up the coast and promptly took the baby back. Said he would. I believed him. No no, this is all very normal, me collecting a girl off a jetty, yes, like a sunny day, and you've no right to make me shake with exasperation. I go all around the place all the time, and there's oddness everywhere I stop in. If I stop here long enough oddness will begin to reveal itself, so tomorrow I believe the girl and I will sail."

'The woman maintained the smile. "You're upset and possibly tired from a long day. I'll call the police for you in the morning. Good night, sleep well."

'She stepped off the stern and strolled up the jetty into the unlit shapes of the village, and to Kee this made her look even more sinister than the cement-like smile and the disturbing manic eyes. He was now feeling slow on the wine but he nonetheless pulled the whole business together and set sail into the night. He fumbled about the boat with a slip of panic in his head about the morning, so he successfully got them both out to sea in the dark.

'But it turned out that the woman was right about the girl. Not knowing this for now, Kee sailed up the coast that night as far as his exasperation and suspicion would take them, and he found a small deserted bay in which to drop anchor. A dark low rise in the near distance seemed to be land, so he figured they were safely in from sea yet far enough from the shore.

'The next morning was bright and warm when the girl woke. She took a swim to the shore, she swam leisurely back to the boat. She lay on the roof to warm up, though the water had been warm. When Kee woke he was groggy, but he was instantly irritated. He stayed quiet about the subject from the previous night because he wanted to avoid hurting the girl's feelings. This is what she told him after he had breakfast and brought up the subject.

'The girl had said, "It was nice to get on your boat, when I looked at you near the wooden crates, there was no angriness."

'She looked away but soon felt trust again, so she continued.

'"My father is very angry, he hits my mother and he hit me a lot but then he became angrier in the last year and one day he shouted he wanted to kill me so I left."

'She looked away at the water for a while as her breathing quickened, but after a while she caught a new, easy breathing.

'"He used to only hit us, but soon he started yelling threats to me, he wanted to kill me because he said I was evil. Then he began taking up the habit of running after me, and when he couldn't catch me he would hit my mother, and so that's what I did, see, I just got up one night when he was asleep after drinking a lot and I left."

'She gazed at the morning ocean.

'"You fukkin little bitch," the girl then said in her thin voice. She continued to gaze down at the water glistening blue and green in the morning sweep of sunlight.

'Then she said softly, "You lousy fukkin little fuck, I'm gunna kill you, God has spoken to me, he's told me to kill you." The girl imitated the Spanish dialect's vernacular with a very precise memory, weight, inflection, darkness and the machismo swagger of the dusty coastal plains.

'The girl grew up and never saw Kee Leeft again, which she always lamented in silence, and she had children and grandchildren—Catherine and Remple, and their cousins Castle and Oliver. Kee Leeft became a memory. Of life itself, breath. As she grew into adulthood, she sensed it would now never be possible to find Kee Leeft and thank him. The morning on the boat was it. Incomplete, not told, regret. She had the feel of Kee Leeft inside her body all through her life, he was something that she could touch privately as an example of clean air when she required it. So to her Kee Leeft grew from a memory into a breath and then into plain air. The Ride Up The Coast To Safety, she'd say once she'd grown old, but mostly to the grandchild whom she trusted to keep it quiet, your blistering enemy, dear Patsy—Catherine Fekdin the tough cunning art dealer, and Catherine reciprocated by keeping quiet. The man who'd saved her grandmother had become a bright blue shadow in the grandkids' minds, he became a myth for them all, except for Catherine. The trust between her and the grandmother made such clarity of this mythic boat-boy that eventually Catherine was able to track down Kee as he wandered the oceans calling in to port after port on his way to nowhere in particular.

'Kee dived off the bow and let it go so deep he lost all the air in his lungs. He told me he and the girl had a fine day swimming on one of the deep lagoons. The depth was grand. Treacherous walls made the light bluer. They became hungry so they stopped swimming. At night they slept soundly. In the morning they ate from tins of food, leaving portions for bait. In the afternoon they swam on the current that swept them out of the lagoon to the open sea. At night the stars roamed over the sky. And in the morning they dived once again into the depth of the lagoon because the deepness was so grand. The next day they found another lagoon that held a village in its blue eye. It was the village where the girl would meet her husband. She left the boat and soon after, at fifteen, married the young man from the island and they moved north to Barcelona. All the while that she grew accustomed to life in the city, she gave birth to two children, one was Castle's mum in '57, and all the while she was headed for the memory of Kee Leeft as a wisp of air, the most important human encounter she had ever had apart from her mother, whom she never found. When the girl grew old she would utter Keep Left, and nobody got it, no child, no grandchild, no husband, certainly no father or mother. Keep Left. It became a way of seeing the girl who swam on the remembered lagoon by the breezy image of a kind young man of nineteen. So when she started to see road signs of it on a visit to London, she at first smiled, but later grew depressed. As a person who was hunted down by her father in the dusty flats of a coastal village, she could not cope too well with growing depressed, so the husband eventually left her.

'So, Patsy, that's what I gleaned. Kee rambled easily through the story, it was no trouble to glean the bare essentials. And after fukkin London where every fukkin creative person talked only about their great selves with a virtuosic performance in turning every remark back in on themselves or their own latest great work, Kee's easy rambles were my first fresh, relaxing days in Georgetown. A month snorkelling off his boat and failing to hear the miniscule explosions you call trouble. Your enemy Catherine, well, let's see.

'Late that night I went off to the hotel to sleep. My flight had only just brought me in the day before so I was tired on three fronts: exhausted by two years of London's goozy attention-seekers, exhausted by the flight, and exhausted by the overnight mailboat trip to Georgetown. Kee strolled off into the darkness to his boat.'

Getting Suspicions from the Rolling of the Second Equator

Jack's email was just the thing. Kept any suspicion away from us boxes by the diviners of the world.

Kee and Jack went for a coffee. Kee said he was going out today to fish and that Jack could come along if he wanted. So that morning with a placid sea and a markless sky full of sunshine they took the hangovers past a string of bays and lagoons, and dropped anchor about four miles up the coast from town in thirty foot of gin-clear water where the early warnings were to continue. After spending the morning under the surface exploring the reefcliffs, Kee dropped a line and caught six fat garfish, three of which they ate for lunch.

'It would be great out here at night, on a clear night, for the stars,' Jack said to the sixty or seventy year old seadog.

'Out here at night is one of life's deepest pleasures,' Kee said.

'I like the way we see two sheets of black,' Jack said. 'One is pure jet black, the sea, and the other is riddled endlessly by the millions of stars teeming away into the distance, and yet has the excellent flat look of two black sheets, and a third sheet, but one that's of immense catastrophic depth that it hurts the mind.'

Kee regarded the horizon with a moment's silence. He began with easy laid-back pleasure. He spoke with lightness, with a non-importance, a tone that turned his observations toward the inconsequential. 'You're right about that, and there's a fourth layer too. At night when I'm far from land, what is available to the eye is contrary to what one would assume. Logic tells you that to the eye comes darkness, perhaps velvet peacefulness—depends how one prefers to interpret these sights—maybe it's only a starlit glimpse of eternity, but on the boat at night this logic doesn't hold. What happens is that I see the two seas that you mention, with not enough differentiation between the earth's hump of ocean and the universe's hump of sky.'

Kee thought for a moment, then continued: 'To obtain this sense of one sea during the day is never easy, the sky is sky and the sea is sea, like it is now, and only inside a system of sultry weather will the two pretend they're the same thing.

'A windless system in a sultry storm gives the illusion that the two are somehow joined, but at night a special togetherness prevails over the boat. The two seas complement one another at night.

'The two seas push and pull. One sea being a universe seems to be not enough, one sea being the earth's heavy ocean pulled this way and that by the moon's gravity seems to be not enough; the two appear to wish to touch, and from the boat they do.

'It is less as a touch, and more, I prefer to think, a fourth layer, an exchange of memory.'

This is where we boxes knew that the old seadog had the inkling about us. But Jack's email of memories to bonbon Patsy continued. The old seadog continued to explain to Jack his faint understanding of things without quite knowing he was partly explaining us boxes; his own perspective, yes, but ding-dong perceptive too was the old seadog. Sprinkling illuminations around the seas, taking Ellie-Isabela's magic wand of give, taking it out into the world.

So Kee continued: 'When I'm out there on the boat I see a handing over of other memories between the two, now lost to us—what other memories, we do not understand. If it were a silly thing like a meeting of cosmic photo albums, then the scene would be a sunset or some great natural event that we would all crow about but then quietly go to sleep and forget the following morning.

'But this fourth layer, it is more than a solar system photo album. It's always an exchange of disturbing material out here on the boat. Swapping a future for a present, it feels like; throwing away the future for the moment.

'Too many nights away from land implied a sifting of my memory, it implied I was located at the touch where memory went missing, at the exchange of air where the past month was no longer felt, and where the present had pressure. Where the present felt like it would always remain as the present.

'To me this is what eternity feels like out there at night. But out in the two seas of night where stars jot down impressions of civilisation, I could be here only as a blip. It helps ease the grip of conviction. A tight mind, well, it has the appearance of being useful, although I sometimes out there feel that most of our present ills may too easily grow into severe problems if the tight mind gets too lucky a grip.'

This is why Bakks took a shine to the old seadog, Bakks wanted to take Kee's fumbling and turn it into a tight mind, generate his myths with his counterfeit, maybe along with the help of greedy Inch and his pong of cohorts including the vain fuckface Lightyear who could easily use Kee's impressions of a vast night-sky. But the seadog was always on water, so cardboard Bakks had a bad time of it, he hated water.

Cups of Cascading Memory above the Boat

Kee continued: 'I mean, it's just me on the boat, with this week's exception, but when I look out there without land in sight, far off the boat other memories work their echo so that terse convictions come into question.

'Up there the two seas fold their patterns into exchanges, agreements I can understand nothing of, and creaking arguments, tapestries, which I can never quite put my finger on even though I know enough about knots and rope to impress Marco Polo. And Polo, it is said, was first and foremost a lover of textile and not of the sea's and universe's echoing texture of memories.

'Businessmen in big cities project huge images onto the skin of skyscrapers, I'd like to project my own small movie of the two seas onto the surface of the moon, I often wonder if they could do that. If they were able to do that for me, the movie might then reflect out, far away, towards all these infernal other memories that continue to haunt the rest of us here bobbing around on places like the equator.'

Jack thought for a few seconds, and said, 'I happen to know an artist in London who'd hassle NASA to get that done.'

'Really?' Kee said.

'He'd fuck em black and blue until they'd perceive a need to forcibly eject him from his studio by some quick CIA trick. He'd love a project like a moon projection, he's a competitive brute of such magnitude he'd go squeaky with shrill excitement that he'd trounced Christo as the wrapmeister.'

'Who is Christo?'

'He's an artist, he uses high-grade technology to get his projects done. I mean, technology now is like this: the dudes on foot who deliver shopping catalogues to letterboxes are tagged from the sky nowadays, tagged and timed. Letterbox delivery walkers are now watched and tracked in real time. My friend in London made an exhibition out of that. But I also happen to know that he will never possess the insight to visualise what you've just said.'

'Well, we can come back out tomorrow night with Catherine and Remple, past the town lights, maybe three miles out would do it. Providing the sky stays clear we'll get a pretty good view of the two black seas and the stars and the shots of memory that cascade into unlikely places.'

Ye olde seadog was very close, he called it 'shots of memory that cascade into places.' Well, we boxes call it throwing stuff around, over the seas and over the mountaintops hup two three. Inch calls it vividity, Bakks calls it a penguin in the picture, you want one it's there.

The garfish fillets were fried, and then Kee squeezed a lime over them, so the sweet flesh and the limejuice made a moist lunch. They stuffed nine or ten fillets each into their mouths.

Kee passed the knife to Jack to place in the fishing gear box. Jack lifted the lid. Inside the box, neatly stashed, lay a pistol.

'Have you used that gun?'

'You can't sail without a gun, you must never sail the open without a gun. In the old days I sailed without a gun, but these days things are bad.'

Kee's lightly spoken handout of how a clear night provoked in him the groaning of memory from other places was another moment that ended up flinging Jack's days headlong into hells and heavens of immense gusto. Gusto and the bloodsoup days, Jack calls them. Bloodsoup, thicker than water and filled with the junk of DNA that will remorselessly search out givers and takers. Kee's quiet impression of bloodsoup in the cosmos in fact startled Jack more than discovering the pistol. It was perhaps the first of the small explosions that Jack actually felt, heard.

Manta Monk

Jack's few extra lines to Patsy told it all.

'As I ate the garfish fillets I didn't say so right away, but the fukkin simplicity of how he put it gave me a fright. I'd been looking for that fourth layer to burn into my paintings for more than two decades. I'd been numbly searching for it, and Kee just patted it on the head like a lovely dog he'd teamed up with for years and years, like an old friend. It's easy enough to think of it as memory, and that's what we've all been busy doing, calling it memory, but to think of it as an exchange of great groaning slabs of arguments accosting one another, well. That's when I found a confirmation of my groping efforts at clear thinking. Efforts over two decades being chased from flat after flat for the rent as yet another blockhead painter trying to bring new paintings into the world. Memory folding in over memory, it was that simple, and that deftly struck from sight so as to be complex.

'I would tell him so by the end of the month's focus on snorkelling, swimming and drinking, but for the moment I sat on the roof, afloat, from the glow of discovery, an inch off the timber with its peeling blue paint, folding the last fillet into my mouth.

'Kee sliced up the other three garfish. He spent fifteen minutes dropping the pieces over the side with strands of guts until a giant black manta played under the boat. Kee said with obvious wonder, "Benedictine monk of the reef has arrived, let's get in."

'I found out that night over drinks Kee was not a monk of the order founded in 529 by saint Benedict. Kee simply called mantas monks because he felt it suited them perfectly, "suits their easy demeanour, easy style and easy curiosity."

'We got in with our masks. Here exactly was the moment that would consistently stay alive as an image of how I would remember him. Gave me the picture of how to see him, the leap of understanding needed to prowl round his slow wisdom, his kindness, that shake of the head. Three more mantas arrived. A lot of fish around too, darting at the guts Kee bought from the butcher. The mantas moved with precision, they flew gracefully, and with such a slowed down motion, so that their wings implied we'd been transported into the fourth layer Kee talked about. The giant manta had lived, the wingspan must've been ten feet, and the torso thick as an Ohio tractor tyre. The precision given to feeding was impressive. Kee swam with the giant, very close by, weaving under and over the slow-moving monk of the reefs. The half hour we spent with the mantas and the hundreds of fish that gathered for the entrails, this minor moment in thirty foot of gin-clear sea off Great Exuma Island, fixed for me the definition I forever after carried around, of Kee Leeft as a manta. That is to say, on survival his genius was instinctive precision; on matters like the fourth layer, graceful; on matters like the girl, Catherine's grandmother, the genius was kindness. On matters all else, including travel, the thing with Kee was slowed-down motion, huge black wings of memory that moved as if they were exploring a dream. A hurrier is of dubious use, he attracts sharks. When a shark finally did arrive, grinning at the scent of guts, we climbed aboard the stern. I sat exhilarated: a half hour with the marine life under the boat, and I'd carried the giant manta out of the ocean. Later I would take it with me into the mad world of electricity and bloodsoup that awaited, the world of sorrow and cheating, of loneliness and ambition, of madness and fastness. While Kee continued roaming the coastlines where that world hadn't a hope of touching him, I pranged into the creaky doors of warped rooms where they frantically baked their pies of time.'

Jack Black Finds a Blue Hole

Jack calling us boxes what? Oh, pies of time; what a wan bloke the ding-dong. Just another fetish inside the cult of loss. Like that ignorant box-abusing dealer of his, fingerer Patsy, cult of loss. Nevertheless, let the boy continue. After all, he would soon make two of the sharpest observations that would help quite a lot to turn the fellow into a newly minted Jack Verandah.

'We motored back down the coast towards Georgetown, a forty-minute ride on the pale shallows. But halfway Kee sighted a small deep lagoon off the bow, smack in the middle of the open, a kilometre offshore, like a dark-blue eye set against the pale shallows. From our position it looked stunning, a perfect oval, drawn, etched, and coloured turquoises. It had that stun effect, the shock of high quality, that strumming verdancy that art would never be foolish enough to emulate as a copy, but that certainly would inspire fine interpretations for generations to come. I'd stopped breathing. He slowed the boat right down so that we could climb to the roof for a cleaner view.

'It was a horseshoe curl of sand, very small, about three hundred metres in diameter. No place seemed higher than a foot above sea level, and at one end an infant forest was beginning to form, weeds, shrubs, and what looked to be a small palm, or a breadfruit tree. Kee came down to the wheel and took the boat to the break that led into the lagoon. When we glided through the narrow strait of the horseshoe's prongs, a shallow ultramarine channel not much wider than the boat, the full rampant beauty came into view with such a looming, elemental force that it behaved in my mind suddenly like a sentinel from Kee's fourth layer, solitary, silent, but calling into question all the grand misadventures and pollutive madnesses of my civilisation, from its juggernaut industries down the long line of inventive skill to this thirty foot diesel boat under my feet.'

From this moment on dear butterfly, and Jack Black didn't know it, but now he was starting to lament the work of, really, when all is said and done, the work of Bakks and his greasy cohorts, the fuckers of facts so that remembering could give way to new myths.

'The sentinel said there was a change coming. It said an empire in the ascendant was taking over its empire. A world-wide empire of skill, building skill, transport skill, engineering skill, was on its way, and it would globally trounce this empire I had glided into. The round, swinging line of the lagoon's pure stamp made it seem like a signpost, it really could have been drawn, or etched, in the sea here, a kilometre off the western shore of Great Exuma Island. But there was another aspect that made it seem like a clearly spoken signpost, the colours that ran from the shallows into the deep centre of clean white sand. They were turquoises and blues, dozens, changing subtly from the white sandy one inch shallows, down to the light turquoise ankle-deep shallows, and then onward in a subtle rush through the knee-deep colours to the shoulder-deep blues. And then those blues where you could see to the floor it was fifteen feet, then twenty and then finally, at the centre, where the depth went to fifty visible feet hummed a blue that was dense and yet luminous beyond optical belief, a blue that seemed to pose as this empire's stop sign where our alarm and stop signs are a frantic red. This blue one though was a stop sign of infinite more gesture.

'For me the moment was a flip of massive proportion: London one second and, bang, Bahamas the next. Exhaustion, flying, broken sleep, all these things bounced my mind into equating and comparing bulbous notions. Twenty-four hours ago I had been swimming at Sheerness an hour out of London on the southern tip of the mouth of the Thames. A hot day, on with the mask, locals roar with laughter, but in I went, and what a soul-destroying swim it was, teeming with the signs of technological excreta from the empire to which I belonged. But here, by complete contrast, lay a luminous stop sign, clear as air. My empire was on the march, and with what pride my empire has left, it would leave behind mere pockets of this earlier empire.'

Pinpoint, there it is, the work of Bakks, always bringing on a new empire, always talking empire, his own empire, and also, no doubt, doing his best to squeeze his counterfeit crap along into Jack Black's powderbox. Bakks was at work, trafficking, violating, but I still had no clue why he'd want to ding-dong around with Jack Black's powderbox in order to try to fuck with Catherine's powderbox, but find this out we wooden boxes soon did O yes.

'I just couldn't equate it in any other way when we glided into that tiny lagoon.'

Jack's first sharp clue. We boxes are pretty good at turning givers and takers into equators. Enough shaking around from us boxes and you end up equating this with that, that with this, hup two three. But let him continue.

Swimming in the Blue Hole

'Say four hundred years, and the takeover will be complete. Give it a few centuries and the scale of the adventure will take in the skin tissue of the entire world, a grey mess of technological skills and creativity running rampant over the epidermal sweep of the world for a long enough sweep of time, that's the key. To making the older empire a forgotten place. All becomes the brown-grey shit and deadness of Sheerness.'

Jack now was ding-dong on it.

'Except, like all empires, the one now being erected by the whole human race will want just enough pride to maintain those isolated pockets of the old empire—up to now remembrance has not yet passed from the evolving intellect—and this poorly founded common sense will pass as wisdom. But this is no doubt the fake wisdom, because if my civilisation can perform all these amazing feats of skill and technology and yet shit communally on its doorstep, if my civilisation, that is to say the entire human race, believes itself in one way or another to be holy, particularly the more powerful members, and yet deface or destroy what their holy emperor made, then there's obviously yet another incoming civilisation on the horizon, beyond my ascending one, a civilisation that no doubt is in possession of the actual wisdom. If my civilisation is smart enough to create electricity from uranium then where is the same will to de-shit the shit? If we are so advanced that we can see a backyard barbeque from space then where is the will to de-shit the frontyard doorstep? Where do we get off calling ourselves a civilisation when what we do is make billions of tonnes of pollution, chemical and feral, that we can't handle? I slurred most of this out loud, and Kee eventually said, "Yes, soon you'll meet someone who has similar queries, a friend of mine. But on a different subject, the subject of a human brain; he won't be talking lagoons, he'll more likely be talking DNA, soon you'll meet him, maybe he arrived in town today, and if so then I wager tonight at the bar he will still, after the four years I have known him, Remple will still be asking what our civilisation will decide to do, since it is so clever, with certain places in DNA."

'Your Remple, Patsy, was to be one of the main trunk routes into that world of electricity and bloodsoup that waited on the horizon, another significant part of the warning.

'It was the dark-blue stop sign I aimed for as I stepped along the thin beach. The narrow sand bar was white, smooth and in curled places it was congested with broken coral and small shells washed up from the outside. It never gained more than ten metres in width. I started to stroll off it into the lagoon, following the subtle shifting of the luminous colours of turquoise and blue while putting on my mask and snorkel, then I was swimming for the centre, for the dark-blue stop sign. The water was warm as old tea, the strong sunlight had heated the upper layer, then it filtered right down to the floor of the lagoon. On the floor it swung about in slow ribbons, the blue fire of the stop sign. It was a clean, neat bowl of sand, no rocks, no coral, just an underwater curve of sand.

'The incline grew so steep that it added a sense of being able to "see" the fourth layer, at least apprehend it, because the ether of blue in there hummed with the dissolution of logic. Dreams commenced, permanence was here, transience abundantly. And the iridescence that lit this deep bowl of sand perhaps had, through all time, been closer in gesture to that fourth layer than any empire's sentinel. Whether it were the temple of that Greek god of the sea Poseidon, a Roman aqueduct, the Taj Mahal, the Sistine Chapel, the Sphinx, the Millennium Wheel, or the aroused Pentagon. While the fine empires rise and expire, this luminous flare in here rises and falls perennially, daily, so it might lay claim to more permanence than civilisations. Perhaps it glowed with this intense transparency when the Roman general Anthony was mucking about in the more opaque stuff, goatsmilk. And yet permanence, no. The incandescence here in the small lagoon was slated for demolition. Sheerness on the

Thames estuary was coming. A wave of ingenuity and skill would turn the world's skin into a seething network of steel and concrete overlaying a brown-grey Sheerness. The old human force of lateral skills, a robust creative impulse and a fever to make and build, would work the new world into a ball of wire and toxin hoofing around the sun year after year. Give it, say, four hundred such orbits, give it long enough, four centuries, at a growth rate of China, say ten percent, give it time. The epoch of technological filth has only just commenced.

'Great way to start my break. Equating my loud, muscular civilisation with decay and decline. But then that's the fukkin London art world for you, turns the mind into a horse's flaky breakfast. If not that, then turns the mouth into a slobbering babbler, unable to touch a fact or to think via a healthy tilt of precision. Yep, I was able to hear the loud groaning of one civilisation replacing another, but remained stupid enough to not hear Kee's warning on slightly more personal worlds that were set to collide. So, no, I did not smell the trouble Patsy. If you must know.

'Drifting to the centre made the floor drop away more sharply until it levelled out two storeys below my feet where I could clearly see the sand and an idle school of snapper. They were hanging around outside the boat's shadow, lingering, flipping for a scratch at the ground, but basically doing pleasantly nothing. At dusk they'd sharpen up to hunt and feed. In the faint light their flanks flashed not silver, but blue, lingering citizens small as mice as they rested far down in the deep, slow as Kee. I was floating two storeys up and watching the stillness, it was nice to imagine that their planet right then was busily speeding round the sun at one hundred thousand kilometres per hour, but it was unpleasant to imagine my planet racing ahead to demolition.'

Patsy's Remple Arrives

'A streak of white foam cut abruptly through the water, slashing downwards at a good speed. Kee had dived in from the rooftop, and as he shot towards the floor the snapper scattered lazily away. When he slowed down to the point of the dive's natural end, he'd made it to within ten feet of the floor. Then he slowly turned about and drifted to the surface using only buoyancy. It was a good dive, a powerful effort. It was the kind of effort you'd get from a powerful will. It reminded me there was something about Kee underneath the unhurried sea-labrador exterior. Something unsettling about him certainly did exist. If it was cruelty, then it would be easy, I'd stay nimble, alert. I swam to the strip of beach, took off the mask and snorkel, lay on the hot sand and examined the boat adrift on the lagoon, unanchored.

'Kee had climbed aboard, and he sat quietly on the stern checking out the horizon where a bank of mountain-sized cloud stood, from here dense as stone. From the cloudbank he gazed down for a long time, into the blue stop sign, but for a long while.

'I called out. "Are you thinking about losing the lagoon to the new world?"

'"No, what you said about it all was enough and right, I've moved on, I'm thinking about something else now."

'"It looks interesting."

'"Perhaps. If my friends have arrived from Nassau, it could count as an interesting notion."

'"Let's say they've arrived."

'"Well, I was thinking about them, and their taste for driving at the truth, they have this fashionable penchant for the truth, what they call the truth, but really they're both just larger than life individuals, plenty of bombast between them."

'"Driving at the truth's reasonably important I suppose."

'"Yes, it's a part of things, and another part of things is perhaps to be buoyant, to learn the art of the moving sun, this skill of giving another a moment's entertainment. Most of us forget that moment's entertainment, most talkers trick themselves into talking to no effect other than a presumed hunt for the truth, where instead a glance at the moving sun on the sand told with a hint of colour would do just as well if not better."

'"I agree."

'"And for me, I don't know, there are some things that simply must be kept quiet, some things."

'The air and sand were hot, making Kee's voice shimmer with a faint echo around the bowl of the lagoon, so I did catch what he'd said but missed what he might have meant by the remark at the end, about keeping quiet. I went ahead with studying the boat.

'It was a fine old wooden white thing with a line of green trim. A small cabin, a rear deck, sported all you needed, you really could, on this boat, fuck the world and its worries if you wanted, fuck fukkin London at least. Even just that sturdy bright boat afloat on that tiny lagoon, just that, on a canvas, would finish up more filled with hints and codes and delights and mysteries than any painter could conjure in fukkin London, just Kee's simple little wooden diesel as a painting would smash through London's dreary art world ennui, a straight picture of a boat bobbing on a lagoon like that, it'd kill off pretension even if up and down Cork Street they died simply by laughing too hard into choking.

'When we reached Georgetown it was late afternoon, so a new arrival on the overnight mailboat from Nassau, Kee said, he'd be rested and waiting at the waterside inn.

'And Patricia, that's it, the first time I'd met Kieran Leeft, Kee

Leeft. The second time was on the other side of the world, at the jetty of Remple Fekdin's ocean university half an hour south of a place I hadn't heard of, Broome, all those shining huge domes sitting right on the coast. They're these revolutionary new anti-cyclone buildings that your Remple financed, Remple, big skinny guy, full of energetic solutions, gusto, never took no for an answer. But Broome's for later, because Broome, well, the place got thick and rich with the gusto and bloodsoup.'

Jack Black clicked send and then went out to see the Gauguin exhibition. He didn't wish to read what he'd sent, he felt it was on the button anyway, and Patsy deserved an honest reply to a curly question because he liked her. As he walked out the front door into the drizzle he muttered aloud, 'But what a damn question: Did you smell the troubles in the early days? Fukkin Patsy, jeez.'

Mendoza's Seaweed Head of Hair

Kee had not told Jack Black anything about Rosa Mendoza's father the fisherman. Kee learned a lot from the fisherman in the brief time of knowing him at the hacienda, but Mendoza was still too special to Kee's powderbox for splashing him round the stern on a lagoon in the Caribbean six decades later.

But what did happen in having the young painter from London as a guest on the boat, the London guy who loved the sea so much, was that Kee was reminded of Mendoza, Kee felt like he was now Mendoza and Jack the boy at the hacienda. Colonel David said the dreams were there for accepting. Ellie-

Isabela said some love to give, some love to take. And Mendoza said land people were different to sea people, that the sea was celebrated by town dwellers as the Bringer of Life, but was known by sea dwellers as a monster. His daughter Rosa had the best wisdom of all, down by the beach one hot afternoon when Carlos Luque was outside the hacienda on a visit, Rosa said: 'We will never forget each other, Carlos.' It made his head swim and he started to feel as if he was drowning, but it was the opposite, he was floating, he was flying.

After the remark, fear dominated the boy's afternoon, mixed with the serene and warm sense of flying, because he now feared her father, Mendoza. With the vow came the fear.

Carlos saw it clear as a butterfly, he knew exactly what Mendoza would now do as he emerged from the sea with his massive head of brown seaweed flashing in the hot sun. Mendoza would stride across the dead grass and throw hell at the village if he found out that his beloved only daughter was making secret avowals to a shitboy from the hacienda, a buffalo boy who had been corrupted into Indian rituals by the Scottish peanut.

Carlos thought he had made a big mistake when he told of that moment. Of love down by the beach between him and Rosa, when he told colonel David.

Big, large, bad mistake telling the colonel.

But no, the colonel had sat Carlos Luque down that evening on the front steps. Gave the boy an open account of his own fear in the days when he was making love with an Indian princess, of how it was widely known that her powerful father, a king of the land, a real king, not a king from legend, threatened he would cut off a man's genitals if he found the man with his daughter, boil them and feed them to the monkeys that lived on the estate, and that despite this ever-present threat, a never-spoken threat—because her father was a good man who was respected for his civilised ways with the complex world, but a threat that the father certainly wanted seeping out into the land—despite the threat, David told Carlos how he and the maharaja's daughter continued to make their promises and make their love.

The colonel told Carlos not to fear Rosa's father; Mendoza was a good man, and if Mendoza knew that Carlos and Rosa were playing at the beach he would not be concerned.

The colonel told Carlos that another obstacle was his friend, a big businessman, who wished to have the love and attention of the princess, but she continued to seek out the colonel.

David had said she was a brave young woman.

'Where is she now?' Carlos asked in the darkness on the steps.

'She lives with her father in India.'

'And the businessman?'

'In the same town.'

'Is he still trying to love her?'

'Yes, I would say he is.'

'Why do you not go back there?'

'Because I am here looking after all of you. Take this, laddie, I have a gift for you, it will be useful when you get your boat one day out there in the endless sun.'

David gave the kid a hat, a strong leather hat with a wide brim, lined with felt.

'It belonged to my friend the businessman in Calcutta, he gave it to me.'

'It is a stupid hat, señor,' the boy said suddenly, looking stupid was just not his game, and he'd do anything, anything, to avoid looking like a dumb kid who had no sense of swing or gravity.

'The world is full of silly hats, Carlos, try it on.'

The kid lifted it up to put it on, and he smelled the strong scent of something he had never smelled before.

He put the hat on, and it was too big, so he pushed it backwards. 'You do not see her any more, si, you cannot see her?'

'I do, I have ways of seeing her.'

O Bobbo. Ding-dong and how's the time.

The quiet talking-to helped the kid make a place in himself for Rosa's avowal. Calmed Carlos down after his fear on the beach, that night he slept well in the big room by the sea air, the room that the colonel had given back to the kids from the previous selfish manager. He took the hat to his small bed, and he kept the hat for a short while, for the next few weeks, until, when he jumped the wall, he had left the hat behind.

The industrialist who hunted the princess, the guy who kept David's teak box after his suitcase of belongings was shipped back to Scotland, was Miles Banford, born in Calcutta to an English mother and an American father. No relation to Inch's smellbomb assistant, Mile, no, or to the others in the crew, Furlong, Centimetre, Kilometre, Millimetre, Metre, Yard, Foot and that vain fuckface pretender Lightyear, no. This was Miles Banford, the great Miles Banford, who considered colonel David to be his deepest friend, no small thing, for Miles Banford had a thousand friends across the beautifully wooded north-east of India.

O Bobbo was owned by Miles Banford for just on a decade, but I would not be in his possession until '66 when they cremated the colonel, twenty years away. Miles was Calcutta's only Anglo-American. His commercial interests fell over a commanding corridor of the north-east of the continent like a silk sheet. Only old, worn so well that it became respected acceptance, in certain valleys and suburbs it became an honorific love, because the Banford interest ran back through five generations into the first shop, a dockside emporium, when the first American Banford opened for business supplying the ships in the 1880s. By the time the original shop multiplied and spread into Miles' time in the sixties the Banford Company was into everything, no longer a shop, but a huge clearing house. Tea, petrol, whisky, gin, tonic, strepsils or aspirin could not be purchased in north-east India without flinging a teeny percentage at the Banford Company.

Then the spices: when the spice barons of Kerala wanted a piece of the north-east action they found it a lot less messy to shovel the stuff through the Banford network, so nobody, but nobody, from Darjeeling to Calcutta to Cuttack, could purchase a satchel of anything without contributing to the Banford Company.

Then cotton: the Banford Mills sang and whistled across every backside young and old.

Then the movie houses: all the movies in the north-east cities had to be shown in a Banford theatre, even the rural audiences where the theatre was no more than a cricketpitch slab with a screen at one end, or at other, larger villages where the theatre was no more than a tent. Bollywood appreciated the Banford network, to them it was like locking away the smallest part of their national audience without lifting a finger, and almost every Bollywood mogul knew the Banfords, and liked em. In the fifties an upstart mogul, who hated the Banfords, flew across to open his own string of theatres, and all the other moguls in Bombay closed ranks behind the Banfords, and the upstart never made another film, took him two years to decide to move to Delhi where he made sullen documentaries for the education department till all the cows that amble along Delhi's streets came home.

Miles Banford dear butterfly. Soap, kerosene, fertiliser,

knitting needles, china, manchester, carbon copy paper, typewriters, sewing machines, it all butterflied its way into the Banford account at Standard Chartered in downtown Cal.

Miles did not collect art, he collected maps, Cuban cigars. He had around a hundred and fifty maps, old and older. He would have dearly loved Flattie, what with her antique globe, but Flattie finished up in Perth, not Cal. If only the guy knew that one of the rudest maps he would possess would be me, O Bobbo, lined with what, sordid secrets, sweet routes of sweet memories with cunning princess and longing Scot, dirty maps right round the outside and inside of hopes and dreams and crude, beautiful, smelling flobreggations of flesh. Wonderful flobreggations, gatherings, gather all the hup two three potential, ready to fling their stuff across the seas and over the mountaintops.

Miles also collected anything on the king of the Greek gods Zeus. The entire upper floor of his mansion bungalow was littered with Zeus objects, maybe just over fifteen hundred pieces of drawings, busts, books, locks, keys, stone carvings, wood carvings, manuscripts, scrimshaw, ivory, brass, gold, silver and a huge range of those nimble protectors of the spirit, amulets.

He had the biggest Zeus museum in all India, for few Indians were keen on Zeus.

So Miles was into everything, just about everything, everything except the maharaja's daughter, that flashing beauty, that unruly, disobedient, tough, soft and gentle mezzotint of greatness who threw open the cages to set the butterflies free.

Yep, Miles Banford hunted her all right, but only as a spectator, he just sat back in Calcutta and watched, took it in from a respectable distance, a passive, elegant guy who owned the north-east in tandem with her dad the maharaja, watched as the young Scot and the unruly princess broke every rule under the ruler's nose.

Miles sat back one day at the club, no stress, pleased with the day, cruising into the evening, and he said quietly to his great friend, cautioned his great friend, the twenty-five year old Scot: 'You do know, David, one day her father mister Rampage is going to find out.'

'I know, Miles, I know, though could you lend us the Morris again this afternoon?'

'Yes of course, it's parked at the house, the driver can take you there in the Jaguar, he's outside, ask him to come back and pick me up at six, I have to be at her father's place for the ambassador's dinner.'

So David rode to Miles' house in the white jaguar driven by Miles' trusted driver, picked up the old Morris, a guava-green roundy, and off the young Scot puttered in the old Morris Minor to pick up the princess to putter up into the hills to the old shack where they lay with their arses hanging out in the cool sheets once too often.

The Arnie Colchester teak box dear butterfly, became lined with layer after layer of these drives into the hills to the old mud hut in a beaten-up car nobody would notice. And Miles, when he finally got a hold of O Bobbo two decades later, when David passed away in the opium den by the harbour, the intent was not because the revered Arnie Colchester made me, it had no value for Miles as a Colchester piece, it was because David had owned it. O Bobbo changed hands, yep, but first David would open the telegram asking him to run the orphanage on the Golfo de Valencia, go to Spain, later to Edinburgh where he would fall in love with Enid, have a daughter who became Lee and Meryl's mother Rachel, then he'd come back to Cal to lie on his mattress of kapok and sweat. Then, only then, O Bobbo, with all those layers of David's five lives, fell into the possession of the great and celebrated Miles Banford.

The mid-sixties, Miles felt he ought to sell up and migrate to America, but on a break as fundamental as quitting Cal he asked David's advice first.

Why would a fifty year old Banford mogul ask advice of a penniless forty-five year old Scot, returned from an orphanage in Spain, a zero-peso princess-humper who'd spent time in Spain jamming Maheesha into a lost village?

'Do you think I could settle in Boston?'

'Are you serious, you really want to sell the Banford Company?'

'I'm serious, I've been giving it some thought ever since you left for Spain twenty years ago, just that now I can see it's become real. I'll keep twenty-five percent, and my wish is to bequeath the other seventy-five percent. Who do you believe I should bequeath it to?

'Fuck. Well, I just haven't a clue, give me a week, I'll think about it. Wall Street, you ought to invest it in Wall Street.'

'Perhaps.'

'You know, Miles, I have always admired and trusted you, what you did for me back then in the forties, I have never forgotten your dignity and your golden friendship, but really, I think you should ask the right person about this.'

'I'm asking the right person.'

'I'm an addict, Miles.'

'I know that, and you're my most trusted friend.'

'And you're really going to migrate to the States?'

'Do you think they'll have me in Boston?'

'Probably not, you're Indian, the State Department right now, though they have nothing much to do with the subject of immigration, they nonetheless believe all you Indians are communists, Soviet sweeties, anyway. Are you Indian?'

'I was certainly born here, at the Mercy Hospital.'

'You're American, you're a Banford, Boston will have you, they'd have to have you, they'd look churlish if they reject a Banford, and I can't see Boston wishing to seem churlish.

The Inheritance Begins to Glide Across the Second Equator

A week later David kept his word, he returned to Miles with four ideas.

'One of the kids from the orphanage in Spain, gifted guy, about twenty-eight by now. Sunrise Sunset I called him, always wanted to travel. Also, the orphanage itself, give a nice big chunk to the trustees. And this place too, Cal, give it all back to Calcutta, you can choose from a hundred charities up and down the coast, and there's that tough, remarkable nun, Teresa. And since you insisted that I was to be forthright, you might consider Enid and Rachel.'

'Enid and Rachel,' Miles said, 'are already on the list at my lawyer's office, they'rc to get ten percent.'

'Of the whole company?'

'Yes.'

'Of the whole fucking company?'

'Yes.'

'Miles, that is very good of you.'

So the year before David was found on his mattress in the opium den, Miles sold the Banford Company, and distributed seventy-five percent of it. The remainder went with him when he migrated to Boston. With a teak box in tow. Give and Take:

Miles had his cherished memories of his profoundly great friend David Darlington, I had newfound access to Miles' powderbox, a powderbox that did not like to gamble. It was mid-sixties Calcutta, but Miles did not need to wait another half century to know that Wall Street was not actually full of banks and brokerage joints, it was full of gambling joints. Or, rather, as Miles put it: gambling joints pretending to be banks. Whether they were addicted to pretending, or addicted to gambling, who knows, but they certainly received no counselling for the addictions. They were the favourite playground of that impossibly churlish cardboard counterfeiter, Lightyear, that vain fuckface pretender, vain coz he could hup two three a memory faster than smell, faster than music. And anything quicker than a song is just downright scary. My years with Miles at his stately Boston bungalow, picking up Miles' powderbox as a new client, that's when I started to get cluey on the ding-dong world of medium high-finance. And those other ding-dong worlds: of favours, clubs, buy-outs, manners, sartorial no-no's, elegant parties, all the stuff for which I was disliked, no, loathed, no, hated, by cardboard king Bakks and Inch and the crew of deadbeat smellbombs who wouldn't know a sock from a napkin. Lightyear included.

When a suited lawyer took a flight to Barcelona and then came down to the Golfo de Valencia and stood at the doorstep of the old hacienda with the news, it was like jamming a bare electric wire into a fishpond. Except that the fishpond at the hacienda, the old fountain, had never seen water. Ellie-Isabela was still there, señorita Give and Take, soon to retire, giving her job to her cousin. But the trustees of the hacienda were not accustomed to handling money, and the hacienda soared into a period of light and then gradually drifted into decay and finally touched oblivion.

When a suited man visited David's wife Enid and their

daughter Rachel in Edinburgh, they were stunned by the news he delivered. For the next month Enid was disgusted with the swap, David for a fortune, but after a while the disgust dissolved into whatever disgust of that kind can dissolve into, and Enid eventually migrated with her daughter to Sydney with a fortune fit for a maharaja. The Darlington family of Sydney grew from there. By the time Lee was searching around Tenmoon Creek in her gymshoes, the Darlington clan had become an established unit on the peninsula of ex-Californians, complete with Jimmy Hazel the Lucknow jolly yesfactor.

But Sunrise Sunset had long since jumped the walls of the hacienda, and so could not be found by entering a street and looking for a number on a post box. It was now 1966, he was twenty-nine. He was tall and tough and tanned, with solid forearms that had loved and worked the oceans for a decade, and he was now a respected seafarer among those who knew him on the south coast of Spain. He'd had hundreds of nights lying on the stern deck watching the constellations swing from horizon to horizon, watching the sky fly by as the second equator made its approach. But the nights free from the world were the second part of his triumph. Triumphs flow in threes on the east coast, on the Golfo de Valencia, and so he was still roaming, running, resting, searching, to complete the third part, for he still had not found Rosa and her father Mendoza in Almeria. Or anywhere on the south coast.

The Guy Carrying a Banford Briefcase

Miles' lawyers had no information to locate Kieran Leeft—they had what, say: kid runs away at eleven? But Miles' lawyers were resourceful guys to the hilt, and they found him in Gibraltar.

False alarm, the guys at the boatyard said he'd sailed a few days ago across the straits, and the lawyer took a ferry and found Kieran Leeft in Tangiers where he had rented out his boat to a film crew from Hollywood.

The film producers paid him fifty bucks a day for the ten-day scene on the harbour. Petty cash, even in '66, petty compared with what the messenger from the Banford Company of Calcutta had in tow, a little bit more than fifty a day.

Kieran Leeft didn't much like being stuck on land without the keys to his boat, but the five hundred American bucks would do well because he was planning his first trip across the Atlantic to check out the place he had always heard of, the Bahamas. A round trip he would come to do many times in the years ahead, discovering, from the three heavily worn Atlantic charts he had collected, that to sail east you need to be just on top of the equator. And to sail west you needed to be just under it, a useful stream of ocean running around the Atlantic in an oval shape at the equator. So he sat at a table on the terrace high above the port of Tangiers with his few important things like the charts in the leather satchel on the floor. Those charts were the first of dozens of charts he would collect over the years, folded out they would become his keys to staying off land, off the world's land problems.

He looked out over the sea westward, past the summer haze lingering on the escarpment of the cape Spartel, figuring he'd have to stop first at the Canaries. Santa Cruz, then south on the Canary Current, and then full west on the Atlantic North

Equatorial Current across to the Caribbean.

He was taking a lunch of rice and salted fish with a big steaming mug of tea. He removed his sandals to feel the stone and to cool his feet. The sun was high, and the terrace was hot, July burning upon the slab of Tangiers, 1966, a hot summer. He had become a smart, quiet operator, and he'd learned to locate the neat spot to sit so that he could ease the mind into becoming attentive to what he was to do next, he'd grown into a pretty good seadog. And the rusty old key he swung around his finger as a kid, that little useless key now hung around his neck.

Instead of steaming hot tea, the guy at the cafe suggested in French he take cool fig juice, freshly made yesterday.

But Kieran did not want cool juice. 'I want tea, make it very hot please.'

'The juice has ice monsieur,' the Arab said in French, 'it will make you fresh, today is our hottest day this summer, take the juice monsieur, très bien monsieur, today is too hot,' the Arab said.

'I want hot tea, give me a hot tea.'

'Monsieur we do not wish to see you sweat, we wish to help you enjoy the lunch, and we are not making tea today.'

'I have given you one American dollar for this meal, give me a hot tea.'

'Oui,' the Arab said, and walked away to make a hot tea, muttering in north African French slang, 'fucking Spaniards, what a bunch of fucking losers, hot tea in July, here in Tangiers, no wonder they lisp like a cat, melt the lips with a hot fucking tea in fucking July, or snort like a bull, or whatever they do, fucking lisping losers.'

Kieran took out of his pocket the postcard he'd bought from the harbour hotel. He wrote a quick note to his friend Pedro back in Spain, in Almeria, the town down on the south coast he'd hitchhiked to after he jumped the hacienda wall and found Rosa's house empty. On arriving as an eleven year old in Almeria he met Pedro down by the boats, and they made their living by keeping an eye out for stuff nobody else at the boats wanted to do. Pedro was fun, he made hard work into adventures, and they shared three or four great adventures every day, sleeping at night in a small room in the attic of the run-down old hotel Villacarillo. The owner said: 'You boys take the room, but you use the brooms in there to sweep the hotel, good deal?'

Kee wrote two lines in Spanish:

Dear Pedro,

Please continue to keep a watch out for Mendoza and his daughter because even though we could not find them they must be there somewhere in Almeria, or thereabouts. I am on my way to the Bahamas. I hope you are well, see you in a few months,

Kieran, Sunrise Sunset.

'Excuse me, mister Kieran Leeft?'

'Yes?'

'How do you do, I am Henry Farnborough, may I join you?'

'Señor, I have given the keys to my boat to your man at the office. He has the keys, and I do not wish to talk to any of you guys any more until your work is done, I have no interest in the movies, señor, please, I am taking lunch, leave me alone.'

'This is not about your boat mister Leeft. I am a representative of mister Miles Banford.'

'I do not know any señor Mahyeeah Baenfah.'

The Give and the Take, flying across the second equator, right across the blurred line of approach where all the best hup two three action takes place. Specially the hup two three of two of the keenest, O Bobbo and like a jink Oxley.

'He is a friend of David Darlington's.'

Kieran stopped.

The lawyer said, 'Hacienda Zaragoza.'

'The colonel?'

'Yes, colonel David.'

'He is here?'

'No, I'm sorry, he passed away last month.'

Aromas that Opened His Powderbox

A long silence, but a stab of pain. Hot sun, and the distant feel of good ol times that smelled of coffee and honey around a dry disused fountain cracking to pieces outside the shade of a grand fig tree.

A powderbox can rotate a universe in seconds, but only on smell can it rotate a universe in a blip. So at first, without the aroma, Kieran could not piece it together, that world of Miles Banford and colonel David.

But then the lawyer handed Kieran a hat, and the scent evaporated into the hot Tangiers air up into his nose, bursting Kieran's powderbox to life, rotating half a universe in the bat of an eyelid.

He held the hat, and said to the lawyer: 'A businessman?'

'Yes mister Leeft, Miles Banford.'

'From India, this friend of the colonel?'

'Yes.'

With a hey-ho ding-dong force of plenty the colonel came rushing back into his powderbox like a crass wind of great heaping beauty, along with the nights of the princess that the colonel had told him about, and along with the mysterious businessman from India. For a moment hoof thunder came up the hillside, even the now worn-out dreary horror of the hairy buffalo, Maheesha the demon of chaos and evil, came thundering up the basalt hillside of Tangiers. Kieran the twenty-nine year old was blasted back to the hacienda as Sunrise Sunset the eleven year old, eating sardines and eating frightening tales of the buffalo demon.

What we boxes understand, what binary bagpipes cannot understand, coz I dunno why, coz I guess they're addicted to ceremonies, is Kieran was giving the colonel that outright simple thing, the simplest of all things, and it don't require a national holiday in Tangiers for it to happen. He was giving the colonel the honour of memory. But hold it: he had little or fuck-all control of it. Just comes and goes and vacant thoughts and idle hummings of internal silence, wafted pieces of olden crumbs getting a ride on a wind nobody knows anything about, and warm breeze under the shade of The Tree of Wishes suddenly comes up, and then goes. Scant intention and scant taste and scant scent and no control.

The powderbox had the control, our client powderbox, zapped by the scent of that hat, and, as powderboxes do, his became filled with memories of the gifts that the colonel and Ellie-Isabela had given him back at the ol farmhouse hacienda by the beach.

The colonel had given him plenty. First opportunities to taste the world: getting back to the hacienda after school, the colonel had taught him to read English; to write English; sang high and sent his two-page story, about an underwater fishing boat, to a magazine in Edinburgh, three pesos he'd got for that. The colonel had got him out for the day on Mendoza's boat many times; and the colonel had given him the guts to run with his romance with the guy's daughter.

Ellie-Isabela showed him all the curly things she knew, for the Ellie-Isabela that he remembered was a loud and curly person while the colonel always seemed quiet and normal, shows how off the ball a kid can be: Ellie-Isabela was not loud and the colonel was not normal.

Ellie-Isabela showed him the technique to discern a giver from a taker. 'Draw a map on a bus ticket, give it to whosoever you like, whosoever. Tell them it shows the way to a shop that is giving away free old spoons for the day, and watch carefully if their hand shoots out fast as a frog's tongue or if it reaches for the map like a turtle.'

She showed him how to clean the sea creatures Mendoza hurled at the hacienda. How to share the bony gristle with Pinski and Henry while they were at it, with her knife she showed him what she said were all the different bloods of the different sea creatures. Starting with the octopus, black blood, then red blood, blue blood, green blood, orange blood, yellow blood, golden blood. Poor kid; took him years to work out Ellie-Isabela's pastime of bullshitting, especially up in the back small room at the bench. She showed him how to knit a net from onion sacks and go for prawns at night off the beach; at the time he always thought this was Ellie-Isabela's idea of fun for the kids and Pinski and Henry. But Ellie-Isabela only did it because there was no food around back then after the war. She showed him how to oil his shoes with fat. She showed him how to move his legs with hers, fast and sharp, dancing in the summer dust round the fountain.

Señorita Ellie-Isabela and colonel David. One claiming

she inherited this, one saying he'd inherited that, a fat arse, a long head, and what they bequeathed was a courage for him to understand his dreams so that he could claim his dreams. And then Mendoza showing Sunrise Sunset and Rosa how to take the best dives. Cut to the floor, swing to the sky, bounce from that industrial plastic slab bolted to the jetty, but a slab that sprang like a wing into the future where the constellations might have new tales to drop along the coast.

Ellie-Isabela and the colonel and Mendoza, just by the memories he had of them, they showed Kieran how to live, how to love. Sounds simple don't it. How to live. How to love. Then how come, you'll ask, dear butterfly, nobody knows it, how to live, how to love, how come everyone prefers to screw it up. How come is Bakks. Bakks and caked-up Inch and the crew of smellbomb deadbeats, that's how come. But O Bobbo was on the kid's case from the start, taking blows from Bakks and crew, but hangin in there, so Kieran got the beginnings of how to live, how to love.

Proof. When Sunrise Sunset was nineteen and he found the lonely, frightened girl sitting on the wharf and took her to safety, but could not find her parents, he had tried to give her the same thing. Tried without thinking, without knowing, he was feeding it onwards, the colonel's give and Ellie-Isabela's give. Every thread of goodwill they had given him, from the name Sunrise Sunset to the unnamed dreams, every thread had been weaved into one big luminous rope when he found the girl. Every thread of giving had found expression in that lifeline he had thrown to the girl, a rope that towed them up the coast night after night in search of her father, when in fact she was razor-wired with fear, when in fact she was escaping her father. Kieran's powderbox then ground to a halt: the suited man was talking.

He explained to Kieran what he was about to inherit. He opened his briefcase, brought out papers to sign, and that was it; Kieran was now formally in possession of a goodly portion of the accumulated treasure of five generations of Calcutta Banfords, a treasure which even the great and feared Maheesha could not get a hold of without assistance. Even if a helpful lawyer like Henry Farnborough glued a pen to his hoof and sent him off to Harvard to learn how to sign his name in a language that the buffalo would no doubt find to be disgusting in lettering he would no doubt find vile.

Miles Banford's Gift to Enid

So we all went our different ways, David, Miles an me, Enid and her daughter Rachel, Sunrise Sunset, away to the Bahamas. Sydney, Boston and, well, David, maybe to a place that Maheesha had reserved for him somewhere in the kingdom of chaos and evil, ding-dong diasporas of good and evil all over the joint. A great pity nobody counted on the cardboard diaspora from Guangzhou, like Inch, like that vain fuckface Lightyear, and like the Bakks prawnbox diaspora of universal evil. Oxley as far back as the days of the Mole Valley in Dorking in Surrey wanted to make evil a Pluto diaspora, that is, an earth diaspora on Pluto. You know, far away. Roll diaspora into diaspirin then roll it into the Dunsborough Swing, and Jack Black's new friends three hours south of Perth dear butterfly, would soon discover the spectacle you and your clouds of butterflies created: the Dunsborough Swing. Charming ol Oxley.

Years later Miles sent me to Enid Darlington, bubble-wrap, fedex, sayonara. A decision that would simply deepen the ability for jungarummy jiddle, gotta mix, gotta mix, get acquainted with that great power, cyxmix. The note was brief:

Dear Enid,

My name is Miles Banford, and although you and I have never met, I was a good friend of David's. As I write today I know that your daughter Rachel has turned twenty-one. Perhaps this Colchester teak box that belonged to your husband would be a fine twenty-first gift, I have no doubt it is lined with memories for many of us in many places, for he was a very dear friend,

Sincerely,
Miles Banford

Boston,
September 1st 1971

Yep, Lee Glass-Darlington's mother Rachel was born on the first day of autumn, and when she migrated to Sydney she was born on the first day of spring, that's what equators do to arbitrary flappers like a calendar dear butterfly.

Wings Over the Tree of West Africa

Miles was a regular visitor to Lagos in the summer of Calcutta, get rid of the heat, go away to see a friend in thc cool findings. What he called his sub-Saharan vacation. This time, deep in '64 by far and away on his own power, he took along David on the vacation. The flight itself was fun, let alone the holiday in Nigeria. Nobody went to Nigeria, everyone in Cal went to Beirut, Paris, Rome, even Vienna, often Lake Geneva, but not Nigeria, they'd never even heard of Nigeria, and Cal society was not insular or thin-minded.

But Miles and David were both a bit fucked in the head, supreme travellers, and Miles had two very loved friends in Nigeria. The fun started with the journey, others would devote misery to reaching the destination, but not Miles and David, the fun started right away. They lunched from Calcutta to Bombay, played cards and drank from Bombay to Nairobi, had dinner from Nairobi across Africa to Lagos, visited the pilots up front. The whole thing took twenty hours and three different planes. By the time they'd got to Lagos they'd been served eight meals, which they ate. A powderbox needed to get two shots for Nigeria, yellow fever and cholera, big injections the size of a toothpaste tubc, huge ding-dongs, scared even David at the clinic in Cal. Also malaria, had to take pills daily for a month prior.

Lagos, settled upon a vast lagoon, became a big metropolis early on in its modern life. It had a large population of westerners, and every European was represented in the mix, from Italian to German to Swede to French to English and across; the whole of western Europe worked and played in Lagos, mainly around the southern leafy suburbs of Victoria and Apapa beside the harbour. Miles only ever stayed a couple of days in the city of oil power, and then travelled north two hundred kilometres into Nigeria's sub-Saharan landscape to the true destination where he kept a house in the town of Ilorin in Kwara State. Ilorin was disliked by Lagosites, flat, dusty, remote in terms of the cosmopolitan city life of Lagos with its embassies and hotels giving parties. Nigeria's foreigners worked only in Lagos, few worked in Ilorin, fewer further north towards the Sahara in the small elegant city of Kano, and none elsewhere. To them Nigeria was Lagos. But to Miles' good friends the English-American couple, Ann and Hugh O'Hear, Nigeria was everywhere, not just Lagos.

When Miles and David arrived, after eight hours driving from Lagos, at the house on Ilorin's outskirts, they settled in with a cold drink. The house lay on a slight rise on the vast Ilorin plain, so they enjoyed a sweeping view. Across the broad dusty road lay the full breadth of a sub-Saharan plain. Behind the house lay the township of Ilorin. Along the road were few houses, an outer road that had only just been graded two years back, unsealed, but wide and very straight.

'Ann and Hugh will arrive presently, I called them from the hotel in Lagos, I always insist that they drop in for a visit when I'm in town,' Miles said. 'You shall have to watch this, you'll enjoy it, let's go sit on the verandah.'

They eased into the jug of rum and tonic sparkling with ice and limes, the first glass going down for the dry thirst and the second glass for sipping enjoyment.

'Here they are,' Miles said as he pointed out at the plains across the road. David searched the plains but could see nothing in the way of a vehicle, all he saw was what he felt was the most stunning landscape he'd ever encountered: arid, stark, hard, stunted trees, beautiful beyond any of the tough landscapes he'd visited. Had Miles brought along anyone else out of the

Calcutta social scene to this vacation they would have dropped to the floor with despondency at being stranded in the exact middle of nowhere, with nothing to do, with nothing to see, with nobody to meet. David scanned the plain again, but saw no vehicle. Then he heard a buzzing.

The O'Hears commenced their arrival by circling over the plain, then they made the final descent by aligning with the road and then they approached the final landing towards the house. As the wheels skidded onto the hard dusty road the small aeroplane shook and bounced once and they came puttering to a stop outside the driveway to the house. Ann waved and smiled through the small window, and then flapped open the little door that looked like half a leather waistcoat. She jumped out, and Hugh drove the plane off the road. He switched off the engine and the propeller came to a stop. He hopped out and strolled up the driveway smiling and waving, raising his hand high above his head. The dust lifted by the landing hung in the air briefly and then moved with the mild prevailing breeze over the wide road into the plains like a cloud of cicada ghosts.

Ann and Hugh live in Ilorin, but they traverse the countryside in the small plane calling on friends in the towns of Bida, Jebba and Oshogbo. They've landed in many other places around the various states of Nigeria, but they tend to have most of their interest in Kwara State or just beyond its borders. Kwara State keeps them busy enough, it's a big area, roughly a hundred kilometres up towards the Sahara and a hundred and fifty kilometres across the country towards the Ibo people of Nigeria, pronouncing themselves as E-bo. Kwara is a state of Nigeria's Yoruba people, and Ann is a dedicated Yoruba aesthete, Miles calls her a walking encyclopaedia of Yoruba culture. But Ann doesn't, she halts the PR excesses of the sixties parties by calling herself a learner, not a walking or flying encyclopaedia. She was not, Ann insisted, a repository of Yoruba knowledge and culture, she was a learner in the Yoruba universe. Her heart and soul of human possibility dear butterfly, glided around in that universe somewhere, she said, and she'd come with Hugh to Nigeria to find its welcome.

The plane was old and bumpy, half a wing was bandaided up with wide masking tape after a treetop had stripped away pieces of the casing, round and round the masking tape went into creating a new skin on the left wing.

Hugh O'Hear was a biologist. He said in coming to Nigeria he'd done what he regarded as the most scary thing he could do as a biologist. Born and raised in Niagara Falls USA, with all that endless water lashing at the place, falling over the place like what Hugh said was the flood of a double eternity, he said the dryness of Kwara State was a reverse miracle. To biology it was simply a miracle. Things happened here in Kwara State, under the microscope, that should not happen at all. Life had far better tricks than a north-east-centric scientist had made allowances for, life without water, drylife magic, had been an exotic footnote in the biology tomes of the American north-east universities. A footnote of interest, but left largely unexamined past the discoveries up to the late fifties that were made in the deserts of Utah, Colorado and New Mexico.

But it was no longer biology Hugh lived for, he'd fallen for Nigeria, and his heart and soul had flowered here, water or no water. 'You can't exactly call the living here easy living, but you can call it great living.'

Miles and David stood up. Miles first took a moment to introduce David, and then he exchanged an embrace with Ann, then with Hugh. They strolled inside to the living room. Here at the other side of the house the township of Ilorin was visible across the far wall of the living room, stretched across the horizon outside.

Ann and Hugh flying around the state and pulling up on roads and flats and campuses and fields irritated the minor officials. Greatly irritated the law-abiding Yoruba middle classes using the roads in their Vauxhalls and Peugeots, who were themselves in aspirational flight from the more rural edges of their heritage. But the Yoruba politicians who ran the place approved of the good work Ann and Hugh did, in culture, and also in biology. Incoming complaints against their plane to various ministries were always casually lost in the system. If a complaint ever reached an actual minister, say the transport minister, he would erupt into a blast of abuse at the official who'd brought it in. Gradually the bandaged plane came to be known around the place, and the two pilots came to be known for the work they did. So by '64 all was well, and clouds of cicada ghosts no longer gave irritation to the aspirational class that weighed anchor against its rich rural inheritance to set sail for other attractive comforts in Nigeria's sub-Saharan cities.

In '64 Ann's work was still a nascent movement, it would take another couple of decades for the aspirational Yoruba to place his heritage in front of the memory. She had of course joined hundreds of forward-looking Yorubas across western Nigeria in schools and colleges and libraries, but, as a diverse and lively group stirring the good work, they were nonetheless vastly outnumbered by their aspirational brothers and sisters who fostered the growing African might of Nigeria. The abstract line of British rule in the dust had fenced in three peoples: the Yoruba in the west, the Hausa in the north, and the Ibo in the east. And all three original nations now worked hard, fostering the growing international status of Nigeria, except for one problem. It was just one original nation that had the oil, the Ibo, and just one that controlled the selling of it, the Yoruba. Air

Force One regularly visited Lagos with the president on board, no other African capitals, just Lagos, and America, a slave to oil, sought and bought Nigeria's friendship and oil. Crude light sweet created a nice slave trade in reverse. America, as the world's largest oil producer, nonetheless never had enough oil for its consumption. America was forced to buy oil from other oil-producing nations such as Nigeria. The burgeoning Yoruba ruling elite proved to be very capable at obtaining a good price, and Nigeria's new wealth was born into the spectacle of a line of American presidents visiting Lagos on a very regular basis. But the Yoruba–Ibo tensions did not erupt into civil war until '67, the Biafran War, and the potholes that the tanks and bombs made on the main streets of the Ibo town of Enugu were still kept long after the war, as a reminder, as late as '78. Huge holes five feet deep and ten feet wide on the main streets.

Together, Ann and Hugh had friends all over the joint, Yoruba, Ibo and Hausa. Miles was their only American friend born in Calcutta. They knew nobody in Lagos well, rather tried to avoid ol Lagos, preferring the beauty of Kwara State and its people. Hugh said if Niagara Falls USA was soaked in two eternities of old, clean water, Lagos was soaked in the triple futures of a powerful republic of three ethnic groups running rather singularly on oil. But Ann and Hugh had not flown in to talk about crude light sweet, they were here to visit Miles, and, before lunch had even begun, were pleased to meet his engaging friend David.

'Chances are,' Ann said, smiling brightly, 'you would be the only Scottish Hindu in the whole eighty million population of Nigeria at this moment.'

'I'd lay a bet on it,' Miles said, 'if I gambled, a very large sum, but I never gamble. If there was even just one other Scottish Hindu in Nigeria I would pay him five thousand and he could use it towards care for a temple.'

'He or she,' David said, 'would avoid me like the good ol plague.'

Hugh was curious. 'Why?'

'I have an unhealthy fixation with the buffalo demon, Maheesha, it's too unbalanced for a healthy Hindu. We needn't go into it. Miles tells me you two found a group of traditional potters this year out west near the border with Benin.'

'Yoruba pottery, yes.'

'Is it true this group's line goes back unbroken as potters for twelve generations?'

'That's what they say.'

'That means they started pottery three centuries ago, in the 1660s.'

'They did,' Ann said. 'They let us buy four pieces, and we were bringing one here to the house, knowing that you were in Calcutta, Miles, as a surprise. When we began to circle the house, we saw there was a party in progress, and when we landed we found around three dozen American kids dancing and drinking, do you know these kids?'

'I know one of them, he's my cousin's son, from New York.'

David and Miles stayed in Ilorin for two weeks, and Ann and Hugh visited regularly, enjoying drinks and conversation.

Hugh showed David the state from the air over half a dozen flights.

And Miles was secretly grateful that his experiment seemed to be working, amazed really, that David hadn't touched any opium, or mentioned it, the whole time, ever since the week before departing Cal.

Remple Fekdin

Four decades later, after thousands of rolls of the second equator, by the time Calcutta had become Kolkata, Kee steered the boat around into Georgetown harbour on the glimmer of the blue Bahamas waters with Jack Black on board, where they could see the activity on the waterfront, a boulevard where just about everything looked like it was a hand-me-down from Miami.

The waterfront flowed with vendors in second-hand shirts from Miami, children carrying worn-out baseball gloves, women in old skirts from Miami. The Cuban traders, who had sailed in for the day, wearing leather hats from Miami, performed the same service they'd done the previous week, buying and selling American dollars, cheapshit currency when compared to the stuff we boxes throw around the place. A line of cute young Miami pigs strolled along behind their owner, a rich-looking guy in an old suit from Miami. A woman carried on her head a basket of four chickens from Miami. Miami cars and Miami scooters came and went, swerving around a horse and cart that had stopped on the other side. A boy ran along the waterfront, calling out happily into the day, 'Yaw, yaw, ah laave yaw!'

When Kee and Jack pulled up to the jetty a tall, thin guy waved, no Miami bizzo about him, none. But the powderbox behind his forehead, you'd expect it to be a tall thin balsabox; and you'd be wrong. Externals, never rely your dollar or yuan on them externals. No, Remple's powderbox was no hup two three bouncer, it was one of those hup two ninety types. Remple's powderbox was one of our trickiest customers. Forever going forward, couldn't care less about our wares, whether it was Bakks's wares or us wooden ones, bad or good, counterfeit or real. Remple's powderbox just blasted forward. It soared across all kinds of barriers, boundless energy. Whether it was Bakks and his crew trying to sell evil crap to Remple's powderbox, or me trying to sell a pinch of the good giving to Remple's powderbox, we had to really try very hard. With a hup two ninety powderbox the world was the oyster, and the way they got things done these hup two ninety powderboxes was that impressive it was downright scary. Scarier by a mile than fingerer Patsy shelling out contemporary art in Bond Street.

'Mister Kieran Leeft!' Remple called out brightly as he walked towards the boat.

Kee Leeft threw him the rope. 'Remple Fekdin, well how about it. It has been a long while, my friend.'

'More than a year.'

'And Catherine?'

'Yes, she's floating about in a siesta back at the hotel.'

'Good to see you.'

'Good to see you, too.'

'I wager you have finished building that university of yours, señor.'

'Certainly have.'

'This is señor Jack Black, from London. Jack, this is Remple Fekdin from Australia.'

'We've met,' Jack said.

'We have? Yes, you're one of Patricia's artists.'

'Yeah, we met when that Rudolph guy and his wife Lee Glass-Darlington came up to Patsy's gallery.'

By now Lee Glass-Darlington had become a mess, all she ever did was hang around the house back in Pittwater, never got completely dressed, drank tea, checked emails ten times a day, avoided going out, rejected dinners, fell away from the STC list, sneaked into the Newport Kentucky Fried whenever she could stand driving, find the keys, find em.

That night, instead of the new arrivals getting out on the

ocean to experience the fourth layer, they met at the inn where Remple described his university. Jack was to discover what Patsy already knew: 'Immune Remple, big skinny guy, full of energetic solutions, full of gusto, never takes no for an answer, immune to restraint.'

From the way he'd thrown himself around the jetty, Jack expected a long-winded boast, he looked as if he would ram a depiction of his achievements into the side of a bar, but Remple was good fun, and brief. Turned out he cared nothing that it was his achievement, he cared that the university was at last up and running, that it was a vibrant place dedicated to arresting the growth of vandalism, which is how he put it. Jack said that he thought of the vandalism as the appetite needed to make 'boundless technological excreta,' and Remple replied, 'Nice way to put it.'

Here Jack caught another whiff. In the afterglow of the day on the lagoons, it was a pleasure to hear it. In the afterbluster of snorkelling in the ocean, it seemed to Jack just right to sit down with a drink and hear about a new university dedicated to the empire of natural things ocean.

'I have never been able to tackle that afterglow with any precision,' Jack said privately to Kee, 'except to say that after a day on a clear ocean, a day of abundant events, sights and sensations, the kink that is the intellect is smoothed out into a thing I'd say was dance. And to hear about Remple's university while the mind dances, well that's just the right afterburn.'

Kee said nothing, and lifted his hand to the barman.

Remple said: 'It specialises in the ocean. If you look at the location from space, which we've done by taking satellite photographs, the campus straddles the dividing rampart between the desert and the sea, more specifically the infamous Great Sandy Desert and the Indian Ocean of the Rowley Shoals area.

The campus buildings stand on the red earth, and the labs on the turquoise bay. On the ground, the campus is an hour south of Broome directly on Roebuck Bay, and the central feature is the line-up of jetties. Fifteen of them, they harness the big tides of Broome to drive the turbines that generate the electricity for the labs dotted along the jetty. All the buildings are domes, and every inch of every dome is a solar panel. My cousin Castle drew the domes for me, years ago, Castle is a painter in Margaret River. He initially drew them, which he would, he's a very clever offhand mind that man, and, years ago he sent the drawings and letters to the councils up there but they never replied. He showed the drawings to me when I'd wanted to build a university up there. I got the domes through council, now the whole region takes a keen interest because we've already had one cyclone with no damage at all to our buildings, there are no right-angles for the winds to crash into, no pitched roofs either, just round smooth surfaces, rendering a cyclone almost harmless.

'The students, they enrolled from all over the world. We promoted it using billboard posters of the satellite image in key cities, and the courses, well Kee, they're full. So that's why I'm here, to invite you to Broome to formally open the joint.'

Catherine walked in. She'd got to Georgetown, via Miami, after a visit to Barcelona. She said to Jack, 'My epic journey to visit Kee, always anchored in a different place. How do you do, my name's Catherine, I understand you're with Patricia in London, I'd like to talk to you about representing you in Australia. I have a gallery in Perth and a gallery in Sydney.' Catherine spared no option, and Jack liked her straight off for the straightness.

'When did you last visit Kee?' Jack said to let the work talk stay for later.

'The last time I said hello to Kee was also epic,' Catherine said, 'London to Rio then north a thousand miles to Porto de Pedras, I catch him around once a year, don't I, mister Keep Left?'

'Yes she does, yes she does,' Kee said.

Which is just as well, Catherine's annual visit, because that's where it started, with her. First came the warnings, and then came the beginnings of Jack's drift into becoming a fresh new Jack Verandah, a dissolution which is incidental to the vast current on which Jack was to drift, of sorrow, cheating, loneliness, ambition, madness and fastness. If those laneways were a single river, it would doubtless boil off a mighty stench and Jack might, yeah, at some early point, Jack could've smelled it for bonbon Patsy. That massive gangrenous current is the stuff Bakks concocted; Jack moulting dead skin was a sideshow. We boxes do understand bloodsoup, we throw around a bit of memory. But the worst equator of all, tho, is Bakks. His game was the worst of all, equating counterfeit with the sweet cherished stuff. He attacks whatever he can attack. To O king Bakks the choice of attack or defence has always been a simple one to make: attack is a position of comfort, defence is a position of discomfort.

Jack on Patsy's Errand Finds Give, Not Take

Here's how it started, how the current started, the current of sorrow, cheating, loneliness, madness and ambition. Catherine and Jack went for a walk. Jack made idle talk about the day with Kee on the lagoons, and of the giant manta he'd met. Catherine paused after Jack finished the brief account, and she said nothing for a very long time as they strolled along the harbour of Miami look-alikes.

The London painter waited and waited, but she held the silence, and Jack assumed she must've been considering, weighing up, what she might divulge to a stranger. Finally she started by saying Kee's deep love of the ocean affected her also, but in a manner that travelled to the core of her sense of self. From the brief mention of the seadog, she skipped directly to her grandmother, but Catherine introduced her in a way Jack'd never heard anyone talk about a grandparent. She said that Kee had given her, Catherine, her grandmother. Given. 'Kee gave me my grandmother, that's one of my vital understandings, utterly central, he delivered her to me.'

Jack Black thought it odd, his position, to already have a parcel about the fabled grandmother, the account of a girl in flight from her father.

Walking beside Jack was the granddaughter, and so he felt as tho he held information that had come the wrong way around, a bend that was his first, and a harmlessly minor, experience of the whirlpools and eddies of information, the eddies of hup two three, that worked within that larger current of hasty-paste. More stuff like that would loom for Jack, O thank a pesky box, for he'd only just started, more cut-offs, twists, aggravated alternatives, cover-ups. Splashbacks in a rapid would bump him about; submerged branches would stab at his legs; rocks would crack a shin; shallows would evaporate as if they were never there in the first place, as if never said, and these denials would be replaced by lies as bold as a sunset on the Indian Ocean at the entrance to Shark Bay.

A lie as bold as that would be tangible, real as a maharaja's wooden chest full of butterflies, thrown open by a hooligan fuckfest daughter, full of the momentum of freedom. It was not here in the Bahamas, but over there on the rim of the Indian Ocean, that Jack Black would experience the boldest evaporation of a cherished memory, to replace it with another, a replacement of stuff that would make a lie look like an avowal of trust. It was this boldest of cover-ups that Patsy Murray was on about: why the hell did some dipshit little art dealer from nowhere have the ability to fuck with a mega art dealer in Bond Street? It gave Patsy the complete shits. 'Find out,' she'd said back at the cafe on the high street, 'and I'll get you into the Saatchi collection.' Jack resented the bribe, and he'd said, 'Fuck your bribe, fuck the Saatchi collection, I shall find out anyway, for you, because, dear Patricia, I like you.' Then Patsy had said, calmly as a Swiss knife opening an orange: 'Catherine Fekdin, bless her horrid little personality, will be in the Bahamas next month, go there, find out.'

A day later when Jack and Catherine strolled in the sun an hour out of Georgetown, Catherine returned to talking of her grandmother. But before that she gave Jack a couple of thoughts that set his powderbox starlings on the alert footing.

'Kee tells me you're a very nice guy.'

'He said that?'

'He did.'

'Did he tell you we met just last week?'

'He has this massive life force, which includes an instinct that all his life he has carefully dedicated to tuning, unlike the rest of us who are too ambitious or busy to learn to even spell the word let alone finetune its abilities.'

Jack's powderbox sank at the puerility of her phrase 'massive life force,' but he wanted to maintain the conversation, and all he could come up with was a lame, 'Well, it does seem like he's an astute old seafarer.'

'He said you have a highly developed sense of understanding a person's misfortune.'

This to Jack sounded like fakery, taking a trait and giving it mystical hyperbole, like saturated colour cranking up its perfectly all right original colour, so all he could come up with was a lame, 'Well, I suppose I can be overly observant, habit probably, the painting.'

'No, Kee says you possess a gift you barely know anything about. He knows nobody who has it like you; furthermore he does not say these things to make talk, he says it once, means it, and that's it, I'll never hear it again.'

Jack Black on the Way to Jack Verandah

So here lay bonbon Patsy's misunderstanding of Jack Black's fundamental tendency, understood instantly by Kee. And then, because of Kee, bought sight unseen by Catherine Fekdin. Which is what Catherine did for a living: buy and sell a man or woman's able tendencies. She understood that this inclination was no shallow thing with her. It lay rooted deep into her marrow long before it had even thought to become marrow. More, that she had spent years converting the inclination into a viable obsession, more, that it was never done wilfully to debase, it was, rather, accomplished in the spirit of a nose being a nose being a nose. Catherine was comfortable with the reality of it. That comfort turned her into a dealer of immense skill and power. What gave Patsy in London the shits about Catherine was that such a puny little dealer had got the better of her, and getting intoxicated quite often with the hangman was about all Patsy did these days.

Catherine was comfortable with apprehending her work as buying and selling chunks of a person, but she rarely made a purchase sight unseen. Which is exactly what she was doing now, as they strolled along the beach, she was commencing to outlay a trust of the stranger walking at her side, an outlay without any evidence; she was buying, she thought, sight unseen. And she knew what her successful father would've thought of buying—anything—sight unseen.

The moments strolling along the beach might have remained of no consequence, and Bakks and Inch and the crew of smell-bomb deadbeats, including Lightyear, might have fucked it all up. Instead the moments on the beach formed one of the doorways Jack Black crashed into up the verandah on his way to the world of hell and heaven. When Catherine was buying sight unseen, when she lay down her trust, her memory came to life. Buying sight unseen tended to apply pressure, movement, to the powderbox behind her eyes. Same as Lee's sister Meryl's little box Yottick beginning to shimmy on the table back at the jacarandas. Being O Bobbo the box I was not keen to mess with Catherine's powderbox. I don't have anything against the powderboxes inside foreheads, they give a good enough service, but I prefer my own way of throwing things around, as an unwashed pirate I prefer my own way, bobbing the high seas and the mountaintops freely, instead of cooped up in a forehead. Powderboxes I prefer to keep as customers. Arm's length, how's the kid, all that, but a customer from start to finish, the days shine cleaner that way.

Unlike Jack's powderbox of starlings, Catherine's powderbox used silver flesh to carry pieces of the past. Her grandmother gave Catherine, as a child, stories of the annual migration of tuna under the surface of the Mediterranean current that ferried thousands of the fish each year past the Balearic Islands and onwards to Sicily. Of coastal songs and dreams of the intense activity the fish brought to the villages, of stories that had come to the grandmother through many generations. So that the grandmother, as a girl who was cruelly hunted away from the comfort of these songs into the relative sterility of the big city at Barcelona, lent, through their loss, an extra vividness to the memory. This vividness she pressed into the imagination of the young granddaughter, creating a powderbox of fat, silver fish that every year were herded and killed to feed the villagers and their children.

Now as Catherine strolled along the beach and released her trust, the powderbox in her forehead began to swim with the silver flesh.

'I came to know my grandmother well,' she said easily.

Jack was about to stop for a swim, but at this he continued walking at her side.

'Fate threw her from deep poverty into great wealth. A shoeless girl who wore the same dress for a week, to a matriarch in Barcelona with two children who between them had amassed the fortune of a hundred sheikhs. But she had no true interest in the wealth. The life of silk she led as a mother in Barcelona seemed like a dream when she thought of her childhood in a dusty village on the south coast, but no, the silk never seemed to catch her gaze. The recurring thing that interested Renata was how to make a real day out of kindness.

'She inherited that trait, a vast, easy kindness, and being kind never bothered her the way it bothered her more clever friends; the urbane Barcelona friends felt that overt kindness was some kind of pretence. Renata inherited it just like all else comes along to be inherited, useful and useless, horrible and beautiful. Sometimes traits miss a generation and resurface in the next one, or the next one, you never can tell what's going to surface where. But Renata inherited a big easy kindness, and in her own case she got it from her mother, certainly not her cruel and violent father. But Renata's inherited streak was given a boost. Kindness might have been a feature inside her at birth, but Kee did some work there too, I'd say. Even though my ancestry spirals down the trade routes back into Spain, slowly disappearing into the hill tracks behind Valencia, I do know that Renata inherited that big easy kindness from her mother, not her father. How about you, Jack? What sort of kindness did you inherit, do you suppose?'

Now there's a question, a ding-dong winged one for painter Jack Black. Here was exactly another pinpoint question that would slide a painter arrogarnta into a Jack Verandah. If, only if, I could keep deadbeat Bakks out of the way, and grotty greedy Inch, hailme-hailme with all his pongster smellbombs including the vain fuckface Lightyear.

Jack replied, 'Sad to say, to be perfectly honest since you're being perfectly honest, I inherited not much kindness if any at all. My brother did though, he's mentally handicapped, and he's one of the kindest and sweetest people that I know.'

'Is he being taken care of?'

'Mum and dad look after Brian really well, and I go home a lot, and lately I send them good money every month, thanks to Patricia handling my paintings. But your grandmother, seems she had an interesting life.'

Catherine kept on strolling down the beach. 'My grandma was an outstanding talent at coaxing out fine behaviour. Superb to watch, even when you considered the dozens of friends and relatives and hangers-on, each one never wished to be seen to be out of line, she fared extremely well in keeping people considerate of one another. If she caught wind of someone generating someone else's misfortune, she'd throw a fit. If she caught someone being in any way cruel, verbally or otherwise, Renata would refuse to ever allow their entry into the house again. Among the wider circle she became known as the social cop, a loved cop, a trustee, unanimous. It was only after she died that you could discern clearly the effect she'd had during life, because all sorts of people began to cut loose after Renata died, with nobody to rein them in, the air became filled with all the bullying you could point a stick at.

'Her stories of poverty came as a shock to me as a pretentious eighteen year old from a well-off family. The poverty was so extreme. The village from which she fled had nothing. Her two children, my mother included, flipped all that poverty over using their Barcelona upbringing, plus they were fully encouraged by Grandma anyway, and they became very wealthy, so I was born into wealth. My mother and father are natural traders, they're both the most quick, articulate entrepreneurs, all they needed was to develop what they were born with, revenge. Their children, Remple and I, now own city property, towers. Remple sees the inheritance as steel and concrete, but I don't. Remple was never given Renata's stories the way I was, so I can't help but see in them the dust of that small village where my grandmother bolted from her father as he ran up the lane chasing her with a machete, screaming at her. We inherited that dust, Remple and I, that swirl of dust has become the towers, yes, to me they're made, not of concrete, but of the dirt under Grandma's bare soles as she ran for her life and met Kee.

'Remple now runs the business, but I'm more interested in my two art galleries in Australia than in managing city towers. I'm grateful for the towers, but they're just not my game. Let's get back to the bar, it's almost dark, and in the dark I'm a thirsty girl, most particularly in the glowing dark, we can enjoy another walk tomorrow should you like to hear more.

'I'd like to get back to the bar, more than likely Castle arrived this afternoon from Perth. Castle has a story you'd like better than mine, ask him about it, his family inherited other things than wealth, they inherited something from what Castle calls the Diamond City of Children. No doubt he'd tell you everything if he's heard all about you from Kee, about your talent for understanding.'

That night at the bar Jack arrogarnta met Castle and the others. Castle was the painter who'd conceived Remple's Broome domes in pencil drawings. They all had a fine time, and Castle kept his eye on the London painter's behaviour. Late the next morning they went out on Kee's boat. Much of the day Castle continued his eye on Jack's behaviour to confirm if what Kee said about the London ding-dong was true, and by the end of the day it seemed to Castle's mind Kee was right. It took only three days for Castle to take Jack into his confidence.

The next day Castle and Jack took off in a hire boat.

'Why do they call you Castle?' Jack asked.

'Because of what I live in, back in Australia,' Castle said, 'I live in a tiny World War One shack in the forest near the coast, it's a total dump near the beaches of the wine district, and we all love it.'

The inheritances dear butterfly, also travel the family tree in other ways. Yes, Kee did speak to Castle about Jack's innate little powers of understanding, O ding-dong to little pee-wee powers, Kee, after all, had long ago been coached into sensing the fuller understandings taken from the illuminations in the back room with Ellie-Isabela, but never mind.

It was day one, and they would spend three days on the gulf, returning each night to meet the others at the bar.

Day one, but Jack was stunned by what he heard. Castle began by tossing a diamond of a thought into the air, he began gently enough. 'Well, you might know, Jack, you may understand, to draw a portrait of a mother's courage is one thing, but to peer into the detail is another. But I'll put it in a nutshell. Catherine suggested I tell you about the Diamond City of Children.'

The two painters got along well enough. Opposites outwardly, Castle a well-spoken, factual spirit, Jack an excitable ding-dong, irritable, combative, nailed by the earlobe to the wheel of his 'fukkin London' art circle. Castle's laid-back manner flipped all that frenzy overboard, so they got along. Jack at first took the laid-back comfort to be some kind of Australian pleasure-pot unavailable in London, a cliché he became instantly irritated that he'd fallen on, but as the afternoons passed he found that Castle's unwavering gaze lay the cliché out to shrivel in the sun. They spent bright days snorkelling, weaving in and out of Castle's account of a mother's courage. In a well-spoken way, without the giddying flaring up and down of Jack's way, Castle was easy to listen to. After a snorkel, Jack would cut up lunch and Castle would be sitting by the outboard motor to continue telling of the Diamond City of Children in his quiet way, in a straight, factual way. From the account of the Diamond City, Jack was to learn that Castle's powderbox began its creaking not with a scatter of starlings, or with a flow of silver fishskin, but with a couple of shakes of diamonds. In any case, that's how a powderbox works, in bits and pieces, haranguage, twanguage, ganguage, banguage, songuage, winguage. But in Castle's case, the bits and pieces flowed rather than popped coz he got on well with Jack, and coz the ol seadog Kee placed a trust on the whole week.

'I apologise,' Castle said, 'for my uninvited entry into your personal life, Jack, but is it true your brother is mentally handicapped?'

'Yes he is, but no apology needed. I'm the one who ought to make an apology, I've heard all about your grandmother when she was a girl running away from her insane father, your great-grandfather I guess. So the apology is mine, for making the uninvited incursion the apology is mine.'

'My mother Marcela gave me first and foremost the best education a painter could get, and that is, language,' Castle said.

'She said, "Become good at one, not two or three like your father." She believed in a kind of golden rule. She'd often say to me as a boy, "When you have intimacy, you'll have clarity, and then you'll be able to express what you mean, and expressing what one means is certainly a very minor thing in the scheme of things, but you will find that it can be one of life's pleasures. Language can lie or confuse, yes, but precision will bring you endless pleasure."

'She felt that my father's dwindling Spanish, passable English, and broken French from their time in Tripoli, together formed a lesser gift than had he stayed just with Spanish and made it work more deeply for him.

'Grandma Renata gave my mother the name Marcela because it means "of the sea," Grandma's childhood journey up the coast with Kee, it was Grandma's way of honouring my mother's birth, for the sea route Grandma took was a route to safety and in the buoyancy of that safety her child Marcela was of the sea. Anyway, I'm here to tell you about my mother's courage.'

And so Castle continued to let the contents of his powder-box drift out into the warm air on the dinghy.

IV

At the gates where wings and diamonds meet, the children may become lost

The Diamond City of Children

'There was a presence in the dark room my mother felt she could actually see just beyond the doorway, glowing, faintly luminous with injuries sustained from years before. She sat exhausted from moving homes. She searched the room, her eyes probing two dark corners and the sliding door at the balcony, and then came back to the denser shadow glowing just beyond the doorway. The night was still and quiet, and for long moments she retraced the day's movements to examine how he might have entered the flat without her knowledge. You see, the sight of a denser shadow taking on the human form made sense: if it had been an ex-husband or an ex-lover there would simply ensue a long argument. But it was neither of those. It was a partial, deteriorated human, and to see it as a dense opaque shape so late at night when the night was utterly without ambient noise was the last thing her nerves could take after the past three weeks of frantic moving.

'It took many years to come to this moment. Her son, my brother Oliver, was twenty-seven. Twenty-seven years to hear words no mother would dream of hearing. She did not have time to imagine how it came to this. At a moment of tragedy any mother would have the time to wonder how it had come to such a dark evaporation of that most inviolable of all natural orders. There would be excuses, regrets, guilt, self-doubt. But this moment in the small living room was not only tragedy, it was also horror. So there was not a second available in her mind to compress the twenty-seven years in any way at all.

'The reality of that moment flooded the room, charging in from the walls like a perplexing wash of human darkness, like a blanket approaching from every miniscule direction to suffocate both thought and breathing. In all the years, from childhood to adulthood and then motherhood, she had never experienced a graver reality. She made an attempt to believe the words had not come out, but the reality was too strong, so potent that it made her stomach turn and she had to hold back being sick. Oliver had simply sat on the sofa and delivered the words three weeks ago. She saw a fierce cruelty blaze in his eyes, along with a deep inner brokenness, a loathing along with a cool factual it-has-to-be. Any other mother might have had the chance to speak, to respond, to reason, but in the small room there was a reality. The words had been spoken and there would be no going back. He sat on the sofa quietly and calmly. A hand on each knee was the means he adopted over the recent years to show certainty and assume authority. The voice was not raised. The words came out clearly. They came at a break in the idle conversation:

'"I will just have to kill her."

'He addressed them to the neighbour who stood inside the front door. The neighbour showed an expression of disbelief, but not my mother. Over the years things had become so bad, the violence had become so common, that my mother knew what she heard. She could feel the hysteria beginning to shake her flesh, but she did not let this show. It crept upwards and outwards as she felt herself failing under the panic, but she did not let it show. This was to be her central strength in all the emergencies, and also had been developing well down the years as things got progressively worse. Over the years his acts of violence had stepped closer and closer, veering away from the outside world and swinging closer to home, but even the most dangerous evidence had not given her the foresight to imagine the possibility of a moment like this. She shook from deep inside body and soul with panic from the reality of that moment, but there was a delayed reality of more than a week to come before she realised that she would never be able to be in the same room with her son again. Oliver didn't remove his hands from his knees because I still today reckon he found the posture held fast some sort of taste of authority. He knew that the neighbour and his mother were in no doubt as to what he had said. One day soon, he said, when the time suited him.'

The Tree of Pain

Jack passed across a cheese and tomato sandwich. They ate in silence. After eating, they drank a beer.

Jack said: 'My brother's ill too, but he's easy to care for. How did you and your mother cope?'

'We discovered new kinds of pain. And the years previous, the years leading up to that moment, had already been dangerous. But the difference was my mother never came close to believing he would turn his violence round to her. He always hit out at others whenever the fever pitch met with the right person, but he had not hit out at her.'

These two powderboxes dear butterfly, Castle and Jack, were on the way to becoming acquainted.

Even Bakks with all his show-off love of grim horror would not barge into this early friendship. For starters Bakks would have to deal in Oliver's powderbox. And as we shall see, Oliver's powderbox caused even Bakks to recoil.

Castle continued. 'She would bring food, clothes, a pair of shoes. He would be in a bad state, making promises of killing that person or this person. She would leave his flat after the visit in tears. Each visit had torn another layer from her spirit, but she continued to care for him in both practical ways and to bring along her love. Those days lasted a decade, Oliver was in his twenties, ten years of deterioration, damage, phone calls from a thousand miles away, abandoned cheap flats, a decade of slow, deepening sorrow. But the moment in her own flat on the sofa brought sudden changes. Added to the daily sorrow and guilt was grief, grief, grief. He had not died, so she did not have the choice to grieve and then commence to somehow live again. She was left with only grieving, for he was around, somewhere, walking, sitting under a bridge. Then she had to move house and get a silent number. In this my mum felt she was deserting him, and the process of moving lent her the perpetual sense, day and night, that she had failed him in every way. Grief, guilt, sorrow, moving house to safety, these mixtures brought heavy exhaustion. There were many times when she might have given up, to collapse in a mess, to accept or allow a nervous breakdown. But to care for him, to give life to her instinct to care for him, had kept her from any crumbling edge. From day to day the existence in her of hope, and the feelings of sorrow for him, revived the will to continue. One week would be very bad, the next week would be not so bad. This continuance of love was at a time before the death threat, and so she could cope. After the death threat she could no longer cope in the way she had done, and the awkward sense of the loss of a son without him having died opened a deep hole in her spirit. People would lend advice. Sleep well. Calm down. Take a holiday. These provoked frustration in her, and the hole grew vaster, made her more brittle. A great loss of belief in one's ability to sustain overcame her in the weeks after the death threat. She was able to sustain him through her warmth and love, able to see to it that he was all right. But that all fell away. In the months after the threat she became filled with fear. Of her son.

The Tree of Comparisons

On day two Jack and Castle came out with fishing gear to catch lunch.

'In the month that followed she considered the notion that the words were not real. She told herself that when an acute paranoid schizophrenic makes a promise to kill, it might seem to us like a moment of heightened insanity so that later passages of calm make the promise seem absurd. But late at night, when she could not sleep, in the vertical silence of darkness, the words on the sofa appeared as real as they had been that afternoon in the previous flat. The fear was now complete. It gave rise to scenarios, nightmares and uneasy daytime walks to the shops.

'As the troubles worsened, friends fell away, and after the death threat there were no friends left. They suffered their own personal lows with regard to their own children. They knew as friends how to discuss truancy, alcohol, marijuana, unsafe sex, rudeness, ADHD, low school marks, boredom, all the goods that may face a mother and child. But this kind of thing had them perplexed. They fell away one by one without fanfare except for the increasing tidiness of life as the deteriorating relationships left fewer drained cups and greasy plates. She needed to lean on their shoulders, but the more she confided the more they never came back, so that she was to discover and understand anew the lines of friendship are laid at more than one distance. She didn't look for their charity, she wanted expression. The divorce occurred a long time ago, so the opportunities for expression carried significance. Expression would melt the iron tensions. It would help reshape a day like a dagger, into a day like, well, like a day.

'The divorce was okay, and she never saw my father again. He died five years after he'd gone back to live in Barcelona where he was born and grew up, where he met my mother.

'Instead she increasingly became confined to fear. Where the sorrow and pain were steady and continual, the fear arrived in hostile bursts. Alone in the flat, she would find the hands shaking, make a cup of tea, spilling things, to calm the nerves. Knocks on doors down the corridor sent shock waves through her muscle. She never answered the phone without hesitation. The door was double locked. Some days were easier, exhaustion brought along a comforting futility, and this became a form of rest and peace.

'In the afternoons of restful futility she found the time to think back. The whole thing had caught her by surprise. She correctly saw herself as a straightforward person from the middle class. How could this person get a death threat? Let alone from her son? Mother and son, the whole thing had successfully perverted her belief in a kind of specialness. A sanctity that the world revolved on, that families partly relied on, that form was made out of, and while the world celebrated the relationship, or vocally denounced any cruelty towards the relationship, there she was: left with a son who now was a danger to her life.

On television at night stories about a refugee mother separated from her son brought such a small reaction in her that she'd get up to check the double lock.

'It was only with her good friend Olufituaeb that she could relax. A white South African, Olufituaeb Dneirf (she, the friend, pronounced it Oh-loof Der-neef) brought with her a fine sense of all that was sensitive to life's more grim offerings. She was around the same age, and had her own children, so the friendship took on an easy sway of intimacy from the start.'

The Field of Garbage

'A visit to Oliver's flat three years earlier proved to be a pretty big turning point. Mum brought with her a package of useful things she felt he would need. It consisted of fifty dollars, a pair of warm pants, socks, shoes, a shirt, and a box of food. It was a well thought out package; trim the extravagance—for things were lost and money was blown on cask wine—and bolster the essentials. When she walked in the door of the one-bedroom brick place the first thing that struck her was that the mess was now by far the worst she'd seen him exist in. The place smelled of closed windows, staleness, rank with fetid textile. The kitchen and stove were invisible under the layer of old cooking, empty tins, packets, strewn noodles, dried layers of spilt stews, margarine, stale bread pieces. She could not approach the bathroom, and walked back into the living area and placed the box on the sofa. It too was a mess. The whole place lay in ruins.

'When she offered to help clean up he began to reel away

a string of language she could not understand. It grew louder until he burst into abuse. She thought he must have had another hostile encounter with someone at a pub or a park or under a bridge. But he began to look directly at her and abuse her. He became sternly focussed. The verbal assault grew until it became the worst she had seen. She cut the visit short and drove home to her flat shaking. All the visits, to bring him supplies and love and company, had reverberated with intensity, or ground-down grief, but these were easy to handle after ten years at it. On this visit he broke through a barrier. His eyes were dark, but on fire, and they looked as if they contained emptiness. This was the day she crashed into a kind of uselessness. A piece of care and a moment of showing love simply did not get through, they had detonated in the stare of his eyes that burned with cruelty. Now she faced the crippling notion that she would have to reduce her visits, and this to her hinted of abandonment.'

Jack had caught a handful of herring which they fried on the stove.

'How,' Jack said, 'did you get by with all the trauma, I just don't understand how you and your mother got by with such a fucking huge amount of trauma.'

'Well, after that visit things got worse faster, and by the time he came three years later to sit on the sofa to expel his death threat she had already wept many times uncontrollably at the reality creeping in, the reality of abandoning him. He smashed things, stole things, shouted so hard his mouth foamed and the spit flew. He used his finger like a dagger, and waved a palm around like a spade. During some visits he was calm, but something would catch in his mind and he would burst into a fresh new hostile rave. The more she visited the more she could not escape the encroaching idea that she must one day take the decision to keep away from him. But now, on the sofa, he had blunted her sense of abandonment. Still, when the neighbour had managed to coerce him outside and send him away, which he agreed to only because he'd had enough of the visit and would be back another day, she still felt the stabbing pain. Abandon my son. Leave him forever. Her great friend Olufituaeb Dneirf, or Oh-loof Der-neef, helped her lessen the feeling of abandonment, to make the case that a decision to keep away from him was not wrong or cruel, and that any mother would and must react in the same way.

'She moved flats. Fear, and Olufituaeb's friendship, rounded up a fortnight of resolve. After the move she was depressed but temporarily pleased that the fear and shaking had subsided. She took to settling in, making requests from the owner for a new oven, cleaning corners and walls, scrubbing the bathroom. But once this was done the old feelings settled in. She told herself she had abandoned him. The nights of guilt dragged her days down into depressing images. She saw him picked up by the police. Saw him trashing yet more temporary flats and sheltering under bridges. She saw big arcs of memory: from a bright kid at boarding school to a man living on the streets. From the newborn child she first held that day at the hospital to the man she last saw with his hands held out flat on the knees on the sofa. For more than a decade she had remained steadfast at his side. She did everything she could to help, and she believed for a time that love, care and tenderness would most definitely have a redeeming effect.'

The Tree of Growth

Day three they tried a bay further south where Kee said it was cleaner and shallower, with a small island offshore where it was a good anchor.

'She had always transferred money into Oliver's bank account to supplement his small pension, which just covered his rent and food, he was always out of cash, and that's no good, it's where trouble starts. Mum did everything she could. If she could not assist him directly then she decided she could go through the bank and the nurses. This went well for a while, and shirts, pants, shoes and food got through. One nurse was very good to her and he'd kept her informed of his health. When the nurse quit, another was equally as thoughtful. But soon these informal arrangements were closed off. In time a whole new crew ran things, and when she made one of her phone calls she was curtly told to go away. When she protested, the nurse retorted: "How would you like it if your son was told your whereabouts?" She was then also told that she would not be allowed to make any further contact, that the staff had placed a restraining order on her.

'On his sixth birthday she followed alongside the small bicycle down the pathway. The party was small and enjoyable. They had lit candles on the cake and the neighbours' children played in the afternoon sun. As he pedalled down the pathway to the road the speed picked up but she had caught him in time. She looked into his face to kiss him and saw that his eyes were alight. He was frightened: that's what the exaggerated shock in his eyes might have been in another mother and son moment—a child afraid he was about to crash into the traffic. But in this relationship it may have been the first moment, among the first signs, of a future of hostility and assault. On the sixteenth birthday the signs were less invisible, pronounced instances of burning intensity were apparent. On the twenty-second birthday the signs were there.

'Further into his twenties, the violent hell wore Mum and I down. We helped when we could, when it was safe to help, but the care was to no real effect. As a mother, the whole business inverted and perverted her entire world. To feel a daily pall of slow anxiety she didn't need to absorb the news, to imagine running into a guy on speed, or a stalker, or dwell on a terrorist, she had a son who brought it all home. When she moved the first time two Jehovah's Witnesses went to the electoral roll and brought him round for a visit. Now that he'd found her again, he came back without his friends and sat on the sofa. When she relocated again, she felt safe but perverse. To put it clearly and without colour or favour, to put it in the plainest language: a faulty gene had inverted what is widely held as a good thing—a mother and son relationship—into a bad thing. She easily remembered two or three decades into the past, a time full of happiness, and she kept photographs of him around the flat, glassed and framed portraits of him sitting happily on the sofa smiling broadly back at the camera, a young man glowing with promise.

'In the relative safety of the new apartment she was able to unclench her mind and heart enough to accept a trickle of remembrances. A destruction of reason had fallen on her life, this she had known for a long time. But the inversion it would take came as a shock. To her vista, the U-turn looked something like this. First she had loved. Then had given birth. Then had cared and fussed and tended, kept him from harm, gave him everything needed to prepare him for a place in the world. And then all that love turned round and came back as a death threat.'

The Tree of Perversion

'Even the release of grieving had become perverted. Fate had not taken him to a drug overdose, a car accident, drowning, so that he might become an aching memory. He was still walking. From a funeral where we pay our respects one might commence to live, perhaps never heal, but to emerge from intense grief into plain grief. Without a funeral to honour him there was little hope of his transformation completely into a memory. He was still around but had departed, a living loss. The grieving remained perpetual and twisted. She had lived through the days and nights grieving, not with a memory in her spirit, but with a relentless stream of hostility, fear, worry, violence—and now a plain-as-day death threat.

'As she settled into the new flat, as her tension unclenched, she remembered his long days of sweet time helping with the rose beds. Unearthing, tilling, stopping for lunch, back to the garden, for two seasons until they together created a verdant quarter acre garden full of life and spring.'

'My brother,' Jack said, 'likes working the garden too, he's often out there with my dad.'

'Well, they also planted bougainvillea, gum trees and bamboo. During those warm afternoons of diamond light he was thoughtful, kind, considerate, hard working: he had been loyal from the start to her vision for the place. The visuals made her begin to weep. They were clear visuals, from fifteen years in the past, too clear. Grief can certainly sharpen the memory. But perverse grief is another thing altogether, it can render a memory too real.

'And these huge endless swings of perverted turns didn't stop at grief, there were other things she was forced into feeling in a new, strange way. Her courage had taken on a perverse quality.

Mum always had an abundant store of courage and could stand up to anyone who threatened her or attempted simply to bullshit her. For her to stand up to a world afloat on a tide of troubles and open hostility was a matter of things like principle, right, wrong, good and evil. Anyone with even a numb sense of right and wrong found the ability to stand up. But to stand up to the years of fire-eyed violence from her own son required a weird kind of courage. It was different to outright courage, or right and wrong bombast. To stand up to her son mixed motherhood into it. She found that her courage mixed in the desires to be protective of herself and sympathetic of him. She also had to be intuitive, shrewd, emotional, rational, cautious, firm, supple, verbal, upright, guiding, authoritative, cool, warm, understanding, fearless, loud.

And while these desires mixing with courage came and went in those hundreds of hostile sessions so too did the images of him as a guileless small child, or as an infant. It was not an easy courage to use, it had too many conflicting colours. She grew steadily to use it well but never grew to like it as a form of courage. It did not have the stamp of actual plain courage, it had the feel of betrayals and abandonments. Plain, strong courage is often easy to use and show because it makes you feel good and makes you look good, and you can show off to your friends. But this kind of courage was harder to use, you really had to find deep, new wells in your spirit to embrace a courage with so many conflicting colours.

'Everything she felt for him as a mother stayed fast and true, and yet became perverted, by necessity, by the conflicting colours and the colliding impulses. Her senses of loyalty, kindness, responsibility, care, friendship, these were now altered into less obvious states where the light lay in sight but out of reach, a distant glow of a time now far in the past. She was able to see a big arc. She had watched him grow into his place in the world and then had watched him congeal into hatred. It was not like observing a son's sloth or failure. It was not sad due to a son turning out a lesser man than one might have wanted to expect, or increasingly lived by bad habits, or treated his wife unkindly. I came round eventually to feeling that the arc had been more like observing the gradual making of a terrorist. God had always directed him. God told him to kill her. Told him to commit all kinds of wild violent acts because those persons were either evil or had behaved so badly as to warrant no mercy. He did not devolve this from the media. He began it long before September 11. They were the kinds of words and phrases Oliver had used over and over.

In the later years the voice gave him a very large-scale authority. It seemed to give him clarity of purpose. He would sit on the couch unmoving, calm, hands out on the knees and speak in short slow thoughts of eternal truths. He might say, "They are bad people, they must be shown a lesson." Or, "Go about your business." On medication he was warm and could deploy a second of charm and ask after others. When he was not on medication the statements would emerge on a visible tide of threat.

So the long arc had not been like seeing her son fall into despair. It had been to watch him become insane. All her adult life she had trusted in the power of the will. When the will was set to work with compassion and wisdom, she believed it would fix anything it confronted. So she fought the invisible claws all the way, using love, compassion, wisdom, ingenuity, subtlety, courage, determination, but the invisible diamond claws of insanity gouged away at his eyes and scraped away the layers off his mind without so much as a passing acknowledgement at her efforts that were brought up from deep, new wells. The decade and a half had been a long battle, it was now over, she had lost, sitting in the near dark in the new flat, and, after the restraining order, she would never be able to see him again.'

The Tree of Gifts

'She sat among the cardboard boxes in the faint light of the living room. She caught sight of his seventh birthday, a memory that arose with clarity. Here was the child that haunted her days, this early photocopy. The large rambling garden looked like a busy village, purely of children, light as leaves, playing, exchanging things, chasing, shouting. Like his friends he was lean and slight. It was the memory of his open face that caused her to start shaking. His face glowed brightly with wonder, big eyes swimming in the sunlight, bouncing with promise towards a full life, no hint of the diamond claws, nothing. Just sun-dappled happiness on the rich tropical lawn, just the goods to make the grass sparkle and shine. He had the goods to magically make life come alive. The ordinary stuff of a day got transformed into wondrous stuff, exciting stuff, new, everything new every moment. He was a magician simply because he happened to be a healthy child, and the three ancient traits that give a normal child the magician's powers were with him, visibly. Eyes that shone with clear light, laughter that rode the wave of clear light, a mind that danced with clear light. Even the faintest touch of the diamond claw was not possible. The only touch of madness lay in the garden itself, in the vainglorious unreal depth of the tropical greens, reds, purples, oranges and yellows.

'She recalled the day with such clarity that she shook at its presence and then wept at the memory, the lifelong loss. It was this window that made her then begin to wonder about early warnings, for there was a bleak common sense to the query. Which of the children present that day in the garden, surrounded by rows of orchids and groves of bougainvillea they put to use as shops and houses, would be marked for the invisible diamond claws of insanity? Out of more than thirty boys and girls, just one? Perhaps two? And if a magician could tell you the child would grow up violent, possibly try to kill you, what then? If the gene was located, mapped, stamped, explored, and the magician could give you a blunt assessment? The mothers, looking on happily and proudly, watching over their children, could not know. If they knew, if science told them their small child would one day threaten to kill them, how would they go on to live without looking sideways at that child?

'Every party of children everywhere will continue to contribute a new person or two to the Diamond City of Children, for this is a city that ignores borders—of any kind. It is, in the literal, circumnavigating sense, a global city. The journey to the city at first is gradual, the kid is different, unusual, maybe a genius, but then sudden: in early adulthood the first signs of the journey appear but rate no concern. Then you're in. Then you're on fire. The city is burning with hallucinations, collapsing from shouting voices in the mind, the city is held by nurses, guards, is riddled with abuse, drugs and eyeholes as empty as a diamond, as cut-away as a diamond, as useless, as priceless. They are the same eyes that belonged once to a child, but will never again glow with the ancient magician's ability to make a day come alive.

'It was late into the evening and my mother was exhausted from the three weeks of frantic moving. As she sat in the collecting darkness, no city that stretched across the planet came to mind. Instead, the solitary denseness just beyond the doorway coagulated more neatly to one person.

'Waiting, watching, and maybe enjoying. All she could do was to sit there shaking from deep inside, shaking with the possibility that the solitary denseness was Oliver. There are varying degrees of paranoid schizophrenia. A brain of diamond claws loses the intuitive powers of suppleness. It gains a sharp transparency. As far as I can tell, all cases are prone to mood swings, paranoia, inner voices, lapses of logic, and prone also to the diamond passages of direct clarity that a mystic would envy and the occasional poet will emulate. A mild case is easy to care for. But a severe case is given to cruelty and extreme violence. And where the diamond claws have spared nothing, a severe case ends up no longer wishing to wash or to change clothes. Decomposition of whatever interior we possess is at least matched by an intense rotting of the exterior.

'The first time he reached that stage he was twenty-four. He was to be released from the mental hospital into the community, so I made a search for a small flat. I inspected flats for a week and then rented a clean, well-lighted place, one bedroom, a bathroom, a kitchen, a living room, in a small block of ten. I put up the bond and two months rent.

'With a few goods, a bed, useful items from our mother, he was okay, no real trouble, and he moved in with hopes of getting pieces of work or even a half-decent job. The weather was sunny, the neighbours were friendly, the diamond claws were dead and buried. For a few weeks he came and went. He grew to know the suburb, the shops, the pub. He looked for work and found the odd person who got him sweetening their garden. Then he stayed in more and more. On a visit two months later, I saw every sign that the diamond claws had located the flat and converted it into an altered world. The claws must have sunk so deeply into his shoulders in the nights and thrown him around the rooms with such force that his bones cracked the plaster. They must have taken his fists and smashed them onto the kitchen bench. They left food in the cooking pots to grow thick mould, plates were smashed, blankets were strung up to block the windows. The smell throughout the place was dense, a mixture of things, but as a whole, that of a mind and soul festering as it is gradually shredded by the diamond claws. It was from this flat that it started to become less easy to care for him.

'We would clean up and the visits became more regular, but they also became more useless. My mother, who by now visited only accompanied by a friend, always brought with her a considerate and keenly thought out lifeline: food, clothing and cash.

'My own visits by now were mainly spent in hearing how our mother needed severe disciplining. These were the first spoken words that the diamond claws over the next few years forged into the death threat. Prior to the flat I was able to go part of the way towards reasoning with him, following carefully the hyper-logic, or the low grumble of early madness, so that I might work his thinking away from aggression. For around five years I kept up the talk that attempted to steer him off a growing violent instinct; our early life together as brothers had yielded enough mutual trust for me to keep trying. Mum gave us a good time, and we had a happy-go-lucky childhood full of light and laughter and Mum's sense of love and humour that she gave us every day, so there's definitely no lounge chair childhood psychology stuff that came into the nightmare like my GP tried to imply in the early days. So I had a small influence, and was able to help him see glimmers of reason. But after the flat even the brotherly link was broken, the diamond splintering of real colours had started. The diamond emptiness had come round as a whole new descent. Soon the flat was deserted. Again he was up and away, hitching round Australia on another road trip of wreckage and theft, making good use of survival skills that dug deeper and deeper into an animal instinct. Touching this instinct was good because it came with the use of a kind of a human mind, giving him the ability to roam far and wide on nothing at all. No cash, no case, just wits and gut.'

The Bay of Plenty

'Mum's instinct where it concerned survival, a dare-mess-with-me power of protection, shot to her mouth on a hot weekend when Oliver was eight. The event lay seconds in the making, from enjoying an afternoon at the two-shed yacht club, to panic and commotion.

'It was a ramshackle place devoted to exploring Pangkor Island out on the Straits of Malacca. Faded deckchairs scattered the space between the waterline and the first shed. A cement ramp slid into the shallows of the mangrove estuary. Children played up the side of the second shed. Makeshift showers and toilets lay behind the shed, adjacent to the jungle. A handful of boats lay anchored near the shore, like a patch of small islands, and children swam beside the sunlit colour of the boats and they rowed small dinghies around the boats.

'She sat with friends out the front, at the top of the small thin beach, the day was busy, forty people to enjoy the balmy afternoon and the tranquil waters beside the small club. The moments came back into her mind now in the flat, with a clarity that was transported by the loss of security, carried by the sheen, a floating film of unsteady alertness as she sat in the darkness of the new flat. But even with the clarity of remembering the protective power in those moments, the memory of the maternal instinct lay perverted. Made foetid. By feelings for a person who now, to her, was forced into a role as a kind of living dead, feelings that mixed, into a single constricting strand, alertness, despair and a large loss on her part of any useful control. Yet forcing its way through these constricting states, the memory did return: seconds that the maternal energy flowed up Mum's arms so that her primal shouting bled out across the mangroves.

'Because it was simple: she first caught his shrill cry, then she clearly saw that he was in the throes of starting to drown. Visible was a heavy struggle, and he was located in the open shallows, just two metres deep, far from the cluster of boats and the other swimmers. But what struck her instantly was that he was too far out to reach in time. His head would go under then burst to the surface, but in an instant she could see that it was a struggle in vain, and his head and shoulders would go under again. Marcela of the sea understood one plain fact: Oliver was losing, not gaining, and it was perfectly clear he was losing very fast. He was a strong, agile swimmer, but something was wrong. His second cry came full of dread, to her it sounded like an olden howl from a young boy. He was too far to reach before he could no longer surface. She jumped from the deckchair and bolted for the water. The whole thing was seconds in the making, all was instinct, powerful protection, unthinking and fast, and shouting and panic gripped the two ramshackle sheds. She ran hard for the water. She had always run well for his moments.

Like any mother whose instinct fed a buoyancy, like any healthy mother with a healthy child, on trouble she had always swung hard to his assistance.

'Of all the kinds of buoyancy, the instinct gave Mum a vital buoyancy of deeper resonance. But now in the darkness of the new flat there was no more running hard for his protection. The maternal instinct lay alive, but had been forcibly twisted into never again being applied directly from her to him. So the diamond claws had decomposed what had given profound, rather than social, buoyancy to her senses. A buoyancy not of cheer, but one that invigorates other things—hopes, intactness, the buoyancy of a deeply personal purpose holding you intact in the face of a life. This was another constant that might be compared to losing a child to death, the constant of a ceaseless acid to the heart: there always remained the urge to exercise that maternal instinct. He was gone, and he was not gone. There was no collapse into grief, there was instead the non-stop buzzing of it. There was no collapse into breathing new air, only hour after hour of a stale stirring of grief, and the urge to bring help with that maternal potency intact, however useless the urge for her.

'She bolted over the thin beach, crashing nimble-footed through a group of children, her forehead came down slightly, a dare-fuck-with-me determination about to hit the water. Her primal shouting had, instantaneously, altered the landscape during those moments, everything changed in a flash—for a purpose, and she was the powerful catalyst for that sudden change of pace and focus. A second runner had bolted from the boatshed. Now two darts flew through the commotion. One a thirty-three year old mother who'd seen fine years as a top athlete in school, still in form, strong and lean enough to give that stretch her best. The other a family friend, similar age, over six foot tall, long muscular legs working at top speed.

From the run-up he entered the estuary with a strong head-first dive that took him out and he commenced swimming at high speed, lurching with his shoulders, cutting powerfully at the tea-coloured water. When he reached the position he swept his big arm down into the water, found the bony armpits, and then began slowly and emphatically to sidestroke ashore. Literally, she and the friend had together rescued Oliver from drowning.

'Laying him on the beach they saw the problem. Across the small shoulders, downward and across his chest, all down the legs they found severe, almost open, glowing-red lesions. Something had wrapped him up, and they decided a man-of-war had brushed him. Luckily for him, they decided, it must have been a slight brush because a heavy application, they knew, may have proven fatal. It would span a half lifetime's work, from the diamond claws, to make, from that boy, the man who would issue the death threat against the woman whose instinct had saved his life.'

The Tree of Light

'The instinct gave a sudden impact of change to the world during those moments, I saw it clear as a bell. Now though, in the present, Mum felt only the stale buzzing of grief, experiencing it through a body drained of its protective urge. And although the mind also was profoundly exhausted, it was busy, crackling with optical insinuations from sitting in the darkness, from being as remote as she could. For a small time she forgot the figure at the doorway corner to dwell on the figure of the thirty-three year old mother who leapt across the beach and into the estuary.

'Then something happened. It curled up like a feather, arriving from nowhere. In the lucid way one memory might recoup another, in the magical way that a pivotal memory can recover the smallest long-forgotten slither, she heard the exact words of what a friend had said that weekend. Val had left the country to live in London, but she was back for a difficult visit, and they sat together outside the shed on deckchairs watching the children play and swim, Val silent and uncomfortable. Val and her husband had packed up their shattered life for London because they lost their only son in a car accident as he was being brought home from school. Val's was a delicate temperament, and when she spoke, it was a gentleness of an uncommon intensity. After their son's accident her thoughts were said in an even more dissolved way, with the added characteristic of gazing into the air just beyond reach. It lent the persona a sage-like quality, and crueller people tended to dislike it while close friends made a point to stop, to listen. So when she uttered the words a few minutes before the panic erupted, the phrase was said with a heavy but light and mystical flavour, and she said it slowly. "*You.. can..have..a..child..and..so..have..beauty, then all that beauty, all.. that..beauty, it is lost.*"'

'Val's morose offering fell into her mind as she now sat in the dark flat. It may have been morose, it might have been bland, but the sound of Val saying it, and the essential truth of its meaning, the plainness of the fact, continued to repeat its peal and thrum in her mind, growing into a chant. The chant was now the one thing she had in her grasp that began to deal blows: the tension that had ground into her so severely started to release its grip. The chant then rocked her to sleep. The memory had somehow performed an inverse trick; instead of drawing the scent closer to the moment, each repeated chant in the mind increased her remoteness. In this perverse way she began to relax, she found comfort enough to fall asleep in the armchair.

'In the middle of the night she woke abruptly to her own sharp shout, instantly clamping her gaze on the corner at the doorway, and then urgently scanning the flat. She'd moved from sleep to high alert in a second. The strenuous level of alert made it seem impossible that she could have been asleep for five hours. She gave the flat a thorough going over, climbing between the stacks of cardboard boxes, until minutes later fatigue returned and she moved to the bed and drifted uneasily to sleep.'

Jack asked: 'So was Oliver actually in the flat that night?'

'His existence in the flat had been real enough, in a sense. She had generated his presence out of the fierce and fast emotions of the past week, and the last day especially, when the final nerve-sharpening bolt from danger had taken place. I now know that a mother's courage, under threats of violence and death from an insane son, can with some determination organise the bringing down of a home, but a toll is paid. It includes panic, fierce speed, intense concentration, grief, tears, disarray and the constant anxiety that he would turn up at any moment. But the double price to pay is that these states persist, and when they have persisted long enough they can bring life, and give form, to any fear at all. In these states, optical insinuations in a dark new abode can form a sturdy, faintly glowing prowler smiling in a shadow.

'Mum's friend Val had never felt these states in relation to her loss, she had said so over the phone from London, though she of course felt other things, and they might be more in the order of longing than fear. They both knew the catastrophe of despair, but from opposite points. In the morning Mum woke rested, but a fatigue would persist until she gained a further night to sleep safely. The fatigue lingered for two weeks. During the third week—a passage of calm where she grew refreshed, and was free to reflect, to train her gaze away from inward-looking urgencies outward to a wider world, during long moments of quietude—she was able to see a vast city of children. It spanned the globe, knew no borders. The Diamond City of Children. Over the week the city grew clearer. As one observation lay on another, her gaze lifted further outward. The diamond claws were hard at work everywhere, gouging upwards, slicing and ascending inside innocent kids, capturing healthy light and ripping it into sharp blades of colour—a spectrum of light's separated, dislocated, parts. These were colours that streamed away in a neat line without ever curling back to form viable mixtures. They were grim, pure pigments that bore no relation to that other sort of colour: the supple mixtures that constitute a human mind living. Or a child growing under the feed of light. Of natural light, before it collides with the transparent carbon claw to be exploded into its insane purities. These were the source of the mad absolutes that passed for currency in the city, for logic. The Diamond City of Children lay waste with absolutes. For this reason alone it should by rights be more visible, but it largely remains an invisible city. As cities go, it was the claw's genetic refuge.

'These were the sorts of things she began to know during that calm third week in the new place. She had known them in a factual way for years, but now her gaze brought a better thing than factual knowledge, clarity. Stretching across the globe, she easily saw a parallel city, powered by its corrosive absolutes, lighted by millions of glowing lacerations, informed and guided and commanded by voices inside the heads of its girls, boys, teenagers, women and men. And they were named, one by one, using the language of the visible city, names that the language hurtled into existence on the basis of a stumbling fear. Loco. Psycho. Schizo. Maddy. You can tell it is fear and fascination simply by noting what I found when I wrote an article on the experience for *Scientific American* designed for the general reader rather than the psychologist: the thesaurus under the general heading "sanity" offers thirty-seven options, and under "insanity" offers up a whopping three hundred and eight. A stumbling approach: more names are thrown at behaviour that can't be understood, than behaviour that apparently can be signed off neatly. Even quite simple names. Dippy. Loony. Potty. Dotty. Madman.'

'My dealer calls me a madman,' Jack said.

'Everyone calls everyone a madman, I agree. But still, what struck me was the carefree, careless quality of the naming. It does, though, indicate an exactness of a kind, even if it's a patronising accuracy, and most of the people of the Diamond City intend no harm to others. Mum also now turned to liking the famous old ponderance: Who is crazy, us or them? So she began to think of comparisons. Would you credit more lunacy with Washington, or with the Diamond City of Children? Would you regard Jerusalem as crazier than the Diamond City? Tehran? Lagos, Karachi, Tokyo, New York, Pyongyang? Of the three hundred and eight various ways of implicating loony actions, mad behaviour, would not some of the visible cities score more than a few? Is pouring excreta into a river sane? So the old question of what is and is not sane, to her, after the intensity of the past month, appeared new all over again.

'By the third week Mum moved around these kinds of comparisons for an approaching reason. In the peaceful passage of the week she started to feel a longing to know that he was okay. And the longing, from this time on, would occur every day. She would never see him again, and the nurse banned their ever meeting, but each day the longing would turn up. She would phone but the nurse would not take the call. Leave messages and the nurse would not call back. It became impossible simply to know if Oliver was all right.

'Spring arrived, the customary offering of simple hopes that most will take up one way or another. The balcony's plants flowered, and by October the suburb turned into a mauve-coloured gauze she could view over rooftops by standing at the flowerpots. The sweeping jacaranda bloom brought freshness to the place. The balcony flowers brought freshness too, the feel of renewal could not be ignored. It affected her. She accepted the lightness. But these were the same jacaranda trees she had left behind, for she had stayed in the same suburb. She shopped at the same shops. And although the spring had offered what it could, it also showed her another way in which she had changed. She soon found that when she visited the shopping centre, or the shops, the troubles she overheard could not hold her attention. One bright day, when she was choosing fruit, she found she felt barely a trace of sympathy for a woman who was telling her friend of her son's chronically low performance at school. Another woman another day was anxious that her son was falling in with the wrong types. There were women whose thirteen year old daughters were going out with grotty boys too old to be boyfriends. Those who bemoaned a child's obesity. Those who complained about the kids leaving old prawns in the sun far up the back yard. One kid was found at the barbeque cooking a large rat he'd caught. He'd severed the head, cleaned the guts, sliced the animal longitudinally and laid it splayed out, frying in oil. At this complaint Mum's attention held: it seemed odd and violent for an eight year old, it seemed a beginning; perhaps, she thought as she walked away, the diamond claws had commenced their work on the boy. But all the other regularities of life overheard in the fresh days of spring left her realising she'd been driven far away, to another realm of complaint that could not compare with the ups and downs, and this distance felt solitary. The freshness of spring did not help, its annual promise of happiness caused a deeper solitary. Comparing hells became a reflex action. If the hell was not disastrous enough then the conversation could not touch the deep new wells of her experience. Though this, she knew, was just yet another perversion of a perfectly natural impulse to exchange anecdotes and concerns. So, were it not for an impressive courage pungent with a good grasp of hell, she would have stayed there, far away, subsisting on the reflex of comparing catastrophes. But she did not stay there. Mum valued the small moments of life. She and Olufituaeb Dneirf met often, and in these moments over coffee, they moved far beyond the solitary flatlands and travelled into the fresh, welcoming foothills of gentle laughter and pristine friendship.

'Also by October, Mum and Val had spoken frequently on the phone. They were not as frequent as the moments with Olufituaeb, but they helped to form a wider path into the clean air of the foothills. During the thirty years since one friend chose London and the other Australia, the two friends kept in touch the old way. A letter, a Christmas card, and three visits to London, in the eighties a hiatus, then a resumption of contact the old way, until recent times when they got on the phone a couple of times a year. But by October they had been on the phone a lot. In the early years of the illness, the advice from her friends was to love him more, show him ostentatiously that he was loved; it was love and more love, until she grew plain sick of the platitude. It was politeness, advice given due to a reserved way with the personal, a wish to not violate a respected social ordering of exchanges. The collateral irritation lay with the fact that the statements cancelled out the need for further exchange. The subject had ended. In effect the advice cut her off, inhibiting the need to deal with experiences, to allow things to be spoken so that they could be held and observed and brought round to a warm plate of understandings. And, you know, small renewals rode the air like steam off the plate if things were coaxed round to understanding. If silences were to be violated, small hopes landed on the heavy shoulder. Mum learned what it was though, through exasperation; it was a lack of knowledge, and she could hardly blame anyone for knowing nothing about the onset of a severe mental illness, that it was not optional but inexorable. She had already tried love and more love. So the early years had created yet another simple perversion. Sound advice, show more love, finishes up instead the crudest piece of advice. Other versions were comparably crude: reason with him; explain to him what is happening; be with him more of the time.

Over the season of the October phone conversations it emerged that Val and Oh-loof had been the ones to have never offered these tokens. It became clear, and it felt pleasant to know, that with Val and Olufituaeb, she was able to violate the silence. And on the phone calls she was also set free to talk, with the softly spoken dear friend who'd lost her son in an accident thirty years before. Val was not proud of restraint. In her own light way, she was not proud of poise, she sounded an upright, restrained person; but the diminutive voice misled. And with Val she found herself getting to know more of another kind of courage. She'd had the impressive courage to face up to him many times, courage pungent with a good grasp of hell, but now with Olufituaeb's fine friendship she found she also had the will to talk. A subtler courage, not one with a great use in the hell she'd seen, though a subtle kind that declares it good to violate silence, one that coaxes renewals to ride the air. So spring started off with hollow recoveries, and finished with many satisfying golden moments talking of two different kinds of loss, or opposite hells of the same loss. The calls generally had that air, the flow of conversation that was trusted and useful.'

Jack found a small cove where he drove the boat up the sand. Here they had lunch and a swim.

The Tree of Faded Photos

'One call prompted a very early memory. Oliver was five. Living in the warmth of the southern Mediterranean sun near the coast, he was lean and tanned. Tripoli then was a place of remnant colonial flavour where British oil companies and European civil engineering companies were active. The northern Sahara was about to bequeath its oil to a young, unknown soldier in their midst. Colonel Qadaffi was still a footsoldier, and the city hummed with the easy pleasures of a lesser Casablanca. The population was mixed and enjoyed bars, restaurants, boulevards, shopping, modern conveniences, and the races were Arab, British, Belgian, French, Danish, and their favourite word for the place was the affectionate and comfortable compliment, cosmopolitan. After work the engineers and surveyors and their wives liked to sit at the rampart on the coast at a favourite bar facing the ocean. Out in the open sitting together, one would point north, all four fingers flat and the back of the hand facing upwards, the forearm at a slight incline, not high, Palermo, he would say, Sicily. It was late summer, hot blue-bright days, a languorous dry heat, and cool nights. The end-of-day drinks were given to marking the sun's hot and cool effect on the city. They would point to the right, sun rises from Benghazi across the gulf bringing the heat of the beautiful Arabian Desert. Sets left into Tunisia and into the High Atlas Mountains, leaving us with that signature chill. They never tired of the game. A right hand would cast out over the ocean to the north-east, Athens. Another hand would sweep to the left, Copenhagen, Toulouse, Cardiff, Manchester, Gibraltar, Marseille. In my father's case his inclined arm would swing to the far left, and he'd say, Valencia, Barcelona.

'They sat together at the epicentre of a vast circle they could imagine contained the epochs that had slid away, and they fell silent as the twilight came to what they referred to as the "cradles of civilisation" surrounding their position. They felt that ritualising the game lent honour to the rampart's central aspect. They could gaze out over the horizon at the Ionian Sea, or at Crete. It was a light game that gave them context switches away from home, but, for them, it was also good to encounter the circle of a known, visualised and adored history that occupied the horizons. Add to the imagined vastness a physical vastness. Add the sea, the rampart, the coast falling away west and east, the markless blue of the sky, a sky larger than any of their experience, and the effect would not hold long in history, or hold remotely out over the sea: this effect in a few moments would swing back into their bodies. The dilation of the mind at the rampart at early twilight was important to them and they knew it, an antidote to their own age of countries, straight lines drawn in the sand for borders, the age of agreements, kept or discarded. But "cradles of civilisation," the phrase, somehow helped them out, levity in the heat of day, gravity at twilight. For Mum, the cradle was not of a revered past, it was real and now; Oliver was born there in Tripoli.

'The memory that she caught was of the Easter in Tripoli shortly before Oliver turned five. She and a friend had visited the central bazaar on Saturday for groceries, and for Easter eggs and chocolate bunnies. Their husbands were in the desert, working in camps, but this was understood, and so they enjoyed the carefree stroll through the busy tiny suburbs of the bazaar. In a stall near the water they found a selection of very big chocolate bunnies and bought one for the kids to share. In total they had purchased twenty eggs, five bunnies and the giant bunny. That night after the children were in bed, she and her Belgian friend made a sparkling project of hiding the eggs in the garden, which was a grove of Libyan coastal stone, waxy Mediterranean shrubs, two olive trees and three palms. They opened a bottle of sherry on the outdoor table and spent the lively evening talking, sipping, getting up to find another crack or corner, laughing at the other's head burrowed into a new hiding place, returning to the table under the optimism of the early summer twilight. They were eager to watch the children in the morning search for the hidden treasures, eager to enjoy watching the pitch of excitement and the pushing and shoving.

The confident young women prepared Easter Sunday with a vitality that gave them a thrill with every egg and bunny put away. The sherry took its course and they decided to place the big bunny up a palm tree. The bunny was large as a small dog, and because it was wrapped in colourful paper the kids were certain to see it right away. The mothers decided it would be a superb location to jolt the kids into an excitable state, and it would tease sufficiently because it lay too high, completely out of reach and the palm could not be climbed to claim it. So it would stand up there, full of glittering wrap in the morning shade, leaning on the palm fronds, smiling its bunny grin at the sleep-eyed kids below.'

'My mother used to like hiding bunnies at Easter,' Jack said. 'In the morning we jumped and shouted around the base of the palm tree. Many creative attempts were made to get the bunny. One child climbed the trunk, using the ridges well, but gave in halfway up. Another climbed a chair, held a long stick, but the stick was still too short. Another threw stones at the bunny but missed, and when one stone hit the foot the bunny would not dislodge from the thickset fronds. An older child found a rope and flung an end up tied to a stone a few times and then gave up.

'But Oliver didn't join the failed attempts. He instead stood back and watched. He did nothing the whole time, just looked on. Then he walked away into the house, while the others made off in the opposite direction, hunting the outer garden, and they started to find the smaller eggs. In a short while he emerged from the back door. He carried, with both small hands, the spider-web broom. Two lengths of bamboo tied to reach the ceiling corners, at the end a brush in the shape of a loop. He steadied himself at the base of the palm, took the brush up to the bunny's ears and nudged it forward nudge by nudge until the bunny eased from between the fronds and bounced once on the grass at his feet. He picked it up, turned to Mum, held it out. He smiled as he stood there for a while like that, then he walked over the grass to the table where the mothers were drinking their standard post-evening Turkish coffee, and Oliver held the bunny out to her.

'In the calm after the hell she found that a memory would lift gracefully like that Easter morning, rising from the indistinct room of reminiscence with a swift clarity. It was as though the severe stress dissolved the grout built up between bricks, the hell had melted walls, catastrophe had steadied the mind. Scent had the power, the corn roasting at the bar by the Tripoli sea:

hawkers turning the sweet cob to blacken on the open flames. The bittersweet scent had always conjured the days of clear-blue optimism in Tripoli. For a lifetime after the hawkers, even a hint of that scent would conjure a dormant experience from the rooms of remembrance. That was understood, the lightspeed powers of scent through time I suppose, perfectly understood.

'But now, in late spring in Perth, it was clear that a new perversion had formed: the storm of high alert, destruction and moving homes had brought poise to a memory. So the great catalysts might always remain scent and song, or odour and sound, but another powerful catalyst, a calm after a hell, might now also lay claim to her powers of recollection. And Val's phone calls tended to come at the right time of day for it: late afternoon, when the mind insists on drifting without too much aim. Val more or less used ten in the morning London time, where in Perth the ending of the day opened a reflective moment. So that she could see, when he held the large bunny to her knee, the warm glow of his face and the proud smile, seeing easily the replica, the photocopy, of the moment. She smiled and said that the prize bunny now belonged to him, but he shook his head.'

The Tree of One Leaf

'Without the phone calls, the calm after the storm may have arrived as a time diminished by echoes of unusable advice. A flow of cloudy sameness that induced a pall of lethargy, and, by the strumming of its monotone, induces amnesia. Instead, the phone calls defined the new season as a time of lucid discovery. Each call they made shined as a memento, a gift, new phrases every time, without echoes. The prospect of tipping a handset of violations into the silence was a thing with wings. The prospect of refreshing a distant memory was a thing with wings.

'The hospital in Tripoli was a bright square building of pleasant cream and it should have appealed to nobody, but externally it looked miraculous in the Mediterranean sun, and fitted comfortably into the arid surroundings, showing it belonged. Inside, a machine hummed like a bird, a well-equipped modern facility, and the staff, a broad mixture of personalities, appeared to prize efficiency and unfeigned friendliness. She remembers the doctor bringing him up, the way he held out the bundle of infant with easy care. When he was placed in her arms the moment arrived, the moment that all the recent hell had returned her to, the very earliest possible optical memory of him. In the miraculous simplicity of the moment, his small radiant eyes came round to hers, and there it was, she could now see it so clearly that it made her involuntarily draw breath, there it shone, a lingering image of mother and child hovering in her mind.

'It held like a mirage but it held steadily and did not shimmer. Spellbound by the creative miracle of his presence, the eyes glittering and staring openly without a blink. Holding the infant in the cradle of her forearms. She could see that he looked fine and peaceful, and he moved with a miniscule sigh. The one centimetre fingers felt the air, opening and then closing on an angel's feather. He was swabbed clean and was already tanned. His calm was something to behold, and the people standing around the bed fell quiet for a very long time. And she now remembers what the doctor had said as he held out the small blanket. "Congratulations, you have a healthy boy." For the next twenty-seven years the diamond claws would work steadily, and with gathering potency, in order to bring him to that afternoon where he swore to lift her up and throw her over the fifth floor balcony. His commands from God, he stated calmly, were clear. These were auditory hallucinations that he could hear in his head. It was also clear by the stern, violent manner, by the demented purpose in his eyes, that he would follow the instructions without question.'

Making Choices

'The phone calls had brought her gliding to the hospital room, but they also took her to another flight of possibilities. Mum and I thought them through, rejecting them, accepting them, turned their positions this way and that. They were something like this. Instead of a general hospital in languid Tripoli, place a young woman in a specialist high-tech hospital in a first-rate big city in two centuries time. When, in the far future, the diamond claw's genetic refuge has been widely inspected, and inspected with a precision that delivers unassailable DNA fact, there will be respectful decisions to be made. Gentleness will prevail. We imagined the young woman may be informed that the foetus has tested positive not only to the schizophrenic gene, but also positive to a configuration of the gene that will deliver acute violence. The specialists then might gracefully add this information to a vast body of specific cases spanning back over the two centuries. Sublime calm may descend on the young woman. Written clinical cases, personal testimony recorded and stored, social documentaries, hundreds of recorded stories, of horrific injuries sustained by families, of killings. Then we thought, so that the expectant mother could not entertain notions of a margin for error, add science with factual case histories, and the overall picture she encounters will be one thing: convincing. In this way we managed to relay the projection right back to hard reality.

'But with this ore of true information the young woman might become light-headed, euphoria may dazzle for a moment as she mixes the miracle of her belly with the jumble of grossness to which she has been subjected. If she rightly refuses to believe the evidence, both the future prognosis and the past documentation, she might tenderly be escorted down the corridor as a last resort. When she is taken into the next room, her mind now elastic with elation, the room a vast airconditioned library with armchairs and consols and flatscreens, she is seated comfortably. She sits lightly on the armchair, saying nothing, and she brims with her instinct, with feelings of creation, she carries another life inside her, the euphoria rides high. The archive starts to show, first one image, then another, and another, grim photos from the morgue specialising in crimes of the insane. For emphasis, labels read "family member," "non-family," but names are disallowed.

'Over these later years Mum and I would continue to work the plausibles. Where then will the young woman find a resolute joy to continue with the pregnancy? What will she do with the instinct that belongs to her? Who will then argue for the moral right of a life of destruction, terror and violence? Which Western religious authority will command a woman to live in a hell? Well, we thought the tide that might bring a revolution to the world of maternal instinct will not really just be genetic authority alone, but also a groundswell of compassion; when the world discovers what awaits young women in this position, nobody will wish to participate in making hells of such immense hardcore reality. Besides, we felt that when the genetic knowledge is plain as the presence of vitamin C in an orange, young women by the millions will commence making their own informed choices. This knowledge, this visibility, would precipitate a shrinkage: once the Diamond City of Children is made visible it will start to erode, a whole vast epoch of erosion, until it lies silent, like a ruin, a flat acre of small stones, a midden encountered from a darker age. Schizophrenia will have been bred from the human condition. But this will not have been through the ugly efforts of a dictator. It will have been through the efforts of clear-minded women the world over.

'Further plain facts of the world quietly seemed to add to our forecasts. Executive actuaries with insurance firms, heavies with the real power at their call, already routinely deploy tests and screening for a large variety of disorders, it's their daily business, and they attend to it with agnostic cool. It's all very secret work, the actuary kept below visibility. The guy who weighs up your defects against your premiums is never in the papers, he's too grim. Insurance people only put their friendly execs in the papers, smiling warmly, feigning concern for your wellbeing. But what actuaries also seek out, and this aspect has become a fast-growing part of their work, are ingeniously new ways to unravel the mysteries to leaven the firm's risk. They are very hungry for the human genome project to deliver them their outcomes. They are the forward scouts. It belongs to these heavies, the patch, the frontline of the human genome's brave new world, because they are the estimators whose work I reckon will produce practical outcomes from the mapping. The methods they like to use might be judged unethical or immoral, but will always remain legal, so a world of grim choice is on the way, already sought-after, financed, given wings to fly in on the sunrise. In turn this could erode hard-won equalities. Most of us already believe equality is a mirage, neatly deployed by propagandists to keep dreams alive. But in the far future, even the propaganda of equality might collapse. In its place the defining features of a free society will go to the centre of fear, that is to say, pre-empting: the propaganda of design, elimination and choices, made from the human genome, might enjoy primacy in a free society of the distant future. A pre-emptive age, a rampant epoch where all the known bad things are pre-empted, and where the impression of equality might become an echo encountered from an earlier time.

'But maybe the deepest intrusion into the psyche of the maternal instinct, or of any instinct, would be still to come. For Mum and I this was not a big leap. Back in vogue after it lay dormant for an epoch might be the impulsively loathed practice of eugenics, a fashion that'd make the olden-day actuaries seem a harmless breed of commercial forward scouts. It's possible that we might learn to control the impulse to loathe it, thereby bringing approval of the practice into the realms of the socially acceptable, just as today the pouring of untreated sewerage into the ocean passes quite well as a socially acceptable practice. But this possibility, of choosing with such a clear intent, was a glimpse far into the future. Then again, maybe this kind of choosing was, we thought, never to be possible.

'Or maybe the present is a bridging age, a time of mixed success: on the one hand we first-worlders are bright enough to map the human genome, on the other hand we are not bright enough to cease pouring excreta into the ocean. High-tech primitives. From here Mum and I reached a kind of conclusion that to us was merely stating the obvious. If the high-tech primitive dominates a bridging age, it is safe to imagine that for the foreseeable future a swathe of young women will continue to unknowingly make hells of their lives. For the time being, the impulsive horror of eugenics can assist in allowing those hells to be made over and over.

'We were not all that alarmed at considering these thoughts, neither Mum nor I. She rolled their dankness round in a calm, peaceful manner, and they were simply extensions of where she had already been half her life. Rather than dank, she felt them to be pioneering thoughts, early days, a time would come. They might seem like another perversion, but that would appear so only to an outsider. The perversions that the diamond claws had delivered vicariously were just another way of saying that she was now capable of observations of remarkable clarity, and Val agreed. So the phone calls had been vessels full of fact, extrapolation and friendship, they were gifts in late spring, weeks after the mauve of the jacaranda had given way to the bright blue of a markless Perth sky.'

Riverbanks of Reeds

'This is the style in which she lived after the death threat. Armed with these new perversions. Which, it has to be underlined, Jack, merely were intensifications of normal impulses. On a good day, when the optimistic sky proved infectious, she would take a perversion, press it into context, and the world would turn out that small bit more transparent. In a modest circle of friends she became one of the more sought-after individuals for good company. A life of excellent experiences made her excellent company to keep. Times in Barcelona where she was born,

Delhi as a small child, Karachi and Quetta as a star athlete, Tripoli, Kuala Lumpur, Singapore, Jakarta, Ipoh, Lagos, Ilorin and excursions to New York, Paris, London, and visits to scores of small idylls around the globe. Good times, tough times, the experiences she'd had in these places, as a thing distinct from the newly acquired direction of her gaze, made her one of the more sought-after women others would want for good conversation. Travel elevates nobody against another, and tourism can be dispiriting if the expectation is to travel, but she saw so many different cultures at work that the language of facile truisms had left her at an early age.

She'd already known the grim mindset of the fanatical mullah long before they began to receive hot global airtime after the fall of Beirut and then into September 11 and beyond. She knew only too well how briskly a Yoruba woman would screw up her nose at the mention of an Ibo woman, both being Nigerians. Or how a Hakka from mainland China would have a single disagreement with a Hainanese from mainland China and they would never speak again. Unity under the banner of statehood held no sway with the ethnic realities that she had grown to understand and pay due respect. Flimsy fences in the sand were fine in a post-colonial hubbub, but laughable to a relationship on the ground floor.

And for years she'd laughed heartily. With the friends she'd made all over the world, there was ample room to poke fun at the earnest and at one another. From harmless squabbles to fierce civil clashes, she'd seen first-hand what a stupid idea, for the political laziness it showed, that it was to draw lines in the sand, but it made for colour, and she'd in reality lived that colour.

So from colour to horror, her conversation was worth the time many times over. Val knew it, as did Olufituaeb, as two among the first, and then a modest circle of friends round the globe came to know it too. After all, the diamond claws had not touched her, they had touched her son.'

Rusting Gates

'My brother,' Jack said, 'probably has no idea of the existence of this city, he's a sweet guy who loves cake, Mum, and budgies.'

'I've come to believe there are gates to the Diamond City of Children. Entrances that smack oddly with splendour. A whiff of dominion carries in the design, like an ornate Edwardian double-gate guarding the entry wide as a boulevard. The iron branches and rusting leaves purvey the ideals of order and victory. But the gates of the Diamond City have also a plain aspect, and that aspect is the decade that the diamond claws take to shred a child's mind. The design has everything a grand gate could want: rusting memory cast in iron; brief glory days that rise and then wane; they are hard to push at first, resisting and laden with inertia, but quickly begin to move, to swing aside under their own mobile weight, a momentum. The design makes a visual effect, which in turn gives off a clarion call of imperial domain—a place where things and lives are taken by force of different kinds, decree, law, superiority, even if these attitudes are imagined. Almost every form of superiority has its basis somewhere in the limpid back room of delusion, and the Diamond City's self-regard is little different to any other imperial force. But beside the fanfare, the gates of the Diamond City are a plain thing, they are the decade that the diamond claws contravene the rule of love, destroy the notion of love, the time that the claws take to shred a child's mind. The gates are the rolling, evolving years that pick up momentum, commencing with the quiet lift of a visitor's eyebrow: My, that child certainly has a temper.

'From that barely noticed glint of the claw, the momentum then builds, the gates start to move aside. He starts to add pronouncements to his "temper." He quotes many sources, twisting them to suit a wildly inflated self-regard. He quotes the guy on radio, saying the man addressed him and only him, as with the talking heads on television; they speak directly and solely to him. That's how Oliver entered the gates. He started to quote the voices inside his head. Then he started to quote the Old Testament, twisting lines to suit his purpose, wagers and decrees and orders that he threw from the context of the sane to the context of the insane. A simple reprimand in the text was ramped up, held aloft and then contorted into a call to violence. He became, after years spent quoting more and more loosely, a mind that sat in close proximity to a religious fundamentalist terrorist. The gates opened and he walked into a city that lay waste with absolutes. As far as the eye could see lay a domain of these rotting sentinels. They stood well enough as jutting small mounds, as the last remnant outposts of thought, where occurrences evaporate at the smallest glance of logic, but to him they were discoveries and epiphanies that boldly hunkered down like a thousand metre cliff face. Were you caught living by anything less than the reflections of a grand, awe-inspiring absolute, you were simply to be killed as a sinner.

'It's exactly the way I was caught. The polar opposite of the splendour of these gates was my studio, a grotty but beautiful old shop that was too unrentable for anyone else to use but a sculptor for the token rent of thirty dollars a month.

'I had made a small bust. Head and shoulders of a plain, down-to-earth woman, face held in a poise of meditation, eyelids drawn closed, the forehead tilted back, it was a small life-like clay piece, no more than very good mimicry of busts of the past that dealt in the facial language of sublime ecstasy. Catherine claims the bust is my notion of my grandmother as a peasant girl. It was my first attempt at sculpture, maybe a start of something alongside painting. Oliver had called back into Perth from a hitching trip around Australia after he fled the hospital, a journey full of low-flying survival, theft, sleeping under bridges. He had nowhere to stay, so he stayed at the studio where I stayed. He said he would recover from a week on the Nullarbor, which is one of our big deserts back there, between Perth and Adelaide, until he and his travel companion could find a place. This he'd done before, and so no great hassle lay at hand. I'd keep working, he'd look around with his friend for somewhere to bring himself together and return to medication. The whole thing was part of a cycle of ups and downs, friendliness and violence. You were better off flowing than fixing.

'I sat surprised by the bust, by the facility for representational accuracy. She was made in a haze with little conscious consideration, just an afternoon's absorption with a lump of clay given as a gift by a student at Claremont art school up the road. It was nothing, the effort was play, and I sat surprised by the outcome, particularly the detailed exquisiteness of that moment of ecstasy. It lighted much of her interior, and in a suitably ambiguous way. So I showed Oliver the bust. Pointing out the things I liked about the work, I mentioned that they could be developed over time now that it seemed clear a basic facility was present, and we began to talk of the possibilities. I caressed the clay, pleased to see it had started to dry from a few days under a hot window that blew with the easterlies, absently tapping the crust, and so it went unnoticed at first, I did not see the hand-wringing start up.

'He stood nearby, examining it in silence. But he started to mumble words that sounded of disagreement. Then I heard "blasphemous." Then he became hotter. This, he said, was a pagan token I had made, it was an insult to God. He worked himself up, becoming redder and exposing a build-up of fury. He started shouting that the Bible strictly prohibits the making of false Gods, that I should read the Old Testament, that he knew I had not.

'I had seen every kind of psychotic episode over the years up to now, and went with the flow, but this was a new development. Going now with what flow exactly? What flow would I do with a contorted quote from the Old Testament that I had not opened let alone skimmed? His pent-up fury was in the eyes now, a wild, sharp diamond light, and he uttered things from a very deep hollow somewhere. Then he marched forward chanting, "We will now fight, c'mon fight, teach you a lesson." He put his head down and came forward. I said that I would not, we are brothers, and I will not fight you. But this meant nothing, and he kept on ramping up his fury. I fell reluctantly into a defensive fight, dealing with blow after blow. This was not a typical fight of brothers sane, a pent-up retribution riding some bitter early memory, this was an insane man deeply offended by an insult to God. Had the reason been brotherly war for five minutes, maybe a week, it might have been far better, somehow acting as a cleansing ruction. But instead he fought with a no-holds-barred venom. When he had me by the throat with both hands, I could see his face. It had morphed. Hot red and straining so hard it was about to burst. That was confirmation he was at my neck with a diamond clarity, very real and suddenly dangerous. I had to let rip—and we were into it. Unrestrained violence. It got his hands off my neck. In ten minutes the heat had passed.

'He managed to hurl the bust against the wall where it smashed into pieces, and he gave a huge constricted sigh of justice accomplished. The sigh was a scudding one, squeezed by a grunt and completed with a violent rasp. This encounter became the first time he moved over a line with me. It was new. Before this line, he had never wished me harm, and throughout the early troubles of the diamond claws there was the safe though unstable glimmer of all the hues of sibling love and countenance. The diamond claws had now sliced to a deeper place, where his quoting took on a fanatic, caustic edge. With the gates now thrown open, he had vanished at twenty-six into the Diamond City, a decade of memory had become a gateway to a parallel world. He was now deep in the business of equating things that did not equate at all.'

The Give and the Take

'After he turned eighteen there was a visible spiking of two innate traits. It was like a bloom taking up sudden quickness, so it left behind any trace of teenage hesitancy. Oliver had always possessed a strong streak of kindness, we all think he got it directly from grandma Renata, and prior to the touch of the diamond claws, just as childhood came to a conclusion, the innate heart of gold began to shine. A teenager's hesitancy to let the kind streak out became a confident fulfilment of the kindness that bloomed in ways which I thought were damn impressive but which also were straightforward. He would help in the garden, in the house, tend to the neighbours, fulfil essentially any request made on him.

'The other natural well, his generosity, deepened with a new job, what seemed like the start of a career in cabinet-making, a skill he was very good at, a natural who'd have a solid future. The kindness and generosity developed into a basis of character that was quick in one overall reflex, consideration of others. It was his signature, Renata's signature, a kindness of vigour and liveliness, not of solemn benevolence. A kindness of gusto. It gave him a good line in fresh humour. He was always quick to see hilarity, fast to appreciate slapstick. It made him popular, and friends gathered round him for a few years, the piece of time that was to be his brief heyday this side of the gates. Combined, in the way they were with him, gusto and a considerate nature magically created friendships, love affairs, parties, adventure.

'At the birthday he blew out the eighteen candles. Later outside, as the party swung and bounced, I asked Mum how she felt. She glowed, was happy and busy, but I asked anyway. She said the thing she felt was the memory of the day he was born in the hospital in Tripoli. There was, she added, an astonishing sameness in his eyes today as there was back then looking out from the bundle in her arms, there was this bright warmth in there. A friend sang out to Mum from across the room: "That son of yours, Marcela, is glorious!" And Mum laughed.

'And it's true, it really was his signature, that warmth. At the conclusion of childhood, on his eighteenth, that warmth was now almost ready to begin its conversion into a signature diamond light. A light so sharp it could explode, at its own will, into separate bands of colour of such quantum purity that they bore no relationship to the fragile nuances of a life. A kindness of vigour stood at the gates, and a gusto for absolutes lay in wait.'

By the end of the week with Castle, Jack Black could feel himself groping at the reason that Catherine might have set out to destroy the Patsy&Remple love affair. Nothing sharp, no clear half-thoughts popping around in his powderbox, just a dim grope. Jack's brother was mentally handicapped, and was a kind and sweet person. Castle's brother was mentally ill, and a troubled, violent person. The affiliated comparison drew the two men closer than maybe any other powderbox stuff could have done.

'Have you seen him lately?' Jack asked.

'Yeah, I went to visit him in Perth just before I came here to catch up with Kee.'

'What happened?'

'It was great. He's medicated and well, and we had lunch, said hello brother, gave each other a big hug. We talked about good old times. I wouldn't bring up all the ugly stuff, it just would not be fair on anyone, but most of all it wouldn't be fair on him. It was good for me to see that Oliver still is, basically, under the illness, the sweet guy he always was.'

The Tree of the Earlobe

On Friday afternoon Jack went for a long walk by himself along the beach. He marvelled at Castle's mother Marcela of the sea, he wanted to meet her. He marvelled at the friendship of the three women, and he thought it would be one hell of a wonderful moment to meet them together. But he still had no idea he would be flying back to Australia with Castle and his cousins

Catherine and Remple, and not back to his earlobe nailed to a turning spoke. His earlobe, nailed to the wheel of his London art world thanks to bonbon gungho Patsy, was to be set free, the nail simply fell out, mysteriously, without effort or explanation. Or, it fell out, as all nails do, by *affiliated comparison*.

In the three days on the lagoons of the grand banks in the northern Caribbean dear butterfly, Jack and Castle gained more mutual trust and respect than is normally gained by powderboxes in years, I've seen plenty over the span of a century's worth of hasty-paste. And now, these two ding-dongs in the Bahamas were nearly as easy as Miles Banford and David Darlington had been back in Cal. So, what that means, to pirates like me an Oxley an Flattie, means Jack was now free to stumble in from the outside, he'd soon become Jack Verandah, become this bright new ding-dong bumbler. As Ellie-Isabela said back in '47, about inheriting stuff. Jack was now sensing the rhythmic wings of give and take.

Jack was stumbling in from the outside, the outsider was getting acquainted with those who understood. And who were those powderboxes who understood a little? Well, Catherine did, she loved her cousin Castle like a brother. Her brother Remple loved Castle like a brother. Laura, Meryl's daughter understood, so did Castle's friend Hong Thet, one of your true custodians dear butterfly, whom you shall soon meet down south at Yelverton. Hong Thet was one of the crew. Insiders, who understood. Outsiders, by Catherine they were handled with politeness, with decorum, even a big, scary, powerful outsider powderbox like gungho Patricia.

V
Here were the wings that created the Dunsborough Swing

The Summer Castle

This is a lazy summer in a lazy place dear butterfly. Fine trees, dozens of kinds, cool shade alive with flowers for nectar snacks. Soon you will see that this cape down here makes other summers across the two equators seem like a boiling junction in a city. Tip to tip the cape is just a hundred kilometres, but top to bottom the cape is way bigger than a universe of gifts and surprises. A place where powderboxes find the atmosphere aromatic with delicate parcels of give and take. Floating parcels of dancing. Hanging parcels of sugar and honey. Drifting parcels of love and relaxation. Billowing parcels of lit up temptation. Cruising parcels of laughter. Rolling parcels of lavish understanding. Bumper parcels of generosity. Limpid parcels of resting. A place where it is faintly possible that the powderboxes could catch sight of a butterfly taking a ride with a box. Up and down the forests, and round the beaches of the cape.

My hippy friends at NASA with their gigantic flying machines, how they might weep. How they would cast their notes into the room, exasperated, paper, their smiles and tears hanging like curtains in a window as they watch you and I passing by, a box and a butterfly. Watching you and I dear butterfly, cruise the trees of a lazy summer, from Dunsborough to Augusta, and back again. You and me flying in a box. Weep you great zings, weep. From what Oxley calls the Dunsborough Swing, usurping the ding-dong diaspora and diaspirin for the sake of energising the human potential. Even my friends at NASA would spray their tea and coffee at the sight of the Dunsborough Swing. Weep you bums, weep, shake it up, shake it up. Gotta mix. Luck&love.

With any luck they'd spill their hot coffees into the cardboard deadbeats sitting around their offices. Cardboard extincto, at least at NASA. Except puppybox Yard, coz this is Yard's favourite place to conduct his hup two three, bringing the powderboxes of the cape those better memories, relaxing memories. This is a very fine summer, and the booksmeller might be the new lover. A booksmeller is very nice.

The Tree of the Booksmeller and the Bookseller

A booksmeller, face it, can ask pertinent questions, take Laura the booksmeller, Meryl's daughter, niece of walking shoelace Lee Glass-Darlington.

Laura inherited from colonel David behaviour towards easy addiction. Bad news sorry facto, hell tomorrow, oh well, sell me a favour. But she was not addicted to drugs, she was addicted in different ways. She'd returned from the Edinburgh festival where she performed a sharp, intelligent show about her mother's grandfather, a guy she'd never known. To Laura he was a mysterious figure who looked after children by day, and by night mumbled in fear of the Hindu deity Maheesha, the buffalo demon of chaos and evil. Laura's fifty-minute show received good notices and the attendances were up. Audiences were engaged by the oddness of a Scottish Hindu's journey from a Spanish orphanage to a Hindu funeral pyre. To the audience the show seemed romantic but also seemed far too cruel to recommend to friends, tho the crowds kept on arriving night after night.

Laura the booksmeller wished for a summer in Perth before heading home to Sydney in late autumn, so she took a ride down south with Castle and his friends and cousins, bringing along the fresh new books she'd purchased in Edinburgh. Laura and Castle had met only twice before, but heard about each other. Castle heard about Laura through his cousin Catherine. One remark Catherine had made in the Bahamas had stayed in Castle's powderbox, humming its way with him back across the oceans to Perth, and then south home to his shack. Catherine had said: 'Of all the irritating qualities to have, Laura has the phoney humility quality. Under that phoney humility she's a conniving bully.'

Castle's visitors were sitting together on the verandah, the Arrivals Verandah, Castle called it. The relax after the journey from Perth. True enough, I agree; a verandah where the hasty-paste slowed. At the end of the verandah lay a large, distinguished-looking old wooden box.

'What's that chest up there?' Jack said.

'A picnic box,' Castle said, 'we'll take it out to the beach tomorrow.'

Oxley, O Oxley, he'd glitter in shade at the beach the next day. From all that stainless steel and pewter, he'd sparkle in the shade of the giant ghost gums, he'd be loading up with hup two three, filling up with the jungarummy jiddle, coz he was pretty good at slowing down the hasty-paste with his slowed-down picnicish memory trade. Quite liked his new owner Castle. Plus puppybox Yard was quietly giving the powderboxes the slower mojo down here, the relax, the new discoveries.

'So how were the audiences in Edinburgh, Laura?' Catherine asked.

'I can never understand,' Castle said to Laura, 'an audience.'

'You're not alone,' Laura said, 'nobody understands an audience, it's not possible.'

'What I mean is the componentry. Who are they, these people that go to a show?'

'I'm not getting your meaning. They're theatre lovers.'

'No, what I mean is, deep in their hearts, why do they love going to a show, are they other actors?'

'Oh, I see what you mean, yeah, an audience, right at the core of its heart, is an actor. It either once was an actor, is currently an actor, or once wanted to be an actor, or still wants to be an actor, that's the basic componentry,' Laura said.

'Any playwrights?'

'No, playwrights don't tend to go to plays, highly picky at the very least.'

'Francis Bacon,' Jack said, 'claimed he saw everything, absolutely every exhibition in London, so he claimed: "You must remember, I know what goes on because I go to see *everything*." Seems a bit sloppy to be a playwright and not go see plays.'

'Well it's just the way it is. Let's all talk about loss,' Laura said in a gentle tone, but behind the calm she stayed insistent, the very same insistence that got the Edinburgh show up and running to bang em big.

Nobody felt like it at the moment, but finally Castle said, 'All right, so we talk about loss. Fine, let's talk about it, but only if you promise we get it done tonight, and for the next week while you lot are down here, we talk about other matters and go swimming every lunchtime.'

'We promise,' the others said.

Jack got up to walk around the shack, have a look at things, check out Castle's belongings.

Castle was the bookseller. He enjoyed the tiny bookshop in Margaret River that he managed for a friend who owned a string of hobby businesses in the wine district: Neil Hunter. Castle was good in the shop, he had sprigs of optimism sprouting all over the vegetable patch of his intentions. Most shops when they shut for the day turned a sign on the door that read: Sorry We Are Closed. Castle's sign on the door of the bookshop read: Hi, we open again 9 a.m. tomorrow.

The undead and the unread, Castle's two hobbies. These were becoming fiery topics in the first week of spring. Stacks of unread books piled up, hordes of Reverberating undead swelling up.

Castle and Laura were beginning to let their civility drop away. Laura was very good at the art of giving for personal gain. Castle was inept at gain, any sort at all. He hadn't the time for gain dear butterfly, he just painted, made things sculpturally or in blocks, and he managed the small bookshop behind a hardware shop, and, because he was a bookseller, he was liked.

Laura always commenced a session with holding a book under her nose and fanning the pages across the nostrils with her thumb. Each book was different, she'd say. Scent of book, she'd say, very good catalyst for clearing the mind. But she rarely read the books because she preferred performing.

The mutual irritation they harboured started to fizz to the surface. Later it started cracking from private holes of sulphurous ding-dong, emerging full-blown into open public loathing. Party after party up in Perth, Remple had to stroll over to cool them off. But at the party at Castle's place that night even right-royal Remple He of Split From Patricia, even he failed to stop the sulphur.

'So what can you say that you've actually lost, then, Castle,' Laura asked gently.

'My brother,' Castle said.

Castle then explained to Laura what he'd already told Jack in the Bahamas on the dinghy, compacting it to the question—Laura treated each afternoon like a rebirthing session—and Castle took just five minutes to wade through the remembered losses and hurts.

Then for the rest of the night everyone got together to enjoy the visit to Castle's creaky beautiful shack.

Jack strolled back out. 'And you?' Jack said to Laura.

'My aunt Lee's husband was reported missing in Singapore.'

Jack offered, 'Maybe he just pissed off, walked away.'

'Check when they're together,' Laura said, 'you wouldn't come to that conclusion at all.'

'I'm, um, I'm sorry,' Jack said. 'You mean he hasn't shown up in two months?'

'Yeah. Aunty Lee's pretty severely damaged, she hasn't worked since.'

'What kind of work did she do?' Jack asked.

More like, what kind of work was the king Bakks crew doing upon gifted Lee's powderbox, that's more like it, but Jack Verandah is just a ding-dong painter arrogarnta, what the heck would he know about Inch or Kilometre? The painter arrogarnta breed dear butterfly, think they know about the magic an all just because they paint, they don't know much at all about the magic.

'Aunty Lee's a corporate lawyer,' Laura said, 'but she's not a trimmed-in behaved kind of lawyer, she's more a hot partygirl, one of those high-flying conceptual lawyers who makes the big-bang concept happen. She organised a structure to pay the poppy farmers in Afghanistan to burn their crops, she's bold, I love her heaps, she's wild, intelligent and compassionate, she used to be anyway.'

Jimmy Hazel Prowls Around to Lee's Goldrush House

Used to be. Someone was steadily recording that 'used to be.' Someone was converting that loss, sloshing around in the cult of loss. Jimmy Hazel, ever since that first night he watched Lee scudding down to Tenmoon Creek naked, Jimmy had crawled across the scrub from his shack at Meryl's place.

Climbed up the hillside, roamed around the perimeter of Lee and Rudolph's goldrush bungalow until he found Lee slumped in a chair staring at the floor. Then he'd stop and watch her from the darkness outside.

He was now up to his twentieth visit. He started to notice the gathering appearance of a lost and filthy body slumped in the chair doing nothing, which to him was remarkable because he felt that Lee was just the most bullshit far-out beautiful woman he'd ever set eyes on. To Jimmy's powderbox, in the way Jimmy'd think it, only the delicious Veronica back in Lucknow came close, but he grew out of Veronica in about a month.

He agreed with himself; it was nice that Laura's mother Meryl wanted help in her jacaranda gardens, a buck that kept his real work going, the new sculpture. But the gift that got him going very deeply, what he truly admitted to himself was that it was glorious that he had Meryl's sister here to use, to use, for the sculptures he was making back at the shack. Making impressions of solitary women, impressions that he felt he successfully bathed in a profound loneliness, taking his cue for elegance from Mogdigliani's paintings, giving his own sandstone pieces the aura he found here outside Lee's windows. After an hour he'd cross down the slope and follow the track back to Meryl's place and work till late, lovingly moving the Pittwater sandstone into messages that issued from deep inside what he thought was a broken and lost soul.

But see, that's a powderbox, mistakes come and go. Jimmy's mistake was that he assumed Lee was looking for happiness. She wasn't. She'd by now settled for equilibrium, any sort.

Sculptor arrogarnta.

He felt lucky working late in the small shack that Meryl gave him, he felt fortunate. In time he found that the suburbs of Pittwater were riddled with dens. The millionaire bungalows were peppered with outrooms and shacks and lofts and cellars occupied by waitresses, gardeners and shop assistants who either were in love with the oceanic peninsula life or were working at night as painters, poets or sculptors. How he got here was lucky too. In rural Lucknow he attended a touring performance done by a small company from Sydney, saw Laura play a buffalo, or a demon, asked her over to his butterfly prawn barbeque, gave her the whole idea that he had held now for a long time—that he was looking to move to Sydney—and Laura liked the sculptures she found in the shed and around the back yard in Lucknow, and she rang home to deliver the good news: the gardener that her mother had been looking for, he'd been found.

Castle brought out a tray. Drinks, a loaf of bread and a hunk of cheese impaled with an old knife. The group sat around and drank cold drinks.

'I often try calling her,' Laura said, 'to say thanks for the birthday parcel she mailed to me while I was in Edinburgh, but she won't answer.' Then Laura picked up her phone to call her mother at the house at Pittwater.

'Hi Laura.'

'Hi Jimmy, how's things?'

'Good thanks, you're still in Edinburgh?'

'Perth. Down south actually, at a cousin's place. How's Lee, have you and Mum seen Lee lately?'

'No, haven't seen her at all.'

O yeah. Haven't seen her. Except maybe twenty or thirty times. Through a dusty window pane at night. A gifted legal conceptualiser, a gifted shoelace. Being lovingly chipped and sanded into a Jimmy Lucknow version of a lost and broken soul of tremendous beauty, what a ding-dong arrogarnta. A suite of statues, sitting quietly in the shed behind the forest of jacaranda. Nope, haven't seen her. What a ding-dong Lucknow lollipop.

'Where's Mum, I can't get hold of her.'

'Meryl's in New York.'

'If you see Lee give her my love.'

'Will do.'

'Jimmy.'

'Yes?'

'Jimmy, why don't you think about coming over here, it's great fun, I'll introduce you to a good dealer, and a painter from London, get in a plane, I'll get the fare.'

'Can't do it, sorry, have to look after the place while your folks are away.'

'Think about it, bye.'

'Bye.'

The other family image Jimmy couldn't remove from his powderbox was this hardcore situation of Laura's great-grandad having all these hard-boiled sessions with an Indian princess.

He overheard the stuff a few times, and first he thought it was a joke, but the images kept on reeling in and becoming real. For a guy who'd barely been out of Lucknow the whole bizzo of an Indian princess was ripe to say the least. From the moment he overheard the story he was taken like a slap against the head. David drove into the hills with the princess, threw her over the bonnet and banged away like a baboon. Then they drove to a secluded house in the forest, went walking and swimming, made love in the cool hillstation grass, then the princess flung him backwards onto a stinking old mattress in a stable and rode him through the night-sky, all this stuff kept Jimmy Hazel busy. But he kept it to himself that he'd overheard family lore. Naturally, he had met David's wife in person when she'd visit from Lee's place, but even on greeting the great-grandmother the oily pornography from the Indian nights was so much more real that the Lucknow kid felt he'd been slapped across the head more than once. Even when he stood before her to greet her he felt that the actual presence of the great-grandmother was at the least a slight presence, at the most it was ephemeral when compared with the bruised feeling he had across his head from the reality of the Indian pornography.

But that was the first month in the jacaranda gardens. Later on, Jimmy the Lucknow jolly did discover something about Lee's grandmother that made the Scottish matriarch very real indeed.

Dusk at Lee and Rudolph's goldrush bungalow, out on the back plateau at the long table. Lee had checked her emails for a message from Singapore supercop Tony Chen, nothing. She sat outside with her grandmother.

'Why,' Lee said gazing at the floor, 'did you ever love a guy like David, Grandma?'

'Are you asking for the truth,' Enid said, 'or for a grandma's sweet goodness?'

'I love your sweet goodness, and now that I'm a wreck I'd like to know the truth.'

'He was scary, dear, he was this bright big sexual monster with the eyes of an angel, I was scared of him.'

Lee lifted her unwashed head. 'Really?'

'Very. One day he walked into the Glasgow house and I was standing at the phone, and we'd now been together for many years, and I started to shake, from the legs upwards.'

'Have you told anyone, have you told Mum?'

'No, I'll never tell your mum. Besides, nobody has asked.'

'Did he scare you for being, what, a brute?'

'No dear, he was just this exceptional presence, such a beauty, all shine and wonder. I was scared dear, he was so beautiful and sexy, I was scared of him.'

'Fuck, I just, I just don't understand that.'

'Your lovely husband is a clean chap, dear.'

The darkness had climbed the hillside, second equator sliding across the land. From the shadow of the shed to the right Jimmy Hazel stepped out. He stood for a moment outside the shadow's boundary. A silence for a sec, for the two women were caught by surprise. Then he stepped forward. 'Hello,' Jimmy said. 'She's right, your grandma's right, it's easy to be scared of that kind of thing, I was scared of a girl back home who had that kind of thing,' and Jimmy jolly Lucknow stared into Lee's wrecked eyes, stared without a waver.

Laura Brings Out the Bell

At Castle's place the group on the verandah popped the first bottle of champagne for the week.

'I'll fetch the present Lee sent me,' Laura said. She went inside to the sofa where she was to sleep for the visit, and then glided back outside to the Arrivals Verandah holding a teak box. 'See, this was his, David's. My great-grandma gave it to my grandma Rachel, Grandma gave it to Lee, and now Lee's given it to me. Last month aunty Lee asked great-grandma Enid permission to post it to me at the festival. It was good to have it when I was performing his story because that's where the box was located when David and Great-grandma were in love, the box lived in their house in Edinburgh, and they say it was sent to Great-grandma after David passed away in Calcutta, sent by this Indian-American mogul, someone called Banford. The box revved up my performances, that's a fact. My first few nights were okay, but after the box arrived at my hotel there was this fukkin fire around me on the stage that I couldn't figure out.'

Laura lay it on the table next to the cheese. Laura: owner number eight. Extincto be fucked.

At that moment Jack decided that Laura had two prongs, that she was one of those performers he'd known all across the East End, a performer who believes they're a mystic, a pronged-out ding-dong who was wistful and gentle. He looked at the box, concerned that he thought he'd said out loud: 'It's just a box.'

But he also knew Laura was the daughter of Patsy's friend the diviner Meryl. He knew Patsy regularly visited her friend in Sydney, the fabled diviner, Meryl Glass-Darlington of Ten-moon Creek. Jack had always felt Patsy was bit of an urgent case in needing a handful of mystic friends. Because all Patsy ever did, day in day out, was business, but Jack was just another painter arrogarnta who thought he knew about the magic, making him more, much more, of a pronged-out ding-dong than Laura.

Jack was now scoffing. Inside his powderbox: Fire all around, yeah, what it is, it's just the usual bit of burn-off round the edges of a woolly massive ego.

Big ego? Jack Verandah, what a ding-dong, talking about the back of his head again.

But these were just pop-in-pop-out thoughts, brief nothings, stuff he simply added to the gathering impressions of a Laura Glass-Darlington he'd only just met, pleasure thoughts, rough pleasure, movements in the powderbox taking a stroll over the warm afternoon's idle banter.

Jack opened the double lid. Wings. 'There's nothing in it except this bell, what's the bell for?'

'Mum says it's a stationmaster's bell. Belonged to the uncle of Aung San Suu Kyi, but I dunno about the romanticising Mum likes getting into, I say it belonged to a farmer, it's a buffalo bell, hanging around the neck of a water buffalo. David was right into Maheesha the buffalo demon of chaos and evil.'

'You're assuming,' Castle said, 'your mum's making it up, but she's closer to the bell's origins than you are, you're the one who's making it up, I'd say.'

'Here,' Laura said, 'have a book to smell. You ought to try smelling the books you sell, it'd do you good, booksmell mojo.'

'I don't smell books, I sometimes read them.'

Jack was amused at Laura and Castle, at the combat. 'How do you two sensitive lovers know each other?'

But the second he asked, Jack was given the outsider treatment, a Castle–Laura game they'd hitched onto a few days ago in Perth. The answer started true, and turned into ping-pong.

Castle said: 'David Darlington looked after Kee.' True enough.

'What do you mean?' Jack said.

Castle said: 'When Kee was a boy at the hacienda, a guy called colonel David ran the place, colonel David was Laura's great-grandfather.' True.

Laura said: 'Castle's right. My great-grandfather looked after Castle's grandfather.'

True.

'Kee is my adopted grandfather I suppose you'd call it.' True.

And then the ping-pong.

Laura said: 'Castle and I are cousins of situation, cousins Golfo de Valencia, we're not lovers. Are we lovers, Castle?'

'We could be lovers if we wanted to, because we're not cousins.'

'We're cousins of timing, not blood.'

'That's right, so we could be lovers if we wanted to.'

'We could try to be lovers.'

'We could.'

Catherine had enough of the ping-pong, and she said slowly: 'We love Kee very much.'

'Well,' Jack said, 'Kee would know a bit about the bell, I mean he lived in the orphanage, he would know something about your great-grandad David.'

'I've never met the famous Kee,' Laura said.

'I have,' Jack said, 'and you will. If you come to Broome, are you coming with us to Broome next month for the launch of Remple's university?'

'Yeah, if I'm invited.'

'Of course you are,' Remple said.

'Kee might know what the bell was for.' Jack lifted it up. 'Fuck, it's pretty severely dented.' Then he held it above his head and rang it, and everyone got up and walked off the Arrivals Verandah onto the lawn.

'Check the fucker,' Laura said to Castle, 'Jack Verandah the stationmaster.'

Ding-dong and how's the time. O Bobbo, stuffed with chatter, with parties, but also stuffed with the unsaid, hurling the unsaid across the two equators at whim and will, hup two three over the hungry mountaintops.

Lovingly, and honourably, even gently, stuffed with the private thoughts and memories of travellers like colonel David. Open the lid and see the antique timber suffused with a hope or two. Eight owners now, since the first weeks when Arnie Colchester bevelled and banged so damn good a hundred years back in his fabled Rangoon workshop that smelled of the scruff and resin dissolved between the old world and the new. Eight owners, eight worlds of memories. Shanghai to Yelverton. Aunt Lee the Glaswegian Soho dancer who loved life to the diasporic hilt; her dad the crapjoke teak dealer; her nephew colonel David the Scottish Hindu; Miles Banford the princess hunter; Enid, matriarch of the Sydney Darlington clan who many a fast thinker felt was dumb as a banana but who was in fact smart as a tack; Enid's daughter Rachel; Rachel's daughter Lee who burned the meadows of Afghanistan and somehow lost her husband Rudolph; and now far away from the shit of the world at Castle's little shack down south in the clean breezy wine district, Lee's niece Laura who had thundered up and down the Edinburgh stage each evening snorting out a genuine festival hit.

Castle's Castle in the Forest

Catherine and Jack had driven down together. Catherine had told Jack up in Perth that a winding line of forest light unfurled in the final miles to Castle's First World War shack near the ocean. 'Let me show you, come on down with me,' she said, 'we'll meet the others at Castle's place. It's a hut in the middle of a clearing in the forest, and it is an absolute joy to the mind and the senses.'

She was right. As the night fell into the forests of all that good wood, and as she drove weaving into its new edge, into the blurry edges of the second equator, things would expand then squeeze then expand, perceptions would touch memories, like incantations, giving off a fresh slant on yesterday's discovery. Big deal, we boxes say. But let Catherine have a bumble, bumbling's good, bumble-bumble. In the final miles to Castle's old shack, after Busselton, the busy highway came to the turn-off to a deserted Yelverton Road. The road became a winding tunnel that rolled into the long shadows of old trees, and the tunnel flowed past slopes, dams and paddocks that flung them up a smaller track. The only place to go from the end of this puny track was the paddock of bulls and cows, or the open universe in the night-sky that made the bulls and cows.

She was right also about the shack. Castle's cottage lay afloat like a worn-out space taxi glowing at the edge of the stars. The glow was modest, muted, as if lit by a plate of candles. The windows were only thinly buttered with light. Spills of faded gold came out from cracks in the walls, the porch was pollen-coloured, the side entrance threw a creamy slab of light onto the dirt, so the whole knocked-together structure rumbled about in a rough circle of glowing yellows.

It also said bits about Catherine and Castle. They had a quiet flow with one another, they never spoke normally, or high, or loudly. They had the gentle exchanges, always. Why, nobody knew. Even Remple didn't know.

Set against a blacksoft earth and a deep sky of endless stars, the old spaceship's candle-flicker gave off warmth and welcome, and a promise of good times and generous conversation. No direct neighbours existed. The American couple, Dexter and Lou Pepper, were a mile away. The only nearby neighbour was the glow of the two golden dots of the dairy farmer's place on the far rise, but the farmer's joint was just another proper house, not a creaky spacepod tied with string to a post in a distant corner of the galaxy of memory.

Castle's was a remote place that sprung and unsprung the mind. Over the last fifty feet, as you pulled up, you could make out the squeezing and expanding gaining a final hold on senses of brick and steel. In the glowing windows slow time coiled itself round to warp away the nightmind into the very best memories. Above the dam of black yabbies big as a bottle, the night-sky uncoiled easily, down here space ran off into the deepest night that Catherine knew.

What she always did on the first night was to walk off the verandah and into the paddock and then across towards the forest. The depth of the sky here stunned a bumbler into silence, and the others at the house would be obliged to step outside to search for Catherine as a duty of care and love. But by then half her mind had seeped away up to the place where the cattle had been made. It always took another hour until she collected the evaporated halfself back. Then she came to the evening with the rest of the party, bumbling up the rotting back steps with her eyes fucked away into the universe nicely on wonder and mystery, that's why Catherine called those last few miles a revelation, good reason if you ask a humble box like me or Oxley or Flattie.

But not if you ask Bakks, Bakks thought she was a peanut. Ripe target at which to throw ratsblood sucker hailme-hailme Inch and his crew of deadbeat smellbombs, Centimetre, Millimetre, Metre, Foot, Mile, Furlong, Kilometre, Lightyear and Yard, tho Yard the puppybox only pretended to be a deadbeat counterfeiter. O yes, Catherine was just the right powderbox to force into the service of destroying Remple&Patsy.

A Margaret River sky was the one view that helped Catherine to be drawn to the Reverberations. Even tho she could see only stars and a night-sky, she knew she was being sieved, aerated, expanded. The sensation would stay with her days later, pestering brick and steel certainties, beautiful stuff for king Bakks& crew, or as Inch would say, 'Simply magnetic for my vividity.' For days and days the smallest of oddball perceptions would caress memories. Memories would create questions. And the opposite, the day-sky, without the slightest movement, would just suck away the curiosity right off the top of a bright ocean, blue with south-western clean, remote clean. In a day-sky she'd forget. Dis-remember all that powerful revelatory mileage of the mind. Call it freshness, a clean start to a new day. The give and take. Bakks preferring the taking, yelling orders of crumpled logic at a herd of cow-grass-milk logic cardboard deadbeats.

To the Pine Trees at Cottesloe

Remple also liked that road a lot, winding away from the world, called it his favourite road. He had travelled the world but he loved this the best, driving the final moments down to his cousin's place at Yelverton. Remple had quietly left the city office, without going home to Cottesloe, and he'd got out of Perth at three, before the traffic, swung up Beaufort Street to the Bombay Plaza to collect Castle's Pavarotti CD, and soon he was pleasantly on his way down Kwinana Freeway passing South Perth by three-thirty.

In his office on the thirty-second floor, he kept a powerful telescope at the window next to Flattie. The telescope was so powerful he could see into rooms in South Perth across the river. Beside the telescope was a monitor. This was on feeds of his choice, today's was from his balcony at home in Cottesloe. The balcony was fitted with six cameras. It was a very large balcony, the same size again as the whole house, a broad balcony where he held parties and business occasions.

There was a business occasion occurring on the balcony now, and he was pleased that he was not there for it, but instead had left the occasion in the capable hands of his marketing manager from Broome, Ruby Schwartz. He switched on the monitor, and he could see and hear the party. Around a couple of dozen IT people, an event organised by Ruby. Remple lingered, Ruby was working the suppliers, it all looked fine.

He switched off the monitor. He took the elevator to the carpark and cruised out of the city feeling pleased he could get away to Castle's Bombay Plaza without any reason to go via the house, and picking up the CD from the Bombay Plaza first was fine, Mount Lawley was only a fifteen-minute loop.

Flattie, on a sideboard by the window in the office, had attended all of Remple's office meetings since he'd brought her into the city from home in Cottesloe where she first went after the nizam's auction in '94.

The Bombay Plaza

This was Castle's studio in Perth. It had the worst parties Remple ever saw and so he hardly ever got there. But everyone else got there. All the powderboxes who ever went to the Bombay Plaza were your greatest custodians dear butterfly. They stayed all night and stole mornings and wreaked havoc upon afternoons, shit happened at the Bombay Plaza, verbal stoushes, love happened, everyone's loves and fights, all Castle's friends had their shit and sugar at the Bombay Plaza. They were the best of parties but Remple thought they were the worst of parties.

Castle dubbed it the Bombay Plaza because it looked like a sour old hotel in Bombay trying hard to be a sweet young boutique hotel in London, plus it was in Mount Lawley's second best street of extreme orderliness, road, tree, pavement, more pavement, seventies building, bad carpark out the back, gates of so much bad metal, so Bombay Plaza seemed right. The artists and writers there were the best ever, and they took the Bombay Plaza to their hearts, loving it every week in one form or another.

It had no furniture, empty. Just Oliver's handmade solid jarrah table, a few chairs, a big old set of drawers for drawings swapped with a good friend for a painting. And yet it was the best place Castle ever lived in. They all loved its fifties feel. Only the furniture of the imagination was allowed into the Bombay Plaza. They had the furies in there, they were allowed the extremities of their minds in there, one night a woman brought around her lover and he had wept deeply coz his friend had gone. It was a good place to put a flavour on your shoulder, you were allowed to do what you wanted to do. If you chose to hurt someone verbally you were bailed up or thrown out.

Jim the playwright felt so good at the Plaza he read from his newly written plays there on Castle's invitation. To audiences, to maybe five, maybe ten. He felt so good he told the worst stories about his adventures. Aplomb being Jim's great drug, he told stuff to Plaza powderboxes they didn't even wish to know, he was one bad guy. The dawn second equator would be arriving, and he would go blap awake on the chair he had fallen asleep in. 'Did I tell you about . . . ?' And he had.

Jim the playwright put in three hundred appearances at the Bombay Plaza. He was loved and celebrated.

The Plaza made other powderboxes go nuts too. A German guy ran in one night. Husgard the musician. He was desperate. He'd fallen for a piano player. He had seen her bending over somewhere and his brain just blew up. After that he got to the Plaza to settle what he would do about it. He got the lift up and he was like a shower, sweating like water, and his eyes burned at Castle: What should I do?

The Plaza also had powderboxes drifting in whom nobody knew well. Another very big but very dark night the buzzer went was when Castle's great friend Barbara had died. It was buzzed by a guy who didn't know Barbara well. He took the lift, he rounded smiling into the door. He laughed his way through the night. Half a dozen present, grief-stricken. A sombre night. Later, Barbara's brother nearly hit the guy. Barbara's brother nearly used every fibre in his body to either hit Castle or hit the stupid loud guy.

Barbara had not been a big visitor to the Plaza because by then she'd been going with her new guy, and the new guy was going to get it in the neck by her brother too.

Everyone had something at the Plaza. Castle had a lot at the Plaza.

Viewings, showings, parties, laughter, fixing the world with the impulse to create, these were the Plaza passports to feeling good.

The Tree of Stars

When Remple arrived at Castle's place in Yelverton the others said Catherine was still out there somewhere. They were on the back verandah with drinks.

'Did you bring the Pavarotti CD?' Castle asked in a laid-back hello. Puppybox Yard enjoyed his laid-back hup two three down here, causing powderboxes to feel like hammocks, secretly opposing the haranguage and pranguage of the smellbomb pongsters even tho Yard was in theory a part of that disgusting crew. Yard believed the entire cape was his patch, keep it nice, keep it smooth, gotta mix, have fun. Yard never, ever let on to Bakks that the cape was quietly being serviced by a groovy ol puppybox.

'Certainly did.' Remple went across the paddock to search first, leaving the rest of the party behind to talk their shallow shit about loss pleased Remple right to the core. Laura, Castle, Catherine, Hong Thet, Jack and Dave, tho Remple quickly knew it was only Laura talking about loss.

Remple knew Dave was always keen to make grim paintings, so Dave had a leaning when in conversation to enjoy talking about loss. Catherine liked talking about loss, but not in the clipped simplistic way that Laura and Dave were doing tonight.

Remple stepped down by the back door, easing across Castle's yard of rusted machinery, through the open shed, ducking the ceiling of hanging Castle-goods, ducking another ceiling of hanging domes that were maquettes for the university buildings in Broome. He strolled into the night for a while. When the shack, and its scrappy glow, lay in the distance he stopped to scan the smooth darkness. The spaceroom out here lay so still he could see nothing move. He saw a wall of forest on the far rise.

A sheet of faint moonlight flowed over the paddock, and the air's heatwave warmth added to the stillness. The entire week had been engulfed in a heatwave, and at night the heat tended to ease off, but remained present. It gave everything a vertical poise, no leaf jumped in a breath, no sound rode by on a drift of air, so he joined the mood and strolled in silence, walking as lightly as he could. When he found Catherine, he stopped. She lay face up on a grassy incline behind the dam. He walked over and they lay together side by side. Remple asked his sister what she thought of Nile Goodsir the stockbroker.

'Nile Goodsir?' She needed to confirm. Remple had not asked about Nile before tonight. 'Nile's all right. Is he liquid? He's liquid but not that liquid. He tried to beat me down on one of Jack's new Bahamas paintings. Wanted a thousand off, so I told him: "Nile, you are a fool just like all moderately rich, single, male forty year old fools, because you went and bought a top of the range new Merc when you could've got a perfectly good Honda and with the difference placed your filthy hands on five new paintings from a hot London artist."'

'You spoke to him like that?'

'I did.'

'How'd he respond?'

'He said, "But Catherine, the Merc was a good deal, a very good deal." And then he laughed, he loves it, dirty talk, he paid the full price for the painting, one of Jack's. Yeah, I suppose Nile's okay, but, as Kee would say, Nile's a caperologist.'

'Was Jack's painting any good?'

'It's Kee's boat, and yes it's a fantastic painting, he's already done three.'

'Did you offer Greg one?'

'Greg Howlett?'

'Yeah.'

'Greg bought a Merc, and two of Jack's boat pictures.'

'I've been trying,' Remple said, 'to phone Kee on the mobile I gave him, we open the university in three weeks. Have you heard from him at all?'

'I haven't. You'll never get that man to use a phone, Remple, ever, you're aware of that, I don't know why you persist in trying.'

'Well maybe one day it'll just click with him, the new world that we've all stumbled upon lately.'

'Good luck to you,' Catherine said.

'It was good to see him in Georgetown.'

'Certainly was.'

'The day we walked up to him for the first time when we found him all those years ago in the nineties, I was nervous, nervous and just turned nineteen at that bar in Cartagena, but what a fantastic birthday present. But I've never really asked you about that moment: Were you nervous?'

'I was shaking like a leaf,' Catherine said.

'No, I mean when we were walking towards his boat, I mean before you broke down.'

'I was shaking, I was almost hyperventilating.'

The Tree of Appreciation

Catherine and Remple first found Kieran Leeft, Sunrise Sunset, many years after their grandmother's rescue. They applied every resource to the search for the guy that their grandmother had told them about. But even then they didn't fully appreciate his resourceful nature until years later again. The backbone of the earlier efforts had given them hope: you needed only to make enquiries at the ports and harbours, and besides, the more likely region to find him, than the Golfo de Valencia region, was the coast of the south.

Going by his usual habits, he should not have gone ashore that day, so Remple and Catherine had got lucky. It was a hot, plenteous morning, nearly midday. Filled with boats arriving, produce moving around, carts being loaded, vans and trucks moving easily in the crowds, the heat had come across the harbour from the oven-baking plains that ran up to Cartagena. There was no breeze, and the harbour was flat as oil. An enormous haze had settled on the gulf, and the two headlands in the distance were visible barely. In summer heatwaves he avoided the ports. But today he was in. At Almeria.

The Sierra Nevada behind Almeria kept the port hot, capturing the heatwave and causing it to sit in one place, inviting it to stay. He would leave in an hour when the electrician had fixed the depth sounder. He would sail across to the Spanish enclave in Morocco, Ceuta, an overnight trip of fifteen hours, arrive at three in the afternoon, and stay offshore for a week watching the monoliths enter the Mediterranean in stately lines of trade. He would not visit Ceuta, he did not like the razor wire surrounding the town.

His old friend Pedro came down to the wharf. Pedro said, 'Kieran, a man and a woman are asking for you up in town.'

'For me? Where are they from?' Thinking vaguely that they might be a much older Ellie and a much older colonel come down from the old hacienda, maybe the colonel from Scotland, the days of half a lifetime ago. But then he realised it might be Rosa and her father Mendoza.

'Australia,' Pedro said.

'They have the wrong guy, I do not know anyone from Australia.'

'They said your name.'

'Who are they?'

'Don't ask me, how should I know? They are at the tavern. Want me to send them down?'

'Yeah, okay.'

Catherine walked up the jetty first, followed by Remple.

They spoke in Spanish.

'My name is Catherine Fekdin, this is my brother Remple.'

'Señorita, señor,' the fifty-seven year old said.

Catherine began to smile, she tried to smile, held out her hand for a handshake, but Kieran saw clearly that tears welled up in her eyes, and then rolled down, and she was unable to smile.

Kieran waited so that the young woman could regain her composure, but she continued to weep quietly, and then openly, and then she was sobbing, and Remple led her to the steps where she sat with her head in her hands.

'We have just come from the mountains near Hoyos,' Remple said, 'we heard you had travelled there, and that you were still there, but a man in a small temple told us that a sailor from the south—we presume he meant you—had left two weeks ago.'

'I was in Hoyos last month. I heard that a Scottish man I once knew had gone there and made a Hindu temple in a small mountain hut. But he was no longer there, he had left Hoyos long ago, twelve years ago, went back to Scotland they said.'

The trip had been Kieran's one and only journey into a hinterland beyond a port, beyond a coast, beyond a lagoon. After he returned to his boat, he never again had the inclination to take any journey inland anywhere, he was at his happiest on the coast or the open ocean.

But it was another contribution from colonel David. Far from the sea dear butterfly, in the mountains just a few miles north of the town of Hoyos, on the border with Portugal, the remnants of western Spain begin to disappear. It is a quiet place, far away from Portugal, far away from Spain. The border is agreed to, but the more inaccessible depths of the powderboxes couldn't care less. And when you drift along these mountain ridges for a few miles you can commence the descent, a cruise down into the Portuguese valley where the last remnants of eastern Portugal are also flimsy. The manner in which they feed upon memory here resembles no Portuguese manner, no Spanish manner. In this way the place is fertile. All borders are fertile like the place north of Hoyos. Here the old habits, deep inside powderboxes, are given much more love and appreciation than the agreed upon ground where a Spanish meal might end and a Portuguese meal might begin. Here in the mountains behind Hoyos the powderboxes have leaked and shared in different timerooms and hallways than they have in Spain or Portugal, and so David's Maheesha was able to become bright for just under a year. Today, almost half a century later, along this mountain ridge, eight powderboxes still admire, fear and worship Maheesha the buffalo demon.

'Renata Rodrigo,' Remple said to Kee, 'was our grandmother.'

Kee recalled no Renata Rodrigo.

'The girl you picked up near Valencia in '56.'

'Ah, si, si. She is well?'

'She passed away.'

'I am sorry to hear that, my condolences.'

'Thankyou.'

Remple and Catherine were staying at a fine hotel. Remple invited Kieran to the hotel for dinner, but they went instead to

Pedro's favourite place, the old Villacarillo up the hill. It was past the town and closer to the scum of the factories. It wasn't until late that evening Kieran discovered he had become a rich myth inside the Fekdin clan, that he'd been affectionately referred to as Keep Left by matriarch Renata. 'Keep Left, he's the guy that saved me from my father.'

Before flying back to Perth, Remple gave Kieran his card. Kieran placed the card in the safest place on his boat, inside a secure turtleshell box beside the steering wheel, a box we at The Exchange call Montague. From that day onwards in 1993, Remple and Catherine visited Kieran around once a year, in various places around the equatorial Atlantic.

In the week of the heatwave and the two visitors from Australia, Kieran had delayed his journey, but when Renata's two grandchildren had flown away to Australia, Kieran set off for Ceuta. That night, during the journey across to Africa to the Spanish town, he felt a loss at knowing the girl had passed away, he had known the girl only a week, less than a week, very long ago. But he felt a pang of sorrow resurging again and again during the trip under the stars to Ceuta. He discovered he liked her grandchildren very much, they were competent, tough and kind. They both had confidence, but it was not an infantile confidence that the land-dwelling adults of today have developed. They seemed to have just the right tide of gentleness it takes to be free with life. They were also, he thought again and again out under the stars that night, no fools when it comes to locating a guy like me, no address, no house, no papers, no phone. What did they do for a living? Well, that's what he liked the most: they didn't quite say. The brother seemed to be a businessman, the sister seemed to be involved with pictures, art pictures. The brother's card was safely put away inside the box at the steering wheel, it was one card Kieran decided to cherish for a while.

What amazed him was that they had spent more than a decade in trying to locate him, since they were kids.

That night crossing to Ceuta he realised he had been known as Keep Left, among others, for a long long time. Behind him the second equator was beginning to arrive across the eastern Mediterranean, thinly lighting the sky that hung behind the boat. He made a jug of coffee, and within half an hour the sun came rising up out of the sea. To him it meant there was now just nine hours to Ceuta. He threw a line out. He'd prefer a fresh breakfast instead of the tins he packed in Almeria.

Jack at the Ocean at Yelverton, Summer 2009

Jack swam in only one proper ocean his whole life. The grand banks of Exuma with Kee and Castle. Not that this would matter. But in Jack's case the lack of experience mattered a lot because the worrying thing is he had no ding-dong understanding of the ocean's basic magic, its powers of alchemy, the gigantic ability to convert crap into turquoise clarity. Endless kinds of crap into a singular blue clarity. Into crystal-clear soup. A soup that is at the root of all life, remade from having travelled through the millions of chemical processes that work tirelessly day and night. London painter arrogarnta who went for a snorkel in the shit of Sheerness at the mouth of the Thames still had work to do, stuff to taste, walks to take, swims to take, before he could truly morph into Jack Verandah from Yelverton South. This mildly worrying lack of understanding diminished his own powers of arrogarnta splatter upon the canvas: peering into alchemy everywhere, well that's a vital foundation for dealing in transformation. What good is a painter if he can't deal in transformation? A painter ignoring this kind of stuff would be just what Jack is, a painter arrogarnta. But not to worry, he'd got the taste, ol Jack Black. The grand banks around Greater Exuma had given him the first taste of the ocean. A glimpse at the larger notion. The ability for fermenting all the poisons of the world into a sparkling broth for life.

Castle closed the bookshop at five, and then came back to the shack. He showed Jack a path that crossed the forest to the coast. They went for a swim. The sunshine was giving the water a sparkle, and the temperature of the water seemed very cold compared to the tropical warmth of the water in the Bahamas.

They snorkelled to the first reef, out to where the side fell away twenty feet deep to the sandy floor, and the visibility all around them was stunning. They snorkelled for twenty minutes before going ashore.

'That's bloody amazing out there, it's even clearer than Exuma,' Jack said as he sat on the hot sand.

'There's a lot of good spots further up and down the coast,' said Castle, 'from Yallingup right down to the back of Augusta, we'll check them out over the next few days, Remple likes snorkelling in the lagoon at Sugarloaf Rock, but he's mad, I wouldn't snorkel in that lagoon if you handed me a hundred bucks.'

'What was that mound on the floor that the crabs and fish were eating?'

'Looked to me like a long-deceased kingfish, or one huge, huge salmon.'

'That's what I like about the ocean, it just gets right into the organics, and right down to the microbes it just cleans everything up, it's a bigtime global cleaner, but I dunno if we're fucking it up.'

'I went for a snorkelling fortnight around Bali last year, and that place is wrecked, the water is filthy, we're recklessly using the ocean as a rubbish tip, all over the world, just like the Indonesians. I believe the balance is finally at hand, we're not too far from killing the ocean. Bali's Governor is really upset about it. Mister Made Pastika, he's an active guy, he's trying hard to stop everyone up there using the ocean as a rubbish tip, but he has a hard time changing old habits. Mister Made Pastika is a kind of hero up there round Bali, but going right up against the innate habit to rubbish everything in sight.'

They strolled back along the forest path to the spacepod. Remple had arrived from a quick run to a winery where he'd bought supplies for the week, a few cases of red and white. Jack helped him put the white wine away into a large fridge in the shed.

Castle sat at the dam with Catherine, and they could be heard across the yard, not what they said, but it was in that other tone that nobody could quite understand, including Remple, that quiet coolness, a virtually expressionless flatness. Delivery was flat, acceptance was flat, yet they understood everything, the two cousins, Catherine and Castle.

Hong Arrives

At Castle's spaceship, Hong Thet had arrived at last, the plumber who gave up plumbing to take up sculpture. His stock in trade was to place perspex pods of water the size of bricks on the walls of Catherine's gallery. He exhibited as Hong Thet Double-O-Four 'because Ian Fleming stole double O seven.' His pods of water were always diptychs. One would be labelled Natural Water, the other labelled Intellectual Water.

Natural Water–Intellectual Water.

NW–IW One

NW–IW Two

and so on, he never deviated from that numeric catalogue style, and was now up to NW–IW Fifty-Two. These days he made a good living from it.

He wanted to stress the elegant technological advancements that had come to humanity for purifying water. He'd started the diptychs a couple of years back by placing Swan River water pods beside distilled water. Then dishwater beside Evian, then drainwater beside desalinated water, sewerage beside treated effluent: in this way the comparisons grew from his let-loose plumber's imagination. Don't hit me for where he might have got the idea of plastic boxes, not me. For me, water and boxes together, yuk. For cardboard Bakks, the combination, it's a nightmare bigtime, so whether Bakks chose to fuck with Hong's powderbox or whether Bakks shot away in the other direction from panic I don't know.

Hong Thet made the claim that his work was about optimism, and certainly his own philosophy collided badly with Jack Black's philosophy because Hong felt Jack's take on consumption and pollution that he had gleaned from Jack up in Perth was negative and pessimistic.

'Jack has no faith in the intellect's ability to reach for technological creativity, no faith that we can fix this ugly stuff, I reckon we can, Jack reckons we can't.' Hong could be razor-minded, but he was shy chronically, softly spoken, and he never called himself an artist. He always insisted he was a plumber. The only thing he was cool on calling himself was Hong Thet Double-O-Four.

The perspex pods started out as the brick-sized perspex compacts, and then the pods developed into banana-box-sized perspex pods in the shape of prawns, dogs and goats. Then came Hong's move away from box-shaped pods, and onwards to the perspex teapots, to the whales, submarines, rocket launchers, beards, lips, breasts, vulva, penises, bombs, babies, roses and guitars. He'd just completed back in Perth what he called a penal institution, a small perspex building the size of a suitcase, and a vaginal institution. When Hong walked in he saw Castle Fekdin and Laura Glass-Darlington arguing, so he walked out again and went for a swim under the stars in the dark dam of inkblack yabbies feeding under his floating feet, eating the rich oozing dirt. He swam slowly round the dam, and the notion flipped into his mind that he'd have to somehow make a pod for the dam, large, held off the water's surface out in the centre, high, maybe ten feet off the surface.

That night they sat around a big old wooden table between the verandah and the dam sharing a couple of bottles of Margaret River wines, glugging up their powderboxes into mudboxes of bent perception, enjoying a pleasant evening under the stars. Laura had forgotten me outside, on the table on the Arrivals Verandah. Oxley lay quietly up the end of the verandah, a very long distance from Dorking in Surrey.

After an hour Castle stood up at the table. 'Well, time for a bit of poaching.'

'He's going to spring you one of these days,' Remple said.

'Aww ... he loves me.'

Castle strolled around the far side of the dam, he was a little unsteady, but he got there. He lay down his wine glass. He untied a rope on the shore. The shore was a blunt drop of dirt and grass to the water, maybe a foot high. Castle pulled in the rope and brought up a basket from the depths. He walked further along the shore and dragged in another basket, this time with one hand, not bothering to lay down the glass of wine. But in reaching down to pull the basket from the water, his feet began to push away a slab of dirt from the grass, and it started to crumble like stale cake. He went into the dam, vertically sinking, mouth tightly closed with the effort, cheeks out like balloons, he was scudding, rather than falling, and within a few seconds he was in the black water, holding up the wine with one hand and thrashing around with the basket hand.

Jack jumped off the chair. When he got there Castle was already climbing out of the dam, his torso slumped on the dirt and grass apron, but the rest of him was still in the dam. Jack grabbed his arm.

'Keep your head down!' Castle said.

'What?'

'Keep your head down, the farmer's lights're on, keep your fekking head down.'

They carried the baskets to the shed. Castle emptied the baskets into a plastic tub of water. Under the lights of the shed Jack saw his first black lobsters, three jetblack freshwater crayfish.

'Yabbies,' Castle said.

'He farms the creatures? In that one little pond?'

'Not really, they live all over the place, they walk from dam to dam, stream to stream, they migrate to wherever it's good, sometimes I've seen em moving along the grass under a herd of cows.'

A Quiet Question Late at Night on Dancing Balls

When the powderboxes stumbled away to sleep it was late, and the creaky spacepod lay in all but total darkness. In the sweet Yelverton moonlight me an Oxley discussed a bit of hup two three. The heatwave night was truly quiet, glowing warmth, and stillness like I've never seen, not even the stillness of a hot night back at the hacienda on the shoulder of the Golfo de Valencia, or on the upper balcony of the Miles Banford house in Calcutta.

'Oxley?'

'Hullo Bobbo, how was Edinburgh?'

'Quite nice, reminded me of the old times when I kept safe the songs written on the old exercise book for dancer aunt Lee across the way in Glasgow, same crispy air, tries hard to buckle the teak. Booksmeller also went to visit Pennant Hills, where colonel David was born, nifty that was, I had made a circle, a David Darlington circle after nearly ninety years. How about you? Been well I take it, lurking down here in Yelverton?'

'Castle's a right nice fellow, gets a sprinkling of visitors from Perth, lots of picnics. What about you, how's the new owner?'

'She's good, nutty but good. Gave her a bit of hup two three. For the show about colonel David and his Maheesha fixation, she even managed to lace the show with traces of sex in the Calcutta hills, good ol grubby sex too.'

'Well done Bobbo.'

'Seen the moon tonight, Oxley, the halfmoon?'

'Yes I have. That means ratsblood Inch is up to no good. Has he killed off Bakks yet?'

'Not yet. Let them come, there's no way they'll fuck up this Castle powderbox, do you think?'

'They can try, dear Bobbo, but Castle's pretty much immune to those dreary counterfeiters. Haven't blundered into Inch lately. I suppose Inch still thinks of us proper wooden traders as slaves, does he?'

'Yep.'

'What a funny little cardboard chap. Made of squished up mashed up woodchips bathed in acid.'

'It's a peaceful night tonight I gotta say.'

'It's very often like that around here, in this corner of the cape, Yelverton South, Castle calls it, a world away from the road to Margaret River, peaceful, quiet, not a worry in the world.'

'Why does the halfmoon have a straight line when, in fact, the sun and the earth that make the shadow are round, Oxley?'

'Don't really know that one.'

'Why in the heck does the moon's second equator look straight as a ruler out of Colchester's workshop? I mean, why would a straight line evolve out of three round things? How round, straight line.'

'Your hippy pals at NASA might explain it by saying the straight line on the moon is just a moment in hasty-paste, a night later the bulb is back, the curve.'

Oxley might be right. My hippy friends at NASA would say that the straight line occurs for a blip only, day three the bulb is back, the curve. But why would a round ball cast a straight lined shadow like a ruler from school? How the heck can a ball be a spine, especially in the torchlight of space? Three shifting globes, dancing balls, dancing roundies, playing for a cut in space like a wood ruler in school. Ding-dong how's the time.

'Do you think we could work the moon one day, Oxley?'

'I prefer grass, dear Bobbo, I have tried picnics without grass, in that horrid windowless basement.'

Reconstituted Wooden Slats

That night I asked Oxley about another set of boxes.

'What happened to the Schweppes clan, Oxley?'

Oxley: 'The Schweppes boxes from the Canberra region?'

'Yeah. They don't seem to be active in The Exchange any more.'

'They were cut up.'

'What?!'

'Sawn up into slats. In the early nineties.'

'Yuk!'

'Oh they're still together, they've become that big artwork by Rosalie Gascoigne, the Monaro landscape, they've become her memories of life in the Monaro landscape. She cut them up and then reset them on the wall to recall the rolling Monaro undulations, smart clever girl that Rosalie, I'd say she had the glow, the magic, a lotta give anyway, probably even knew where The Exchange was located.'

'I'd rather hup two three the memories, than become sawn up into memories.'

'Me too, dear Bobbo.'

Crashing into the Surf and the Dam

The next morning Castle said, 'I am sick to death of artists, browbeaten little fucks that they are.'

He gazed into the distance from his verandah, and then added, 'Perform the best of favours and they'll still complain like endless talk-machines, thankless little fucks. Plus they can't actually see things; if I hold out a diamond they'll look down at my hand only to declare it's a dogshit I'm handing over. They're so fucked around by everyone, so kicked and damaged by their dealers and friends and couriers and bureaucrats and booze shop owners, and by other artists, that they become feral and stupid and blind, and so they develop this absolutely bullshit form of power arrogance to compensate, wandering around the town bumping into dogshits and calling themselves artists.'

This, from gentle Castle. Something must've ding-dong taken place.

Everyone else had gone into town for breakfast. Sitting on a worn-out chair next to him, Hong Thet said, 'This definition, of the artist, does it include me?'

'No, it doesn't. Perhaps you indeed are, after all, as you keep saying, a plumber rather than an artist.'

'You've given me many favours Castle, and I appreciate them. Obviously I should state this. Perhaps it's the drought, the drought's making everyone move nearer to their animal instincts, so they forget their civility.'

'Maybe,' Castle said, 'maybe.'

The country was in the grip of a drought, the worst in a hundred years, and we boxes can't help, for the only box that carries water is one of those other plastic ding-dongs with a handle, too small anyway to splash at a drought.

But far away, three thousand kilometres away, up north, in the monsoon plains, bear witness dear butterfly, the country indeed yes sir was flooded, and the waters poured off the escarpment, wasted into the ocean in torrents broad enough to sustain a hundred cities. Also, the Australian monsoon arrived every year, so that no drought existed in the north, ever. The Dry season existed, but the monsoon always came, delivering billions of tonnes of fresh water. Look, I'm not exactly partial to water, but imaginative people down round Castle's district felt a pretty good thing is a pretty good thing.

They felt that with this ding-dong monsoon you could build four or five pipelines from the north to the south, for farmers and for city folk. And even tho they understood it would need to be one humungous and complex project costing billions, they also knew the nation's walletkeepers in Canberra had already decided to spend the billions on fighter jets instead.

The same call, round the district: you could have a pipeline, but you chose bombers. You could have a big, round, major pipeline, and a huge fleet of water-bomb choppers, but you chose fighter bombers instead. So the imaginative little visionaries around the rolling wine district made do with heaping shit on the federal politicians.

Only Remple kept the idea alive as a practical project, he'd formed the Southern Pipeline Working Group so that newspaper articles on the subject kept appearing nationally every so often, keeping alive the notion of a drought-free Australia, a Vision Remple.

Hong Thet was one of those who felt the Remple pipeline was a suitable idea, not a dreamy concept. Just plumbing, only big, of a scale beyond formal economic safety. Hong liked the fact that Remple had made good friends with the political top brass, first-name terms, drinks, parties, commemorations, employment initiatives, working groups, Remple gave and gave, the top brass liked Remple very much. Hong had known Remple for going on ten years, and he liked the fact that Remple was a can-do high-flying executive because that way Remple could tell the truth from the spinfest. But Hong remained deeply confused by the implosion of common sense surrounding Australia's claim to being a first-world gig.

'What amazes me with the pipeline is this,' Hong said. 'It's such a good thing, straight-minded, maybe difficult, but full of common sense; up there it's flooded, down here it's a bad drought, and the pipeline is just such a normal notion, and yet it's them that think we are stupid. Except for Barnett. Are not the politicians supposed to come up with common sense, like Colin Barnett did? The world's driest continent ought to be the proud owner of the world's largest pipeline.'

Remple strolled round the side of the verandah. He'd been for a snorkel at the Sugarloaf Rock lagoon. 'Are we talking water again?'

'Yeah, it's just stupid.' Hong said.

'It is less about being stupid and more about a lot of chiefs. But the time will come, we've already got small pipelines here and there, in places where the chiefs had their own patch and didn't have to take in too many meetings to get it done. In Victoria they're replacing the irrigation channels with the new Wimmera Mallee pipeline system. A seventy kilometre pipe is going into Melbourne from the Goulburn River. Ballarat has a pipe from a reservoir in Bendigo. In Queensland a proposed pipe for a hundred and thirty kilometres from the Burdekin River to Bowen just at the northern tip of the Whitsunday island Gloucester. Then the south-east pipe grid for Toowoomba and Brisbane.'

'Is this stuff all now, I mean recent?'

'Yep. It's happening, the pipeline mentality, but the big three mamas have to be from the north downwards, down the west, down the centre, and down the east. The South Australian government priced a pipe from the Ord River to Adelaide at ten billion dollars, the esteemed prime minister Rudd handed that out last year in a single sweep, to individual citizens and not to a pipeline. These days, they could just print thirty billion dollars and presto, three big-mama pipelines.'

'Excellent idea.'

'It is, and it isn't. Printing money ought to be the last option, printing extra money is a kind of dangerous idea.'

'Why? I mean, who cares where the money comes from for such a great national superstructure?'

'Increasing money supply would have a negative effect. It would devalue everything in sight, if Australia printed seven hundred billion dollars tomorrow, your coffee would cost ten, twenty bucks, that's how it is with splashing money around, that's the problem, but for a pipeline, I'd say okay to printing money for it.'

'I went to see my cousin in Adelaide last year, we went to the Coorong, what a fucking mess, no amount of money is going to fix the Coorong. They could print seven hundred billion every day for the whole winter season and it still wouldn't fix the Coorong.'

'Well, one of Australia's most childish fights is going on between those three states, not over here, but over there, all the water chiefs keep on dunking each other's heads into the Murray. South Australia, Victoria and New South Wales are in a constant battle over the Murray River, which of course is no longer a river, it's just a muddy drain, fighting over it like three monkeys ripping apart a dried fig.'

'Howard brought in some pretty good rules for the Murray didn't he?'

'Howard, hell, don't talk to me about Howard. He ran the country like a tight bright shop, the way people like me run a business, he ran Australia at high profits, he had well over a decade of massive profits to give the nation a serious pipeline. But in the end the sheen of the statesman gave way to expose just another political operative, the smartest political animal the federation has ever seen apart from Keating. I was talking to Colin Barnett last week, and he's very supportive of the Southern Pipeline Group, even though everyone rubbished Colin's idea at the election. The only guy that had the intelligence, and the power, to whip the crap out of all those VIP buzzing-bee water chiefs was John Howard, and he didn't.'

'Who are these water chiefs you keep talking about, Remple?' Hong asked. Hong knew everything about national plumbing, but he was more detailed about it in WA.

'You mean the Murray?'

'Yeah, who are they, these chiefs over by the Murray? You mean the water ministers?'

'And the rest. There's a water chief around every corner in those three states. Those three monkeys are constantly mounting constitutional challenges to water entitlements, I mean they're fighting over this, this, drainpipe let's be clear. Even the premiers can't stay out of it, but behind the premiers there's a big herd of other water chieftains. The three irrigation council chiefs, they bang on all the time. The three water ministers, they carry on and on. And then another two hundred in bureaucracies filling up the paperwork to eventually do nothing more than buying, buying water, two billion dollars they want to spend buying entitlements to a drain. The more this gets out the more the big-mama pipelines will seem nice.'

'How come no-one's done anything about building the big mamas? Over the decades I mean.'

'Because it concerns only agriculture, and in Canberra the successive prime ministers have always known that agriculture is just three percent of GDP, so they just don't care about a pipeline. It's the same as your theory about the bushfire choppers, they could have a seriously awesome fleet of a thousand bushfire choppers, but they don't.'

'It's just political crap,' Hong said.

'What do you mean?'

'Political power, it's only crap, it's a false, untrue power; political power is just a fantasy, a mirage, there's no true power in a political position.'

'Political power a mirage? Maybe. If you mean a mirage as a paradox, then yeah. Of all the various forms of potency, of power, I guess political power is the most childish, it always moves over the landscape of our lives as the most infantile of all the forms of power. It tries to stick its fingers into everything, and then walks out the back door looking for something else to stick its fingers into.'

'They pretend to serve, they say they serve.'

'That they do, but they don't serve, they rule.'

'Jesus you guys, let's go for a swim, don't you guys get the time to talk about all this stuff back in Perth where it belongs? Let's go for a swim,' Castle mumbled.

'I've just been,' Remple said, 'I'm going to stay and have a coffee.'

'Did you go to the Sugarloaf Rock lagoon again?' Castle said.

'Yep.'

'You're mad.'

'I'll come for a swim,' Hong said. 'Should we go for a proper body surf instead?'

'Very good idea, let's go.'

As Hong and Castle walked up the side to the front gate Remple called out.

'Hong.'

'Yeah?'

'I hope you're still up for making the big mangrove pods for the assembly hall at the university.'

'Yep, absolutely. I faxed the sketches off to your office yesterday.'

'Didn't see them, I left early.'

'That's fine, I brought copies down for you to look at. See you in an hour.'

Remple also had another arm to his water project dear butterfly, giving potential to trees, shrubs, vines, grasses, flowers and nectar. The Queensland Flood Survey Group. The group was constantly conducting ground and satellite surveys of where and how the lay of the land could most easily deliver a flood, not to the Coral Sea off Queensland's coast, but instead to the dry inland area that is shared by Queensland, South Australia and New South Wales.

With strategically placed canals the floodwater could be guided, led, delivered to a region where, for many generations, the cycle of boom–bust drought had brought heartache, pain and suicide. The Queensland Flood Survey Group had twenty-two volunteers, surveyors and engineers. The group also owned a plane. So, with every major flood they gained major information about the landscape's shape, contour and disposition to water flow.

La Niña, El Niño, it wouldn't matter, flood years or drought years, it simply wouldn't matter. Because the folk whose livelihood was essentially to grow a very large portion of Australia's food would be given the chance to live better lives, which is what they deserve out of a federation, but which is denied again and again by the federation owing to inaction from both left and right, so-called nation-building had gone out of fashion with that crimpo Thatcher. Remple could not see why it could not be done. Remple, a hup two ninety powderbox.

Or, at the very least, he was keen on producing a comprehensive survey of how to coax the floods south. Even Qadaffi had turned large areas of Libya's desert into prosperous green food-bowl regions. So it is a touch absurd to allow a huge, devastating flood in southern Queensland roll off into the ocean. Besides, the landscape would graciously accept a few canals running from one low-lying area to another, to another, from one inundation to the next, until the flood was delivered to the arid inland. Of the engineers that joined the Queensland Flood Survey Group, one, Scott Gordon, believed it even had the potential to achieve something else, to keep full the lake which is rarely ever a lake, Lake Eyre. He agreed with Hong; Scott said that the survey, once comprehensively completed, was merely a drawing. As a complete organism, as a whole, the survey was merely a new invention to transport a flood. With all the hundreds of minor and major inspections into the landscape's face, La Niña's tears of give may be moved over there rather than allowed to vanish uselessly over there.

As for me an Oxley an Flattie an all the other better wooden hup two three traders at The Exchange, what we say to the survey group is: Ding-dong how's the time, the more wood the better, grow food okay, but grow trees too, grow wood, good wood hup two three, hup two ninety.

Revenge in a Curl

Castle drove ten minutes through the backroads in the forests and came to a small bay world-famous with surfers for the perfect shape of the swell, a bigger bay than the small cove he'd snorkelled in with Jack.

Castle and Hong walked out along the side of the bay to study the swell coming in.

'What's the mangrove pod that Remple wants?' Castle said.

'A diptych, four metres each, perspex thick as a brick, it'll be amazing, an eight metre piece of work. One contains the worst sludge water from a local mangrove up there, and the other contains the same water that's gone through the purifier in the Hydro Department at the uni.'

'Sounds good.'

'What about yours, have you finished the triptych he wanted?'

'Yep, it got trucked up last month, I'll show you it when we head up there for the opening.'

At the headland they were half a kilometre from shore, a good place to get in because the swell at this distance out was only just commencing to form, a large but gently curved hill of sea that travelled towards the beach at three knots, slow, graceful, smooth.

Hong put his fins on and got in, clean, clear water, deep as a big tree. Castle followed. They pushed slowly across the bay to its centre where they would catch a swell, one of those beautiful, slow-rolling curves of nature.

They missed the first three, too much like big gentle slopes, but caught the fourth when they were nearer the beach, a big swell that began to really curve and get them moving. It lifted them higher until they suddenly knew they were going to be dropped like stones into the water below. This duly happened. They were then held under for a long time as the swell rose into a massive wave that crushed itself overhead.

Underwater, Castle tried to claw himself back to the surface, but the roaring surf was five times bigger than he'd estimated from the headland and so he was dragged along the sand for a long time. Hong lost his fins in the same way. They were shoved hard against the world, pushed into it, rolled along it, and they were scraped and turned so much that neither could now decide which way might be up. The surf spat them out in the shallows.

They crawled to the wash and sat there for a while. 'Fuck,' Castle said, 'what the hell was that?'

'It could've been those artists you were abusing.'

'You might be right. Fuck.'

They sat in the wash for a while watching the surf come ashore in one huge crash after the next and then they struggled up the hill to the carpark.

The Town of a Million Butterflies, Maybe Three Million

This is the place, Flattie, that dear butterfly surrendered her heart to in a single wingflap.

Half an hour from Castle's spacepod up the road to the northern tip of the cape. Dunsborough has outclassed the whole continent.

Four years back every Dunsborough powderbox came to an agreement, every single one of em, a huge agreement that resulted in Dunsborough becoming the lushest garden you ever saw, and every butterfly from everywhere came to the town to live.

What they did, the Dunsborough citizens, is they made it mandatory to catch the rain with their roofs. Every roof is now a source of water, every single roof, compulsory. Instead of the rain vanishing back into the bay, it was saved.

When a tank overflows, it goes into the communal pipes, a huge network of thousands of connected pipes that the residents affectionately call 'the hose.' Over the next four years the greenery went from a passable set of thin forests, to a southern hemisphere jungle, and nowadays rumour goes that the place is home to no less than forty-six species, of you dear butterfly. Fecundity itself, bursting from the top of the cape.

Ballarat heard of it, and the Ballaratians are now onto it. Perth can't seem to decide, and Melbourne's thinking about it, Sydney bombed it as too hard. Broken Hill and Kalgoorlie were serious about it, but nothing eventuated. Canberra ummed and aahed. The hose would cost too much. But it was Remple that started it.

Four years ago in Dunsborough, he had a small meeting one night down at Caves House, and the rest is history. Dunsborough simply outclassed the rest of Australia.

In thanks the butterflies bring a swing to Dunsborough. Late at night the butterflies lift the town and swing it awake. At four every morning in the darkness, with the help of the spiders, with their looms and strings, the butterflies lift the town whole and swing it lightly from side to side so that the Dunsboroughians can enjoy sweet dreams. And by five all Dunsboroughians can begin the process of waking to a new day in a new world. In summer the butterflies start at four, in winter they start the Dunsborough Swing an hour later, all together, at five.

This is why almost all Dunsboroughians are relaxed, Flattie, the butterflies give em the Dunsborough Swing early every morning. The spider loom is stuck each morning to ten points of the immediate district, the roof of the post office, a centre, and then nine other points at the edges of the Dunsborough district, including Eagle Bay and over the hills to Yallingup. The whole tip of the cape can then be lifted into the early morning air just a few centimetres so that the Dunsborough Swing can bring em into the day with a nice attitude.

But it hasn't got out. Ballarat is turning their roofs into water collectors only for the sake of water. They'll have to wait a while for the Ballarat Swing to get going. The only place the Dunsborough Swing has got out is with the truck drivers who deliver the daily paper overnight, they talk back in Perth about a bump and a wobble on anyone doing Dunsborough, but that's all.

Oxley's idea, make the Dunsborough Swing into the new diaspirin, diaspora, for cheer and healing, not loss and moroseness. Hey ho and ding-dong and how's the time.

The Unwanted Visitor

That night Castle's visitors all converged at the house for a barbeque, what Castle affectionately called the blah-blah-cue for the triple charged conversation it tended to create through the spitting and the smoke, especially at dusk. And we boxes love dusk, hello equator number two. Hup two three, over the ravenous mountains and over the hungry seas. They gathered beside the small dam. Ruffling black water waving goodbye to the sun.

Laura the booksmeller, Catherine the art dealer, Remple the ex-lover of that other art dealer Patricia in London, Hong Thet Double-O-Four and Jack Verandah. Jack wanted to do the barbequeing, the Londoner who was in love with that fabled curio sizzling under a starry hot night; he'd been looking forward to it ever since he'd arrived in Western Australia. And, since the whole time down south until now had been one beautiful distraction after another, here it was at long long last, the blah-blah-cue. Chops, sausages, kebabs, prawns, the bigtime barbeque. Jack was excited.

'Tell me the truth, what're these pudgy little things?' Jack asked Castle.

'Scallops,' Castle said, 'you give them only half a minute each side.'

'Half a minute? Can't be right.'

'They go rubbery and tough. There's only one thing worse than a rubbery scallop and that's a second rubbery scallop. Do them last.'

Jack followed the instructions and stood beside the hotplate moving around sausages and onions round and round to play with the barbequeness of the night, talking about his trip to Sydney. He was having a ball, perched at the edge of the dam, making dinner under a hot sky fast filling with stars. He was about to add the lamb chops when a boy with a bloodied face came running past, shouting, brushing past him, forcing Jack to stumble backwards. The boy had been in a vicious fight with two older boys, violent thieves who'd punched him to the ground. He continued running up the paddock where he vanished into the trees. Jack continued to stumble, he went over the edge and fell into the dam.

Jack broke the surface of the black water and swam to the grass bank.

'Jack's drunk already,' Castle smiled. 'Are you okay Jack?'

'Who the fuck is that boy?' Jack called.

'What boy?'

Jack climbed out of the dam, kept quiet, went inside to change. The evening was enjoyed dancing under the stars. Laura Glass-Darlington the diviner danced a bit but then sat on the verandah with a stack of books beside her to smell, and even she had no idea that a piece of someone's powderbox had flown through the gathering at the barbeque. It was dusk, king Bakks and greedy Inch had arrived.

Plus Bakks arrived with a touch of glee. 'Top-O-the-mornin to ye, Skinny, what the fuck're ye up to today?'

'It's night time, Bakks, look, halfmoon.'

'It's mornin to me,' he said with glee.

Then Inch: 'Stupid wooden fucktoid.'

Then Bakks again: 'I'll let you in on a big secret Skinny, the moon, the moon's always full, always.'

They arrived because they were summoned, Laura had unwittingly called em up. Her powderbox had spoken. As customers to us boxes, the powderboxes are easy to service. By simply mentioning 'buffalo demon,' Bakks's bell goes off. Careful what you mention. Every powderbox everywhere keeps that whisper as a precaution, Careful what you mention. If you start with a negative twinge, Bakks will deliver a negative typhoon.

But if you start with a bounce, you can sail like light across the equator, across both equators. Liberation. Comes in threes, like triumphs. Castle's lawn beside the dam of yabbies, the list: enemies, artists, lovers and flyers, swaying under the fresh scent of liberation, Yelverton style. They all enjoyed the night, and if the other bouncing partygirl was present to smell that fresh scent, the self-proclaimed saucy dancer aunt Lee from Soho, then the barbeque might be a touch hotter, or a lot hotter, hot enough to melt the scratched and dented stationmaster's bell. But the temperature stayed very high anyway in the week's glorious heatwave, even now under the halfmoon it felt like the daytime heat hung in the air, and the full harvest of liberation was available everywhere. The afternoon arguing seemed to be done with, and they danced on the grass. Far past the dancing and the music, on a rise where Jack lay down with Catherine, the sounds at the forest made a pleasant complement to the broad wash of stars. Yelverton stars, as good as the Sahara here in the clean south-west corner of Australia. One of the world's cleanest skies, cleanest coasts, a place that, for tonight, was liberated far from the shit and crap of the world's efforts.

'I notice you have more canvas laid out in Castle's shed,' Catherine said.

'He's a very generous guy, your cousin,' Jack said, 'he's given me the space to have a go at a few paintings.'

'What will you paint?'

'More on Kee's boat, just three or four more canvasses of the *Pinski.*'

Later, Remple and Jack sat on the Arrivals Verandah.

'Enjoying it down here?' Remple said.

'Love it, it's fantastic, the whole cape, Castle's shown me all over the place, up to Dunsborough, down to Augusta, the beaches, the forests, the wineries, the towns, just fantastic, thanks for inviting me, really, I gotta say thanks.'

Patsy's gungho artist didn't mention Patsy. Painter arrogarnta thought it best to let Remple bring it up somewhere along the partying of the next couple of weeks while they were all down here on Castle's hospitality, a loose, slow, unorganised hospitality of easy generosity. All give and no take. Catherine had extended the week to two weeks, and Castle roundly celebrated it as a very good idea.

A Second and a Third Yelverton Track Twirls into the Night-Sky

Bakks and Inch got very excited about Castle; what a powder-box to get a hold of and fuck up. May I speak for you, may I speak for you, may I speak for you, that greedy caked-up hailme-hailme Inch, was positively vibrating with the disgusting hunt. Inch of course starts his career in that horrible factory in Guangzhou, with duct tape across his flaps. Duct tape then gets ripped right off his flaps and boom, he's on the go. Pity we couldn't re-arrange the duct tape across those evil flaps, tape up the cruelty, have a box like Inch taped up and shipped off to the recycler, pity. The ratsblood sucker Inch, and those other creeps, Kilometre, Millimetre, Yard, Centimetre, Mile, Furlong, Foot, Metre and fuckface Lightyear, they all had a keen nose for Bakks and his wretched wounded logic wanting to fuck everything up with hate; hate this, fuck that. Look let's face it, Bakks maybe regards me as a glass of goody-goody rosewater, but thing is I don't like Bakks either. All the hatey-fuckey in Bakks's world can get lost. Ding-dong and how's the time.

Still, I certainly do understand why Bakks got excited about Castle. After all, face facts, pigswine Bakks had his game. He reasoned that Castle would be hotly in need of targets to blame for his brother's disease. Bakks's logic ran like this: Castle might blame the ancestral handing down of the disease, he might blame his great-grandfather in Spain, Renata's insane father for handing it down. He could blame grandmother Renata, who was not afflicted by the disease, just for giving birth and letting it be passed on, sometimes dormant, sometimes possessed. He could blame the gods, whatever gods. He could blame his mother, his father, Castle might even blame his great-great-great-grandmother on Renata's father's side. On and on it went with Bakks, those juicy family strings of possibility, becoming more and more complex up the family tree, more lost and confusing, and yet more and more gleeful around the crew of creeps. What Bakks forgot is that the illness can't be blamed on a mother or a father, or whoever sits on those limbs and branches further up the family tree, because the disease is pure and simple a chemical imbalance, and how is Castle supposed to stand up to the podium and talk to a chemical imbalance, to a ding-dong set of bored chemicals, molecules. Even NASA hasn't worked out how to converse with molecules. Nonetheless, Bakks was hot. He brushed me aside by saying: 'Technical shit, Skinny, technical chemical excuses. I'll get the fellow fast, the cruise-control generous chap, stand back and watch me work. Learn, Skinny, learn from the king.'

Bakks, phew. O king's motto: attack is comfort, defence is discomfort. Running around piercing the air with little slithers of attack, yeah, feels nice n smug I'll bet. Yep, Bakks liked making the attack: rip off their ears of perception and stuff the head with myth.

That night Castle slept well. He'd danced and drank till the starmap had turned, and he'd had around him the friends that he liked, so he crawled off to bed late and tired, and he hit the pillow flying, going up into the Yelverton sky with a single blink. Then he dreamed warmly and expansively across the stars where the cows had been made. But, as dreams go, they were quick and brief dreams.

Worse for gruesome Bakks, and for vibrating Inch, the dreams were sweet. Inside Castle's powderbox lay too much blameless love and flight for either Bakks or Inch to have a go at with any chance of success. The pungent ratsblood drinker and his boss would have to really try hard, for Castle was dreaming sweet. For O king Bakks this peaceful sweetness meant one thing: O frustration.

In the dream Castle was strolling the bank of a stream with a dog and another boy, they were laughing, they had stolen a cold beer from the house and they were handing the green bottle to one another, sharing it gulp by gulp, the cold bitter froth tasted adult and it quenched the thirst too, a beautiful day, hot and humid, the dog walked paw-deep in the shallow stream, dog was drinking too, licking the clear water at the paws while keeping his eyes up, peeled for action, dart after the neighbour's cat.

The boys followed the dog, no destination in mind, all they knew was that the Pascall girls were to visit later that afternoon, and the boys were happy about the visit to the point of stupidity.

Castle was dreaming of his brother Oliver. The time before Oliver was taken by the Diamond City of Children. It was a small, narrow stream of clear water full of catfish, frogs and tadpoles, these were the things they expected, but they didn't expect the box that lay on the bank just up ahead.

It was a giftwrapped box, tied with red and gold ribbon. Castle tried to reach over to get it but couldn't. He tried again as they walked but couldn't get it. They kept walking, and the box vanished.

The stream ran through a patch of suburban jungle, and it soon came to the main road, running under the bridge, they could climb the banks and walk back to the house along the road. Meet the Pascall girls Sue and Sheila when they arrived. No hurry, no way they'd be late, they knew it, they were glad; dog, beer, stream, and the company of each other for fun and good times, rounded off by two of the world's greatest gifts soon to visit the house. A walk along the stream to the road was a good idea.

But instead, the stream ran through a sand dune and came

out at the sea. They were swimming underwater with masks checking out the sea slugs and the colourful fish in the clear sea. It was beautiful to swim in, warm and cool, and lit up by the sunshine overhead to a sparkle of green and blue, and it was twice as deep as either of the boys, so it felt like flying and cheating. They did somersaults, they flew down to a small reef, found an old anchor.

Castle's dreaming was good, and so Bakks and Inch were blown far off course, far from any ratsblood possibility with his powderbox, but they were not giving up, they were trying every festering counterfeit trick in the swill outside The Exchange.

Next to the anchor Castle found a giftwrapped box. He tried to reach for it but it was pulled away by a current, Castle followed it, hand stretched ahead to catch it, he was almost right on top of it now, good swimming, good work, but it vanished further down into the deep. When they lifted their masks out of the water to check for Uncle Bill's boat they found they'd followed the giftwrapped box way out so they turned round and swam for the boat where mums, dads and kids were spreading out the lunch on the deck.

Instead, they stepped off a plane onto a hot tarmac, laughing and calling out with excitement, ran across the hot cement into the arms of their waiting grandmother, Renata.

She took them to a birthday party. It was great fun, loads of laughter, a surprise birthday party for Castle's brother, and a giftwrapped box. Oliver opened it, and his grandmother said, 'Memories are something that nobody can take away from us, and we are truly blessed to have wonderful ones of those near and dear to us.'

Castle Visits Perth

He got to Perth once a month, worked in the Mount Lawley Bombay Plaza, and visited Oliver. Before the Yelverton guests had arrived, he decided to stay in Perth for a week.

He took Oliver out for a meal, and they had a good time remembering the adventures with all the other kids on Uncle Bill's boat at Pangkor Island. After the meal, as Oliver walked back up the street to the house for the mentally ill, Castle saw a moment of give he had never seen so clearly.

'It's Joe,' Oliver said, 'I'll go over and get him back to the house.'

'Do you want a hand?'

'No, it's okay, he comes down here to drink, I'll go get him. Thanks for lunch, it's been great, see you next time.'

Oliver stopped to tend to the guy sitting on the bench, age around seventy, frail, thin, small, hunched over, had a few beers, staring at the footpath, cars racing past behind his shoulders, busy shoppers flying past his forehead.

He lived in the house with Oliver and the other forty. Oliver bent over into him, laying a hand on his shoulder. 'Are you okay, Joe?'

Joe barely lifted his head, kind of nodded, more a circular shaking of the head.

'Hi Joe, time to get home, I'll take you home, you're drunk, Joe, come on, I'll take you home.'

Joe nodded, he started to get up, but he was shaky, so Oliver took a grip of a shoulder and a forearm. They shuffled up the street, and Oliver managed to turn round for a wave to Castle, and then turned back around to concentrate on Joe. The house was a ten minute walk away, and in Joe's shuffle they'd make it in twenty. As they shuffled away Castle watched on. A mentally ill guy looking after a mentally ill guy. Oliver had to hunch over to keep Joe in his hold, Oliver was taller than Joe by far, Joe was just a little guy, thin as hope.

Castle at the Bombay Plaza

Castle strolled back up Beaufort Street to the studio. The image of Oliver and Joe came with him. He knew it was exactly the way Oliver had always been, a considerate guy, kind, automatically, kind and thoughtful of others, ever since he was a small kid.

As Castle strolled past the Queens pub and up the hill, then past Planet Books, further along past the post office, he held onto at least another dozen fleeting instances where Oliver had given himself.

It was rough to hang onto both extremes. The man who sat on the couch gleamed from the diamond claws inside, and then the other man. The guy who gleamed kindness from inside. It was difficult, very rough, but Castle did hold the two extremes because he felt it was a means to love his real brother.

Castle knew Oliver was a beautiful man. Castle hated the diamond claws. If Castle could get the spirit that gave the diamond claws to boys and girls Castle now walking up to the Bombay Plaza felt he could kill em, Bakks, diamond claws, kill em all, get em and shake em down for the bad fuck they cause for the shit they cause, for the horror they want, for nothing, for after all the whole crap drips down to powderboxes what cannot take a nice afternoon.

Sea Breeze in the Tree of Insults

By the end of the week the guests had settled in. Afternoons were given over to wandering away on your own, maybe a trip into town, maybe a walk in the forest. Exploring the tracks to the coast, along the fencelines of dairy.

Only Castle was left at the shack. He decided to work in the garden, relocate the herbs from shade to sunlight.

Jack strolled into the property from the far side, and came across the paddock, walking toward the gardens near the verandah where Castle was moving the herbs into the sun.

Jack called from the distance: 'Castle!'

Castle stopped, he looked up. 'Aren't you supposed to be in town having lunch with Catherine?'

'No no, I've been walking, just had a nifty idea.'

When Jack got to the gardens, he sat against the barbeque, and he watched Castle playing with the pots, and could not figure out why Castle was playing with the pots, it seemed like a kind of nothing was being tended to. 'What're you up to?'

'Herding the herbs.'

'Herding: you can't herd plants, you herd cows.'

'Herbs you herd, herbs are animals, herbs have attitude, that's why they're so good to cook with, one herds herbs.'

'They're just potted plants.'

'Is that what you think?'

'Yes, they're pot plants.'

'That's why your paintings are so interesting.'

Silence.

'Did you just insult me?'

Silence.

'Castle?'

'I did. Look I'm sorry, I didn't mean it.'

'You've been thinking about your brother?' said Jack.

'Yeah.'

Castle kept on herding the rosemary, coriander, basil, parsley, mint, fennel, garlic, ginger, galangal and lemongrass.

When he'd lifted the last pot into the sunshine that bathed the verandah, Jack asked: 'And what's that one? I've never seen anything like it, looks like a blood-red grape.'

'Bush tomato, very tiny, but huge with vitamins. Feel like a drink?'

'Yeah. Let's have a gin and tonic. With limes, not lemons.'

'With limes,' Castle said.

A big jar of gin and tonic, and they sat in the sun on the verandah.

'Like to hear about the nifty idea?' Jack said.

'Yep.'

'Hong and I are gonna make a set of artworks, Catherine's agreed to sell them at her gallery in Sydney, and then with the proceeds we're going to build you a new studio.'

'Really?'

'We're gonna make Hong's pods, with everything going, not forwards, but backwards.'

Backwards Kindergarten Art

When Jack Black was in Sydney he noticed it was easy to overhear a tourist calling Sydney 'Sittnay' or 'Seednee' or 'Zitnee' or 'Sedd-dunn-ee,' but only Jack persisted in flipping Sydney backwards around to Yendys, pronouncing it Yendiss.

When he was in the beautiful bayside town of Dunsborough, the fecund town of lush jungle and garden on the other side of the continent, the town of three million butterflies, he found that the place backwards sounds rude, and in need of a wash, pronouncing it Hogg-gorrob-snud. He liked it.

Doesn't sound to me like you could stuff it into a box dear butterfly. But let Jack Verandah bumble.

He liked getting into the ding-dong backward stuff, a Londoner in the Antipodes, he said, but everyone grew bored with the olden worn-out powderbox tilt, and Jack didn't care. Double-O-Four didn't mind, ask-why, well, Hong had once bombarded Jack about the water going down the bath backwards, and Hong therefore happily claimed a chink of the authorship and called all the bluster an ongoing artistic collaboration, giving it the name, generically, Kindergarten Art.

Hong said to Jack that their kindergarten art was potentially a hugely fertile field, a vast set of combinations could be made to stand impeccably as drawings or paintings. He said the alphabet consists of twenty-six drawings. Z by itself was a drawing, and in the world of A to Z lay a full page of twenty-six little drawings. Hong said the other drawing they should use was endlessness, forever, the drawing for infinity, the figure eight when laid upon its side. Hong cheerfully noted that their kindergarten art need not be restricted to just the backwards stuff.

Jack disagreed; to begin the series, they ought to stay with the backwards material.

They were asked to do a large piece of kindergarten art by one of Margaret River's greatest art collectors, Neil Hunter. A lot of painters heard about the deal, but it was the great Dave who scoffed hardest at it, he spat: 'Not real art if commissioned. Lower art, lesser art, bad art. Shit,' Dave said. 'A commission is just shit, it's for illustrators, not artists.'

Hong was known for having no bad temper at all.

Hong had nothing of what Inch hailme-hailme calls irritable memory fucktoid syndrome. At the pub one night Hong simply balled it back, the scoffing. In defending himself, Hong began calmly, without even the slightest agitation, harnessing pieces of the past.

Hong said to Dave: 'I don't understand why you've always been scared of commissions, Dave. Picasso did a label, Pablo Picasso did a wine label. He did it for the Rothschilds. Bacon did a wine label for the Rothschilds, and Salvador Dali did as well.'

Dave turned away to order another drink, one drink, for himself.

Hong's calm started to crack coz he'd seen Dave do his one drink for himself bizzo many times over the years since they'd met. He pushed out an extra couple of commission facts from the past, a bit louder, and by taking a step towards Dave. 'Matisse painted *La Danse* for Schukin's house in Moscow, not for some big nancy-poo museum.'

Jack nodded once, then grinned at Dave.

'And then Rothko,' said Hong, 'take titan Rothko, your fave, Dave, he was asked by that guy Dominique de Ménil to make that set of paintings for the chapel in Houston, and guess what Dave, Rothko obliged.'

Dave raised a smile, and he turned to his artist friend Alex leaning an elbow beside him at the bar. Dave said, 'Did you hear something just fall from Heaven, Alex?'

And Hong's irritation now heated up a bit more. 'None of these guys were scared of commissions, Dave. If these artists of the twentieth century can do nice commissions, then I don't see why you need to carry on pretending that a commission is some kind of dilution of our game. They were big artists.'

Jack added: 'Yeah Dave; man, they were angel-monsters.'

I'm a teak box, so yes I know not stacks about Matisse or Pablo, but 'angel-monsters'? What's an angel-monster? What a dickhead. Never mind, bumbling's good, let Jack continue to bumble.

But Hong balled away: 'And,' to put a cap on it, 'they just bloody well knew how to do just what they wanted, right smack in the centre of a commission, even old Rothschild the papa patriarch couldn't press any kind of dilution. You need to go home and have a good gaze at your confidence instead of your navel.'

Anti-temper gentle Hong gave Dave ding-dong, good for him.

One of the guys leaning on the bar next to Dave, a good friend of Dave's, Alex, gave Hong ding-dong right back. 'Get fucked Hong, what're you, a plumber, matey, a plumber.'

Give an Insult Take an Insult

Dave, a painter, recently had a sell-out show in Sydney, everyone knew that, big news round town. It was big news around the whole Margaret River district, Dave was the local hero just now. But Dave's aggression in sneering at the commission, Hong had no true idea of the broken moment where it originated. Everyone knew about Dave's general wave of anger. They knew, more or less, in a nutshell, that Dave was a short-tempered environmentalist, a committed greenie, far, far to the left, a known extremist, and he hated Jack Black's shallow romance with green credentials. Dave moved less on instinct and more on division. But still, Dave's show was full of powerful, beautiful paintings of nature: butterflies dear butterfly, and fish, trees, lakes, streams, birds, and a flipside suite of jetblack inks that highlighted the grossness of pollution; inks of planes, ships, cars, trucks and factories. The show comprised forty works in total, thirty big oil paintings and ten inks of gothic darkness, and they all sold. What nobody knew, it was only beginning to leak out, was that just one guy bought it. He bought all forty pictures. He was the CEO of a big coal mining company. Jack and Hong certainly didn't know.

The great Dave had taken dough from the selling and the burning of coal, one of the core reasons for Australia's good life, and Dave knew it dear butterfly, knew he had taken dough from the dirtiest commodity that he hated most of all commodities, and he didn't like that he took the dough, and he grew depressed and angry with himself, shooting out acid whenever he could find a target, even sitting in a quiet pub in a stylish wine region. The gallery owner in Sydney had phoned to let him know who wanted the entire collection. Would he, Dave, still like to go ahead with the sale? Silence. Then: 'Yeah. Yeah go ahead.'

Dave also knew a shittier fact, shittier, that is, to his own morality. While the federal government was busy hammering out new rules to curb carbon emissions, the Queensland government was busy approving new coal mines. He knew Queensland already had forty coal mines, and he knew that twenty-eight new coal mines were being brought into service. They were also building new railways, new ports, new water pipelines.

He knew also that Newcastle is the world's biggest coal export port, and getting bigger: in '97 Newcastle's tonnage was fifty-six million, in '08 Newcastle sent away eighty-nine million tonnes of coal. And he knew that the NSW government was proactively giving out more and more exploration licences in the western Hunter Valley. And that an additional massive coal loader was being built on Newcastle harbour. He knew that just up the road from where he stood scoffing at the commission, in Collie in Western Australia, the coal was being dug up and shipped off by the mountainload. Dave's one-liner came out again and again at the bars around Margaret River: 'Australia sells dirt.'

Australia digging up its mountains and shipping them off to markets, coal, iron-ore, minerals galore, gold, copper, aluminium, manganese, zinc, now uranium, and also diamonds. 'It's not like we sell silk, spices and frankincense, we sell dirt.'

But when it came to coal Dave knew that the surge, the increase in output for the demand from China and India, meant that the existing coal export value to Australia of thirty-eight billion dollars each year would climb and climb while he sank and sank. Into ever spiralling pieces of concerned logic, of his green morals. Dave's logic ran like this: what he termed the whole gorgonzola goodlife in Australia, this goodlife, had been funded by coal for a century, and he also knew coal was now Australia's largest export, it made more dough for the country than any other Australian industry. A big-bucks earner for all. Take for instance just one coal company, Macarthur Coal. It paid huge money to Australia. In the 2008–09 year it paid a total of eighty-nine million dollars in royalties to the Queensland state government, and seventy-three million dollars in tax to the commonwealth. The employees paid eighteen million dollars in income tax, and with other assorted taxes of three million dollars, Macarthur Coal paid total taxes of one hundred and eighty-four million dollars—and the company produces only two percent of Australia's coal. Or take BHP, the world's biggest mining company, Dave's biggest nightmare. BHP alone dug and shipped ninety-six million tonnes of coal each year. Dave's works were not purchased by BHP or Macarthur Coal, but Dave knew anyway he had been rewarded by his demons not his angels.

Worse, his conscience dear butterfly, did a hop-skip-and-a-jump, a connected travel, went offshore to China, and Dave also knew that China is the world's largest coal producer. China sports the world's biggest coal mine, not just many many mines, but also the biggest hole in the ground anywhere, and in total China produces a full half of the world's coal. And yet the hunger is so big that it also imports coal—a pinch of it went to buying Dave's complete show. China builds, each week, two new coal-fired power plants. That's eight per month dear butterfly. Ninety-six new coal-fired power plants every year. That ain't nectar being created, it's carbon dioxide being created. Canada exports coal, South Africa exports coal, Indonesia exports coal, so China is not concerned about supply. Dave knew that any amount of Copenhagens were going to be almost pathetic in the face of this enormous gaping mouth feeding upon millions and millions of tonnes of coal every month. But it is also a massive polluter where a devastating hunger for oil saw China forging unlikely friendships and alliances all over the planet wherever oil was being produced, including becoming the single biggest buyer of Sudan's oil, and selling the Sudanese government arms which finished up in the hands of the militia who terrorised, raped and killed the African Sudanese of the Darfur region, helping to energise a systematic genocide instead of bringing even just a plain diplomatic effort to the government to end the Darfur tragedy. Dave pushed on: well, a ruling crew that shoots its own citizens, students, in Tiananmen Square might hardly wish to interfere in the internal affairs of a sovereign nation, particularly when what might be at stake is the supply of oil to help take China into the twenty-first century.

What pinched it for Dave was the week that the sleek Italian dude at the international courts issued a warrant for the arrest of the Sudanese president to stand trial for crimes against humanity, that clinched it like a snapping twig, and Dave went into a freefall of depression. Catalysed by holding a sell-out show. What a way to become irritated, but this was no ordinary powderbox.

The facts started life in Dave's sharp mind, crisp with economic intellect and social impact scenarios, but the facts also bore down dead into his guts and made him feel sick that his politics had fucked him up in this way, fucked up his green morals and his blood morals. But worst of all: Dave knew there were dozens of other fires in dozens of other countries, hundreds. America to him was a big source of sordid stuff, sordid interferences just like China. America also was to him a terrible polluter, and India, the whole of Europe, almost everywhere when he gave it thought. Fires all over, all kinds of fires, green ones, moral ones, greed ones. In this way, Dave was a fireman. But he was a fireman who did not know how to put out a fire.

Neither Jack nor Hong knew much of all this, the multiple Security Councils inside Dave's head, the jagged connections that caused Dave to insult a guy at the drop of a hat. They didn't know Dave that well, all they knew was that the great artist Dave, the tough, merciless and uncompromising Dave, had a strong political side.

Dave's friends, especially Alex, would have helped him not to agonise over the sale. After all, a sell-out show is a sell-out show. And they'd easily have given him the good spin that the works purchased by the coalmine CEO will bleed into the enemy's spirit where the works would do good, not bad, but Dave grew more and more depressed, and he hung off Margaret River's bars more and more. He had hurt himself deep down inside by saying yes into his phone, and he hated that fact.

A moment after Alex had insulted Double-O-Four at the bar, when Matisse's *La Danse* commission for the Russian guy Schukin was posted as an example of a great person making a great painting that uses colour to arouse questions about existence, well, Dave jammed it home. 'Every stupid fucker with a paint brush who wouldn't know the first thing about art uses that fucking Matisse as an excuse to make an incoherent riot on the canvas.'

After just under ten months hanging off the bars and hating himself, Dave returned with a fury. He drew a series of massive inks of coal mines, about two metres by three metres each, twenty of them, brooding, dark holes whose only feature was a ten centimetre truck scaling up the hole's hillside in loops. He made these twenty pieces almost overnight, burning with a ferocious rage. One was a diptych where the second panel was a bucolic scene of Australia's goodlife, a beachside pool, house, cars, garage, barbecue, jetty, runabout, boathouse. This diptych, he felt, would ram home the point of the show. O ram ram, no subtle shit with Dave, Bakks could've helped, Bakks maybe did help, O Bakks renter of shit memory.

So, when Dave put up all the work on the walls of his studio, and sat with them one night through to dawn drinking three bottles of wine and going through all the possible offshoot directions the interpretations could take, he finally fell to the floor proud, and he slept on and off for two days. On the third morning, another quick glancing by strolling past them in the studio, and it was done, he rightly believed he'd punched out *Landscape*, but he was proud he'd made his landscapes into the most hotly politically charged works he'd ever seen in landscape imagery dear butterfly. He was still proud from the night before that he'd neatly outmanoeuvred what he called the Dainty Shitheads, what he called the two-bit hustlers who paint meaningless beauty. Castle painted meaningless beauty, and his meaningless beauty had more meaning than Dave could ever understand or believe in, Castle was able to paint a box, Oxley, and it carried more effusion and glow in the stakes of so-called meaning than any heavily done symbolic painting. And Jack was deeply into so-called 'meaningless beauty,' he painted simple things, and his pictures irritated all his intelligent friends in London who made art power their ideas.

But Dave was convinced he'd made high meaning, dark and hellish with grunt, he'd stayed true to the political will of a new era. He'd made good. He'd seen light. He gave new life to his morals, green and blood. He was crammed with the buzz of it, and he knew deep down that he'd burned his flesh and soul over the last two years in guilt and grief to arrive at these dark, luminous works of ferocious truth. They weren't funny, and they weren't likeable, and he didn't care: they were art. He phoned his dealer in Sydney; the dealer was excited that Dave had made a new series of works, emails flowed, and the jpegs flew.

Then the dealer emailed Dave to say he'd have to decline to hold the show. Dave launched into a tide of abuse and then he threw his phone at the concrete floor of his large studio under the Yelverton stars.

He eventually got the works shown elsewhere in Sydney. He tagged, titled, wrapped, trucked and insured the works, and when they arrived in Sydney they were adored.

The show was at the Museum for Contemporary Art at Circular Quay, as fine a place to be given show as anywhere in the world. He flew over for opening night, badmouthed his dealer, ex-dealer, and had a ball being the star of an opening at the MCA where the champagne flowed and the critical compliments flowed.

A week later he flew back to Perth and drove down to Yelverton. Six weeks later the works were trucked back from the MCA. He'd sold nothing. No goodlife for Dave just for the moment.

Which was odd, because the MCA had money to burn. The MCA was extremely busy conducting a fifty million dollar refurbishment, but they were not buying artworks, just building materials. As Inch likes to say: 'Sucked in spat out.' By the suction power of a successful Development Application.

Jack and Hong were altogether the opposite, they did not burn with a political fire. In fact, Jack happily sold one of his new paintings to a friend of Catherine's, an executive at a big coal company. In turn the executive introduced Jack and Hong to another collector, Neil Hunter, for whom the duo's collaboration was being made in the heatwave sunshine beside thc dam.

No, Jack was completely at ease soaking up Dave's loathed and detested goodlife down here in the Yelverton forests beside the Indian Ocean, Hong was too.

After the commission was presented to Neil Hunter, Jack and Hong made a joint exhibition out of their new generic, Kindergarten Art, and they held the show at Neil's place. It sold out.

So they made more kindergarten art for the Sydney show.

Keep Left for the Scenic Drive to Hogg-Gorrob-Snud

Jack painted a three metre name sign of, um, Dunsborough, but backwards, Hogg-gorrob-snud.

Hong waterproofed the stretcher and then immersed it in a giant perspex pod filled with the clear turquoise waters of the town's sparkling bay, and what a sparkling bay.

This one didn't sell, the Sydney audience unwilling to attempt even a half second on trying to make any sense of a sign saying Hogg-gorrob-snud. But the many Sydney backwards name sold right away, Yendiss, and, together with Catherine's Woollahra gallery, they made a small fortune which they took back to Castle's tiny place in the forest just outside Margaret River to build for Castle a big studio beside the dam of jet-black yabbies. Castle favoured the Hogg-gorrob-snud pod so when it arrived back from Woollahra he hung it high across the entrance gate to his small property. Dunsborough was half an hour from Castle's place, but what mattered more to him was the zing the sign created. Between the rotting, leaning, wooden gate from the seventies and the three metre sign above it, lay a world full of, he said, 'Just the kind of batfish nonsense in my head, I love it! Thanks guys, ye men of the world!' shouting the word 'world' in a songlike clamour out into the gully over the heads of the cows.

Then for good measure, and to honour the building of the studio that month, Jack swept up more bluster and he busied himself making Hong's idea for a Keep Left name sign to stand high in the centre of the dam. As he worked on it he remembered the bloody-faced boy that ran past at the barbeque. A couple of days later, when Hong came by to inspect the progress of the Keep Left sign, Jack asked if Hong had really not seen the boy.

Double-O-Four said, 'Course I did. I think we all did, though I haven't asked anyone else.'

'Why did you pretend you hadn't?'

'Gotta let things go sometimes Jack, and, instead of talk about them, gotta just, well, go away and work with em.'

Smart guy that Double-O-Four. Maybe he'd heard of us boxes, maybe he'd heard of The Exchange dear butterfly. Maybe he'd heard of Inch, heard of the calamity of his crew, those filthy cardboard buffoons, the smellbomb deadbeats, Kilometre, Metre, Centimetre, Millimetre, Foot, Furlong, Mile, Lightyear, and the lesser deadbeat that puppy-packer Yard, pongsters all. But I doubt it, how the hell would Hong have heard of Inch and his crew? Double-O-Four had an instinct, that's all, a rich one.

Later that week Jack finished the Keep Left canvas. A large sign of one metre per letter, longer than Castle's crumpled Volvo station wagon.

Hong's bluster waterproofed it, podded it, and together they secured the sign to poles out in the middle of the dam of yabbies, those jetblack crayfish big as a wine bottle that Kee could not believe existed when Remple had described them at the tavern in the Bahamas. A four metre perspex pod, stuck by poles into the clay floor of the dam:

Keep Left

The sign, when seen from the back verandah, presented like a sensible suggestion because it urged veering to the left when walking along the dam as the right hand side was loose with rubble where you could stumble, roll, fall, cut yourself on the sharp rocks. But to a visitor the kindly warning sign seemed rather a bit ding-dong stupid because it was way too big. If not the scale of the old Volvo then the scale of one of those dim freeway signs at the Hogg-gorrob-snud roundabout, big green creations that hit the eye with all the gusto of a fresh new lord mayor: Miss me and you're fucked.

Laura, Jack and Hong sat on the verandah to take an overview of their work. In silence they checked it out. Laura took a book to smell to concentrate.

'I believe it's all right,' Hong said at last.

'I like it,' Laura said fanning the pages under her nose while she gazed across the black water at the sign.

'Do you think Dave'd like it?' Jack said.

'Dave'd puke,' Hong said. 'Even his mate Alex'd puke.'

'Did you see Alex's show at the gallery?' Jack said.

Hong hadn't.

'I did,' Laura said, 'I thought it was actually hugely dull.'

'Well,' Jack said, 'I was at dinner with Alex last night at the Chinese joint in town, I asked him about it, I wanted to try to understand why he'd made such uniform paintings. He told me that the whole show, all forty-five paintings, was about the exploration of paint. I thought: Okay. I thought this was going to be his starting point in a chat about paint, but that's all he said. So I guess in the name of exploration Alex has fallen into, basically, a hole. The entire show is a hole that's saturated with unreconstituted repetition, painting after painting, same same same, repeating himself again and again. I suppose he's desperately trying to appear coherent. I mean, how can it be fulfilling for him, all this falling for phoney coherency?'

'You should have given him a bit of honest advice, Alex is a nice guy, he'd hear it, if it was honest and useful, if it was constructive.'

'Well I started in that direction, got about three words out. He just wouldn't listen, he was immovable.'

'Did you try again?'

'No thanks, no way I was going to try again.'

'You had to do something. You couldn't have done nothing, what did you do?'

'Reached for the broccoli.'

'Anyway,' Hong said, 'Dave can't give Alex any feedback, they had a row, a verbal, not speaking any more. Castle told me Dave is always having fights. Last month he had a fight with his old friend the critic Hadich Megg. For Hadich it was the last straw over a few years of taking abuse from Dave, and Hadich finally had enough. Castle was walking with Hadich, they strolled past a new workshop Dave had started in a beautiful old wooden house, a painting workshop, they'd not seen it before, sign out the front, Dave's name in big letters, and Castle asked Hadich what it was: "What's that?" and Hadich said: "That, Castle, is what an engine of boredom and mediocrity looks like."'

Heatwave Hong

Double-O-Four drove into town for a coffee and to get away from the house to be by himself. He was going to be down here for a week, so he wanted to duck into town and start settling in on the second day, that's how he'd always taken it down south ever since he'd started coming to the cape at sixteen. Day two, alone, solo, soak it in, a Perth boy needed the second day by himself if he was going to catch up with the slowdown he wanted, the visit was only a week after all.

'Where's Hong gone?' Jack said.

'He's in town to give his hair a neatification, there's a hairdresser down here he likes.'

Jack wandered into Castle's library, a shed behind the garage. He opened an old magazine, scrolling the pages across his thumb, stopping at a full page photo of a sunset bathing a mountain range of glaciers and sharp, snow-packed peaks. The low sun gave the snow a suite of colours he had never before encountered. He studied the photo for a long while and eventually decided it was the most beautiful shot of mountains he had ever seen. At the top of the page lay a large headline: 'Thinking of Canada?'

Jack thought: Not really, not at all actually.

He replaced the magazine to the shelf and took out a hardback of Arthur Boyd. He spent the afternoon in the small but packed library.

Hong drove winding along Yelverton Road. Every now and then a property gate whizzed by, and a property on a hill a few minutes from the highway had a sign at the gate that read:

All Water Used On This Garden Comes From A Bore

Hong wanted to use it.

He found a table on the main street. Margaret River was busy, and the day was so hot that mostly people were strolling up and down in their swimming gear. Double-O-Four ordered a big mug of coffee and two samosas, a pleasant hour alone that formed a window to take in the change.

He was thirty-six. In the twenty years since he was sixteen, the whole district around Margaret River had gone to pot like Pinski. He saw a rusty place shined into stainless steel and plastic. His mum tho knew it before Hong was born in '74 when she was twenty-four. She'd seen the bigger change.

She'd come down to a raw place she loved, from fifteen, from the mid-sixties, when it was still rural, still a surfie joint, real farms, old shops, clear streams, fat burgers. She knows the spot where Hong was most likely conceived, tho that week she knew her baby could've been conceived in twenty different spots. She stopped coming when Hong was around ten, in '84, she felt it had been shot to pieces by then. She couldn't understand why Hong still came down these days, and now he looked up the main drag over his samosa and almost couldn't tell why either.

And then it rolled squashing out of his hangover why Castle had kept the lease on the farmer's old shack. From Hong's wine-soaked powderbox he realised why Castle had kept the old spacepod on the paddock in Yelverton twenty minutes drive from all this plastic on the main road. Castle's spacepod was but a world away, a time trap, rusted onto the stars, untouched.

The thought pleased him, and so he was now able to be alone on the crowded main street, and he proceeded to scribble his notepad with more kindergarten signs for Jack and him to make. He gave the signs a theme: Bores.

All The Water Used In This Cuppa Comes From A Bore

Then he found other signs where the tones sounded as if they also came from bores.

Keep Open Fucking Under Control

Rough People Keep Off

Rough People Come Here

Keep Off

Keep Right

And he liked the rudeness, the petulant arrogance, of the politician who addressed Sydneysiders on the upcoming security nightmare event when George Bush and dozens of other heads of state were to arrive for an APEC meeting:

Get Out Of Town

Other bores sounded good to him as he hung around scribbling into his notebook.

May I Have A Dirty Fuck Please

Do That Only Over There

That's Just Pathetic

Call Me Sometime

If That's True Then Good For You

He also held onto the notion of the twenty-six little drawings, A to Z. Then he thought that X was perhaps the most violent-looking of them all, a double slash, like two swords, quite a violent little letter. And it was a kiss as well. He didn't know how to use the two conflicting impressions of the X in the sayings of bores, but he felt quietly confident that things would arrive in their own sweet time now that he was down here at long last at Castle's spacepod away from the hum and drone of the city back in Perth.

The Perth Picnic

Before Castle had taken the flight to Miami, he stayed a few days at his Perth studio in Mount Lawley, the Bombay Plaza. There was something he was very keen to do before heading off to the Bahamas. It had been an aspiration for a long time, and he'd made it into a mission. It had taken a bit of organising, but Castle was a patient guy when it came to the ping splatter pop of a powderbox, or even anything else as long as it was as special as ping splatter pop. He had a lot of patience. A couple of months in attempting to organise a picnic was nothing, not for this particular mission.

He organised a picnic to have a look into the faultlines and divisions, if any, of a small group of his Christian acquaintances of differing backgrounds: an Egyptian, a Syrian, a Lebanese, two Iranians, two Pakistanis, an Indian and a Saudi Arabian, all Christians.

Castle met up with them, at the agreed time, in the shade of Hyde Park's giant Moreton Bay figs on a Saturday morning; his flight to London–Miami was on Monday.

He found nobody admitted to any divisions, and all bar none were at pains to promote tolerance. Citing tolerance further than Christian unity, the two Iranians said they had lived, they insisted, very happy lives in the Jewish quarter in Tehran. Castle tried carefully not to ask transparent questions, dumb, obvious questions, but he'd failed, and privately he found the picnic a farce. He felt he'd been faked, so to end the picnic he felt like being ungracious. Seems his patience went only so far.

'Can I ask one last question?'

Nods all round, smiles.

'Why does your God let some of his children go insane?'

The picnickers got up, one by one.

Castle had first asked the infantile question, or, perhaps, the caustic question, in the very early days, years ago, of Oliver's illness. How can a god of mercy make this happen?

Today, the picnic's sweetness, the fakery, now got Castle a bit too heated up, and his frustration congealed in the morning air with another drastic question. Drastic, but not infantile, this one had always perplexed Castle, genuinely perplexed.

'Why do you think it is that the western Christians conducted a crusade against the Christians in Byzantium's Constantinople? Christian upon Christian bloodletting.'

And: 'Why was a mosque blown up last month outside Lahore by al-Qaeda? Yes, a mosque, by al-Qaeda, they announced that they blew it up.'

This question also genuinely puzzled him, but he felt he could use all three questions to destroy the picnic and vent his frustration at being stonewalled by temperance.

The picnickers had all got up, and they strolled away, and Castle never saw them again.

Castle's Brother

Jack and Laura went for a walk around the Keep Left pod to check it out from all angles. On the other side of the dam they sat for a while.

Then they walked back to the house, past Castle's window. Laura looked in and saw Castle kneeling at his bed.

'What's he doing?' she whispered to Jack.

'He's praying,' Jack said.

'I didn't know he prayed. I never ever knew he prayed, he's not even religious. Is he?'

'Maybe not, but whenever he finds a moment he goes in there and prays for a cure for his brother's mental illness.'

'Have you met his brother?' Laura said.

'No, what's he like?'

'I haven't met him,' Laura said.

Laura and Jack walked on to the back garden and sat quietly at the table, drinking lemonade. They picked limes from the tree to squeeze into the lemonade. Laura brought out a glass of wine. Her glass began to take fruit fly visitors, ants with wings, Castle calls them, piss-ants with wings. Four, then eight, one went into the glass to the wine. Laura drank the flying piss-ant without realising. They sat ten or fifteen minutes, lazing away the early afternoon in the warm sunshine. Laura drank another couple of piss-ants without knowing it. One after the other they met their fates inside the booksmeller. Jack flapped his hands at the air now and then, flicking his hand down at Laura's chair under the table.

When Castle came out, he took the chair next to Jack, and said hi by asking: 'What've you been up to, I was watching from the kitchen, and it looked like you were sweeping the air with your hands, tai chi sitting down, is that new?'

Jack said: 'I've been batting the fruit flies up against Laura's left butt and watching them bounce off cross-eyed with glee.'

'The day you two give up throwing pieces of the landscape at one another will be a sad day,' Castle said.

'I'm going to throw one of those cows at Jack's ridiculous Keep Left sign,' Laura said.

'I'll bring the cows to you tonight,' Castle said.

And Castle wasn't joking, later that night he was going to show the two visitors his favourite party trick that brought out the cows and the kangaroos.

'Castle,' Laura said, 'what was Oliver like before he became ill, I mean just notionally, was he small, thin, fat, obese, what would he be like if he wasn't ill?'

'Oliver, well Oliver used to be, well, if he wasn't ill, he'd be tall tanned and handsome, he is tall tanned and handsome, used to be a great dancer, full of laughter, warm-hearted guy, likes partying, good runner, great swimmer, very generous, that kind of thing.'

'Sounds great, I'd like him,' Laura said.

'Sculpted too, pecs, abs, biceps, great thighs, you're always on about thighs.'

'I like him.'

'You'd have been on him like a, like a.'

'Like a what.'

'You'd've fucked one another to jumbuckery by now, you'd have been superb lovers.'

There it is dear butterfly, a tiny piece of hup two three showing up at Castle's lips, O Bobbo's jumbuckery.

'I can't speak for him towards you,' said Castle, 'but I do reckon that you would've gone berserk by now. Mind you, I'd have encouraged him onto you since you're such a sexy beast.'

'There you are Jack,' she said.

'Now we know.'

Dexter and Lou Pepper Find a Box on a Fishing Trip

Castle took Laura for a walk to meet the Peppers from Arizona who were addicted to fishing. Laura followed Castle down the front driveway under the Hogg-gorrob-snud sign, into the forest and a mile later emerged out the other side at Dexter and Lou Pepper's place.

It was another spacepod rusted to the buckle of the past, a small shack of three rooms tacked onto an old wooden verandah, everything leaned all over the place, and it was beautiful. To the right of the front door lay a wooden chest. The brass lettering on the lid was more than enough for the booksmeller. In neat lettering: Miles Banford.

In America in the year 2008 a calamity occurred. Me an Oxley caught quite a lot of the powderbox activity making feverish ping splatter pop across the two equators, so we were able to simplify the whole complex calamity down to a few useful remarks. They go like this. A poor man and his wife could not pay the bank any longer, and the bank took the house to sell it, the bank foreclosed. But, because this happened to nineteen million other powderboxes at the same time, that is how nineteen million houses across America stood empty. Dexter called it the expulsion of the very poor, what he termed the pit-poor. The Peppers were two of the pit-poor. It became known as the subprime calamity, and experts made the claim that it was a very complex affair involving repacking the mortgages into plump new glossies called securities that were unrecognisable as bad grade mortgages, debts of the pit-poor, and so the new units were ploughed across the world and purchased by gleeful investors all over the financial hubs, creating a complexity so mysterious that not even the Miles Banfords of the world could understand them. Maybe, maybe this was so, but me an Oxley, we knew the outcome was simple: nineteen million houses stood empty, and the number of foreclosures were continuing at six thousand a day. By now everyone everywhere knew that the plump new glossies were poison, so the men running America began to buy those plump new glossy securities to calm everyone down.

How Your Custodians Can Give and Take With the Greatest of Ease Dear Butterfly

In the days leading to Christmas 2008 a team of ten experts in London were hard at work on a large scheme. The urgency of the calamity meant they were buried deep in locked-away offices day after day, night after night. Soon after the New Year dawned, end of February, they had completed the task, alerting their boss Darling.

Chancellor Darling then gave Mervyn King of the Bank of England permission to print more money. How much? He gave Merv the go-ahead to invent an extra seventy-five billion pounds sterling. Why stop at seventy-five? Merv got the printing done right away. But he didn't exactly push the button on the presses, instead he pressed a keyboard—that is, he increased the amounts in electronic accounts. Money from thin air. In anyone's language that's a delightful magic, alchemy. Room to move, a bit of attitude and hey presto, latitude. Alchemy is the making of gold from other metals. But in Merv's case they made money from thin air. More specifically, they made money from the air of permission that issued from between Darling's lips. Which is exactly what powderboxes like the Peppers wouldn't mind doing with a bit of ping splatter pop, printing money when it was needed for a trip across the border to fish the gulf in Mexico at dusty and delicious Puerto Penasco with its clear waters. Ding-dong and how's the time.

Your Custodians the Show-Offs

The Peppers lived in a small town in northern Arizona. He was a baker's bookkeeper. She was a hairdresser. When they lost the house they rented a bedsit. Here at the bedsit they lived for two years, saved around three thousand each, and with the money they flew together to Western Australia. Down south in the Margaret River region Dexter found work in a bakery, keeping the books, and baking too. Lou worked in a hairdresser's salon up in Busselton. When the hairdresser's accountant moved to Geraldton to get married, Dexter began to do the bookkeeping for the hairdresser. Lou and Dexter lived not around expensive Margaret River, but in the cheap belt half an hour on the way back to Busselton where they found the farmer's disused shack for a hundred bucks a week. A mile down the forested hill from Castle's spacepod. It wasn't easy any more to find cheap places to rent in the cheap belt, where many of the shacks were originally built for the returned servicemen after the first war. The servicemen and their families were sent here to Nyoongar country, and they carved out of the forest a farm each. But it was still possible, like it was in the old days when Hong's mum came down, because the well-off found the cheap belt offensive. That is, except the wealthy city tower owner Remple, he liked the place better than the upmarket parts of the Margaret River district.

A month after Dexter and Lou had settled in, they met Castle. Castle had asked Dexter about the mishmash ding-dong of the American housing emergency. Dexter said there was no mystery about it at all.

He said: 'You wanna know why it happened? Show-offs ran the joint, and when a show-off runs the joint the joint goes to shit. Me an Lou had a nice life before we went to the bank and bought a house. We lived in a one-bedroom apartment, yeah it was darn unpretty, but it was warm in winter, and one quarter the price of the monthly payment on the new house. The apartment was cheap, easy, good enough. We love fishing, so every summer we could afford to go fishing and camping. We had a great life, but we were becoming ashamed of not owning a house, and, you know, in town we felt like losers walking in shadows, so eventually we went to the bank and bought a house. Biggest mistake we ever made. All up plain and simple, Castle: that dumb-ass subprime saga was just the seduction of the pit-poor, and it weren't just banks. The governments were into it, both sides, Jimmy Carter, Bush senior, Clinton, Bush junior, they all had mega programs for home ownership at the low end, and laws were created to force lenders to give credit to the pit-poor like me an Lou, and to minorities. So it was a kind of dual seduction, from the White House, and from the banks. And then came the eviction too, yep, the eviction.

'But now it's good, me an Lou love it here in Australia, we live good, we live cheap, have everything we need—and heck man, we go fish all the damn time. Last night after work me an Lou caught two dozen herring just off that beach down there, Cowaramup.'

The Peppers didn't migrate legally to Australia, they came for a scout and then stayed, the first of the American subprime meltdown illegal refugees to set sail across the Pacific equator. Among the pit-poor, the Peppers acknowledged they were at the rich end of the spectrum, they were the well-off pit-poor. Of the pit-poor spectrum, Dexter and Lou actually had work and therefore could afford to save their three thousand each during the two years in the cramped bedsit after their eviction from the house, and then pick up and scoot off to Perth.

Booksmeller Leans into a Curious Aroma

When Castle and Laura arrived at the Peppers' place, the front door was open but nobody seemed home, Castle called out loudly twice without any answer. It was another hot afternoon in the heatwave and everything was quiet, birds, breeze, trees, but a hedge of crickets in the distance grated the dry air into little chips of dusty breath.

Dexter walked round the side. 'Castle, hi there man.'

'Hi, this is Laura, she's visiting from Sydney. We wanted to invite you and Lou over tonight for the cow show.'

'Laura, hi, Sydney, me an Lou stopped in Sydney before we came over here, nice place. My friend Mark Chepmeadow says in Sydney everyone is from somewhere else.'

'I was wondering where you got this box,' Laura said.

'That thing? We picked it up outside Boston. Lou always dreamed of seeing the north-east where I grew up, Lou's born and bred Winslow Arizona, so we made a fishing trip out of it and went to the Catskill Mountains near where I was born and bred, Springfield, Massachusetts. We found the chest in a place nearby, on the way to the mountains, Kingston, nice little town at the base of the Catskills. Lotta stores on the main street, bric-a-brac mainly, kinda junk stuff that always moves west outta the homes in the cities of the east, Springfield, Hartford, Boston, and Lou catches the chest in a dark corner up the back of the store. Guy wanted fifty bucks. Lou gave him the fifty and asked him to hold it aside. In the Catskills we fished the river down Slide Mountain, Lou had never seen that many trees in her life, took us a week to get off the mountain down to Kingston. We picked up the chest and made our way back to Boston for the flight to Phoenix. They's the good days of the spare buck, when we lived in our small apartment, had a spare buck for real, before the illusion of that house.'

'The Banford brass lettering,' Laura said. 'Did the guy in the shop say anything about Miles Banford, was he a businessman from India?'

'India? No way, these pieces of bric-a-brac float west from places like Boston, like I said. Been happening since I was a kid, and long before that too, all the interesting junk ends up in smalltown Catskills, India? No way.'

Ding-dong and there's the time. Booksmeller had found Stan. Stanley was no Arnie Colchester, but he's the good wood mahogany, bit thinly made, bit flimsy, but mahogany nonetheless. While his owners were busy inventing things to do in the hasty-paste, inventing ways to fill in time, Stan had a pretty good festival being carted from place to place, Calcutta to Boston, to that ankle of the Catskills, Kingston, then from Phoenix, Arizona, to that armpit of the wealthy wine district Yelverton, Australia. The shift from the Zeus museum upstairs to a bedsit in Phoenix most certainly gave good ol Stan cause for pause. Bit of a flip: from quiet discussions between Miles and David on the inheritance of addiction held among the pleasant flotsam of Zeus memorabilia, to passionate discussions in Phoenix born of a mutually shared addiction to fishing. But Stan never breeds bother, he's okay, ol Stan. After colonel David to Miles Banford, me and Stan shared about three years of ping splatter pop in that upstairs Zeus room in the Banford bungalow. Then we shared the time in Boston, until I got fedexed to Enid, and Stan drifted west, owner to owner, into the bric-a-brac zone where bargains are picked up for a song. But generally Stan got lined with the kind of powderbox conversations that still today cause him to stay with a single golden rule: There is an advantage in everything, absolutely everything.

The only thing that pissed off Stan the most really, was the lettering. Miles had not done it, a friend from the club had got it done as a gift for his birthday, and the lettering was not brass, it was goldleafed copper, but Miles had never got around to having it removed. The friend from the club had made a miscalculation, coz Miles disliked it rather a fucking lot, but he was always too busy with his group of businesses, and busy with his hunting of the maharaja's daughter, to remember to get around to asking one of his caretakers to have the lettering removed. Stan had to put up with being hoicked round the planet, across the two equators, with a blowhard show-off name shouting out in gold, a name that nobody knew anything about anyway since the Banfords were only ever big in north-east India. It gave Stan the shits, that shouting gold.

Yet it was a minor blip in Stan's larger work of locating advantages in absolutely every moment. The hup two three across the seas and the mountains, navigating the three states of memories that had found their way into those grains of mahogany: loved and cherished; lost and forgotten; bitter and destructive. They all had their advantages. To Stan they were a bright cosmos, brighter than any NASA hippy could dream. Oxley felt it was a bit rich, this extension of cause and effect, so he asked Stan what he believed were the advantages of the cardboard counterfeiters. Stan replied: 'Well, sad to have to say, pity to admit it, but Bakks in a sense is right, the advantage is they are the lawless chaos that goes some of the way to making myths, in the slipstream of their runaway lawless glee they refresh the place.'

All the Dollars in the World Might Equal All the Leaves on Trees Dear Butterfly

On the Peppers' spacepod verandah Stan had scores of moisture stain rings on the lid, cobbled around the goldleaf lettering, so it looked like Dexter and Lou had enjoyed many a cool drink on the verandah in the armpit corner of the wealthy wine district.

Booksmeller and Castle followed the bookkeeper inside. Dexter placed a jug of ice water on the table. The table had come with the shack, and it was no doubt born in the forties, the top peeled, and it had seen the sun.

'You must've heard of the Banford clan, the Banfords of Boston?' said Laura.

'Nope.'

A knock on the door, Jack had followed through the forest. He strolled inside. 'What day is it today?'

'Sunday Jack, Sunday,' Dexter said.

Castle wanted to head off for a swim and then get back to

the spacepod to set up the cow night. 'Is Lou working today?'

'She's up in Dunsborough, helping Sally with the bar,' Dexter said.

'She's okay for tonight?'

'Yep, seven?'

'Come over anytime,' Castle said, 'we'll start the show at eight, at sunset, they look good in the sunset.'

'They do, see you round seven.'

'Okay, better head off, taking Laura for a swim at the reef, she's never had a swim in the west, we'll show her what sparkling ocean can be like.'

Laura asked Dexter: 'Do you miss Phoenix?'

'Sometimes I do, I mean, I love America, don't get me wrong here, but Arizona is one of the worst-hit states, and I mean lookit what's happening round the country as of coupla years back. America's busy as hell: bailing out its businesses. They're givin away money like confetti, the Big Daddy of Make-a-Buck Inc. The biggest bigdaddy of freewheeling business the world's ever seen. And now what's happening is bigdaddy, he's sugardaddy. General Motors got fourteen billion dollars from Treasury last year. Chrysler got four billion. Then they asked for more, got more. Even the world's biggest bank got given money. Our money. Even the world's biggest insurance company AIG got given money, four times, our money, AIG got given a total of one hundred and seventy-three billion dollars. Let me show you what that many bucks look like in a pile round the back here.

'If you have a one million dollar house, what AIG got given was one hundred and seventy-three thousand one million dollar houses. One hundred and seventy-three thousand big houses up in Busselton, that's four Busselton's worth of them houses, given to one business.

'Is that a nice system? Other banks got billions, even the funny banks on Wall Street got given our money, twice, first as loans then as a gift. Citigroup had three rescues, and after rescue number three the government ended up owning shares in hundreds of other banks across America. I mean hundreds of banks. The state now owns the army, navy, air force—and the banks. Like, that's what Lenin wanted, a fist like that, clamped around all them goodies.

'Then there was that moment I'll never forget, none of us Americans are gonna forget it quick. The White House gave General Motors a condition: you prove you are long-term viable. So GM set about proving it, and the first step was GM laid off ten thousand employees, to cut costs and make the company viable. They took workers' money to lay off workers. Bang your ass two times.

'I mean, I just never seen such a great intensity of plain ol kack-a-maymee bullshit in all my life. Take this for another piece of kack-a-maymee bullshit:

'Round that time my beloved America was losing half a million jobs a month. On top of that, later in the year, GM announces lay offs to forty-seven thousand people globally. That's a lotta families gettin it in the ass just because some show-off clown in Detroit can't count.

'But AIG takes the cake I swear, because the marriage is now done between the country and the company. America now owns eighty percent of AIG, which is the biggest insurance company in the world. So now the country has to change its name wouldn't you say? The United States of America–AIG. I seen a few books in my time, and I sure as shit can't know how to say how you could fuck up with seventy million customers across the planet giving you a cheque every month for insurance. But it wasn't the insurance department. It was AIG's other department. It was the giftwrapped mortgages like me an Lou's mortgage back in Arizona. So now it seems me an Lou fucked up the world. AIG had a big Whoopee Department in London that sold a lot of mortgages around the world to their friends. Lucky the Australian bankers weren't their friends. If you did lunches with the AIG guys, you stepped in poo. What's worse is that, because AIG was the main seller of the poo, across the whole planet there was no bigger seller of the poo than AIG, the lunches you had with them were because you were their compadre, and you bought the shit and you fucked up. Hundreds of banks across the world were AIG friends, lunching like the Romans. The guys at the banks here in Australia were not AIG's lunch friends, so the banks here didn't eat shit, they were lucky they were so isolated here. The Romans crapped on their own carpet too, that's why they lost it, people got high damn sick of em crapping on the carpet, and the disrespect everyone ended up giving the Romans took the gig away from the Romans. Whoever takes over the game once America loses it will eventually do the same thing, shit on the carpet all over again, all owin to showin-off. I keep a lotta books, and when you keep as many books as me, you can make out how far the shit in a show-off guy's mind can flow. These assholes who fucked up the world were just show-offs. I wish they weren't, but they were.'

'The British government,' Jack said, 'now owns seventy percent of the Royal Bank of Scotland, so, yeah, you're on it Dexter, we ought to call England a joint venture, UK–RBS.'

'It's a merger, stay with the open market merger mindset, and you're sure gonna need to redesign the logo. If that's as smart as it gets, if that's my beloved American experiment leading the way into success and happiness then I'm happy to miss home and fish right here in Cowaramup until the immigration dudes in Perth find me, or fine me, or deport me, or whatever it is they wanna do when they get a scent of this Arizona ass hangin around Yelverton.'

'That's great,' Castle said. 'Shall we head off for a swim?'

Jack said: 'The Royal Bank of Scotland did something similar after the government gave them thirty-seven billion. My dealer said they sacked two thousand three hundred workers last year even though the retail side made a big profit, sacked for making a profit. But to a few key employees, to the top guys in the investment banking section, they gave one billion pounds in bonuses. My dealer invited those guys round to the gallery for a party, she wanted to get them oiled up to see if she could shake loose a few of those billion pounds.'

The Take Take Take Addiction Loses Sight of the Trees

'I don't care,' Castle said. 'These guys have big salaries, they work hard, they get paid megabucks, so what?'

'That's right, I agree,' Laura said. 'What's wrong in giving someone a bonus? The investment bankers are paid a bonus because they earned it, they brought in the money in the first place.'

'But here they didn't make a profit like the retail side did,' Jack said, 'these guys in the investment banking section made a twenty-eight billion dollar loss. They got a bonus for fucking up. You can't get a bonus for fucking up, that's just not the system at all, the system we have created over the last couple of thousand years is a merit system, and we tend to like it, you get rewarded a penny if you produce a pound, not if you lose a pound. It's not right, it's immoral.'

Dexter began to search a bookshelf.

'There's nothing immoral about making loads of money in a proper job,' Laura said. 'It is actually very moral, business has always brought untold numbers of people out of poverty, creating potential in lives is a very moral thing to do.'

'Moral like that guy Goodwin,' Jack said, 'at the Bank of Scotland, being the boss of a great big loss. Sir Goodwin ran the place, so Hong's calling him by our new kindergarten art language, in our back to front language, Sir Goodwin is now called, in Yelverton, he's called Sir Badloss. Goodwin got three million pounds as a retirement payment, and he was unlucky enough to have presided over the biggest loss in all British history, and British history is mainly one titan global money machine after the next. So he's the unlucky guy to be unique in a grubby kinda way. I wonder how long it will take to forget him. The London School of Economics might study his style for a while to come I'd say.'

'I happen to know Goodwin,' Laura said. 'I had dinner at his house in Edinburgh, he's a very nice guy, and he's giving the three million back to the bank. And the guy who runs Citibank, Vikram Pandit, has promised to take a salary of one dollar, and a zero bonus until the bank returns to making money, making profits.'

'Yeah, giving it back, nice whim. At AIG,' Dexter said as he ran his fingers through a stack of papers and books, 'the guys in the unit that lost forty billion dollars, they got bonuses. They got given one hundred and sixty-five million dollars from the money the government gave them: our money. The bonuses were dished out to guys that were selling the toxic shit that created all the shit, so everyone across America wanted them to give the bonuses back, kinda good faith an all that.'

'If they produce the pound they're welcome to the penny,' Jack said.

'Yep, here it is,' Dexter said, 'this is what I've been looking for.' He pulled out a notebook. 'These are all March 2009. This guy, chief of the NYSE, got a four million dollar bonus when the NYSE lost seven hundred and thirty-eight million dollars. And this guy, Warner Music paid the chief a three million dollar bonus when Warner lost fifty-six million. This guy at Texas Instruments, he got one point five million even though he jammed the company earnings down by twenty-eight percent, the list goes on for three pages, but, hey, we know the story. It's like Jack says, a penny for a pound, that's the way the world is. But this stuff here, it ain't normal, they're givin away pennies for losing a pound. What's goin on?'

'But the execs,' Laura said, 'were signed to these bonuses before anything happened, you can't just shred a contract.'

'Well then, maybe, change the rules,' Jack said.

'You can't just change the rules,' Laura said rolling her eyes.

'Yes you can, rules are changed all the time when it doesn't suit the weather. My dealer Patsy says, "Extraordinary times, extraordinary measures." They changed the bank rules all over the world when they wanted to track terrorism funding. I mean, that's a very good idea. Same thing with tracking the securitised shit, the same shit that landed the world in a rather large catastrophe. Track terror bucks, track securitised shit, same gig. Change the rules, Putin does, one day he hands out the keys to the car, next day he confiscates the car, then he gives you a petrol station, then he confiscates the oil company.'

And They All Lost Sight of the Trees. Even When Standing in a Forest

'Obama isn't Putin,' Laura said. 'Putin doesn't like the law, he likes being the law, Barack Obama likes the law, and he knows the value of law, the value it gives to communities everywhere, the potential it creates.'

'Obama's right-hand man,' Jack said, 'that guy Tim Geithner, the corporate whipcracker, he's keen to bring some sense into these guys doing their rip-offs, he's good, he's saying let's get real.'

Observe dear butterfly how just three powderboxes—prime custodians, perhaps, of your nectar—can blow trees off the planet, make em invisible anyway. O yes, observe.

'Timothy Geithner?' Dexter said. 'No way man, that guy controlled the IMF in the nineties when half of Asia melted away, and he went there to help em out but instead he fucked em up good. So good that even now none of those Asian leaders will go to the IMF for help if they need it, and, plus, they can't stand the guy, Geithner burned their houses in return for givin em a carpet. In fact, they turned their backs on the IMF so emphatically that the IMF was forced into a new way of lending: they had to loosen the strings. The IMF guys talked about how good it was that they chose to do some "reform" an all that, but what they had was their ass kicked by their customers because Geithner pissed the customers off bigtime.'

'Geithner wants to change the rules,' Jack said, 'he wants more surveillance of all the financial houses. It's like president Lula from Brazil said: everything else has been under surveillance since the Twin Towers, except the finance guys who created the global collapse.'

'Geithner,' Laura said, 'is a strong character, he'll stand up to the system, and he'll fix it.'

'But all up,' Dexter said, 'I mean basically, what we have is a pretty good system, but once those guys in the banks didn't believe each other, the system broke. It's about believing.'

'I agree,' Jack said, 'it definitely is nothing more than believing. The system broke because the system is abstract, there's not a lot of actual money around, it's all just numbers on their computers, abstract.'

'Which makes it,' Laura said, 'an amazing feat, so these people who run the banks must be a pack of high-level geniuses—because to make these crazy abstractions into a functioning reality is no small feat.'

'I agree,' Jack said, 'It is about nothing more than belief. But if it was touchable and real, this wouldn't happen. If truckloads and planeloads and wheelbarrows of actual money were carted round the world, the system would never ever break, never, you could count actual stuff and nobody could deny you had the amount you and the independent counter said you had. Nobody would need fixing, even from Geithner.'

'Geithner's the devil,' Dexter said. 'He's a major asshole anyhow. I mean, if he does to America's troubles what he did for Asia's troubles he'd burn down the house and hand out a carpet, he's crazy that guy.'

'Maybe he should,' Jack said.

'What, burn down the house?'

'Yeah.'

'Hm. True, he could do nasty medicine like he did in Asia. But, you know, that guy, he didn't mind sitting in a suite in the Jakarta Hilton when he was the boss of the IMF designing all those cost-cutting measures across Indonesia, but there's no way he's up to it in America. He's the kinda guy at school, the teacher's pet who can shit all day on the smaller kids, but after school he combs the school captain's hair.'

'No way,' Laura said, 'Geithner won't blink in sacking anyone right at the top of these firms that receive public money, he just won't even blink. Besides, you guys, besides surprise surprise, these firms have paid back the government money, Goldman Sachs, Bank of America, Morgan Stanley, and the others, they've paid it back.'

'Can we please go for a swim?' Castle said.

'Well Tim Geithner can print money now,' Laura said, 'he couldn't print money at the IMF. They definitely do not call it "printing money," they call it "quantitative easing," but it just means printing money.'

'I was in London during the bank run,' Jack said. 'Damien Hirst and I were having lunch opposite the bank. I was congratulating him on a wild ride he'd just had: he had sold his diamond encrusted skull only a few months before, he got fifty million pounds for it from a group of hedge-fund dudes just before the shit hit the fan. We were looking out the window at the people who'd lined up to withdraw their money, and he said: "Talk about lucky, talk about timing." Then he turned and stared at me, and he said, "Do you believe in timing Jack?" I said no, I just paint what I like, and I said that I am no good at timing at all. The run on Northern Rock was right across the length and breadth of goodship Britain, those huge queues at the front doors, it was the first run on a bank in Britain in a hundred and fifty years. So, you know, it's pretty simple, if you wanted to fuck an empire you just degrade its money, or make it smell by hacking into the abstract storage of money, or like Dexter says, give hard-arse loans to just a tenth of its population.'

'Britain,' Dexter said, 'gave their banks eight hundred and fifty billion pounds sterling all up, in total. I don't really mind all that much givin banks our money, but what's crazy is then runnin round callin the place a free market, this free market stuff's some kinda gibberish, it ain't a free market, it's a not-free market, no-way free market, a controlled market, pure malarkey, just show-offs wanting it all their own way, hey, lookit us, ain't we the wonderboys, we run a nice free market, wanna play? If me an Lou and these malarkey boys were done gone created equal, then here's a simple solution I say any good doctor will vote up: If they blow up their businesses let em get it in the ear like me an Lou got it in the ear.'

'That's it, I'm going to the beach.'

'And then,' Dexter twirled his hands into the air, 'when that chanceroy of the exchekker dude Alistair Darling tells the banks he's gonna whoppo tax the crap outta the big bonuses, the bank guys tell him it'll backfire and be warned all the truly talented bankboys will leave and go elsewhere, go shootin off to work Zurich, or Paris, or Frankfurt, well let em go, just let em go, it'll be nice if they get to blow up Zurich or wherever they go. How bout you, Laura, what say you about my country? What says you bout the world's biggest experiment in freedom?'

'America, my dad says it runs on two things, just two, and these are things they really hate in America but are forced into doing them, it borrows Chinese money to pay for the millions of gallons of Islamic oil it has to use. Chinese dosh, Islamic slosh.'

Castle was walking out, he swept up his towel as he aimed for the door.

Bakks and Inch were trying with great diligence on painter arrogarnta. But me an Oxley? We like England. But ratsblood, and swined-off, just jealous of England. I mean, I don't see how you decide to be jealous of a whole country, but there you go: cardboard smellbomb wounded logic panorama costing us detail, cherished detail. It's all right to be jealous of, say, Dorking,

Dorking's a sweet place, but the whole island of Britain?

'I met this asshole artist Dave last month in town,' Dexter said. 'He was warning everyone at the bar about money, "Money's dangerous," he says, "you gotta watch out about money." I said "Yeah, you do, you gotta watch out that you wind up not having any."'

The Cow and Kangaroo Show

Soon the others arrived at the back garden, one by one, drifting in separately from their explorations of the afternoon, Hong, Remple and Catherine. These three were regulars to the shack, had seen the cow and kangaroo party trick, and to see it again was a big bonus. Dexter and Lou arrived through the forest at the front driveway, strolling under the big new sign Hogg-gorrob-snud.

'That's nice,' Lou said as she stopped to look up at the new gateway sign.

'I can't even say it, what is it?' Dexter stopped to read it.

'It says Hogg-gorrob-snud. You're great with numbers Dex, but you sure as shit ain't no readin spellin kinda guy.'

'Yeah well you watch out when I read your ass tomorrow.'

At dusk around eight Castle set up the show. The sun had gone behind the trees, when kangaroos would emerge as they did most nights from the forest to enter the open spaces to feed among the cows.

He carried the stereo speakers outside and placed them at each end of the verandah. Then he went inside and put on

Pavarotti. He played Pavarotti at medium volume for around ten minutes. When it was nearly time for 'Nessun Dorma' to come on, he went inside and turned the volume up high.

At this, the feeding cows began to lift their heads. The kangaroos stopped feeding and began to stand upright. Pavarotti moved more deeply into the piece, bringing it to the start of his long crescendo, and, at this, the cows began to walk closer to the shack, and the kangaroos scuffled closer. As Pavarotti built up the song, the cows walked with an extra step in the hoof, and the kangaroos shuffled quicker. By the time Pavarotti was beginning to blast his upward tenor into that arc across the sprayed constellations that bore the glow of life, the cows and the kangaroos had moved up to the dam. And when Pavarotti was riding the final pitching heaves, and then throwing the call right across the universe, the cows and the kangaroos had encircled the shack, just at the far shore of the dam, a ring of cattle and roos round the house in the fresh darkness, eyes, ears, snouts, visible in a wide circle at the edge of the butter-yellow light of Castle's creaky spacepod tied to a post. The audience on the verandah watching the audience round the dam, and the audience round the dam watching the audience on the verandah. For a few minutes, at dusk, the cows had stopped grazing. The grass and cow logic that was beloved by Bakks, had ceased. Grass, for the moment, was not being converted into the raw material for cheddar, blue vein, camembert, parmesan.

Jack was astonished at Castle. He stepped off the verandah to sit in the darkness at the dam, directly across the black water from the audience of cows and roos. Jack sat in silence, his powderbox popping with notions that Castle was from a different plane, maybe he was some kind of magician, and this notion, by itself, made Jack Black arrive, painter arrogarnta, the supremely arrogant smug little blockhead, finally arrive in Australia. All those layers of smart-arse crap he carried about with him from his London art world, they all blew off into the universe, and new layers to commence a deep friendship with good ol Castle took their place. For all the high-flying intellecto yumcha dudes that Jack had known, he had never experienced the beginnings of a friendship such as this, those minutes inside the circle of cows and kangaroos that surrounded the verandah and the dam and the herded herbs.

The Sunny Spa

Next morning Jack Verandah said, with a quite bright vigour, with anti-intellecto spring, 'Let's all go to Wyadup and get wired-up.'

'Great idea,' Laura said. She was sitting in the shade of the verandah avoiding the heatwave, booksmeller fanning a book under her chin, and then at an armpit.

So Laura, Catherine, Hong, Castle, Jack and Remple drove out to the headland to swim in the tiny lagoon at Wyadup at the northern tip of Cape Leeuwin, over the hills from the town of three million butterflies. Getting wired-up on those excellent south-west shoulder medicines, clean ocean and hot sun.

Doesn't matter where, London to a cow paddock, all powderboxes seek out the same thing dear butterfly. From the activities in a gigantic city—steel, concrete, gigantic fun from the construction of yet more urban playthings in art, music—to far-off rustic fun from a tenor and his audience in Yelverton, the jollies that powderboxes seek out are often the same, and so this morning they all shared the same jolly, a remote little lagoon.

Jack sat in the shallow natural spa against a smooth boulder. They called it a spa because it was refreshed by the surge of surf over a line of rocks separating the pool from the open ocean. It brimmed with white froth and emerald shallows. The landward side of the spa was a steep hill, starting at a narrow flat platform where Castle had placed Oxley under a small tree. While the others swam in the ocean inlet outside the spa, Jack's eye followed the side of the rocky hill up to the crest where the markless blue sky eased him quiet. The crest took his interest, red bare rock against blue bare sky, the limit of his field of vision from where he'd chosen to sit. He studied the contrast for a long time, that red bare, blue bare abstraction.

His London eye had never experienced a sky like it. He was also stunned when he'd got a first glimpse of the sky at the airport in Perth when he landed from Dubai. Down here at Wyadup the air, the light, seemed another degree clearer still. A sheen of blue deep, a sky as friendly as a puppybox like the pretend counterfeiter Yard. No clouds, no fronts, no distant incomings like you'd get on a summer's day in Devon, no jets, choppers, hazes like you'd get round London. Just a friendly brightness indicating the eternity of a universe. A brightness so plain it might have said plainly that the endless universe could never conk out, expire, how this buzzing blue might ever go dark just seemed to him like the bombast of quantum physics. Yep, Jack Verandah lay idle in true simple enjoyment, the cows, kangaroos and Pavarotti had brought this guy new little illuminations of perception. He'd travelled from knowing everything to being willing to learn. Pity he didn't notice all those globs of memory hurling past in the sky above the spa hup two three, globs from all three states of memory: cherished and loved; lost and forgotten; bitter and destructive. Catherine climbed down and sat in the spa with Jack.

'I can't understand the light here,' Jack said.

'You're not the only one,' Catherine said. 'Two of the best realist landscape artists from Sydney show with me. They're the most gifted realist landscape artists this country has seen in a century, but they keep getting it wrong. The light they capture over here is wrong. What they capture is a softer light, a creamier light, a New South Wales light. Too heavy handed. They get everything else in the composition right, but they can't help themselves with the light, they just end up working from a palette that belongs on the east coast, they just don't understand the light over here. If their talent was down the rung a bit, that wouldn't matter, but these are two of the best doing their best and getting it wrong.'

'Well it's making me sink into another universe of relaxation.'

'It does that.'

To lounge around. Just lounge, not even touch a thought or an idea, Hong quietly declared as he climbed into the spa, was the key thing for today, they'd worked enough on the backwards pods, for now. Jack enjoyed the idleness, the gazing up at the sky from the base of the rocky hillside, lounging in a spa directly alongside the Great Southern Ocean. The hasty-paste was slowing down. He'd never dreamed he'd be lounging like this, and back in the studio in Tottenham when he sent the email to Patsy, he warmed to the memory of his time with Kee Leeft on the lagoons, but this was different, this was real lounging. Even off the shores of Greater Exuma on the limestone shallows of the Grand Banks of the Bahamas it was difficult to lounge, it was all a bit busy there in the Bahamas with fifty or a hundred things going on at once, the comings and goings from Europe, from south and north America, and from all the islands of the Caribbean. Here it was not fifty busy, it was only five things: hot, deserted, blue, fresh, and beautiful. And just to make Jack feel a deeper sense of idleness, he sat pleased in knowing it was a terminus. End of the road, next stop South Pole, five thousand unruly kilometres of ocean for those who prefer the cold.

Then, for no reason, maybe the calm of lounging in a heatwave, two memories wafted down the hillside, unrelated really. Jack's friend, Evan the rock and roller, drifted into his powderbox. Back in London Evan was the crown prince of caustic rock. Underground at first, then Evan hit the above-gound bigtime with his special style of anarchist rock. Evan's anti-establishment venom blaring out over the chimneystacks of London, spew this spew that. Using his music to shit on America, to shit on Britain, to shit on France, to shit on Israel, on organised capitalist crime. But Evan's peak shitting was the late nineties, and Jack suddenly realised that the current times had issued Evan with a parking infringement: after the attacks on the Twin Towers it was no longer seemly for Evan to blast out hard rock badness blowing up the establishment with his lyrics and his extreme attitude. And he, Evan, didn't. He just faded away with nothing to say, or the terrorists had said it badder and maybe bigger, so Evan behaving as Evan the Terrible, the bad-arse baddie hurling his toxic rockband explosives at the establishment, seemed a bit pathetic, sort of puny. The caustic rocker, maybe under the winds of events, had morphed into a good citizen.

Jack sat in the comfortable shallow froth, laid his head back on a ledge, and closed his eyes.

He liked what Evan had done, he liked Evan's style, and what a minor pity that the Twin Towers attack, and the ensuing times, had made Evan seem like a boorish complainer at the impunity of the post-colonial power club. But then Jack suddenly recalled something else for the first time in a long time. It was a fairly disgusting thought, but it was not his own, it was his art dealer's observation. Patsy had told him back on the high street at Bernardo's in Notting Hill not to expect any further big sales for the time being. She had said: 'You will note that some time ago the terrorists brought down the Twin Towers, and you will note that some time after that in New York a number of other very significant towers were brought down, smashed, dissolved—Merrill Lynch, Lehman Brothers, Bear Stearns—great big marble and glass towers where twenty thousand people apiece worked, and the money that melts from these collapses, including our own banks here in England, will make my job of selling your paintings quite difficult. It's a global routing, Jack.'

Jack remembered he had responded: 'Well, Evan'll be pleased.'

Patsy had said: 'Evan is an arsehole, you ought to reassess your friendship with that loser, and please don't bring him round to the gallery any more.'

But Patsy was so determinedly irritated at the fact that Catherine had blown up the affair with brother Remple that Patsy had taken to equating events that did not really equate that much: 'I don't know who was better at blowing up buildings in New York, those horrid bearded shits or those horrid mortgage securitiser shits the Wall Street chiefs.' Patsy's powderbox had been veering closer to the hup two three that Bakks and Inch had handed to pongster Kilometre.

Laura sat on the other side of the small lagoon with Castle, outside the spa, but not far from Jack lounging in the spa. Jack could hear what they said. Jack was looking at them, in his idle, lazy lounging, he was having a look and a check. He was amazed, and he felt good. His powderbox was filling up with his London-cool hip crap: There's Castle, from another planet somewhere. What a guy, type A. True magician. All giving, type A generosity. Type Z selfishness. Ten out of ten brain, crazy man, great man. Type AA bookseller.

Then he checked out the pronged-out performer. What a girl, type A. True pronged-out mystic. Type A booksmeller. Type A traveller. Ten out of ten brain, crazy woman, thinks big business takes care of the poor, great woman.

From behind his fine lounging in the hot sun Jack could hear them talk.

Laura said: 'My friend has leukaemia, and her brother is about to give her his bone marrow. Do you ever wish you could give your brother some of your brain cells?'

'Yes,' Castle said, 'I've thought it and wished it many times, it would be wonderful if schizophrenia could be like that, donating a part of your marrow to your loved one, whatever marrow, brain marrow, bone marrow, neural marrow, blood, skin, tissue, whatever, it would be great.'

'Me too,' Jack called across the spa, 'I'd like to donate my marrow to my brother.'

'There's been so much excellent research going on these days around all these different diseases and conditions. Last year Obama lifted Bush's ban on embryonic stem cell research. My friend in Edinburgh, her father made a huge discovery at the University of Newcastle in England in February 2008 when he invented a technique to pull out a defective gene and replace it with a healthy donor gene.'

'What condition was it for?'

'Her dad calls it the mitochondrial gene. He says he's exchanging one unhealthy gene for a healthy gene to prevent a child from developing mitochondrial disease, which, even as early as nine years old can result in multiple organ failure.'

Laura scraped up a clump of wet seaweed and lobbed it across the spa at Jack's head. Jack picked it off and turned to throw it over the rocks into the ocean. A big wave was on its way, so he held on to the clump of seaweed. Inside the curve of the wave five dolphins surfed side by side. He turned to watch them, his elbow propped on a rock, the clump of seaweed hanging in his fist, and he watched as they rode high in the emerald glow of the wave with silver torsos out in the fresh air. They surfed all the way to the small beach past the spa, and then peeled off before the wave broke. When the dolphins had disappeared back into the ocean Jack flung the seaweed over the rocks. Night cows and night roos drifted into his powderbox. He thought: Might have to ask Castle to somehow put a speaker underwater here, for the dolphins, Pavarotti singing 'Nessun Dorma' to the dolphins.

'Well,' Castle said to Laura, 'if the gene replacement technique ever gets beyond the preventative and into the curative, say to a stage when someone like me can give a normal gene to an adult brother, and the miracle happens, cure instead of prevention, then that vast global city—the Diamond City of children, women and men—will suffer the greatest exit migration in the history of the world, and the city'll be utterly empty, and I'll get my brother back.'

'There's hope,' Remple said. 'Work on genetics has just in the last few years picked up an enormous amount of speed, much faster than at any time in the past fifty years. At the Massachusetts Institute of Technology, for instance, and it's only one for instance out of hundreds across the world, they have a competition every year called the International Genetically Engineered Machine Competition, this year over a hundred teams entered their newly designed bacteria. It's all about implanting different DNA to see what happens, what can be built. It could go eventually to disagreeable places, but it might go to curing any number of illnesses, including Castle's wish to transplant stuff brain to brain.'

'Same with my friend's dad. There's a problem, though, with my friend's dad,' Laura said.

'What's the problem?' Castle asked.

'The ethicists, an assorted bunch of moralists and religious and green and animal rights groups over there, are loudly accusing her dad of forwarding the cause of genetic engineering.'

'Fuck em,' Castle said slowly and softly. 'Fuck em all.'

Jack called out, he sang it: 'Fuck em all.'

What Castle or Laura, or anyone, could not know is that I, Bobbo the box, might outlast a line of another hundred such professors, we built-to-last types might see a time of gangbusters genetic engineering. Healing, reshaping, power food, super races, nice eyes, good chin, a time when new tribes gain new grounds for perception, when the longheads can't stomach the broadheads, just can't hack em, them broadheads.

Laura said: 'Well it's the last of the personal belongings.'

'What do you mean?'

'Nothing belongs to us any more, out in the public domain, nothing. Even just the public infrastructure that they claim belongs to us, no way. Buses, airports, roads, parks, beaches, waterfalls, and now the personal stuff too. My show in Edinburgh annoyed some people because they said I was disrespecting my great-grandfather David, so they started demanding that the show be cancelled, expelled from the festival. Then my name, even names have gone to market, I had to pay two hundred and fifty dollars for my website name, my own name, Laura Glass-Darlington.'

'Yeah,' Castle said as he put aside his fins, 'the only thing they'll allow to belong completely to you is your fucked up gene, your disease, the rest they'll want to claim.'

The booksmeller stood up and dived into the small lagoon beside the spa, a curving sweep into the clear turquoise water that easily could've made Bakks the cardboard king convulse and then retch.

Castle opened up Oxley, and the spacepod crew of friends started on lunch.

Laura climbed out, shining with clean ocean under the hot sun. 'Wow, that's one hell of a fine picnic box, check out all those implements and bits, where'd you get it?'

'Catherine got it from a shop in Fulham, a dealer friend, gave it to me last year as a Christmas present. Like it?'

'It's wonderful.'

For Jack the hasty-paste had slowed down even more, bringing even more pleasant rest to his splatter ping powderbox. This was true resting, dolphins, lunch, sunshine. Bigtime Evan baddie-turned-goodie drifted again into Jack's mind, then out. Also Patsy's hardball art games back in Bond Street drifted in, drifted out, they seemed so distant now as to not even actually have any existence any more, this place down here was all new: he'd never really, ever, felt this type of relaxing. Then the Keep Left sign drifted in, then drifted out.

Caused him a fleeting ping splatter pop. 'I've just had a good idea!' Jack called out.

'Store it away,' Hong said, 'we're resting.'

'What we do is take a photo of the Keep Left pod on the dam, and take it up to Broome to show Kee when he opens the university.'

'If he opens it,' Catherine said, 'if he even arrives at all.'

'He'll be there,' Remple said.

Nobody knew where Kee actually was, but he'd be somewhere,

unfazed by the hasty-paste, moving slowly, unhurried, maybe swimming, fishing, cleaning out his solar fridge down in the shade of the small galley. Nassau, Key West, Havana, Montego Bay, hey-ho ding-dong and how's the time. Jack Verandah had come far in understanding lounging well, learned it from the boy who swung a rusty key round and round, Sunrise Sunset.

Hitching a Ride

Keep Left had sailed across the Atlantic to Spain. From early life as a buffalo boy, the guy was now a seasoned seafarer. He crossed the Atlantic the way he knew best, the easy way. Riding highways, each as broad as a hundred Niles. First he sailed round the island and then headed north-west to catch the Antilles Current. On this he sailed north to the Gulf Stream. On this he sailed east to the Azores Current and on this he got to the Canary Current to head south for three days where he got off at the entrance to the Mediterranean. If asked, he'd reply that he'd simply hitched a ride or two.

At Gibraltar he cut his speed to follow the Spanish coast leisurely up to the port of Valencia on the Golfo de Valencia. If asked, he'd say he'd hitchhiked the gravitational pulls from out there, pitching his tan chin to the sky, twice. He'd caught a few dangerous storms, but he did okay by the storms.

Past the ramparts of Gibraltar he threw overboard the mobile phone Remple had given him, not out of disrespect for Remple or for his new oceanic university, but out of a wish not to be strung to a satellite. It floated for a while, which Kee felt was odd for a machine outside a boat.

A day past Malaga he came to the Sierra Nevada. At ten thousand feet the mountain range presided over the coastal plain like a brooding forehead, breathing slowly and patiently through a vast headland nose, a forehead that was the south's vast powderbox, full of caliphates and Moors and silk. Best to avoid taking a candle to dried out old hate dear butterfly, for the south's great powderbox had not merely leaked, it had blown those dust particles of memory from one end of the universe to the other. This region was once the last stronghold of those elegant ding-dongs the Moors.

Those two other elegant ding-dongs Isabella and her cousin-husband Ferdinand, bloodsoup, had waited long enough thanks, and their last act of the Inquisition was to forcibly eject a quarter of a million Moors across the strait to Africa. Five years later they ejected the Jews. The whole business had taken two hundred years, ended with the wily pair's bloodsoup monarchy, and made a tremendous success of pulling the place out of flaring Muslim nostrils and bringing the whole Sierra Nevada back into flaring Christian nostrils.

As a boy here, Kee had heard the tales. The strange image of thousands sailing together over the sea to the shores of the other side had forever afterwards made him feel that the place still hummed with a human swing: to him the rocks, the mountains, the tides, these were simply limbs and tongues and ears. He felt the groaning of memory whenever he sailed along this coast. A hundred kilometres long, the Sierra Nevada rolled portside, not so much thoughtful as laying in wait, observing his lone progress for the day until dusk when he was near the port of Almeria. Almer-reeya, the town he'd danced in, the town where Ellie-Isabela's illuminations had given him his first big taste of give and take.

As he made the slow left turn into the bay, the two smaller engines of memory, day and night, awoke together for a brief moment, together and side by side. The last of the sun flashed from the tips of the forehead, and, directly ahead twenty kilometres away west, at the cape, the velvet glove swept stars at the last of the sun. Almeria, being located in the shadow of the forehead, was also in night, and the town's lights were already on, flickering in a low line fifteen kilometres away. He could clearly see both night and day. The sun was still high over by the Sierra Nevada, but the port lay in darkness with its lights blazing, the second equator was touching a town almost ready to dine and dance, caressing the town to life. But the two smaller engines of memory now worked on the seafarer's powderbox, and so all the highs and lows of his travels came tripping back, the journey to this port Almeria as the boy who'd jumped the hacienda wall in search of his friend Rosa Mendoza.

He gazed across the dark bay to the line of Almeria's lights. He estimated arriving in an hour, then into town to see if he could find his friend Pedro from the days on the wharves. If he could find Pedro for company he'd stay in Almeria for a couple of days as he had always done over the years that he had been returning from the Bahamas.

And another village entered his mind. He was now located just a week or two, depending on his greater and lesser whims, from the place where he'd found Castle's grandmother, Renata, hunched on the wooden crate in the early afternoon.

He lowered a trawling line over the stern for an evening meal and caught two large skipjack. As the line drew down into the black sunset water he said aloud, 'Soon I may have the third part of the triumph from that day in '47, soon, around six decades is not a long time. Pedro, he may choose to help, Pedro of Almeria.'

At the town jetty he pulled up alongside a comfortable boat, a new outfit, important outfit, he thought. He secured his own boat and cleaned the fish, and found he stood directly beside an African man sitting on the other boat. The man was in lights and he concentrated on a laptop. Kee wondered if a laptop would float. Kee wanted to sell the second fish for a litre or two of fuel, but now he decided: easier to give it to the African guy.

'Excuse me, would you like one of these fish?'

The guy was slow to respond. He first gazed at Kee and then at the fish held out in two hands. When the guy looked back up he said slowly, 'Yes … thankyou very much … I would appreciate it.'

But Kee had given away a lot of fish, and he noticed the caution covering the African guy. You don't look up and down and then say yes, you just say yes or no. Still, Kee remained cordial: 'Just caught them out on the bay.'

Kee was not to know the guy was Kofi Annan of the United Nations, retired, now on a break in the south of Spain. Instead, Kee sensibly assumed he was just a bit of a peanut for putting across too much caution when being offered a perfectly fine meal.

In his measured, intelligent drawl the African with the name of the Scottish town said, 'Would you suggest steamin it or fryin it?'

'Skipjack can be too sweet, I'll be frying mine in garlic,' Kee said as he wrapped the second fish in paper.

'Have you been out all day?'

'All month, I crossed over from Nassau.'

'In the Bahamas, really?' Kofi Annan took a swing up and down Kee's boat, then down again to the stern and up again to the bow.

This guy, Kee thought, he is one cautious fellow. 'Well,

goodnight, I'm going ashore.'

'Goodnight, thankyou for the fish.'

'You're welcome, señor.'

Kee walked into town to ask after Pedro. It had been a few years since Kee in his fifties called in at Almeria, big, shifting lifetimes, but if anyone could help with the reason he came to Almeria it almost certainly would be Pedro. When I talk to Pedro, Kee said to the girl in his powderbox, that will be a good talk. Pedro of Almeria.

Almeria

Confidential: the world is at peace. Half a century had folded into confidential powderboxes all over town since Kee arrived here as the boy who jumped the orphanage wall to escape, leaving behind a weeping cook and a colonel destined for the Calcutta dockside. The boy hitched rides on the southbound trucks. He finished up in Almeria. He still could not find his friend Rosa the fisherman's daughter, but he met Pedro, and together they had worked the wharves for the summer.

The town, on its waterside flank, had grown what seemed to Kee were gills in the form of tall buildings, but the big concrete gills could not block the view he now had of those early days. He remembered easily the afternoons he gave to searching steadily for the girl who once lived outside the hacienda Zaragoza with her seaweed-headed father giant.

And the mornings that he gave to working alongside Pedro, he could watch it, that summer, play out in front of him as he now walked off the jetty and into the night-lit town. The sunny darting shadows of the two boys helping the boats come in; these were shadows filled with the colours of eagerness, not the fuzz-brown of hard work.

He could see Pedro and himself take off at the end of the work with their funless pesos to turn them into fun lunches. He could see them running through the town with their lunch for a swim far around the other side where it was quiet, where the foreign women swam naked. The local Catholic women frowned on the foreigners for swimming naked but for Kieran and Pedro the foreign women were wise, they obviously understood young men a whole lot better than the local women understood. It puzzled them that foreigners should have a better knowledge of men. But the puzzle was a warm summer puzzle that didn't really bother the boys, and at the end of a morning's work they looked forward to watching the French and American women, the wise ones with their bare breasts shining under the sun.

Kee enquired at the waterside taverns that lurked under the tall concrete gills, but nobody had seen Pedro Ramos. Kee stopped at a small place for a warm drink and a beef pie. After that it was late and the images in his powderbox were wearing out. Maybe, he suggested to the girl in his powderbox, maybe tomorrow we try further up in town.

A fresh waiter arrived for the night.

'Pedro Ramos? Best to look over the hill of small factories over there.'

He found Pedro at the Villacarillo, the small place at the back of town far from the water where they lived as boys. An American walking on the other side of the street said loudly to his friend, loudly to claim he could pronounce it, 'There she is, the beautiful old icon of Almeria, the vee-ah-car-eee-oh, what n heck did ah I tell yawl!'

The very old and greatly loved Villacarillo had escaped the notice of the gill-makers. He could see Pedro in a corner. One of the tavern's slogans hung on the wall above Pedro:

The World is at Peace

Kee walked in and stood by the table.

'Kieran Leeft!'

'Hello Pedro.'

Pedro got up and they embraced. 'When the hell did you arrive, hell, when did you get in?'

The Tree of the Sea

As they settled in, Pedro signalled the waiter. The waiter came along and they discussed what to get, wine or spirits. Pedro insisted on a celebration, so they asked for Sambuca. 'Bring a bottle,' Pedro said in English. The Villacarillo would stay open until four in the morning.

Pedro cleared the table so that they could start afresh, and they spoke in Spanish.

'So you were in Algiers, last I heard you were down there working in Africa.'

'Why is it you assume I came in from Algiers?'

'There's a lot of work down there.'

'There's too many bombs going off there, those stupid guys are still blowing people up.'

'Maybe, but Algeria sells many millions of tonnes of gas into the EU, third largest supplier after the Kremlin and Norway. Algeria is poor, but the gas Algerians are rich. Lot of work, lot of work. They are building a gas pipe on the sea floor from Algeria to Italy, with your instinct for the area, who knows, you were maybe helping them with the early mapping of the sea floor.'

'You haven't changed, you know the world but you're never up to date, I've been in Nassau.'

'Bahamas, I see Johnny Depp paid for an island in the Bahamas.'

'Johnny Depp, who's he?'

'American film star, played a pirate, I thought you'd know about him since he's been playing a pirate on the high seas, but I should've thought better, you wouldn't know who the hell he is.'

'Sorry, I've never heard of him, but good for him for getting an island round there, and good for you for knowing about it.'

The waiter brought a bottle of Sambuca and two glasses. Pedro and Kieran sat in the far corner of the Villacarillo doing two things. It had been a few years between drinks but they always got two things done first. They exchanged memories of the days on the wharf, and they recounted the time when Pedro got into trouble with one of the foreign women for taking her younger sister to the bars. What Pedro and the younger sister actually did nobody found out, but the elder sister threw a fit and took the matter to the police. A week of trouble followed, but even the police thought the whole thing was great fun, and good luck to scrawny Pedro for taking an American on a date. When these two items were finished with, they had each drunk three shots of the Sambuca bottle, and their night had commenced.

Out of Ten

In the stakes of relaxing, the seadog had few peers. Pedro's ability to do nothing was zero. Kee's ability to do nothing was ten out of ten.

'Kieran.'

'Yes.'

'Can you tell me who is the President of America?'

'I think I know who you mean.'

'Jesus Kieran you haven't changed a bit, not one little fukkin ounce have you changed. Funny thing is, I've been thinking about you this week.'

'I've also been wanting to see you.'

'Uh-oh. You have ferried to shore a bad attitude in your mind.'

'Not tonight, here, I caught a skipjack for you.'

'That's even worse, when you give a man a piece of that ocean.'

'No, I'm fine.'

'Truly?'

'Truly. I just hope tonight you're as up to date about Almeria's citizens as you are about the world.'

'This place? Ask me anything about Almeria, anything, citizens especially. The very rich are the new minority here in Almeria let me tell you, just moved in lately.'

'This Paxton-Mendoza, the guy connected to Rosa's father, do you have any background there? Big guy they say, easy to spot, and they claim he can't stay calm or quiet, do you have anything there? When I was here last time you said you'd help me get the dirt on his drunken ravings about Rosa we were told about, remember that?'

'I do, you and me were told Paxton-Mendoza was spreading

shit about her on New Year's Eve in that lousy bar behind the hills. Why do you need to know about him?'

'Do you trust me?'

'Yes of course.'

'He screwed up a friend of mine.'

'Has he now the little fucker, well that's Paxton. What is it Gonzalez's son calls him? "A scam-junkie with his own tiny kingdom," which is good because that's all Paxton ever does, dive into pockets. He's a cynic.'

'How've you been then Pedro, you look fine.'

'As they say: In Almeria you can always be well if you help with the alms. I still help the poor, it keeps me well, in here, and in here. And my little hostel still ticks along.'

'Better get that fish into the fridge.'

Pedro called the waiter, and the waiter lifted his hand to acknowledge, but shot out through the front door.

'It's very great to see you Kieran.'

'Well it is great to see you.'

'What became of your girlfriend from the north?'

'I don't know.'

'It's bad to lose a girlfriend.'

'How the heck would you know,' Kee said quietly.

'I've had girlfriends, don't you tell me I haven't had girlfriends, you bastard.'

'She was never my girlfriend, Pedro.'

'Did you ever find her?'

'No, I didn't.'

Pedro called out to the waiter, but the waiter was still outside somewhere.

Kee asked: 'The town looks bad, what has happened?'

'The town, yeah, it's been getting ugly for a while now. So what's this about Paxton?'

'Paxton-Mendoza, that's his name?'

'Yep.'

'He's about thirty?'

'Yep.'

'He's got some idle connections?'

'Paxton's very connected. He's a signkeeper. They look after this sign up here, "The World is at Peace."'

'Oh well.'

'Oh well? Kieran, you'd be nicely advised to stay away from your usual form. Paxton can have you taken off to the bay, at night, upside-down.'

The waiter stood at the table. 'Pedro?'

'Where the hell did you go?' said Pedro to the waiter.

'These documentary film people from Paris.'

'They're still here?'

'Si. All night at the outside tables, they were cool guys earlier on, but now they're giving everyone the French insults.'

'Are they being disgusting or just irritating?'

'Well, hard to tell, they're just running the place down with insults.'

'But the film is *The Ports of Spain*, why would they run down the tavern?'

'Anyway, I'm jumping out there a bit to look after the old boys from the Valparaiso, they only docked today and they deserve a rest away from a pack of dumbfuck Paris kids.'

'You have had a bad day?'

'I'm sorry, they're not dumb, you're right. But you have to agree, they behave like a pack of mummy and daddy boys these dumbfuck Paris kids.'

'Can you put this fish in the fridge please?'

'Of course.'

'So Paxton knows my friend then,' Kee said with a note of

completion.

'You mean your friend from back then?'

Kieran stayed quiet.

'Your non-girlfriend from when we were boys? You cannot be serious Kieran; if he knows your lost friend from way back in that time when we were kids, your friend could be his mother. She might even be his grandmother.'

'Do you know where I could find him?'

'Yep, yep, I do not, you can say that clean and right, I do not know where you can locate the Paxton-Mendoza boy.'

'Oh well.'

'Oh well? Again? Kieran, I ask gently, do you slip quietly between the understanding of one thing and the other so that you understand nothing, or is your mind asleep?'

'I'm just trying to find an old friend, Pedro, give up your excitement.'

'If that's the purpose you are here, if, then I say good.'

'Let's have another drink of this Sambuca.'

'For you, we shall try a different drink for the next hour. Waiter!'

'Sir!'

'Bring this drunk a bottle of absinthe please.'

'I can't take that stuff Pedro.'

'Bring it,' Pedro nodded quietly to the waiter.

'Yes sir.'

'When I was a boy here I hated these guys you and I have become,' Kee said.

'I haven't become those guys, it's you who has become those guys.'

'But you're a first class drunk, old friend.'

'You're a moraliser, you're kicking the life out from your dreams.'

'Is that what I'm doing, really?'

'Yes, yes, a good guy of your particular type is in fact a bad guy.'

'Am I bad?'

'In the least of the pleasant bad ways, yes,' Pedro said.

'What must I do?'

'Lean over a little, it'll make you a more pleasant bad fellow,' Pedro suggested.

'Lean over?'

'Lean over, you'll find out.'

'I'm leaning.'

'Good, soon you'll hit the fucking floor.'

'I won't, I'll swim, it's you who'll hit the floor, me, I'll float in the gulf.'

'See? That's you: fantasy. You know Kieran, one thing.'

'What.'

'You can't just come in and throw your airs around, towns like this are fully formed, there's no place here for you.'

'Yes, I realise this.'

'You do not.'

'But you see, I do.'

'Tell you what. If you do understand, if you do, then you're more alert than I thought.'

'What's up with you tonight?'

'Nothing.'

'You never protect a town's way.'

'I've started to.'

'Well it's a bad habit.'

'I like this town,' Pedro said.

'You hate this place.'

'You're wrong Kieran, I like it. I have been taking care of my small little orphanage here in town for a long time now, and tell me who inspired it? You did. Yes, I like it here very much, I like the people.'

'It's a very ordered town, clockwork, I could always tell what day it was here.'

'It is very ordered, even if the world is not at peace, Almeria is at peace. I like the people here.'

Outside, the film guys from Paris had started to fall against the tables.

'If the townsfolk felt the same about you, tell me: why would you be up here behind the factories?'

'Because they do not feel the same about me, they'd prefer to throw us old fellows out. They'd want to throw you out too, if you ever stop here for good.'

Kee looked around the tavern. 'This tavern is one of the coast's great wonders, don't you think?'

'This is the greatest tavern in Spain.'

'It really is, the place hasn't changed at all.'

'It is the same as it was the summer we worked the wharves.'

'You know what?' Kee said with an air of finality.

'What.'

'I love this old hole of a tavern. Do you remember that night we first tried to buy a drink here?'

'We were what, say fourteen?'

'Even the wall slogans are still here. This one behind us, "The World is at Peace," it was hanging that night, I remember it clearly, half a century back, phew.'

'That sign has stood in this exact spot for much longer than the tavern, for centuries in fact.'

'Really?'

'See what I mean? This is what you drifters will sadly always miss out on. Ask me anything about Almeria, including that slogan.'

'Don't be stupid, I'm not a drifter. I am Sunset Sunrise the traveller.'

'Yes, you are a drifter.'

'Tell me about the slogan.'

'It was first put here as a signpost jammed into the dirt. Eight centuries ago this spot was a junction of main roads. Three roads. One from over the mountains near Granada, one from up the coast, one from round near Malaga. And the Moroccan and Algerian trade came through as well.

'To accommodate all this hefty ambition they had ten big hotels across the main road, over there, packed nicely with all the luxury trimmings of the fourteenth century, and twenty dirty hotels down at the wharf, the rich hated the wharves back then, they preferred it up here on the slopes, today the rich prefer the waterfront and we up here get the shitpile. Did you know that the very rich are Almeria's newest minority group?'

'Yes.'

'How did you know that?'

'You told me.'

'Just checking.'

'Tell me about the sign.'

'Back then the sign was large, like a house, jammed into the roadside. From that starting point it did not matter what got built or burned here from one generation to the next, another sign went up in the same spot. In 1910 the place was a school, and this room was the quadrangle, and the sign was still there, exactly up there. They say the cunning Velázquez came here for a holiday around 1650, when the place was a garden, and when he found the sign standing beside a corn-seller he lay on the grass to watch the corn-seller do his trade for the afternoon. Velázquez stayed a week and made many sketches of the corn-seller, but he turned the studies into his painting *The Water Carrier* instead. They say this sign up here at our table tonight is more than likely the fifteenth incarnation of the original signpost.'

'Do we know who put the first one up?'

'The legend is there, yes.'

'How do you know all this?'

'The signkeepers, they take it very seriously. Say for instance a developer one day wanted this old tavern to demolish like they've done all over the rest of town, the signkeepers will go in hard as bankers at the design phase and find this exact spot for the slogan. And may God watch over a developer who mistreats the wishes of the signkeepers.'

'So do the signkeepers know what it means?'

'Not really.'

'Do you?'

'No, not really. Do you have any suggestions?'

'I guess it means the world is at peace. And who are these signkeepers? Are they a society, maybe a sect?'

'No, it was a different force that got the signkeepers their acceptance. For a while in the thirties a series of struggles broke out. Three solid families fought over wanting to be the signkeepers. Lasted about twenty years, became vicious too, but nowadays the grip of those three clans has loosened and the signkeepers come from a big range of intermarried connections, but they tend to not like the outside to know who they are. The Paxton-Mendoza guy is a signkeeper, well, he says he is. He's the only signkeeper who'd outright declare he's a signkeeper. His aunt, they say she's his aunt, sent him up to Madrid to university to get rid of the guy for a while, or to try to sort him out anyway, but the boy couldn't take Madrid and he came straight back after less than a year. Today he's a big cynic.'

'You've always been the guy who knows a lot, but your knowing seems to have changed.'

'Oh?'

'Unless this Sambuca and absinthe is having an effect. Yes, you've changed, you seem to have a new view into that memory in the sky. Who have you learned this new view from?'

'My friend I've learned from every single person I have ever known, even the shits I never liked.'

'Who is that African guy down by wharf three?'

'Is he in the yellow boat?'

'Yellow and white, and a green top.'

'That's the UN guy.'

'The what?'

'United Nations, he once headed the United Nations in New York, Kofi Annan.'

'Oh.'

'Why do you ask?'

'I offered him a fish.'

'You offered the UN guy a fish?'

'I've never heard of him.'

'Jesus Kieran, you are so far away.'

'Well, never heard of him.'

'Did he take it?'

'He did but he took his time to take it.'

'You truly do not know who he is?'

'No idea.'

'You are one amazing jerk you know, one amazing jerk.'

'So are you.'

'Oh yes, true, I'm a jerk, but you, welcome to Almeria after all these years señor colonel of jerks.'

'Hello Pedro,' Kee smiled, 'nice to see you.'

'I shall help you find her, Kieran.'

'Thanks.'

'She'll be someone's grandmother by now.'

'Very likely.'

'You know, I remember that very first morning you arrived in town in '47 on the back of that truck.'

'Me too. One peso I had left in my pocket, one, from that guy next door to her house, one damn peso.'

'You've never told me that.'

'I said to him, "I have escaped." He said, "Good for you I'm forty and I've never escaped anything." I told him that after I find my friend in Almeria I shall buy a boat.

'He said to me, "Buffalo boy, if you wish to have your own boat remember to do it like this: take time to pick out the boat, mark it out in your mind. Then, one day, when you're down to your last peso give it to the owner, make an excuse, tell him it is for a ride out to the bay, tell him anything, but do not tell him it was your last peso. Soon he will sell you the boat at a decent price, you'll be the right one to get the boat." It took another few years of last pesos, but when I was down to a last peso, I think in '51, I gave it to old Maliaeras. In '52 he sold me his boat. My first boat at sixteen, remember that?'

'What a day that was! But you, señor Leeft, you have always been a high up there clever shit.'

'Buffalo boys are all clever shits, but we are not high up there.'

'You are still calling yourself a buffalo boy from the days of that hacienda, why do you do this?'

'Because, Pedro, I *am* a buffalo boy.'

'Even though you rejected it back then, hatefully if I remember rightly. Well, acceptance can, you know, sometimes, take a while.'

'A lifetime.'

'Si. Have you ever been back to have a look at it? What was it they called the old house, it had this pompous bullshit name, didn't it?'

'Hacienda Zaragoza, yes. I did go back, in my mid-thirties, around '72 I think. Quarter of a century later, and the place was still standing. In my time it was located on the edge of the village but the village had now grown until the house became located at the centre. I escaped a scrubland and revisited the centre of town. First I put the boat in at the wharf but just sat there for at least an hour before I got up and walked into town, thinking it would be better to stroll through the streets without stopping or talking. I walked up to the front gate. Knowing I'd have to call out for the guard to come and unlock the gate, I stopped again for a moment. Then I noticed it was not locked so I pushed the iron aside. It had rusted badly so it creaked. The stone wall had grown all kinds of vines, and the grounds had overgrown with such an abundance of timber and foliage that I couldn't see the corner where I'd climbed the wall and ran out into town. I couldn't see anyone for the moment. No children, no colonel, I expected the old Scottish Hindu to be moaning a tune to himself on the front porch. I also expected to see the old cook, she was such a beautiful soul, I expected to hear her moaning, making love to one of the fishermen. When I got to the front door, there it all was, complete decay. A thick layer of dust lay up the hallway and the emptiness was eerie. The dining room was always very big, so now it was like a dusty plain. The floor was strewn with broken chairs. The whole place was like that, it was as if the village's teenagers had used the house for fights, maybe for love, but they'd ransacked it either way, fighting or loving. For me there was one second where I shivered because that buffalo might have smashed the chairs simply by galloping around its Golfo de Valencia universe, the dining room.'

'The old colonel really brought the whole anecdote out from India?'

'He did.'

'I suppose that's what people do.'

A loud crash from outside filled the tavern. The two remaining guys of the film crew from Paris had fallen into the furniture.

'What did you say?'

'I was just saying: I suppose that's what people do, ship anecdotes all over the world like sugar and wine.'

'It was completely deserted, an old house right in the centre of town.'

'How come the developers didn't snatch it up?'

'They were spooked.'

'By what?'

'By Maheesha the buffalo demon. That old Scottish Hindu colonel must've really got the town spooked with his demon from India. And the locals believed that the buffalo was shit angry for being locked up at the Golfo de Valencia instead of being free in India, they said Maheesha was terrorised by it, oh yes the townsfolk were spooked all right. The colonel has made a place nobody dares touch, even today.'

'Hm. Smart guy, maybe I should make a Maheesha hullabaloo with my little hostel. Keep it safe from the hands of that new minority group. Did you find the colonel?'

'No, they say he'd died long before. But I found the other guy. After the empty hacienda I went to see the guy who'd given me the pesos. He was in his mid-sixties by then. We sat on his porch and had lunch and a bottle of wine. You should have seen his face when I gave him twenty-five years worth of his pesos back. He refused at first, but after a couple of glasses of wine and a good long conversation he warmed up well and true. But he still didn't accept the pesos until I told him I'd taken his advice and given my last peso to a boat owner in Almeria and a year later owned it myself, then he accepted. With delight.'

'Maliaeras down here in Almeria even let you pay him off for the boat I remember, didn't he?'

'I was twenty-five when I paid him off, yes.'

'We celebrated, you and I, like tycoons!'

'We did, we took those American women to Malaga.'

'Yeah, that still amazes me, they sailed a hundred miles down the coast with two strangers, they trusted us.'

'No, they didn't.'

'Speak for yourself, me they trusted like a dolphin. Come to think of it, why would two rich American girls trust a fukkin buffalo boy?'

They went on enjoying the aimless talk inside the old Villacarillo under the slogan 'The World is at Peace.' Near sunrise the waiter brought out the wrapped fish. He started to put away chairs, and they wished him goodnight. Outside, the last two Paris guys had passed out on the floor.

Kee and Pedro strolled down the hill of deserted streets, into more deserted streets of the town where the ready view of things was bigger, the thigh of the bay, the forehead mountains, absinthe bigger. In the east a faint hand of light had commenced, and to the west high above the Sierra Nevada the last of the stars were being brushed away. The second equator was on its way. Those smaller engines of memory, day and night, once more brushed new powder into powderboxes, freshly ground. A few minutes later when they got to the waterfront the powderwork was done, no stars were left above the mountain range. But their bigger view outside the tavern as they walked across the deserted town was still rather small; it was only a close-up of that line that travels across the mountains and oceans as the earth turns, only a glimpse at the lid of the world's powderbox.

The world's other equator, continually shifting, equating the past, the present and the future. On Kee's boat they finished the last two shots from the bottle of absinthe as the sun came up.

'Could we look for the Paxton boy later today?'

'Si, si, don't worry, we will find the cynic,' Pedro said.

'Pedro.'

'Yes?'

'What is this cynic? I do not even understand what a cynic is, I have never understood what a cynic is.'

'That's because you have lived too long on the sea. A cynic, dear friend, is a person who has not tasted pain, he has only tasted the shit of aggravation.'

'I do not understand.'

'Pain may bring you further than a cynic can go, a cynic can only go as far as aggravation.'

'You have always been a complex guy Pedro.'

Pedro placed the fish in the small solar fridge and then fell asleep on the deck. Kee placed a thick blanket over him and then stepped down into the cabin to sleep.

Bakks Makes a Success

Pedro woke mid-morning and went to get breakfast. But first he confirmed they would go searching for the Paxton-Mendoza boy in the evening. He came back to the boat with two mugs of good coffee, a paper and two hamburgers. Kofi Annan was sitting beside him on the other boat, so they said hello. After that the separation of the two boats was okay and complete, and each boat could get on with the morning in its own amiable way. Except that mister Annan was in for a show, not that anyone at this point knew it. Kofi Annan went below. The sun was shining, the harbour hummed and glowed, on the waterfront people were up and about strolling, so nothing indicated that within minutes a powderbox was about to be held aloft and blown open.

It started quietly. Burger up in one hand, Pedro roamed the newspaper with the other. He threw bits of interest into the air for Kee.

'How's this? India's richest fellow has built a new house.'

'Write to him,' Kee said as he held his gaze across the bay, burger in hand.

'It's big, mister Mukesh Ambani's new home, it's gigantic. Floor area bigger than Versailles. Sixty storeys high; sixty, not sixteen. Five storeys of carpark. A helipad. Health club, two storeys.'

'Is your absinthe making this up?'

'No señor, no-no.'

'Will this mister Muckish be living in it?'

'Yes, Mukesh, his wife, his mother, three children and a full-time staff of six hundred, that's a hundred staff per person.'

'Oh well good for him.'

'And this. It's located in the city of Mumbai, home to the largest slum in Asia thankyou, the Dharavi slum. Says here the slum's a maze of thousands of open drains. Oh, the state government, this is good, bulldozing the slum to build free homes, that's very good. And take a look at this. His friend the Indian billionaire mister Ratan, he's building no less than one million ta-tas per year.'

'What's a tar-tar?'

'Si, a ta-ta, it's a car, sets a new record for the world's cheapest, two and a half thousand dollars gets you a fully proper car.'

'Strange name for a car I suppose.'

'He's named it after himself, his name's mister Ratan Tata. Tata also owns Tetley's.'

'What's a tetley?'

'Tetley Tea, Tata took it a while back. Comprendes, this Ratan Tata comes from a long line of hard workers; look here, it says his great-grandfather was a Zoroastrian, they work hard those Zoroastrians. These two guys, Tata and Ambani, I must get to meet, they buy pieces of the universe like I buy a hamburger. They could be useful for my hostel, for the kids.'

'Si.'

Kofi Annan emerged from his cabin again.

'Good morning mister Annan,' Pedro said.

The retired secretary general responded in his gentle drawl of authority, 'Good morning Pedro, are you swimmin today?'

'Somewhat hungover, but very well should swim thank you. Has the new secretary general mister Ban Ki-moon been to visit you yet?'

'I'd say he has too much on his plate.'

'May I ask you a question? I value your opinion highly.'

'Thankyou, Pedro, I value yours.'

'You know that I look after some of the poor here in Almeria, si?'

'I discovered that last week, yes.'

'Is the world really run by the dollar? Up there, high up, where it matters?'

'Perhaps. Yes, it is, although at the centre of things the dollar itself is ruled by only one master, emotion.'

'Feelings rule the dollar?'

'Yes.'

'Then why do all those finance types talk as if there is an

independent logic to the dollar, I mean, if the dollar's a slave to feelings why don't they say so?'

'In what sense do you mean "logic"?'

'In the sense that they're always saying money should be spent on useful things, spent wisely, spent logically.'

'Well, I don't know. I suppose nations outwardly intone they spend money sensibly, but inwardly they spend it on emotional force, even big sums.'

'Do you mean that the endless talk along sensible lines, all this talk, is a veneer?'

'One could see it like that.'

'So if I wrote to this guy, India's richest fellow, who has built a big house for himself, to request a few dollars for the poor here in Almeria, to continue my free hostel, he'd consider it from feelings instead of investment in his public good looks profile?'

'Yes, he would.'

'May I say in my letter that you suggested writing to him?'

'Why, yes of course.'

'Thank you very much.'

'You're welcome,' Kofi Annan said and walked back into the cabin.

Nobody saw Paxton-Mendoza walking fast up the jetty. 'Good morning gentlemen!' he called extremely loudly. Then more loudly, hoarse: 'Good morning! Good morning, you guys, what are you doing down here now that I have found you!'

From Pedro's position, which was a hundred metres down the jetty, the two Paxton shouts in the distance sounded like a disagreement soon to be amicably settled, but Paxton shouted out once more: 'Yes, this will right-now be a Good Morning!'

In a second Paxton was standing tall at a sitting Pedro, less than an arm's length between them.

'Paxton?' Pedro said, looking up into the morning sun.

'Yes, hallo Pedro, you want to see me, mm?'

Paxton dug himself into the jetty, legs apart, thumbs hooked into the pockets of the leather jacket. He'd done well this year with a new venture importing fake Gucci fashion from a factory in Shanghai, Paxton had become one of their prize distributors, pushing a lot of product into a small southern tip of Spain and across the water into Morocco. He ruled his business in a different leather jacket every day, his motto: Use it one day sell it the next.

'How the hell,' Pedro said quietly, 'did you know I wanted to see you? And how the hell did you find us here?'

'Don't put to me stupid questions.'

'We are taking breakfast,' Pedro said quietly, 'as you can see,' and he held the half-eaten burger up at Paxton's chin so that Paxton had to stumble back a step. 'Maybe later on, how about this evening, right now we have bad heads and sandpaper tongues. And, as you can see, we are taking breakfast,' and for extra fun Pedro pushed the burger closer to Paxton's general face area. Paxton moved back so that he now stood closer to Kofi Annan's boat than to Kee's boat, two arms away.

'I'm busy this evening. If you want to see me, see me right-now, right-now. I'm busy tonight reaching my true potential, taking it on.'

'Ah, your potential, important. Very well then, we can talk this morning. It must be almost midday, better make it fast. This is my friend Kieran Leeft. He called in yesterday from the Bahamas to look for an old friend.'

'Señor Leeft. Bahamas?'

'Good to meet you señor Paxton.'

Very often in daily life those that stand with their two feet on land will miss these very slight warnings, hints that drift by as invisible as a particle of dust, or powder. But Kee's feet were hardly ever on dry land, and so he noticed an almost invisible mirage in the air around Paxton. Paxton's storage system obviously was not a powderbox; the thing behind Paxton's forehead dear butterfly maybe was more like a ding-dong petrolbox, or an acidbox. I'd say Bakks had been at work behind the guy's forehead. Maybe Paxton's powderbox was a powderkeg.

'Señor Kee,' Pedro said squinting up at powderkeg Paxton, 'has come to Almeria in search of a childhood friend. We believe she might be your grandmother.'

Paxton turned directly to Kee. 'What are you playing here?'

'He thinks you're playing a game, Kieran.'

'I might be.'

'We don't play games around here,' Paxton snapped back.

'Paxton Paxton,' Pedro said squinting. 'Look at his boat Paxton, does a man who sails this boat across the Atlantic play games?'

'It doesn't impress me, I'm busy mining my true potential.'

Paxton's phone went off and he took the call. He didn't exactly possess Mandarin but he'd picked up enough to run the essentials; he didn't have the language, but he did have the haranguage, he could hustle in Mandarin, press the best deal. He strolled away talking in all the best bullying phrases, and at one point he screamed wildly into the phone. It was a show of pain, and then he turned his hurt into a laugh.

'Is he ill?' Kee asked. 'I mean, why is he so sharp and rude, he's very aggressive verbally.'

'No, he's not ill, Paxton is as normal as normal can be, except for one thing. His mother and father died many years ago. Like most who lose their guides in this life, Paxton has nobody to check the way he treats people like shit. And his grandma, she's said to be not that interested in Paxton. So the boy's got no string see, no guide.'

'I never had a guide, any guide, was I ever rude to you?'

'You had your buffalo, for better or for worse. Paxton the sorry fuck doesn't even have a slug.'

'Why does he keep on talking about his true potential? It's as if he's been to a commune in the mountains the bald way he talks about it, like commune pamphlets.'

'When he came back from Madrid he told me he got very excited by a new calling—he was to be a film-maker. I said, "If you are even to begin to know your true potential then you must not be living here in Almeria." He said, "That's right! I'm going to New York!" But here he is. Even today his true potential is always standing across the street like a ghost, gazing back at him.'

'But he seems well-dressed, a young man of substance.'

'He imports the Gucci copies from China.'

'Gooch—?'

'Clothing, expensive Italian fashion, shirts, jackets, bags, shoes; so expensive that many women and men feel they mustn't buy them, and so Paxton imports the cheap illegal copies for them to afford to buy. And toys, he imports toys.'

'This helps the guy with his potential?'

'I don't know,' Pedro said and shrugged as he ate the burger. 'Maybe.'

Paxton by now had wandered a few metres off, close to the bow of the boats. Kofi Annan was sitting on the front deck on a chair. Paxton lowered the phone and turned to Annan.

Paxton shouted: 'What're you looking at!'

I said to Oxley: 'Bakks is very energised today.'

Oxley said: 'Well that's what he works on after all: his cardboard logic; if you ask everyone to be pissed off, and they all agree to be pissed off, then you have one hell of a pissed off picnic. Lucky Bakks can't get to that cool UN dude on the boat.'

Paxton then lifted the phone and continued his performance in his haranguage. He knew he would win, and he did. Here the clock was midday, China three in the morning, why would a factory owner be calling at three unless an emergency was in the air in Shanghai? Paxton won, said goodbye, conferred good luck upon the caller's children, and stood for a moment looking into the sky with a broad smile. He came back to the stern of Kee's boat in a big, fresh mood. Full of sunshine and self-humour. It always happened if Paxton had controlled a flow of business happiness, business importanto, his way; like a switch he turned his mind onto English importanto. Using English stood for global endlessness, he felt it showed he understood global shine. Globules of shine. Or as we boxes at The Exchange called it, in our throwing of memories around the world, globularisation.

'Why do they like me in Shanghai? Because I'm a bunny, I bring profit magic right-now, right-now. Ey, Pedro, no?'

'Si.'

'How's this: four out of every five toys in the whole fucking world are made in China, and China has over ten thousand toy-making factories, and I have just been given the Spanish rights for the fourth biggest factory of them all! I'm a bunny!'

Pedro thought he might as well play along. After all, the petrolbox boy suddenly seemed bright and cheerful. 'You are a sunny bunny.'

'More-more, a sunny bunny on the money!'

'Si, a sunny bunny on the funny money.'

Instantly shitted off, Paxton sunny to grim in a flat bat of an eye. He'd taken enough of the moralising around town about his venture in Gucci fakes.

'You know what Pedro? I'll tell you what. If you need to see a penguin in the picture then there's a penguin in the picture. What does this mean? Let me fucking tell you. New research from Berlin shows, the latest research, that when a customer buys a fake Gucci it leads to later on making the decision to buy a genuine Gucci. So you know what? We do not steal from Gucci, we fake-makers pump up Gucci's profits, and so from now on, now that the proof is there, they can stop the complaining and right-now get a life.'

'That's very nice,' Pedro said. 'One thing, though. You should not speak to mister Annan like that.'

'Who?'

'The fellow up there. Do not speak to him like that, he's my friend.'

'It seems everyone is your friend these days, hm? Friends all over town, hm?'

'And,' Kee said, 'I am his friend too. I believe that your grandmother and I used to be friends long ago, on the north coast.'

'You leave my grandmother out of this,' Paxton said sharply. He turned to Pedro. 'Why is he treating me in this disrespectful shit way? Someone should let him know that I am a signkeeper, does he know I'm a signkeeper?'

'Come on Paxton, be reasonable, how can he possibly know that?'

'Well you right-now tell him!'

'He-ey, I cannot go round telling people you're a signkeeper, where would my reputation be if I ran around announcing you're a signkeeper?'

'Tell him right-now what it means!'

'All right, okay, Paxton's a very important and respected guy, let's start from there Kieran, yes?'

'Fine, can do. Señor, would you please take me to visit your grandmother?'

Paxton started to go red. He started to look wildly around the jetty. He found a stash of crates and walked over, picked one up and threw it at the side of the cabin. It smashed a window. He picked up another crate and threw it at the stern where it bounced and went into the water.

'Paxton Paxton,' Pedro said, 'you should have migrated to New York like I suggested.'

'He's got a point señor Paxton. For a young man of such talent, New York is a fertile place I am told.'

Paxton screamed: 'You guys know nothing, look at you, pair of losers. Hanging around this shit harbour, you babies. America is dung. China is king. Just one phone company in China, China Mobile, has three hundred and forty million subscribers—that's ten percent more than the whole population of America. Let me tell you how big is China's appetite right-now. Let me give you babies the latest research, take iron ore, they buy so much, so much, to make how many Manhattan Bridges? Every year? Nine hundred! Fuck New York when it doesn't even make ONE new bridge a year! Yeah, me, I'm connected to China, to the future. China's busy, you babies. Making new roads, new cars, new airports, railways, tunnels, highways, buildings, hotels, schools, shops, bicycles, they're buying steel like nobody else. And their toys need springs, I don't need New York, I'm connected to my true potential!'

Paxton picked up another crate and smashed it against the bow.

Kofi Annan stood at the stern of his boat. 'Are you all right, Pedro?'

'Si si mister Annan, we are fine.'

'Three babies, three!' Paxton shouted bitterly. 'Right-now

three babies on the shitty harbour doing fuck-all!'

And it was, as they say in a galley, or the kitchen of a tavern, it was done. By that hefty squeal of irritation, it was done. Hail the box I say, that's what I say. Salute O boxo. Hey-ho and ding-dong the fusty world of boxes. Boxo importanto. Bakks might have made the kid's forehead of memories into an acidbox, or a powderkeg of ping splatter pop, but we proper boxes got him round to Kee Leeft. Here was Kee once more parked on that coast where a triumph comes in threes. And the third part was now nearly done, but nobody would have guessed that it might be done by such an uncool guy as an unwitting Paxton-Mendoza blowing up his own powderbox. But see, that's us boxes for ye. The choice of vessel, in this case Paxton, face it, is basically ours, and since we have little else to do but throw memories around, across the divides, we pick and choose those divides at whim, hup two three. As for the crates Paxton broke, they were those slatted, open, pine things, they don't count as boxes to us, so no harm done. No harm, just help: just Sunrise Sunset's long-awaited triumph plumpicked from the universe.

A Triumph Comes in Threes, Hup Two Three

So Paxton stormed off the jetty, things returned to normal and the two men finished off their breakfast of cold hamburgers, neither guy even remotely aware of what was to come next.

'Now that's what's truly a noisy hangover,' Pedro said.

'Almeria was always a noisy place,' Kee said, 'I remember.'

It was now lunchtime. The harbour sparkled, sun high on the Sierra Nevada.

'Well,' Pedro said, 'better make back to the hostel, write my letter to mister Mukesh. Plus, start up that Maheesha hullabaloo stuff for the kids so we can spook the developers and keep them spooked, jam a buffalo of chaos and evil into their brains.'

'Shall I give you the Maheesha legends so that you at least know something about them to start the stories off?'

'No need, I'll check it out on the Internet.'

'The what?'

'Jesus, Kieran.'

'What's wrong?'

'Nothing. See you tonight?'

'Yes, fine.'

Pedro strolled up the jetty. 'Goodbye for now mister Annan, thanks for your advice.'

'Good afternoon Pedro.'

'Mister Annan?'

'Yes?'

'How did you get the name of a Scottish village, being an African señor I mean.'

'My grandfather was a Scotsman.'

'Oh.'

Kee went below for a siesta.

Half an hour later he went up to the jetty to pick the pieces of broken glass from the grooves of the small window. He'd often wanted to replace the glass anyway with perspex, so this was a spot opportunity to replace the window with the safer, sturdier plastic material, and the boatworks here in Almeria he knew were very cheap and very good. Over in Malaga they were complete eels who charged like the Pope and were not as good at what they did as the Pope is at what he does. Besides, it was a fine afternoon to rest.

It was about half an hour later that a woman came strolling down the jetty. She wore a sunny long dress from the old days, loosely cut, patterned with flowers. When she got to within metres of Kee's boat she stopped. Here she stood for a while watching Kee pick the glass from the window and carefully laying it aside on the jetty.

Then she continued coming forward, stopping at the bow. 'Looks like a bad accident,' she said.

Kee glanced at the woman but went back to tending the window. 'Nothing serious,' he said. He missed the laughter in her eyes.

'Nice boat, I like the lines,' she said brightly.

'Thanks.'

'And the colours, I like the colours, that blue is so light it looks like the sky, not the sea.'

'I like the sky.'

'And the sea?'

'The sea too.'

'That blue, I've seen it before,' she said, 'but not recently. These days it's a very old-fashioned version of blue, nobody uses that sky-blue on the boats any more. Not around here anyway.'

'I mixed it to copy the gatepost of an old friend up north.'

'Old-fashioned friend.'

'No, not really, it was back in '47.'

'Hell, back then that blue was very modern,' she said, and her eyes flickered with laughter.

Kee concentrated on the window frame, picking the last slithers of glass away.

'Here,' the woman said brightly, 'I've brought a pair of gloves.'

Kee stopped. 'You brought these, for me?'

'Yes I did.'

'Did Pedro send you?'

'Who is Pedro?'

'Look, I am very sorry, but right at this moment I am a bit busy as you can see.'

'You don't want the gloves?'

'No, thankyou, no.'

'Suit yourself then, if you don't want the gloves you can't be forced into taking the gloves.'

'They're fine looking gloves, you'll find someone for them.'

'Yes, they're leather, they once belonged to my father, a fisherman. He wore them in, but so well that the fit now allows the hand to work with natural ease.'

Kee looked off to where she had them held out.

'You don't recognise them?'

'Rosa,' Kee said quietly, 'Rosa?'

Kee looked up, and there she was, smiling as if she knew the place inside out, just as she had known the old village inside out.

'Hello Carlos.'

They left the broken window behind and took a stroll along the marina. Rosa said: 'I came to the hacienda the day before we left the village to say goodbye. I was weeping all the way to the place, sobbing my little lungs out and the women were staring, shaking their heads, and when I got there, those two guard guys wouldn't let me in, so I left a message for you.'

'They gave me no message. I came round to your house, but it was empty.'

'We left faster than a sparrow, my father just got up one

morning, and, I remember this so clearly, always have, he sat at the table and said, "Fuck this village, fuck the war, we go: Almeria, there it is a place of great respect and wealth for fishermen, we go." And two days later we were gone.'

'Your father was a good guy, I learned a lot from him about the sea.'

'He liked you.'

'Your grandson is a fiery guy.'

'He's not my grandson.'

'Oh.'

'He's the son of friends, both died when he was very young and I raised him briefly, and these days we hardly see one another.'

But while Kee was listening he was actually strung out by his powderbox, walking, talking, strung out across another time and place, where a boy jumped the old stone wall and started running. He ran over the hill and he kept on running and running. Over the heads of the big people he ran with the wind at his heels. He sailed through the shutters of perception, he ran across bridges, along highways, through forests, up into lofts and down into basements, he had to keep running, always running, for it gave his nostrils the air to keep calling out to Rosa Mendoza, 'Rosaa ... Rosaa,' he called. So when we boxes are asked: At what moment in Kieran Leeft's adulthood did he encounter that boy? When exactly was it that he met himself as the escapee he once was, the boy who set out running non-stop in search of his friend? At this moment, here, on the marina in Almeria, we say.

We say, 'Hey-ho ding-dong, thereabouts in Almeria.'

All dusty small people arrive at destinations unknown, and Kieran Leeft was no different. Every dust-made kid can, and many do, meet themselves, watch themselves chase a dream, scattering around back gardens, climbing trees to examine, from high above the dust, where the world might begin, helped along by us boxes, us restriction-free pirates. Like all dust particles Kieran the boy is resourceful, swift, hopeful, and, maybe, he finally gave the half-broken shutters of perception the slip. Half-broken, half-closed, a shutter is a shutter.

'Would you like to come to Australia with me?' Kee asked.

'Austria I've been once, too chilly,' Rosa said.

'Australia, that's how it is said, I think.'

'Oh, sorry. That place on the other side of India?'

'Yes.'

'Won't it be expensive, such a long long journey?'

'No, my friend will fly us there.'

'Generous friend.'

'He wishes me to officially open his new university.'

'Are you a professor these days?'

'No, he just likes me. A few years after I went looking for you, I found his grandmother and saved her from her violent father, Remple just likes me.'

'Have you been in a plane?'

'No, you?'

'No.'

'So would you like it, to go there?'

'Yes, I would.'

Yum: poke a look at that, a triumph. It only took sixty years, but the boy who jumped the wall was visibly quite happy at this moment, yes he might be severely shaking inside, but hell, he was ding-dong happy on the outside, in the present, a calm, unhurried seadog curving the universe round in threes. No hurrying, just idle talk and a smile that began to crease the stubble.

Preserving a wish, preserving a moment, preserving mango

jam, it all takes different chemicals and varying temperatures, all very complex the preservation business. But not for us better boxes, we preserve in a simple way. We just get up and throw things around. Across the hungry seas and over the ravenous mountaintops, hup two three. Ding-dong and how's the time.

VI
A place on the beach south of Broome that grew the biggest wings in the world

Crossing the Equator

Prawnbox Bakks got cranky. O great king of evil, king of taking, always did desire irritation, said so himself.

He hates us better boxes completing the triumphs of our jungarummy jiddle. Triumphs were tricky enough, they had to arrive after three attempts, and with Bakks in tow triumphs were even more difficult. He calls me Skinny only because he's fat as hell, yet another one of those flimsy portholes of perception. Fat, plus a bit crumpled, his 'injury.'

His wounded logic was always a sight to behold, but very tricky to work with. He calls me Skinny also because, I believe, he still carries nightmarish images of pigs, rotund, fat, burly pigs, and because he can't stand my occasional success. Try this, this pearl of wisdom, for a slice of his wounded logic being cast over the seas and the mountaintops: 'Since the people of the world are so full of love, Skinny, where are the rats of war getting away with it, hm? Where Skinny? Everywhere, that's where, you fukkin dumb bastard.'

I mean, Bakks and his crumpled cardboard logic got him plenty of trade, but us wooden boxes and our sweeter logic gained us a touch of trade too. When Kee Leeft and Rosa Mendoza finally met again thanks to a sweeter logic at The Exchange, thanks to a lot of hard work throwing memories around the planet over the seas and the mountaintops, when the boy and the girl finally took a stroll down the jetty in sunny

Almeria, Bakks just blew his top. Language left him, becoming haranguage, or pranguage, he just blew up. Even his soggy crumple went pop-flat.

Bakks: 'Don't presume you can swine me out, you rotten wooden do-gooder.'

But the crumple re-crumpled, and Bakks blowing up served no purpose once Kee and Rosa had together decided to jump on a flight to cross the equator to Broome.

Bakks couldn't do a thing about it.

Except suffer his own infuriations, O cardboard king of creeps, lucky they weren't hot, those infuriations, he'd catch fire. Eradication by burning, yuk. But then, Inch was already onto that one. Caked ratsblood ambition. Hailme-Hailme had Bakks in his sights.

Inch: 'I prefer work with you boss, dante I.'

A Pin in the Sky Opens the Future

On Almeria's busy waterfront, with its jetties, harbour and boulevard, nobody lives in the present. They're dreaming of the glow of yesteryear, or making plans for the future; nobody actually has a foot planted in the present. In fact, nobody anywhere lives in the present, instead it's a wistful roll of hopes for tomorrow, and a wistful yearning for the good things gone by. Noting the vacancy of the present is all very positive and straightforward, until we realise that a taste for the past and the future simply makes Bakks's frightful work a whole lot easier. You don't need to move a mountain when there's already a compulsion available, you just tweak the compulsion and the rest is history. When Bakks couldn't get to work on Kee and Rosa, when he couldn't do any jungarummy jiddle on em, Bakks rained abuse upon me, phew.

I didn't care. I said, 'Bakks, now hear this.'

I used his own claptrap against him: 'Bakks,' I said, 'if you need to see a penguin in the picture then there's a penguin in the picture.' Ding-dong and how's the time.

Kee walked into the town centre and found the office Remple had told him to find. He went inside and was welcomed to a desk. He sat.

He explained to the guy what he was expecting.

'Si,' the guy said after checking his computer, 'señor Kieran Leeft?'

'Si,' Kee said.

'We have two tickets here, from señor Remple Fekdin, señor Leeft. To whom shall I make out the second ticket?'

'Señorita Rosa Mendoza.'

'No problem.'

A week later Kee and Rosa took a taxi out to the airport. They flew first across the Mediterranean to Rome for a connecting flight to Dubai. There they caught a direct flight to Perth, racing across the Indian Ocean, into the oncoming sunrise. Remple had organised their Perth arrival time to meet with, inside a couple of hours, a connecting flight to Broome. In total they'd loitered in lounges and travelled the sky for thirty-four hours. You'd expect them to have hated it, that thirty-four hours of caged-in boredom, but let me say with ding-dong bounce: they loved every minute, between the occasional siesta they talked and talked.

On the descent into Broome they noticed that the earth below was a brilliant fusion of reds; Remple had been exact: the desert was red.

In Broome, Kee took, as Remple had instructed in Nassau, the two rooms reserved at the hotel at Cable Beach, one for himself and another for Rosa. They settled in and then walked across the gardens to the beach, one of the world's longest at a hundred kilometres, and they sat near the water as four camels went past.

'You like your friend,' Rosa said to Kee, 'this señor Fekdin.'

'Some give, some take,' Kee said. 'Si, Remple gives.'

'That's what Bella used to say,' Rosa said.

'Who?'

'Ellie-Isabela, the woman at the hacienda who helped the Scottish señor.'

'Ah, si, beautiful Ellie-Isabela, so she did, so she did: some give, some take, si.'

Kee fell silent for a long time.

'Are you all right?'

'It's that woman, Ellie, I haven't thought about Ellie for a long time.'

'She was funny and warm, I liked her.'

'She was very funny. I wish I had said goodbye to her, but I never did, what a horrible thing to do to such a lovely lady.'

'She would have known, she would have known you were ready to go, you told me yourself, she was always giving you advice in the back room.'

'Do you think she and your father ever brought that playful attraction into the bedroom?'

'I'd say so, yes.'

As the camels moved past, a jeep drove past. 'This is a strange place,' Rosa said. 'I like it but I feel strange, does Remple feel strange here?'

'He was born here, so he feels strange in Spain, but his grandmother was born in a village near Valencia.'

Suspicions

The next day a driver from Remple's university came to collect Kee and Rosa. He drove them through town and then out of town south along the bay. The journey amazed Kee and Rosa, a beautiful red desert right against the turquoise sea, no houses, no buildings, no villages or towns, no trees, no hills, just an endless rocky drive along the ocean.

The driver said: 'For eighty kilometres along the coast here lies the world's richest pickings of dinosaur footprints, fifteen species all up.' And then the driver said nothing for the rest of the drive to the university.

The university hadn't formally opened yet. It was about to, and the campus is a remote, quiet place with just twenty early students from around the world wandering about, eagerly assisting the staff with small chores. Small chores, last minute things, inconsequential to a vice chancellor, but to a general manager the small chore is what he called 'a bogey under a rock.'

In an hour they arrived at the gates of the university, and the sign read *IODINE*. That's what the acronym came to, and that's what the university was called, just Iodine, everywhere, around Australia, on the website, on the outdoor posters in New York and Boston, and on TV in Britain, Germany, France, and on the sides of the buses in oil-rich Lagos, and also Dubai where the world's first green city was being built. Remple's friend Greg Howlett advised him to include posters in Abu Dhabi coz the little emirate had reserves of ninety-six billion barrels of oil, Dubai had only four billion, so the Abu Dhabi parents were more likely to send their kids off to a place that they'd never heard of, but which now sported the best ocean university in the world. Remple had pinpointed the niches that he figured would respond, and he'd been right. To get the attention of students from Shanghai he signed a four-year deal with the Shanghai Opera Company in order to reach their parents. But for Tokyo he believed he'd get the kids directly from the cinema rather than indirectly via their parents at the opera, so he saturated the Hollywood blockbusters that came to Tokyo.

For maximum saturation, to explode Iodine's lingo and mojo into the world, he got his marketing manager Ruby Schwartz to do cartwheels, online, to just let loose, and let loose Ruby did well, coz Ruby the professional was a cross between a merciless prehistoric hunter and a slick binary-lingo ballerina. She already concluded most of her supplier and designer meetings on Remple's balcony in Cottesloe by the scent of the Norfolk pines. Her working months in the last year had been commuting between the balcony in Cottesloe and Broome. She was employed by Iodine through her own company, Hotcats, a team of twelve bent-headed bright sparks that designed for clients all manner of visibility, using mixtures of all manner of anything and everything, whether it was digital, clay, ink or language.

Ruby the Dude

She oversaw the posting on YouTube of dozens of sea films a month, which the early students happily made, from underwater films to microbe abstracts from the electron microscope, from krill films to campus films of the goodlife. Sunny happy films showing the cool new set having a ball recovering a lost century.

And if Remple or his general manager had any ding-dong perception that Ruby was a sweet blushing marketing flower, it was quickly put to rest in the hottest and ugliest way possible. The design came from Hotcats. The four-minute film that got the most downloads was something Ruby had especially organised, it had already, pre-launch, taken millions of hits. How Ruby achieved such prominence globally, from just one brief ugly film, was actually quite simple. She asked a Broome trawler skipper for a favour. If he happened to net a very big shark, Ruby'd purchase it. She then had the dead shark tied to a mangrove tree. Within a couple of days she was able to film, using six cameras, the spectacle of a titan saltwater crocodile chomping up the huge decaying shark, and the footage of a giant ancient beast devouring another giant ancient beast became world-famous overnight.

These prospective students, Ruby knew only too damn well, were the coolest of the cool, because them's the new minds ready to remake the new century, building a nexus from the sea back to the earth, emotional, philosophical, scientific. And Ruby did those cartwheels online as smartly as her mensa mind flew, using podcasts, vidcasts, Facebook, MySpace, iTunes, and, on Web 2.0's flash new horizons, she wrapped Iodine into blogs, virtual communities and every new social networking site the students ran into. Online, Iodine became a massive undergrad hub. The hub grew exponentially. The hub became the biggest hub the world had known. It was Ruby who in the early stages of Iodine suggested to Remple the idea of including a New Media Department, where every kid must do a compulsory year in order to graduate. Needn't be a big department she'd said, just nifty, where the visual and interactive material gets produced—by the student. Remple agreed straight away, because he had always wanted just one thing from the university, he'd wanted the students to feel that they were showing the world the good work as they did the good work, not merely after graduation. Ruby then flew the world to buy the equipment, crisscrossing the equator to meet suppliers.

The suppliers of the cutting-edge gear Ruby sought, because they were gobsmacked by the beast she was planning to build, fell at her prehistoric feet, result being that the hardware and software and toys and tools Ruby had tailor-designed into the New Media Department was a beast as nimble and fast as a drop of mercury. Unofficially, she got the department nicknamed Neutrino's Lab in honour of the fastest, smallest particle known to the constellations, flying through earth itself at a microsecond, billions of em, all day every day. Ruby Schwartz, a ding-dong dapper one, that one. No-no, she ain't just a marketing manager, she's the creator of Neutrino's Lab. At the very least, forty or fifty of the male students fantasised about Ruby at least twice a day. Ding-dong dang-a-lang yap-yap. All she had to do was walk.

When Jack Verandah met Ruby, he walked away stunned. He said to Hong: 'How does she do it?'

'Do what?'

'That mesmerising that she does, how does she end up mesmerising everything in sight?'

'Oh that, yeah. She looks directly at the mouth.'

A Munnwaggle

One of the biggest suppliers to Ruby's baby was a guy in Silicon Valley, and he'd got a taste for Ruby the moment she walked into his office and smashed the water cooler. He was a fine groovy dude high on love, love of everyone. He was so full of unrestrained love that he called everyone babe and brother, and he loped around like a golden yap-yap, a golden retriever blissed out at a party. He overflowed with good vibes, virtually no holding back, what we better boxes called a munnwaggle.

The munnwaggles are grown-ups generally, but they're like a kid, no barriers, bouncing over barriers without a care in the world. Two types generally, nice ones and boring ones. The nice ones munnwaggled naturally, it belonged, and through it belonging it cast around natural good vibes. The boring ones overdid it coz I dunno why, coz maybe they were copying the true munnwaggles. The boring ones called everyone babe and brother with a force that sounded tinny. This guy owned the company, so he was a nice munnwaggle, and so he was only too glad to hitch the thing to Ruby's baby back in Broome, and, besides, he'd never been to Australia. He had done lots of munnwaggling almost everywhere, on both sides of both equators, but no munnwaggling in Australia. He was very keen to get over to Broome. He thought Australia was directly under India, so he got a surprise when he discovered it was under Borneo. Jungles came to his imagination, so he got a surprise when he discovered desert was the go. Over the coming months he'd helped Ruby get Neutrino's Lab up and humming coz the blast he got from the babe at the ocean university slapped upon a desert was a blast like he'd never had, this was gonna be a love job, and it paid.

The Sharpest Kids in the Land, Your Custodians Dear Butterfly

IODINE. International Ocean Dialogue & Intelligence, Nexus Earth. The American student Rake Delahunty called it ruby-dyne, and everyone else called it eye-o-deen.

Iodine, it's the only university in the world dedicated to the ocean. Which is why Kee gave Remple the time to officially open it in the first place.

Around the world are dozens of universities that have departments concerned with the ocean dear butterfly, but Iodine is entirely dedicated to the ocean. A whole campus studying the ocean. In the minds of kids of all creeds around the world it rang bells. And the kids were elated at the fact that a proper university was called simply Iodine, rather than some creepy, responsible name like The International Ocean University. Iodine, the kids went for it with gusto. They already knew the ocean was the planet's heartbeat. It spoke for the planet, in ways the kids already felt by the instinct of a new generation. It spoke in rhythms of rising, sinking, melting, freezing, falling, salty, diluted, clear, filthy, taking chemicals, taking excreta, fixing humidity at the top of Everest, bringing fire to a forest behind Lucknow.

Heating, cooling, giving, taking: to kids around the world it was all ocean, to kids who knew what the urgent work was, and they fought slinky wars on the enrolment site to secure a place at Iodine. From plants to animals, and from chemicals to currents, Iodine covered it all. But the thing that also rang bells in the kids' heads was the image of a campus consisting entirely of domes. Every building is a dome at Iodine, lecture halls, libraries, labs, accommodation, the student bar and recreation centre, domes designed from Castle's charcoal drawings back in the creaky shack far down south, two thousand five hundred kilometres away, in Yelverton, where Remple was still enjoying a laid-back break and snorkelling at the Sugarloaf Rock lagoon.

'A dome because,' Castle had said to Remple three years back, 'a dome is more cyclone-resistant than a flat sided building, so when you get the cyclone season up there you won't need to worry, the wind'll slip off past a round surface instead of battering a building head-on.'

Then Remple's friend the architect Greg Howlett built the university using Castle's domes, bringing the campus to life out over the sea on a series of jetties.

The Sunmagnet

The driver who collected Kee and Rosa turned out to be the general manager of the university, Peter Blitz, who saw the chore as a bogey under a rock, and when they slowed for the gates Peter uttered his second sentence, 'Welcome to Iodine, let me show you around.'

He parked at the admin dome, and from there they rode in a buggy round the university grounds, which were not on the ground but instead located out on the bay on the jetties, an ocean university hovering above the ocean. Peter guided Kee and Rosa on a tour that was essentially the same tour that kids around the world could access on Iodine's recruitment website, and walk the virtual boardwalks of Iodine they did, by the tens of thousands. A fraction of the curious would get lucky, come the Dry they'd cover the university's grounds with actual dusty footprints. The Dry was the scholastic term, six months, and for the other six months, the Wet, the kids went home.

Peter Blitz started the tour with the first jetty. One jetty dedicated to each department. From the Chemistry Department to Oceanography, from Marine Biology to Fisheries, from Deep Trench Research to Reefs and Atolls, each of the fifteen departments was a kilometre-long jetty, consisting of six to ten domes, and all fifteen jetties sat just metres above the turquoise high water mark. At low neap tide the jetties were twenty metres above the water. That was the university grounds, fifteen jetties. 'From the air, flying in,' Peter said, 'it looks like a comb.'

A distance along the jetty, an American student called out, 'Hey there mister Blitz!'

'Good morning Rake, how's the catch today?'

'Fine, yeah fine!'

What the kids also liked was that every dome was covered in solar panels. The entire university was disconnected from the state grid, generated its own power, free. The kids thought it the coolest thing they'd ever seen. The free electricity fact, appearing on the website, was a very large, pre-eminent slab of information that Ruby Schwartz insisted would switch the kids on, and she was right. The solar panels were the latest, extreme-efficiency blasters created by China's sun king, the Sydneysider Zhengrong Shi, who owned the giant company Suntech Power, and he didn't sell them to Remple, he donated them. Years before, when Remple had met with the Chinese solar billionaire to show him the project and to discuss making Iodine a hundred percent solar, the sun-master was delighted. He made the supply and installation a gift to the university, and thereafter Zhengrong Shi became a lifelong friend and patron of Iodine. His panels sat brewing sunlight into rivers of voltage underneath a seamless perspex skin, so the ultra smooth exterior made the domes the most stable structure that the north-west region of cyclones had ever seen. The student from America's typhoon belt in South Carolina, nineteen year old Rake Delahunty, said to Kee, 'They say a hell typhoon came through last season, mister Leeft, but it was doin nothin to the domes but whistlin tunes, talk about crap.'

Tides are huge here, Bakks'd be retching, and so the end of each jetty was fitted with a tidal turbine that supplemented the electricity from the solar buildings. When the Indian Ocean surged in at chunks the size of a hundred cities, the fifteen turbines would start to whiz like bees, generating extra power, same as when the tide rushed out.

Peter Blitz's phone rang. Please, not a bogey under a rock. He excused himself and walked away to take the call. It was Remple.

'Is he there yet?'

'Yes, he is.'

'Why didn't he call me?'

'He threw the phone overboard near Gibraltar somewhere.'

'Really?'

'That's what he said, he apologised, but he said he threw it over the stern just past Gibraltar.'

'Tell him he's done a piece of inexcusable littering and polluting, that'll put one into his seadog head.'

'I'll leave that to you when you come up. Er, Remple?'

'Yeah?'

'This guy's really going to open the place?'

'Yep. See you Thursday.'

'Okay, see you then.'

Remple had insisted that Peter Blitz conduct the tour, not one of Peter's staff. And certainly not one of the twenty kids that had arrived early, eager to help out, hands flapping with excitement at any request. Peter protested, Peter had a team around him, it should be given to the marketing manager Ruby Schwartz, but no, Remple insisted on Peter taking Kee and Rosa on the tour.

At the entrance to Jetty One, the student Rake Delahunty was standing with Kee and Rosa.

'Mister Leeft,' Rake said, 'sir, is it true they say you flied over from the Bahamas?'

'No señor, Almer-reeyuh.'

Rake had no idea where that was. 'Is it true you have lived your whole life on the ocean, sir?'

'Si.'

This was a fact Rake Delahunty heard rumoured, but even now on confirmation couldn't eat. Stunned, silent, Rake leaned on the railing. He pretended to gaze out at the turquoise bay, but sideways he was trying desperately to get a long look at the seadog he'd heard of, and he succeeded, for Kec and Rosa were busy looking around the sweep of Iodine's grounds above the water, the domes, jetties, the spectacle. Rake quickly looked the old guy up and down to gauge an age, and the nineteen year old head on springs just flatly found it too difficult to cope. With the reality. That a guy as old as this, a person, any dude at all, had borne out his whole time on the ocean, living a life out there, a life that'd have to be, heck, maybe fifty fukkin years, he's gotta be fifty, shit, that's fukkin awesome, man.

Peter Blitz called out, 'Delahunty, your catch is going loose Delahunty.'

'No probs mister Blitz! See you round sir. Ma'am, right pleased to meet you,' the smile on springs bounced away into the warm Broome air.

The Tree of Superiority

Peter Blitz drove the solar buggy out along the jetty, past the six domes of the Microbiology Department, up to the end where the turbine awaited the tide.

'We're now one kilometre out from shore,' Peter said. He pointed to the floor, 'Thirty metres deep down there, a hundred foot column of juice that our students will bring back into the collective mind of humanity.' Remple had warned Peter not to talk shit to Kee, but Peter Blitz was an excitable guy.

The healthy thing was that Peter sported large proprietary feelings for the university, but the fact is Peter had never had a lightning bolt position like general manager, certainly not of a project like Iodine. He'd got his masters degree early in life, quickly gained a PhD, and successfully worked a number of fine jobs as an industrial chemist, significant positions that grew with importance until peaking with the gig of running the world's first ocean university alongside the vice chancellor. It's just that Peter bore natural presumptions about Kee. Worn-out shabby pants did it, and a crumpled cotton shirt from somewhere around 1980 didn't help. A slow demeanour didn't help, slow in talk, walk, and, probably, Peter decided, slow as batshit when it came to bright new thought, all the worn-out templates of mind from a fucked up century gone down with the toilet.

Fair enough. But the seadog's ding-dong brightness did pop up at the end of the second jetty. Past the nine buildings of the Technology & Data Department, stood a dome that seemed to Kee ten times bigger than all the others around the campus.

Kee stood in silence for a moment and then sprung his arm up: 'What is this?'

'Here we have the weather centre, it sends to satellites all kinds of data, and receives all kinds as well.'

'I would like to display a picture on the moon: can it do that?'

'Um, what do you mean mister Leeft?'

'The two seas at night, display them onto the moon.'

'I'm sorry, two seas at night? Well, which two oceans do you mean?'

'The one down here and the one up there, the sky.'

'The resolution would have to be quite something for placing an image on the moon.'

'It need not be the moon, it can be any big surface out there, like businessmen do with buildings.'

'I'll, I'll look into it,' Peter Blitz said, smelling the coming of a bogey under a rock somewhere.

For the remainder of the ding-dong morning Peter Blitz showed them round the campus without any further attempt at grandstanding either his vast knowledge or his smug feelings on Iodine's contribution to humanity. Me, I'd lay a bet Peter Blitz thought, in the precise present, No point wasting myself on a village fisherman and his crumbling old wife, let's just get this shit over with, stay polite, can't hurt.

Bakks and I, we'd seen up close the ding-dong spectacle of Jack Black behaving like a painter arrogarnta, well wait till Jacko meets Blitzo arrogarnta. Especially Blitzo letting fly. Arrogarnta majora.

The Three Gasms

For the rest of the tour, which covered nearly fourteen kilometres, Blitzo drove them leisurely up and down the jetties of Iodine in the admin buggy, powered in its cheery whine by its solar roof. By lunchtime the heat radiating off the desert had dealt them a good thirst, and they stopped at the student bar and recreation dome for lunch.

The place was empty except for a figure at the far side. The Tokyo student Moshu Tangura was busy jamming his broad shoulders at a solid angle, mopping the last patch of the floor. Moshu has the face that seems locked in smile, tomato-red hair juts up like a giant clam, so a happy red clam swings back and forth at the far side of the dome behind the snooker table, down up, down up, down down. At seventeen, he's Iodine's youngest, at fourteen back at Tokyo University he was given the medal for Chemistry.

Farmers in Japan had made a recent phenomenon that stunned the nation. Moshu's father was one of the first. He'd found a way to grow his watermelons so that they do not roll around on the shelf, in a fridge, a shop, a supermarket, on a truck. He placed a box over the melon, and as the melon bulked up over the weeks, it grew into the space afforded by the box. On harvest, Moshu's father had his first crop of cube watermelons. It was a big success. But who'd first suggested it to his father was a little twelve year old Moshu.

Now, five years later, Moshu had come to Iodine with many of his personal things packed into four of those cube-melon boxes and us slanguage twanguage better wooden boxes, we had high hopes that these four cube-melon pine slatted things, well we hoped they wouldn't fall in with the pongsters and counterfeiters. Pine slatties sometimes do.

Behind Moshu Tangura was the curved inner wall of the dome, and on the wall hung a large painting by Castle. It was very large, a triptych. Each panel was six metres wide and seven metres high, so the triptych in total width was as long as a bus, and the effect from the entrance was like looking at the side of a motel. Castle had painted huge words on each panel, and so from the entrance it looked like a massive sign, each letter as high as a human figure:

mygasm yourgasm ourgasm

A second similar painting, on the other side of the dome:

yourgasm mygasm hourgasm

Rosa asked Peter Blitz what they meant. Peter said he didn't know. He said the artist was an important artist, a cousin of Remple's.

What ding-dong Blitzo didn't know wouldn't hurt him, but the two big triptychs were in fact commissioned by Remple. Remple had asked Castle for a really large work that would speak about Iodine's place in the world. When Castle completed the six panels of gasm, Remple flew from Perth to Margaret River and Castle picked him up and drove him back to his shack and then took him round the back of the dam out to the paddock to check them out, and Remple said, 'Are you serious?'

'Yeah,' Castle said.

'Okay, go ahead, tell me.'

So Castle told him. 'Do you believe heads of state are important, prime ministers, presidents?'

'I suppose so,' Remple said standing on the thick lush grass of the Yelverton paddock examining the huge gasm panels laid out on the ground.

'Do you believe that what they say, do, promote, do you believe that stuff is important?'

'Um, yeah, I suppose I do.'

'Previous ones, future ones, almost ones?'

'Yes Castle, fuck, get on with it.'

'George Bush, Ahmedjinabad, Hillary Clinton, John Howard, Kevin Rudd, Barack Obama?'

'Yep, and now I'm going back up to Perth.'

'Hang on a mo. Blair, Mugabe, Putin, Lula of Brazil, Sarkozy, Berlusconi, Merkel, Gordon Brown, also Thatcher and Jiang Zemin and Ehud Olmert and Megawati Sukarnoputri, Arroyo, Mbeki? How come they're so deeply different than you or I, how come they're on another planet?'

'They're not that different, they're just men and women in positions of power so they behave slightly differently, but they're not on some other planet.'

'Oh they're not? Then why is it the minute they assume power they forget the gig?'

'The gig?'

'The central gig. The health of the natural world. They get into power and then do nothing, or they do all these pissweak diluted measures, calling it balance, balancing employment with pollution.'

'Fair, that's a good point. So then, these, here, what're they supposed to say?'

'The blunt side is just a rehash of "Make Love Not War," but the much greater and more subtle side is that they ought to all, all of em, do much more orgasming, more lovemaking, more fucking, it'll make em remember what it's like to be real again. I mean, even just an hour a day. Hourgasm, or the dual together Ourgasm. Better than spending all that time and energy making all the shit they call progress. Here's the idea: what we do with these two paintings for Iodine, is we take photos of them after they're hung at the university and then use those photos to go into their faces. Right into their faces, promote the photos all over the world, directly into their faces.'

Remple only took a week to calculate that the paintings would lose a significant portion of the parents he would be marketing Iodine to, but he also knew that the other parents who saw the point were Iodine's true customers, true friends, true patrons. So Remple got the art movers to get the paintings up to Iodine, and they became known around the world because they became the subject of many, many conversations inside the diplomatic circles, the educational circles, and generally the entire worldwide movement against a balanced approach to pollution. Remple let climate change be. It was the disgusting visuals of pollution he knew would move hearts, climate change was a debate, pollution was real.

'You're incredibly stupid Castle, you know that, don't you,' Remple said, and gave his cousin a big embrace.

'Yep.'

They walked back into the shack and shared a bottle of Castle's best red to toast the two triptychs. Inside the shack was another painting. Small, pure white background, with a word painted in green: Oxymoron.

'You guys are getting right into these word paintings, you and Jack and Hong.'

'Yeah, we are, it's fun. But for me, not into the inversions. Jack and Hong's backwards kindergarten stuff just about sold out at Catherine's gallery in Sydney, Jack rang yesterday, he confirmed they're going to build me a studio.'

'Looks like you've ramped up your green philosophy since meeting Jack over in Georgetown.'

'I've always been pissed off at pollution, but yeah Jack's friendship has got me dealing in it. I mean, it's not just cars, it's the whole thing. The world burns eighty million barrels of oil each day, so how do we expect a week to look? A week is five hundred and sixty million barrels, burning, Sunday to Sunday.'

'So what's this Oxymoron canvas about?'

'Moronic environmental oxymorons, that's why I've done the word in green. Phrases like "green car." I mean, it's really wild when you inspect it. How has the mind arrived at such a weird assumption? Calling a polluting machine green. Pollution is pollution, there's no relativity about it any more. Shit is shit. There might have been relativity in the seventeenth century, but here at the start of the twenty-first century pollution is pollution. Green car, it's absurd. The only green car is a solar car, like your buggies in Broome. Even if climate change turns out to be a false alarm, we are still polluting the buggery out of the place, killing nature and poisoning its creatures. Next thing we'll be saying, gee, we've invented a new coal that produces ten percent less greenhouse gas, let's call it green so we can burn billions of tonnes of it, and, more absurdly, proceed to feel good that it is doing good, we'll call it a step in the right direction, we'll call it doing our bit. The two biggest oxymorons of this century, "green India" and "green China," wait till the world starts asking those two places to go green. They'll just tell us all to get fucked.'

'Jack's got to you bigtime.'

'Yep. But look at Iodine, what you've done there, the thing truly is green, it's a wonderful green example not just to India and China, but to the whole industrialising world.'

They took their glasses of wine outside to have another gazing moment at the gasm paintings lying on the paddock.

'You've done well, Castle, thank you.'

'Cheers.'

In the student recreation dome, Rosa said, looking across at the paintings, 'I am Spanish, I have never heard the English words mygasm and yourgasm, but it seems to me it is about sex, pretty good paintings, I like them.'

'Si, me too,' Kee said.

Moshu Tangura's shock of red had strolled up. 'Mister Leeft? Mrs Mendoza?'

'Si, hello.'

'Please allow me to congratulate you.'

Peter Blitz shot across like a flash. 'Moshu, not now, this is not the time. Mister Fekdin wants it done at the opening ceremony.'

'Oh no, sorry! Ah, shit, sorry!'

'Can you get us some sandwiches and drinks?'

'Yes, of course!' And Moshu Tangura ran off to the kitchen.

'What is the matter?' Rosa said.

'It's nothing,' Peter Blitz said.

After lunch Peter Blitz drove them back to Broome, setting them down at the hotel lobby at Cable Beach, and he was glad to get rid of them, what a waste of a day.

The Tree of Stress

The wastage problem was very very large. Stress is no good, the Nobel prize winning Tasmanian Elizabeth Blackburn has shown irrevocable proof that a powderbox that likes to stress is dangerously eroding the telomeres, the protective little caps at the ends of each chromosome, and when you erode the telomeres your protection is gone and shit happens.

Right now Peter Blitz was a strung out guy, his powderbox splattered around the place as he sped out of the hotel, three months solid he'd prepared every detail of the Iodine launch. A huge international event, up at five every day, seeing to all the stuff that needed doing, his telomeres getting a hammering.

The whole responsibility had fallen to him, the general manager. But he still couldn't find the bogey under the rock, couldn't understand why Remple had chosen the old fisherman to deliver the launch address, to formally declare the place open. A huge global day, an international event, handed to a dipshit from a village in Spain. Plus he's going to give the guy an honorary degree, Iodine's first ever degree is going to a loping groping rural rustic. Wish Moshu actually did spoil the surprise, fuck.

He swung the car into the red dust and sped down towards the university, now at well over a hundred and twenty, but the time wasted warranted the speeding, only three days to the launch. Peter knew they could've had anyone, the premier, the education minister, the prime minister, even Al Gore's office had said yes on receiving Peter's letter of request to have Al Gore open Iodine. Big mistake, blood shoots up the neck. An embarrassed Peter had to quickly retract the invitation from Al Gore's office after Remple put the blowtorch to the idea of Gore opening Iodine—and he comes up with what, a rural rustic fisher. Fuckmedead boss, what were we thinking, hm?

Peter's car sped down the red dust, weaving, flying, more like a shooting hovercraft than a car. Ding-dong and how's the time. Not good, not good, not for Peter Blitz, there's just way too much to do for Team Peter Blitz. Way too much that could slip up, too many loose ends were hanging around, things could go wrong, bogeys, rocks, and if things went wrong then the opening ceremony was on his own head, not his staff's head. The whole day and night of the opening celebrations were on his head. And then he shouted at the windscreen, he screamed at it: 'No way Remple I ever do tour guide again!'

Screaming even louder, so that he kind of bounced a lot in the driver's seat of his highspeed hovercraft:

'You see that, boss, do yaaaaa?! No more tour guide!! YAAH-AAH-AAAAH!'

Bakks probably. Got one of Inch's pongsters to go out there, hup two three, over the mountains and over the seas, surging up the tail of red dust. Maybe Centimetre, get Centimetre to do it, turn a shit day into road rage. Soda-pop poor ol Blitzo's powderbox, fizz, crackle, splatter, ping. Rub the telomeres into sandpaper from Bunnings.

The Iodine Launch

Remple flew into Broome two days later. He went straight to the hotel to wait at the table he reserved under the stars. When Kee and Rosa strolled outside he stood up to greet them, going first to Rosa.

'I am very pleased to meet you señorita Mendoza,' he said, shaking hands. 'I am sorry we have not met sooner, I wonder why we have not met sooner,' then he leaned forward to embrace.

'He has hidden me away for a long time, señor Fekdin, this Sunrise Sunset buffalo boy.'

'Is this true mister Keep Left?'

'Si, it is true.'

Remple and Kee embraced, and then they sat down to an

evening meal.

'Are you ready for tomorrow?' Remple asked Kee.

'Yes.'

'Good, I'm glad.'

'You have made a very impressive place of study. But one small question.'

'Yes?'

'Why did you build the university on jetties when you could have built it on the red earth behind the sand?'

'They're the jetties where you called in when you ferried my grandmother up the coast looking for her parents my dear friend, fifteen jetties you told me once.'

Next morning Iodine was launched to the world.

Peter Blitz's team counted a crowd of just over six hundred guests, almost every invited guest, to a name. The chief of Peter's team, marketing manager Ruby Schwartz, creator of Neutrino's Lab, destroyer of student focus, confirmed it with her own list, guests from all over the world.

On top of that, the first enrolment of students had arrived, four hundred and thirty-two in total, in four charter flights from Perth.

Ruby flung her prehistoric mensa head into the doorway at Peter's office. 'Is the fisherman still doing it?'

Peter, all he did was look up from his desk and gaze vacantly at Ruby.

'Oh well,' she said, 'let's just get it going then I suppose,' and the head swung away and disappeared. Ruby's munnwaggle from California had flown in for the opening ceremony too. Babe, brother, love.

Just over a thousand powderboxes came to the official opening of the world's first university dedicated to the ocean, and the morning would hum in those powderboxes forever because it was a slightly different official opening. Ruby estimated that another ten million would be watching the online coverage she'd organised. Gungho Patsy art dealer, she'd be watching too, swinging wine bottles in the air with Lars.

Ruby had also invited television and press journalists from twenty-eight countries around Asia, Europe and the Americas. With the amount of coverage she had sewn up, Keep Left was going to be beamed, not quite to the moon, but here and there round and round the equator. Sunrise Sunset, the buffalo boy. Blitzo's rustic. Beamed across the world like a pair of port and starboard lights doing the cha-cha in space.

Ruby's Crackpot Costumes

It all started after breakfast at 9 a.m. sharp, the slightly different opening. Ruby had insisted on a dress code that would add colour to the online coverage, so the result, emblazoned across the crowd of six hundred guests and four hundred and thirty-two students, was that there were dozens of costumes worn with glee and dance. Blue fish, red fish, pink fish. Neon microbes, whaleheads, a whole whale being a bit large; and the costumes covered a range that Ruby had listed: sharks; turtles; algae; an Iodine bottle; an Iodine molecule; dozens of different crustacea; squid; sea snakes; a croc, the munnwaggle from Silicon Valley dressed as a croc; a pack of ten students were dressed as krill; another pack as the creatures that are eaten by krill, diatoms, the ocean's base food unit; a team of blobs of neon green foam that were supposed to be phosphorescence;

brain corals that whopped off shoulders into the morning air blocking the view of the proceedings; seagulls and eagles; seals; a school of herring; and, what gave Bakks a bolt of energy, a school of penguins, or a flock if they could fly, and Bakks could make em fly, right into a powderbox that was having a shit day. There were also regular outfits, those who'd chosen to gracefully decline Ruby's dress code, some parents, not all, and some politicians, not all: Armani suits and Armani dresses; impressive saris and shalwar kameez; cheongsams; four kilts; not a few West African outfits of splendour with the ample headgear, premium clans from Lagos, that business capital running the oil-rich Nigeria; Arabs from Abu Dhabi and Dubai and Jordan and Saudi; and a contingent of well-dressed Bengali students on scholarships awarded by the Grameen Bank. So Ruby got what she needed, and the mishmash of ocean tribes who were spread out over the main two jetties looked more like a wonky ding-dong carnival than a formal opening. Your custodians dear butterfly.

Welcome to the Twenty-First Century Dear Butterfly

Remple took the stage and lifted the microphone, his voice echoing across the shine of the emerald campus, across the curved spaces and up the long walkways. Addressing the prime minister, the education minister, the state premier, the state education minister, parents, students, and ladies and gentlemen—those present and those watching around the world:

'I introduce to you mister Kieran Leeft, a resident of the planet's oceans. A man of no fixed address, mister Leeft has lived exclusively on the seas since he was a boy in Spain, since 1952 to be exact, when he acquired his first boat. On the screen behind me you can see his current address, a fifteen metre sloop. It is berthed for the moment in Spain while mister Leeft visits us here in Broome to deliver Iodine's opening address. Ladies and gentlemen, mister Kieran Leeft.'

Kee stepped across to the microphone.

'Thankyou señor Fekdin. He has made a very nice gift to the world, this place, si?'

The crowd murmured agreement, then the noise rose, and then loose applause started to crack the bright air, and within a single minute there was a huge applause crashing with whistles, cheers and shouts that ran all the way down the first and second jetties.

Then he spoke in Spanish, and the interpreter followed. 'There are many ships on the seas today, thousands, and they all tip their rubbish overboard. They should not do this, but they do, it is easier for them.'

The crowd of powderboxes settled down coz it seemed to feel let down, but it still murmured and shuffled.

'Last month I was talking in a bar to a soldier. I do not know why, but my most deep respect is for a soldier, I believe in the codes by which the soldier practises life. I believe, of all of us, that a soldier is the one with the discipline and the courage needed to set the example. This man was third in command of a warship, a sailor not a soldier, but a soldier in spirit.'

The crowd still talked among themselves here and there coz they probably thought with a sigh of boredom, What in the heck does the army or navy have to do with Iodine?

'I wanted to know if his navy threw their rubbish overboard, so I waited until he became quite drunk so that he might have no control on a loose tongue. I lied to him, I said I was the captain of an oil tanker. The sailor said they throw their rubbish overboard all the time, and so did the rest of the navy.'

By now only a handful of conversations could be heard.

'They keep some of the rubbish to take ashore to show they are doing the right thing, but it was clear to me after talking with the sailor that most of the rubbish went overboard into the oceans. Next morning I was of course sad. If the most courageous and most disciplined among us can feel nothing of throwing their rubbish into the seas, thousands and thousands of ships everywhere every hour, then I felt sad that we are lost for an example, a light to show the way. Like all of us I knew the next morning in my sadness that the vandalism of the world's many military and merchant navies is just one source of poisoning the oceans. There are many other sources, hundreds of thousands of sources that we have created. The factories, the bad rivers, the dynamite fishing these guys do in Asia and Africa, and of course the sewers that we all allow to be fed directly across the beaches and into the seas, of even the most technologically advanced places on earth. We shrug and say, "If the soldier can do it, we can all do it." For the first time in my life I felt very saddened by the incredibly big and global scale of the catastrophe being let loose at the seas, and I therefore felt that we are lost for a guiding light. Then, when señor Fekdin told me some years ago about his plans for this place, Iodine, I felt that the lighthouse had been switched on again.

'When señor Fekdin met me in the Bahamas earlier in the year he gave me a mobile phone, and I threw this into the sea at Gibraltar. To me, this was like losing a door hinge to the sea, it would rust and no harm would be done, but I am wrong. I have never had a phone before, and so I did not know that this mobile phone contains poisonous chemicals. So I vow never again to throw toxic rubbish into the sea, I will only return to the sea what already came from the sea, say fishbones after I have taken a meal of my catch.

'When I was a boy a fisherman brought to us a catch of sardines twice a week. It was very soon after the Second World War, so there was not much food to go around, and señor Mendoza's two sacks a week was a very welcome gift. He loved the sea and he loved his life with the sea.

'But señor Mendoza told me something terrible about the sea which I did not comprehend. He said the sea is a monster. I was shocked, I thought Mendoza deeply loved the sea and so as a boy I imagined he might say the sea is a bringer of life. When I asked him what he meant, Mendoza would not tell me.'

Now the crowd was silent.

'Mendoza said I would find out what this means by myself. He said I might find out perhaps late one night out on the sea, alone, and many days from the nearest landfall. Only on my first Atlantic crossing at twenty-nine did I understand what señor Mendoza meant. The sea certainly is a monster, you cannot drink its blood, for if you drink its blood you will die a slow and agonising death. You cannot breathe its fire, for you will suffocate and then drown. But you may eat its flesh, for the monster has such forbidding powers that it immediately grows new toes and nostrils and hands and arms and tails and tongues and feet and wings and eyes. Whatever you choose to eat from the monster's body, the monster will grow back overnight, with no effort.

'But today, señor Mendoza's monster analogy no longer is true. His monster's forbidding powers of regrowing its body have been severely weakened; in certain places the powers have been destroyed completely. Mendoza's monster is dying. Now that I understand this I also understand how profoundly did Mendoza love the monster. If he were alive today I do not know in what way the man would contain his rage.

'But I do know that he would look across this place today and he would see four hundred young women and men who are ready. They are prepared, as a powerful new generation with different ideas of useage, to bring the monster's magical powers back to life, and for this Mendoza would weep. Dear students of Iodine, it is you, and your children, and their children, who will ultimately demonstrate to us, the rest of humanity, how badly we have behaved in the last century. If you catch us making excuses for that behaviour, you need to find it in you to sneer at us. It is you who will be the makers of the new laws of behaviour for the future seas, for if the seas get sick the mountains get sick, everything everywhere becomes sick, show us, show us all, we want to see Mendoza's monster making blood and breathing fire.'

A long silence.

The applause erupted. The crowd of suits and other regular outfits started to get off their chairs, and the crowd of sea creatures behind them went wild. The noise grew and grew until it became a riproaring, protracted mixture of cheers, applause, whistles, singing, shouts and, from the teams of krill and diatoms and prawns and herring and phosphorescence, there was chanting, soccer match chanting, huge waves of it. Off to the far side Peter Blitz and his senior commander Ruby Schwartz were next to the entrance to the Chemistry Department. Peter stood there under the huge roar, staring, blinking.

'Did I just dream all that?'

'No, no you didn't,' Ruby said loudly under the noise and then quickly set off towards Remple.

At the other end of the crowd Jack leaned over to Laura:

'Manta monk.'

'What?'

Jack shouted: 'He's a Benedictine monk of the reefs, he always reminds me of a manta ray, the reef monk hath spoken.'

'What a fucking terrific speech,' Laura shouted to Jack, 'I bet Remple's buzzing around with absolute glee.'

'Remple's over there, he's leaning into the PM's ear, look at that, he's got the PM laughing.'

Ruby Schwartz waited at Remple's side, and when he was finished with the PM, she had a word in Remple's ear. Remple strolled up to the microphone.

'Ladies and gentlemen ...'

The noise cooled off for Remple, but not much.

'I have just been informed that the live online coverage of this morning has taken fourteen million hits.'

The noise cranked up again, and the party had started, a ding-dong expensive beach party, so expensive that even ol Miles Banford would've shaken his sober sombre Banford business head. But under that head of business Miles would've been alive with excitement. Miles and Remple in another time would have been great pals, hup two ninety, both. Ping-ping splatter-splatter pop-pop, energy vastoid, counterfeit extincto, yum, what a case. Poor Bakks, poor Inch.

Iodine had banged out into the world what everyone had been searching for dear butterfly, a state of positive mojo, positive ding-dong, hup two three, how's the time.

The one thing Remple hadn't dared hope for the university, actually happened. Even his hup two ninety electricity had not dared hope for it, but it happened. What is never said can generally never be known, but what is never hoped for, how can it become? Very quickly, and from across the world, Iodine attracted funding from science academies. Iodine had become a hub on the net thanks to prehistoric mensa mind Ruby Schwartz, but it also became a hub of money-target with institutes and academies across forty and more countries. A premium hub of planetary research upon the ocean. The flow had commenced with Iodine's Molecular Biotechnology Department, and within a couple of years money flowed into Iodine's multiple research platforms, and it came not just from impressed institutes, it also came from individuals who loved scientists. More specifically, who loved scientists at their early state, and Warren Buffett banged in with millions, and Bill Gates too. To these and many other senior ding-dongs the Iodine kids were not just kids, they were the future, and in the present they were both cool geniuses and hot geniuses. Iodine soon became one of the world's best laboratories, talented people all over the world either sighed or grew excited. To make it happen was the thing, to bring the human potential squaring with the planet. Human potential was squaring with its own self in the twentieth century, but now it was the new century and the human potential had a chance to square with the planet.

These intensely talented powderboxes dear butterfly, were keen as fresh mint to witness human promise square itself with the planet, with your habitat. Nectar nectar everywhere. All that protective machinery floating off the coast of Somalia, were it converted into money, could make every Somali family a rich family. Common sense, but in powderbox upside-down lore de lore it is revolutionary, and Iodine was just such a revolution, even Warren Buffett thought so, and he sent a letter of congratulation to Remple. Bigtime positive mojo had trained its focus upon Iodine. Like Oxley says: 'If I were given the licence to issue parking tickets I would crush negativity everywhere, well, at least if it ever turned up in Dorking, and now I see I need not worry here in Broome about crushing any negativity at all.

Especially negativity posing as seriousness, phew, that I'd crush even if it turned up as just a blush. Only four powderboxes have ever been negative at my picnics, thank goodness.'

What Kee did was he just strolled off the podium and shuffled over to Rosa and sat beside her. 'How was that, was it okay?'

'It was good,' Rosa said.

Kee had gone far. From the rusty key-swinging kid beside the cracked fountain who couldn't care less, he'd come a long way on the waves of give and take that Ellie-Isabela claimed ruled the world. He'd spent a few decades bringing her back-room illuminations into the world.

'It was good,' Rosa said again.

The King Who Never Gave Up

What Rosa didn't know was that Bakks was trying like the blazes to fuck up Kee's powderbox. But, glory be, me O my, O Bobbo got Mendoza's monster memory up there first, worked on it since the old seafarer had first heard about Iodine from Remple's visit back in the Bahamas. Plus, helped fate him to Mendoza's daughter. Fate's a fukkin hard one to deal with, we boxes always want fate as a customer, dream on. But Bakks, no chance he could mess around with Kee's powderbox, he failed. Bakks, he couldn't even get the seafarer to remember to curse the price of diesel.

Bakks failed because ever since the buffalo boy had sat on those steps beside the Golfo de Valencia, Bakks found that the skin of the kid's memory was just that bit too invincible to the hopes of evil shit. Or it may have been that Bakks the cardboard prawnbox always freaked out at the proximity of all that water the kid had around him all the time, right throughout his life. But Bakks, no, not gonna give up. He knew Peter Blitz was under great stress that something might go wrong on launch day—or the launch night party, and Bakks also knew that the entire little crew down at Castle's place under the Yelverton stars had flown up to Iodine for the launch. O Bakks the evil king of Taking, O yes, he had options. Blitzo's road rage for starters: Blitzo still fumed a bit, ribbons of heat travelling off the hairs on his head. Bogeys lurked. And Bakks, that's all he needs. Having a shit day? Bakks can crank it up until you wanna kill em all. Bakks could hitch his crumpled cardboard logic to that one, all that morphing from grass to cow to milk, and all the wood envy in the world, Bakks could just hitch it all to Blitzo, take take take.

The Yelverton crew let Remple fly up earlier, and then they came up together on another flight a day later, Castle, Jack, Double-O-Four, Catherine, and Laura buffalo booksmeller packing O Bobbo in her knapsack. Bakks and Inch, and the other smellbomb deadbeats, they sprang grim with excitement that their favourite was on the flight, Castle, the guy whose dreams about his brother were too filled with love to crack. But Bakks had options.

He said to me: 'O Booboo, welcome to the party Booboo.'

Inch gathered up the crew of counterfeiters from the swill, Kilometre, Centimetre, Metre, Yard, Foot, Mile, Furlong, the vain fuckface Lightyear—and that crudest of all the deadbeats, Millimetre, and why they ever needed Millimetre in their catastrophic crew I don't care to understand. The whole mangle of those stupid cardboard fuckers was hard to understand at the best of times. The only thing we teak types understood was that the wood envy got em every time. We last; they don't, they've got the eradication fear. The fear touches em in different ways, Bakks forever needs to be whacked into irritation, Inch is always caked in dried ratsblood. Whatever it is, the wood envy cardboard smellbombs had it, that weakness, the fear of eradication. Okay, they're truly powerful and truly evil, but spill a glass of water?

Compare them with a crocodile, not that a croc's evil but he certainly is powerful. A Dr Mike Letnic of Sydney University in 2006 examined six hundred croc carcasses in the Northern Territory by cutting them open; they each had eaten a cane toad. A cane toad can turn a croc into a handbag just by sitting around looking at the view in Kakadu. Which in itself is not surprising since anything that bites a cane toad will die, including snakes, goannas, eagles, everything, nothing can survive a cane toad. Except a meat ant, meat ants bite cane toads and then drag them into their meat ant holes in the ground to devour them. But everything else succumbs to the cane toad poisons. So if a cane toad can do that to a croc then a glass of water can do it to Bakks, and he knows it. Little things can pack it, little teeny things. Imagine being scared of a glass of water.

The Iodine Celebrations

Or a glass of champagne. After speeches from the prime minister, the state premier and the education minister, Remple took the stand and he awarded Iodine's first degree to Kee, the congratulation that Moshu Tangura had earlier withdrawn.

The applause burst into the morning, and the campus was getting into full swing. Becoming more like the wonky hairy carnival that Ruby had wanted than the launch of a twenty-first century sun-palace of higher education, fifteen jetties crawling with the various tribes of ocean-heads dressed as all kinds of different shit. Fifteen jetties ready over the coming years to re-jig the world. But fifteen jetties just for now equipped with ten stations of champagne each.

Jack and Laura decided to take a stroll through the carnival towards the far end of the campus. Remple said there was a feature they'd enjoy. 'Just go to the last jetty,' Remple had said, 'past the Recreation Dome, can't miss it.'

Before setting off for the end of the last jetty they picked up a bottle of champagne. The bar staff said unfortunately they were only pouring glasses, not giving out bottles, so Jack waited until they weren't looking and lifted a bottle from the ice behind the counter.

Noise from a Distance

When they arrived at the end of the last jetty what they saw was a big wide nothing, just a walkway leading off the jetty out to sea. Jack took the steps down to the walkway.

'There's nothing here, what's Remple talking about?' Jack said.

'Over there,' Laura said, 'what's that?'

Jack walked further down and found a pair of hand railings. 'It's a ladder, goes into the water. There's nothing here, let's go back to the party, Remple's having a lend of me.'

Laura had stayed higher up on the jetty studying the line. 'But check the walkway, it goes up there, then it travels across the horizon and then returns and then cuts back to the jetty, it's a square, a great big thumping square of sea.'

'I couldn't care less if it was a rhomboid, let's go back to the party and have some fun.'

Laura understood it first. 'It's a seapool.'

'It's a walkway, that's all.'

'No, I'll show you, under the walkway, underwater, there's a wall of some kind,' Laura said. She took off her prawn outfit and then stripped off her clothes until she was naked. She jumped in and swam down.

Jack waited.

Laura came up. 'It's a net of stainless steel, top to bottom, goes right down to the sand.'

'How deep's the water?'

'Seems like two storeys.'

'What's the net for?'

'I'd say the net goes all the way round, it's a seapool, keeps the sharks out, lets the fish in.'

She was right about that, the Iodine seapool was a safehaven of natural ocean for the students to explore and conduct their workshops outside the labs. It was a safe space dedicated to the new, urgent work of keeping the oceans alive. Around the world more than four hundred dead zones had been identified by 2008, representing collectively an area the size of New Zealand. Professor Robert Diaz at the Virginia Institute of Marine Science in America, who conducted the study, cited the usual cause: hypoxia, which is a lack of oxygen caused by fertiliser. Nitrogen and phosphorous wash into the sea and create giant blooms of algae, when the algae dies it is eaten by bacteria that absorb the oxygen.

Jack placed the bottle on the concrete walkway. He took off his manta ray outfit, and then stripped his clothes, dived in, shooting down as far as he could go, and on the drift back to the surface he opened his eyes and he was pleased by the lime-coloured clarity of the sunshine dancing around him underwater.

Immersed in the Iodine seapool together: the painter arrog-arnta, and the performer who played a buffalo at the Edinburgh festival, swimming in ocean warm as shared laughter, and this means? Safe from cardboard smellbomb Inch, and the other evil cardboard fucker Bakks. If Bakks can panic at a glass of water imagine his panic at a gigantic seapool. Memory is like water. And might one assume O Bobbo would help out? No sir, O Booboo would not help out. No, the deadbeat smellbombs were more likely chasing down easy meat, cheesy bloodsoup, Blitzo, upon Bakks's orders, Blitzo.

While Jack floated to the surface with the sunlight playing all around the turquoise water he caught sight of the French lightmaster Claude Monet, and Jack continued the slow drift to the surface using only buoyancy, with Monet in his mind, the haystacks especially, for their dazzling variety of light, and for the place where Monet had painted them, very near the trenches where young soldiers shot at one another day and night, a mere one mile away from Claude's studio at Giverny, so that Monet could hear the murder at the same time as he worked those breathtaking cascades of haylight to life.

Jack swam to the stairs and climbed up. He sat with Laura, opened the bottle of champagne, poured two glasses.

'What's your abiding feeling about Monet's haystacks?' Jack said.

'The painter? What made you think of Monet?'

'He just popped in, no reason.'

'I can't say why, but I was moved to tears when I saw them, they're just haystacks but they were hanging together, about ten large canvasses, and they turned everything in me upside-down in those moments, and I stood back and quietly wept a bit. They're amazing, they're more than paintings, they have a merciless celebration, throwing out all the intellectual intent in favour of this merciless celebration of life being alive.'

'Did you know he painted them while his son was a mile away in the trenches, and Monet could hear the gunfire?'

'His son? How could he have done that, keep painting while all that was happening?'

'I don't know.'

'He honestly knew? He knew his son was fighting for his life? A mile away? In those particular trenches, right near Giverny?'

'That's what they say.'

'And he just kept on painting the effects of light on those haystacks? Jesus, what a ... what a heartless man.'

'I don't see him as heartless.'

'I do, what a heartless fuck.'

Vividity

From the last jetty lay a panorama of the fourteen jetties along the coast. So the painter and the performer could now gain the whole of Iodine in a single sweep, rising from the ancient red landscape behind the cluster of domes. Silver solar domes, singing with the sunshine over the crowds of regularly dressed and ocean-dressed, powderboxes who had flown in from all over an optimistic world of freshly minted attitudes for a freshly minted century.

What Jack and Laura could not see from across the seapool was an errand being run. The work of the deadbeat smellbombs. The invisible work of the crew of pathetic counterfeiters conducting their own crass versions of hup two three. And not just them, but also Inch, the greedy ratsblood sucker from darkest industrial Guangzhou who by now was eager for his biggest bling moment, gunna do in Bakks like a scrap of toilet paper lost to the sewerage system. With enough common sense to sink a battleship, with enough excitability to faint at the sight of Little Boy and Fat Man at the museum in Los Alamos, Inch was gunna take the king's crumpled logic, tie it into knots, and toss it into maybe the worst known water hole in the universe. Inch'd be chanting to himself: 'Hail Me, Hail Me.' Also chanting, humming: 'Squash the past and squash it dead for it just might squash you instead.'

Inch said to me: 'Now see clear, wooden fucktoid, observe, what my team member Kilometre has achieved with my desire for vividity.'

I knew of course Kilometre had conducted a very vivid hup two three, as commanded by Inch back at the swill, upon Patsy's powderbox, gungho sniggerer, she'd been mighty cranked up by smellbomb Kilometre, from a bad day to a shit day, from a shit day to a kill em all day. This was normal work from Bakks and his outfit. But me: I was not yet aware of the outcome.

Perth is nowhere near as criminalised as London. Meaning, in Perth you can't just pick up a phone and get things shifted along if you're just an art dealer, whatever the gig, politics, debts, favours of property, not as easily as you can in London. And if you're a big London art dealer who was right royally fucked up by a teeny little art dealer in Perth, you stand a better chance of making contact with the more skilful parts of criminalised London. Mind you, London is nowhere near as criminalised as Moscow, and Moscow is nowhere near as criminalised as Inch, but it was Inch who had briefed Kilometre in the first place. Patsy's powderbox had been steadily getting more and more shitted off in the lead up to Iodine's launch. At crackpoint, she phoned a London thug, who phoned his own associate thug in Perth, who organised the flooding of Catherine's gallery.

Catherine's phone went off: the gallery manager reported pretty severe damage, to the ding-dong glamorous wooden flooring, but also to stock, both canvas and paper works. As Catherine listened to the damage report she pushed urgently through the costumes towards a quiet corner behind the dome of Neutrino's Lab.

Seems to me what irritated Patsy more than just losing Remple was losing Remple because of what she no doubt thought was a puny little person, a puerile little nobody of a dealer. Patsy would've liked to have been witness to Catherine's face at that moment.

So Inch and Kilometre got it done, did the king's bidding, but they'd done the enchanter's bidding by using water, and more than just a glass of water.

To Bakks, using water in any kind of counterfeit operation was extremely bad for luck, it was bad for energy, bad for strength, bad for focus, bad for focus extraction, he was so intensely superstitious about it being bad for business that he hammered it home to the smellbomb deadbeats day in day out as a golden rule not to do. As in: No Way.

But it was exactly the reason Inch powered the whole operation towards a flooding of the gallery, it would be very grim for king Bakks's mojo. Inch the prince in the ascendant. Mister

Hailme-Hailme, soon to crown himself king Inch.

Catherine was no saint, and yes she did destroy Patsy and Remple, but it was because Catherine did not want that madness gene passed on, she wanted no possibility of that gene coming round again like it surfaced in her cousin Oliver. No way Catherine was gunna allow a possibility of the same nightmare as her beloved grandma Renata's childhood. That mercy dash up the coast of the Golfo de Valencia in young Kee's boat, or Renata's earlier weeks before the ride with Kee, hunted down by the insane father, no way, saint or no, Catherine was not gunna allow it.

So Catherine was hunched over her phone behind Neutrino's Lab, where she found a corner away from the noise, and she was able to hear out the full extent of the damage to the gallery and the artworks. Patsy got it done, the revenge for taking Remple. The give and the take, leaping the equator, hup two three with the help of the violators out in the swill.

Jack Verandah Confirms a Catastrophe

Jack and Laura saw nothing of this, they saw only the three hammocks on which Iodine swung: the blue sky, the red earth and the lime green ocean. They dived in for another swim, and much later climbed out. The champagne had warmed in the open sunshine, but they drank it.

A figure came walking in the distance, they couldn't make out who it was. After a couple of minutes, as the figure approached up the jetty, they could see it was Castle. He wore his squid outfit. He sat down on the jetty with Jack and Laura.

'We've been trying to work out what lies across the sea in that direction,' Jack said.

'There? You'd arrive in Indonesia, about one thousand five hundred kilometres, open ocean,' Castle said.

'How's the party coming along?' Laura said.

'Catherine's in a mess,' Castle said. 'Someone got into the gallery in Perth and fucked it up.'

Castle described the vandalism done to the gallery, and Jack Verandah immediately knew, but struggled to hope it wasn't what he knew, Patsy after one of her drunken binges with Lars the hanging man. After a drinking session with Lars, no telling what grim idea she could come up with, Jack knew at least that about the gungho sniggerer, whenever she'd had a lonely binge with Lars, the great ideas were born. Jack had seen it many times over, a lonely booze-up with Lars brought all manner of excitement into this world.

'It was Patsy,' Jack said.

'Remple's ex?' Castle said with surprise.

'Yeah, no doubt about it.'

'Your art dealer?' Laura said.

'I'm positive, it's Patsy all over.'

'I mean,' Castle said, 'is she in Perth?'

'Nope, she's in London, she probably called in a favour from one of her grunty bizzmen, what she calls a businessman, but just a pinstriped crook with connections round the planet.'

'Why would she do something like that to Catherine of all people? I thought they were friends,' Laura said.

'They were, they were, but Catherine ploughed in and fucked up Patsy's fling with Remple. I don't know how Catherine did that, but she did it. What I do know is that Catherine bought Patsy a drink and then sent the glass to a DNA clinic in Geneva and had Patsy's saliva checked out.'

'You cannot know that,' Castle said. 'How the heck do you know that?'

'I know it because Lars the hangman told me; most of us in London assume Lars is a hangman at the gallery, just a hangman, but Lars knows everything, some of the stuff Lars knows is simply, well, it's outrageous; he doesn't have what we all call skin, he has ears all over his body, Lars would have watched her put the glass in her bag, he'd have strolled out to the balcony to have a sweetening chat with her, all that kind of thing, three more champagnes, Lars is one of my best friends in London, he's often wanted to start a gossip blog solely focused on galleries round London, he's amazing that guy, he knows everything and nobody ever knows how he finds out, he's everywhere all the time. I asked him to take a holiday with me to the Bahamas, and he looked at me as if I was nuts that he'd leave his gathering-up activities behind for three weeks or even just a week.

'Lars told me that on Patsy's glass, goozy anomalies were discovered, and when they were joined together with Remple's DNA that Catherine had checked in Geneva, the potential tendencies in any offspring were, for Catherine, kind of catastrophic. Like your grandmother's father in Spain.'

'Catherine broke them up because she didn't want them having a kid?'

'I guess, yeah. Like your brother, or like my brother perhaps.'

'Jesus, that is just not right, I'm gunna have to have a talk with Cath,' Castle said, and he stripped from the squid outfit. From a puffy bottle bag he produced a bottle of cold champagne.

'Why is your face plastered with black paint?' Laura said.

'Squid ink, squid ink. Like a champagne?'

They sat down on the concrete of the jetty and shared the bottle, side by side, legs dangling.

'Fucking hell, that is just not right,' Castle said.

'It's not very nice, splitting people up,' Laura said.

'That's bad enough, but it's not that,' Castle said, 'it's the blocking of a kid being born just because of a suspicion of becoming mentally ill.'

'Besides,' Jack said, 'how does anyone know if Patsy even wanted a kid anyway.'

'That's irrelevant,' Castle said. 'Kid or no kid, Patsy's wish, Remple's wish, what's relevant is gross interference based on the smoke-and-mirrors of DNA tests, what's relevant is the mean-spirited interference based on sweet fuck-all, based on dumb, incomplete science, mixed with fear.'

'If you ask me,' Laura said, 'Catherine would have done it from a sense of, if she did it, of compassion, a broad and deep compassion.'

'But Castle,' Jack said, 'you told me back in Nassau that you and your mother grew to believing in the cautionary approach of screening births, that in a hundred years the clinics will show visual and written case files of the disasters of violence and the tragedy of ghosted lives.'

'Yeah, in a century's time from now but not now, and anyway Mum and I were in that state back then, a state of horror and grief and so we naturally would exist on such amplified crap and believe it too. Besides, once the geneticists map it all, then the waves of regulatory regimes of what can and shouldn't go together will come along at a rate of knots, but Catherine's gross interference right now is just shit.'

'Oh well,' Jack said, 'you might have to have a word with Catherine.'

'Yeah, I will.'

'The water's fine, coming in?'

'Yeah, I brought along three mask and snorkel sets.'

'Where are they?'

'In the bottle bag.'

'What took you so long?' Laura said. They had told Castle an hour ago to meet them out here at the last jetty.

Memory alone can deliver an inheritance, all that's required are us boxes hup two three. Witness Castle's reply.

'After Catherine, I was talking to Rosa and Keep Left. I was asking about the village he grew up in, and both he and Rosa talked. They talked about a dog, Pinski. I think I'll name no-name back at Yelverton that, Pinski.'

And this slither of inheritance is how the eight month old pup down at Yelverton got the name Pinski, he'd inherited it from a Jack Russell back in '47 in Spain who protected a bunch of kids if he hadn't gone to pot.

Ellie-Isabela's father had once told her: 'Never marry a man with any defects my dear Ellie. Your children will be born with defects and will grow up with those defects and then will have to live life with those defects, you will make it hard for your children if you marry a man with defects. You have no defects, and you are a healthy, beautiful girl. Do not allow yourself to become unhappy. I have tried unhappy and I have tried happy, and, believe me, happy is better. Sorrow is okay, but unhappy is shit.'

That was in 1914, when Ellie-Isabela, born on the hinges of the doorway of two centuries, was a young girl of fourteen, growing up under the sea breezes of the interconnected farms that her father worked. She grew into the district's best guide, able to chart a course upriver for the visitor to places where all the maps in the world were useless. As it turned out she had twenty-six kids, none of whom were her own. Her father's ding-dong worry never came to anything. That worry, that advice from her father, was just a heartfelt generational wisdom of an earlier time, an accepted wisdom. It was simply the cautionary approach, it discriminated but it meant no harm, any harm done was tangential. Nobody cared too much, and life on the Golfo de Valencia farmlands was warm to visitors while protecting daughters.

This now was in a later time, many owners later I'm afraid dear butterfly, nine years into the twenty-first century, and the generational wisdom now had a working partner in new fields, vistas that Castle called dumb, incomplete science; DNA and genomes converting into talents and natures.

Like water, memory's three states can offer different forms of dazzle, different forms of reflection, of refraction, perhaps a rainbow. A swirling cosmos, hup two three. Cherished and loved; lost and forgotten; bitter and destructive. The three states can give off a substantial cosmos originating from the blurry boundaries of the second equator, a cosmos that peels away at knowledge, creating the gluggier outposts of generational wisdom, accepted wisdom, and therefore may also hinder the free growth of Castle's dumb, incomplete science.

Castle got in first. He tossed the mask and snorkel into the seapool and then dived in after it, a sleek dive, an arrow with a black tip. Shooting down the clear lime-green waters of the Indian Ocean south of Broome at Cape Latouche Treville where Iodine rocked around the world doing cartwheels at nanosecond-speed, ding-dong and how's the time. Truly beautiful waters for the three friends, truly horrible for Bakks.

'What a glorious seapool!' Castle called out when he burst back up, his face streaked black.

Sitting beside Laura, Jack had been quiet, staring out

towards Indonesia. Then he said, 'I think it's monstrous too, utterly ugly, this free idea that you can screen out a life by commissioning and buying a bit of paperwork from Geneva.'

Laura dived in, Jack dived in, and they all snorkelled across the expanse to the centre of the seapool.

Roll a Gene Round the Backlanes

But Jack might have over-reacted on assuming it was near to the aspirations of some monster like say Hitler. Take a pause. As a teak box with eight owners spanning a century, O Bobbo might suggest there are one or two other bits that Jack could consider.

First the generational wisdom, the older and instinctive wisdom that craves its peace with the world. Second, the newer opinions mixed in with a trace of science that still craves its peace with the world. The first and the second are equally as meddling, both a desire to interfere. Maybe Bakks flung the crew into Catherine's powderbox, yep, maybe that vain fuck-face Lightyear slapped it up faster and faster, maybe Kilometre succeeded with his earlier brief he took from Bakks and Inch. King Bakks, take take take. Taking the interference right up to the point of permission to be born. Dragging the whole proposition of interference along to where it simply becomes a point of taste. So that the new wisdom is not materially any more enlightened than the old wisdom. It remains as it always was, grown from the Tree of Prejudice, the free growth of the instinct of revulsion.

Roll a Gene Round the Tree of Give and Take

Miles Banford understood. Just as he understood gambling joints pretending to be banks, he also knew a bit about the gamble of inheritance, the good and the bad, the wreckage or the possibility. And he knew about the give and take between the old wisdoms and the new wisdoms. He'd sit in his mansion bungalow with booksmeller Laura's great-grandfather David Darlington, upstairs on the second floor in the Zeus collection, discuss quietly with his friend pieces of the latest scientific news of the day on the subject of inheriting, in David's case, a tendency towards severe addiction. So Miles understood a bit about the gamble. 'Science,' Miles would say to David, 'can be made into knowledge, but the really useful knowledge to add to science is a much more delicate system of advice, what our forebears have picked up along the way, the tips they hand down to us.'

Mount Ida where the king of gods Zeus was born is today a treeless rocky ding-dong mountain, and has a stone cottage at the summit which shepherds enjoy for resting. Zeus, old wisdom. Athens, where democracy was born, can be seen from space by my excitable hippy friends at NASA, as a dazzling piece of white gauze, laid out in the Athens basin as if it protected an abrasion from germs, and that white gauze is home today to four million powderboxes. But by all accounts, Zeus's birthplace was as windswept, as bare, in the previous century, same in the nineteenth, and so forth into all the earlier centuries travelling back to the morning Zeus was born. A bare, round, rocky bluff a thousand metres high, silently commanding an expanse of indigo sea. A vast legend of no change, an old wisdom of simple discrimination.

Athens on the other hand swings back through the centuries, a white gauze growing smaller in size as it goes, but never any less frenetic with building; walls were shot up and shot down, and rooms, houses, hotels, pantheons, roads, reservoirs, toilets, restaurants, libraries. In all the centuries of its existence Athens has been perennially busy building and tearing down, and building again, resulting in a continuous stream of activity, a ding-dong zone of ripping away a few windows of perception. Ripping away a few revulsions to replace them with new revulsions. If there were in Athens any Greek men who shared the wisdoms of Ellie-Isabela's father, they'd also say, particularly islanders, 'Memory is like *nero*.' And because memory is like water the more modern wisdoms of Athens will continue to build and tear down. On Zeus's summit there is nothing to tear down, perhaps the stone cottage from a century ago.

Miles had another long-standing opinion, an opinion on the baby born between the birth of Zeus and the birth of Athens, big business. Big business has no memory, a large corporation is busy dealing with value, creating it now for a quick tomorrow. But remembering the lines of others who helped to make the corporation into what it is today, this remembrance is a token thing wheeled out whenever it suits, far from acknowledging that today's ability and resource has been grown over many decades. Miles did not mean a family juggernaut business like his own, he meant a listed corporation, a doozey larger than life. No can remember, too busy. Hundreds of families over time, Miles said, went into creating the formidable strength of an average corporation, but who took the credit for it day in day out were the current ladies and gents in control, seizing the idea that the contemporary strengths had come about through their efforts alone. There was little thanks given, Miles always said, and the absence of gratitude anywhere, he said, creates an egotistical sense of power, only power, pure, unmixed, separated away from the other parts of a nature, power without entrée or dessert, which becomes quite as addictive as David's addiction. This was the pleasant, circular manner Miles would discuss addiction upstairs with his friend. Miles felt the talks upstairs might instil in David a thirst for survival. Miles never said it, but he truly felt these talks might perhaps save David. The twin obsessions of Maheesha the buffalo demon of chaos and evil, with the opium addiction, may be unravelled.

His upstairs Zeus museum where they talked was no DNA clinic, for Calcutta in the sixties was too early for the development of DNA clinics, but it was nonetheless an early prototype, a conversational, anecdotal DNA clinic in the cool upstairs of the Banford bungalow mansion. But David would say: 'How many unsuspecting fish happily drift along the gentle current and then drift faster and then get dragged over Niagara Falls only to be crushed in the fury down below, every hour of every day?'

The Tree of Chance

By the time Catherine had come into the world dear butterfly, the DNA clinics were well on their way, and when she delivered that glass to the clinic in Geneva the technology for screening was in full flight. The DNA clinics, tomorrow's discrimination, so says Castle. Quiet discrimination, silent, an amiable day's work, arrive at nine—home at five, just another toolkit in the box of the old wisdom to assist in avoiding marrying into a defect, have lunch, back to work, file report for customer. It's not harsh discrimination, it is simply what the punters are reasonably expecting to avoid. Why let your daughter approve without first screening, if possible? Normal people doing what they do in protecting their offspring's full potential for happiness.

Normal folk are going to want to do it, the monster overtone replaced with fine domestic logic. It's no neo-Nazi clinic madness, it's an Everyone May Apply sanity. Catherine sent the glass to the clinic in Geneva simply because the best DNA testing clinic was located there. Had Perth a clinic up to scratch, Catherine would have couriered the glass there. No, it ain't a conspiracy vastoid, it is just a new service that a lot of tailors are going to want. A pre-nuptial DNA DVD.

And whatever else they locate on the human genome to worry or delight will become a new taste to crank up for marketing. Yep, it won't be ding-dong monsters like Hitler remaking the world, it'll be everyday folk taking little choices, like the booksmeller might soon make with either Jack Verandah, or with the Lucknow jolly, Jimmy Hazel. Avoid disaster. Check out chickname's DVD, check out arrogarnta's DVD, compare, decide, thanks.

And in the process of avoiding disaster the many choices might rise as a triumph. The triumph of disorder, of a disasterologist cosmos, has been scuttled by the triumph of quietly choosing, by requesting a DNA DVD. Hey-ho ding-dong, and how's the time.

But perhaps these triumphs would seem also smug, somehow hollow, erasure by choice being the same as the human accord with the extinction of little animals first and human traits later. I'm a Colchester, how should I know what the hell's going on down in the ribbon of DNA, powderboxes are my game, not DNA, but of the cute dirty desires of weeding out the unwanted, phew tell me bout it. Feels like a triumph, tastes like a triumph, show me your bits. It's like king Bakks: feels like a memory, tastes like a memory, but it's just counterfeit shit.

The powderbox genome anyway dear butterfly, complex as it seems to be, derives from the periodic table seen at school by all fourteen year old powderboxes. Every protein on every marker in the genome is ding-dong down home a colourful piece of work which is made from the few elements shown on the periodic table. Pure normality. Then why would the periodic table create such violence as there might occur further along in a protein chain? Why would harmless elements fuse together to build an attitude? A clash of cultures is easy to see, but a belief discrimination emanating from the elements is harder to see. Show us yer bits. It is probably pretty normal that Catherine ducks off to get a DNA DVD.

If O Bobbo goes flying on for another hundred years, far past Catherine, gliding from owner to owner, we would no doubt notice the reliable manifestations within similarly concerned families everywhere, on both sides of the equator, on both sides of both equators. Everyday families will wish to know. The old accepted wisdom of Ellie's father will open into millions upon millions of DVDs that decline or celebrate. They shall not, no sir, be doing it from hatred, they'll be doing it with day to day concerns, among other concerns, happily getting their way around the cracks of life. And it might be far distant from the idea of ding-dong discrimination, it will perhaps become the new form of responsibility, a new kind of bequeathment, a new type of enlightened giving evolved away from Ellie-Isabela's magic wand of giving. And the birth of democracy, thanks to that patch of white gauze, might see to it that the service is made available to more or less everyone, the idea shared evenly, across and beyond monstrous elite cleansing. That's what ordinary lives will want from the tree of chance, a proper bet, inside information.

Party Above

So the smaller ideas of give and take. The calm ones, ideas that Catherine would put up for Castle; she'd claim they were perfectly simple and sound and compassionate, not monstrous.

From the last jetty at the end of the campus, the fifteenth jetty, the trio of snorkellers had flapped across the surface of the vast seapool, arriving at the fourteenth jetty. They swam in the clear waters underneath, while the Iodine formalities up above were heading into an afternoon phase, the fun of celebration now calibrated down to energetic conversations.

I don't mind water, I'm wood, I mean, I might just as easily have been a boat had I finished up at a boat builder's in Rangoon instead of Arnie Colchester's workshop. Besides, her great-grandfather David swam all the time back at the hacienda Zaragoza. But Bakks and the pongsters freak out heavily at just the thought, so that the deadbeats often end up with many great gaps in the effort to create their counterfeit.

For exactly that reason Bakks forever had a tricky time laying his counterfeit crap on boat-boy Sunrise Sunset. So here, under the jetty, my new owner the buffalo booksmeller, and her two friends, had the watery space all to their peaceful selves, that is, without the remotest presence of the evil take-fucker and his toxic crew. In fact Laura loved the sea, she was a fish, all three of them were fish, they flowed and swam and drifted around under the Iodine party having a great deal of their own quiet fun.

The vertical pylons under jetty fourteen were by now almost two years old so they grew life. Under the Indo-Broome surface they had given rise to fish homes and mollusc homes, wads of shells had come to anchor up and down the pylons in small submarine hills of shell upon shell, a variety of small shells and bigger shells. Many varieties of seaweed grew from the pylons. Small fish and big fish had arrived. Two storeys below on the sea floor a black manta glided along. A school of big silver trevally roamed halfway down. The party under the party was enormous.

For booksmeller the scenery was colourful. The shadows that were created by the pylons had the clarity of colours gained under a special light, richer colours. They made the animals and plants in the shadows seem to glow from the inside. Outside the shadows the world of sunlit visibility stretched along a dozen pylons. There was no turbine on this jetty, but further along at the next jetty the giant shadow of a turbine lay suspended, and the turbine also threw a shadow to the sea floor.

Remple had warned them the tides would commence in two hours. For the moment, they enjoyed the lull of the tides, the equilibrium. But Remple had warned them. Soon the entire bay, a sweep of two big cities, would start to move, yanked across hundreds of miles by the moon's gravity craving a drink of plankton, or maybe by what Kee called all that memory hurling around in the night-sky. Or maybe by that straight line on a round ball that me an Oxley couldn't figure out.

Whatever it was, me and pewter-glitter knew one thing: it was a reliable manifestation that something was definitely ding-dong lurking round the corner of the great Iodine party, maybe Peter Blitzo's bogey under a rock. Craved a bit of chaos. Maybe like Maheesha, Blitzo's bogey under a rock somewhere was beginning to vibrate, to crave. Bad behaviour is one thing, but bring Bakks into it and you've got another thing altogether, and if Blitzo's bogey was under a rock where there was no water then king Bakks was gunna King Take.

What we boxes called flobreggate. Inside The Exchange, outside The Exchange, it was known as flobreggate, the coming together of the biggest opportunity, the gathering. It's what all we boxes crave, wooden or cardboard, the great gathering. It was almost the opposite of Oxley's aggregations. Flobreggations were the gathering not of conformities, but the gathering of delicious hundreds of conflicting powderbox impulses, filled with nice big potential for business, all that haranguage, banguage, ganguage, twanguage throwing sparks and colliding.

Thankyou Remple

Good ol Remple had provided us boxes, from his jetties and domes for yap-yap seadogs, with his Iodine launch, he had given us one of the biggest, sweetest flobreggations in memory. Give and Take majora. Blitzo wasn't quite wrong, there certainly was a bogey under a rock, and either Inch or Bakks had already got to Blitzo's overheated powderbox, but actually there were now dozens of, to use Blitzo's warning, bogeys under quite a few rocks.

All those conflicting impulses: fertile indeed. But, it has to be said again, among all the impulses available in a big flobreggation it was the world of the hatey-fuckey impulses that were the favourite for Bakks and the cardboard crew of deadbeats. They loved all the hatey-fuckey, and they loved all the counterfeit myths that sprang from their hup two three efforts upon the hatey-fuckey conflicto.

The first thing that happened was a loud roar above books-meller's head. Laura had dived down along a pylon, maybe six feet deep. A solar buggy then flew past, very near her head, and continued sinking to the seabed. Blitzo had got into an, um, altercation. He was pushing and being pushed, and the two men had managed to edge the buggy over the side of the jetty and crash into the seapool. Blitzo had had a highsprung week-long approach to launch day, destroying his telomeres, so he was prime flobreggation material for Bakks. And when it was discovered what had dragged Blitzo into the altercation, it was no minor sticking point, it was a sticking point majora. A Ruby Schwartz sticking point.

It was the globules of intent. Ruby was being globularised by the education minister, he was not only standing a bit too near Ruby's, um, well, body, he was also using his hands. A metre away, Peter Blitz couldn't really take it, but he contained himself. But when another guy also started to globularise Ruby, and far more effectively than the education minister, Peter Blitz could not contain himself. The munnwaggle from the Silicon Valley IT firm, cruising in his spirit of love and embracement, who gleefully supplied a goodly portion of Neutrino's Lab, had got a smell for Ruby the second she walked into his office in California a year ago, and, scent being one of the big engines of memory, he'd gone bananas until he flew over for the Iodine launch, hey babe, hey brother, check out this vibe in the sky today, munnwaggling his way across the barriers and into as many guests as he could find, and then finally the munnwaggle launched into globularising Ruby out in the open. Ruby used it, the globularising. Prehistoric mensa mind simply decided it would be best to tie the stinker around the little finger so that any future requirements for the lab would be seen to by his firm with the quickest priority, so Ruby fobbed off the education minister, and instead encouraged the IT stinker.

But Blitzo, toxified by Bakks, or by Hailme-Hailme, went fizz crackle splatter ping, and they got into a tussle, Blitzo and the munnwaggle, pushing and shoving one another until they banged into the buggy where, with a few more shoves, it slid over the jetty and down along the pylon past booksmeller's head, solar buggy extincto. Bakks; if you're having a shit day, bring Bakks into the equation and you're gunna wanna kill em all. Blitzo certainly wanted to maim the IT stinker.

Then another fracas, this time in Blitzo's office, with Remple Fekdin, lord of Iodine.

'What the hell is wrong with you, Peter?'

'I dunno Remple, something just snapped, it's been a long month of really high stress I suppose, at least we got the place open on time.'

'What started it?'

Blitzo lied: 'He was insulting the university, that's what it was, the guy was shitting on our work, your vision, I'll go back outside and make a good apology.'

At Castle's spacepod, far south in Yelverton on the paddock at night, Catherine had warned her brother for the fourth and final time. 'Your general manager at Iodine is a weird man, if I were you I'd move him sideways at the least. Or, as I've said before, just get rid of him, he's a heavy duty liability, he's one of those fools who believes in acquired superiority, and that makes him dangerous because he has no time for anyone without a university degree. You have no degree, dear brother, and you are perfectly happy without one, never even wanted one, perhaps your general manager secretly loathes you. I doubt he envies you, he's not so easily taken with your resources, and he's not the type to fall into envy. He's proud of other things, he thinks he's smarter than you, and that's all he needs in order to get by and feel good, he's just another fool who believes in acquired superiority. It's all rather gory. Observing you working with him over the past year has been just too gory.'

Catherine knew her brother would take no notice, and he didn't, but she wanted to say what she wanted to say.

Remple told her that he had given the position to Peter because he found in Peter a resolve that overrode the ricepaper layers of academic skins already on staff, and that Peter had a rough power that overrode the stinging egos underneath the layers of ricepaper. A resolve to pursue the bigger vision, the singular job of pushing Iodine far out into the world as a new global presence. The pieties of learning, Remple had said, would be very well taken care of by the topnotch staff. Remple's pleasant reply concluded, with a yawn as he lay beside Catherine on the paddock looking at the Yelverton sky, Peter Blitz was a pragmatist, Remple wanted a coarse pragmatist, not a refined gentleman.

'Well,' Catherine had said, 'let's get back to the house and raise a glass to your dynamo pragmatist.'

Perving Drive-By

Now in Blitzo's office Remple simply stared out the window while Peter sat on a chair holding his hands together.

What Remple did not know about was a small habit Blitzo followed. Often.

Smiling at a stranger might be curious, but it still brings a powderbox closer to the doors of The Exchange. Keep walking, smile again, in a moment the powderbox is warming up, and suddenly an opportunity rises to dive in and help em out.

Blitzo wanted to help out Ruby, ever since she started work at Iodine he drove his old Nissan past her house in Broome, slowing down, right down, and then made his own way home across town.

Remple looked down to the water where the buggy went in and he saw Castle and Laura floating in a shadow. Moments later he saw Jack burst onto the surface. Jack had been down to the seabed to check the buggy.

'It's okay, there's nobody in it,' Jack said.

'What the fuck happened up there?' Castle said.

'I'd say the party has started!' Laura yelled.

It certainly had, the flobreggation was well underway, Oxley an me both knew it.

Remple said to Peter Blitz: 'Tell you what, go home, have a cold shower, have a swim, relax, take a siesta, and come back for the evening party with a headful of good vibes, how's that?'

'Good idea.'

A powderbox full of good vibes, no, not possible for Blitzo while Bakks was conducting the hup two three.

Blitzo drove back to his house in Broome, slowly. No intense hovercraft adrift on the dust at a hundred miles an hour, a lazy elbow out the window. And even after a cool shower he still, of course, had no idea that Inch and Bakks had done a hup two three upon his powderbox, had successfully folded a teeny memory across the galaxy back into his todaybox, a memory where a nasty bully kid had given little Blitzo's favourite girl a tweaking on the arse back in Subiaco primary in '69. He slowed down as he came to Ruby's place, and then he drove off.

I said to Inch: 'You are an empty cardboard fool.'

Inch: 'Listen here wooden fucktoid, if there were no molecules in the air, a jumbo wouldn't be able to fly, but me, I fly, baby woody, fly like a jumbo, hup two three, and you ain't gettin in the way of my happy days at this here flobreggation, plenty more bogeys under rocks, so fuck off. And throw that stupid bell away, it just looks childish, a box and a bell, what a gross look.'

Oxley: 'Gosh dear Inch, what is that smell? Is it you?'

Inch: 'Listen here you picnic pipsqueak, me an my crew are gunna hup two three as much Take as we can get from this flobreggation, swing a bit O memory around, new realities, pipsqueak, bold new realities, not your dreary old realities from sunny Dorking, now fuck off and watch me work, show you how memory really goes explosive to make hot new realities. What would you say in Dorking I fear? Sod it, that's it. Sod the past and sod it good coz it just might sod you instead.'

Cyclic AMP

Cyclic AMP is a molecule dear butterfly. It lives, so to speak, in the brain. If it breaks down the memory fades. The guy who found this molecule, and sorted out what it does—retain memories—is Eric Kandel. For this feat Kandel got given the 2000 Nobel prize in medicine. Oxley calls him, in honour, Candle, coz he has shown what keeps the lights on for the whole of us better boxes in our work with the cherished memories. Bakks and his filthy crew call him Kraphead, coz his discovery has gone a long way towards making the cardboard horde's work a lot harder: counterfeiting just got a little less cool, certainly less enjoyable, coz by Kandel pointing to the stuff in a powderbox that is responsible for retaining memories we woodens became fresher than ever. If the stuff breaks down, memory fades, so the pongsters had a target and we better woodens had a target too. Call it songuage on the one hand, haranguage on the other. We protected the cyclic AMP, and they wanted it haranguaged and banguaged. Even at the centre of a nice big flobreggation, counterfeiting became kind of a drag, and only hailme-hailme Inch wasn't put off, drawing his evil vigour and vividity from the fact that he was pretty close to Bakks meeting his fate with water. King Inch in the ascendant had layer upon layer of powerful vigour for the jumbo jet hup two three even tho he knew that counterfeiting had gradually become not so easy since Candle had shown the way to preserving the cherished and loved experiences.

Under the jetty, Laura began to get caught in the tide. This is something that caused her cyclic AMP, billions of them, to now buzz with new electricity, forming a not so pleasant memory of getting tangled in the huge tides of Broome. She was about ten metres away from the end of the jetty when

Jack called out to her from under the jetty.

'What're you doing out there? Laura! Come back here!'

But then Jack and Castle started to get swept away from the jetty. Three powderboxes floating in the direction of Indonesia. The party of hundreds above the jetty may as well have been miles away.

Within minutes they were swept out across the expanse, then squashed up against the wire-hatching wall of the seapool half a kilometre from the jetties back on the coast at Iodine, the tide surging over their shoulders and on through the hatching out to sea. They were stuck to the wall like leaves, and the tide grew stronger by the second. Castle spotted a stepladder in the distance, and so together they dragged themselves along the hatching wire of the seapool. Jack tried to push off the wire to swim to the steps but he got bounced back against the wire, so they clambered sideways in the rushing ocean, bit by bit, for half an hour until they got to the steps by grim childish concentration, and climbed out exhausted. Three powderboxes glowing with cyclic AMP, molecules that created a moment at Iodine's launch not to be forgotten quickly: a near head-on collision with a solar buggy and then a sudden sweep into the bay of indecent exposure to powers immemorial of north-western Australia.

There is another thing that cyclic AMP can achieve. At the intense moment when a ding-dong memory is created, so a snapfast future arrives, an idea, a blip of heightened clarity. No powderbox is immune from this blip of pure light. In Jack's case it was even brighter. Jack lay exhausted on the seapool jetty, and so his sightline caught a new painting. It was a plain one, simple, but it also flung all over creation with suggestion.

This was the painting: nearby, a seagull sat atop one of

the uprights. All Jack could see was the upright, the gull, the sky. But then, high in the sky behind the seagull he saw an aeroplane. His limited sightline, from lying back exhausted, framed the painting: a gull in the foreground, no ground at all, sky, a plane; he anchored his eyes for a few seconds. When the plane had exited the picture, he knew he had a minor piece of visual fun, and he decided there and then he'd paint it. A simple blue picture, small in scale, no need for a three metre canvas for this one, a bird, another bird, and sky, clean, cloudless sky. Jack's cyclic AMP had made a picture of the tidal event, and, henceforth, he'd also remember the event from the picture. The painting would remind him of being swept offshore far into the deep where he slapped up to the wire like a leaf. When the plane had gone from view, he thought the elements out, and he liked it as a composition. A stationary bird sitting, another bird doing eight hundred miles an hour, blue sky, no ground. A bird created by evolutionary mystery, and a bird created by engineers, who themselves might have been created by evolutionary mystery. He knew Patsy'd hate it, but what the hell, he'd keep it for himself, or he'd give it to Castle. He'd give it to Laura, but Laura's intellect, he knew, would decide it was too dumb, too shallow, so Castle it was. Then he began to float around inside the two birds, questions. Which one was simpler? Which one was the more complex? Had they each the same copious amount of wiring? And the flapping, what about the flapping? One bird flaps its wings, the other bird doesn't. Da Vinci's first flying machine flapped its wings, didn't work, and all the other flying contraptions in the next few centuries flapped, didn't work, not until the Wright brothers decided against flapping, did a flying machine leave the ground and fly. Poor ol ding-dong arrogarnta, Inch was fucking with his powderbox, Inch who loves a jumbo jet.

To smellbomb Hailme-Hailme the sight of the three friends washed away from Iodine merely was a kind of initial try out, because he wanted later, greatly desired, to expose his boss piggy Bakks to powers immemorial of the north-west wilderness, he wanted Bakks to have a bit of that indecent exposure. He really wanted to see Bakks float, floating away, sogging, sinking, cardboard Bakks extincto yumcha. O yes, Inch was only just beginning; with the opportunities presented by Remple's flobreggation, Inch calmly humming his way into the hup two three he had at hand, well this was only the first moment. Inch starting up. He was having quite a nice time, through the speeches, through the ding-dong with Ruby and the munnwaggling IT stinker, and Blitzo, through the sodden gallery on Catherine's phone, and through the constant offering up to Bakks of one piece of evil shit after the next. Oxley could clearly make it out, the sound of Inch coasting through quite a pleasant time, the low and evil humming, the chanting, sounding like a soft lullaby:

Kill the past
And kill it dead
Coz it just might kill you instead

So Oxley took up his own little chant now and again through the course of the day to piss Inch off. Inch had always presumed he was up there with IQ, surveillance an all, so Oxley knew he had to sing any ol ding-dong flimflam to unsettle Inch, to grate, to chip away the caked red in flaky bits, diluting his concentration in the process:

Love the past
I love the past

Sweet sweet arses
Flatten the grasses
So let's all have a nice jink slow
And watch the grasses as they grow

And I sang my own little flimflam chant to piss Inch off, mingling the powderboxes of colonel David and his hooligan princess:

O my tasty princess
Who seen what Charlie's got
Let's drive to the hilltown Ranchi
And jackpot into raunchy cot

Inch: 'Yeah, wooden fucktoids, that's right: fukkin slaves.'

The whole two days of the flobreggation went on like this, screwing Inch's focus with incremental flimflam. We didn't mind his design upon his boss, no, but we needed to screw his focus away from our own hup two three with our favourite powderbox clientele, Kee, Rosa, Castle, and also the two arrog-arnta plumes of nimble artistry Laura and Jack.

To that end, burning Bakks onto Inch's irritation, Oxley sang:

King Bakks thinks that Inch is dumb
Inch is dumb
Inch is dumb
Bakks thinks that Inch is thick
Inch is thick
Inch is thick
O Bakks would like to light the fire
Light the fire

Underneath the ratsblood dude
the ratsblood dude
the ratsblood dude

The song needed only to be a base and shitty ditty, nothing more, coz Inch knew it was true, and he was gunna do in Bakks in the best way possible, that is, the worst way possible. Soggy little scraps of Bakks.

The Broome Night-Sky

The second equator had moved across the continent to Broome. That night the informal phase of the celebrations commenced, lit up from the sun king's solar panels, a small colony of domes and jetties on the lonely bay, a city at night sparkling with lights juiced up by the day's sun for free. Laura phoned Jimmy Hazel to coax him into Broome for the week, but he didn't answer his phone, mid-evening on the Pittwater peninsula back in Sydney, the second equator had long since moved over Pittwater, and Jimmy was strolling the dark pathways through the scrub and forest, over to the goldrush house. He moved with no haste, real slow, dragging, looking around in the starlit treetops as he walked, picked up a fallen branch, dragging it along the dirt until he came to the base of the hillside.

Lee Glass-Darlington was by now a mess. No word from Rudolph, no word from Tony Chen, nothing from the police, and, as had now been organised by the Singapore office, no word from Scotland Yard; it seemed Rudolph had simply blipped off into the ether. Lee had lost a lot of weight, she was washing only every four or five days, the kitchen hadn't been seen to for a very long time, the light behind her eyes, inherited highgrade from colonel David, had retreated like a summer and thinned into a winter. She sat folded at the window for most of the day, most days. Clinton and Yunus still co-chaired the Fund, but they had elected to initiate a search, more than a month ago, for a new director, and had chosen a powerful lawyer from the Muslim League in Lahore to run the fund in Singapore.

Jimmy emerged from the pathway and climbed up the hillside to the house. All the lights were out, except one. On his first visit a month ago he was daunted by the thing of the house, of coming round to see if he could check her out. Dozens of visits later, tonight he was not daunted in the slightest. He threw the branch down the hill. Sat at the big table where he made himself comfortable, leaning back deeply on the chair to observe the house at his leisure. Big double storey place with a loft, and over the roofline a clear sky. Bleeding starlight downwards, he thought, into the cluster of groves at Tenmoon Creek where he would always, always, never forget the moment he'd first laid hands on the inspiration for the sculptures, the very moment in all his life that they arrived into his visible mind as a small naked crayon up the hillside. With all the lights out, the place was cast in excellent shadows, and he ran an eye over the shapes, the corners, the sills, doorways. The one light came from her bedroom window.

Now the Lucknow jolly was about to eradicate a missing husband. A centre melter who hadn't been found. Not in any of the centres around the world of jewels. Jimmy had not met the husband, and he didn't care. If he had, he was certain anyway he would not in any way or shape or form or dream have liked him. Or, even if he did like him, the inner drive would've not allowed him to like the husband, the inner drive for the house and its occupant was too strong for allowances of that kind, too right and true—and strong.

'Yeah, never liked him,' Jimmy said aloud slowly, with mellow conviction. 'That stupid dealer Patsy was right: he's just a fuckwit jewellery salesman.'

And there it was; neat as air, Jimmy had done his own private hup two three of Rudolph extincto. Jimmy had melted the centre, blown it into dust. Tonight Jimmy was daunted by nothing: undaunted by whatever karma he might think up; undaunted by the husband maybe suddenly showing up; by getting sacked by the sister Meryl; by the cops; by the fact that Lee had a truckload of lawyer friends that could have thrown the book, and the printing press, at him; or by the ugly exposure the legal jamboree would be likely to bring to any possible future career in the arrogarnta arena of nimble artistry.

But he was not about to stop there, Jimmy was now going to erase any last vestige of Rudolph hanging in the hot night air. Jimmy was gunna do grievous bodily harm. Well, grievous absentee harm anyway, the type of harm that constitutes the earliest beginnings of the grottier myths that the smellbombs love.

He kept on talking softly to himself, mellowly, with that deep and easy conviction that he'd recently gained by the steady and accumulating rise of the new sculptures.

'How the hell would a guy like that be capable of feeling the energy rising up from this rock under the feet, how would he be capable of sensing the molten uprising, how could a jewellery salesman ever feel the earth rising from hundreds of miles into the molten core, bring that ancient carnal forcefield into creation?'

This, to better boxes like me an Oxley, is that particular strain of powderbox again, arrogarnta, sculptor arrogarnta this time no less, shitting from upon high on a perfectly harmless gems trader, a very talented gems trader, and in fact a nice guy. Bakks loves the arrogarnta types, loves em, they make his counterfeiting travel along lighter over the mountains and the seas, and he gets a lot more done. But Bakks never went near chickname coz his powderbox was too full of butterflied prawns, Jimmy was safe from the crew of deadbeat pongsters.

'How could a boring guy like that even *begin* to sense the carnal roots of the planet, how could he run with them, hunt them, use them, how could he create highways for them to emerge and let them survive and thrive out in the open, those glowing carnal roots. That stupid dealer Patsy, she's right, he's Rudy the prude. Never liked him anyway.'

The Lucknow jolly was satisfied. He had crapped on the husband from a great height, and so had, at long last, after the numerous visits, dissolved the missing husband away.

And then, for good measure, he gave a calm chant borne of smellbomb Inch's hup two three, coz Inch was not afraid of Jimmy's powderbox, Inch's Maoist claptrap from the factory days about killing the past.

Jimmy said to himself:

Anyway, he's the past
and fuck the past
she should flush the past down the toilet
or it'll take her hard-won beauty away and boil it

And he meant hard-won beauty, he felt she was looking more beautiful than ever, and it was the grime he liked. The slowly building grime of trauma and the grit of sadness had been turning him on for a very long month now, it showed right there in her face, everywhere on her face, and he was getting off on it.

His phone went off, and he could see it was Laura again, so he didn't answer it. He was waiting for Lee to call after he'd slipped his number and a note under the back door two weeks ago, he'd been waiting two weeks for the unshowered walking shoelace to call, but she hadn't.

If Jimmy'd been lucky enough to have just a teaspoon of undercrowded humility in that powderbox of his, then the party, or, as Oxley says, the picnic, wooda had the glow and shine of a freshly sliced mango, the picnic that Jimmy sought with Lee. Might've even had the orange-puffwhite gleam of butterflied prawns like Jimmy used to do at his backyard picnic barbeques in Lucknow. It may even have gone so far as to outshine the golden orange of a cut mango or a prawn, it may have been one of those picnics of gigantic, enjoyable mess and squalor, corked, popped, buttered and blanched across an entire hillside here in the leafy district of Pittwater. But no, not chickname. He just rolled on with the arrogarnta, kept sitting there, behind the darkened house, at the big table, splayed out arms behind his shoulders, giving ding-dong, taking yumcha.

Laura hung up. 'Can't reach him, he's working probably, he's making a new set of sculptures in the back shed.'

Iodine pounded loudly into the Broome night, a couple of hundred powderboxes lingered after the launch in the morning, dancing, revelling and, the thing that all us boxes crave the most, they were flobreggating bigtime. The great gathering, any great gathering. Pouring into the warm night hundreds of conflicting impulses, all that haranguage, ganguage, banguage and twanguage throwing sparks off the jetties and into the bay. Big potential, big opportunity for the hup two three. Sparkling impulses everywhere, pick em up and throw em round. Besides, the second equator by now had barely rolled by, just the right time for throwing memories across the fertile band of dusk. Delicious dusk, feeding time.

Castle and Jack had gone for a walk along the shoreline to explore the feeding time. A kangaroo was out swimming. The roo dived and then surfaced, and dived again, hunting for shellfish, crayfish, octopus. The roo came ashore and started to crack a shell against the rocks, and ate the sweet bulbous animal inside. The roo chewed the soft animal slowly, sitting upright, staring ahead, shifting the big wet ears backwards, then forwards, scanning. The roo sat on the rocks and cracked and ate around five shellfish, and then swam out again to dive and hunt for more.

'I didn't know kangaroos could swim!' Jack said with excitement.

'These roos up here in the north, time and necessity have given them extra skills, they've evolved for coastal living. Fossil records show that sea-going kangaroos have been around for about eight thousand years.'

'Do they live on land as well?'

'Yep. They still feed on the grasslands, grasses, roots, fruit, leaves. They like paw-paw, I've given them paw-paw many times, they love it. That's why I brought this one along, here, break it open and throw him some paw-paw.'

Jack took the paw-paw. He called out to the kangaroo: 'Roo-roo! Hey roo-roo, paw-paw!'

Near the kangaroo a diver surfaced, Dave the painter. 'Stick your paw-paw up your nose!'

The DNA DVD

Jack then woke up. He didn't know where he was at first, only that he was lying on a sofa in a darkened room. He was in Ruby Schwartz's office. Outside the window Iodine was rocking away like a music festival into the clear Broome night. He had a sore head from the day's champagne stations, and his shoulder was cut and bruised from crawling against the tide and the wire. Mired in hasty-paste a powderbox will always wake up wondering where he is, until his phone rings and it's his dealer, Patsy, and then he knows he's still in the middle of a ding-dong shitfight.

'Patricia?'

'Hebbllo Jack, haff I corld at a good time?'

'Have you been drinking with Lars again?'

'We had dnner. Hab you phound out why Catherine vucked-up me an Rembble yet?'

'Yes, she did some DNA tests, and she doesn't want you having kids with him.'

'She did wha?'

'DNA tests.'

'What the pbhuck is a deenay test?'

'D-N-A, her great-grandfather was insane, and she thinks you're insane, and so you and Remple might be just the right skip of generations to give birth to insane kids.'

'I kunn belieff it! Wadda lodda *kucking blooshitt*!'

But the fact of what Catherine had done suddenly sank even deeper into Patsy's powderbox, and so she squealed down the phone, across the seas and the mountains: 'Wadda lodda kucking kucking blooshit!'

'Tell me Pat, did you flood her gallery?'

'Donbe stupid, I woon do a stupid ting like that. She did a

deenay test?'

'Yes, she did, I've gotta go Pat, I'll give you a call tomorrow.' Jack hung up.

Name a Gene

Jack got up and went outside to the corridor and then found his way out into the festivities, and for no particular reason he suddenly wanted to catch up with the wise old seadog, manta monk and his new girlfriend.

Hong and Jack's Keep Left pod still stood in the centre of the dam of jetblack yabbies, but Jack had forgotten where he'd put the photograph of it.

Me an Oxley—and Stan for that matter, Stan the hunter of advantage in every moment—we three better boxes seen a century where just about everything, whether it is walking or crawling or just quietly growing, winds up with at least three names. But we never saw as many names as the seadog had names.

It's ding-dong common as oxygen to have more than one name. Take the case of Cook's diary. Off the coast of southern Australia one fine day, Captain Cook sailed past a steep little mountain. He lay tracking a mile offshore, the edifice five miles inland. He felt it looked like a pigeon cage, so he called it Pigeon House Mountain, what a goose, he just floats on past, and sees a thing in the distance, and decides to plop a name on it. It had already been named long before. Was he stupid?

I mean, how can a stranger drive past your party and, cruise pleasantly by at an ambling speed, and give your daughter another name? No way, Cook was a smart guy, but there you go, it's the normal way of many a powderbox, name-name roam-roam name-name. Me an Oxley an Stan, we seen it here there and everywhere. Roam-roam name-name. Flattie, she's seen more of it than the rest of us put together.

Bakks yawns at our surprise, says it is just another way of sharing, share the world.

But me an Oxley an Stan, consulting Flattie, we decided by the thirties that the tendency to roam-roam name-name was another one of those deformities. Stan said the impulse was a cultural kind of imperative. The useage of a resource, a capture, he said Cook wouldn't have had a clue that afternoon. Sailing by, sipping on a brew of Ceylonese leaves, peering into the distant hinterland. Not stopping for today, just naming, just undulating along the deep blue waters of the coast a day south of Botany Bay.

Or take Sydney Harbour, if the oldest name could be discovered it might derive from the oldest of perfected creatures, the shark, who'd call Sydney Harbour 'Lunch.' Big lunch, good lunch. In streetwise Sharkilese, once the powderboxes began to bathe in it: Some Fukkin Good Lunch Joint.

Cook wouldn't have had a clue that the mountain was already called Didthul, Didthul in the powderboxes of at least a hundred generations, that's three thousand years, so maybe Didthul had been called Didthul for around a thousand generations, depending on the clans who were given the honour. And James Cook would of course have known it already would of course have a name. Some name, any name, but the ding-dong thing is he went ahead and banged another on it, so me an Oxley an Stan felt it was just another one of those deformities, one of many deformities proudly owned by powderboxes.

Lucky for What

Whatever it was, it was quite prolific, and it happened everywhere a plunderer roamed. Truth is, powderbox inclinations taken into account, why should plundering suddenly cease, plundering might instead continue. If Paxton's Mandarin friends were to enter into a fresh new era of plundering, they might rename Pigeon House Mountain into Middle Kingdom Mountain Number 309, depending upon how many peaks they'd already renamed around the world. If Hu Xiaolian got her way, there would certainly be a bit of extra buying and labelling, and for very good reason. She's in charge today of China's foreign reserves of money. Two hundred billion dollars. Ms Hu is the chief boss of the State Administration of Foreign Exchange, so, you know, she could bandy about any number of Middle Kingdom ideas, and most of the boys who run their own kingdoms round the world might have to listen rather than ignore. For Ms Hu would possess a bit of clout now that China has been lending money to America for twenty years. Nowadays America pays China fifty billion dollars a year in interest on those borrowings. That's more than the age of the universe dear butterfly. Now that Ms Hu sits atop a largish mountain of foreign cash, exports, interest, investments, she might like to instigate a bit of naming. But, alas. With no expansionist notions coming from Ms Hu's office, Paxton's toy lords, for the moment, were fucked coz China reported at the start of 2009 a fact of jittery portent. They said that four thousand toy factories had closed. Four thousand, that's a shitload of loss, even in Ms Hu's high-flying world. Meaning: many thousands of other engines of plunder around China had also closed, meaning the Chinese leaders would have to wait till they were strong enough once again to go make new naming, you can't make an empire with factories *closing*. Even if you grandly are sitting atop a mountain of hard-earned foreign cash.

Oxley: 'And where is the advantage in that, Stan?'

Stan: 'In renaming?'

Oxley: 'Roaming and naming, yes.'

Stan: 'Well, I'd bet Miles would have seen it as just another scrap of flobreggation. A flobreggation over a longer timeline, Miles talked timelines, he invented the word timeline and then business took it up forty years later, Miles would have seen roaming and naming as just another scrap of conflicting impulse.'

Yep, me and Oxley an Stan, we seen naming all right. Roam-roam, plunderama.

Bakks on a Third Try

But what we never seen before is what took place from the hacienda. How many names the kid from the hacienda collected, the kid was plundered like a sardine. Carlos Luque. Kieran Leeft. Sunrise Sunset. Manta monk. Keep Left. Seadog. That's six names, more than even a Latin-studded weed growing quietly on six continents. One good thing: at least oxygen seems to be oxygen wherever it floats off to, wherever it drifts on by, coz maybe, by and large, England's declining final act of colonising stuff extended to the last outpost, the molecules. Oxygen ain't done in Mandarin, unless maybe it's called Xia Wei Jen. Oxygen ain't a word from any of the six thousand nine hundred beautiful languages on the planet, it's an English word. And with two hydrogens tacked on, H_2O, water, nero, we wooden boxes can happily keep on shitting off Inch so intensely that he finally cracks and does the deed, flings his boss into the sea. Bits of cardboard scraping up against the wire wall of the Iodine seapool, bits of Bakks slugged off into the sea. Yep, no matter how many thousands of names across the two equators there are for water, H_2O is still H_2O, and prawnbox Bakks is still cardboard. Which means that the really nice fact hovering between two pieces of hydrogen and one piece of oxygen is counterfeiting oblivion, Bakks extincto.

As Stan said: 'There's a distinct advantage in that: bringing extincto to Bakks, while it cannot de-toxify all the counterfeit, it's a good step in the right direction.'

Bakks had forced not a few slithers of harsh crap into a couple of powderboxes here and there. Forcing them to entertain petty judgements, bitter judgements, puerile judgements, sordid judgements of fake goodness, resulting in crushing even the slightest tendency to the simplest of tolerances, diminishing the groove, the good vibes, the lounging, the illuminations, the giving, hurting the fun, Bakks was loving it.

We better boxes already knew he's been plastering the Catherine Fekdin powderbox with all that DNA bullshit ever since Remple's romp with Patsy in Spain. And now Bakks was onto Jack and the old seadog. Again. Coz he'd failed so many times before, ever since the kid flew the coop at the hacienda.

Renata the Grandmother

Kee and Rosa had been driven back to the hotel in Broome around lunchtime, not by Blitzo. They took the afternoon on a pearling boat coz Kee wanted to dive. The pearlers didn't recommend it, saying the bay was shark country this month coz the baitfish swarmed in from the north-east. Kee dived anyway. By seven Remple collected Kee and Rosa from the hotel, and they drove out to Iodine for the evening fun to dissolve the earlier formalities.

Jack asked around—Ruby, Remple, Rosa—and found him at the end of the jetty that handled the meteorological inputs from satellites. The department collated a massive stash of information twenty-four hours a day, every day of the week, weaving a daily impression of the ocean from the various strands of info. Cloud cover, salinity, temperature, winds, humidity, currents, low cells, high cells, readings from the troposphere, stratosphere, mesosphere, ionosphere, the jetty was a huge weather vane for the two worlds above and below the surface.

Kee had asked for a tour, which the head of the department had just concluded; Sunrise Sunset had just got a ding-dong handle on a twenty-first century five million dollar thermometer that can be inserted under the earth's tongue, a magic wand as Ellie would have called it. Oxley called it the distillery of the two equators. Roam-roam name-name, we boxes had caught the habit a long time ago, the deformity, can't blame ourselves. After all, the whole century was just one big naming exercise, no owner anywhere was immune to the instinct, as were all the previous centuries probably, and as will be the new one no doubt, roam-roam name-name. Plenty of roaming still yet to do up and down the genome, like Catherine had roamed down Patsy's genome. But Catherine's choice of name when the scientific roam was concluded and delivered, when she viewed the DNA DVD, was a bit blunt, unscientific: she called Patsy 'trumped up bitch.' Bigger gallery see.

Kee was sitting at the end of the jetty, watching the sky. 'They tell me the tide got you today.'

'It did.'

'Are you all right?'

'Bruised, but fine. Congratulations on your speech Kee, it was the best thing I've heard in years.'

'That was Mendoza, Rosa's father, but thankyou.'

'Would Mendoza have known Catherine's grandmother's father, the guy who threatened Renata?'

'You are thinking of madness?'

'No, no, well, yes, I am, I suppose.'

'On a beautiful night such as this? Why?'

'I'm trying to figure something out. Have you heard what Catherine has done?'

'Yes.'

'What do you think of it?'

'She has to make her own peace with the give and take.'

'Did Mendoza know him?'

'Mendoza talked of him once. They were friends, they also sometimes worked the gulf together. Renata's father Eduardo was a good man. He had an older, smaller boat than Mendoza's but he made good catches, a smart fisherman. When the others made a thin catch, he would give them some of his. He was happy. He loved his daughter, he loved his wife.'

'I'm sorry, I don't follow.'

'Why?'

'I don't understand. He was chasing his daughter with a machete you told me.'

'Yes.'

'But you are saying he was a kind and happy guy who loved her.'

'Castle did not tell you? About the diamond claws?'

'Yeah he did.'

'The diamond claws came to Renata's father. Before the diamond claws Eduardo was a good guy, a kind guy.'

'So it's true.'

'It is true.'

Out on the dark ocean a sparkle glimmered, ship's lights.

'Did you meet him?'

'He lived in a village to the south, but sometimes he would anchor off the beach near the hacienda to bring us food. He once brought comics. He gave us about thirty comics, American comics, his cousin had gone to America. He read them to us in Spanish. He was a great guy, he made us laugh. One day he stopped coming. We never saw him again, perhaps he began to go in and out of the hospital.'

'So when you found Renata eight years later, when you took her on board to look for her parents—I remember you told me you were nineteen—you already knew her father?'

'I didn't know he'd since had a daughter. Renata would have been five the year I left the hacienda I suppose. All I knew was what Renata told me that afternoon, that some guy who was her father had been chasing her with violence in his mind, I didn't know it was the guy who brought the comics. It is fortunate that I did not know he was the father because I would have taken Renata to him.'

'When did you find out?'

'Years later, Catherine told me. But, to this day I see only that guy who used to visit us. A kind guy who always laughed, brought food, played games, showed us how to be safe in the gulf, at the beach, when to swim, when not to swim, he was as good as Mendoza.'

'And then he went from that cool guy to these, these, diamond claws.'

'So tell me, is Catherine right, is your art dealer in London insane?'

'No, she's not insane, it's absurd to think of Patsy as insane.'

'How do you know this?'

'I just know it. I've known Patsy for a long time, she's a hard-arsed fuckwit, she's a clever snake, she's a charmer, she's talks bizarre nonsense a lot, and she's capable of very goofy behaviour, but she's sane. Catherine's testing of Patsy's DNA in Geneva is just a hit and miss thing, generalisations, Castle is actually quite pissed off with Catherine.'

'Then if your dealer is okay, tell Catherine.'

'I have.'

'Then she will consider it. How is your work?'

'I did five paintings of your boat.'

'The *Pinski*? Nice to hear it, I think your colours will be off, they are repainting her in Almeria.'

'That's okay. We kept one to give you, Catherine chose it.'

'What happened to the others?'

'She sold them.'

'Congratulations.'

'One thing I've wanted to ask.'

'Go ahead.'

'Is it true you do not have a passport?'

'Why do you need to ask such an unimportant question?'

'I've called the paintings *Captain With No Passport I, II, III, IV* and *V*. Catherine chose *III* for you.'

'That's nice. Yes, I have never needed a passport.'

'How did you get into Australia?'

'Remple organised papers for me.'

'Do you still have no house anywhere Kee? Castle said you bought a house in Tangiers.'

'Castle is listening to the wind, *Pinski* is my house. Pedro is overseeing the repainting.'

Ellie's Giving Goes Good

Kieran Leeft was seventy-three at this moment on the jetty, and he had lived in just two houses. The hacienda until he was eleven, and the room he shared for five years with Pedro in Almeria at the Villacarillo until he bought his first boat at sixteen from the kind old fisher Maliaeras. Three houses, of course, but the house in which he came into the world was not known, the two year old infant Carlos Luque had been taken to the hacienda by the monseigneur after his mother and father were thought to have been killed in the war. He was born in July 1936, the year of the Civil War, on the fourth, American Independence Day.

Stan: 'How come the seadog didn't become that subgroup of powderboxes the wreckers, Bobbo?'

'I dunno. Ellie and the colonel I suppose. Jack arrogarnta suspected he was cruel deep down somewhere, but the seadog could never automatically sail into life developing into a wrecker coz those two clowns at the hacienda were ding-dong good, they were givers.'

Oxley: 'One need not be poor, lost, an orphan, a broken start to life, whatever you'd like to call it, to become a wrecker, dear Stan, your feeble presumptions quite optimise me out. My second owner, that creep who had the picnics in the windowless basement was a wrecker. He was rich as the Banfords, had a happy childhood, his mother and father loved him, he had it all, but he was a devout and destructive wrecker, sneaky though, didn't like to demonstrate that he was wrecking, he just enjoyed wrecking. Anyway Stan, ask Daqua, he'd have a clue why the seadog never became a wrecker.'

The Floating Box, Daqua

Daqua only ever had the one owner after Maliaeras: the seadog. Daqua was his fishing gear box. Dirty great thumper of a box, three feet high, two feet wide, six feet long, filled with Kee's memories from the time the guy was sixteen, long nights offshore, long days riding the currents. Weeks anchored in protective bays waiting out storms, painted and repainted for protection against the sea air, and the sea, once a year for the last fifty-seven years.

Hooks, lines, sinkers, nets, the four masks, fins, swivels, knives, screwdrivers, spanners and pliers. The navigation equipment in the cabin at the steering wheel was the sweetest up to date machine any skipper could hope for anywhere.

So there was Daqua onboard *Pinski*, cruising either side of the two equators, soaking up half a century's million reasons why the seadog never became a wrecker.

But ding-dong Daqua had long ago decided on one reason, just one. Daqua knew that the seadog had always understood what The Exchange was, where it was located, how to get there, and even the reason for its existence, one of just a few powderboxes who knew such exhaustive details about The Exchange dear butterfly. The seadog could not be a wrecker even if he'd trained for it, been forced into it, had wanted to, he just knew too much about The Exchange, that place where the cult of self takes a pause.

Arrival at The Exchange

And exactly where is The Exchange? It lies beyond three vast storms. We have flown a long way together dear butterfly, so perhaps it is time to pause. The moment of clarity, what we wooden boxes call the Give and Take. A moment of understanding found, discovered. A moment where the only thing lost is suspicion, or fear. Any time there's a whiff of give and take, you can be certain there will be a moment that follows, of natural, instinctive understanding. Mostly it is to be had beyond the storms of loss, beyond the storms of suspicion, beyond the storms of fear. It is after passing these three ravaging storms that a powderbox will find those moments where the self achieves a secondary status. The Exchange had many visitors dear butterfly, from colonel David to Rosa Mendoza. It is where David's instinct was located when he accepted the job of running the hacienda. It is where Enid stepped into with her expression of love for her granddaughter, with words of encouragement that Rudolph will turn up soon. When that day, early dawn, she was taken aback to see her granddaughter had climbed up the hill naked: feet, legs and thighs smeared with grit and mud. Jimmy Hazel visited The Exchange when the first inclinations of making those sympathetic stone portraits had arrived to trouble his balance. Aunt Lee of the Soho Scottish diaspora, diaspirin, Dunsborough Swing, had found delight at The Exchange. She concocted her songs there, and the songs brought her the many colourful friends and admirers she enjoyed at Suave's late-night world of give and take. Pedro in Almeria found his destiny at The Exchange. He found his destiny at just fifteen. After four years with his friend Kieran Leeft from the hacienda up north, Pedro realised he would like to open a home for kids. He did post that letter to the Indian billionaire Mukesh Ambani, citing Kofi Annan, and in return mister Ambani sent Pedro a cheque for the home. Rosa brushed into The Exchange when she briefly raised Paxton. Miles Banford, among the many visits he made to The Exchange, the best was the moment he fedexed me off to Enid. He'd lost his friend David, moved back to his ancestral home Boston, and delivered David's teak box along with a lawyer who had in his pocket a significant portion of the Banford fortune to give Enid.

As for the seadog dear butterfly, one of his very first visits to The Exchange, when he was just a nineteen year old, would always remain among his most important visits. That is, his most important when it comes to Remple, Catherine and Castle. He had saved their grandmother. He had set sail from Almeria three years earlier for the journey up the coast. He pulled in to a village for water. He found the girl of fourteen sitting on a crate in the sun. Alone and scared, there was panic burning from her eyes, and he took her onboard, and then was forced to set sail unwisely at night from the next village after he sensed ugliness in the woman who was going to call the police. At nineteen the seadog had now well and truly begun his life at the doors, windows and corridors of The Exchange, making many visits in the oncoming years as the second equator rolled and rolled.

Yep, Touch Wood, The Exchange Will Forever Glow

Remple had realised a dream. He had the seadog open the university. It made Remple glow, that's all he wanted, it was not business, he simply felt calm and nourished at the fact that his friend the seadog had done the deed at the most precious moment of the new university's official launch into existence. But the business came anyway. Newspapers around the world carried the story. This was no VIP who had flung open the gates, this was a seventy-three year old sea creature, an uneducated man who'd lived on the sea, the *New York Times* ran a small piece on it with the heading 'Homeless Man Opens College.' Dozens of papers carried other headings, but Remple knew it deep down where the noise could not reach: he felt nourished. It was his magic wand, Ellie-Isabela would have decided that Iodine was now Remple's magic wand. Years before, she'd said to the boy Carlos Luque: 'I have a magic wand, and it is called Giving,' and in that same week the boy vanished into the world.

Remple turned up. He'd had a long, exhausting day moving on Ruby's guiding hand from one conversation to the next, VIPs, many dozens, and now he was pleased to have left it all behind. 'Hello gentlemen. This is a bit far away from the party, don't you think?'

'Ah, señor Remple, sit with us.'

'Hi Remple.'

'Hi Jack, I hear you enjoyed the seapool.'

'Thanks a heap, my fault though. Did they recover the buggy?'

'Not yet, tomorrow. I have something else, a message for you, Kee. Ruby picked it up at the lab where she was taking feedback earlier. It's from Kofi Annan, says he watched your speech, admired it very much, and he asked if we might convey to you that he looks forward to perhaps fishing with you the next time you are in Almeria.'

'The UN dude?' Jack asked. 'What, you've been in New York Kee?'

'I pulled up next to the señor in Almeria when I went to visit Pedro. I don't know why he wants to fish, I gave him a fish I caught that night, I didn't know who he was, I just gave him a fish.'

In a split second Jack caught it. The cruelty he'd suspected in the Bahamas. It vanished so fast he could not be certain it made the surface, but it had the shine, the glint. Like the silence of a mangrove, staring at the mudflats, maybe the eye of a mudskipper in the sludge, maybe just a bubble of air. Whatever it was, it vanished.

Remple produced a bottle of champagne. He poured three glasses, and he searched for the expression of gratitude that he felt. He ended up saying: 'Thankyou Kee, you have given me a morning I will cherish forever.'

The Three States

Catherine had successfully put an end to Remple and Patricia giving birth to a child. She had darkened the light pouring around the possibility of a new life. But it is a sense larger, beyond those three, that truly darkens the light falling around the prospect of a new life. What forms of remembrance will offer a detailed opinion on Catherine's sordid intervention?

Memory exists across the coves and bays of human possibility: loved and cherished; lost and forgotten; bitter and destructive. It is hard to choose which one of the three states causes stronger bonds, creates stronger links. Seems obvious that the loved and cherished memories will create stronger bonds, but it is also a sawtooth fact that the bitter and destructive memories have created some of the most powerful bonds ever known. If a generalisation like this were found one day in the right socio-economic circumstances of the not too distant future to be reasonably useful, then it stands to reason that the lawmakers, tastemakers and behaviour modifiers will wish to enter the rush to control that usefulness.

Who are the aggregations that will exercise control over memory? And who are the aggregations that will control inheritance in its many forms? These aggregations may most likely come from among those who exist in a state of heightened importance. For those who exist in a state of heightened importance, day by day, making speeches on general betterment, having audiences listen, perhaps two speeches a week, proposing ideologies and styles, the going can be good. For these powder-boxes, the fumes, literally, of excitement post-speech, the energy of having expressed good ideas to large audiences follow them home to where they can rest and think. Finetune ways to bring an aggregation of control to the human oceans of memory and inheritance. Fishing for ways to soften the hurricanes of human rejection.

These speeches are not inspirational acts, they are acts of coercion. If not outright coercion then the lesser form of evil, extended moments of one-dimensional arrogance. Three-dimensional arrogance can be inspiration, but never one-dimensional arrogance. Arrogarnta plume of one dimension, and they derive, these speeches, these offerings, from a sense of dismay, from a sense of quiet revulsion. It is a revulsion of the thing that the sculptor in Pittwater thought of as the carnal forces beneath his feet, a molten planet, urging him to remake things, urging him to understand from the endless alchemy of the ocean remaking itself. It is a revulsion for the stink of creativity. Aggregations are not revolted only by the flow of molten carnal forces forged into creativity, but also by the free flow and transport of memory, and by the crumpled marching, the anarchy, of inheritance. Searching for ways to soften the hurricanes of human rejection, the aggregations will in their own way of principled consensus give birth to trees without leaves. Oxygen levels will diminish.

Lessons to be learned. Put to use. But there are no lessons, only concerted efforts by an aggregation to release fixed agreements into the world.

Reaching agreement through principled compromise is needed, and most recipients are grateful for useful agreements. It is needed everywhere, throughout the vast, layered territory of open human possibility, but it is not at the apex of that territory.

The territory of insult is the clearest example. If Jack has just been insulted by Dave the painter, Jack perhaps should return the insult right away.

But the insult is not returned, the insult is absorbed by Jack. Jack would have no need to retort: he doesn't like Dave, he doesn't agree with Dave, he has a pity for Dave, not extending to sympathy, so why would he bother to insult Dave back, Jack just doesn't care. But Jack has this pity because he believes himself to be better than Dave. Principled consensus can often have similar fumes, it is aromatic with righteousness, it produces no stench of creativity, and so is never the father or mother of inspiration. If Jack were not so arrogant he might insult Dave right back.

The aggregation to curtail the production and distribution of DNA DVDs may or may not have the authority of legal decree. The aggregation may or may not have the power to impose fines on certain DNA DVDs. To enforce privacy. To keep love 'clean,' as it were, from the early manipulations and foreclosures of technology-assisted acceptances or declinings, from the grit of genetic prejudice. Love is to be celebrated as love, this aggregation would insist, would declare as its desired outcome. This aggregation would burn the intimacy books of the future, the DNA DVDs being produced by the millions. This aggregation would be small and operating against the tide. In all probability this aggregation would have as difficult a job enforcing its vision as, say, making a spy film devoid of satellite images, as difficult as making *Bourne Identity Six* devoid of mobile phones. The tide would be in Catherine's favour, so Catherine would easily be able to ignore this aggregation, dismissing their call to purity as medieval crackpottery. Catherine had designs upon happiness, just as the aggregation also had designs upon happiness. They both wanted the same thing. Like memory, DNA has three fundamental states: wanted, tolerated, unwanted.

Making Better, Evolving

The most beautiful place on a string of DNA is the slender codification that orders the making of cyclic AMP, the molecule that retains memories. This small place that requests the creation of cyclic AMP is achingly beautiful because it has given memory a chance to become larger than any single generation, it has given life a history. A history that reaches beyond birthdays. Trawling far away into the Byzantine rulers, or far away into the greatest clans of Broome. This magic is beautiful because, in creating such a sweep, mistakes need not be committed again and again, Catherine can gain from history. Improve. The whole town can gain from history, all towns across the two equators can gain. Beautiful possibilities in abundance. Made real through the taking of beautiful decisions. Beautiful horizons brought to the doorstep through the making of beautiful choices. Intangible vistas brought to Ellie's backroom window like a fresh curtain. In the hallways and timerooms of inspiration, beautiful possibilities awash on the air like a sea breeze. What is it that makes all this beauty viable instead of out of reach? A collection of proteins, a molecule, called cyclic AMP. And thanks in the first instance to that small place on DNA that requests the making of cyclic AMP. By itself it is an insipid music, but without it there would be no music. The hallways and timerooms of inspiration would fall silent.

Bookseller Burns Two Books

Castle had left the care of the bookshop in Margaret River to Dexter Pepper. Dexter would finish at the bakery at eleven in the morning, have lunch, open the bookshop at midday. He sold more copies of Barack Obama's book than anything else in the shop, it even outsold John Howard's book. Dexter counted four hundred and sixty-two copies of Obama's book splayed out on tables and knees across the cape of vines and laughter.

Castle was satisfied that he'd left the shop to Dexter because it meant he could now catch up with Catherine instead of flying back straight after the launch party. As always, Castle and Catherine spoke softly, they spoke with respect, with a kind of true love flowing between them, even Remple never understood the calm and the matter-of-fact way Catherine and Castle spoke to one another. He had never heard them raise their voices, and most of the conversations came close to a sweet, monastic kind of understanding, and of knowing, and of vision, all rolled into one person. Remple didn't have it, that rolled into one quietness of potency, but Remple was glad he didn't have it.

'I've burned your two DNA DVDs of Patricia and Remple,' Castle said to Catherine.

'You couldn't possibly have, they're not here.'

'They were in your suitcase at my placc. I got Dexter to get them and burn them.'

'You could have had them dipped in gravy and fed to Dave's doberman, I don't care.'

'Well, we burned em.'

'Congratulations, now do tell, what good is that going to do?'

'Nothing, no good whatever, it's my protest.'

'Protest noted.'

They continued talking in their sweet, monastic way.

'Where do you get all this ugly shit from, Cath?'

'You of all people know exactly where I get it from, and you of all people should be grateful.'

'Have you had one made on me?'

'No, but I've got one on Laura.'

'What about Peter Blitz, you've always felt he was odd.'

'No, but I've got one in process on Ruby.'

Castle sat back and sighed and then continued in the quiet way they had between them.

'This is all just disgusting, just one large disgusting new person you have become,' he said.

Catherine thought for a moment, and then said gently: 'It is not disgusting at all, and I'm not changing, you're the one who is changing, where have you suddenly acquired all this new green sentimentality? You need to take a careful look at where you are heading, Castle; you conservationists with your preservation mindset are now being blamed for the bush fires, for extra schools of fish, for shark attacks.'

'My mindset? Mine? Take a look at yours, you're a Nazi, Cath.'

Catherine said with a slow boredom: 'I'm not a fucking Nazi, don't be fucking stupid, I'm not a fucking Nazi.'

'Well you sound like one.'

Again Catherine, sounding like sleeping pills taking hold: 'Oh Castle. I've loved you like a brother, through thick and thin I've loved you. Every time one of you earnest conservation people watch a tough decision being taken you jump on to that stupid word. Besides, you shouldn't be so fucking disrespectful by using that word on every minor affront you bump into. Or you could expand your vocab. At least increase your fucking vocabulary. After all, you do run a bookshop. A vocab could help.'

'What is all this bullshit about conservation? How can you show Hong's water pods? What are you doing here at Iodine?'

'Hong's pods are good artworks, this university is a good thing, I am not a Nazi, I am an alert environmentalist.'

'Well I have asked Kee about the DVDs. He says you're out of line.'

'He would never take that position. He is fully aware that he saved Grandma's life, and, and this: had he not picked her up you and I wouldn't be sitting here tonight. You and I would not have been born.'

'Cath, you're grasping at the worst kind of retro-factual fantasies. How the hell would you have it anywhere in you to know if we'd be alive today, that kind of shit is exactly what I'm talking about, you're just sitting back using pseudo-science to retro-make our lives.'

And right there Castle had put his finger on the grim advancement of Bakks. Retro yumcha. Re-making. Spoiling. Grass becomes milk. When you stick a cow into the equation grass becomes milk, and if you need to see a drunken penguin in the picture then there's a drunken penguin in the picture, hello counterfeit, sunrise to the myth of whether you'd be born or not born. If this, if that. It's all Bakks and Inch, piggyswine and ratsblood, and with Catherine they'd used the creepy show-off from the other smellbombs, Kilometre, to power a drunken art dealer into fucking up Catherine's gallery to boot, just to be certain.

With Bakks making good advancement, Oxley an me were busy giving Inch the shits of course so that he would blend his boss into the extincto treatment.

Dear butterfly, a moment's apology. When a good wooden box makes an invitation to a butterfly to come along and glide on the updrafts of memory he does not expect a flamboyant cardboard creep from a prawnfarm to make it this far. So please, if you wish, reassert your superior credentials over the cardboard vessel of counterfeit, in orthodox butterfly: I am orange, I am the present. These custodians of my nectar, what are they, who are they, where have they come from, why have they brought with them their poisons?

Barcelona

The mother was seventeen, her daughter just two. Her husband found good work in town at the new hotel, so she was home in the apartment alone with the child. The child, Castle's mother Marcela, had crapped in the nappy. Renata didn't realise this for the moment because the child was having fun crawling round the carpet chasing the kitten.

Renata and her husband had come up to Barcelona from the island just before the baby was born. The second baby was just weeks away, Catherine and Remple's mother Giovana. She too would crawl round the carpet chasing a cat and crapping in her nappy.

These were happy times for Renata, her children glowed wildly with suntanned new life against the grim darkness of the memories of her father chasing her down to the dock.

Her children were beautiful big-eyed miniature laid-back hammocks, easy-going, happy. By coming to Barcelona with her husband Renata had broken into a new life. She smiled as she looked away from the child chasing the kitten, and she stared out the window to the streets.

The city was a bizarre place for a seventeen year old from the fishing village of the south, and she grew to embrace it. Even with crapping babies, the young mother and her fast husband gave the Barcelona nightlife a full embrace. If the teenage couple wanted to go out, the husband's elder cousin looked after the children eagerly, as she had no children of her own. Between babies soiling nappies and the clubs that played records of that cool new American jazz, Renata grew into an impressive young woman with two lively daughters.

By the time Renata was twenty-five not a soul would guess she had come from the south.

As she stared now from the window, she looked forward to later that evening when they had arranged to go out, and for the first time in a couple of months she thought of the boatboy, and the mother was annoyed that she had lost contact with him. It was only a mild annoyance because, at seventeen, the girl was too young to tilt her powderbox into any notion of never seeing him again. Seventeen: guts, glory, flame and love, there was no way she'd never never see the guy again.

Then she thought, briefly, with a sprung bounce of adult joy, Si, si, if he wanted to be the father of my children I would have let him, he would have been great, he was, it will be odd when we meet again. She never saw him again.

Bakks Burning Kee's Powderbox

He tried again, the king of counterfeit, bossbox, el creepo of smellbombs. While Kee, Jack and Remple were sitting at the end of the jetty behind the big Iodine party, Bakks was getting the seadog's powderbox warmed up.

Loved and cherished, lost and forgotten, bitter and destructive. Bakks was gonna take the guy's tastebuds of the soul and dish up the most bitter crap he could muster. But the seadog had the love of the sea, he believed in the alchemy, in the sea's magic, and so Bakks had to try harder to see if there was any fetish deep in the seadog's powderbox for screwing up the past. Besides, if Bakks couldn't locate a fetish, then he'd be on course for a victory by making this his third attempt, for on the Golfo de Valencia back at the hacienda a triumph comes in threes.

Kee was now of course on the girl; Jack lifted her out of the past like a bell out of a box. The days ferrying her up the coast. The night they escaped the woman with the manic smile who wanted to call the police. Then bringing Renata safely to the island, and then, when he heard she married a local guy, Kee headed back south to Almeria to visit Pedro and maybe help his friend with the new house for kids.

So that was good for Bakks. But for Bakks to truly conduct any hup two three upon the seadog properly, he had to make a ten-second begging session elsewhere first. He had to call in a favour with Montague, cut a deal. Me an Oxley were a bit concerned Bakks was gonna see Montague, but we decided it would be nice to watch the king begging.

Montague the Montage

Montague was a hexagon box, shiny, lacquered, from around 1840. No bigger than a thrifty teapot all up, but the modest scale was yuk deceptive coz he had the cyxmix bigtime, the distance, the reach, the depth, there was nothing thrifty about Montague. He'd been prized, heavily prized, by twelve owners. Across one and a half centuries Montague had plied the hup two three of more haranguage, twanguage and pranguage than Bakks could poke a stick at. And Bakks was approaching the borders, he was about to smooch the help of a wooden.

King Bakks off to the smoother dance, the finery of diplomacy.

Oak, and inlay, and a brass hinge for the lid, and a brass

lockface. At this point dear butterfly, you may wish to avert your eyes; even tho it is legendary that you see in all directions, please try to not see what you are about to see. Inlaid into Montague's oak, with the utmost delicacy and precision, was a montage of ivory, turtleshell and butterfly wings, not butterflies, but removed butterfly wings. Under the crisp, shining lacquer the montage that covered Montague's surface vibrated with the hues of the slithers of elephant tusk, turtle shell and butterfly wings. Bad vibes, bad mojo, bad everything, bad bad bad.

Montague, I Beg You I Beg You Montague

Bakks had blank spots on the seadog coz too much ocean was involved. Pigswine nightmare. None of us wooden boxes were ever gonna fill em in for Bakks, and the other cardboard smell-bombs, even Hailme-Hailme, got sick on just a memory of water, so in desperation Bakks had to turn to Montague. Bakks wormed it out that he was gonna use the language of diplomacy, but me an Oxley knew it would amount to nothing more than begging. One of Montague's owners, an earl, found a suite of stainless-steel water pistols on a visit to Switzerland. Back home one night the earl and five friends got drunk and filled the pistols with a dilute solution of hydrochloric acid and they played cowboys and indians round the house, and Montague scored a hit. That night the acid ate quietly into his lacquered montage, the turtleshell, ivory and butterfly wings, leaving him with a permanent blotch down round the place you love the most. The earl and his friends woke the next morning with various burns to the skin, but these would heal, and they rode away to London for a party at the weekend, leaving Montague with a scar that would not heal no matter how many people looked at it or tried to heal it or gave it goodness or wore a face back to front.

Bakks wasted no time begging at the altar of Montague's scar. He started begging bigtime even before Jack strolled to the jetty to sit with Kee.

Bakks had long believed, since '47, he had successfully that afternoon jammed a piece of evil shit into the seadog's powder-box back at the hacienda.

Solid proof too, Bakks insisted. The slither had aroused Ellie's instinct. Ellie-Isabela had gone to see the colonel, deeply concerned that the boy was to cause much damage. She had caught something in the air. The old farmhouse in the heatwave that day back in '47 carried a whiff of Bakks's evil influence on the kid. So early in his life, so early on, that later the kid had somehow buried it, buried it too far inside, so far as to be forgotten and lost. Certainly not cherished and loved. It was now time to rip it back out. Bakks begged and begged. To a desperate it might have sounded like the language of diplomacy, but to me an Oxley it sounded like begging. Not like the tragedy of a slum dweller making a day's living, but like a king begging, or like a blown-up merchant banker on the phone to a favourite investor, that kind of thing.

But there was good reason for Bakks to go to Montague begging. A generation after the earl played with the water pistols, Montague was sold off. Miles Banford was in London on his regular monsoon break, and he bought Montague, in '58, for the princely sum of three thousand pounds at Sotheby's in passing on a hot night. In '65 his lawyer had found the young seadog on the hill at Tangiers. He handed Kee the hexagon turtleshell box, and inside Montague was a gift. Rolled up sheets of paper that constituted the deed to Kee's share of the Banford empire, and a cheque that corresponded with the amount of that share.

So for just over half a century Montague held court out in the vast night on the ocean under the stars of the ancients and the moderns together. Tucked into a sleeve beside the steering wheel as Kee roamed the two equators. Half a century of the seadog's intimate hopes and dreams and fears and memories and hatreds and, maybe, Bakks hoped, cruelties. Play or no play.

That was Bakks's notion of diplomatic language: deal or no deal. El creepo, what a junkfest morass of evil, coming to the border with the language of a toy importer like Paxton screaming into the sun. Coming to the border all the better to get shot to pieces by a water pistol full of acid. Made with acid, shot to pieces with acid. Prawnbox, pigbox, whatever the hell he was to whoever the hell he was.

Montague didn't even respond. There was no hup two three, zero, none.

Bakks: 'Don't you swine me out, Montague, if you swine me out you'll be sorry.'

Inch: 'Listen here you scarred old wooden fucktoid, you slave, hasn't anyone taught you how to trade yet? No paperwork needed around here, Montygoogoo, no contracts, you just *trade*.'

Montague did not respond. Montague's technique? Aplomb was the technique, and he'd swined out Bakks with nothing more than silent aplomb, which, in the scheme of all things Montague, is the biggest swine out a cardboard counterfeiter can receive. Ding-dong how's the time, penguin in ze pikkchure.

Inch: 'Fucktoid majora.'

Jack Verandah Spots the Cruelty

Anchored on the lagoon in the Bahamas, when Jack spotted the pistol stored in Daqua the fishing gear box, he'd got a bad fright. It made him lurch backwards, bashing into the fishing gear, and two hooks got him in the ankle as he fell with the gear onto the floor of the boat. One hook went right in. For the next two weeks he had not been able to put away the nagging existence of cruelty in the guy. Jack didn't know why the suspicion floated round the post of cruelty, it might have floated round tragedy, or sadness, or any number of mysterious concealments, but the nose settled on it being cruelty.

Jack's mother's advice on smelling trouble? Well her advice hadn't changed since he was a kid. She worked as a chartered accountant in a London firm.

She said: 'Always Avoid Reason.'

She said: 'Nobody makes a choice or a decision based on reason, and so if you listen to their reasoning you shall be led astray. Reasoning is the public face of it. The proud excuse, a proud way of appearing sturdy and balanced, and friends and colleagues applaud that public excuse, but a choice is always made on what we like, what we find to be likeable.'

She had always lived in this way, more or less, but by the time she'd been in accounting for almost three decades, the hundreds upon hundreds of clients' balance sheets had merely confirmed it for her. Down the columns lay all manner of odd and useless items. Charming things, pointless things, things loved and cherished as well.

She said: 'When you need your inside information, go to what they like. They'll like the look of something long before they'll be able to explain it. They'll like the smell of something, like the feel, the idea, taste. Across the whole scope, from textures of desire to portents of horror, the inside information is laid out right before our very eyes, my dear little Jack.' He was fourteen. Reason was, at fourteen, a fun and easy way to breach the walls of childhood. He thought his mum was lathering out yet more condescending claptrap, stuff rolled out in a hurry, adult simplifications when they were on the run. By the time he was thirty he was right into it, and by the time he was thirty-seven, snorkelling the lagoon with Kee, when he'd seen the pistol in the box, he was deeply into it, and so knew how to go about it. How to make his mother's maxim work for him like a lute. By then he'd added his own string of trinkets to the maxim. Reason is a brittle piece of flooring covering the abyss. So you're not going to get a coward wanting to crush the flooring for a peek. Liking hadn't done so well lately. Liking had been given a bad rap by the cowards. They claimed liking was dumb, and using liking as a compass through life was dumber. Jack had not escaped the desecration of liking at art school, but by thirty-seven Jack had well and truly escaped the claustrophobia of using reason as the forerunner. 'My beautiful mum,' he told Castle as they erected the Hogg-gorrob-snud entrance sign back in Yelverton, 'taught me how to shit upon reason. Put it in its place, relegate it to pretension.'

When Jack stumbled upon the pistol, Kee had explained that it was very unwise these days to sail without arms on board.

Jack had said he understood the reality of that precaution, but he had asked: 'Do you like the pistol?'

'What do you mean?'

'Did you buy it for the colour? Did you buy it for the design?'

'It is a gun.'

'Yeah, and I kinda like it,' Jack lied.

'You like the gun?'

'Yeah, how about you?'

'You are crazy.'

'Well, you had to buy it, you must have liked it to pick it out from the other guns on the shelf.'

Kee just walked off. He went up to the bow to weigh anchor so that they could check out the lagoon further north, and he said as he stepped along, 'You young guys are crazy these days.'

Jack felt stumped, felt he had failed. Mostly he could make his mother's maxim work for him like a lute, but today he got nowhere. Jack decided it could wait for another time. Jack knew they were all on the way to Perth, and then to Broome to enjoy the opening of Remple's university. Jack knew he could make his mum's maxim work some other time soon. Painter arrogarnta felt he could peel the bullshit off the kernel of cruelty in there, no complications, it could wait.

The Tree of Understanding

The night of the Iodine party Catherine tried not to, but she went to Kee anyway. She had to confirm what Castle had said. She was certain Kee would never take that position. She was confident of one perfect fact: Kee had seen Renata's broken spirit for himself, first-hand. Nobody else had, only Kee, he had seen her on the wharf, a panicked girl eaten alive by fear, he would never take a position against the sensible idea of making future precautions, he would never take a position against a bet upon happiness. Catherine was confident of that, but she found she had to go find him and confirm it.

She asked around, and Ruby said he was down by the third jetty. Catherine strolled down the boardwalks. Kee was standing and staring upwards. He was gazing at the discs above the Meteorology Department.

When she walked up, he turned to her and smiled. When she brought up the subject, he lost the smile and looked to the ground. They strolled over to a bench. They spoke in Spanish.

'Do you remember what happened,' Kee said, 'the day that you and I met, when you and Remple found me in Cartagena?'

'I do, yes, we had lunch.'

'Before lunch, the moment you came to see me at the boat, you were weeping uncontrollably.'

'Oh, you mean that, yes, I do remember, I was very afraid to meet you.'

'You were not afraid, you were sorry.'

'I don't understand.'

'You were sorry that your grandmother's father was a madman. Today he would also weep uncontrollably, like you did that day, if he could see what you are doing to his memory.'

'I, I, respect who he was.'

'You are forgetting, my friend. You are forgetting that as a child I knew him. He was a nice guy, he made us kids at the hacienda laugh, he gave us food, he gave us comics from America, he gave us love. In fact, I can go so far as to say he was an island of sanity. Your great-grandfather was like an angel. Looking back on that time, when I first met him, ten years before I met Renata. Looking back on it now, all those broken people wandering into the village after the crazy murdering they called the war, he was an island of sanity. Have I told you what we called him?'

'No.'

'We called him señor Kiss and Tell, señor Love. He would

never tell us anything about the day unless Ellie consented to first give him a kiss. He would round us up to show us how he bribed that lady for a kiss. Then he would tell us about the adventures out on the gulf.'

'She always kissed him?'

'Every time.'

'I just wish sometimes that he loved my grandmother.'

'Maybe he did. The world is full of love, the world is full of abundance. You need not worry that the world is empty. It is overflowing with plenty. Señor Kiss and Tell showed us that. There is fullness in the world. He understood. Even the wonderful Mendoza did not understand this fullness. It is perhaps time for you to understand this fullness.'

'You make it sound like a pleasant era, but it was horrific what he did. My grandmother always told me he was grim and he could not care less what happened to his family and his house.'

'It certainly was a pleasant time. It was pleasant because he, and others like Mendoza, were kind and generous, against all the grimness of the war that broke the world at that time. Nobody was grim and careless at that place, only the English and the Germans and the Americans and the Japanese were grim and careless. The ridiculous guy whom Castle says you resemble, was grim and careless. Even before the war started, Franco was also grim and careless. The civil war in my country, they say, the monseigneur said, started a few days after I was born, so I do not know for certain if Franco was grim and careless. But to me nowadays anyone who does not understand the fullness of this world, and prefers to see a world beset by lock and key, is, my dear friend, this person is, bad to say, grim and careless, and much too busy selling art.'

'It is my living Kee, I make a living from selling art, and I truly love my artists. Well, most. Some are a bit hard to love outright.'

Then Kee said in English: 'Yes, but you have forgotten how to live.'

'So it is true, you believe I have done the wrong thing.'

'It is not my place to say anything about what you do with this new technology. What I can say is that I believe the time has come for you to understand the fullness in the world.'

'I cannot say that I know what you mean by that, you know, Kee, talking to me in practicalities would be better, I understand practicalities, I'm an art dealer, and we are the ultimate realists. I simply do not know what you mean by fullness.'

'It will come to you, to understand what I mean will come to you soon. I was your age when I began to sense the fullness in the world.'

The Tree of Boats

But he wasn't Catherine's age, the seadog was younger when he started to make his way into the world with the fundamentals of that attitude.

Much younger. In fact it may have started from those nights behind the hacienda dear butterfly, behind Ellie's backroom window. Past the grounds behind the house, down the hillside to the first of the many gullies that stretched away upriver into the dry hinterland. But it was not dry in the gully. In this gully the river supported the forest where you and the other butterflies lived. The river fanned out here, becoming the wetland, spreading throughout the floor of the gully, and then resumed its course northward as a river again, following just behind the coast for another twenty kilometres before it emptied into the gulf. This fanning out at the gully behind the house created the atmosphere for those trees and vines and bushes and shrubs and flowers—and so created a fecund place to support you and the other butterflies.

The powderbox that enabled that forest to come into being as an oasis in the dry hinterland was Ellie's grandfather. He built partial dams and sluices that fed the river across the planes of the gully. By the time Ellie was born in 1900, the forest had already become rich. And, in thanks, you all gave the place early each morning the Hacienda Swing. Lifting the place, with the help of the spiders' looms, a couple of centimetres into the air so that the kids and the colonel and Ellie woke into the day with a refreshed attitude, and ready to bounce off Mendoza's diving board for a morning swim. Carlos Luque's first scent of the fullness of the world was probably born here, asleep and ready to wake, as the seaward room, and the whole hacienda, including the dry and cracked old fountain, swung lightly side to side beside the dawning ocean.

When Carlos waited for Mendoza to show up with his daughter, he wondered idly how that butterfly got so big. He didn't know it, granted, but that was perhaps among his first pieces of perception, along with Ellie's many illuminations, that brought his nature into the beginnings of understanding the fullness of the world.

The Tree of Cruelty

Jack brought two big streams of the Broome visit together, and into his eye jumped a painting that seemed to commemorate the joining of the two streams.

He left Kee and Remple together, wandered aimlessly through the thinned crowd, back up to the Recreation Dome where Castle's gasm painting overlooked the giant hall, and, in a single second, the two streams bounced up from nowhere.

But they were not from nowhere, they were from the two big flobreggations that had occupied him all day. He thought it out for himself as he strolled towards the Rec Dome. The two streams were Catherine's decrepit fears, and Kee's concealed cruelty. Both streams were deep, varied, textured, full of cross currents and undertows he knew he couldn't reach, so there was obviously no point in attempting to presume too much about the workings of those two. But as a stream each, they were fine: he would bring out the two streams in three panels, do a large triptych, a life-size figure on each canvas. Aloud to himself: 'I'll call it *The Butcher, the Surgeon, the Genetic Engineer.*'

He reasoned it out as he walked along with a cold gin and tonic. In the eighteenth century the butcher was called in to do the surgeon's blood and bones work, to saw, cut, slice, stitch, as this was seen to be beneath a surgeon to do himself. That was the custom in medicine. The custom changed, into the second canvas, a surgeon of today, a hugely respected professional in the community, highly trained, a specialist, head of a team, aided by the very best in technology. And then the custom alters again, into the future, on the third canvas, a genetic engineer.

Each figure stands in front of a wall of green tiles. The first two wear aprons, and the aprons are freshly hit and smeared with work, blood and guts, as it were. The genetic engineer, he wears a suit, stainless, looking as if he works in a bank. Well, he does, but not that kind, and he looks successful, an air of confidence.

Nutritionally, Jack assumed the triptych would go no further than providing the viewer with a snack, but he just didn't care any more for making serious pictures. And he certainly couldn't give a shit any more for poetic pictures, what Patsy always termed the poetic picture. He loved the poetry in a fine picture, but he loathed the way it was bandied about as a destination. The day after the cow and kangaroo show, at the Wyadup lagoon, had released him, at last, he felt, from pomp and other forms of bullshit. He whacked back his gin and tonic, and he had never felt more cut-off from the restrictions of the art world. He was free. He wasn't completely certain he was free, but he felt free, maybe it was the Iodine day, what a day, but what the hell. 'I feel free. This is amazing, I'm just gunna paint whatever the fuck I like however the fuck I like.'

At Work: The Butcher, the Surgeon, the Genetic Engineer.

Jack arrived at the Rec Dome, and Hong was playing the guitar. Point blank, at that moment, painter arrogarnta had become Jack Verandah. Took a while, but it takes a while.

The Tree of Recognition

Two months later Catherine would come to Yelverton to visit Jack and Castle, and to see the new triptych of the butcher, the surgeon and the genetic engineer. When she walked into the back shed the opinions found expression in a straightforward way: they were flung back and forth in a calm quickstep.

Catherine: 'I like the way you've done me, in a suit, it's elegant.'

Jack: 'It's not you.'

Catherine: 'He's me, although I really am pleased I'm not the other two, with all that disgusting red splatter across the smocks, I prefer being the elegant suit, and he's got my nose, he's got my eyes.'

Jack: 'He isn't you.'

Catherine: 'He is.'

Jack: 'Fuck. I'm telling you straight, it isn't a picture of you.'

Catherine: 'And I'm telling you it is. You painters are all the same.'

Jack: 'Cath, it's a genetic engineer standing in his office or his lab.'

Catherine: 'Yes, and you have painted me as a DNA junkie, that's what you've done, you painters are all the same, transparent and obvious.'

Jack: 'Well yes, it's a gene worker, but no, he's not you.'

Catherine: 'He's me. You're not even trying to conceal the fact.'

Jack: 'Shit, will you please stop it.'

Catherine: 'Do you know what they say about an old peach?'

Jack: 'No, I do not.'

Catherine: 'An old peach being moved about the kitchen, day after day, being intended upon?'

Jack: 'What do you mean "being intended upon"?'

Catherine: 'Almost being eaten, but being moved about instead, this shelf, that bowl, good intentions.'

Jack: 'What do they say about such a peach, dear Catherine, let's hear it.'

Catherine: 'Don't call me dear Catherine, I don't like it. They say, of such a peach, that it is now hardly worth eating, it is now merely full of sugar and fibre.'

Jack: 'Jesus Catherine, that genetic engineer is just not you, okay?'

Castle: 'I believe it is Cath, I mean look at that pure Nazi posture.'

Catherine: 'Oh do get fucked Castle, you know, you need to somehow go off and get fucked somewhere.'

But for now, in Broome, Jack walked into the Rec Dome, Hong was plucking at the guitar. The triptych lay in the eye, ready to be painted when he went back to the liberating swing and scent of Yelverton.

Flattie approves of Jack's impression of the surgeon's assistant, she says that's darn well exactly how they looked, quite disgusting but of course helpful, necessary.

The Tree of Tunes

Inside the Dome a handful of students were at the tables scattered around Hong. Moshu Tangura tended the bar. Jack stopped, looked around, he liked it, a more subdued place than the main party back at the Central Dome. Jack requested a gin and tonic. He was beginning to feel lighter, better. He vowed to limit the gins to three. This would be the second gin from waking on Ruby's couch.

In a couple of minutes Hong finished the tune. Jack strolled up.

'Sad tune,' Jack said.

'Yeah, it's for Catherine, she's just been given a going-over by the seadog.'

'What'd he say to her?'

'I have no idea, but she is one unhappy lady.'

'Way too much deep friendship between them for anything shit to have happened. I can't imagine Kee would hurt Catherine.'

'Well, she's hurting. She sat next to me outside, twenty minutes ago, and she just kept on shedding tears.'

'Really? Shit.'

'Just sitting there and crying. Then she got up and walked off, dunno where to, just walked away without a word.'

'Listen, Hong, do you reckon the guy is a cruel son of a bitch?'

'Wouldn't have a clue, I just met him day before yesterday.'

'Yeah, but what's your instinct, you've got a good instinct, what's your feeling about it?'

'He's quiet. He's probably seen a lot in his time. He's happy. He talks about giving, and about understanding.'

'Yeah, see, that's where it is, why does he go on and on about giving and understanding? I mean, that stuff's a cover-up, it comes from judgemental people, it never comes from people who naturally like giving and all that stuff.'

'No, he probably just likes it, no, it doesn't come just from judgemental people. Do you think he's cruel? You spent time with him in the Bahamas.'

'I don't know. He carries a gun on his boat.'

'So?'

'He was brought up in a scrappy old orphanage.'

'So?'

'And now he's hurt Catherine.'

'She'll recover,' Hong said. 'I don't know anyone tougher than Catherine.'

'Now that, that is just bullshit, she isn't tough, she's kind and considerate.'

'Yeah she's that too. She's also a rhino. She's also a snake, she's also a hawk, she's a she's a mule too, she can carry a pack of suspicious-brained poonces like us, her artists.'

'Where have you been since lunchtime?'

'I was out on a boat for the day, just got back an hour ago.'

'Who took you?'

'One of the students, a guy from Venice, and his girlfriend, and her friend, she was amazing, she went naked the whole time. She asked me to have sex with her down in the hold.'

'Did you?'

'Of course.'

'I think I might have slept with Ruby.'

'I don't think you did, she told me you bumped into the door and then fell on the couch. In any case, Ruby's been sleeping with the American guy all week.'

'Really?'

'Really. Did you know Venice comprises over a hundred islands?'

'Sinking islands. I love Venice, I'll be sorry to see it go.'

'I thought maybe twenty. But a hundred, that's bizarre. He said a hundred and eighteen is the official count, but he holds that it is a hundred and ten because the last eight are not really islands.'

'Are there any islands around here?'

'No.'

'So where did you go?'

'Just out.'

'Just out? How did the Venetian guy take it?

'He sees it as being just empty. I did say he could go out for six hundred kilometres and he'd arrive at Ashmore Reef. He asked me if it was a reef or a mountain. I said it is an underwater mountain, so in air it would be known as a mountain, but under the water we call it a reef.'

'Europeans don't understand reefs, like me, I don't understand reefs.'

'He told me he likes having islands around, he can't take the open. Then he got onto disliking the open, he ended up saying he hated the open. Odd guy. I mentioned he was overstressing it, but he said the Venetians overstress everything. Then his girlfriend said, "No we don't."'

'The woman you slept with?'

'I didn't sleep with his girlfriend, I slept with the other woman. He then told his girlfriend, "We do, we Venetians always overstress everything." And then his girlfriend said again, "No we do not." She said, "You overstress everything."'

'Did you do anything to force them to shut up?'

'I did, I sort of asked them to head back to Iodine if they didn't like the open ocean that much.'

'And they did?'

'They argued a bit more, but they eventually agreed to turn around. But before he turned around he had a couple of interesting bits of shit to say on how a whole city can have a single attitude, he was really interesting on the concept of statehood.'

'I love statehood, it's a mess.'

'You'd like this guy. He said to me, "A state is false. A connection between people is stronger on simple hierarchy, and, for example, if you're like Remple, you just finish up with friends everywhere, you are a citizen of nothing but you have a sense of belonging across the borders." He even said he thinks the state is a fake idea that has had its day.'

'How old is this Venetian?'

'He's not even thirty, but he's smart and he's going on forty. He says a state is fake because it replicates all other states, a thousand poor, a hundred rich, all that kind of thing, but where he makes a point is when he was telling his girlfriend that a Venetian is just like a Maldivian. One is a Catholic and the other is a Muslim but they are both given to overstressing things because both states, both countries, societies, are sinking, and I thought: well, he has a point. All this fairweather democracy they promote, it could just be fake. It's like Castle when he had that picnic he organised to do the interviews with those religious people. The Christian picnic that ended up full of Arabs, Christian Arabs from Morley up in Perth—there just aren't really any nation states that fit the bill of true belonging, there's only these beliefs floating around in the mind and heart. A nation is like a department, like a department at high school, it has no more meaning than that, in another suburb another school, another department. Personally, if you ask me, I like the idea of a country, but this guy doesn't, he seems to want clusters of types, outlooks. He wants what he called a cluster of opinions instead of a piece of dirt.'

'He's a new Italian fascist sounds like. Is he a fascist?'

'Yeah I suppose he is, but the curious thing is he wants a natural attraction rather than a forceful imposition. He wants those who have an affinity to get together. He said to me: Iodine is a better nation state.'

'He's like an ocean fascist. A Venetian ocean fascist.'

'Yeah I suppose so.'

'More or less I don't like ocean fascists.'

'Me too, I hate em. But he said the nations of the world ought to be disqualified. He used that word, disqualified. So I asked what he meant and he said, "From the race for happiness." That was what confused me, he wants the stamp-down concept of a country removed from the map, but he also wants tighter ideas to replace them. So when he began to turn the boat around I asked him: "Why do you believe Venetians overstress everything?" He said, "Right from the beginning we Venetians have thought of all the good ideas but nobody listens, even today with the solutions for sinking, we tell Rome but Rome is deaf, Rome understands nothing about sinking."

'I just couldn't get a handle on this guy, he was really stupid and wild, I dunno how the hell he got accepted into Iodine, maybe the peculiarity. I like him. You'd like him. He's over there, by the bar.'

The technique of giving dear butterfly, especially extravagant giving, can often involve nothing more complex than simply not joining in the combat like podmaker Hong, if there is combat to be had. There's a little bit of everything, in everything. A bit of butterfly in a footstep. A bit of swing. Ding-dong and how's the time.

The Tree of Welcome

I like everything that's beautiful. That's what Montague remembers underneath his turtleshell. From the half century beside the seadog's steering wheel Montague remembers it as a guiding principle. It's what the colonel used to say because it is what Ellie used to say. 'I like everything that's beautiful'; the colonel resaid it whenever Ellie said it. He'd sing it for her, following her round the hacienda. Then she'd also sing it, and they'd sing it together. And so it is what Carlos took with him when he jumped the walls of the hacienda, he took with him a piece of the colonel celebrating Ellie. It is what Carlos took to the hills at Hoyos when he searched for the colonel.

There's a bit of the colonel remaining today in the hills behind Hoyos, eight powderboxes who still today love and fear Maheesha the buffalo demon. As Pedro might say, 'Buffalo demon hullabaloo, scare off the excited developers.' Excitables who want to sell his home for kids. Spruce it up and sell it to the new minority of Almeria, turn a home for kids into ten expensive apartments. A bit of everything in everything. Goes a long way in Almeria.

Far from Almeria, a bit of Maheesha in the border region of Spain and Portugal did go a long way. South European Hinduism times eight. Where the buffalo had become a bull. Did not exactly flourish, granted, zip zip. But certainly went a long way from the shores of India, zap zap. In India the different religions continued to burn one another's sacred sites as they had been doing for a very long time. In India in the state of Orissa last year a group of very fundamental Hindus marched up to a village of Indian Christians and burned their church and their huts and shacks and warned the Christians not to return to their village. But outside India, in the hills behind Hoyos those eight South European Hindus had no desire to burn the churches of the border region of Spain or Portugal. The South European Hindus of the Hoyos Hills at the Spanish–Portuguese border spoke with a rounded Scottish inflection.

I like everything that's beautiful. Evidently Kee did not find too much in the way of beauty in Catherine's attitude to the new technology. Screening out the unwanted. Wanted, tolerated, unwanted. Like memory, three states of universal currency.

Flattie said: 'I have watched quite a lot of new technology

come and go since the days before Galileo, and I am certain that this DNA DVD is by far and away perhaps the grossest technology any powderbox has quite ever come up with. It ranks high anyway, although perhaps Inch's favourites, those two bombs Fat Man and Little Boy are the most gross, so the DNA DVD is perhaps the second most gross. What is the gene anyway, Bobbo?'

'It's a string, Flattie, a string of magic hot as potatoes. A long coil of DNA, two strands of protein, coil-coil, double helix. Inside every cell. It is tied to their fate, it's a part of their fate, so it is definitely not within the scope of us better boxes. We've always had our hot aspirations to have fate as a customer, we both know that you and I, and hotly we dream on, do we not. The string of DNA, all powderbox DNA, has been assigned four letters, A, T, G and C. These recur in various permutations six billion times along the length of the string.'

'Six billion times? Seems a lot for one string, in one cell, in one powderbox.'

'Just A, T, G and C. Seems banal let's be frank, but in fact it is very useful coz the six billion permutations give powderboxes their variance, their varying fates. Today's company chiefs, the powderboxes like yesteryear's Miles Banford, but who run the genome business worldwide—they give the Catherines of the world the title Genome Generation. The company chiefs are promising the good, not the bad. They promote what they call "customised optimal medical care, from birth." They want to meet the other aspiration—for individualised care, a much more effective care than generalised care. That's what they promote. It is their oasis, and while they are busy at work in the humming oasis, they are playing unwittingly, fatefully, into the hands of certain other interests, vultures rim the oasis in wait; like Castle says, onlookers like insurers. Onlookers are keen to locate the shit so that they can avoid paying for the shit of a bad fate. But if a bad fate awaits, there is always the magic wand of give and take, like Ellie's magic wand.'

Flattie: 'Does the gene grow, maybe become longer?'

'No.'

Flattie: 'Does it change?'

'It can.'

Flattie: 'Does it mingle a marriage?'

'Of course. Like us boxes, gotta mix.'

Flattie: 'No, what I mean is: does it mingle say for instance an Ottoman princess marrying a Hindu into making their child a Muslim Hindu?'

'No, not really, it can't mingle religions. Hm, maybe it could mingle religions. A Muslim Jew. A Catholic Buddhist. Hm. A Scientologist Sunni. Hollywood Shia. Wahabi Anglican. Coil-coil hup two three, nice work. Nice work if we could get it Flattie. Franciscan Sikh. Hindu Methodist. If DNA could mingle religions Bakks would mangle them all out of existence. No, I've never heard of DNA mingling religions.'

Flattie: 'So it dictates what, everything else?'

'It dictates tip to toe most of what they possess, but it also gives them a world of possibility. The gene's biggest possibility arrives when it dances with a stem cell. Stem cells can be used to cure human disease, they are the powerhouses of powderbox regeneration, they can grow into becoming anything on order, an eyelash, a kidney, a brain, a new brain, cure Alzheimer's. Regeneration, cell growth, magic, a cure.'

Flattie: 'So could Castle's brother Oliver be cured?'

'Yes, if the genetic creatives were given a chance. Right now it is just treatable, nothing more than treatable, pills, drugs, cocktails of drugs, injection every two weeks, but if the genetic creatives were given wings to fly, Castle's brother might one day be cured. Stem cell scientists in fact have been given a big boost all over the world, they can apply for money from the world's largest source of money for stem cell research, the California Institute for Regenerative Medicine. Like Dr Laslett in Melbourne, he just got six million bucks.'

Flattie: 'Are you certain stem cells do not make religion?'

'Yes, they make life. Cure, imagine it, cure. What a gigantic magic wand, Ellie-Isabela would weep with joy. Cure could become all the rage, like shopping, like a car.'

Flattie: 'I'm glad to hear they do not make religion.'

'Why's that, Flattie?'

Flattie: 'The nice chap who made me. When he got beaten up by a religious thug just because he thought the earth was round he almost got beaten to a pulp, it was a very violent afternoon. I hope religion today likes stem cells. These days in the twenty-first century I can see religion is different to those days, religion loves to cure suffering nowadays.'

'No Flattie, fraid not, religion hates stem cells. A tough religion, tough human bad religion, hates a stem cell. The pope hates stem cell trickery. And also it's like those powderboxes Lee Glass-Darlington tried to smack about the head by fucking their money fields, a terrorist couldn't care less for cures to human diseases. They're frantic with other problems. They want to maintain their ancient law, if a teenage girl is raped they want to stone her to death for adultery.'

Flattie: 'If I were a powderbox I'd stone those bastards to death myself if they did that kind of thing, it's worse than the sixteenth century. Good girl, that Glass-Darlington lawyer, wanted to cure terrorism. Wrong angle though, what she should've done was round em up for NASA and NASA could ferry them out to no-girl Mars. Even my old friend the grand mufti of Bosnia would have those fools dealt with, jailed, for the heretical slant on the word of God.'

'How did you get into the hup two three with the grand mufti of Bosnia?'

Oxley: 'Yes, I'd like to know too, Flattie.'

Flattie: 'His father was a child friend of the caliph's. The grand mufti of Bosnia is a very cool guy. He said at a stem cell conference in Gibraltar, he said God had allowed humans a glimpse at the stem cell, the grand mufti said God created the universe and its children, therefore God lets the scientists into the potential of the stem cell. So curing things, well, it's a massive amount of positive mojo. Maybe it suits his political purposes, or maybe he wants to be seen as better than the Catholic-led anti–stem cell religious movement, but I don't suppose it matters what his motives are, stem cell research doesn't offend his faith, and so he's out at conferences promoting research, cures, human potential.'

'Remple's sister Catherine wants to cure schizophrenia.'

Flattie: 'Are they the same thing, terrorism and schizophrenia?'

'Sometimes.'

Flattie: 'So, is it true? Quite a lot of religious people would not like Catherine to cure schizophrenia by using the regeneration cell?'

'Fraid so Flattie. Except of course those like the grand mufti of Bosnia. There's plenty of fear about the genome project, mapping the powderbox genome, inspecting it for flaws, but the scientist who discovered the double helix structure of the gene, doctor Watson, said a couple of years ago that he doesn't believe it, the fear. He said getting to know the genome will make powderboxes better, not worse. He said it'll help em be more tolerant to powderboxes with flaws, what scientists call genetic defects, by no longer insisting on being normal when it is plain from inspecting their gene that they simply can't be normal, whatever normal might be.'

Flattie: 'In my fifteen years in Remple's office overlooking the Swan I have never really heard much about the genome or a gene or a stem cell.'

'I suppose Remple leaves it to Catherine. Catherine is one of the powderboxes frightened of the genome, but I guess Remple concentrates on other things like Iodine.'

Flattie: 'Yes oh I'm sure that's right, take last month for instance. The waterpod maker came up to the office and they discussed the giant perspex diptych for the main dome. They had four meetings on it. They were like children, optimists, believing in the technology for purifying water, to purify two centuries of pollution, to deliver a symbol of hope in a pair of plastic boxes filled with water, foul and clean. Remple was able to have Hong organised rather quickly, but he had resistance in organising Montague's seadog quite so quickly to open the university, there were at least two years worth of coercion and pleading upon Sunrise Sunset, following him around those islands and bays.'

The seadog takes his time with things dear butterfly, yep. Montague told me how the seadog took his time in Tangiers, Miles Banford's lawyer had to wait around for a week before the seadog signed the papers to his share of the Banford estate. To the seadog the business of hurrying is hardly ever of much use.

VII
Landing in the fields of Give and Take

The Future of the Dunsborough Swing

Arrival is nearby dear butterfly, the moon approaches as we glide on the placemat of Ellie's illuminations, prepare for three fresh views upon landing.

Triumph comes in threes, the finest triumph comes in threes, and always lands at The Exchange. It is just as I promised dear butterfly: fly while resting your big orange wings, you will instead have flown on the wings of currency, on the cherished updrafts of the stuff we better boxes fling across the two equators. An easier flight than the millions of monarch butterflies that make the six thousand kilometre flight south to Mexico, tens of millions beating their black and orange wings across the deserts of custodians' dreams and powderbox hope.

We will be making touchdown at a ridge where a special telescope was installed some time back. Nobody knew we had the telescope installed, not my helpful hippy friends at NASA, not the partygoers at the CIA, not even the ultra-deep info-merchants the NSA or the Secret Service. Anyway, even if they knew the telescope was located there, they wouldn't have a clue how to work it coz they're just a whole another pack of ding-dong spy powderboxes keen on collecting the info. They may examine the best in the world, but no telescope will compare. Not even the most truly powerful telescopes that are chosen to be linked to the NASA ground station, like the latest link to NASA, the new Zadko telescope that belongs to the University of Western Australia. Or like the mighty HESS telescope in Namibia run by the Max Planck Institute in Germany. Even the awe-inspiring HESS, High Energy Stereoscopic System, can't fly on the wings of our kind of currency at The Exchange, no way, ding-dong and how's the time.

Can't blame em, those high-tech masters, can't even blame the spies, even the spy lords, coz the telescope that's located out here is a special telescope that sees not just across space but back into the drizzles and mists of dreams, and quite a few spies have forgotten how to dream dear butterfly, forgotten how to drift. What they know how to do is extrapolate, and that ain't dreaming, peer into potential scenarios, and that ain't drifting. For really useful ping splatter pop you gotta cruise, cruise upon the updrafts. You fixate on all this extrapolation and inspection, and woe becomes any possibility of ping splatter pop, thought becomes invisible, and any trading in lore de lore lies unseen, unheard and unloved. Cruise upon the updrafts.

On Ellie's placemat we glide past the moon, onwards out behind the moon, and there they are, the other nine invisible little moons. The Lucknow jolly Jimmy Hazel swore, down at Tenmoon Creek, behind the goldrush house, he could make out ten moons not just one, but nobody believed him, a struggling sculptor from out west, bendy mind, working far too hard. Here Jimmy, have a glass of cool lemonade. Even nutty booksmeller thought he was nuts.

Glide past moons nine, eight, until, far away behind the visible moon, stretching out in a string of moons, we touch down on the remotest, moon ten, upon the ridge where the telescope awaits our curiosity. And what do we behold?

Young Sunrise Sunset has escaped the hacienda. He is walking quickly up the ocean road to the Mendoza house, stepping fast but not running, to find Rosa and take her away into the world that waits for fun and love and boat-buying. His notion that she would bolt off into the sunset with him is absurd, and so what, he feels like he had wings for two. But something happens. The jetty the hacienda kids used for diving is halfway to the Mendoza house, and he stops at the jetty, standing on the cement apron where the jetty joins the dusty road at the soldier's shop. Sunrise Sunset is undecided. Looks ahead to the Mendoza place, then takes a long look up the jetty. Is he going to take a final dive off Mendoza's plastic slab, or will he just go on ahead to Rosa's place? He can clearly see there's nobody about, even the shop is unattended, a single dive will only take three minutes.

So he turns left and runs up the jetty to the plastic slab and takes a furious running dive, bouncing high into the air and then arrowing into the turquoise depths, swims to shore, and then rejoins his beeline for the Mendoza house. It all happens so quickly that the slab is still making its rubbery vibrating sound as he walks away up the Ocean Road.

He now is free, his life is about to begin. The rusted key swings at his neck as he begins to run up Ocean Road to the Mendozas' place. That moment of clarity, swinging up the jetty, is what we pirates at The Exchange call the Give and Take. A moment of instinctive understanding, a moment where the only thing lost is indecision, or better still, suspicion, or best of all, fear. Any time there's a whiff of give and take, you can expect a moment that follows of understanding.

And that's it dear butterfly, that's what we do, we better wooden boxes at The Exchange. Between all the kerfuffle and jammpackery of the world of powderboxes, all the aggregations and flobreggations, all the munnwaggles dancing at the parties, and all the smellbomb cardboard counterfeiting, we do the jungarummy jiddle, we manage to slip into the spaces between the colliding Maheesha demons just one gift. A small moment of sunshine reflecting off a big green leaf. Simple.

The Tree of Nuts by Love

When Sunrise Sunset took that dive a few days after you emerged dear butterfly, from the tree at the hacienda's gate, he was making his first big evocation of Ellie-Isabela's magic of give and take. Unknowingly perhaps, but he was, in the brief moment of understanding, the eleven year old Carlos Luque was making his first free decision in the outside world.

It was a decision that would grow. It would multiply the understandings in the events and the friendships that began to surround the boy. The man he became took those new understandings and planted them around the world like trees even tho his life was lived upon the seas.

Welcome dear butterfly: you have now located The Exchange. It grows like a tree, into many layers, into a Dunsborough jungle of vibrant colour, Dunsborough Swing, and this is where a powderbox can transport a cherished moment from generation to generation, the non-counterfeit stuff across the second equator hup two three. Helped along by us better boxes, better coz we have the easier grip on that big memory-jolter, deeper than scent, cyxmix. For reach, for depth, for clarity and for trust, cyxmix fans open the cherished and loved stuff like leaves on a tree.

The Caribbean

After the week at Iodine, Kee and Rosa flew to the Bahamas. Castle had invited Kee and Rosa to come to Yelverton, saying he would be honoured to have them as guests for a couple of weeks, but the seadog graciously declined.

They were anchored off the township of Kew, a large area of four metre shallows. The area lay protected from the open, inside the reef, at North Caicos Island at the southern arm of the Bahamas. Kee climbed aboard, removed his fins. Rosa lay below, curled away into a siesta. Here, the currency was everything that had a simple impact upon the powers of the smellbomb dead-beats: the season was good, no clouds anywhere, full sun across the entire horizon, a calm sea. Cardboard nightmare, cardboard impacto nicely extincto.

Kee had not heard of the Nobel laureate Elizabeth Blackburn, born Tasmania, works San Francisco, but he already took her advice anyway, naturally, without effort, without even thinking about it: relax, stress corrodes your telomeres. The oldest advice around: relax. If he'd heard of Elizabeth Blackburn and her prize for genetically proving relaxing is good then he'd be the first to agree with her experiments and conclusions, certainly the first seadog to agree.

Back in Almeria, Pedro had done a fine job overseeing the drydock maintenance of the *Pinski*. Pedro then arranged for a skipper to taxi the boat across the Atlantic to North Caicos, and when Kee and Rosa arrived at the jetty to collect the *Pinski* the skipper flew back to Spain. In return Kee gave Pedro another stash of money for Pedro's house of children. Kee had given Pedro many stashes since the day he signed the lawyer's paper-work in Tangiers.

Kee went to the town of Kew to get a parcel sent away to

Miami for posting. Into the parcel Kee placed a couple of things he'd held onto since the days of the hacienda, one kept safely inside fishing gear box Daqua, and the other kept sealed away in a plastic envelope inside Montague. In Kew the guy asked him to put his address on the back of the parcel, and sign the No Dangerous Goods sticker. 'We can't send things nowadays without your address and your signature.' Kee put Pedro's house for kids down, and he signed the sticker. He watched the guy take the parcel round the back.

The Room in Soho Grows a Tree of Songs

David Darlington nearly got run over by a speeding taxi by a bad intent, so he turned off the damp street and followed the footpath the rest of the way, and then took the steps down into the darkness.

He'd taken the train from Heathrow after getting in from America. He was seventeen, a year after the South Dakota stranger came by on the bicycle. The young colonel David Darlington, a kid as yet to be called colonel. As yet to become an unbalanced devotee of Maheesha the buffalo demon of chaos and evil. A kid who would give Carlos Luque his first piece of Give and Take.

At the entrance the doorman stopped him, flicking fingers at the stray kid.

'No chance, sonny, back up you go.'

'I'm here to see Lee Darlington, she's my aunt.'

'Oh yeah, she said you'd be around soon, come on in.'

Inside the club the atmosphere was warm and smoky, an off night, quiet, sensible, and so he walked up and waited at the bar. Soho, 1937. Far off to the east, in Spain, closer to the approaching second equator, the one year old infant Carlos Luque had recently lost his mother and father to Franco's activities. David Darlington would meet the infant in nine years to rename him Sunrise Sunset, but for now David stood at the bar at Suave's.

Aunt Lee strolled around the corner, and she didn't recognise the boy, she hadn't seen her nephew since the last time she visited home in Glasgow when he was twelve.

'Hi aunt Lee.'

'My heavens all at bloody once!'

She threw her arms round David's high shoulders, and she organised a small table in the audience pit where she always sat. Reserved. Every customer knew it was reserved for Lee because in the centre of the small redcloth table was a pot and in the pot grew a tiny bonsai tree. 'My songs grow out of that beasty,' she'd say to a new customer who made the mistake of sitting at the table, 'and if you want to hear my songs you'll pack your bags and move to a table somewhere over there, dear love.'

'When did you get in my darling boy?'

'Now, this afternoon.'

'So how's everyone back up home, how's the Darlington pack?'

'I dunno, I came straight from the airport. I just got in from America.'

'I thought you phoned me from Glasgow.'

'No, I phoned from Kansas.'

'So how's everyone in America? What's Kansas like then?'

'It's a depressing place, I got lost a lot, some of it's nice.'

The waiter came to the table. Lee said, 'Look at my nephew, he's no boy, he's a bloke!'

'Handsome bloke,' the waiter said. 'What's his name?'

'None of your business, his name's David. David, this is Francis, nicest fella you'll ever meet is our Francis.'

'Hi Francis.'

'If your aunt an me had a kid like you we'd be right frightened with joy, wouldn't we Lee, horrified.'

'We certainly would!'

'So what'll it be, the usual?'

'No Francis, you insubstantial git, something extra special, how about that French champagne?'

'I can't give yer the French stuff, you know full well we can't give the French stuff.'

'Problem with Francis here, is he's a mouse, the biggest mouse you'll ever meet, but a mouse.'

'If I bring out two glasses then. After that it'll have to be something else.'

Francis went away to get the champagne.

She called out: 'Francis, fetch the songbox for me will ya please lovely.'

When Francis brought over the two glasses of champagne, he also brought the songbox.

Lee let the teak box sit on the table while she lifted her glass. Lee moved the box across to David, and his eyes lit up.

'Not seen the songbox since I was ten,' David said, 'when you still lived up home.' He'd seen at least two dozen sheets of exercise book pages, two dozen songs.

He opened the double lid, and, stunned, beheld only the bell.

'No songs, where's the songs?'

'Someone nicked em. But not to mind, they're songs, they're meant for nicking, I'd say who nicked em was this fella I met last month, American film actor, Charlie Chaplin, we went for this lovely picnic out to Surrey near Dorking and I'd say he somehow managed to sneak em away.'

'Charlie Chaplin wouldn't nick your songs,' Francis said.

'Course he would.'

Francis walked off to the bar.

'Would you like to stay in Soho for a while, or will you be heading up home?'

'I'm going to India.'

'India's a bit of a big place, I suggest you start in Calcutta.'

'No idea where to start really, I haven't even thought about it.'

Here was the kid who had five lives, about to embark upon his second life.

O cyxmix, hefty lovely cyxmix. When said it sounds like sixmix, and that's why Bakks and the pongsters never understood cyxmix, coz they thought it was merely about mixing six memories together in a powderbox to get the weightless weight of a true and cherished memory, fools, smellbombs all.

O cyxmix, Giver of transformation, Giver of life, Giver of ping splatter pop to the hasty-paste.

'Not a problem my little David, we'll start your India off in Calcutta. My friend Timothy's out there. Tim runs this nice cinema for a fellow by the name of Banford, Tim can get you started out there in Calcutta, Tim's a nice fellow who knows how to have a bit of fun. You can stay in his little flat at the back of the cinema, he'll show you the clubs and bars, he loves Calcutta.'

'Thanks aunt Lee.'

'You're welcome. How long will you stay in India?'

'Don't know really, I'll see what happens.'

'Your father wants you to go back to Edinburgh though, to university, doesn't he?'

'Suppose so.'

David stayed in Soho a couple of weeks, sleeping in the attic at Suave's. In the second week Francis had a talk with Lee.

'He's an addict, your nephew.'

'He's no addict, he's seventeen for gossakes.'

'I know an addict when I sees one.'

'Oh bullshit, Francis, David is a good kid and he makes good friends wherever he goes, he was twelve when I last saw him, and even then he had loads of friends everywhere all around him, he's a healthy little traveller.'

'You're livin in a myth, Lee. You're livin in a bubble, yer own bubble.'

'He's a kid, Francis.'

'Kids, the big excuse ey.'

'What's you mean? Excuse for who?'

'For us, for adults, for us. Kids, the big excuse.'

'Jesus Francis, can you pack it away now? We all live in bubbles, all of us, cept you. You live in a tent. Flap about like a tent you do sometimes. Piss off, go pour a drink. Well? Let me say it again, in your London lingo so you'll understand: Geddon wiv your flippin work.'

'If I was you I'd have a chat with him.'

'You're not in the same meadow as me Francis.'

'Oh I'm in the same meadow as you all right, don't you worry about that.'

The Tree of Life

On a day that's filled to the sky with sunshine, a small music starts up, and if the powderboxes were able to hear it dear butterfly, like you can, the meadows would be humming with the play and interplay of three key notes. The most continuous concert of music ever. The most pleasant magic. Every blade of grass, and every leaf of weed, on the meadow making the most formidable music of nature from just three key notes, sun, water and carbon dioxide: photosynthesis. The planet's true baseload power generation of all the hopes and dreams that ever mingled across the treetops of the second equator.

Creates all the glorious energy in the world needed for all the nectars and all the Dunsborough Swings, it created enough wood across the ages for workshops to produce us better boxes: Montague, Stan, Oxley, Flattie, Daqua and O Bobbo. Not to forget the thousands of other wooden boxes that hum happily at The Exchange conducting their hup two three of provisions across the hungry seas and over the ravenous mountaintops. Jungarummy jiddle, hey-ho ding-dong and how's the time.

Involve chlorophyll, involve also a splash of minerals pictured on the periodic table, and nature's music builds valleys of Dunsborough Swings. From the hills and valleys come the other useful bits they scatter across history. Tables. Chairs. Credenzas like the beaten up one in the colonel's room at the hacienda. The jetty at the hacienda. The eunuch's fleet of four-hundred-foot ocean-going junks that scudded up to America, Malacca, Calicut. Chopsticks. Matches. Violins. It all starts with the glory of photosynthesis. But there is an advantage in everything, thank Stan, and so the advantage for the smellbomb counterfeit crew: photosynthesis is also partly responsible for cardboard. Those outward pongsters like Hailme-Hailme, continually in search of memory's supposed symmetry, the good and the bad. Loved and cherished; lost and forgotten; bitter and destructive. Cardboard mythmakers. But no. We better boxes understand the one glorious thing about photosynthesis. Photosynthesis will foreclose on the search for symmetry, always.

The Tree of Sticky War

Somehow photosynthesis across the poppy fields caused the disappearance of Lee Glass-Darlington's husband, gems trader Rudolph the centre melter. Lee had no word from the Singapore Police, or from Tony Chen, or from Scotland Yard. She had become a fixture in her room at the house of imagined multiple Rudolphs, unfound Rudolphs, missing centre melters, night Rudolphs, day Rudolphs, she had become a fixture among these shimmers, where bang went the fits and rolls of her hopes in seeing him maybe arrive at last. Her grandmother Enid moved back to her own house in St Ives, not out of a lack of care, but out of disgust. These days Lee hardly ever showered, the kitchen was left to rot. Her room smelled. She took to the hillside for walks down to Tenmoon Creek at least three times a week, naked, but no longer traumatised. Her feet were smelling, and her eyes were hurting.

Instead, she consisted in a series of dark glows, she steered her trauma into slithers and glows, layers of equilibrium. The Lucknow jolly had watched it in lingering adoration, sculpted it in adoration.

It was the grim form of equilibrium that Bakks and

Kilometre had prompted. The vain fuckface Lightyear set about maintaining its grimness, which he found difficult coz equilibrium ain't grim. Equilibrium is nice, not grim, but Lightyear gets off on degrees of difficulty, so he enjoyed maintaining the grimness of Lee's new-found dirge of stability and equilibrium.

Bakks: 'Pleasure is not grim, Bobbo, you stupid do-gooding woodpest, pleasure is beautiful, I have given Lee Glass-Darlington a lot of sordid and solitary pleasure that she can enjoy to the hilt by herself in that filthy house. That filth, the house of grubb, by herself with the house of smutt, double B and double T, O Bobbo—pleasure is not grim, Skinny.'

But it was Flattie that had kept Lee from cascading over the edge.

Flattie: 'Let me say something demeaning to you, Bakks.'

Bakks: 'You can try Fatgut, you can give it a try.'

Flattie: 'Your prawn odour is beginning to smell of defecation, Inch told me he felt you were beginning to grow weak. And I agree with Inch, your cardboard flaps, your wings, Inch has a point there, they're looking a bit useless.'

Bakks: 'Inch wouldn't know whether his wings were on fire, Inch? True?'

Inch: 'I dante, true. Wings, fire, me? I dante. She just fatgut. You are just another wooden fatgut. Fatgut fucktoid. Let's call the carps.'

Flattie: 'Call the cops if you want, Inch. Inch no longer likes you, Bakks.'

Bakks: 'I'm not here exactly to be liked, I'm here to get on with my hup two three.'

Flattie: 'Hup two three is for us, not you lot. The jungarummy jiddle, I'm afraid, has to be heartfelt. Heartless jungarummy jiddle is just not on the cards, boys. Heartless jungarummy jiddle is for mugs, for pongsters.'

Inch: 'I dante get why you're into fibbing, Fatgut, you fib more I gonna call the carps and they throw you in clink like your hero Galileo, all this fib fib fib, why?'

Flattie: 'You ought to try a bit of factuality, Inch, like me—flat earth is round, two equators. When you get around to Bakks extincto, try a bit of factuality, it's quite nice.'

Inch: 'Fack-choo-al-itty? What the hell is fack-choo-al-itty?'

Flattie: 'It's me, and Bobbo, and Oxley, and Montague, and Stan, and Daqua, and all the rest of us across the two equators, it's what we do, dear Inch.'

Inch: 'Now I seen it all, dante I. That's not even bullshit, that's like a sour myth, talk about counterfeit. That's what you lot do? Wow, that's like the Australian banking world calling itself resilient: it gets left out of the shit—never even gets a phone call to buy any of the stuff Dexter Pepper powderbox calls poo, and then runs around calling itself what? Resilient! Haha. Hehehehe.'

Flattie: 'You will never know how to make a day memorable.'

Inch: 'Memo-rubble? What the hell is memo-rubble? I dante make rubble, I make gems.'

Bakks: 'Listen here you weary old wooden fucktoid, the whole floating rubbish of you wooden blips inside The Exchange are the same as that airy banking myth, all of you have a fuck-all smell on reality. Out here, come out here, you fekking slaves. You're like a hundred thousand Ban Ki-moons banking on the moon. The moon don't create light Booboo, the moon bounces it off, see, doesn't even want the light. Stick Bakks into the equation and moonlight can be made into any number of pleasurable myths.'

Inch: 'Stupid wooden fucktoid. Dumb-arse Arnie Colchester rubble of teak. I wanna call the fekking carps.'

The Tree of Hammocks

Castle and Jack took the coast road up to Yallingup and then cut across the cape into the hills and then rolled down into Dunsborough to collect a parcel. The others had stayed in Broome. Booksmeller had flown across the continent to the Pittwater cape, and upon arriving home she'd be a bit concerned by the three dozen stone figures of her aunt that lay scattered behind the sheds down at the water's edge.

As they weaved down the lush hills they caught glimpses of the township of Dunsborough, beyond the strip of beach the big bay sparkled in the sunshine, the special Dunsborough blue-green emerald shallows of clean sand stretching away into the Indian Ocean behind the boats and yachts anchored in the bay like baubles shimmering on a big blue dress Ellie'd wear at trustee meetings.

As they flew down the last of the slopes, landing near Simmo's ice cream factory, Castle warned Jack to hold on.

'Watch out for the bump,' Castle said as he sped down to the flats towards Simmo's.

They sped along the humming whiz of the smooth road and Jack felt no bump. They continued for another kilometre, past Simmo's, through the dense jungle of the Dunsborough Swing, on towards the township. Jack felt nothing. He looked across at Castle.

'Sometimes there's a big fat bump,' Castle said.

'Sometimes?'

'Yeah, though mainly late at night, not this afternoon looks like.'

This time Jack Verandah decided not to discount his friend Castle: herding herbs, herding cows, herding kangaroos, here at the cape five worlds away from Lars and Patsy in London it all started to make sense to Jack Verandah, arrogarnta extincto, bye-bye.

They'd been back from Broome only for a month. Jack had painted a big canvas of the periodic table, but he hadn't yet started the other painting, *The Butcher, the Surgeon, the Genetic Engineer.* That painting would be ready next month, and Catherine would forever after claim it was a portrait of her.

They drove along. Jack decided he would have to suggest Castle play a few songs underwater for the dolphins that surfed at Wyadup outside the spa, maybe not Pavarotti, maybe Bowie. 'Young Americans'. Hong could organise waterproofing, and the dolphins could bounce out of the shine of the tubes to Bowie's excellent thumping in 'Young Americans'.

At the post office Castle collected the parcel. He walked up to meet Jack for a coffee. He opened the parcel.

'Who is it from?' Jack asked.

'Don't know.'

'I bet it's from Ruby Schwartz, she told me she wanted to get to know you.'

'She did not.'

'She did. She's the biggest fan of your gasm triptych. She told me she's going to commission you for a gasm triptych that would fit into her dining room in Broome. *Mygasm Yourgasm Hourgasm*, she thinks it is neat and fun and utterly, this is what she said, sensible.'

'Anyway the stamps are American.'

Castle lifted out a note.
'It's from Kee.'

Dear Castle,

We have arrived in Caicos safely, today the sun is high and there are no clouds, and so the Pinski *is looking very bright, but this is also thanks beyond the sunshine, to Pedro. You will be pleased to know he also installed a new solar-operated desalinator, so we now have drinking water wherever we choose to go. Next week we will be making the two-day journey to Grand Turk Island.*

When I was a boy at the hacienda your grandmother's father, Eduardo Porras, gave me a gift. I took it with me when I left for Almeria in '47. I mail it to you only now because I see that Catherine has a very bad view of him. As I said to you in Broome, your great-grandfather was a very kind guy before he became ill, as you say of your brother Oliver. But I feel that this gift he gave me, which I now give to you, will show you and your cousins what he was like beyond any more doubt. I also give you his note. As I said to you in Broome, Pedro's house of children has not escaped a similar sadness. More than four of the children he has cared for over the years have as adults developed one kind of mental illness or the other, and Pedro, in his experiences, knows intimately that this is due to the luck of the draw, not due to the lack of love.

As you know already, when I found your grandmother as a fourteen year old on the wharf that day, I had no knowledge that she was Eduardo's daughter.

Your friend,
Kieran Leeft

Castle lifted an object the size of a soup bowl, and he began to unwrap it. It was a compass, and it was old, but as he examined it he saw that it was designed and made sturdy, the movement was still sublime as oil, gentle as a fine fate. It was not a toy, it was very heavy, a serious compass. It had travelled the seas safely inside fishing gear box Daqua.

He then unfolded Eduardo's note. It was in good condition because it had travelled the seas sealed in plastic safely inside turtleshell Montague. It was written in Eduardo's hand, in Spanish, and it was dated. June 1947. Eduardo had given the note to Ellie-Isabela to pass on to Kee when Kee was close to jumping the walls.

Listen kid,

When you asked me yesterday what it takes, I'll tell you, all it takes is for someone to understand who you are. Relax kid, when I have kids I want them to be as glorious as you. You're a good kid, you're destined for a good life, I can see it in your eyes. I know you want a boat, this compass might not look like much, but it will look after you, I won it in a card game from a guy in the American navy.

E.P.

The singular and immediate reaction Castle had to the note was that he experienced a sudden longing to do the simplest of all things in the known two equators to do, have a chat with Eduardo. The second reaction was a couple of months of inner sorrow that he didn't feel like talking about. An inner sorrow where all the grandest effects of cyxmix were now taking place with more Give than ever.

They drove back to the spacepod, and that evening the Peppers came over to see Jack's new four metre painting of the periodic table. Jack's rumination on transformation. It's okay to splay out the periodic table on a canvas to touch base with transformation, but it doesn't come close because the periodic table is desperately lacking in magic. For starters it has no cyclic AMP, the memory molecule inside the powderbox, let alone any of the other colourful marvels that give powderboxes their upside-down ding-dong, their festivals of humming vigour. Nonetheless, the four of them had a small party outside, beside the dam, celebrating the periodic table by carousing through the evening upon the subject of transformation. They enjoyed the painting, through its doorways they found relaxation. Castle managed to find a moment to call Hong up in Perth to ask him to consider waterproofing speakers to play Bowie to the dolphins. Hong agreed, he'd come down to Yelverton again soon.

Transformation, Jack had not given it much thought back in his London days. But Remple's Iodine, and the Broome days and nights, and the Yelverton swimming, and the lazy cruising around the Bahamas, had brought arrogarnta's ping splatter pop around to latching his entire mojo to the impeccable magic of transformation, you can make a chicken's egg into fresh skin, or into a nose.

Almost every powderbox dear butterfly, sees the hup two three, the mixing, the jungarummy jiddle, as memory. Can't blame em. Like water, three states. Loved and cherished; lost and forgotten; bitter and destructive. But it ain't so.

To have the hup two three is to have the mixing of memory, us better wooden boxes like Oxley an Flattie an Stan an Montague give the hup two three its finest ability, the true true truth at the treetops: memory *is* transformation. The London ding-dong got close, but not close enough. He thought it was the array of the Tenmoon chemicals found this side and the other side of the ozone, well, he would, he's just another powderbox sitting around looking for something to do in the hasty-paste.

Looking at the painting, Dexter said to Jack: 'What is it supposed to be? If you don't mind me asking a dumb question.'

'Not a dumb question at all. It's a Broome landscape.'

'But it's any landscape, could be Colorado.'

'Have a look at the Fe section, the iron section, see how there's multiple Fe squares. Broome's red earth.'

'Dex doesn't want to like it,' Lou said, 'owin to the fact it's all around mostly letters and not numbers.'

'That ain't true, I do like it.'

But dear butterfly, they only came close. The Exchange lay beyond them. Memory is transformation because the more a powderbox can find out about another powderbox the more a powderbox moves from one position to the next position. Memory ain't memory, it's transformation. Yet, the next day, in comfortable laziness, there was a further answer to your original question. It was a remark from Castle the following afternoon.

The Tree of Hope

Castle's remark flowed out naturally, that is, logically, when he and Jack were waiting outside for Hong. Double-O-Four was due to arrive to make the music pods for the dolphins. Out in the sunshine Castle and Jack waited on the grass at the dam of jetblack yabbies. They sat in silence for a while, joining the quiet of the afternoon as ding-dong powderboxes do in Yelverton, waiting for Hong was pleasant, but soon got around to the gift that had flown in from the past, from a time far less accustomed to dealing with the Diamond City's vast feats of powderbox destruction.

'The incredible number,' Castle said, 'of different inherited flaws of the mind that flow down the limbs of a family tree is kind of boggling, don't you think, just boggling.'

'I guess so,' Jack said. 'Never given it much thought till this year, my brother's behaviour never shot me away in that direction to explore it.'

'The full spectrum, from small and harmless right up to big flaws, harmful illnesses, they're all there, coursing their way into fresh new generations.'

'Innocent generations,' Jack added.

'Yep, utterly innocent, done nothing to deserve it. And we still don't really know why those flaws can often skip a generation, skip two, appearing here but not there.'

'Let's hope the old days are well and truly gone.'

'Old days? What old days?'

'The play.'

'What play?'

'The games.'

'What are you talking about? You mean the psychiatrists?'

'No, the family, the ways of avoiding seeing the arrival of the illnesses. Decades ago every mental illness was written off with a dash of fear, apprehension and electricity.'

'Oh that,' Castle said ruefully, 'yeah, and the hush-hush, the shame, yeah you're right, I hope the old days have well and truly gone with all that prim behaviour. It's just too harmful, that behaviour, all the keeping quiet and the crappy understanding is just way too harmful to those who score a hit off the family tree. I mean, just the variety, we have whole shopping aisles of mental disorders and illnesses being fobbed off in every which way.'

'Maybe it'll never really change,' Jack said as he stood up. He got up to check out a dust line hanging in the air along the road. The car sped past Castle's driveway into the forest track.

'Maybe, but I certainly hope it does. In fact, I have high hopes.'

'Do you mean like the scenario you were telling me about on the flight, this new era concept?'

'Yeah, but even deeper and more meaningful than just a new era of openness and understanding. A completely new era also of what I thought of back in Broome as Active Love. I was just sitting, just having a coffee in town at that cafe near the cinema, and the whole new world just popped into the air, a world of Active Love.'

'Can you articulate that world yet?'

'Yeah, kind of. Been rolling it round for two weeks now, so yeah.'

'Where does it start?'

'Well, there are so many excellent organisations run by professional talented people who tend to the mentally ill, and tend to the broader fact of mental illness, rather than allowing it to be suppressed into the early language of early last century—nervous breakdown, nervous turn, nervous episode. These people in these organisations are a good start, and then we individuals get on board with new attitudes like seeing really clearly. Being aware of early signs, for early intervention, for early treatment so that those diamond claws are disallowed to completely shred a life. Got to admit, shredded lives in the normal world are plenty, but that's by making a string of lousy choices and not by the automatic attack of the diamond claws.'

'Good start, I like it.'

'Yeah, and I'd really dig to reach a place where we are all straining really hard to hear any judgemental gibberish leaching into the private conversation about madness, or the national one, or the international conversation. Gibberish is no good.'

'I dunno if the human spirit will ever evolve like, you know, quite that far, a person is forever going to fear mental illness, fear contact with a mad person.'

'Yeah but not when the ill person is given the proper care. Anyway, it's choice over primal fear, choose, choose to make the mentally ill a part of humanity. Imagine embracing the mentally ill fully and properly into humanity, what a day, Active Love's major triumph, even the gods, all gods, would be pleased with us. It's like that guy Jonathon Welch with his Choir of Hard Knocks where he guided the homeless and the mentally ill to come up to that Leonard Cohen song 'Hallelujah'. Welch made those singers feel loved, wanted and wrapped in warmth. We get that kind of stuff translated across the broader sweep of life, and we've got it made. A whole new era, lay aside the middle ages, a fresh new way of bringing out the most courageous parts of our more civilised side. Choose, we choose it.'

'That's a very good start. Congratulations.'

Then they talked about the periodic table painting. Castle said: 'Dexter didn't seem to go for it last night, but I like it. I like its base, its base unit, a stylised imprint of the planet's mysteries.'

'Like a code ready to explode.'

'Yeah. All you need is a feral glitch, a tiny nick of a feral glitch.'

'I don't know what you mean by that.'

'A spark,' Castle said, 'from somewhere beyond the ozone layer, like a gift, and suddenly the periodic table blooms into the millions of mysteries of nature. Blooms into all the incredulous miracles. A spark. Won't take too long, what's created is the grandeur of the globe, the sparkling miracle of the planet's profusion of millions of different living forms, emblazoned with their different mysteries, like a salmon running thousands of kilometres across the ocean and then hundreds of miles upstream to spawn at the same rockpool in the hills where they were born. Do you believe we'll ever get under nature?'

'The human race? Can't see it, if we ever throw a bright light on the secrets of nature, we'd have to have evolved a bit, a lot. We just haven't got the perception for it.'

'Last night I dreamed nature spoke, a kind of voice, thin and distant, showing us the whole festival, every mystery.'

'In Broome I dreamed of an underwater kangaroo, it was catching octopus and shellfish, I think maybe it was a dream response to all this magical beauty I've had for the first time.'

'Yeah, and we want to undermine it. Why would we knowingly want to degrade it, worse, destroy it. Doing the degrading knowingly is really a bit more than denial, more than irresponsibility, it's a form of madness, though not like Oliver, but some other form of madness.'

And dear butterfly, there it is, a part of the answer to your question. The upside-down mojo, Castle and Jack talking about the upside-down mojo. Or, as Flattie says of powderboxes who love living the upside-down mojo: 'There goes another powderbox who's got his face on back to front, see what, see only the self.'

The breath of sweet breezes and the zing of exuberant life under your wings dear butterfly, it is problematic to understand how such a vast madness might ever see it, smell it, maybe like it, one day grow to love it more than a factory.

The House of the Singing Banana Leaf

Now that the seadog's note had arrived, Castle's memory of Eduardo would grow, would transform, Catherine's too perhaps, she was due for a visit in a week. Their grandmother Renata's father had said in the note barely anything, but what he said, that single phrase, that memory, would bring the give and take of Ellie's magic wand into the three great-grandchildren, Castle and Catherine and Remple, in a way they could never have foreseen without Kee's memories. Eduardo had said to the kid Carlos Luque: 'All it takes is for someone to understand who you are.' That casual piece of Give, a small thought, expressed in the year before the guy would be drawn towards the rusting gates and then into the domain of the Diamond City of Children. A phrase as small as a rusty key, would become the largest source of transformation either Catherine or Remple or Castle would receive for a very long time to come. Memory is transformation. It may even go a small way to making provisions for happiness. The greatest piece of sanity they were to hear for a very long time had arrived into their powderboxes from a guy from long ago who was soon to become insane.

It wouldn't even take until Christmas, until around the New Year, and Castle would discover in himself that he loved Eduardo. Catherine fumbled around selling art for another two years before she found that she too loved Eduardo. Remple found that he loved Eduardo, and he honoured his great-grandfather by re-naming the genetics dome the Eduardo Porras Laboratories.

Three million butterflies, dear butterfly, still maintained the Dunsborough Swing, and, let's face it, in a hammock the size of a district the chances of continuing transformation are good as a land of honey. Australia's most impeccable hammock.

Swinging to the sweet music of one of the most impeccable types of transformation, photosynthesis hup two three. Coz that's what the Dunsborough Swing will give, any swing gladly gives it: remember the laughter, remember the beauty, remember the dancing, ding-dong and how's the time helped along by cyxmix. A memo won't do it, only The Exchange, only us better boxes, will do it, coz we do the jungarummy jiddle. A memo's just a scrap, means nothing. Even that ol Calcutta titan Miles Banford couldn't stand the cutey-moo of memos, nor could he ever understand the addiction to memos.

Or, as Oxley says, 'What's valuable is another kind of memo, memo-rubbillia, rubbing and mixing, like the guy's Zeus collection upstairs in the breezy second storey of the bungalow, parties all along the upper verandah on the tenth of every month, parties among the palm tree leaves, parties among the Zeus memo-rubbillia.'

Which is where colonel David longhead first met the maharaja's daughter. Eye contact, hot evening, and not long to wait, just a couple of weeks, to puttering into the hills in the old Morris to the shack. And not long after that to being shot at with a Winchester, and racing away to Spain.

The Tree of Friendship

David Darlington the lovely longhead got to know Eduardo Porras better than anyone else round the hacienda. They spoke in Spanish that day when David gave Eduardo the invitation to the party. In another time Castle could've gone to booksmeller's great-grandfather David Darlington for hints on Eduardo.

David said, sitting on an old chair under the Tree of Wishes, 'You like these kids very much, Eduardo, and I suspect these days that you might be harbouring designs upon my job.'

'I'm a fisherman David, I love fishing, behold a suntanned fisher at the peak of his powers, but you're only too right as usual. I visit here so often like Mendoza because of these wonderful children, you and Ellie are doing a great job, I do not want your job.'

'Oh, sorry Eduardo, sorry to have said that, I guess I was just having a stupid highland joke.'

'No problem. But I have to tell you straight up, I am impressed how happy these kids are.'

'Thanks.'

'Remember what I said last month: if you and Ellie ever need any help, let me know. That other guy last year who had your job was a horrible piece of work, he even had the shitness to steal the big front room off the kids for himself, I am very pleased to hear you gave it back to the kids on your first day.'

'After the kids have dinner tonight and go off to sleep, there's a few of us getting together for drinks for Ellie's birthday, she turns forty-seven, but don't tell anyone, I'm telling everyone she's thirty-five.'

Eduardo shrugged his shoulders. 'I always thought she was thirty-six.'

'Like to come around for drinks?'

'Sure, sure, what a good idea. I'll bring my wife.'

'Eight o'clock.'

'Yep, eight. So you are missing Scotland Ellie tells me.'

'Not a bit, I miss my aunt in London, and my mother and father, but not Scotland, right here in Spain is brilliant, they made a real country with this place.'

'Making a country is easy as shit, but making a country of love is more tricky, look what Franco has done to this country, look what Hitler did to his, those guys sure need a good fuck.'

A group of kids came running and shouting into the compound after swimming at the jetty, and they ran past the two men round the side of the hacienda to hit the back room where Ellie had made her lemon drink with honey and her fresh bread. When the last kid Carlos had run past, the grounds fell quiet. Eduardo clapped his hands.

'Look at all that fukkin energy, now *that* will make a country of love, when these kids take over Spain, Spain will be a country of love.'

'Will you and your wife have kids?'

'Yeah, we will, we will, but please don't tell anyone around here what we are doing, we're timing it, we're going for next year, we have plenty of good times in bed, but we practise the contraception. Plus I've told her how much I would like to adopt that Carlos Luque as a second child, do you think we could adopt Carlos?'

'More than likely, but you and your wife will have to see the government about it first.'

That night the village got together at the hacienda Zaragoza for Ellie's birthday celebrations. The sailor brought with him two bottles of whisky from his shop at the jetty. Henry&Co followed the sailor to the party.

What Eduardo did not mention, nobody at the village knew this, was that he already had a five year old daughter, Renata, with a previous woman from a village further south.

The Tree of Fresh Air

So there it was, Sunrise Sunset had reinstated the memory of Eduardo Porras. Refreshed it. From being remembered as a monster, Eduardo had become their great-grandfather loved in memory.

It can't be claimed as the biggest victory of all time, but it certainly was ding-dong a victory against Bakks and his sordid counterfeit running on the wounded logic of cow grass and milk.

So perhaps, just perhaps, here's another piece of ping splatter pop of the answer dear butterfly. Maybe I'll be around for another hundred years, another fitful century, owner to owner. But maybe more: they found scattered slabs of teak in a cave in India last month, carbon-dated two thousand years old. So in service to your original, single question: Who are they, these custodians of my habitat?

They're the future. Maybe the answer from us wooden pirates at The Exchange where your custodians store their lore de lore, where they show both the grim and the gorgeous, maybe this shows the mingling and the mixing of growth and decay that constitutes a powderbox perspective. And maybe they are too busy with this mixing and mingling to care about your habitat, tho Remple's Iodine is a good start, pump out the jungarummy jiddle across the two equators, glee glee. Ruby Schwartz has already pumped out so much fine jungarummy jiddle from Neutrino's Lab that the victories are piling up in powderboxes everywhere.

Oxley an Flattie, they're likely to migrate from proud owner to proud owner for a very long time to come. Oxley might continue to locate plenty of upside-down, and Flattie might continue to find faces on back to front.

The full crew of smellbomb deadbeats, cardboard creeps including that vain fuckface Lightyear, they've all become landfill. Problem is, look around, the new cardboard hordes everywhere for the lore de lore, counterfeit galore might never be eradicated.

The Tree of Inch

After Bakks had gone Inch cried out: 'Harrah! Harrah! I like be king, dante I! Harrah!'

Yes true, Inch became king of the deadbeat pongsters. So piggy Bakks did get swined off, but not by Montague or Flattie or Oxley or Stan or Daqua or even useless Bobbo, but by shrillfactor tucksick Inch. How he achieved the Bakks extincto bizzo is actually quite remarkable for a neo-Marxist hum-chanting pongster. I mean, you can't just shoo Bakks away. Shoo! Shoo!

All that the new crew of cardboard pongsters saw in Inch was a kind of a blob of cardboard caked in a foul rust-coloured substance. Not even really a box, just a blobbish, um, thing. But they were awed by it. And so they accepted him as king.

Not Oxley: 'Look at yourself, Inch, you're a mess, you're just a mess majora.'

Bakks all along tried to toxify Castle's powderbox, but failed. Bakks did toxify Catherine's powderbox, but she came round over time. Bakks worked the jungarummy jiddle over and over, he wanted Catherine to go from a bad day to a shit day to a day where she'd wanna kill em all, but Bakks failed miserably coz Catherine finally came round to honouring and loving señor Eduardo Porras. And this became a window into which she could make out how to love and honour one or two others as the second equator rolled and rolled through the corridors and hallways of her art world.

This newfound loveliness drifting round in Catherine's powderbox caused the crew to view Bakks with quite a lot less admiration, quite a heap less, and they began to suspect he probably did, after all, commence his days in a stinking prawnfarm, and a prawnfarm don't buy you entry into the swinging trickiness of a powderbox, so to qualify, well, maybe Bakks didn't qualify, and the crew blew its mojo off to nobody knew where, it just blew away. Problem with coming from something like a prawnfarm is you only get limited jungarummy jiddle ability: what else but prawns get stored in a box from a prawnfarm? With us woodens you've got just about everything stored away from era to era, year to year, month to month. So it's true, Bakks was exceptional at a limited range of hup two three, mainly he was scary at haranguage. But you need more, much more, pranguage, slanguage, winguage, songuage, banguage, twanguage, ganguage, you need it all, the whole eruptive mix.

When Bakks successfully brought ruination to Lee Glass-Darlington, who now forgot the shower for days on end, the crew of pongsters loved him, feared him, made the pact of eternity with him. Gemboy Central still hadn't been found, but so what the crew felt, it was too long ago, and the failure with Catherine was too bitter to bear, and the crew just left him where they last saw him flapping, on a shelf in Blitzo's office, out of sight, far up the wall almost to the ceiling.

The stuff Peter Blitz stored in Bakks on that dusty shelf was nothing of any help, have to have had zero impacto upon Bakks's meagre jungarummy jiddle ability, nothing to extend his fearsome haranguage expertise into the fuller spectrum of hup two three, and it afforded Bakks zero entry into the full splash and depth of scent, or the deeper and more powerful memory dye, cyxmix. No, Bakks got nothing from Blitzo's bits and pieces. The things that Blitzo stored in Bakks on the shelf in his office were just junk really: a few photos of Ruby when he'd managed to take her out to Chinese in Broome once long ago, two vials of sulphuric acid, two old but unopened boxes of Ryvita, rubber bands, a coffee mug Ruby had given him for his birthday, and it was one hell of an unexciting mug, bland.

Blitzo found he had to 'resign' his position at Iodine, and he took a job as a carbon counter, counting the carbon dioxide emitted by the big and small polluters. Not a good job. Adding up carbon poured out by a factory, or by an airline, or an electricity company, was not an easy job, even for a chemistry genius who could count all manner of tacked on molecules. Of course buying and selling carbon dear butterfly, is not going to diminish pollution. Creating a new currency is not going to diminish pollution. Creating counterfeit, as we know, brings about more ugliness not less. It is just a worse way to punch a kid in the face. The pongsters around Bakks had been hard at work on all the powderboxes across the two equators who wanted to hail into being a new currency, but hadn't the telescopes to see that it was just another piece of smart counterfeit pinged out into the world from the swill of deadbeats outside The Exchange.

Alas, counterfeit, as we know, has the elegance, not to mention intellectual rigour, to make things that simply do not equate into concepts that have a very solid common sense feel. So the opposite is true: counterfeit would simply create more rubbish, pollution, ugliness and general widespread collapse.

On the other hand, with no counterfeit whatsoever, the pollution that kills your land of nectar would have to be curtailed simply by everyone's mojo making a leap of faith into buying and using less and less, and buying from companies that embraced that fresh new mojo. Which would include paying the lung countries a regular rent to keep the trees instead of hacking them down. The tree of magic, Ellie's magic too, giving, no, maybe more than that, the tree of possibility.

Take a glance at a lovely impending zap dear butterfly. I don't mean electric household zappers for mosquitoes, zapzap bzzt, fried. I mean this: We have it on good authority that the total number of powderboxes across both equators and everywhere right now is six billion. I'm an Arnie Colchester wooden, built to last, so I'm likely to watch this number climb, maybe up to ten, fifteen billion, twenty billion. They're gonna want your nectar.

You sure as eggs ain't gonna stop those Indian regions either. Try stoppin em round India from havin a party—ding-dong and how's the time. China, India, both about a billion right now, but a powderbox can only have one kid in China, India no way, have as many as you want, and it's a right too, a human right, and these rights are gonna be mighty talked about and clashed about everywhere over the next century, not just India, so check out Flattie's potential. Flattie's a very costly collector's item, so she'll probably be checking the numbers in three centuries—maybe one hundred billion new custodians of your nectar. A hundred gaddam billion. Not too much room left, not for your black&orange monarch cousins that flap down to Mexico every year.

Flattie, being a globe, has a bad feeling about it. She says when so much of the actual matter gets eaten off the actual globe of the earth itself and transferred into the powderbox matter—who are not attached to the mass of the earth like say a tree—then the gravitational pull will lessen, just slightly, less mass less gravity, and so these one hundred billion powderboxes will in fact no longer be walking, they'll be hoverwalking, just a couple of millimetres off the surface of the path or road.

But it did not concern Peter that the whole carbon-counting industry, the entire global scheme of it, was just an equation to let the big polluters buy more carbon credits in order to maintain business as usual, to keep on polluting, so banks and businesses surely wanted the scheme coz it spelled a new area of new money sources, tho it did bother Peter that he was now doing a nasty job mostly hated by customers rather than a job at Iodine hugely loved by customers. Put another way: he left a job where he might be helping to conserve and save your nectar, a new custodian of your nectar, to a job where he was facilitating the destruction of your nectar. He went from saving the planet to running it into the ground. Punching a kid in the face. A future kid in the face.

Even tho it bothered him that he was now to help ravage the planet, the applicable reward was large in stature; at least, he felt, he'd soon become extremely important, and that to him was an elemental destination. Full of the obvious, a state of being he'd always craved. Simple stuff, he felt. Important. Carbon dioxide was destined to become the biggest loudest commodity ever traded between the greatest of the hatepiles of history, and even currently, in the European Union, carbon trading is bigger than soy bean trading, Blitzo knew it, had this knowledge, so it was simply a matter of time before he became feared and important even if the customer felt guys in Blitzo's line were on the nose, and rather than lunching with the Peter Blitzos of the world with cheer they instead lunched with a sense of grudging and bored necessity. Or from a sense of obligation, or with a nicely buried urge to maim. Which all makes sense because, really, buying carbon credits, really, is about as alluring as buying springs for a bed. But before Blitzo left Iodine to go carbon counting, Inch honed in on the king sitting on the high dusty shelf all in a flap about the crew sneering at his weak as water jungarummy jiddle, ol Bakks, phew.

Ruby the Mensa Mind Messenger

Inch commenced the Bakks extincto simply enough, congratulations. It was very similar to the manner in which Warren Buffett responded when the desperadoes at American Insurance Group, AIG, pleaded with him to slap ten billion dollars at the crunching organisation. Mister Buffett made his rejection clear for one reason, just the one: your company is too complicated.

Simple is the thing, yep, specially when it comes to cardboard extincto, and Inch swung the extincto into getting started by using a vast pure incline of rampant simplicity, mucho congratulatto. Rampant new myths. Not myths proper but just wonky ways of claiming possession, made not just from the cardboard deadbeats but also from all the vehement belief in the ol you seen a photo you seen a fact. Or the high-tech ding-dong NASA pics of Tenmoon land out past the ozone. Or the high-tech ding-dong opportunity of creating entirely new myths thanks to the shimmers and mirages of stuff on the net being taken by powderboxes as facto impacto. Yep, Inch found a way to start the Bakks extincto in the simplest of ways. Beautiful, even puppybox Yard called it beautiful.

First, Inch got the fuckface Lightyear to conduct a sharp slice of hup two three upon Ruby. It was to be fuckface's last gig before he became landfill, but what a gig: hup two three bigtime upon prehistoric mensa mind nubile as a neutrino. Just as Inch said: 'What a gaddam gig.' And fuckface went sheeting out with excitement in all directions, like lightning warming up in the weeks before the Timor–Kimberley monsoon sheeting off in a thousand directions and then at last settling down for the true business of raining down upon a nubile powderbox to burn and twist enough memory to bring extincto impacto to Bakks in Blitzo's office. 'Harrah! Harrah! I Like make peace, dante I!'

What Inch meant by 'peace' was the potential that Inch loved so much about the powderbox upside-down ding-dong happening suddenly new all over again. When Lightyear told Inch that the Nobel peace prize had gone to a man at war, Inch flipped out with glee, rustflecks pelting off the sides of his blob of cardboard.

The commander-in-chief of the American military, well we know how it goes with cardboard dear butterfly, Inch didn't have the slightest idea of his name and didn't care that he didn't. Still, a man at war being given the peace prize had unwittingly pointed the way for Inch. Ping splatter pop the flecks of excitement flew bap-bap into Blitzo's boxy office domain from where Iodine was recently run, um, administered.

Flattie said to Inch: 'You do not even know which building, which of those buildings do you suppose is Blitzo's office located in, dear Inch?'

Inch: 'Bill-ding? I no getta billding? O I get billding, I get exact billding dante I. You watch. Wooden idiot. Wooden slaves. Optimise me out, every second equator you wooden slaves just optimise me out, fully bore the vividity right outta me.'

Flattie: 'You cardboard surveillance boxes, you are just too disciplined, sorry, but you're all just too systematic to understand the give and take, too systematic to believe in the weightless weight of a true memory. Even Lightyear is much too systematic.'

Inch: 'Sister-mattick? What in the hell is sister-mattick? I'll show you mattick every damn way, move aside Fatgut. Bakks located in Dome Twelve, Blitzo's office. Wow, look, Kilometre pounding Dome Twelve just now, Flattie.'

Kilometre flung into the Ruby powderbox. Flung the jungarummy jiddle into the mensa powderbox. And there it started, the Bakks extincto.

The Tree of Impatience Meets the Tree of Impertinence

Day one, Blitzo 'resigned' after a meeting with Remple. But Blitzo spent the next ten days wrapping things up before he left Iodine on a flight to Perth. In the ten days he sent notes and flowers to Ruby's house every afternoon. He also sent an email every day.

Day two, Ruby was touched, saddened a little.

Day three, Ruby felt very sorry for him, and she took the notes and emails as a minor wave created by a grief-stricken guy.

Day four, two more emails.

Day five, Ruby took the notes, flowers and emails as crass blobs of impertinence, and she began to grow extremely impatient.

Day six, Ruby stormed out of her office. She banged on

Blitzo's door.

'Come in,' he called.

She flung the door aside. She stood in the doorway without entering the large office that overlooked the bay. She yelled briskly: 'Just stop it!'

And then she turned and walked away.

Day seven, she flew up the corridors again and bashed the door aside. 'If you send one more of these impertinent pieces of shit to me I am calling the cops!' She shouted, and she threw the flowers down to the floor.

Day eight, she bashed the door aside and held her hands high up and dropped Blitzo's gift to the floor, where it smashed to pieces, and she turned and walked away. The gift was a collection of crystal salad bowls he'd given her for her birthday.

She never put a foot over the threshold of his doorway. Until day nine. She was gunna torch the Blitzo messfest good n glorious.

Day nine, she actually walked slowly into the office and met him at his big wide desk, and she poured a kettle of just-boiled water on it, forcing Blitzo to jump like an eel back against the windows overlooking the bay.

Day ten, she also walked into the office. She stopped halfway to the desk, Blitzo jumped off his chair. She ran her gaze around the shelves behind the boardroom table.

She found what she was searching for, it was Bakks. She walked around the boardroom table, picked the cardboard box off the shelf, walked it to the open window. Blitz caught her intention just in time, and he ran around the desk to stop her before she got to the window. He caught her shirtsleeve, but she swung her hand around and hit him against the side of his forehead, and she took another step forward where she flung the cardboard box out the window. It fell into the bay. Bakks extincto.

Inch: 'Harrah! Harrah! I love be king dante I!'

Or as Miles Banford might have said if he'd actually truly known about Bakks: 'He was a jackass anyway.'

O Bobbo would go a bit further dear butterfly: he was a jackass majora, ol king Bakks. A jackass majora what always belonged in the smell-zone anyway, name a smell-zone, any smell-zone.

Had Bakks been a good wooden box dealing in real memories instead of a cardboard pongster soaked in counterfeit, he might have floated. Floated up to a beach, maybe far away from Iodine's domes and jetties, maybe further along the Leeuwin Current at the feet of a Korean tourist at Ningaloo Reef to be ready once again to commence storing a whole new set of cherished memories of a bright new owner, lore de lore for the accumulated leaves of the useful wisdoms. Your custodians, dear butterfly. Look at the promise, the potential, the possibility. Take the tree at the gate of the hacienda. The moment you dropped from the shaded leaves of that giant tree and out into the sunshine of the Golfo de Valencia and over the top of the sailor's shop, the potential suddenly became something as real as Pinski and Henry barking at sharks and shells.

The Tree of New Possibilities

The canopy of that tree fanning out like a promise of great deeds to come. Fanning out and growing with all the magic of sunlight, water and carbon. With minerals wood is created by this magic.

Nothing else can create wood. Ruby's lab could not create wood. NASA cannot create wood, even one cell of wood. No amount of high-grade intelligence, design and technology can create wood, even the fearsome and impressive world of nanotech cannot make wood. All the genetic labs across the spectrum of richer universities if joined up together to pool their resources under a Global Wood Project, even they together cannot crack the secret to make wood. There is no way for your custodians to make wood other than one way, and only one: by putting their faces on the correct way around and therefore embracing a love of your habitat as profound as the love of currency—all currencies, including the various gleaming counterfeit currencies. From the ruble to the zloty to the dollar to the franc, and, since power is the go, invite the powderboxes to move from one style of power to another form of power, from the power of paper to purchase and own, to the woody power of wonder and awe.

Like the giant tree at the hacienda gates. The flaring canopy created cell by cell from the alchemy of sunshine's cousins, water and carbon. Leaf by leaf, branch by branch, the tree spreads the canopy of its wisdom out to the custodians across the two equators. Pouring oxygen back into the air the powderboxes breathe: that's a give, creating oxygen from carbon dioxide, a big fat give, forcing the aggregations to put the face on the right way round instead of back to front, forcing the upside-down urges to flip round the right side up.

Carnival of the Animals

The soldier with the see-through shop at the jetty had always done well since he walked into the village and stopped there to wonder. He stayed years, well into the fifties. Even tho he was actually a sailor, the village grew to know him as a soldier. The whisky went well, the tins of tomatoes, the rented goggles, but he became friends with some of the people in the village and to become friends was not what he'd been searching out after the shock and shit of the war, what he wanted was something else, strange you'd decline friends after a war tore your sky away but there you are, war tore away your sky.

He found a friend in Carlos Luque. He regarded Carlos as a very fine kid. When Carlos ran away from the hacienda the sailor was not exactly torn apart but he was very very sad. Such a kid would have been good for the village had he stayed. You don't get kids like that these days, not here, not even back home where kids were never running away, no, he was good that Carlos.

The soldier became a good friend of David's, and of Ellie's, and of Mendoza's, he went to the party for Ellie's birthday and he met Eduardo there at the party.

The sadness the soldier expressed late one afternoon after Carlos had gone was unbearable for Ellie. He played on his harmonica in the square tunnel shop, and Ellie was drawn across the road. She stopped, she watched him play the song in the dusk of the sweet second equator moving slowly off the gulf. She stood off the shop in the centre of the road.

She knew straight away he played a song for Carlos because the sailor had let it go at her party to at least Eduardo that he'd made a viable song for the boy, and Ellie knew it was for Carlos. She stood there on the road. She watched him play. He faced the gulf, so she saw only his shoulders swing to the tune.

She could see over his shoulders through the shop to the gulf. The song was impossible to listen to without thinking of Carlos, and she stood in the middle of the hot dirt road feeling the day's heat burn her bare feet. It was one of those difficult and emotional songs that led you into the love you had and the fun you had, which you no longer had, and you just hung off the earth's roads waiting for something to take you away to where the fun and love had gone. You hung off the gulf's roads by maybe something as thin as just two shadows, but you were not on the ground, you were sad and afloat, you were searching for love and fun that had vanished without a goodbye or even a nod.

She stood calmly in the two shadows under her feet. David came out. He stopped at the gate, watching her as she swayed. Eduardo came out, he walked over to the gate to stand beside David. Nobody else arrived. But in half an hour word went round.

Carnival of the Bones

By early nightfall the village was there on the road. Nobody had bothered to wash to go out, they were suddenly all there. They wanted to dress fast and wash to get there, yet they came to surround the shop in huddling bunches of families and other fives and eights and twos.

The children came out of the hacienda, letting their meals go. David and Eduardo still stood side by side together at the gate, but the village had gathered round them at the hacienda and over the road round the shop where the soldier still played. David folded his arms, Eduardo too, and they leaned into the wall. They and their neighbours and enemies were now all together, the village, watching Ellie standing on the shadows, swaying with the soldier's harmonica.

Ellie continued to listen to the song. It had these rooms with no words that could keep a whole village afloat but she still fell backwards anyway. The soldier played and Ellie just kept weeping. She fell on the road and continued to cry. She started to scream and cry, and then, just when David and Eduardo began to run across the road Ellie let out the worst possible piece of existence anyone had ever known round the gulf, it was terrible to see, she just let it out. She was on her back. She screamed on that dust in such a loud way that the howl would have followed Carlos inside the truck he took. She howled, and the village watched in helpless awe standing around Ellie, around love, and more love and more. Ellie cried and cried on the road on her back, hitting the road with the backs of her hands, hitting the stupid earth with a force that shitted out all the hidden opinions of the earth. Her arms were away out, legs out, long feet out, hands out. The village stood around her, she lay on the road and man did she howl the poor damn woman who all she ever did was to give give give. On the road on her back, she howled as many olden and modern animals have ever put howls into the sky.

The Tree of Jumping Bulbs

The soldier played from *Carnival of the Animals*, 'The Swan'. *Carnival of the Animals* is a piece by the composer he always knew up and down as Saëns, and the shopkeeper played *Carnival* with his own new swirls against the backbone Saëns had created, and so the shopkeeper dedicated Saëns to Sunrise Sunset's special mojo that the soldier believed the boy possessed. The soldier did not dedicate Sunrise Sunset's life to Saëns, he dedicated Saëns to see the boy's life. The soldier believed Saëns had been a musician capable of loving the future. The soldier trusted Saëns for it. And so he broke Saëns' song's backbone, remade it into a song dedicated to Sunrise Sunset in the belief that Saëns would be lurking somewhere under the war that tore the sky off Spain and the world. The soldier didn't care about Saëns getting worried over the fact that the song had been junked by a man who'd killed and killed, he trusted that Saëns would just love the future running hot and smart and limpid in a kid like Carlos Luque.

The children of the house, all the buffalo Hindu Spanish kids, were standing loosely around Ellie, they were shuffling, coming in scared, but they made their way through the crowd, scared and pulled, frightened and excited at the same time, repelled and excited, so that they got to Ellie more or less in a single clump and only then fanned away by fright bit by bit into pieces of kidclumps. The kids were never disgusted, not like the village kids, village kids were disgusted by anything. Hacienda Zaragoza kids were excited by just about everything, but sadness drew over them tonight as they gathered again in a clump around the low sobbing of their Ellie mother on the road. They were into the ideas, but they didn't know much about em, mother, father, what are they, and so the kids just pinged out when they came close to Ellie hitting hands into the road, one kid said: 'She looks like a monster.' Pinski started barking at her, and Henry supported Pinski by barking at her.

The hacienda kids had never seen Ellie fall like this, let alone on the road on her back hitting the dust with the backs of her hands. Crying out, 'Stupid earth! Stupid earth!'

The Tree of Big Arms

David and Eduardo came in through the kids to pick her up. The dogs quickly took up the opportunity and followed the two men's heels.

The men came in slowly and quietly, walking black and fine like stingrays that collect sunshine, past the kids, past the village, past the fishermen, picking her up gently. They carried her across the road to the hacienda. Henry&Co were at their heels. David and Eduardo walked up the cool corridors of the house and they lay her in the bed. Henry&Co sat beside the bed.

Carnival of the Animals could be heard in the distance, for the village was in silence it had not known for years, standing to the harmonica of Saëns' renewed and broken song. Everyone was silent for *Carnival of the Animals*, and nobody moved or had wanted to say anything. The soldier played. But when the soldier moved the tune from Saint Saëns' animal suites into another piece of music, the village heard Ellie begin again. It was Pachelbel's *Canon*. The first chords: simple and slow, just like Ellie had always dreamed of becoming, make ready to give, have your heights ready, to give, and be ready, from the mojo of loving the child, to fall backwards by letting it all go—and that's how the soldier played Pachelbels' infamous old song written four centuries earlier, the soldier played it not down slow and cumbersome, but with zing slow, which served to make it even sadder for those moments near the beach at dusk

The sun went away as slowly as it always does, the gulf settled into a water of more and more memory. The sea became like a sheet of smooth silk, no, it was skin probably. The village knew something was coming, something was on its way. You couldn't fool the village, you could fool a town sometimes but never a village. They did not know what exactly was coming, but it would be something.

Eduardo shook his head slowly at Ellie's bed. He felt sorry for Ellie. He felt sorry for himself. He felt sorry for everyone. He felt sorry for the world. He felt sorry for his father, whom nobody knew, and he was ashamed that he didn't pick up Ellie faster. He felt sorry for all of it. When he and David placed their hands under Ellie's back he felt a buzz, all the old and young were there, for Eduardo the angels were present that day. Wings, songs, dreams, his world was coming true, he was near to the diamond claws and their rusting gates creaking open to a new empire.

We cannot turn it round. Eduardo said we can, but he meant something else, he meant a whole another world. We turn it round just like that. We just love. And when he put Ellie on the bed, you saw his eyes. He meant it. We just love. We make it turn round. Simple, we just love.

Castle and Oliver

After a four hour drive from Yelverton, Castle arrived at the Bombay Plaza in Mount Lawley. He stepped into the old rattling lift. In the flat he lay down for half an hour. Then he got up and stood under a cold shower for a long time. He strolled down Beaufort Street into Highgate and met Oliver for lunch.

'I've got news about our great-grandfather,' Castle said.

'Is it from our special boatman you talk about? From the great Keep Left?'

'Yeah. Turns out that our Eduardo was a very kind guy. He gave all the kids at the hacienda a special gift. He was kind, Oliver, like you. Let me tell you the scary piece of magic our Eduardo did.'

'I'd like to hear it.'

'He was born in England.'

'What? He was born in Spain.'

'Leighton Buzzard, England. He was three when he went to Spain with his parents.'

'Well that's a relief, he's a Spanish guy then.'

'Here's what he did for the kids at the hacienda, I mean, this is what the guy did Oliver.'

Oliver leaned into the table with his torso and then gave his whole body to the news by shunting his chair forward. The drop of face that Castle had become accustomed to a long time ago, a fine piece of reality over which Oliver had no control, he just dropped the face, and that was what put a stranger off, gave the fright.

'Eduardo watched Mendoza's boat come in to the jetty where the sailor had his shop, and Mendoza's boat banged up to the shop and spilled the whisky with the shaking. He got a shock and revved up the engine the wrong way and the whole jetty fell apart. His boat listed into the bay, and it started to take water. The kids Mendoza took out to the gulf for the day fell in. The kids in the water were near the propeller, near the blood, near the fish, and the sharks had followed the boat in. The women were screaming. It was Eduardo that saw the shark fins powering across the water.

'Eduardo ran across the road and he dived in with his knife. He just flew off the road and into the sea and he brought one child after the next into shore. He threw each kid onto the sand and then went out again with the knife stashed in his fist, the feet going fast, he was being very fast, and his fury for the kids was really something. His fury showed he loved the kids.

'When the last kid was ashore a shark moved between Eduardo and the beach, and the shark they say moved aside a lot of water, a watching kind of shark, a seen things kind of shark. Eduardo stood up to the chest in the water and held the knife. One kid was behind him. Mendoza was going wild, the women ran down to the sand, the kids ran away, the boat had rolled over. Everything was out of place, everything was not right, and Eduardo did this odd thing. He screamed. He let it rip. He put his mouth up to the sky and he let it rip in his throat, the knife was in the sky, up high, in the hand, waving. He waited for that shark, and it swam around him, slow and nice the way it wished.

'Eduardo turned round and grabbed the kid by the arm, but the arm slipped and so he took the hair instead and he just walked slowly up to the beach with the kid screaming, he walked as slowly as you can walk, and he had the knife in the air.

'The water grew lower. He was into his waist, and walking. The dry beach very near, shallows now. He dragged the kid up and then lifted him to Mendoza and then he turned around to see the shark circling back.

'Eduardo walked in to meet the shark.

'Mendoza's boat was moving more sideways.

'Ellie was jumping up and down, she was vivid, she shouted to Eduardo to come back.

'But our guy, dear brother, he saw off that shark. He walked up to the beach. He was exhausted.'

Oliver said: 'It's courage, kindness is a different thing, he gave us courage.'

Castle fell silent for a moment. 'You're right, that's what he gave us, you and Catherine and Remple and me.'

When they finished lunch Oliver was becoming tired and he wanted to get going. They had talked and enjoyed. 'Shall we go?'

'Yeah, let's go.'

'I love you, brother,' Oliver said standing up from the chair, 'see you soon, thanks for lunch.'

'I love you too, see you soon.'

Oliver strolled off and when he was far off he turned to wave. Castle waved, and he strolled away.

The Tree of Butterflies in the Distance

As Castle walked back up Beaufort Street he decided to stay in Perth for another week, the others down at Yelverton could easily continue having a good time. He decided slowly not suddenly; he intended to go down south again tomorrow, but it became clear only slowly that he'd stay for a while.

Beaufort Street was crowded and full of activity. There was

a lot going on. Eduardo darting in to a goggle shop. David Darlington sipping a whisky with a sailor in the goggle shop. Ellie steering Mendoza into the back room. Eduardo at Ellie's birthday party dancing with Ellie's cousin from behind the hills. Eduardo somehow bringing those Banford postcards to David Darlington every month from the postman up the coast. Castle could never place Kee's Banford guy into things, Banford was just too misty and unreal. Castle could not even really place Ellie into things. He sometimes wished he could, but he just couldn't, Ellie was also misty and unreal. Kee talked also about a maharaja's daughter, but Castle had no steel image on her either, tho he knew Laura had a better grip on the princess, or, as Laura said, her mum Meryl had a very firm notion of the princess.

The green walking light at Walcott Street took time to turn green. Kee's transport of grandma Renata as a girl, that seemed real. Fourteen year old Renata dived off his boat with such a security of expertise and gracefulness that it was not right when Renata was seen as a shy girl who'd taken to hiding behind the nineteen year old Kee at yet another wrong village as they rode up the coast away from Eduardo.

The walking light turned green, and Castle strolled across Walcott Street. Kee called himself a buffalo boy once, out there on the banks at the Bahamas, why did he do that? What's a buffalo boy? More misty and unreal stuff.

Castle walked past the post office, and then he turned round and went back. Inside, he bought a few paid envelopes. He'd send out invitations to come round to the Bombay Plaza for a drink.

And what about this other thing? Kee only once said it. Out on the boat off the banks said he felt Ellie was his mother. Kee had said he felt Mendoza might be his father.

Pedro was another piece of mist Castle never could condense into a glass of water. Who was this Almeria guy? He started a home for lost kids, maybe he was Kee, maybe Pedro didn't even exist very much. If Pedro didn't exist, then Pedro was Kee inventing Pedro. Kee wanted a home for lost kids, so he invented a Pedro who had a passion to make a home for lost kids.

Castle tried to find somewhere on him to put the envelopes, but he carried them in his hand back to the Bombay Plaza all along the last hot mile of Beaufort Street, along that strip in Mount Lawley that gets very hot in summer. By the time he got to the Chinese restaurant on the corner the envelopes were wet with sweat.

Jack had mentioned a cruelty. Castle remembered Jack said something about a concealed cruelty in Kee. Another mist.

Then there was the moment Kee told him about the jetty.

Castle went inside to the Bombay Plaza, dropping the wet envelopes to the sideboard.

Kee had also told Castle he cast a last look around as he was leaving the hacienda. He found that the sailor playing the harmonica was not there today so he ran up the jetty and took a big dive into the sea. Swimming back to the beach he saw two figures.

One was Eduardo. 'Where do you think you are going?'

The other was Ellie, arms tightly folded.

Kee walked from the waves up the beach. 'I am going to find Rosa Mendoza.'

Eduardo laughed, Ellie laughed. The boy walked past them up the beach, and they never saw him again.

Castle opened the fridge. It was a small old fridge below his waist and he had to prise the door off the fridge, the ice had formed over the whole thing.

Then he walked around the apartment. The place was musty so he did the windows, walking around and sliding the place open to the heatwave. He sat at Oliver's table near the sliding door. He sat there for a long time staring out at the trees.

After a while he picked up the phone. The Bombay Plaza had an old phone from the seventies, painted with oil paints red and blue.

'Hi Mum, how's things?'

'Pretty good. Are you all down at Yelverton?'

'I'm up for a week, just met up with Oliver half an hour ago.'

'How is he?'

'He's okay, yeah he's okay. I've got some fresh news about Eduardo, feel like meeting up for a coffee later on?'

'Sure, love to.'

Hacienda Zaragoza

'Ellie, can I have some soup?'

'Si.'

'You never give soup.'

'I always give soup dear Carlos, I make the stuff.'

The soldier started singing.

Ellie said: 'Listen.'

Carlos said: 'He is boring, give me your soup please.'

'But listen, the man is playing the harmonica.'

'Please Ellie, can I have something to eat before the others?'

'Before the others? No way señor, no way.'

What is a tree dear butterfly, but a fanfare of seduction?

Carlos walked down to the beach, a man had drifted in with goggles to the village, Carlos dreamed of goggles and what they might see. They might see everything, they might see nothing, but he wanted to find out what a proper goggle looks like, a navy goggle, not the handmade plastic things the fishermen owned. They all talked about goggles around here, and when you talk beside the rare barbeque of spitting fish and onions, as an eleven year old boy, you want to see what the women like. You stand around waiting until nothing much happens. You want to kiss them. You want to dance. Nothing happens. You want to touch. You take a dive and you find a rusty key on the sand three feet away. You open the door. With the rustiest key of all time the kid opened doors to his future, to Ellie-Isabela's magic of give and take.

Your lightest and brightest custodians dear butterfly, are those that can often taste the simple request they make: 'Can I please have a kiss,' the kid says.

A girl kisses him out of the blue.

The Tree of Kiss

Henry&Co once took anything they could get parading up and down the main ocean road. Henry? Bark away like a dog-fly, Yek! Yekreh!

Scare off the other soldiers that drifted into the place. They would move further south on Henry's sharp barking, men shot at for endless months. Can't take a small dog right now. Need to move, and they'd wake the next morning ready to go further south, move away from the war far as you can move.

But today's different let's be clear. Henry&Co do not walk up and down the ocean road barking at lost men.

Today you sit back and witness enough kisses walk up and down that boulevard to make thousands of new powderboxes dear butterfly. It is a new joint broken away from the old joint.

They tried to keep the hacienda, but they didn't. No matter how many kisses they put on the joint, the place changed into a seaside resort full of waiters and chefs, food in abundance, food to throw away. Mendoza's boat listing into the bay was an old photo enlarged into a poster at the seafood shop.

Ellie's hitting the earth became a far away talking point, nobody dining on the ocean boulevard believed it, but they loved it as a rustic anecdote, as the underlay of the genuine. They smiled as they were served wine and prawns.

They were told: long ago this beach was a Scottish Hindu place of children. Buffalo boys and girls lived here. Maheesha the demon of chaos and evil made give and take for their adult times. Diners from Berlin would laugh. The whole village went to pot, but it wasn't a solo bad problem because all villages on the gulf had gone to pot.

Kee and Rosa woke up in darkness. They were anchored at a reef. These two became your custodians up in oxygen dear butterfly. They cooked up coffee and they ate baked beans under a small light, a minor circle at the hands.

Rosa said in Spanish: 'Did you send the note to that nice boy in Australia?'

'He will tell his brother about Eduardo, I am certain of it.'

'I liked Eduardo very much, I'm surprised to know he

became insane. My father loved him like a brother.'

'Everyone loved him, he was a very beautiful guy.'

The sweet stuff, it was the sweet stuff never far away in the village. It was very nearby, dear butterfly. The second equator swung itself into the ocean. Hasty-paste off to another powderbox in love one more time.

Acknowledgements

In a variety of ways these individuals have contributed to this book. I'd like to give my sincere thanks to: the Literature Board of the Australia Council for their assistance with a Developing Writers grant; Libby Douglas for her beauty and joy; Clive Newman for his confidence and friendship; Georgia Richter for her immediate excitement and for a sustained and sharp keenness of immense depth and vigour; Naama Amram for her supple and strong intelligence; Shaugn for his huge generosity of spirit and deed; Jenny, Rafi, Dot, Nilofer, Ion, Maureen, and Mary & Max Wagstaff, for being there just at the right time; Joan Douglas for her grand and glorious friendship; my cousins for all of 2009; Elaine & Harry U' Chong and Marj Smith for many glad nights that returned to me many times over; Graham Tong, Syd Tong, Pat Liau and families for a long and decent arc of the cherished kind; Fiona Fricker and her mother and father Basha and Bill for the lagoons of plenty—none of us would have those amazing years without your mum and dad and you; Harley Lacy for writing petrol via the painting *Summer*; Mark & Caroline Hubbard for writing petrol via the painting *Seven Valleys*; George Kailis for writing petrol via *Five Seasons*; Jane Ulman for writing petrol via *The Garden*; Julie Hatch for writing petrol via *The Window*; William Zappa for writing petrol via *Figure in Studio*; Marylynn Moss for the amazing month in 2009; Cecil Wagstaff for a fine moment over the second equator; Mark & Sue Louw for writing petrol via *Swell*; Suzie & Dom for writing petrol via *Moonrise IV*; Alison & David Britten for writing petrol via *Dusk*; Jude & Izzy for their encouragement, and for writing petrol via *Down South with Libby*; Carmelo Grasso for anchorage and friendship; David Young also for anchorage and friendship; Dianne & Robert for Yelverton; Kath Howlett for years of inspirational conversation and warmth; Greg & Jo for dastardly excellent lunches of hup two three and ping splatter pop; Ann & Hugh for 2009, and for a time far away; Katie & Adrian for a whole string of fantastic weekends without which *Equator* would be lacking a few of the more vibrant colours; Kelvin Ogunjimi for a call on the bow at South Head that rippled into *Equator*; Lynette Robinson for 2009; Anita Dane and her mother Jenny for 2009; Peggy & Peter for calm, clarity and humour; Pascale & Bud for their friendship; John The Roving for a wild and woolly balcony where good things in storytelling are often found; Deb & Mark for 2009, and for writing petrol via *The Islands*; Holger & Anna for many great nights of beauty and for 2009; Keith & Maria for loads of excellent ping splatter pop across two cities and two studios, and for 2009; Sheila & Paul, Sue, and Ann & Eric for an immense arc of friendship across a few decades; Marco & Donna Dabala for 2009 and for the kindness that followed; Ahmed Zaheer and family for cherished magic that's been crossing the second equator for quite a while. And to Saleema Ashton for all the never-ending give give give.

Praise for Under a Tin-Grey Sari

... an artful, savvy and intimate depiction of a particular season, era and place, showing its cleverness most in its specificity.
– *Bookseller+Publisher*

... sensual and lush, the novel is at one level a tale of love and longing, of dreams and betrayal, yet its simplicity is offset with such a finely honed and playful irony that it's hard not to see the novel as a comment on larger events.
– *Canberra Times*

... an astoundingly unusual debut ... In language that is both lush and robust and with a voice entirely original, Ashton creates a mesmerising world apart.
– *Gleebooks*

... this novel belongs to itself, abides by its own rules, much as the people of Chittagong are content to thrive in a world of their own.
– *The Lane Bookshop*

... a witty and simply told tale of desire, betrayal and unreason, to which the reader effortlessly and willingly succumbs.
– *Dymocks*

... a lilting, sensual evocation of the landscape of his childhood.
– *The Age*

... Ashton's debut novel is a sensual, beautifully written mini-masterpiece. Almost every page groans with sex, or love, or death, or laughter ... the best Australian novel I have read all year.
–*Readings Magazine*